M○ON

CHOSEN

P. C. CAST

MOON

CHOSEN

Tales of a New World

ST. MARTIN'S GRIFFIN
NEW YORK

MOON CHOSEN. Copyright © 2016 by P. C. Cast. Illustrations copyright © 2016 Dr. Hilary Costello, N. D. All rights reserved. Printed in the United States of America. For information, address St. Martin's Press, 175 Fifth Avenue, New York, N.Y. 10010.

www.stmartins.com

Designed by Jonathan Bennett

The Library of Congress Cataloging-in-Publication Data is available upon request.

ISBN 978-1-250-10072-6 (hardcover)
ISBN 978-1-250-12578-1 (international, sold outside the U.S., subject to availability)
ISBN 978-1-250-10074-0 (e-book)

Our books may be purchased in bulk for promotional, educational, or business use. Please contact your local bookseller or the Macmillan Corporate and Premium Sales Department at 1-800-221-7945, extension 5442, or by e-mail at MacmillanSpecialMarkets@macmillan .com.

First Edition: October 2016

10 9 8 7 6 5 4 3 2 1

This book is dedicated to my editor, Monique Patterson, because of her enthusiasm for this new world, her belief in me, and her mad, crazy brainstorming skills! May our partnership live long and prosper.

ACKNOWLEDGMENTS

I am deeply indebted to my agent and friend Meredith Bernstein. Thank you for your unflagging belief in me, your integrity, and your friendship.

Thank you to my dad, Dick Cast, and my brother, Kevin Cast, for their biology and botany help. I don't say it enough, but your enthusiasm for helping me create my worlds means so much to me! And it's very handy to have experts in my family! Love from Bugs!

I am so appreciative of the gorgeous illustrations for this book created by my friend Dr. Hilary Costello! Thank you for your amazing talent, your friendship, and your incredible knowledge about homeopathic medicine. Any mistakes Mari makes are mine and mine alone.

Thank you, Christine Zika, for helping me lay the foundation for another rockin' series!

Huge thanks to my publishing family at St. Martin's Press! It is a gift to have a publishing house that gives me the freedom to follow my heart. Sally Richardson, Monique Patterson, Anne Marie Talberg, Jennifer Enderlin, Steve Cohen, and the rest of Team Cast totally rock!

My readers are the smartest, coolest, most loyal fans in the world. Thank you for coming on another adventure with me. I heart you!

And last, but always first in my heart, thank you to my best friend and daughter, Kristin Cast. You always believe in me. You're always right there by my side—even when I lose my path and am stumbling around in the wilderness. When I can't hear my own, it's your voice that reminds me to trust myself. I love you, Ja! Now let's go to luncheon!

M OON

CHOSEN

I

The contagious sound of women's laughter filled the warm, tidy burrow.

"Oh, Mari! That is *not* an illustration from the myth I just told you."

Mari's mother held the sheet of handmade paper in one hand and pressed the other hand against her mouth, unsuccessfully trying to hold back another bout of laughter.

"Mama, your job is to tell the stories. My job is to sketch them. That's our game, right? Our *favorite* game."

"Well, yes," Leda said, still trying to fix her expression to a more sober one. "I do tell the stories, but you tend to sketch what you *think* you hear."

"I don't see the problem with that." Mari moved to stand beside her mother and studied the newly finished sketch with her. "This is exactly what I saw as you were telling the story of Narcissus and Echo."

"Mari, you made Narcissus look like a young man turning into a flower. Awkwardly. He has one hand that is a leaf and the other that is still a hand. The same with his—" Leda stifled a giggle. "Well, with several other parts of his anatomy. And he has a mustache and a silly look on his face—though I do admit it is an amazing talent you have that can bring a silly-looking half flower, half man, to life." Leda pointed at the sketch and the ghostly nymph who Mari had somehow made to look bored and annoyed as she watched the transformation of Narcissus. "You made Echo look—" Leda hesitated, obviously searching for the right words.

"Fed up with Narcissus and his ego?" Mari offered.

Leda gave up all pretense of admonishment and laughed out loud. "Yes, that is exactly how you made Echo look, though that is not the story I told."

"Well, Leda." Mari used her mother's given name as she waggled her brows at her. "I was listening to your story and as I was drawing I decided that something was definitely left out of the ending."

"The ending? Really?" Leda bumped her daughter with her shoulder. "And stop calling me Leda."

"But, Leda, that's your name."

"To the rest of the world. To you my name is Mother."

"*Mother*? Really? It's so—"

"Respectful and traditional?" This time Leda offered to finish her daughter's thought.

"More like boring and old," Mari said, eyes shining as she waited for her mother's predictable response.

"Boring and old? Did you just call me boring and old?"

"What? Me? Call you boring and old? Never, Mama, never!" Mari giggled and held her hands up in surrender.

"That's good. And I suppose Mama is fine. Better than Leda."

Mari grinned. "Mama, we've been having this same discussion for eighteen winters."

"Mari, sweet girl, I can happily say that even though you have known eighteen winters, you haven't been able to *talk* for all of them. I did get a couple of winters respite before you started, and never stopped, speaking."

"Mama! You said you *encouraged* me to start talking before I'd known much more than two winters," Mari said in mock surprise as she reached for the sharpened charcoal twig with which she'd been sketching, and took the drawing from her mother.

"Yes, and I also never said I was perfect. I was just a young mother trying to do her best," Leda said dramatically, releasing the sketch to her daughter.

"Really, *really* young. Right?" Mari said, sketching quickly while she cradled the drawing so that Leda couldn't see it.

"That is absolutely right, Mari," Leda said, trying to peek over Mari's arm. "I had known one winter less than you when I met your wonderful father and—" Leda broke off, frowning at her daughter as Mari couldn't contain her giggles.

"All fixed," she said, holding up the sketch for Leda to inspect.

"Mari, his eyes are crossed," Leda said.

"The rest of the story made me think he wasn't too smart. So I made him look not very smart."

"You sure did." Leda's gaze met her daughter's, and both women dissolved into laughter again.

Leda wiped her eyes and gave her daughter a quick hug. "I take back everything I said about your illustration. I decree that it is perfect."

"Thank you, *Mother*." Mari's eyes danced. She took a fresh sheet of paper and held her charcoal at ready. She loved the ancient stories her mother had shared with her for as long as she could remember, weaving wisdom and adventure, loss and love into them as deftly as the talented women of Clan Weaver wove baskets and clothing and tapestries to trade with Clan Fisher, Clan Miller, and Clan Wood. "One more story! How about just one more? You're so good at the telling!"

"Flattery will not get you another story. It may get you a basketful of early blueberries, though."

"Blueberries! Really, Mama? That would be wonderful. I love the color of ink I make with them. It's a nice change from the black stain I get from walnuts."

Leda smiled fondly at her daughter. "Only you could be more excited about painting with blueberries than eating them."

"It can't be *only* me, Mama. You like the dye you make from them, too."

"I do, and I'm looking forward to dyeing a new cloak for you this spring, but I admit freely that I would rather eat a blueberry pie!"

"Blueberry pie! That sounds wonderful! So does another story—the Leda story. And, Mother, can we take a moment to discuss your name? Leda? Really? I'm assuming your mother did know that story," Mari teased. "But as her name was Cassandra, I sometimes question her ability to name sensibly."

"You know very well that Moon Women always name their daughters whatever is whispered to them on the wind by the Great Earth Mother. My mother, Cassandra, was named by her mother, Penelope. I heard your lovely name whispered by our Earth Mother the full moon night before you were born."

"My name is boring." Mari sighed. "Does that mean the Earth Mother thinks I'm boring?"

"No, that means the Earth Mother thinks we should make up a story to go with your name—a story all your own."

"So you've been saying for all the winters I can remember, but I still don't have my own story," Mari said.

"When the time is right you will," Leda said, touching her daughter's smooth cheek, her smile turning sad. "Mari, sweet girl, I cannot tell another story tonight, though I wish I could. Sunset is not far off, and tonight the moon will be full and brilliant. The needs of the Clan will be great."

Mari opened her mouth to plead with Leda to stay just a few moments more, to put *her* needs before those of the Clan, but before she could speak her small, selfish desire her mother's body twitched spasmodically, shoulders trembling, head jerking painfully and uncontrollably. Though she had already turned from her daughter, as always trying to shield her from the change night brought with it, Mari knew too well what was happening.

All teasing fell away from her as Mari dropped the paper and charcoal and went to Leda. She took her mother's hand, holding it in both of hers, hating how cold it had become—hating the pale silver-gray tinge that was beginning to spread across her skin. And wishing, always wishing, that she could soothe the pain that visited her mother with the setting of the sun every night of her life.

"I'm sorry, Mama. I lost track of time. I didn't mean to keep you." Mari kept her tone light, not wanting to send her beloved mother into danger and darkness burdened with more worry than she usually carried. "We'll make up my story another time. And I have work I have to do while you're gone. I still haven't gotten the perspective perfect on that piece I've been trying to finish."

"May I see it yet?" her mother asked.

"It's not done, and you know I hate for you to see my drawings before they're done." Another tremor shivered across Leda's skin and Mari's hand automatically tightened around her mother's, supporting her—understanding her—loving her. Mari forced herself to grin. "But I suppose I'll make an exception tonight, especially since you're my favorite model, and I like keeping my favorite model happy."

"Well, I think it's safe to say you like me more than Narcissus," Leda joked while Mari went to the simple wooden table that sat in the corner of the main room of the little cavelike burrow she and her mother had shared for the eighteen winters of Mari's life.

The table was framed by the sides of the burrow that held the thickest of the glowmoss, and sat beneath the biggest and brightest cluster of glowshrooms, which suspended from the ceiling like organic chandeliers. As Mari approached the table, the strained smile she had adopted for her mother relaxed, and when she turned to Leda, holding a sheet of thick paper made from meticulously hand processing plant pulp, Mari's smile was genuine. "No matter how many times I look at my drawing table, the way we've grown the glowshrooms and placed the glowmoss will always remind me of your Earth Sprite stories."

"You have always so loved the stories passed down from Moon Woman to Moon Woman to entertain and teach their daughters, though none of them are any more real than Narcissus and his unfortunate Echo."

Mari's smile didn't falter. "When I draw it—it's real to me."

"So you have always said, but—" her mother began, and then broke off with a little gasp of delight as her gaze went to the unfinished sketch. "Oh, Mari! It's lovely!" Leda took the sketch from her daughter and looked at it more closely. "Truly this is one of your very best." With a wondering fingertip, she carefully touched the image of herself, sitting at her usual place beside their hearth fire. On her lap was a partially woven basket, but she wasn't looking at the basket. She was smiling lovingly at the artist.

Mari took her mother's hand in hers again and smoothed her skin. "I'm glad you like it, but your hand is much more delicately boned than I drew it."

Leda pressed the palm of her hand against her daughter's cheek. "You'll fix it. You always do. And it will be as exquisite as the rest of your drawings." She kissed Mari gently on her forehead before adding, "I have made something for you, sweet girl."

"Really? A present?"

Leda smiled. "A present indeed. Wait here and close your eyes." She hurried into the back room of their burrow, which served as Leda's bed-chamber as well as a drying and storing room for her fragrant herbs. Then she hurried back to her daughter, standing before her with her hands behind her back.

"What is it? It's small enough to hide behind your back! Is it a new quill?"

"Mari, I said no peeking!" Leda admonished.

Eyes screwed tightly shut, Mari grinned. "I'm not peeking! I'm just smart, like my mama," she said smugly.

"And beautiful, like your father," Leda said as she placed her daughter's gift on her head.

"Oh, Mama! You made me a Maiden Moon Crown!" Mari took the intricately braided coronet from her head. Leda had woven ivy with willow to create a lovely circle, which she'd decorated with bright yellow flowers. "So this is what you've been doing with all of those dandelion blossoms! I thought you were making wine."

Leda laughed. "I did make wine. I also made you a Maiden Moon crown."

Mari's delight dimmed. "I'd forgotten that tonight is the first full moon of spring. I'm sure the Clan's celebration will be joyous."

Leda shook her head sadly. "I wish it was so, but I'm afraid this spring moon won't be as festive as usual. Not after so many Earth Walkers have been recently captured by the Companions. The Earth Mother feels unusually restless to me, as if uncomfortable changes are coming. Our women have been filled with more sorrow than usual, and our men—well, we know the anger the Night Fever brews within our men."

"They won't just be angry, they'll be dangerous. Damn Scratchers!"

"Mari, don't call your people that. It makes them sound like monsters."

"They're only half my people, Mother, and at night they *are* monsters. Or at least the men are. What would happen if you didn't Wash them of the Night Fever every three days? Wait, I know what would happen. It's why a Moon Woman's burrow has to always be hidden, even from her own Clan." Frustration and fear caused her words to be harsh, and as soon as she'd spoken them the sadness that filled her mother's eyes made her regret such harshness.

"Mari, you must never forget that at night, even I have within me the capacity to be a monster."

"Not you! I didn't mean you. I'd never mean you!"

"But the moon is all that keeps me from becoming more Scratcher than Earth Walker. Sadly, our people cannot call down the moon as can I, so I must do it for them at least once every three nights. Tonight is a Third Night, as well as the spring full moon. Our Clan will gather, and I will Wash them so that their lives may be open to accept love and joy instead of mired in melancholy and anger. You know all of this, Mari. What troubles you?"

Mari shook her head. How was she supposed to tell her mother—her sweet, funny, brilliant mother—the only person in this terrible world who knew what Mari truly was and loved her still—that she had begun to ache for *more* of everything?

Mari could never tell her mother, just as Leda could never allow the truth about her daughter to be known.

"It's nothing. Probably just something to do with the full moon. I can feel it, even here in the cave, even before it's risen."

Leda's smile was proud. "You have my power and more. Mari, come with me tonight. Wear your Moon Crown. Join the Clan's celebration. It is easiest to draw down the power of the moon when it is full, and tonight it will be as spectacularly full as the sun has been bright today."

"Oh, Mama, not tonight. I'm tired of failing, and I definitely don't want to do it in front of a crowd."

Leda's smile didn't falter. "Trust your mother. You have my power and *more*. It's that *more* that makes your training difficult."

"Difficult?" Mari sighed again. "You mean hopeless."

"Such melodrama! You are alive and healthy and *sane*. Day or night—rain or shine—moon or no moon, you show no sign of madness or pain. Trust that the rest will come with practice and patience."

"Are you sure there isn't an easier way?"

"Quite sure. It's much like how you practiced until you attained the ability to make a flat drawing seem to live and breathe."

"Drawing is so much easier!"

Her mother laughed softly. "Only for you." Then Leda's smile faded. "Mari, you know I must choose an apprentice soon. I cannot put off the women of the Clan much longer."

"I'm not good enough yet, Mama."

"And that is another reason you should join me tonight. Stand beside me before the Clan. Practice calling the power of the moon, and while you practice I will be showing our Clanswomen that they may rest easy. Though I have not named you as my official heir, I have begun your training."

Mari's lips tilted up. "*Begun* my training? Leda, you've been training me as long as I can remember."

"You've always been a good student. And stop calling me Leda."

"Good and slow aren't the same thing, *Mother*."

"I'm well aware of that. You're not slow, Mari. You're complex—your mind, your talents, your power—all complex. Someday you will make a fine Moon Woman." Her gray eyes were wise as Leda studied her daughter. "Unless you have no desire to be Moon Woman."

"I don't want to disappoint you, Mama."

"You couldn't disappoint me, no matter what path you choose for your life." Leda paused, grimacing as a new tremor of pain swept through her body, and the silver tinge that had begun to appear on her mother's delicate hands spread up her arms.

"Okay, Mama! I'll come with you," Mari said quickly, and was rewarded by her mother's brilliant smile.

"Oh, Mari! I'm so glad." Pain temporarily forgotten, Leda rushed into her room and Mari could hear her clattering through the pots and baskets and precious glass jars that held her vast collection of herbs, tinctures, and poultices. "Here it is!" she called, and then reappeared with a familiar wooden bowl. "Let me touch up your face. We'll need to dye your hair again soon, but not tonight."

Mari stifled a sigh and tilted her face up so that her mother could reapply the muddy mixture that kept their secret.

Leda worked in silence, thickening her daughter's brow, flattening her high cheekbones, and then, lastly, smearing the dirty, sticky clay-like substance down her neck and arms. When she was finished she studied Mari carefully, and touched her cheek gently. "Test it at the window."

Mari nodded somberly. Followed by Leda, she went to the far side of the cave's main room and climbed the rock steps up to a niche carved meticulously through layers of rock and dirt. She slid aside a long rectangular-shaped stone. Warm air swirled from the opening, caressing Mari's cheek like a second mother. Mari stared into the hole to the upper world and the eastern sky, which was already reflecting the pale, washed-out colors that night painted over brilliant day. She lifted her arm so that the wan light from above touched her. Then she met her mother's gaze.

Leda's eyes, just like Mari's, were so gray they were almost silver. Mari focused on the beauty of their shared trait.

Under the full moon, like her mother, Mari's eyes would glow silver.

Like her mother, Mari's skin would glisten as she basked in the full moon night and let its cool, silver light fill her and calm her.

Thinking longingly of the moon and the power it held, Mari's hand stretched farther up into the hole, as if reaching for moonlight. But instead of finding the delicate silvery beams, her fingertips caught the yellow light of the fading sun. Her hand trembled at the inrush of heat and Mari pulled it quickly back to her, spreading her fingers and staring at the delicate filigree pattern that even such a small amount of sunlight had the ability to call to the surface of her skin. Mari hugged her hand to her chest while the sunlight-colored pattern faded like a lost dream upon waking.

Unlike her mother. She was so unlike her mother.

"That's okay, sweet girl. Let's take your summer cloak. It's light enough that you won't be too hot, but—"

"But the sleeves will cover my arms and hands until the sun has fully set," Mari finished for her. With slow steps, she climbed down from the window and went to the basket that held her cloaks.

"I wish you didn't have to hide. I wish it could be different." Her mother's voice was soft and sad.

"I do, too, Mama," Mari said.

"I'm so sorry, Mari. You know I—"

"It's okay, Mama. Really. I'm used to it." Mari schooled her expression into nonchalance as she turned to face her mother. "And I may grow out of it."

"No, my sweet girl, you won't. Your father's blood runs as truly in your veins as does mine and I wouldn't change that. No matter the cost, I wouldn't ever change that."

I would Mama. I would. But Mari only thought the words as she wrapped her cloak tightly around her and followed Leda from the safety of their burrow.

2

Side by side, Mari and Leda topped the rocky rise in the land and looked down at the Gathering Site. At first glace the site appeared no different from any other small clearing within the swampy southern forest. There was a stream that wound through the willows and hawthorns, holly and ferns—the stream and the lazily waving boughs of the trees and shrubs were what purposely drew the eye. It took more than a glance, or even a second or third look—at least from the distance of the rise—to see the truth cunningly hidden among the ferns and foliage. In neat clusters early kale, lacy endive, fat tufts of butter lettuce, and late-winter garlic flourished under the care of the Clanswomen.

Leda paused and drew a deep, satisfied breath. "Thank you, Earth Mother," the Moon Woman spoke as if the Goddess, and not her daughter, was standing beside her. "Thank you for gifting your Earth Walkers with the ability to coax living things from your fertile bosom."

Mari breathed deeply with Leda and smiled, used to the intimate way she spoke with her Goddess. "I can smell the lavender oil from here," Mari said.

Leda nodded. "The Clanswomen have done a good job readying the Gathering Site. No wolf spider pack will get anywhere near here this night." She paused, pointing to the carefully situated campfires. Only one was in the center of the Gathering. The others were strategically placed all around the circumference of the space, with torches planted nearby. "And the firestarters are ready in case a swarm is attracted by so many of us in one place."

"I know the fires are for protection, but being lit up like that makes the whole clearing look happy."

"It does indeed," Leda agreed.

"I hope the purple kale is ready to harvest soon," Mari said as they began picking their way down to the Gathering Site. "I can almost taste how delicious it'll be mixed with those capers we pickled."

"It has been warm early this spring," Leda said. "I wouldn't be surprised if a bunch will be ready tonight."

"That alone will be worth the trip," Mari said.

Leda's glance was sharp. "Mari, I didn't force you to join me."

"I know, Mama. I'm sorry I sounded like that."

Leda squeezed her hand. "Don't be nervous. Trust yourself."

Mari was nodding tightly when a mini-whirlwind hurled herself into her arms, hugging her tightly and almost knocking her off her feet.

"Mari! Mari! I'm so, so glad you're here! You must be feeling well."

Mari smiled at the younger girl. "I am well, Jenna. And I'm glad to be here, too." She touched the Maiden Moon Crown that circled Jenna's dark head. It was woven beautifully from lavender and ivy. "Your crown is really pretty. Did your father make it?"

Jenna giggled, looking more like six than sixteen. "Father? No! His fingers are like stumps and he says they all turn into thumbs when he tries to weave. I made it."

"Well done, Jenna," Leda said fondly, smiling at her daughter's friend. "You did a wonderful job of weaving the lavender into the center pattern of the crown. You're showing real talent."

Jenna's cheeks flushed an adorable pink. "Thank you, Moon Woman." Her smile was bright as she bowed formally to Leda, arms down and spread, palms open and facing outward to show she hid no weapon or ill will.

"Oh, Jenna! You don't have to be so formal. It's just Mama," Mari said.

"She's *just* your mama. She's *my* Moon Woman," Jenna said cheekily.

"Who is also your friend," Leda added. "Which type of weaving are you most drawn to—thread work or something less intricate?"

Jenna spoke softly, shuffling her feet, "I—I want to weave beautiful scenes, like the Earth Mother tapestry in the birthing burrow."

"Then thread work it is," Leda said. "Tonight I'll speak with Rachel about being sure you are properly apprenticed."

"Thank you, Moon Woman," Jenna said quickly, her eyes bright with unshed tears.

Leda cupped her face and kissed her on the forehead. "Your mother would do the same for my Mari had I passed on to join our Earth Mother before her."

Mari moved closer to her friend and linked arms with her. "Only I am as hopeless with weaving as your father, which would have baffled your mama."

"But you can draw anything!" Jenna gushed.

"Moon Woman! Our Moon Woman is here!" From the Gathering a strong, male voice called

Leda smiled and acknowledged the greeting with a cheery wave. "As usual, your father is the first Clansman to see me."

"Father will always be first to see you—first to be Washed by you. It's because he loves me so much," Jenna said proudly.

"That he does, Jenna," Leda said.

"Xander is a really good father," Mari agreed, smiling at her friend, though to herself she acknowledged, *lucky for Jenna that Xander seeks out Mama without fail every Third Night. If he didn't she'd be worse than an orphan. She'd be raised by a monster.*

"Our Moon Woman is here! Light the torches! Ready the Clan!" The women of the Clan took up the greeting and the Gathering Site exploded into activity. From all directions they came to take their proper places. The movements of the women were practiced, and though they weren't in perfect step with one another they wove a serpentine pattern through the trees, vegetables, and foliage with an earthy grace that reminded Mari of the rhythm of water flowing over river rock.

The Clan formed a semicircle to welcome their Moon Woman. Aged women first, then mothers with the Clan's young beside them, then maidens of mating age all crowned with gaily woven headdresses, and then, finally, the Clansmen, who held torches and stood protectively around the edges of the clearing. Mari could feel their predatory presence—a barely controlled chaos that she could imagine drifting in dark, roiling eddies of unease throughout the gathering.

Mari couldn't help glancing nervously at the men. Ever since she'd first realized as a young girl the changes that Night Fever brought to the Clan—the deadly melancholy it caused in women, and the dangerous madness it caused in men—she kept a watchful eye on any Clansmen, especially as sunset drew near.

"Don't stare at them. It is Third Night. We will Wash them and all will be well," her mama whispered to Mari.

Mari nodded tightly. "Lead the way, Mama. Jenna and I will be right behind you."

Leda took one step forward and then paused. She held out her hand to Mari. "Not behind me. I would rather that you were beside me for all to see."

Mari could feel the excitement in Jenna, but she hesitated before taking her mama's hand. She searched Leda's gray eyes, looking for reassurance.

"Trust me, sweet girl," Leda said. "You know I have your back."

Mari let out a long breath she hadn't realized she'd been holding. "I'll always trust you, Mama." She grasped Leda's hand.

Beside her, Jenna whispered, "You're practically a Moon Woman already!" Then, before Mari could respond, Jenna bowed respectfully again—this time to Leda *and* Mari—before taking her place behind them.

"Ready?" Leda asked.

"As long as I'm with you, Mama," Mari said.

Leda squeezed her daughter's hand and then strode confidently forward, head held high, shoulders back, with a wide smile beaming joy to her people.

"My daughter and I greet you, Weaver Clan, and wish you bounty the spring full moon brings times three!"

Mari felt the weight of the Clan's curious looks and heard the muffled susurrus of speculation. She mimicked her mother's stance, pulling back her shoulders, straightening her spine, and lifting her chin. She tried to look at everyone and no one, but her gaze was drawn to another pair of gray eyes. These were lighter, more blue-gray than the silver-gray of Leda's and Mari's eyes, but they were still remarkable, and still, definitely, belonging to a Clanswoman who carried the mark of a Moon Woman ancestor.

"Greetings, Moon Woman," the girl said. She bowed low to Leda, but the position of her body made it clear that it was *only* Leda she acknowledged. When she straightened she tossed back her mane of dark hair, and the feathers and beads that hung from her Moon Crown fluttered around her as if she wore a living veil. Her gaze flicked to Mari dismissively before she added, "I didn't realize you were acknowledging the Moon Women candidates tonight."

Leda's smile was serene. "Hello, Sora. Actually, this was an impromptu acknowledgment of pride in my daughter." She lifted the hand that she'd linked with Mari so that the Clan was sure to see. "And part of that pride is that her gray eyes mark her as a Moon Woman candidate."

"As do mine," Sora said.

Mari stifled her irritated sigh and spoke up before her mother could respond. "Yes, but you're usually so busy fluttering your eyelashes at our Clansmen that sometimes it's hard to remember your eyes are gray."

"Of course I pay attention to our Clansmen. It is only logical to show appreciation to our protectors. Mari, jealousy is unattractive, especially on someone who pays so little attention to her appearance," Sora said.

"Arguing among Clanswomen is unacceptable," Leda said sharply.

Sora and Mari shared a look of poorly disguised annoyance before they bowed their heads respectfully to the Moon Woman.

"You're right, of course," Sora said. "I apologize, Moon Woman."

"It is not to me you owe the apology," Leda said.

Sora turned to Mari. She smiled silkily, though the expression did not reach her eyes. "I apologize, Mari."

"Mari?" Leda prompted when her daughter remained mute.

"I apologize, too," Mari said quickly.

"Good," Leda said. She held out her other hand to Sora. "And you are correct, Sora. Your eyes do mark you as candidate for Moon Woman apprenticeship. Please join me."

Eagerly, Sora took Leda's hand, but before stepping forward into the heart of the Clan, Leda raised her voice, calling, "All maidens with gray eyes present yourselves to your Moon Woman!"

There was a rustle in the crowd before them, and then a young girl stepped from the group.

"Mari?" Leda prompted under her breath.

Mari smiled at her mother and then extended her open hand toward the girl, welcoming her with, "Hello, Danita." The younger girl was smiling tentatively at Mari and sending nervous glances to Leda as she moved to take her offered hand when a flush of light caught at Mari's gaze. She glanced down to see that the sleeve of her cloak had fallen back, so that her outstretched forearm had been caught in a single, fading beam of sunlight and the filigree pattern of a fern frond was glowing brightly through the concealing clay.

In one swift movement, Mari jerked her hand free of her mother's, rearranged the sleeves of her cloak, and wrapped her swathed arms around herself.

"What is it, sweet girl?" Leda quickly stepped between her daughter and the Clan, careful to conceal her.

"My—my stomach pains are back." She met her mother's gaze. Mari could see that Leda was trying valiantly to keep the disappointment from her expression, but her smile was melancholy and it didn't lift the sadness in her eyes.

"Jenna," Leda said. "Could you please take Mari to the hearth fire and ask one of the Mothers to brew her some chamomile tea? It seems she isn't as well as we hoped."

"Of course, Leda! Don't worry about anything. I'll take care of our girl."

Jenna linked arms with Mari, pulling her into the crowd as Mari watched first Danita, and then another gray-eyed girl and another, take her place with Sora beside her mother.

"Don't be sad," Jenna whispered. "Some tea will fix you up. You can sit with me and we'll gossip about those silly feathers in Sora's hair while your mama Washes the Clan." Jenna pointed to a log not far from the central campfire of the Gathering. "Sit there and rest. I'll get your tea and be right back!"

"Thanks, Jenna," Mari said, sitting on the log as Jenna scampered away. She felt the pitying eyes of Clanswomen on her, and managed to school her face into the impassive expression she put on for the Clan—never letting them know how much it hurt to be held apart from them—never letting them know how difficult it was to hide the truth from them.

She watched as her mama made her way to the center of the Gathering Site. She stopped before the single idol that decorated the clearing. Leda dropped the girls' hands she'd been holding, bowing deeply to the image of the Earth Goddess who seemed to be emerging from the forest floor. Her face was a smooth, carved river stone, creamy white and flecked with quartz crystals so that as light hit it—sunlight or the softer, cooler light of the moon—she glistened as if she had been formed from wishes and daydreams. Her skin was thick, soft moss. Her hair was a verdant fern that had been lovingly coaxed to cascade down the curve of her back and over the roundness of her shoulders.

"I greet you, Great Mother, as the Clan greets me—your Moon Woman—your servant, with love and gratitude and respect," Leda said reverently. Then she straightened and faced the watching Clan. "Men of Clan Weaver, present yourselves to me!"

As the men made their way forward, Jenna joined Mari, handing her a wooden cup filled with fragrant chamomile tea before sitting beside her on the log.

"Oh look, there's Father." Jenna smiled and waved. The powerfully built man who led the men acknowledged her wave with a nod, though Mari could see that his face was set in lines of pain, and his eyes were narrowed against the anger that boiled within him with the setting of the sun.

It was an anger that would overflow if his Moon Woman didn't Wash the Night Fever from him at least every Third Night.

With the other Clansmen, Xander dropped to his knees before Leda, and as he did so, the sun sank beneath the far western horizon. Mari saw her mother's arms lift, as if she would cradle within them the full moon that wasn't yet visible to the rest of the Clan, but which a Moon Woman could always find—could always call—as long as the sun had fled the sky.

Mari watched the gray tinge that had begun to spread up Leda's arms fade and disappear. Her mother's smile was radiant as she tilted back her head so that her face and her arms were open to the darkening sky. Leda's breathing became deep and rhythmic. Automatically, Mari's breathing deepened with her as she practiced the grounding exercise that preceded the drawing down ritual. Mari saw her mother's lips moving as she communed privately with her Goddess and prepared herself.

Mari's gaze drifted around the semicircle of Clansmen and women who surrounded her, counting them and consigning to memory the twenty-two women, ten children, and seven men who were present so that she could help her mama make the proper annotation in her journal when they returned to their burrow.

Mari frowned as her eyes paused on Sora. *Unbelievable!* She fumed silently. *Everyone else is praying and readying themselves with Mama, but not that girl.* Instead of praying or studying Leda, as any other candidate for Moon Woman was expected to do, Sora was smiling at one of the young men kneeling before Leda. Mari craned her neck and saw that the young man she recognized as Jaxom kept glancing surreptitiously at Sora, a heat in his eyes that seemed to have little to do with Night Fever.

Mari felt a stab of jealously. It was so easy for Sora! She was bold and confident and beautiful. *What would it be like to be her—just for one day, or even one hour? What would it be like to have a young man look at her with such heat and longing? It would be wonderful,* Mari thought. *It would be unimaginably wonderful.*

Then into the Clan's silence her mother, her magickal, loving Moon Woman mother, began to speak in a voice sweet and strong and sure, and Clan Weaver lifted their heads to face Leda.

> *"Moon Woman I proclaim myself to be*
> *Greatly gifted I bare myself to thee.*
> *Earth Mother aid me with your magick sight*
> *Lend me strength on this full moon night.*
> *Come, silver light—fill me to overflow*
> *So those in my care, your healing will know."*

As Leda spoke the invocation, her body began to glow. Not the sickly gray glow of Night Fever, but the sublime silver illumination of the pure, icy power of the moon. Mari had watched her mama call down the moon more times than she could begin to count, but it never ceased to thrill her. And though Leda's Earth Mother had never, ever, so much as whispered one word to Mari, she imagined that if the Goddess were to truly rise from the earth, she would look exactly like her mama.

> *"By right of blood and birth channel through me*
> *the Goddess gift that is my destiny!"*

Leda spoke the final words that drew from the sky the invisible threads of power that only answered a Moon Woman's call, and as she did so she began to move from man to man, touching each upturned head. Mari thought Leda was a living paintbrush whose touch stroked moonlight and magick into the tableau of the Clan, so that in turn each man glowed silver for an instant. Even from where Mari sat, she could hear the relieved sighs of the Clansmen as their Moon Woman Washed the pain and madness of Night Fever from their bodies.

Beside her, Mari felt the tremor that went through Jenna's slight form, reminding her of the public role she must play. Mari drained the last of her tea and then wrapped her arms more tightly around herself, pretending a pain she had never felt.

"It's okay, Mari. She's almost done with the men," Jenna said.

Mari opened her mouth to say something distracting to Jenna, but the sight of Sora moving beside Leda, smiling flirtatiously at each of the newly Washed Clansmen before they drifted back to their watch places surrounding the Gathering, had her gritting her teeth in irritation.

Jenna followed her gaze and snorted indelicately. "She's so bold! I'm surprised Leda doesn't put a stop to that."

Mari said nothing. She was afraid she knew why her mama didn't put a stop to Sora's shamelessness. *The Clan needs their Moon Woman to name an heir and choose her as a formal apprentice—and that apprentice can't have mutant skin that glows in sunlight. Yes, Sora was arrogant and annoying, but she was also popular with the Clan and obviously determined to be Moon Woman after Leda.*

Leda paused before them, smiling lovingly down at Jenna and Mari. With the rest of the Clan, Jenna lifted her head and Leda pressed her hands over the delicately wrought Moon Crown. Her words were for the Clan, but her eyes met her daughter's.

"I Wash you free of all sadness and gift you with the love of our Great Earth Mother."

With the rest of the Clan, Mari murmured, "Thank you, Moon Woman." She shared a secret smile with her mother. Leda touched her daughter's head, bent quickly, and kissed her forehead before moving on to the next group of waiting women.

Mari longed to join her mama—to show the Clan that she wasn't sickly and she could be a help to their Moon Woman and, possibly, someday *be* their Moon Woman.

"Better stay seated. Wouldn't want your stomach pains to return."

Mari looked up to meet Sora's gaze. There was nothing wrong with what the girl said, but Mari felt the mockery hidden in the polite facade. She wanted to leap up and yell that she didn't really have stomach pains! She was just different! But Mari wouldn't, couldn't say anything without jeopardizing her safety and, more importantly, her mother's. So, all Mari said was, "Better hurry and catch my mama. Wouldn't want one of the other gray-eyed girls to take your place."

Sora's frown marred her smooth forehead as she turned her back on Mari and rushed after Leda.

"She's not much fun," Jenna said.

"That's not what the Clansmen say," Mari quipped.

Jenna put her hand over her mouth, stifling a giggle. Mari grinned at her friend and leaned closer, ready to talk about how birdlike the feathers in Sora's Moon Crown made her look, when she felt her mother's gaze. She met her eyes and, over the heads of the Clan, Leda mouthed one word, *kindness*.

Mari sent her mama a quick, apologetic smile. As Leda moved from the maidens and children to the mothers and elders, Mari sighed. Her mama was right, of course. A Moon Woman was the Clan's matriarch, and as such was Healer, counselor, leader, and mother to them all. Leda didn't just act kind—she *was truly kind*.

But was Mari truly kind? She didn't know. She tried her best to make her mama proud. She tried to do the right things, but no matter how hard she tried she still felt as if she was lacking—or maybe lacking wasn't entirely right. Maybe it was just that she was so unlike any of the Clan, even her mama, that she never felt as if she belonged. Mari watched Leda with bittersweet longing. If only she could be as easy in her skin as was her mama and Sora and the rest of the Clan.

Automatically, Mari checked the sleeves of her cloak even though the sun had left the sky. She realized what she was doing and stilled her restless hands as sadness washed over her, making her feel suddenly short of breath.

What am I doing here? I don't belong and I'm only causing Mama to look weak and indecisive. I shouldn't have come.

"Mari? Are you okay?" Jenna asked, and Mari realized the girl had been chattering a nonstop commentary about how she had helped the women from the nearby burrows ready the Gathering Site for tonight's celebration.

"Sorry, Jenna. No, I'm still not feeling well. I'm going to head back to the burrow before it's fully dark. Would you tell Mama that my stomach pains made me tired and that I left because I needed to rest?"

"Of course! Hey, I found a whole grove of blooming purple irises. Didn't you say they make great dye?"

"Yeah, they do," Mari said.

"Want to harvest them with me tomorrow?"

Mari wanted to say yes. She wanted to laugh and talk and gossip with her friend and not constantly be on guard, worrying about what the sunlight might reveal.

But she had to worry. She couldn't predict or control if her skin would begin to glow in the sun, but glow it did, more often than not. And the recent days had been too bright and clear for her to chance disaster.

"I don't know if I'll feel well enough tomorrow, Jenna. But I'd like to—I really would."

"Hey, don't worry, Mari. It's no big deal. I'll be here at midday. If you feel better meet me here, okay?"

Mari nodded. "I'll try." She hugged Jenna, and silently prayed that the morrow would be overcast before adding, "Jenna, thank you for being my friend, even though we don't spend as much time together as I wish we did."

Jenna hugged Mari tightly before stepping back and grinning impishly. "It's not about how much time we spend together. It's about how much fun we have when we do, and we have lots of fun! We're Clan, Mari. That's all that really matters. I'll always be your friend."

Mari smiled through tears. "I really will try to make it tomorrow," she said. She snuck a quick glance at Leda before she hurried away. Surrounded by Earth Walkers, her magickal mother bathed the Clan in the healing power of the moon, not noticing that her daughter had slipped silently into the darkening forest, alone once more.

3

F ar to the northwest, just beyond the boundary of the ruins of the
City, Dead Eye made a decision that would alter the fabric of
the world. Recently the restlessness that had punctuated his entire life
had grown to an almost unbearable level. He knew why. He was well
and truly disgusted by pretending that his God, the People's Reaper,
was alive. Dead Eye had known the God was dead from the day the
Caretaker had presented him to Her.

The day of his presentation he had been as excited as the rest of the
younglings who had survived the sixteen winters it took to be proclaimed one of the People. Dead Eye had fasted and prayed and brought
his living sacrifice. Naked, he and the other younglings had entered
Her Temple in the heart of the City and climbed the stairway up and
up to the Watchers' Chamber.

The chamber had been filled with the sweetly pungent smoke of
cedar wood. The bones of the Others who had been sacrificed for the
People were stacked against the walls of the large room, forming intricate decorations to show the People's pleasure in their God's bounty.
Sleeping pallets were interspersed between metal pots filled with fragrant, always burning wood, curtained by walls of vines that had been
coaxed to grow from cracks in the Temple's ceiling.

Then the Watchers had included young women, as well as the crones who chose to end their days in service to the Reaper. Dead Eye remembered that the day he had been presented to the God many of the pallets had held young Watchers, their bodies actively accepting the Reaper's tribute from young, virile men.

"Best concentrate on the God. If She accepts your sacrifice and answers your question, there will be time for pleasure later." Dead Eye's Caretaker had reminded him when his attention had strayed too long to one of the more vocal couples.

"Yes, Caretaker," he'd replied, instantly averting his gaze and refocusing his thoughts inward.

Even then—even when Dead Eye had barely known more than sixteen winters—he'd believed the God had a plan for him. Believed it. Known it. Never doubted it. Yes, the People were suffering. No, Dead Eye did not understand why. He didn't understand why the Reaper, the beautiful, ferocious God of the People, allowed death and disease among them. He didn't understand why their God told them to flay the skin from the living Others so that the People might heal their own shedding skin and absorb the Others' power, and yet the People still sickened, shed their skin, and died.

But Dead Eye had planned on understanding that very day.

The God would accept his sacrifice, and then She would answer him, and he would be eternally in Her service.

A youngling ran past him, clutching a tiny gutted creature to his naked chest as he wept brokenly.

"His sacrifice was not accepted! The God is not pleased!" The lead Watcher's high, reedy voice came from the balcony.

With a jolt, Dead Eye had realized he was the only youngling left in the chamber. His gaze flew to the balcony as he cradled his sacrifice close to him, praying his instincts had served him well—that he had chosen wisely when he'd spent days trapping and then rejecting all except the pure white pigeon that rested in his hands.

"Caretaker, present the next youngling!" The lead Watcher stepped into the chamber, standing before the huge glassless windows that separated the room from the balcony on which the enormous statue of the

Reaper perched, looking out from Her Temple and beckoning Her People to come to Her.

"I present Dead Eye," his Caretaker said. Then she stepped aside, allowing him to walk the rest of the length of the chamber alone.

When he reached the lead Watcher, she turned and together they walked out to the sacred balcony.

Though he now knew the statue was just dead metal, and the God an empty shell, Dead Eye would never forget the first time he approached the Reaper. As always, metal pots arranged in a semicircle around Her were filled with fire, illuminating Her, warming Her. Dead Eye had stared up at Her, taking in the magnificence of Her presence.

She was everything a God should be—strong, terrifying, beautiful. Her immortal skin was made of metal that glistened seductively in the firelight. She was taller than ten men and more magnificent than any woman Dead Eye had ever beheld. She knelt above the entrance to Her Temple. With one hand She reached down, calling Her People to Her. With the other hand She held aloft the trident—the deadly three-pronged flaying knife with which She gifted Her people after the Time of Fire.

"What sacrifice have you brought our God?" the Watcher had asked him.

Just as Dead Eye had practiced, he said, "I offer this creature's spirit to our God, the Reaper, and its body to our God's chosen servants, Her Watchers." Ritualistically, Dead Eye offered the pure white pigeon to the old woman as he bowed deeply.

"Yes, this might do. Come to the pit." The lead Watcher had gestured for Dead Eye to follow her to the largest of the metal fire pits. It was directly in front of the God. Around it, other Watchers, all ancient crones, hovered greedily, licking their lips and whispering among themselves.

Dead Eye shivered in remembrance of the stale smell that had wafted from them and of their rheumy, restless eyes.

The old woman had lifted the ceremonial trident and slit the struggling bird's belly, from crotch to chin so that it had looked like a beautiful scarlet flower had blossomed from its body. Blood had spewed so high and fierce that a few drops had actually touched the skin of the statue.

"Ah! It is a sign of the God's pleasure with this youngling!" the old woman had croaked, holding the bleeding, twitching bird aloft. "What role would you take among the People?"

"I would carry Her mark, and be a Harvester," Dead Eye had said. He remembered with pride that his voice hadn't broken and that he had stood proud and tall before the old women and the statue that dwarfed them all.

"So be it!" The Watcher had nodded to the other women. They'd surged forward, grabbing Dead Eye's arms. With surprising strength, they'd pulled him off his feet and pinned him to the floor of the balcony, arms spread. Then the crone had pulled a small trident from the God's fire pit. The deadly metal of its triple-edged blade had glowed like fresh blood. With a flourish, the Watcher lifted the weapon, asked for their God's blessing, and then knelt beside him. "From great pain comes great knowledge. As you are accepted into the service of the Reaper, you may ask Her one question—and the God will answer." Then she pressed the burning blades against the skin of Dead Eye's forearm.

He hadn't flinched. He hadn't cried out. He'd stared eagerly up at the face of the God and asked his one question.

"What must I do to make the People strong again?"

Dead Eye's fingers found the raised, trident-shaped scar. He stroked it as what happened next replayed through his memory.

Nothing.

The God had not spoken.

Dead Eye lay there, ignoring the blazing pain in his arm, waiting for the God's mighty voice to fill his mind.

"She answers Dead Eye!" the crone had suddenly shouted as she stood, holding up the trident that was covered with his blood and seared skin. "She accepts him!"

"I heard Her speak! She accepts him!" cried another of the old women.

"She spoke! She accepted him!" cried another.

"Behold!" the lead Watcher shouted, still brandishing the smoking trident. "He is no longer a youngling! He is Dead Eye, one of the God's Harvesters!"

The women tried to help Dead Eye to his feet, but he shook off their skeletal hands. Swaying only a very little, he stood before the God, staring up and into Her face, searching for any sign at all that She had spoken.

All he saw was a lifeless statue surrounded by dying old women.

He'd looked at the leader of the Watchers, asking, "The God spoke to you?"

"As She did to the rest of her Watchers and to you, though She is difficult to hear if you do not have the ears of a Watcher," said the old woman. "Did you hear nothing, young Harvester?"

"Nothing," Dead Eye had said.

"Do not fear, She will always speak through her Watchers, and we will always be here to guide the People to act according to Her will."

Dead Eye had looked from the lead Watcher to the other crones, who were taking sharpened sticks and picking through the body of the pigeon, plucking out steaming entrails and sucking them into their greedy mouths as they laughed and whispered to one another.

Then he'd looked up at the God once more—really seeing the statue for the first time. And that was the moment it had happened. He had met the God's metal gaze with his own, and with all the force of his mind, shouted at the Reaper.

If you were alive you could not tolerate these vile old women. If you were alive you would make your People strong again. There is no Reaper. There is no God. You are dead.

Dead Eye remembered how he'd stood there, wishing he was wrong, even if it meant that the God chose that moment to strike him down for his blasphemy.

But She did not.

Dead Eye had turned his back to the statue, drawing cries of shock and anger from the Watchers, who were not too busy sucking the bones of the sacrifice or pleasuring the men to notice. He had ignored them all and strode from the balcony, the chamber, and the Temple, promising himself that he would only return when he had an answer—and as his God was dead, he was determined to find the answer himself.

Which is why Dead Eye found himself there, five winters later, entering the forest that belonged to the Others.

It drew him, that ancient pine forest, as the moon draws the tide. Unlike the rest of the People, the forest had long fascinated Dead Eye. Since he had discovered that their God was dead, he had come to believe the forest could very well hold more than enemies and death—it could hold answers.

It was difficult, though, to be out there alone. There were no slick walls of glass and metal—no mazelike pathways through buildings that hid sanctuaries and escapes in equal measure. There was only unrelenting sky and the forest and the Others.

Dead Eye stroked the puckered scar shaped like a trident on his forearm. The movement called attention to his skin. Cracks in his skin had begun to cluster around the creases of his wrists and elbows, radiating pain into his joints. A terribly familiar lethargy had begun to seep throughout his muscles. He set his teeth against its seductive pull.

"I will not succumb." Dead Eye forced the words from between his clenched teeth. "There will be more to my life than this never-ending cycle of disease and death. The Others do not come to the City, so I come to the forest instead. There must be a way, and since the God is dead, I must create the answers myself. I will find my own sign—my own sacrifice." Dead Eye went to his knees, bowing his head. "Yes, there will be a sign, and when there is, I will take word to the People."

The forest around him went completely silent. Then, with a majesty that was second only to the image of the God that beckoned from the heart of the City, a stag stepped from the underbrush before him.

With no hesitation, Dead Eye hurled himself at the beast, catching it as it leaped back, trying to scramble away from him. Dead Eye wrapped his arms around the stag's neck and set his heels into the damp loam of the forest floor. The creature tried to rear and strike Dead Eye with his cloven hooves, but Dead Eye grasped his antlers and, using all of the strength in his massive arms, he began twisting the stag's head—pulling it back and back—until the creature lost its balance and fell hard on its side where he lay struggling for breath and trembling.

Dead Eye worked fast. He rammed his knee into the point between the stag's head and neck, pinning it to the ground. Then he drew the triple-tipped dagger from the sheath on his belt and lifted it, preparing to drive it into the sweet spot on the stag's spine that would paralyze the beast. But before Dead Eye could strike, the stag's dark eye met his. Dead Eye saw his own reflection there as clearly as if he was standing before a mirror. With one hand he held the trident aloft. With the other he reached down, in a gesture that beckoned as if he had called the stag to him. In that reflection Dead Eye saw not himself, but the image of Her—the Reaper—the dead God.

The power of understanding coursed through his body hot and rich and exciting.

The sign was clear. Dead Eye had become the God! And he knew what he must do.

"I am a Harvester! I will not slay. I will slake but not kill. Harvest but not cull. That is how I will make the People strong again. Then the Harvest can spread beyond the City—beyond the People—to the entire world."

He sheathed the knife and pulled a length of rope from the travel pack slung over his shoulder, tying the stag's front and back legs together by the creature's ankles. With the beast unable to struggle free, Dead Eye used a second rope to wrap around the stag's neck, then he looped the end of that rope around a low-hanging branch of a young pine, stretching the creature up so that it was more interested in struggling to breathe than struggling to escape.

It was then that Dead Eye unsheathed his flaying trident again. But instead of turning it on the stag, he pressed the triple blades against his arm, slicing across the cracks in his skin so that they wept pink fluid. Only then did he begin to fillet the flesh from the living stag.

Dead Eye worked quickly and efficiently. He accepted the screams of the stag, drinking them in as if they were water to a man dying of thirst. He cherished every inch of the stag's flesh, anointing the creature's raw wounds with the tears from his own before packing each strip of the creature's bloody hide carefully into his cracked skin. Though the stag's flesh was alive and warm to the touch, it felt cool against his wounds, soothing the pain and inflammation there almost instantly.

The stag came to the Sacred Place that marked the line between life and death much faster than Dead Eye would have imagined, but there was no mistaking the signs. One more strip of flesh and the beast would pass beyond life and begin embracing inevitable death. Dead Eye bowed his head, pressing his bloody hand against the trident mark on his forearm.

"I thank you, my stag, for the gift of your life. I absorb it with gratitude."

But before Dead Eye could cut one more ribbon of scarlet from the creature's hide, his gaze was again caught in the stag's mirrored gaze. Dead Eye paused, mesmerized by the mighty image of himself as God.

Slowly, Dead Eye began to understand.

What would he expect from his God? Truth—righteous anger—compassion. And through his reflection in the stag's eye, he found the answer.

I am a Harvester, not a Reaper. I must deny myself the final stroke. I must free my messenger to complete the fate I have set him to by sharing my life and my wounds with him.

Dead Eye brought the dagger down in two motions, cutting the noose around the stag's neck and around his legs. Then he stepped back, watching the creature struggle to its feet. Eyes flashing white, skin raining a trail of scarlet tears, the creature staggered away.

Dead Eye watched it go and his gaze was drawn to the distance where the sugar pines grew to mammoth heights, great sentinels that stood guard over the mystery and magick that waited beyond the dead City with the Others.

Dead Eye smiled.

4

It was an uphill climb to Mari's burrow, but she was used to the effort it took to reach the safety of their home. As she came to the first of the nettle thicket Mari shed some of the constant watchfulness she, or anyone who wasn't looking for their death, had to maintain in the forest at night. Instead of avoiding the knife-tipped bushes, Mari entered their domain boldly, stepping easily around the thickening clumps of stinging plants. She only paused when she came to what appeared to be a wall of thorns. She bent and picked up one of two well-worn walking sticks hidden beneath the branches, using it to hold aside thick arms of the sticky nettles, only to release them to fall back into their protective wall after she'd passed.

It was slower going here, though still uphill. The hidden pathways through the nettle grove were labyrinthine, but Mari knew their secrets. The grove had been planned, planted, and nurtured by generations of Moon Women to conceal their burrow.

Earth Walkers all lived in burrows they created from the living earth, usually choosing difficult, hidden places for their homes. Women tended to group their burrows together. Men, even those who were mated, lived apart from the Clanswomen, as Night Fever made cohabitation as dangerous as it was difficult. But the Clan didn't hide from one another. The women simply controlled day-to-day life—raising children, growing crops, weaving and counseling and lawmaking. Men hunted and served as protectors.

In the matriarchal Clan world, the ultimate leader for each Clan was their Moon Woman. She not only held the power to Wash the Clan of Night Fever, she was their Healer—legend even said a Clan's Moon Woman held the true Spirit of the Clan within her protection, and as long as she thrived, the Clan thrived.

As Mari made her way through the maze of nettles she felt as if the grove embraced her, hiding her and protecting her much as did her mother. Gently, she lifted aside the last thick nettle branch and stepped within a moss-carpeted entryway behind which was the high arch that framed the thick wooden door to their burrow. Carved into the arch was the lovely figure of the Earth Mother. Her sides were worn smooth and shiny from the reverent touch of the generations of Moon Women who had lived safely, securely, and happily within the cave.

"And that's why it is forbidden for all except a Moon Woman and her daughters to know the location of her burrow," Mari spoke to the silent carving. "The Spirit of the Clan must be hidden and safe if the Clan is to continue to thrive." She approached the door and, mimicking her mama's movements, touched her fingers to her lips and then pressed them to the side of the Earth Mother. "Please watch over Mama and bring her safely home," she murmured.

The inside of the burrow welcomed her with familiar sights and scents and she shrugged off her cloak and went straight to the washing bucket. Mari dipped her hands in the cool water and splashed it over her face and arms, scrubbing off the hardened clay and the concealing dirt, sloughing off the uncomfortable disguise she was forced to wear daily. She dried her face and arms, ignoring the matted feel of her hair, and muttered to herself. "I wish . . ." she began as she went to her desk and sat. She picked up the unfinished sketch of Leda, speaking the words to it that she would never allow herself to be so unfeeling to speak to her mama in person.

"Mama, I wish you'd never met him. I wish you had loved one of the Clansmen. I wish I could be like everyone else. Then I could truly stand beside you without it causing us to be banished, or worse."

Mari mentally shook herself. "This isn't helping. It's only making me sad. I need to snap out of it before Mama gets home. She'll already be worried about me and exhausted from Washing the Clan. She's always worried about me—and the Clan always exhausts her." Mari paused and then whispered the thought that was never far from her mind every Third Night when her mama was gone. "I hate them. I hate the Scratchers. They use her and use her. Someday they're going to use her up."

Sweet girl, don't hate your Clan. You hold my heart, but I hold the Spirit of the Clan. It is my fondest wish that someday you will hold their Spirit, too.

Her mother's admonishment drifted through Mari's imagination, and she forced her thoughts to lighten, and focus on the one thing that always brought her joy—her sketching. She studied the drawing of her mother, really seeing it with her sharp, artist's eyes. Yes, the hands were out of perspective, but that was really an easy fix. What she had done perfectly was to capture her mother's face. Though Leda was Moon Woman, and the soul of the Clan, she was as plain in appearance as were most of her people. Leda was thick-browed, wide-nosed, and narrow-lipped. But in Mari's sketch, her mother's thin lips were lifted in a brilliant smile that was reflected in the one feature of hers that was truly remarkable, her wide, silver-gray eyes.

"Now that, I got perfect."

Automatically, Mari turned to the hand-sized oval of precious glass that sat in its place beside the pots of ink, quills, and charcoal pencils on her desk. She lifted it and gazed into its magickal surface.

The newly scrubbed girl that looked back did not have her mother's face, though she did have her wide, silver-gray eyes. Mari touched her hair, feeling the familiar stiffness of it that was caused by the thick dye her mother applied to it weekly, keeping the color of it dark and muddy, like brackish water. "Like the rest of the Scratchers," Mari said with resignation. She shook her head and spoke to her reflection. "No. You shouldn't complain. It keeps you alive. It keeps them from knowing the truth about you."

The motion of her head made her hair move, and even in the dim light of the glows her excellent night vision, inherited from her mother, caught a flash of daylight within the mirror. Staring in the reflective surface, Mari pulled a long, errant curl from under the matted mess. She wrapped it around her finger, reveling in the softness of it. "It is the color of sunlight. I'd almost forgotten."

Mari studied her reflection more closely. Yes, she'd been right to look carefully. Her brows shimmered in the light of the cave, their true blond color peeking through the dark dye.

"Mama was right as usual. Time to dye it again," she mumbled.

Not that it mattered all that much. When she went out tomorrow, *if* she went out tomorrow, *if* the sun was covered well enough by clouds, Mari would be sure she camouflaged the true blond of her brows and her face with the muddy paste she and her mother had spent eighteen winters perfecting—thickening her features and transforming her into that which she was not—a full-blood Earth Walker.

Mari traced the line of her clean brow, delicate where her mother's was thick, down her face to her high, well-formed cheekbones, then over her small, straight nose.

"I see you, Father," she whispered to the mirror. "It's the only way I will ever see you, but I do. I see you in me, and I know the story. Mama will never forget. I will never forget. How could I? Every day my differences remind me of you."

Mari put the mirror down and began to sort through the pile of what her mother believed were unfinished sketches—sketches Mari knew Leda would not look at without her permission. Near the bottom of the pile she found it, and pulled the long, slim sheet out.

The sketch was done in black ink, made from boiling walnuts. She'd used only the sharpest of her quills to produce the intricate lines needed to bring the scene alive. It showed a tall man whose facial features, except for his eyes, mimicked Mari's. He was standing beside a waterfall smiling at a plain young woman who gazed at him adoringly through her mother's eyes while she held an infant, swaddled in the soft, thick fronds of a Mother Plant. And beside the man was the rough outline of a large, ever-watchful canine.

"You met by accident," Mari said softly, tracing her finger over the sketch of her father. "She shouldn't have allowed you to see her, but she did. She shouldn't have loved you, but she did. She said that she knew your heart the first moment she looked into your face because she saw such kindness there." Mari paused, her finger moving from the sketch to her own face again. "She says she sees you in my face, too. But we have to hide—we have to hide what was between you because Companions and Earth Walkers cannot join, cannot love." She smoothed the paper carefully with her hand, as if she would touch the father she could never meet. Then she chose her favorite quill, dipped it in the ink, and began to sketch over her father's skin the delicate patterns that would glow from just beneath his flesh as he absorbed the sunlight that gave Companions the ability to turn that which once had destroyed the world to that which had created a new world order.

The same delicate patterns that glowed from beneath Mari's flesh, but would never, ever glow from beneath Leda's skin, or the skin of any true Earth Walker.

Mari bent her head over the paper and worked through the night perfecting the sketch and thinking of the story her mother had told her over and over again—how she and this man who should have captured her, enslaved her, and been repulsed by her, had instead loved her. How they had met in secret, discovering the hidden beauty of Leda's body, and the miraculous kindness of Galen's heart. How Mari had been created from their love, and how Leda had been planning to run away with him—to begin their own Tribe somewhere far away, deep in another forest where there were no Companions or Earth Walkers, there were only Leda and Galen and the baby they swore to love.

"Oh, and you, too." Mari paused in her contemplation of the sketch and touched the rough outline of the canine. "I know your name,

Orion, and I know your story, too. But I don't know your face." In her life, Mari had only glimpsed canines four times, and then from a distance so great that she saw only their silhouettes, never their faces.

"*Fear canines—flee felines—take to the ground or you will be found.*" Mari whispered the warning all Earth Walkers knew. "But there is more to the story than that," she mused as she worked on shading Orion's fur. Leda had told her that the Companions reflected their canines—that the Leader Shepherds were noble and brave, and that the Hunter Terriers were clever and true, and that when they chose the person that they would be bonded with for life, that person also had those wonderful traits.

"Then why do the Companions enslave us and treat us as if we are animals?"

There was no reply in the silent cave and Mari sighed again, wishing she could get real answers to her questions. Her mother, of course, told her that her father's canine had been a mighty Shepherd, that he had not been evil or mean. He had been everything a noble beast should be and everything her father, his Companion, had been—loyal and loving, kind and brave. "She says your fur was thicker than a rabbit's and softer than a fawn's. I wish I could have known you. I wish I could finish your picture."

As if she'd just broken the surface after a deep dive, Mari shook herself. That was an impossible wish.

"They killed you before we could get away," Mari said. "You and my father." Her gaze went to the infant version of herself swaddled in the life-changing fronds of the Mother Plant. "They caught you taking the Mother Plant's fronds for me, and they killed you because you would not betray us to them." Mari closed her eyes, for once wishing her imagination wasn't so vivid, and that she couldn't picture the death scene so perfectly in her mind. Even though eighteen winters had passed since the terrible thing had happened, Leda could not speak of it without weeping.

"*They followed him to our meeting place, trying to trap me and you, sweet girl. But your father had told me to always, always remain hidden until he called for me. That horrible day, he must have known something was wrong, because he did not call me from my hiding place. I had waited silently with you, smiling and thinking that he was testing me, being sure you and I would be safe.*

"But it wasn't a test. The Warrior sprang on him and tried to force him to give us away to them. My Galen, your noble father, refused. He and Orion died for that refusal."

"You didn't give us away, but you left us to this life of hiding." Mari pushed her matted hair back from her face. "I know it wasn't your fault. And Mama, she's done her best. She's kept me safe all this time—loved me and been my best friend—given me a life, even though she mourns you every day." Mari smiled sadly at the man in the sketch, wondering for the millionth time how either he or her mother could have ever believed they could make a life together. "Not in this world," she told him and his ghost. "Not in this lifetime. I know you don't want to hear this, but the truth is I'm sorry you and Mama met. Mama would have found a Clansman to love, and I would have been born looking like, feeling like, a normal Earth Walker. Mama wouldn't be so alone. I wouldn't be so alone."

Mari worked awhile longer, and then finally put her quill down and studied the sketch critically, waiting for it to dry. Would she show this one to her mother?

Probably not. The first time she'd tried to draw her father she had only known a little more than nine winters. Proud of the scene she'd brought alive from her mother's stories, she'd shared the finished piece with Leda. Her mother had told her it was a wondrous thing—that she'd captured a miraculous likeness of Galen. But she had also gone pale at the seeing of it, and her hand had trembled so violently that Mari had had to hold the sketch for her. For many days after that, Mari had listened to the muffled sobs that had drifted like lost dreams from her mother's room.

Seeing that Leda's hair needed more shading, Mari bent back to the sketch, working on bringing the younger, hope-filled version of her mother to life while she wished that she didn't have to live a lie and live in fear—always, always in fear. "And I wish I could finally find my own story . . ."

In finding his answer, Dead Eye had become a God. He knew it because of the power that coursed through his body as he had begun to shed his skin! It should have been impossible. The stag hadn't been one of the Others. Absorbing his living flesh shouldn't have worked. Even absorbing the living flesh of the Others hadn't worked for the twenty-one winters of Dead Eye's life. No matter how many of the Others the People trapped and reaped, none of the People had ever been healed—not truly. Always, always, within a season the People would sicken. Their skins would crack, shed, age, and eventually they died. They always died.

But no more.

Dead Eye stretched out his mighty arms, flexing his muscles and laughing. He had asked for a sign, and the stag had given him one. Let the old men slink about the City begging the Reaper to make their skins last longer, or—if all else fails—to draw more of the Others to the City so that their pitiful lives could continue.

No. Dead Eye would not beg a dead God for those things. And if the People wanted to live, to thrive, they would stop worshipping a metal statue and acknowledge the God who walked in their midst. The proof was as obvious as the power coursing through his body.

First, he must make the People understand. Dead Eye had thought a very long time about how to approach the People. Though he longed to proclaim the truth he knew that the People would not be ready to hear it. No, they would not be ready for a new God, but perhaps they would be ready for a new Champion.

Ineffective old women had been speaking for a dead God for generations. How much easier would it be for a Champion to speak for God?

As dusk fell Dead Eye made his way to the Reaper's Temple. At first he was glad to see so many of the People gathered there among the bonfires that littered the entrance and the great, broken bricks that paved the way to the Temple. Then he saw that most of them were old, with broken skin and slack, lifeless eyes. He thought they looked like beaten animals that waited witlessly to be slaughtered.

He stepped forward, and then turned to face the People.

"Will none of you approach Her? Will you all be content to die here, in the shadow of Her Temple?" he asked the group, his voice echoing from the massive walls of the crumbling Temple behind him.

"We worship the Reaper from here," said a white-haired man who was naked except for patches of ragged moss pressed to his oozing skin.

"Turtle Man, She beckons, yet you are content to worship from a distance?" Dead Eye scowled at the old man.

"She beckons for Her Watchers, and they are with Her," said Turtle Man, scratching at a sore on his arm. "We wait here, as the Watchers tell us, for the next group of Others She draws to the City. If we pray and make enough sacrifices, the Others will come."

"I think She beckons for more than that! I think the Watchers are wrong. Our Reaper is tired of old women and is beckoning for Her Champion!"

The crowd erupted in shocked shouts. With a flourish, Dead Eye flung off his tattered cloak and stood, bare-chested, before them. He saw the People's amazement as they took in his shedding skin, and the strips of stag flesh he had cut and packed into the open wounds on his arms and torso. The wounds were completely healed and pink with healthy new flesh that was closing around the stag's flesh as his body absorbed and digested the creature's strength. He flexed his arms, reveling in the power that flowed through him. With a grace that was more stag than human, he leaped against the side of the Temple, grabbing one of the thick ropes of living vines that cascaded from the Reapers' perch, and using it to scale the slick green-tiled outer wall. When he reached the balcony, he jumped easily over the ledge, and automatically dropped to his knees before the huge statue.

"Though She is not pleased by your abrupt appearance on Her balcony, the Reaper acknowledges her Harvester. Present the sacrifice you offer," demanded the leader of the Watchers in her thin, high voice.

Still on his knees, Dead Eye pulled the rodent from within the pack slung over his bare shoulder. Free of the confines of the pouch, the fat creature began to struggle.

But instead of offering the sacrifice to the Watcher as expected, Dead Eye abruptly stood, brandishing the triple-tipped dagger he drew from its sheath at his waist. As the Watchers gasped in horror, he bent the rodent back so that its body strained to form a crescent, and with a deft motion slit the creature's throat. Hot scarlet blood spewed, arching up and up so that it splattered the Reaper's face.

"She cries! Dead Eye's sacrifice has made the God cry!"

From the corners of the balcony on which the statue perched, Her Watchers rushed forward, jostling one another to get a closer look.

"Why? Why have you caused the God to cry?" several of the old women asked fearfully.

"Can you not answer that question?" Dead Eye's voice was filled with disgust. "Does She not speak through you?"

The lead Watcher's eyes narrowed. "Do you dare to question the Watchers of the God?"

Dead Eye stood, tossing the still warm body of the rodent onto one of the many fire pits. He ignored the lead Watcher. The rest of them were mute, staring at him with a mixture of horror and fright, while others poked sticks into the fire pit to retrieve the burning rodent entrails, sucking them noisily into their ravenous mouths. They were revolting. What were they but fear-filled old women in sick, wrinkled skin sacks that proclaimed they were past fertile years, past harvesting, past life? Lithely, he jumped up on the lip of the Reaper's ledge and looked down at the People.

They were milling with nervous excitement, having taken up the cry of the Watchers, "She cries! She cries!" They stared up at Dead Eye, their eyes catching the reflection of the flickering firelight and sparkling like glowworms in a sea of pale faces.

"She cries with joy because Her Champion has finally appeared!" Dead Eye's voice was a clarion trumpet that silenced the People. "I have prayed for strength. I have prayed for guidance. I have been answered!"

The most ancient of the Watchers approached him, her sallow, sagging face set in disapproving lines.

"It is only for the Watchers to say whether the God has spoken." Her voice was so shrill that Dead Eye felt it like daggers. "Now go! If the God needs a Champion, he will be chosen as all is chosen for the People, though our reading of the sacrificial entrails."

"You mean through what you decree. And what is it you old women decree except the same things you've been saying for generations? But are the People better for your words, or is it only a select few, you Watchers, who gain from them?" Dead Eye said.

"Blasphemy! Blasphemy! Blasphemy!" the Watchers began to chant in their pathetic old voices.

"I agree! Blasphemy has been committed against the Reaper, but Her Champion will right this wrong that has gone on far too long." Dead Eye's deep, powerful voice cut through the whispering women, as easily as his trident sliced through living flesh. "Look at me! Look at my skin! I did not sit idly by, waiting for one of the Others to wander close enough to the City to be taken. I Harvested a stag and our God rewarded me. I have absorbed it. I am the stag, just as the stag is me!" He held open his arms for all the Watchers to see. "Bare yourselves and prove that our Reaper shows you favor as well."

The old woman made a dismissive gesture with her long, skeletal fingers. "I am a Watcher of the God. You are a mere Harvester. I need not show you anything."

"Did you not hear me? I am Her Champion!" With no hesitation Dead Eye sprang forward. Lifting the Watcher by her scrawny waist he hurled her up, impaling her on the three-tipped spear the statue held above them. As the old woman shrieked and writhed in the agony of her death throes, Dead Eye closed on the other Watchers. Panicked, they tried to flee from him, but he caught each easily, throwing them from the balcony to the broken pavement below.

Filled with righteous power, Dead Eye leaped to the ledge again, this time standing intimately within the curve of the Reaper's beckoning arm, as if She embraced him.

"Does anyone else dispute my right to be Champion?"

Scattered around the bleeding, broken bodies of the dying Watchers, the People fell to their knees. Dead Eye memorized each face, noting who remained and who had disappeared into the shadows of the night-shrouded City. He was pleased to see the younger People had stayed. He was equally pleased to see that Turtle Man and the rest of the old ones were absent.

Good. He had no use for the weak and dying.

"We do not dispute you!" First one voice lifted, and then another and another. "We do not dispute you! We do not dispute you!" the People took up the chant.

Dead Eye basked in their worship, smiling down at them beatifically as his mind whirred with the limitless possibilities the future held.

5

High above the forest floor, the female stirred. She uncurled herself from around the last of her littermates—the only other pup who had yet to choose a Companion. She snuffled at him, breathing in the familiar, comforting scents of their whelping nest, their mother, and the raw rabbit on which they had both recently fed. The big male pup sighed, yawned, and rolled a little toward her before putting his paw over his nose and drifting back to sleep. For a moment the female almost allowed the pull of sleep to reclaim her as well, but the *call* sounded through her body again, and this time it was more insistent.

She must not sleep. The young canine must find the one who would be her partner, her life, her Companion.

The door to the whelping nest was closed against the coolness that was coming with the lengthening of shadows. She sat before it and barked twice, two sharp bursts of sound that were far from the puppy-like yaps that had been her norm until that evening. From a cozy spot near the opening, the man who had been drowsing came instantly awake—as did the big Shepherd that lay curled beside him.

"Finally!" Pleasure filled the Guardian's voice as he quickly patted his canine's head and then untied and lifted aside the pelt curtain that served as door to the whelping nest. The man's expression telegraphed excitement to the pup. She met his eyes, body trembling as she waited impatiently. Then the man smiled and gave her the most important command of her young life, *"Seek!"*

With no hesitation, the female leaped from inside the nest onto the narrow walkway outside and began to run. The Guardian, with his canine close behind, called ahead of them, "The female has begun the choosing! It is time!"

The Tribe often debated what it was that compelled a pup to find its Companion. Was it something in the look of a particular person? Something unique about their scent? Or was it luck mixed, perhaps magickally, with fate? Had the Tribe been able to share the moments just before choosing with the pup the factions would have been surprised to learn that neither and both were correct.

"Clear the walkway! Clear the walkway! The female is choosing!" The Guardian cupped his hands around his mouth and shouted, warning the people who were slowly meandering to their nests thinking more of the beauty of the waning sunlight and the aromas of simmering meals than of the young canine who ran silently and swiftly along the winding walkways with a single-minded goal.

"It's the female! She chooses!" The cry was caught up and the Tribe began spilling out of warm nests, eagerly watching the pup, whose pace was becoming increasingly more frantic.

"Light the lanterns. Won't do for her to slide from a walkway before she's made her choice!" A voice boomed and torchlight began to blossom as sunlight faded and shadows continued to lengthen.

As the pup scurried around and around the vast walkway system that tied nestlike dwellings together, the Tribe followed the young Shepherd, knowing smiles on the faces of those who were accompanied by their own canines—and eager, hopeful looks of anticipation on those who lived, thus far, Companionless.

Within a very few moments, the pup's quest was joined by music. First so faint that only the deep, sonorous sound of drums came rhythmically, as if to goad forward the tap, tap, tapping of her feet on the wooden walkway planks. Soon the drums were joined by flute and strings, and then, lastly, by the crystal beauty of women's voices raised together in perfect harmony.

> *"Verdant you grow—verdant we grow*
> *On and on and on*
> *Secrets you know—secrets we know*
> *On and on and on . . ."*

The sweet strains of the Tribe's most sacred music surrounding her, the pup came to a drawbridge section of the walkway and sat, impatiently bouncing up and down with her two front feet and barking in time over and over, as if trying to hurry the song as well as those tending the drawbridge.

"She's not even waiting for the lift to catch!" the Guardian shouted, trying unsuccessfully to grab the pup's scruff before she gathered herself and jumped from the partially lowered bridge. There was a collective sigh of relief when, instead of plummeting to her death on the forest floor more than fifty feet below, the young canine's front paws caught the far side of the bridge and she scrambled onto the wide, solid platform.

The music and singing fell silent. A dozen women of different ages had been lovingly tending the Mother Plants—singing to them—pruning them—worshipping them. At the young Shepherd's very noisy entrance and the trail of eagerly watching Tribesmen and women that followed her, eleven of the twelve singers turned to greet the pup. The women who had canines close beside them watched with smiles and soft eyes, hands automatically stroking their Companions' fur. Four of the women had no canines. They were young, having barely known eighteen winters. They watched the pup, expectation and desire clear in their rapt expressions.

The pup ignored the eager young women, inexorably making her way to the only woman who was *not* watching her.

As the pup drew closer to the woman her frantic energy calmed and the female slowed, moving with a maturity well beyond that of the scant five and a half months of her life. The woman who was the focus of the pup's attention was sitting cross-legged before an enormous Mother Plant that looked as if it was close to opening. The woman's head was bowed. The pup lifted her muzzle, touching the back of the woman's neck where the thick mass of her hair, golden except for a few streaks of gray, was tied up in a loose but tidy knot.

At the touch of the pup's nose, the woman's shoulders began to shake and she put her face in her hands.

"I—I don't think I can bear this. Not again. My heart may break." The woman's voice was muffled with tears.

The young canine scooted closer to her, leaning against the sobbing woman and whining softly in shared distress.

"Your heart *may* break if you choose to accept her," the Guardian said from behind the pup. "But if you reject her, it is a certainty that her heart *will* break. Can you bear that, Maeve?"

Maeve turned to look up at the Guardian. Her face was still beautiful, even though it showed lines of age, loss, and regret.

"You know none of us understand why some are chosen more than once, but it is a blessing, Maeve."

"Speak to me of this blessing when your Alala is no more," Maeve said in a voice that was sad rather than angry.

"I dread that day," the Guardian said, his hand automatically reaching for the head of the big Shepherd that was never far from his side. "Yet I would not change one moment of my life with Alala. Remember and honor the love you had for your Taryn, and for her blessed life as your Companion, but do not allow your mourning to stop you from living."

The older woman's shoulders slumped, and still she did not look at the pup. "It is time for others to take on the mantle of Leader."

The Guardian chuckled, but not unkindly. "The Mother Plants flourish under your care. Your voice remains as crystal and true as it was two decades ago, and now this young female has sought you out—*you*—when she could pick from anyone in the Tribe. Maeve, think!

A Leader's pup is choosing you as her Companion—and that choice is never wrong, can never be undone, and will never be broken."

"Until death," Maeve added, her voice cracking as she tried to stifle another sob. "At death the bond is broken."

"True, at death," the Guardian agreed solemnly. "Remind me—how many winters did you have with your Taryn?"

"Twenty-eight winters, two months, twelve days," Maeve said softly.

"And how long has Taryn been dead?"

"Three winters, and fifteen days," Maeve responded without hesitation.

"And though your pain in still raw, in the three winters and fifteen days you have been without her, have you ever regretted that Taryn chose you?"

"Never," Maeve said firmly, her eyes flashing with anger as if even the asking of the question was offensive.

"To be chosen by one Shepherd is a wondrous thing. To be chosen by two is a miraculous thing. But only you can decide to accept her—only you can decide to open yourself to the miracle."

The Guardian's gaze went to the pup, who had not moved since Maeve had turned, but was staring at the woman as if there was nothing else in the world except the two of them. "Even if you do not need her, Maeve, this young one truly needs you."

Maeve closed her eyes and tears spilled down her cheeks. "I do need her," she whispered.

"Then do what many of us before you have done, borrow strength from the Companion who believes in you more than you believe in yourself."

A shudder washed through Maeve's body. She drew a deep breath, opened her eyes, and finally, finally looked at the pup.

The pup's eyes were gentle and brown, and reminded Maeve heartbreakingly of Taryn. But that is where the similarity to the other canine ended. This young canine was darker than Taryn had been, with beautiful brindle stripes of unique silver fur around her chest and neck. The pup was larger than Taryn had been—so much larger that Maeve was surprised by her size. She knew the litter wasn't yet six months old, though she hadn't known the pups were so large and well formed. She had not once visited the whelping nest, nor had she visited any of the Companions chosen by the other pups in the litter.

I couldn't stand it, Maeve thought as she studied the pup. *Until this moment I have avoided each of the Shepherd litters that have been born since Taryn's death. The Guardian had been right—since Taryn's loss I have not truly been living.* Maeve steeled herself and met the pup's gaze again, only this time she released the sadness that had been shadowing her for more than three winters, and opened herself to the possibility of joy.

The pup did not move. She continued to return Maeve's gaze and suddenly the woman was filled with warmth. The pup's emotions poured into Maeve, finding that which Taryn's death had broken within her, and soothing her damaged spirit with unconditional love.

"Oh!" Maeve gasped. "Mourning Taryn for so long I had forgotten the love, remembering only the loss," Maeve admitted more to the young canine than herself. "Forgive me for making you wait." Tears spilled down Maeve's cheeks and her hand trembled as she gently cupped her face and completed the silent oath that all Companions swore to their canines. *I accept you and I vow to love and care for you until fate parts us by death.*

Neither woman nor pup moved for a long moment, and then every canine in the Tribe began to howl at the exact moment Maeve opened her arms and the young Shepherd hurled herself, wriggling, into her Companion's embrace.

"What is her name, Companion?" the Guardian asked, shouting over the exultation of the Tribe's canines.

Still keeping her arms around the pup, Maeve looked up, her face flush with a joy so great that it made her appear decades younger than her fifty winters. "Fortina! Her name is Fortina!" Maeve laughed through her tears as the pup enthusiastically licked her face.

"May the Sun bless your union, Companion," the Guardian said formally, bowing his head in acknowledgment of their bond.

"May the Sun bless your union, Companion!" the Tribe took up the familiar cheer.

Making his way carefully through the controlled chaos of celebration, a tall man crossed the drawbridge. At his side padded an enormous canine, whose coat gleamed with the same silver highlights as the female pup. The women who had gathered around Maeve and Fortina parted respectfully to allow the Sun Priest passage.

"Welcome, Sol," the Guardian said, moving aside so that the man and canine could get nearer to Maeve.

"Ah, Laru, your daughter chose wisely." The man ruffled his canine's thick scruff. Then he smiled kindly down at the woman, who cradled the pup in her arms. "What is her name, my friend?"

"Fortina," Maeve said, kissing the pup on her nose.

The Sun Priest's smile widened. "May the Sun bless your union with Fortina."

"Thank you, Sol," Maeve said.

"It is a fortuitous choosing indeed that is completed just before sunset," Sol said.

Maeve's gaze found the western horizon through the thick branches of the closest Mother Tree. "I—I hadn't realized."

"Come, Maeve. I invite you and your pup to receive the last beams with me."

Maeve's eyes widened with surprise, but Fortina had already moved off her lap and was nudging Maeve's knees in encouragement. Laughing breathlessly, Maeve stood, then she and the young Shepherd fell into step behind Sol and Laru as they strode across the wide platform and hurried up and up the steps that wrapped, helix-like, around the cluster of Mother Plant–laden trees, leading to the exquisite landing that had been smoothed and oiled to an amber sheen. The platform jutted above the canopy of ancient pines, its baluster carved in the shape of howling canines on which a gleaming, waist-high rail rested.

Maeve gazed around her, seeing the beauty of her Tribe anew. On other smaller platforms, both near and far, Companions, each with a mature Shepherd or Terrier at his or her side, turned and bowed briefly but respectfully to acknowledge Sol's presence before their sharp eyes returned to their task, constantly scanning the land around and beneath them. A thrill went through Maeve, skittering down her spine like a cooling summer rain. When Fortina was old enough, Maeve would once again have the privilege of mounting her own platform and taking up her own watch.

Alive with anticipation, Maeve gazed to the east toward the island the Tribe called the Farm—the fertile isle that kept them alive with its abundant produce. From the distance of the hillside on which the Tribe had fashioned their homes in the sky, the island appeared to be a green jewel surrounded by the Channel on one side and the Lumbia River on the other. Sunlight played on the closer of the two waterways, the Channel, turning the green water golden, and even lighting the rusted bones of the ancient bridge—the one way on and off the island—from the color of dried blood to amber.

"Beautiful," Maeve whispered to her pup. "I'd forgotten how beautiful it all is."

Feeling blessed and fulfilled, Maeve looked from the island to the Tribe that spread like a secret promise around her. Large round family nests, and smaller individual pods clustered in the enormous pines, perched among their sturdy branches as if they had been created by a huge and magickal species of bird. Jewel-like, strands of shells and bells, bone and beads and glass fluttered from the latticework walkway system. In the setting rays of the sun, the decorative strands winked a myriad of colors among the variant greens of pine needles, orchids, mosses, and ferns. On the graceful walkways below Maeve, the Tribe gathered, choosing places near the great, glistening surfaces of the precious mirrors that were mounted carefully, with the utmost consideration, fashioned for form and function—as the Tribe fashioned all things. Maeve blinked, marveling at the size and strength of her people—*when did there become so many of us? Little wonder the Mother Plants have been hyper-productive. Babies were being born one after another, swelling the Tribe's numbers, but I hadn't stopped to realize how great those numbers must be.*

Sol flung out his arms to encompass the vast maze of nests, walkways, platforms, and pods that stretched below and around them. "Behold the majesty of the Tribe of the Trees!"

First, the lookouts mimicked the Sun Priest's actions, spreading their arms wide and facing the setting sun in the west. And then the people below them raised their faces and their arms to the reflection of the last of the sun's brilliance as light struck the perfectly positioned mirrors, careened from the glossy surfaces, and filled the Tribe with the glowing essence of life.

Joining her Tribe, Maeve opened herself to life. The ancient pines swayed gently, as if joining her in an exultation of joy, causing the sunlight to catch the strands of strands of beads, bone, and crystals that the Tribe's artists draped all around the cluster of massive trees, making them to appear as if they, too, were celebrating life anew. Maeve thought she had never seen such an exquisite sight.

"And behold the last beams of our lifeline—our salvation—our Sun! The Tribe of the Trees shall drink them in with me!" Sol's voice was amplified by the power of sunlight, and as one, the Tribe embraced the light that the mirrors caught and reflected among the people.

Above the Tribe, Maeve watched enraptured while Sol's gaze locked on the setting sun. His eyes trapped the day's last beams and they changed color, turning from the mossy, muted green that marked all of the Tribe's eyes, to blaze a brilliant gold as the priest began to absorb the power of the sun. Laughing joyously, Sol spread his arms even farther apart, and as the sunlight coursed through his body, the filigreed patterns of the fronds of the Mother Plant became visible, glowing beneath his golden-hued skin.

Maeve bent and caressed Fortina before her greedy gaze went to the light, and she, too, opened her arms to embrace the sun. Maeve was well used to gathering within her the life-sustaining energy the sunlight provided for all of the Tribe as each morning and each evening its power was trapped and reflected through mirrors, glass, and beads, and shone onto the Tribe within the protective canopy of their home. But it had been more than three winters since Maeve had risen above the canopy to taste unimpeded light, and she was not used to the brilliance of unfiltered sun. She gasped in pleasure as a rush of heat and energy coursed through her. *Thank you, oh thank you for bringing Fortina to me,* Maeve sent the heartfelt prayer to the Sun. Her own eyes glowed and the delicate patterns of the Mother Plant lifted through her body to mark her skin with the power of the golden beams. Maeve glanced down at her pup and felt another thrill of pleasure. Fortina's eyes were glowing with the same golden light that radiated from hers, proving beyond any doubt that she had been chosen—that they were now linked forever through the bond of sunlight and love.

"Movement by the Channel!" a strong voice called out. "South of the bridge. At the edge of the wetlands."

"I see them!" came anther voice, this one farther away than the first and faint. "Looks like a big male is trying to grab two females."

Jarred by the interruption, Maeve's eyes automatically went to Sol. He issued a single command, "Stop them!" He did not take his gaze from the setting sun. And Maeve understood that he didn't need to. The lookouts would do as they had been trained. The Tribe would have it no other way. *All must have a purpose. In fulfilling the needs of the Tribe, the individual's needs will then be fulfilled.* Maeve knew the truth of that saying in more than words. She registered the right of it throughout her blood and her body, her heart and her soul. So she did not turn her gaze from the sun because she questioned the fidelity of the lookouts, but rather because she valued the certainty with which they would perform their duty.

Movement on the platform halfway down the hillside to her right drew Maeve's gaze. She smiled as the lookout lifted the beautifully carved crossbow, notched it, and aimed. Maeve followed his line of sight in time to see three figures emerging from the golden Channel. With a grace that was fluid and effortless, the lookout fired rapidly three times, *Thwack! Thwack! Thwack!* Each of the escapees crumpled, one after another. The largest of the three and then the two smaller figures disappeared into the tall grasses that grew green and thick near the

Channel as if they had come to the end of a beautifully choreographed dance and were bowing to kiss the ground.

"Three Scratchers down!" the lookout reported. "Should I fetch them?"

Without turning his face from the sun Sol answered. "I will not risk a Companion this near to dark. If they are not dead now, they will certainly meet death within the night, may the Sun make their passing as pain-free as possible."

The lookout saluted Sol and returned to scanning the distance.

Maeve faced the sun as the priest spoke softly, "That they run shows the futility of trying to domesticate them."

Maeve felt a start of shock. "Domestication? Of the Scratchers? I haven't heard the Tribe speaking this madness."

Sol shook his head. Maeve was surprised to realize he sounded sad and weary. "The Tribe does not speak of it, but sometimes I think of the Scratchers and the horror that must fill their lives, and I am troubled."

"Sol, we care for them. We give them purpose. We protect them, even from themselves. Yet they are so base that over and over again they flee our safety and care and, heedless, rush to their destruction. And at sunset! They know what waits with the coming of the night. What can be done with such creatures?"

Just when Maeve despaired of the priest responding, the cool evening breeze brought the muffled sound of the words he whispered more to himself than to her. "*Yes, what* can *be done with such creatures . . .*"

6

"S he made her choice! She made her choice! Another Companion is
complete!"

Nik dropped the knife he'd been using to carve the finishing designs across the stock of the crossbow, and narrowly missed slicing his
own foot.

"Nikolas—concentrate. No matter what is happening around you.
No matter the distraction. You must *always* retain your focus when
handling a blade. You know this well. I should not have to remind you!"
The Carver frowned at him and the small, wiry canine that was never
far from the old man raised his head and pointed his gray muzzle in
Nik's direction, giving the young man a scornful look.

Nik opened his mouth to protest—the knife had just slipped—it had
been a harmless accident! But his gaze had been drawn to the old man's
right leg, the one that was completely swathed in bandages. Nik knew
all too well the ruin that lay beneath the poultice wraps, and he silenced his excuses.

Accident or no, the end could be the same for him had Nik's flesh
been sliced—blight and a death sentence, with no chance at being healed
and whole again. Nik looked away from the old man's admonishing
gaze, nodding his head. "Yes, sir, you're right. I'll be more careful."

The Carver was grumbling a reply when O'Bryan stuck his head inside the doorway to the Woodworking nest. "Cousin! What are you doing in there, slug sitting?" The excited young man sent the Carver what would have been a respectful nod had it not been belated. "Beg pardon for the interruption, Master Carver, but the last female of the litter has chosen."

"Yes, so we have already heard," the Carver said, then in a tone that showed that even the old man was unable to keep his curiosity in check, he added, "We heard she had chosen, but not *who* the new Companion is."

"Well, she's not really new, but she is definitely a Companion once more," O'Bryan said, smiling sardonically. "The pup chose Maeve."

"Maeve! She lost her Taryn three winters past." The Carver sounded as pleased as surprised. "Well and good—well and good. I am glad for her. It is a terrible thing to lose your Companion." He looked down at the canine who leaned against him and ruffled his ears fondly.

Too distracted to be fazed by the emotions of the old man and his canine, Nik scowled in irritation and blurted, "Maeve? The female Shepherd chose Maeve? But she's old!"

"And making a comment like that has you sounding like you're a callow youth and not the fully grown man you so loudly proclaim yourself to be," the Carver snapped.

"I meant no disrespect, sir," Nik said. "But I can't be the only one who's going to wonder at the waste of having a Leader choose someone whose life is more than half over."

"Nik doesn't mean—" O'Bryan began but the Carver cut him off.

"I think you should let Nik explain what he does and does not mean."

Nik lifted his hands in a noncommittal gesture. "I think it's obvious. Maeve's seen, what? Over fifty winters? There is no doubt that she is gifted at tending the Mother Plants, and has a voice that is still crystal and true, but shouldn't she be passing her gifts on to someone younger? And there are so many younger people who are waiting to be made Companions and Leaders, but now that a Leader pup has chosen Maeve, there's no chance of that—no chance for anyone else to take her place for at least a decade or two. Plus, she'll probably die before her Companion's life is over, which means the Tribe will have to deal with the mess Maeve leaves behind."

"By *mess* do you mean her grieving canine?" The Carver asked the question in a deceptively cordial voice.

"Yes, but I also mean that the Mother Plants and the birthing women of the Tribe will have lost an experienced Caretaker who might not have passed along all of her knowledge because she was still taking the active part of a Leader long after she should have retired to teacher."

"And yet the pup still chose Maeve."

"And yet I still think it's a waste," Nik insisted. "I'm not being callous. I'm being practical."

"Practical, you say? Nikolas, do you know how many canines have chosen me?" the old man asked abruptly.

"No, I don't," Nik said.

"Two?" O'Bryan answered hesitantly.

"Paladin is my third canine."

"Three!" O'Bryan grinned at the Terrier, who wagged his tail in response at the young man. "That is impressive."

"Yeah, but none of them have been Shepherds. None of them have been Leaders," Nik spoke quickly, as if his response was automatic.

"Do you think that makes a difference to the depth of the Companion bond?" The Carver skewered Nik with his moss-colored gaze. "Do you think the life I share with my canines is something less worthy because they are not Shepherds, are not Leaders?" The hand that had been resting benignly on Paladin's head slapped against the workbench with such force it made the bits and pieces of half-carved wood tremble. "Without Terriers we would have no Hunters. With no Hunters the Leader canines and their Companions would starve, and then what would happen to your *practical* notions about class and worth?"

"*All must have a purpose. In fulfilling the needs of the Tribe, the individual's needs will then be fulfilled,*" O'Bryan spoke calmly, attempting to diffuse the tension that was building between the old man and his outspoken cousin.

Nik and the Carver seemed not to have heard him.

"You're missing the point. I didn't mean that you and Paladin lack worth," Nik said, sounding more frustrated than contrite. "I just mean that I care about what is best for the Tribe."

"Your father's Laru is the second canine that chose him," the Carver said.

"Carver, everyone in the Tribe knows that," Nik said.

"And how old was your father when Laru chose him?"

Nik frowned, realizing what the old man was getting at. "He had seen forty-seven winters when Laru chose him. Everyone in the Tribe knows that, too."

"True, and even though I am an old man with failing health, I can easily remember back seven years to Laru's choosing of your father. You rejoiced then with the rest of the tribe, did you not?"

"I did, but that was different. Sol was our Sun Priest then, and he's still our Sun Priest. The Tribe needs him, and there's no reason for him to retire unless—" Nik broke off, realizing what the old man was baiting him into admitting.

"Go ahead. Continue. Unless what?"

Nik drew a deep breath. He would not let this sick old man get him to admit aloud what the entire Tribe gossiped about—that the only child of their beloved Sol, who had been groomed to become Sun Priest after his father, and who almost everyone thought should be Sun Priest when his father retired, could not be considered for that Leader position *because he had not been chosen Companion by a Shepherd. He had not been chosen Companion by any canine.* And so the Tribe and Nik waited—perhaps for Nik to be chosen—perhaps for another to be groomed by Sol to take his place. But instead of voicing his shame, Nik said shortly, "All I was saying was that Father has many years left to him before his successor, whoever that might be, will enable him to retire from his Leader duties. Maybe you're right, though, sir. Maybe I shouldn't be so quick to judge Maeve because of her age." Nik shrugged his shoulders nonchalantly, as if dismissing the subject.

"You can't fault Nik for believing that his father is unusually strong for a man of his years," O'Bryan said, as always supporting his cousin.

"We all want to believe that about our fathers, and in this case Nik is right!" O'Bryan grinned.

The Carver was studying Nik as if O'Bryan had not spoken. "Remind me, son of Sol, how many winters have you known?"

Nik narrowed his eyes at the old man, wondering about this sudden change of subject. He should, perhaps, pity the Carver. His gaze returned to the man's wounded leg. Maybe his mind was beginning to fail along with his health. "I have known twenty-three winters, sir," he said, making an effort at sounding respectful.

"And remind me, what age are the great majority of Companions when they are chosen by a canine?"

Nik felt as if the old man had punched him in the gut, but he made sure his answer was no more than an emotionless retelling of that which all of the Tribe of the Trees knew. "Most canines choose Companions who have known eighteen to twenty-one winters."

"Indeed. Indeed they do." The old man's sharp gaze skewered Nik. "And you, the son of the Tribe's Sun Priest, Sol, Companion of the sire of the Tribe's last six Shepherd litters, have passed twenty-three winters without being chosen."

"No one knows why canines make their choices," Nik said, hating that he couldn't stop himself from sounding defensive and desperate.

"True, we do not know why canines make their choices, but we do know why they do not."

"Not always!" Nik tried hard to control his anger. "My mother was the most talented artist of the Tribe. She was beautiful and smart and loved by all, and she was *never* made a Companion."

"Ah, but did it eat at her spirit as it eats at yours?"

"You were her favorite teacher. You know the answer to that question as well as I do, Carver. Were my mother here she would say the asking of it was unworthy of you."

"I have no doubt that she would. I also have no doubt that she would have words for you as well, Nikolas. Words that you might not want to hear." As if their exchange had wearied him, the old man deflated back on his chair, slowly stroking the Terrier, who stiffly climbed onto his lap. "Ignore this old man's musings, the both of you. Nikolas, you are free to join the Tribe in celebration."

"Nik, let's go! The sun has almost set. We're going to miss the last of the rays, and there'll be a celebration tonight. It's going to be ridiculously crowded. We need to get to the Gathering before the best perches are taken." O'Bryan bowed his head to the Carver. "Sir, do you need help to make it to the Gathering?"

"No, son. Paladin is all the help I need. We shall follow you—slow and steady, slow and steady." His sharp gaze went to Nik. "Nikolas, I need not see you on the morrow."

Nik frowned and his hand went to the crossbow he had been carving, tracing the intricate design he had begun. "Sir, the stock isn't finished."

"The stock will wait."

"Should I return the day after tomorrow?"

"Perhaps. Perhaps not. Wait for my call. When I believe you are ready to resume your training I will send Paladin for you," said the old man.

Nik felt his cheeks grow warm. *Did the Carver think to punish him for speaking his mind?* "You expect me to just wait for your call? Like I am a novice in training and not a skilled artisan?"

"I expect you to do as you are told, Nikolas. And no one would dare to question your skill as an artisan—it is indeed as vast as your skill as a bowman. It is only your skill as a human being that I dispute. Perhaps with a break from your carving duties you will discover a way to apprentice more successfully for your humanity."

Nik felt his hands fist in impotent fury. If the Carver wasn't four times his age and half dead already Nik would make him regret his harsh words.

"Cuz, it is past time for us to go," O'Bryan prodded.

"You're right, cousin," Nik said, turning his back to the old man and his gray-muzzled Terrier. "I'm more than ready to go."

The familiar excitement that filled the Tribe after a choosing was bittersweet for Nik. It was hard not to be caught up in the celebration.

Another Companion had been made. A Leader had been chosen, demonstrating once again that the Tribe continued to thrive. Five Shepherds had been whelped and all five had survived to be weaned and grow to almost six months of age. And now four of the five had chosen Companions. Nik's father's Laru was siring strong, intelligent canines—a sure sign that the Sun was blessing the Tribe of the Trees. That made Nik feel secure in the strength of his people. And yet Nik was heading into his twenty-fourth winter and no pup—Leader or Hunter—had so much as given him a glance during a choosing.

"The old man was right."

"Huh?" O'Bryan called from over the laughter and music of the Tribe's celebration. He lifted the wooden pitcher from a convenient niched fork of branches in the massive pine. "Ready for more beer?"

"Sure, why not?" Nik held out his barely touched beer mug to his cousin.

O'Bryan grabbed a jutting branch and pulled the little hammock-like swing toward his cousin, topping off his mug with frothy, yeasty spring beer. "Don't let what the Master Carver said get to you. You know he's not well."

Nik looked away from his cousin's kind gaze and repeated, "The old man was right. It's winters past when I should have been made a Companion. There's something wrong with me."

"That's beetle shit and you know it. There's nothing wrong with you."

"Then why haven't I been chosen? An old woman gets a second chance," Nik thrust his chin in the direction of the group of the jubilant people who surrounded Maeve and Fortina in their place of honor near his father. "And I sit here with my dick in my hand."

O'Bryan grinned. "So *that's* a dick. And all this time I thought you were holding a mug in your hand. No wonder I can't get one of those pretty maids to take me seriously."

"I'm not joking," Nik said, scowling.

"Cuz, did you ever think that you haven't been chosen yet because the perfect Companion for you hasn't been born yet?"

Nik opened his mouth to respond, but his words were stopped by the sight of the big male pup trotting through the Tribe, making his way confidently to where his littermate was cozied beside Maeve. He touched noses with Fortina, and then affectionately licked Maeve's offered hand before settling next to his littermate. He put his nose on his paws and yawned. Then, before he closed his eyes, the male gazed across the Gathering platform, unerringly finding Nik. The pup's unique amber eyes met Nik's. Nik stopped breathing. The pup held his gaze, and held it, and then held it even longer. Slowly, the pup closed his eyes and slept.

Nik gulped air.

"He's a fine-looking young canine," O'Bryan said.

Not able to find his voice, Nik nodded.

"I heard your father talking to one of the Guardians. He said this pup is even bigger and stronger than Laru was at his age. He said that he expects him to choose a Companion who is going to be a great Leader."

Nik took a drink of his beer and wiped the foam off his mouth with the back of his hand, saying, "I've heard him say the same."

"Nik, the pup doesn't have a Companion yet. He's almost six months old. He must choose soon. Maybe he *will* choose you," O'Bryan spoke softly but earnestly, his words for Nik's ears alone.

Nik choked out a sound somewhere between a laugh and a sob and started to say, *I would give anything—anything at all if he would choose me,* when there was a roll of drumbeats, like the pounding of an excited heart.

The crowd that was perched around the drawbridge to the platform parted, and with a swirl of her rabbit pelt cloak, the Storyteller made her way to stand before Sol and Maeve. By her side padded her Companion, a tall, black-faced Shepherd whose chest and neck were so massively muscled that the Tribe had nicknamed him Bear—a nickname that had stuck so firmly that not even the Storyteller called him by any other. The woman and canine stopped before the Place of Honor, nodding respectfully to Nik's father.

"It is a blessed day, Sun Priest." Even speaking this simple sentence,

the Storyteller's voice was spectacular. It carried easily across the platform, up and out into the protective canopy of the mammoth pines,
spreading like winter fog to fill each hollow, pod, and nest.

Sol smiled warmly. "It is, indeed, Ralina. Do you have a new tale for
us? That would be the perfect ending to this day's blessings."

"Perhaps. Perhaps not," Ralina said. "You know the dictates of tradition, Sol. Tonight our newest Companion chooses my tale." Her
emerald gaze went to Maeve. "May the Sun bless your union with
Fortina," she said with uninhibited warmth.

"Thank you, Ralina. It has been an unexpected, but magickal day."
Maeve lovingly stroked the young canine sleeping by her side.

"So, tell me my dear friend, which tale would you have me tell?"

With no hesitation Maeve said, "The Tale of Endings and Beginnings."

There was a pleased murmur through the Tribe that reminded Nik
of the sound of pine needles rustling in the wind, but he couldn't
stifle a moan.

"What?" O'Bryan whispered.

"That old tale again. Why didn't she chose the new tale we all know
Ralina's been working on?"

O'Bryan shrugged. "Maeve's all about tradition. And it's an old tale,
but a good one." He muffled a burp before pouring himself another
mug of the rich beer. "When you get chosen—"

O'Bryan's whispered support ended mid-sentence when Ralina took
her place before the largest of the metal braziers that formed a semicircle around the Mother Trees and their precious cargo, the Mother
Plants. The Tribe went silent with hushed expectation. With a dramatic
flourish, Ralina threw off her cloak and the confined fires suddenly
blazed high, changing from the yellow flames of the sun to a mystical
green-blue. As one, the Tribe sighed in appreciation of the Storyteller's
loveliness. Under the cloak Ralina wore a simple knit shift that had
been dyed a golden yellow to match the rich fall of her hair. Every inch
of the shift was lovingly decorated with a rainbow of beads and mirrors

and shells, so that as Ralina spoke her tale was set to a score created by the music of her graceful movements.

Even Nik, who knew every word of the familiar tale, couldn't look away from the spell the Storyteller began to weave.

"And so it shall be the Tale of Endings and Beginnings." Ralina gestured with her words, causing the fringe that cascaded from her sleeves to flutter beautifully. "Once upon a time, the world was much smaller than it is today. People covered the surface of our green earth, choking out the trees with cities of stone and metal and glass, and filling up the spaces in between with labyrinths of concrete over which they traveled. These labyrinths did not grow, did not breathe, did not live."

While Ralina told the beginning of her tale, she moved liquidly to stroke the bark of the nearest pine. "The trees were lost, unnurtured, unprotected. The people did not know they breathed and did not care that they struggled to grow. The people believed in only one thing—nurtured only one thing—protected only one thing—a dead, deceptive thing called *technology*." Ralina whirled with sure, quick steps, moving across the platform, saying, "The world continued to turn. Winters were seen and easily survived. People lived for the dead, deceptive thing, secure in their dominion over all." Ralina stopped spinning, once more at her place before the centermost brazier. Her lowered eyes lifted and she cast her gaze to the east as if she could look through the verdant canopy of ancient pines and see the distant, dark horizon. "But the people could not hold dominion over the Sun!"

"The Sun!" the Tribe echoed Ralina's words.

The Storyteller smiled and her hands once more began to move in a slow, graceful pattern around her.

"It began gradually. Our Sun belched displeasure, warning the people and sending rays of power to disrupt the things that fueled technology. Far above the earth, though not as far above it as the Sun, the rays of power first destroyed the orbiting things that were man-made. Did the people heed the Sun's warning?"

"No!" the Tribe responded as one.

"No, they did not," Ralina agreed. "Then the Sun, ever vigilant, spat more rays of power at the people, and the thing called *electricity* was burned away. Did the people heed the Sun's warning?"

"No!" the Tribe intoned.

Ralina's voice dropped and deepened until, eerily, she sounded as if the tale possessed her and was now telling itself. "So then the Sun belched its power at the people, over and over again—day after terrible day—until *all* was destroyed. *All!* That which fueled technology, and the technology itself. In a beautiful, fiery blaze—all that was dead and deceptive burned and burned and burned." The power of the Story-teller's voice echoed through the silent Tribe. She spread her arms wide. "But our Sun was not sated yet, because the people still did not heed the warnings. As they raced to rebuild their dead and deceptive technology, our Sun sent one last warning, so bright—so hot—so filled with righteous power that it caused the very firmament above us and the earth below us to change."

Ralina's swaying movements stilled.

"The air became hot and thin. The people began to die. The animals began to die. As if in mourning for the dying world, the earth trem-bled. Much of the land disappeared into the ocean's depths, hiding from the anger of the Sun in the cool waters, and taking the heedless people with it."

The Storyteller bowed her head and her voice was filled with sadness.

"Cities became chaos. Chaos became death. From that death new danger was born. That which once was the smallest, the most insig-nificant of things—creatures that crawled and crept—simple bee-tles, diminutive spiders, irritating roaches—claimed dominion over people."

As one the Tribe shuddered. Even Nik sent a quick glance over his shoulder, as if the Storyteller's voice could conjure a crawling thing from the night.

"The good and wondrous things of the world were dying, leaving only that which preyed on others—that which was the most base, the most sinister." Ralina paused, and then her bare feet began slowly, gracefully, to tap out a pattern. *One two three—one two three—tap tap tap.* The shells and ancient coins that were wrapped in row after row around her ankles made music with her steps and her shift shimmered with new life in the light of the brazier. Her magickal voice turned lyrical, changing story to song.

> "But before all could be death
>> all could be death,
> from the ending came the beginning
>> came the beginning.
> For not all of the people were deaf,
>> not all were deaf.
> Some left the soulless cities,
>> the soulless cities.
> And followed the promise of green,
>> of healing green,
> To the forest they turned!
> To the forest they turned!"

Ralina's feet still tapped out a musical pattern, but her body stopped swaying and her voice changed again, becoming soft and sad.

"It was slow and painful for the people who had so recently only nurtured that which was dead and deceptive to learn a new way of life." Ralina bowed her head. "In the beginning they tried to follow the old ways—to build their homes on the forest floor. And in daylight all seemed well. The trees helped the people breathe and shielded them from the anger of the Sun. But as the new world turned and learned, with each night new horrors grew, new horrors slew.

"First came the beetles—the bloody beetles—destroying with their jaws of blades. Next came the spiders—the hunting wolf spiders—trapping with webs like fisher nets. Finally came the roaches—the gnawing roaches—bodies swollen to tenfold in size they swarmed and

covered all that remained on the forest floor after sunset, endlessly killing, endlessly craving."

Ralina lifted her head. "But the people did not give up. Instead they
finally, finally took to the trees!"

The Tribe murmured, nodded with her unfolding tale as they
watched and listened, rapt with attention.

"The first winter was upon them, and many, many died. But the
small group who lived, that first Tribe who survived, *discovered . . .
learned . . . delighted* in the life opening to them in a way that had been
lost to the people who had worshipped technology." Ralina turned and
with a graceful flip of her wrist, she tossed a handful of herbs into the
brazier nearest to her, and the flames leaped blue-green again. "The
strongest and bravest and wisest of the first Tribe took to the trees with
more than their mothers and daughter, fathers and sons. The best and
brightest of the first Tribe took to the trees with their canines."

Ralina dropped to a graceful curtsy before her thick-chested Shepherd, continuing the tale as if only for him. Bear's tail thumped against
the wooden platform and he gazed at his Companion with absolute
adoration.

Nik sat up straighter, forgetting his irritation at not hearing a new
tale as the storyteller came to his favorite part of the telling.

"Many of the people complained
Many of the people demanded a change.
If you choose to keep your dogs
You go from here! We have no food to spare!
The first Tribe refused
They had lost much—but this, this they could not bear to lose.
So, they went from the others and traveled deeper into the forest
Farther from the ruins of the chaos and death of the past.
And climb they did, the first Tribe and their canines—up and up."

Still kneeling before her Companion, Ralina began moving her
hands in delicate, grace-filled motions.

"Winter came with sleet and cold and darkness.
The first Tribe was naked against winter relentless.
They wept with despair, they cried it is hopeless!"

Ralina's hands changed movement, turning from snow to the soft-est, sweetest of caresses as she smoothed Bear's muzzle and followed the swirls of his thick, shining coat.

"It was the Tribe's canine that found their salvation.
Among the boughs of six sentinel pines, grown together to form a heart,
a Shepherd pup discovered a fern that opened its fronds to him as if he was the sun.
The pup nested within its fronds, warm and dry and safe.
The Tribe made nest with the pup, covered by thick, loving fronds divine.
And as the winter passed the first Tribe understood what that Shepherd had discovered."

Ralina stood and faced the Tribe once more, her entire body alight with joy.

"They discovered safety in the verdant boughs.
They discovered beauty in the verdant boughs.
They discovered power in the verdant boughs.
They discovered the Mother Plant in their loving, verdant boughs!"

The Tribe, unable to contain themselves, cheered. "They discovered the Mother Plant!"

Ralina lifted her arms, extending gracefully posed hands upward. The trees above her swayed with a whisper of night wind, allowing the lambent light of the newly risen full moon to flicker across her body so that to Nik the Storyteller took on the appearance of a beautiful young pine tree stretching up to capture a caress of moonlight.

"As Spring awoke the first Tribe and dark days turned light and bright they understood the depth of the miracle the Sun had provided for them and their canines." Ralina traced a graceful dance to the Mother Trees and the Mother Plants that rested within their boughs, heavy with huge fronds silvered by the delicate dusting of hairs that covered every inch of the thick, supple leafs. She crooned to a Mother Plant as she caressed a fat frond, much as she had so recently caressed her Companion.

"You had become one with the Tribe.
Your spores entered us.
Forever changing us.
Forever bonding us.
As Companions, as beloved of the Sun, as the Tribe of the Trees!"

The Tribe was shouting, repeating the familiar line when O'Bryan nudged Nik and whispered, "Hey, what's up with the male pup?"

Nik's gaze immediately found the young canine, who had woken and was padding directly toward him! Nik felt the small hairs at the nape of his neck lift and a shiver of anticipation skittered over his skin as the pup reached him, sat right in front of him, and stared up expectantly.

7

Bloody beetle balls! Is he choosing you?" O'Bryan whispered.

Nik didn't want to move, didn't want to look away from the pup's intelligent amber eyes, didn't want to answer his cousin in case he broke the spell of whatever might be happening.

"Hey, pup! I'm back here." The Guardian materialized at Nik's shoulder, resting a hand heavily on the tree and swaying slightly. "Have to go down again, does he?"

At the Guardian's appearance, the pup turned his attention to the older man and wagged his tail expectantly, sending a little yippy bark at his caretaker.

Nik sucked in a breath, realizing then he'd been holding himself so still and concentrating so hard that he'd forgotten to breathe. His gaze, no longer held by the young canine, automatically went across the platform to the place of honor where his father sat. Sol was watching him so intently that he didn't have time to school his expression before his son saw it and registered every emotion Sol was feeling—anticipation, sadness, disappointment, and finally, ultimately, pity.

Nik's chest burned with embarrassment, and he looked hastily away lest he see that the entire Tribe watched him with his father's eyes.

"Well, pup, I knew I shouldn't have let you drink all of that water so late, but it is a celebration!" The Guardian swayed and belched, and Nik got a whiff of something a lot stronger than spring beer.

Trying to cover just how rattled he was, Nik nodded and said, "Yeah, he just showed up here, obviously looking for you."

The Guardian sighed and blinked blearily down at the pup. "Don't suppose you could hold it until Ralina finishes her tale?"

"I'll take him down," Nik heard himself saying.

"Are you sure, Nik? The sun is well set," O'Bryan said.

"Cuz, we're just going below for a piss a few paces off the platform. We aren't going for a picnic," Nik said.

"That's right! It's no problem. No problem at all," the Guardian slurred. "The pup's smart—brightest and biggest of all the litter. He never goes outside the torchlight at night."

"Want me to go with you?" O'Bryan offered.

Nik gave him a quick once-over. His cousin was well into his second pitcher of beer. "No need," he said quickly. "I'll take him down and be back before Ralina gets to the part about swaddling the babies in the Mother Plant."

The older man slapped Nik's shoulder companionably. "Good man, Nik! You mind if I keep your perch warm while you're gone? Better view from here than from behind you." He didn't wait for Nik to answer, but half sat, half fell into his seat as soon as Nik stood.

"No problem," Nik said, and then handed the Guardian his almost untouched mug of beer. "Might as well keep this warm for me, too." When the Guardian gave him a confused look, Nik smiled and added, "That means you can drink it."

"Well, thank you Nik! Always did say you're a good man, Companion or not. Oh, you should probably take this with you. Better safe than sorry, you know." He handed Nik a crossbow with an arrow notched in it.

"One arrow?" O'Bryan said.

The Guardian laughed. "One's all you need if you're good enough, and Nik's damn sure good enough. Pup, go with him!" the Guardian commanded, pointing at Nik.

Nik held the crossbow comfortably, well accustomed to the fit and feel of the weapon, and patted his leg, encouraging the young canine to follow him. Then he slipped as quickly and quietly as possible through the tightly packed people, the pup heeling obediently while Nik ignored the curious looks that were cast his way.

It didn't take long to get to the winding walkways that spread like spokes of a giant wheel from the Mother Trees out to the mazelike sprawl that encompassed the Tribe of the Trees, and once Nik was free of the prying eyes of the people, he allowed himself to relax and to—if only for just a little while—soak in every moment of his time alone with the pup.

"You are good-looking, no doubt about that," he told the pup, who padded at his side and glanced up at the sound of his voice, tongue lolling in the canine version of a smile. Nik returned the smile. "And clever, too." *If only you'd choose me*, he added—but silently. He wouldn't say aloud what his soul shouted. It would do no good to tell the pup—he would choose his Companion as his instinct dictated, and that choice couldn't be manipulated or coerced—but what if someone heard him pleading, begging, praying for that which might never happen? Nik shook his head. "Not going to say it—never going to say it. It's bad enough *they* all say it when I'm not around."

The pup yipped at him and moved restlessly around his feet. "Oh, sorry boy," Nik said, realizing that he'd reached the lift and had just been standing there, talking to himself. "My head must be full of moss. No wonder you haven't chosen me." Nik sighed sadly and patted the pup on his sable-colored head before turning to the door of the nest hanging closest to the lift and using the stock of the crossbow to rap twice on it. "Need to take down a pup," he called.

The door opened quickly and a young Terrier bounded out, enthusiastically greeting the pup, followed by a lean young man who was wiping stew from his chin. His gaze shot from the pup to Nik, and his face broke into a brilliant smile.

"Nik! Has the big male chosen—"

"To drink too much water too late. Yes. A lot like his Guardian has chosen to drink too much whiskey too early," Nik interrupted, laughing softly as if he hadn't given a thought to anything except taking a young canine down to relieve himself. "I don't have much of a taste for drinking tonight, so I offered to go in his place. Do you mind, Davis?" Nik gestured to the door to the lift.

"Not at all!" Davis hurried from his nest to the lever that released the massive pulley system that served to lift and lower the Tribe and their canine Companions to and from the forest floor more than fifty feet below. "Any time you're ready." Then Davis called to the Terrier, who was trying to follow the pup into the square wooden lift cage. "Not you, Cameron. You've known a full winter and more. You're old enough to wait until sunrise."

"I don't mind if Cammy comes with us," Nik said, bending to ruffle the Terrier's big blond-furred ears. "He can help me keep an eye on the pup."

"All right, but be quick. It's well past sunset, and I don't have to tell you what that means," Davis said, handing him a lit torch.

Nik nodded, his expression turning somber as he latched the door of the cage shut. "That's why I have this." He lifted the Guardian's crossbow.

"I hope you don't need it, but I'm glad it's you holding it," Davis said, adding grimly, "Hey, don't know if you've heard or not, but some of us Hunters have been finding some pretty strange signs out there lately."

Nik was taken aback. No, he hadn't heard of anything weirder than the usual mix of deadly insects, poisonous plants, and mutant humanoids. "Strange signs?"

Davis looked uncomfortable. "I shouldn't say anything. Thaddeus ordered that I keep my mouth shut about it."

"Hey, no worries. I won't say anything. What strange signs are you talking about?" Nik felt a crawling up his spine.

"I found a stag. He was half skinned."

"Someone wasted something so precious? That is strange."

"It's worse than strange. The stag was still alive when I found him."

"What?"

"The only injury he had was that he had been partially fileted alive."

"Skin Stealers! Why were you hunting so close to the city?"

"That's just it, Nik. We weren't close to the city. And we didn't see any other sign of Skin Stealers. It was terrible. Truly awful." Davis paused, shuddering. "I put him down. Quickly. It was just Thaddeus and me on a training Hunt. The stag practically ran into me, appearing in the middle of the trail all of a sudden. I took the shot with my crossbow, and then followed up by slitting his throat. The poor creature was mad with pain. It struggled. Its blood was everywhere . . . everywhere." Davis shook his head, looking pale. "When I hit the stag's artery Thaddeus was close by, and the spraying blood spattered his face, actually getting into his eyes and mouth. He said there was something wrong with the blood—that the rancid taste of it gagged him."

"You didn't bring the meat back to the Tribe did you?"

"Absolutely not. You should have seen the creature, Nik. There was something very wrong with it. We built a pyre and burned its body."

"Sounds like you did the smart thing. It probably was sick and wandered too close to Port City and the Skin Stealers attacked it. Bloody beetle balls those mutants disgust me! Though I didn't think they messed with animals. I thought they only skinned—and ate—people." Nik grimaced, his stomach roiling.

Davis shook his head. "They're completely insane. They do skin people alive and eat them, which means nothing they do makes any sense." He paused and then added. "Hey, thanks for letting me get that out—and thanks for not saying anything about it."

"No problem." The pup yipped imploringly and jumped against Nik's leg. "Okay, sorry, I see you." From inside the lift Nik looked through the wooden slats at Davis. "Hey, don't worry. I'll be quick and careful. The three of us will piss and then I'll wave the torch for you."

"And I'll bring the three of you right up. Piss fast."

Davis released the lever and there was a series of clicks and the clattering of the great chain salvaged decades ago from the wreck of what, centuries before, had been a thriving city of two rivers—but was now a nightmare of death and danger. The platform lowered slowly and smoothly while Nik peered down into the forest blackness, trying to see if anything waited or slithered below them.

Here the moon had a difficult time reaching its delicate silver fingertips to the forest floor, and the best that even the fullest of moons could do was to touch the green beneath the canopy only slightly, not truly illuminating anything, but rather adding an eerie, underwater quality to the night.

The lift came to rest on a well-cleared circle of ground, covered with thick moss. Nik reached through the cage slats to place the torch in the upright log that had been slotted as a holder. Cautiously, he studied the surrounding forest, already feeling the prickling just beneath his skin that always came when he left the sanctuary of the city in the trees.

The torch cast a small globe of yellow around them, which lit the pine needles and moss that carpeted the forest floor. No underbrush was allowed to grow near the lift, though Nik noticed a thick log that lay recklessly close to their circle of light.

"Must have come down in the windstorm last night. Strange that no one cleared it today," Nik said, hesitating to open the cage door as he studied the broken bough.

The pup whined plaintively and jumped against Nik's leg again as Cameron huffed and snapped playfully at his heels. "Okay, okay!" Nik laughed. "I get it. You two have to go." He unlatched the cage door so that the two canines could spill out. "Stay close!" he voiced the familiar command. The Terrier instantly complied, circling back to Nik and lifting his leg on the stump that held the torch, almost getting Nik's feet wet. "Well, maybe not *that* close." Chuckling, Nik went a few strides away from the lift and untied his pants, not far from the pup, who cocked his head to watch him, and then squatted to relieve himself, reminding Nik of just how young he was. *Maybe it isn't too late. Maybe this one will choose me.*

"All right then, let's go home," Nik said, gesturing at the cage with the crossbow and feeling doubly relieved as he headed to reclaim the torch and the Terrier that waited beside it. "Inside!" he called the command that all of the Tribe's canines learned to obey before they were fully weaned from their mothers. Cameron jumped into the cage, and then stared behind Nik, whining softly.

Nik turned, and a sickness began to fill his stomach.

The pup was exactly where he had been when he'd relieved himself, only he wasn't watching Nik anymore. He was staring out into the blackness, ears pricked, and tail up.

"Pup! Inside!" Nik commanded.

The young canine turned his head slowly and met his gaze. Nik was suddenly filled with a flood of emotions—happiness, confidence, and, lastly, regret. And then, before Nik could move, the pup sprinted into the black maw that was the forest at night.

"No, pup! Stop!" Holding the torch in one hand and the crossbow in the other, Nik rushed after the pup, trying to keep him within the circle of light.

And he did. Nik did keep the pup in sight, until he reached the fallen log, which shivered, morphing from a harmless broken branch into a dozen deadly beetles, each almost the size of the Terrier, whose panicked barking was filling the circle of light. The insects turned their dripping scarlet-colored mandibles at Nik, and with a terrible clicking sound, descended on him.

"Pup, come!" Nik shouted, forced to stop his pursuit of the canine by the blood beetles. "Inside!" he called again, but the pup didn't pause. He sped forward. Without another look at Nik, the forest swallowed him. "No!" Nik screamed in despair.

Two of the giant beetles broke from the group descending on Nik and skittered after the young canine. Nik automatically ran to intercept them, but the rest of the beetles had closed around him, cutting him off from the pup and from the safety that waited with the lift.

Nik raised the crossbow and aimed, trying to find a shot that would take out more than one of the bugs, but they were coming at him—fast and with deadly intent. He only had seconds to make his decision—if they reached him, if they broke his skin with their disease-filled jaws, chances were very good that Nik would die.

Shouting his anger and frustration, Nik turned from the forest and shot the biggest of the creatures that crouched between him and the lift. As it writhed in agony and shrieked its piercing death song, Nik ran to it. With a rush of stinking gore, he jerked the arrow free from its body, and vaulted over it. The two bugs following close on his heels fell on their wounded brother and began to slice him into devourable pieces.

Nik sprinted across the clearing to the ancient brass bell that was mounted beside the lift and pulled its rope, once, twice, thrice, sending a clarion of warning pealing up into the trees. Then he slammed closed the door of the cage, latching Cameron safely inside, and waved the torch wildly.

The lift immediately began up and, resolutely, Nik climbed to the top of the torch holder log and faced the blood beetles that were closing a circle around him.

"Come get me, you bastards! Let's see how many of you I can kill with this one arrow!" Nik notched the crossbow and waited until two of the beetles fell into line and he squeezed the trigger. *Thwap!*

"Three down. Seven to go. I like the odds." Nik jabbed the torch at the mandibles of the first of the creatures to reach his log, and it screamed, skittering back. "Fried bug! You know, the Lynx Tribe says it's a delicacy—can't stomach it myself. Just like I can't stomach cats!" Nik shouted the words as he swung the torch like a bat. He connected with the armored head of a beetle, cracking its skull. While the bugs feasted on another of their brothers, Nik glanced up at the lift. He thought he could see that it had reached the landing, but before he could be sure a noise pulled his attention back to the carnage around him and his stomach tightened in horror.

The forest floor had begun to quiver as the true carnivores of the night crawled within the circle of Nik's light. Bigger even than the blood beetles and drawn by the scent of gore, the death's head roaches swarmed, covering the bodies of the first bug Nik had skewered and the two who were still tearing its body to pieces. More shrieks of agony filled the night as the roaches began moving closer and closer to Nik, devouring everything in their path.

Nik weighed his chances quickly. The lift would be sent back for him, but probably not before the fucking roaches reached him. He'd sounded the emergency bell, so Companions would be answering the summons, but probably not before the fucking roaches reached him.

And then there was the pup. Was he still alive? Was he being attacked by beetles or devoured by roaches? Or had something even more dangerous lured him into the forest? Could Nik save him?

"Well, I'm sure as hell not leaving him out here," Nik said grimly. He'd have one chance at getting past the roaches while they were distracted by the beetles. He gathered himself, preparing to launch from the log and over as many of the damn bugs as possible, when the sky above him opened, raining fiery arrows into the seething mass of insects.

The shrieks of the roaches and beetles were deafening, and the stench of burning bugs almost made Nik gag. Then Companions began rappelling from the trees, each with thick wooden clubs in their hands and their Shepherds strapped to their backs. Legs covered by bark armor, the Companions formed a tight circle around Nik and began beating back the insects and clearing the way to the lift, which was careening downward to retrieve them all.

"With us, Nik! Move to the lift!" A Companion named Wilkes, Leader of the Warriors, smashed his club into the skull of a beetle and then kicked it so that its body was tossed backward into the horde of roaches while his Shepherd lunged, grasped a roach in his strong jaws, shaking the insect until its body ripped in two, spraying blood and insect parts around him and his Companion like macabre rain.

"I can't! The pup's out there!"

"The pup? The male pup?" Wilkes said.

"Yes! He took off when the beetles attacked. I have to go after him."

"No time. Get on the lift, Nik," Wilkes said.

"*But he's still out there!*"

"Wilkes, they're swarming. We can't keep holding 'em off much longer," said Monroe as his Shepherd ripped open the belly of a beetle.

Snatches of the light from the full moon touched the flesh-colored wings of the roaches and the rust-colored armor of the beetles, and as they roiled together the forest floor became a sea alive with insects.

"Nik, there's no time. Get into the lift," Wilkes ordered him.

"I can't leave him!"

"He's already dead! Nothing could survive that!" Wilkes gestured out at the writhing forest floor. "Get into the lift. Now."

Nik allowed the tide of Companions to force him into the lift and as they began the laborious journey up to safety, he clenched the wooden bars in his hands, stared down at the seething horde below them, and shouted his misery into the night. "No! Pup! Noooooooo!"

8

Mari stretched the aching muscles of her back, rubbing her shoulders and rolling her head from side to side. She glanced at the dawn hole, and thought she saw a slight lightening. On the heels of the rush of happiness the thought of her mother returning home brought, Mari realized that time had utterly escaped her, and she had spent the entire night working on perfecting the sketch of her father, which was the one drawing she absolutely could not show her mother. Hastily, she set the drying piece aside and replaced it with the one Leda would expect to see. She exchanged the quill for sharpened charcoal. Clearing her tired mind, she pictured her mother's delicate hands in her imagination, and got to work.

The sound of rustling undergrowth outside the cave door pulled her attention from her almost finished sketch. Automatically, she checked the hole and then smiled with pleasure. The weak light of foggy dawn was finally filtering gray from above.

There was more noise outside the cave door, and then came one, two, three scratches against it.

Worry had Mari dropping the small piece of charcoal and hurrying to the door. Had Mama been hurt again? She usually knocked, but not always—not if she'd shared too much of the healing power of the moon so that it left her weak and vulnerable.

"Mama! I'm coming!" she called through the door as she unbolted it. "Sorry, I lost track of time while I was drawing. I'll have your tea brewing right away." Mari swung open the door and her world was forever changed.

Instead of her mother, a panting canine was sitting in a pool of blood outside the door.

Mari shrieked and stumbled backward, trying to close the door against the creature. But the canine was too fast. Though he limped and whined pitifully, he managed to slip inside the burrow.

He was still whining, but his ears were pricked forward and his tail was wagging as he followed Mari. Backed against the moss-covered wall of the cave, Mari froze, unable to look away from the canine. Now that she'd stopped retreating, he sat not far from her, gazing up with eager, amber eyes that seemed to see through her skin to Mari's heart.

He's big, but he has to be young. Mari's thoughts were clear, but felt detached from her body. *His paws are huge, but they don't look like he's grown into them yet.* She looked from his paws to the rest of his body, and gasped. The thick sable fur of his chest was matted and covered with fresh blood.

"What happened to you? What are you doing here?"

At the sound of her voice the young canine wriggled joyfully, and then started forward again toward her, only to yelp in pain and stagger to a halt, pitifully lifting and licking one of his oversized paws.

Mari moved without thinking. She went to her knees before the pup and reached out to him. He limped to her, falling into her arms and resting his head against her chest. Then he looked up at her, again meeting her eyes, and Mari was flooded with emotions: relief, joy, and an unconditional, unending current of love.

And then Mari knew beyond any doubt what the pup was doing there. "You came for me," she said, unable to stifle the sobs that had been building within her.

Mari and the pup might have stayed that way for hours, curled together, sharing a bond that was miraculous and indescribable and life-altering, but her mother's voice, hushed as if she was speaking a prayer to the great Earth Mother, interrupted them.

"Mari, what is his name?"

Mari looked up through her tears to see Leda standing in the open doorway and smiled as if her heart would explode from happiness. "Rigel! His name is Rigel, and he has chosen me!"

"Of course he has. You are your father's daughter," Leda said matter-of-factly, but the tears that washed down her face belied the nonchalance of her tone. Leda wiped them away briskly. "Do you think Rigel will mind if I come in?"

"Oh, Mama, please come in!" As Mari gestured with one hand for her mother to enter their home, she stroked Rigel's thick fur soothingly with the other. The young canine had shifted in her arms at the sound of her mother's voice so that he faced the door, and he was watching Leda carefully, but Mari could feel no tension in his body.

Leda entered the little burrow they had fashioned into home, and slowly bent just inside the door to put down the basket filled with the tribute the Earth Walkers had paid her that night, before she closed and carefully barred it once more. Then she turned to face her daughter and the pup. "Mari, your father's Orion seemed to be able to read his mind. Galen explained to me that their bond was an intuitive one, an ability that a canine and his Companion would always share."

Mari glanced down at Rigel. "He reads my mind?"

"In a way." Her mother nodded. "Mostly Orion sensed Galen's emotions, sometimes even before your father had fully thought them through himself." Leda's smile was sweet and sad with remembrance. "Orion knew Galen loved me long before he admitted it aloud—or, I think, even to himself." Leda shook herself and continued. "So, though your bond with Rigel is new I believe we are going to have to test the strength of it."

"Test? Mama, what do you mean?"

Slowly, Leda approached Mari and the pup. "Ah, I thought so. It is his blood I followed to our door and not yours." Leda paused and smoothed back a sweaty tendril of hair from her face. Mari noticed her mother's hand was shaking, and her eyes widened in realization. "Mama, I'm sorry Rigel scared you. I'm okay—I promise. I didn't go outside. *He* came to *me*."

"Yes, I see that now. There was just so much blood, and it led straight here. I didn't see you leave the Gathering, Mari. Jenna said it was before it was fully dark, but when I saw the blood . . ." Leda's voice trailed off as she wiped quickly at her eyes.

"Oh, Mama! I really am sorry."

"There is no need for you to apologize, sweet girl. You have done nothing wrong, but I am very much afraid your Shepherd has been severely wounded."

Mari's arm tightened automatically around Rigel, who whimpered in pain. She loosened her hold on him instantly. "It's okay! It's okay!" she soothed, petting him and letting him nuzzle closer to her. "I'm such a fool, Mama. I've been sitting here, holding him and petting him, and the whole time he's been bleeding and in pain."

"Don't be so hard on yourself." Leda squatted in front of them. "This isn't something you were prepared for."

"He was limping when he came in." Mari lifted one of his front paws and turned it so that she and her mother could peer at the pad. "Look, Mama, his paws are punctured and bleeding."

"It was our brambles that did this," Leda said. "You'll have to teach him how to get safely through them, *after* you be sure there are no thorns embedded in his paws." She pointed at Rigel's bloody chest. "I'm more concerned about what's causing all of that blood."

Leda quickly wiped her eyes and nose with the back of her sleeve and then gently, oh so gently, brushed aside the thick, soft fur that was soaked with blood, wincing as she exposed the deep lacerations zigzagging Rigel's chest. The pup began to shiver and pant, but he didn't so much as whimper, though he did press closer to Mari.

"Mama?" Her gaze found her mother's as she tried to think through the fear that suddenly seemed to press down on her, smothering her joy.

"It looks like your brave Rigel fought his way through more than our brambles to find you."

"But will he live?" Even to her own ears, Mari's voice sounded childlike and pitiful. Rigel whined and licked her face.

"He will live. I will not consider any other alternative, and neither will you—especially as your Rigel knows your fear before you speak it. Be strong for him, Mari."

Mari nodded and stifled another sob.

"Think of how much you love him already, and not how afraid you are of losing him," Leda said as she scooted closer to study his wounds. "And also think of what a brave fellow he is."

"He *is* brave. He's brave and beautiful and incredible. I know it—I can feel it."

"He is all of that and more," her mother agreed, smiling at Rigel, who thumped his tail in response. Leda extended her open hand to him. With no hesitation, the pup licked her and allowed Leda to stroke the sable fur on his head. "Just as his chosen Companion is brave and beautiful and incredible." Her mother's voice shook with emotion as she caressed the pup briefly, and then stood, brushing off her skirts.

"But your Rigel is losing a lot of blood. Those chest wounds must be closed so that he may heal."

He'd begun to tremble and Mari hugged Rigel closer. "He's shivering like he's cold, but it's warm in here."

"He's going into shock. You know this, Mari. I've drilled you over and over again about how to treat injuries. Now you must act."

"But this is so different from listening to your stories and answering your questions. And he's a canine—not an Earth Walker; I don't know what to do!"

"Mari, pull your emotions together. We have no time for fear. Dawn is near and the sun is encroaching upon the night's sky, but a full moon cannot be so easily usurped, especially on a morning as foggy as this one. I can still call down enough energy to stop the bleeding and make him comfortable, but only with your help. *He'll* need your help."

"Anything. I'll do anything to help Rigel."

"That's what I need to hear. The first step of a Healer is to—"

Leda paused, and Mari automatically finished the sentence for her, "Take action over panic."

"Excellent. Then let us act. I don't think it's good for him to walk. Can you carry him? We must go above and seek out the energy that sustains us."

"He's big, but I'm strong. I can carry him." Mari scooped Rigel more securely into her arms. Holding him carefully, she used her legs to lift, and stood. The pup made no sound, but rested his head against her shoulder and continued to shiver and pant.

"We're ready." Mari panted, too, with effort, but her face was set with determination. She would carry him, and he would heal.

Leda nodded in approval and then moved purposefully to the door, lifting aside the heavy wooden plank and stepping outside.

Her mother took her walking staff. Just as Mari had, Leda used it to hold aside the razor-tipped bramble bushes that thoroughly hid their home. Leda led the way down, around, and then up another winding path, until they came to the cleared circle built into the ridge above and behind their burrow. Here the old, lovingly tended brambles had grown to a height that towered above their heads, exposing a beautiful clearing and a round section of sky.

"Sit here, in the center, in the arms of the Earth Mother," Leda said. "Hold Rigel in your lap."

Wordlessly, Mari obeyed her mother and approached the figure that seemed to be a woman emerging from the earth, half reclining in the very center of their cleared circle. This idol was much like the one at the Gathering Site, though older and even larger. Her skin was the softest of mosses. Her hair, a cascade of verdant maidenhair ferns. Her round face was a perfectly carved piece of obsidian, serene and ever-watchful. Mari automatically bowed to this image of the great Earth Mother, the Goddess with which Leda had such a strong connection, before sitting cross-legged facing the figure, arranging the pup on her lap and hugging him closely. While her mother walked around their clearing, picking from the aromatic beds of herbs that grew in such proliferation there, Mari stared at the Goddess's perfect face, wishing as she had so many times before that she could feel the connection with the Earth Mother that Leda had.

Leda rested her hands, fragrant with protective rosemary, on her daughter's shoulders, and as if she could read her mind said, "You do not have to hear her voice or feel her presence to know that the great Earth Mother is here. She watches you closely, my sweet girl."

Mari drew a deep breath, letting her mother's scent of rosemary calm her, and nodded her head. She may not feel the Goddess's presence, or hear her voice, but she definitely trusted her mother. Mari leaned back, resting against Leda's legs and taking comfort from her nearness.

Mari looked up, trying to see through the dawn fog to the sky— trying to get a glimpse of what was left of the night's brilliant full moon. But all she could see was the bland grayness of a shrouded morning.

"There's no moon left at all. It's too late," Mari said, trying not to cry.

"The moon is there. Seen or unseen, the moon is always there. And with the aid of our Earth Mother, and your help, I can call down her power."

Leda didn't waste time seeking that which she knew was there, and Mari didn't need to look behind her to know what Leda was doing. In her mind's eye Mari could see her mother spreading her arms, low and wide, and focusing her gray eyes skyward. She knew that, even the slight amount of night not yet chased fully away by the dawn was already causing her mother's skin to take on the silver flush that cursed all Earth Walkers—except Moon Women—to madness from dusk to dawn. Then her mother began to repeat the invocation in a voice sweet and strong and sure.

> "Moon Woman I proclaim myself to be
> Greatly gifted I bare myself to thee . . ."

Against Mari's back she could feel her mother tremble. "Ready yourself," Leda told her as she paused in the ritual. "And give me your hand. Place the other on Rigel and focus, Mari. As we have so often practiced, so this night you must do."

Mari squared her shoulders and set aside her fear and uncertainty. Blindly, she reached up. Her mother's delicate hand took hers in a firm, sure grip.

"Now speak the final words with me, and see it, Mari, see the silver power pour from the moon and Wash through me into you, then through you and into Rigel."

Mari squeezed her mother's hand and nodded. With her mother she spoke the familiar words that drew from the sky the invisible threads of power that only answered to a Moon Woman's call.

"By right of blood and birth channel through me
the Goddess gift that is my destiny!"

Mari braced herself, and as she had so many times before, felt her mother stiffen while energy surged through Leda and into Mari, sizzling through her palm, down her arm to swirl around and around inside her, growing in power with each second that passed. Mari's heartbeat began to hammer and her breathing suddenly increased until she was panting as hard as was the pup. In her arms, Rigel whined uncertainly.

"Focus." Her mother's voice was only a whisper, but Mari could feel it through her whole body. "You can do this. The power is not yours to keep—your body is merely its channel. Borrow serenity from the image of the Earth Mother. Though you may be surrounded by chaos or sickness or injuries, find the true you within. Release that which belongs to the world—fears, worry, sadness—so that the silver stream may Wash unimpeded through you. It is a waterfall at night. Rigel is the basin that must hold it."

Mari stared at the beautiful image of the Earth Mother that Leda pruned and cared for so lovingly. But as always the figure was only foliage and art to Mari. She couldn't feel the divine presence her mother revered. She could not find her true self—her center. "Mama, I c-can't. It's s-so c-cold. It—it hurts," Mari stuttered through chattering teeth.

"Only because the healing power is not meant for you. Release the fears of your body, Mari. Focus! Find your grounding and become a channel for the moon's energy. Tonight you must succeed. If you do not, your Rigel will surely die."

Her mother's words exploded through Mari's body. "No! He can't die. I won't let him." She gritted her teeth against the cold and tried to focus past the pain—to release the cacophony of emotions that swirled through her body unimpeded—and to be the channel for the moonfall of water. Yet, still the power was a whirlpool within her. It terrified Mari and threatened to suck her down to drown in its freezing depths.

This was when she usually failed. This was when she dropped her mother's hand and allowed sickness to claim her so that she vomited, dry-heaving misery and moonlight while Leda stroked her back, consoling her with calm, loving words that reminded Mari there would be a next time—she would do better the next time.

But there was no next time for Rigel, and Mari refused to lose him. *Think! Focus!*

"Mari, slow your breathing. Calm your heart. This is no longer practice. You either heal Rigel, or fail and he dies from shock and blood loss. *This is your reality.*"

"That's it, Mama! I need to make this my reality!" Mari squeezed her eyes closed. *Could that be the answer? Could it really be that simple?* Mari imagined that she was in their burrow, alone, sitting at her desk preparing to create a sketch. Her gulping breath slowed. Her hammering heart quieted. Mari found her grounding as she envisioned a blank sheet of paper. On that paper her imagination began to quickly, easily, sketch an image of herself, sitting cross-legged with Rigel spread across her lap. From above her silver light cascaded into her lifted palm, Washing through her body in a glistening wave to spout from her other palm, which was pressed against the pup's bloody chest. Eyes still tightly shut Mari worked on the scene, creating a picture of Rigel's body that was Washed clean of blood by the liquid light, leaving behind wounds that were neatly closed and already healing.

Suddenly the cold tide within Mari was controllable. Instead of drowning her, it used her as a conduit, passing through her harmlessly as she let go of the energy. *I'm doing it! I'm doing it!* And just that quickly her concentration shattered. The picture she'd been creating disappeared along with the tide of power within her.

"No! No! Get it back! I was doing it—it was working," Mari gasped, gripping her mother's hand like a lifeline.

"It's too late. The sun is fully risen. Even with your help I cannot call the moon back to me." Leda knelt beside Mari, gently disentangling her daughter's hand from hers. "But it was enough. You did it, sweet girl. I knew you could. Praise the Earth Mother and the blessed moon! You have saved him."

Feeling dizzy and disconnected, Mari looked down at Rigel. The pup wagged his tail animatedly and sat up, licking her face. Even though she felt light-headed, she laughed weakly and put her arms around him. He nested there, curled against her body and, sending her waves of contentment, Rigel fell sound to sleep in her arms. With a trembling hand, Mari brushed aside the blood-matted fur on his chest. What had only moments before been deep, seeping, whiplike lacerations were now pink lines of newly joined flesh that had ceased bleeding.

"I knew it was true. You do have my powers and more." Leda's voice was filled with happiness. "Rigel has changed everything."

Mari kept staring at Rigel, trying to take in her victory while she sifted through the emotions that bombarded her. "He has changed everything," she said as the morning breeze awoke and, with a warming gust, the fog above them swirled and then parted, allowing yellow sunlight to fill their little clearing. Mari felt the light instantly, and her eyes automatically lifted, dilating as they absorbed the brilliant rays. Warmth filled her body and, unable to stop herself, Mari breathed deeply, accepting the heat and power and light before she slowly, sadly, looked down at herself. The golden pattern was forming just under her skin. It glowed and expanded, spreading with the warmth that coursed through Mari's blood, to cover her entire body.

At that moment Rigel opened his eyes and looked up into the sky. As Mari watched, they began to glow, changing from amber to the color of sunlight.

Mari knew without the precious looking glass that the eyes she turned to meet her mother's gaze had gone from silver-gray to a brilliant, blazing gold—the same color as Rigel's.

"Oh, sweet girl, the two of you look so much like Galen and Orion!" Leda smiled through tears.

"Yes, Mother, Rigel has changed everything and nothing. Everything *and* nothing."

9

I don't think this is quite right, Mama. Could you check it for me?" Mari offered the wooden bowl up for Leda's inspection.

Leda pinched a small amount between her fingers of the concoction Mari had been muddling and sniffed it. "You have enough comfrey and chicory, but you're correct—the salve needs more processed plantain, and not simply the dried mixture of leaves you've used."

"The processed plantain is in the medium basket mixed with cooled beeswax, right?"

Leda nodded. "Right." She threw a smile at the ball of fur curled on a sweetgrass pallet beneath Mari's desk. "I think Rigel is a better teacher than I am." The young Shepherd seemed to be sound asleep, but when Leda spoke his name his eyes slitted and his gaze automatically found her. His tail thumped thrice lazily against the ground before he closed his eyes again, and with a contented sigh began to snore softly. "You've learned more about healing in the past nine days since your canine has been here than I taught you over eighteen winters of your life."

"Well, I hate to admit it out loud, but I don't think I have been the best of students." Mari smiled over her shoulder at her mother as she looked through the medium-sized baskets that lined the wall of their burrow's well-stocked medical pantry. "Here it is!" She carried the basket back to her desk and carefully began to add the gelatinous mixture to the muddled herbs.

"Not the best of students, perhaps, but the best of daughters," Leda said.

"Mama, you're totally biased." Mari laughed. "That's like me saying Rigel is the best of canines."

"Well, he is, isn't he?"

"Absolutely! So, I guess that makes you right again!" Both women giggled, and Mari thought how girlish her mother suddenly seemed. As Leda laughed, the worry lines that had begun to trespass on her face softened, making Mari realize that her mother, who was also her best friend, was aging. A little shiver of trepidation skittered down her spine, and she blurted, "Yesterday, when I took Rigel out, I noticed that the wild carrots in the clearing by the west stream are ready to be harvested, and you know they're always sweeter pulled at night. It's not Third Night until tomorrow. The Clan can get by without you tonight. Why don't you stay with Rigel and me, and we'll go together to pick a big basketful?"

Leda's smile was distracted as she returned to the basket she'd been weaving. "Not tonight, sweet girl. I have called a Gathering of the Clan before sunset, and afterward there is much Clan business to which I must attend."

"Keeping them from eating each other isn't Clan business—it's charity work," Mari muttered.

"Earth Walkers do *not* eat other humans, you know that."

"Not as long as you're there to Wash them of Night Fever, they don't," Mari said in an exaggerated whisper.

"Skin Stealers are cannibals, and not to be spoken of with sarcasm and flippancy. You know better. Recite the teaching rhyme, Mari."

Mari stifled a sighed and recited by rote, "Of cities beware—Skin Stealers are there."

"Always remember the rhymes that have punctuated your childhood. I didn't teach them to you just to pass time." Leda paused, obviously collecting herself. When she spoke again her mood had shifted. Her patience had returned, but so had the weariness that caused shadows under her expressive gray eyes. "Mari, being a Moon Woman isn't charity—it's destiny. You've felt the power and understand that your gift should be cherished and used well, for the greater good of the Clan."

"Mother, I know what you're saying, but I don't feel like you about it. Over and over again you save the same people who would condemn you *and me* if we didn't hide the truth from them."

"The Law was set long before I met Galen, when the first of our Clan migrated here from the coast and the Companions discovered our connection to the Earth Mother, and all that she grows. We were willing to help them, to aid them in coaxing crops from the fertile ground of their island, but instead of thanking us, they captured a group of women, holding them against their will. Without their Moon Woman, the Clanswomen were overwhelmed with Night Fever, and the Tribe refused to release them, killing or enslaving any of the Clan who attempted to free them. Henceforth, the women of the Clan forbade any contact with the Tribe of the Trees."

"Yeah, and if they found out about me, according to Clan Law, you and I would be driven into Companion territory and abandoned there. Let's just say that doesn't endear them to me."

"So you would have me withhold from the Clan that which soothes them and keeps them sane. You would have me stop healing the wounded and sick who need my touch and my skill. What about Jenna and her father? Would you consign your friend and her father to sorrow and madness?"

"No, I didn't mean that." Mari frowned.

"Mari, I often wish your life could be different."

"Well, I wish *our lives* could be different," Mari said firmly.

Leda looked up from her basket and met Mari's gaze. "I can imagine no life I would have savored more than the one I have shared with you."

"Oh, Mama, I love you so much! I just wish our lives could have more happiness to balance the sadness."

"Sweet girl, thanks to Rigel, I believe your wish is coming true. Since he chose you, I have seen you filled with great joy."

Mari grinned and reached down to caress Rigel's head. The half-grown canine yawned happily and stretched, then nuzzled her hand and looked up at her adoringly. "He does make me happy. But, Mama, he's changed everything and nothing," she repeated the sentiment that was never far from her mind.

"Mari, if something happens to me, I want you to promise that you will take Rigel and go to the Companions."

Inside Mari went very cold. "Mother, nothing is going to happen to you!"

"Promise me that you will remember my wish is that you go to your father's people."

"No, Mama! I won't make that promise. The Companions kill us or enslave us. It doesn't make any sense for me to go to them."

"Mari, listen to me. It is different for you because Rigel makes you one of them. You are bonded to a Shepherd—a Leader canine. That is a sacred thing. You are valuable to their Tribe, and what benefits the Tribe is always what is most important to the Companions."

"My father was bonded to Orion, a Leader canine, and important to the Tribe. They killed him."

"Because he broke one of their most sacred tenets—he stole from the Mother Plant. But you have broken no tenet. I believe they will accept you."

"Mama, how much do you know about the Companions today?" As Leda started to answer her, Mari lifted a hand, halting her mother's response. "Before you speak I think we should look at what we *really* understand about them, and not the stories you have been told in the past. It has been eighteen winters since you've spoken to *any* Companion. For my entire life you've told me that my father was a good man—kind and loving. You've also told me that he was different. He loved you instead of capturing and enslaving you, but the two of you knew that you would have to find a new place to live if you were to have any chance to be together."

"That is true, but Galen told me many stories of his friends and family, and though he admitted to being different, he also said that there were good people, wise and just, who made up the Tribe of the Trees."

"What if he was telling you stories like you and I tell each other?" Mari's frustration finally boiled over and she gave voice to the nagging worry that was never far from her mind. "What if Galen made his people into living myths to amuse you and to keep you from worrying too much?"

"No," Leda almost whispered. "I don't want to believe that. I can't."

Hating her mother's pale, strained look, Mari amended. "Okay, okay. Let's say everything Galen told you was true. But that was then, Mother. *More than eighteen winters ago.* And even then those *good* people weren't wise and just enough to allow him to live. Imagine the changes that might have happened during the winters of my life. In that time a lot of things could be different for the Tribe of the Trees."

"Some of the differences could be for the better," Leda said.

"But from what we can tell, that's just not true. Mama, you told me that you've felt a great restlessness in the Earth Mother. Well, I believe you. Something is happening. The Companions' hunting packs have grown. They have begun to search for us outside the confines of their Sugar Pine Forest. They capture more, and not fewer, of our people as the winters pass. They continue to kill us. But I do agree with you in part. I believe they have changed, just not for the better, and Rigel is proof of that."

"Rigel?"

"He's a Leader canine, revered and protected by the Tribe, right?"

"Yes."

"Then what is he doing here?"

"Choosing you as his Companion, of course," her mother said.

"No, Mama, I don't mean literally. I mean how could he have gotten away from a people who revere and protect their canines with their very lives?"

Leda blinked and then stared at the pup as if seeing him for the first time. "I had not thought of it until now, but you may be correct, Mari. The Tribe your father described would never have allowed a valuable Shepherd pup to run loose, especially not after sunset." Leda shook her head, as if clearing dark thoughts from her mind. "Yet you are a Companion, just as surely as you are my daughter. I understand it must seem dangerous and frightening to go to your father's people, but sweet girl, when I am no more you must find a place for yourself and for Rigel in this world, and that place is not in a burrow, hiding from half of your birthright."

"Why are you saying these things? I thought I was going to be Moon Woman after you. What has happened?" Attuned to Mari's mood Rigel whined softly and she petted him reassuringly.

Leda sighed and set her basket aside. Folding her hands in her lap, she faced her daughter. "The women of the Clan announced last night that I must name my heir and proclaim her my apprentice so that her instruction may begin."

Mari felt as if she'd just lost her footing and tumbled, headfirst, into a freezing stream. "Because they're tired of waiting for me to grow out of the supposed sickness I have and claim my powers."

"No, sweet girl. Because the Earth Walkers need to know that there is a young Moon Woman among them who will care for the Clan after I am too old to draw down the moon."

"Let me try again. I know more about controlling my powers now. I helped you save Rigel! Let me be your true apprentice. It's my right as your daughter, Mama."

"The only thing I would love more than choosing you as my apprentice is knowing that by *not* choosing you I am keeping you safe."

"But I will be safe! I'll be sure that I never seek out the Clan before sunset or after sunrise. I'll pay better attention to keeping my hair dyed, and I'll be sure I cover my features. Always."

"I wish I could say yes. You know that, Mari, but it is simply too dangerous, especially now." Leda glanced at Rigel. "The Law is clear. Moon Woman or not, you would be banished from the Clan if they discovered your secret."

Following her gaze, Mari said, "He'll stay here. I'll tell him to. You know he'll listen to me—he always does." Rigel thumped his tail, and scooted closer to Mari, as if in agreement.

"There is much I do not know about the Companion-canine bond, but I do know this—though your Rigel will do as you command, it will cause him pain to be separated from you, just as it will cause you pain to be parted from him. Mari, it has only been nine nights since he chose you, and already the two of you are inseparable." Her mother shook her head. Her eyes were sad, but her conviction did not waver. "I have chosen Sora. I make the announcement before dusk this very night."

Mari bit her lip against the disappointment her mother's decision caused her. "Sora! She's too selfish and arrogant to be a Moon Woman."

"Sora is young and self-absorbed, but she also has power aplenty, and a strong desire to be my apprentice. I believe with guidance she will mature into a Moon Woman who will care properly for the Clan."

"You don't like her," Mari said.

"It is true that I am not fond of the girl. She has been given too much too early, and that has made her difficult. Yet she has a certain logic about her that will serve her well in her dealings with the Clan. Also, I can feel that she has the power to draw down the moon and to wash the madness of night from Earth Walkers. Those things make her the right choice as my successor."

"I—I know I should have expected it, but I didn't think it would hurt this much," Mari said softly, looking away from her mother.

Leda was at her daughter's side in an instant, putting her arm around her and drawing Mari's head to her shoulder. "Don't let it cause you pain. Were I given free choice of all of the children on this earth, I would have no daughter except you. And could I choose between every Earth Walker who has been gifted by the great Earth Mother with the power to draw down the moon, I would want no apprentice except you. But fate has sketched a different scene for your future. Perhaps someday fate will allow you to stand naked in the sun, as well as to draw down the power of the moon. Until that day I will do everything I can to protect you from those whose ignorance would do you harm."

"And all I want is for fate to let me be with you and Rigel forever."

"Then you have been granted your wish, as you have him and me for as long as we draw breath. And think of the positive—once Sora is well and truly trained there will be more time for us—for the three of us," Leda said, kissing Mari on her forehead. "Now, let's apply the poultice to your young Shepherd before I have to go about the business of the night."

Mari sighed, but nodded. Side by side they examined Rigel, pulling off the moss that was packed over his chest wounds while he wagged his tail and lolled happily in Mari's arms, his gangly legs all a-splay, his paws too big for his body.

"I am so pleased by how fast he is recovering. The wounds were deep, and his blood loss truly concerned me," Leda said, prodding the neatly scarring lacerations on Rigel's chest. "But his appetite is excellent. His eyes are bright and his nose is wet and inquisitive." Leda laughed as Rigel stuck his nose into her armpit and sniffed. "I see no sign of infection whatsoever. All I see is a healthy, happy canine who is growing at an incredible rate."

"And look at his paws." Mari lifted the pup's paws, one at a time, offering them to her mother for inspection. "He doesn't limp at all anymore."

Leda passed her hands over each of Rigel's paws before she ruffled the eagerly watching pup's ears, saying, "His feet are completely healed. I proclaim that by the new moon his chest wounds will be naught but faded lines hidden by his fur." He licked Leda's face enthusiastically, making her laugh. "You are quite welcome, young Rigel."

"Do you think he looks thin?" Rigel went to Mari and leaned against her, watching her mother as if he, too, was waiting for an answer.

"Perhaps a little, but he is a swiftly growing young canine. We're doing our best to keep him at least semi-full of rabbit." Leda's gaze returned to the pup's paws. "I think he's going to be bigger than Orion, and Orion was an enormous canine."

"Mama, what if I change the snares?"

"Change them? How so?" her mother asked.

"Make it so that they don't kill the snared rabbit. I've been thinking about it a lot during the past few nights, and look what I came up with." Mari hurried to the pile of sketches on her desk and pulled out a long sheet of paper that was filled with drawings of a strange-looking rectangular-shaped basket. "Do you think you could weave a basket like this?" Mari pointed at one of the more finished sketches. "With an opening that allows the rabbit to go in, but closes once the trap is tripped and won't let him come back out, like this drawing, here."

Leda studied the sketches. "I believe I could."

"Good! Then all I need to do is to catch a male and a female, then it won't be long and Rigel will have all the rabbit he can eat. Actually, we will, too!"

"You are remarkable, Mari," Leda said. A small shiver passed through her body. She sighed wearily and the happiness that had been in her voice dissipated like dew before a summer sun. "I feel dusk approaching. The Clan will be at the Gathering in expectation of my announcement. I will be glad when this night is over."

"Well, Rigel and I will be here when this night is over, waiting for you like always, and I promise to have your tea brewed and ready." Mari purposefully lightened the mood, hating that as night drew near her mother looked more and more burdened.

"Then I will leave you early and, hopefully, return early as well. See, sweet girl, there is positive already happening in taking on Sora as apprentice. I will begin tonight in passing a few duties on to her."

"You're right, Mama. All will be well."

"No more sadness and fretting?"

"No more," Mari said brightly. "What can I do to help you get ready?" Mari said, determined to only show her mother support. *Maybe Sora will be good for Mama, and for us.*

In no time, Mari was saying good-bye to her mother and sliding the barring plank into its well-grooved slot. Though this night she did not take up her usual place at her desk. This night she stood, listening carefully at the door with Rigel sitting expectantly at her side. Mari glanced down at her Shepherd. "That's right. Tonight is different. Tonight we follow her."

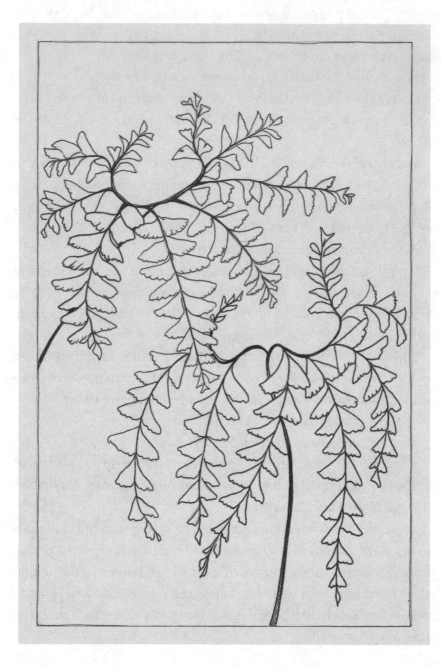

I O

Mari hurried to the pallet she shared with Rigel. From the ledge beside their bed she took down three small wooden cups. One held a thick clay substance, another charcoal mixed with dirt, and the third a dark dye made from walnut shells. Going to her desk she quickly used the mirror to check her reflection, reapplying dye and clay and dirt to cover her delicate features and camouflage the true color of her hair. When she was happy with her reflection, she rechecked Rigel's chest wounds, being sure the sticky poultice was securely in place.

The pup had, as always, been watching her and moving around the burrow with her, preferring to stay as close as possible to Mari. He definitely felt Mari's shift in emotion, and reflected her excitement with his own puppyish nervous energy—bounding around her, tongue lolling in expectation.

"Okay, we're going to take it slow, but we are going after Mama," she told him. "We're just going to watch—to be sure everything is okay. She's been talking so much about the restlessness in the Earth Mother that I can't shake the feeling that something's going to happen, and if it does we need to be there for her." As she spoke, Mari went to a large basket full of smooth, robin's egg–size stones. Carefully choosing several of them, she filled a leather pouch. Then she took her favorite leather sling and stuffed it into the pouch as well.

She paused before their collection of sharpened flint knives, picking the one she liked to use best for chopping, and added it to her pouch. Next Mari unhooked the precious goatskin bag that hung near the door and was a match to the bag her mother took with her every night. Out of a lifetime of habit, she lifted it, testing its fullness. Satisfied, she hung it across her shoulder and neck. Then Mari met Rigel's bright, intelligent gaze and focused her thoughts into soothing emotion, which she telegraphed to him as she spoke. "It's different tonight. We're not just sneaking out so that you can relieve yourself. We're going *out*. We have to be silent. We can't let them see us or hear us. No one can know we're there."

Rigel understood; she knew he did. It wasn't like the canine answered her with words—that was impossible. It was a sense she had—a feeling of completion and understanding, one that grew and strengthened every day she spent with Rigel.

"Okay, we're as ready as we'll ever be. Let's go."

Mari opened the door and took her walking staff from its resting place. Rigel waited patiently for her to lead the way, holding aside the thick arms of heavily thorned brambles so that he could follow her without injury through the maze of hidden pathways around their burrow. As if he had been with her for years and not days, Rigel remained silent and close until they cleared the bramble thicket.

From there Mari had several choices of which way to go. Leda would be proclaiming her heir, which meant she would go to a Gathering Site that was larger and more easily accessed than the full moon site. Mari began to sift through the possibilities in her mind, trying to anticipate which would host that night's important announcement.

It might seem as if the Clan was a ragged group of people, barely scratching out an existence from the earth, but that was far from true. Earth Walkers were highly social, with a complex system of Gathering Sites that had been molded into the skin of the earth between clusters of burrows. Mari's Clan were skilled weavers, and they filled those burrows with hemp tapestries, dyed with delicate beauty, just as they wove incredibly intricate baskets, nets, traps, and even clothing. Clanswomen

were undisputed rulers, making all decisions, from where new burrows and gardens should be built to which other Clans they should
trade with and how often. They taught the children to read and write
through the telling of ancient myths from a world that no longer existed anywhere except in the imagination.

And above all—Moon Women were revered as the physical incarna-
tion of the Great Earth Mother, and as the Spirit of the Clan.

So where would the Weaver Clan gather this night? Near which
cluster of well-concealed burrows? Mari knew where each of the Earth
Walker sites were located, she and Leda mapped them frequently,
keeping scrolls updated as well as committing them to memory. But
there were many Gathering Sites, and Mari had no time for a wrong
choice. She couldn't watch over her mother if night fell before Mari
found her. Only a fool or an Earth Walker fully in the midst of Night
Fever would wander the forest alone after dusk.

Which way had she gone?

Mari paused, listening intently, hoping she might hear a rustling in
the distant underbrush that would give her some indication of which
direction Leda had gone, but the only sound was that of a jay in a nearby
tree, calling his displeasure at Rigel.

Mari glanced down at the pup. He sat beside her, ears pricked, looking off into the distance knowingly, as if the wilderness around them
whispered secrets only he could understand.

That's it! Mari realized. *He does know things I don't—smell things
I don't—hear things I don't.* Mari crouched beside Rigel and took his
face between her hands. She and the young Shepherd locked gazes as
she sketched within her mind an image of Leda.

"Find her," she told him. "Find Mama!"

Instantly the pup went to work. Nose to the ground he began to
weave a serpentine pattern back and forth, side to side, until suddenly
his tail went up and he stopped, sitting expectantly before a small pathway that led to the northwest and looking back at Mari.

"You're so smart and handsome!" Mari kissed and hugged the
pup. "If this is the path she chose, then the Clan must be Gathering by

Crawfish Creek beside that big grove of cherry trees. Okay, remember—silently and swiftly. No one can know we're watching."

Then it was Mari's turn to lead Rigel as she left the little path—not trusting that latecomers to the Gathering wouldn't overtake her—and made her way northwest, halting only when Rigel pushed ahead of her, whining softly, ears pricked and tail up.

Mari knelt beside Rigel, listening intently. The faint sound of water was carried to her on the wind that brushed against her face, and within the voice of the creek she heard the familiar sound of her mother speaking calmly and slowly. On her hands and knees, Mari crept forward, Rigel beside her, until she came to a holly bush that had grown fat as a spring lilac and tall as a tree. Ignoring the stinging spikes that tipped each slick leaf cluster and scratched at their faces and arms, Mari and Rigel burrowed their way beneath the concealing branches of the needle-like foliage. From the impromptu hiding spot under the holly, Mari peered down and over the steep bank.

Crawfish Creek was usually a lazy stretch of clear water with enough river rock in its bed that it made for easy crossing, as well as an excellent breeding ground for tasty little crawfish, though as Mari studied the area she noted that the creek was filled with spring rain that made it swollen and muddy. The opposite side of the creek had a gentle bank that smoothed gracefully down to create a beautiful little clearing, behind which was a grove of mature cherry trees that were just starting to bud into their pink and white flowers. The Gathering area was one of Mari's favorites, and she smiled in remembrance of the foggy days she and her mother had spent tending the Earth Mother idols that appeared to miraculously materialize from the ground. There were six images of the Earth Mother in the glade, each easily thrice the size of a human woman, and each in a different pose. Some of them were lying on their sides, stone faces carved with serene smiles and closed eyes, as if in eternal, dream-filled sleep. Some were leaning against boulders that had been carefully placed so long ago that how they had arrived there had been utterly forgotten. And one idol, Mari's favorite, lay on her stomach, with her head resting on her hands, smiling as if she knew a particularly fascinating secret. Her face had been carved from an enormous gray stone. Her long, thick hair was made of ivy that Mari had pruned just weeks before on a lazy, rainy morning. "Magick or not, they *are* beautiful," Mari told Rigel softly. Then the people of her Clan drew her attention from the idols as Earth Walkers greeted one another and chose places to sit around the circled images of their Earth Mother.

Mari blinked in astonishment. She had never seen so many Earth Walkers together at one time! Though it wasn't long until dusk, the Gathering was not a somber waiting, but had the atmosphere of a celebration, and the Clan's excited voices lifted easily to her hiding place. Mari quickly counted forty-five women, twenty men, and seventeen children—including Jenna, who was rushing to greet Leda.

"Leda! Leda! Is Mari with you tonight?" Jenna asked eagerly.

Leda hugged Jenna. "No, Jenna. Mari cannot join the gathering this night."

"She's been really sick lately," Jenna said sadly. "I miss her."

"And she misses you," Leda said.

"Is Mari still not well?" asked Xander, bowing respectfully to Leda.

"Mari's health is always precarious. You know how delicate she can be," Leda said, repeating the words that had become a lifelong excuse to keep her daughter separated from the Clan, and to keep her secrets hidden, even from Mari's only friend and her father.

"But she has your powers," Jenna insisted. "I know she does. Her eyes are just like yours."

"That they are, child," Leda said kindly. "And Mari does have power, but it is as unpredictable as her health."

"So it is true. You are not choosing Mari tonight," said Xander.

"I am not choosing Mari tonight," Leda said firmly.

"I'm really sorry," Jenna said. "I was hoping she would be strong enough."

"I was hoping the same, child, and so was Mari," Leda said. "But it is not to be."

Mari wrapped her arms around herself as if to keep her heart from bursting from her chest. She wanted to run down the bank, take her place at her mother's side, and once and for all claim her birthright without being frightened that she would be cursed for her fair hair and sunlight-absorbing skin. She closed her eyes against the wave of long-ing, feeling so weary of being different that she felt unimaginably sad and alone.

Rigel pressed against her, lending silent comfort and reminding Mari that she wasn't truly alone, and that her emotions no longer only affected herself. Mari hugged the pup to her, focusing on releasing her sadness, imagining that it washed over and then through her, dissi-pating into the fertile ground beneath her before Mari returned her attention to her mother.

Leda had moved to the center of the mossy clearing. She lifted her staff and then brought the end of it down on the felled log before her, once, twice, thrice. An expectant silence fell over the Clan. Leda raised her chin and stood straight and strong. The wind caught her long hair, lifting it in a dark, silver-tinged curtain around her.

"I am your Moon Woman. It is my destiny to care for Clan Weaver, and it is because of my destiny that I have heard and considered the concerns of our people. I agree. It is time that I name my heir so that she may begin to walk the apprentice's path."

Leda paused, looking from Clan member to Clan member, allowing each one time to nod their agreement and to feel as if it was because of their concerns, in particular, that the Moon Woman spoke. In the dimming light of encroaching dusk, Mari thought Leda looked full of power, wild and beautiful and wise, like one of the forest fae from the tales her mother had told her as a child.

"All Earth Walker women with the silver-gray eyes of the moon-touched, step forward and present yourselves to me!" Leda commanded.

Mari gritted her teeth against her desire to answer her mother's call and to step forward along with the four girls who moved quickly into the center of the gathering to bow before Leda.

Three of the four girls bowed deeply, respectfully. Sora, of course, was different. Though she, too, bowed to their Moon Woman, it seemed to Mari that her movements were too languid to show the proper respect. When Leda released them and the four straightened, Sora instantly lifted her head and tossed back her thick black hair. This night she wore no crown, but her hair was ornately braided with feathers and beads and shells, cascading down her back almost to her curving waist. Mari scowled. Sora's entire demeanor radiated an arrogant confidence that was wholly inappropriate for one who someday would embody the Great Mother Goddess and hold safe the Spirit of the Clan.

"Before I begin the naming of my apprentice I want to honor these four young Clanswomen." Leda smiled warmly at each girl. "All have potential. All have talent. I will name only one to train and to eventually take over my responsibilities, but any of the four of you could mature into a wonderful Moon Woman. If I do not name you, you are free to look to another Clan and to set your name forth as one who wishes to apprentice. Do you understand?"

The four young women nodded together. Mari thought three of the four looked nervous. Sora looked like Sora—beautiful and utterly sure of herself.

"Isabel, I see you and acknowledge your willingness to serve your Clan," Leda began. "Though I do not name you as my heir, I ask the Great Mother to bless you with strength and safety."

"Thank you, Moon Woman." The girl named Isabel bowed again to Leda before hurrying with obvious relief back to her place among the Clan.

"Danita, I see you and acknowledge your willingness to serve your Clan. Though I do not name you as my heir, I ask the Great Mother to bless you with health and happiness."

Danita didn't look as relieved as had Isabel, but she bowed deeply and smiled at Leda before rejoining her mother and sister on nearby logs.

Though Mari knew her mother was going to name Sora as her heir, she could feel the Clan's excitement and expectation as the two young, gray-eyed women waited silently for Leda to continue.

They don't know, Mari realized as she studied the people. Then her gaze went to Sora, who was staring at Leda with such intensity that even from her vantage point above them Mari could feel her desire. *Mama hasn't told any of them that she's choosing Sora, not even Sora herself.* With a jolt Mari understood why. *She really did want to name me her heir, and it was only nine days ago that she truly gave up hope of doing so.* Mari stifled a sob and put her arm around Rigel. The pup leaned into her, lending her comfort and strength. Mari whispered into Rigel's ear, "I'll never be sorry you found me, but I wish it was possible to be both— your Companion *and* Mama's heir." Rigel crawled into her lap. Mari wiped her eyes and kept watching the scene unfold below them.

"Eunice, I see you and acknowledge your willingness to serve your Clan. Though I do not name you as my heir, I ask the Great Mother to bless you with love and laughter."

Mari didn't watch Eunice bow and retreat to the clan. Her attention was focused on Sora. Standing before Leda, the girl seemed to blaze with a fierceness that boarded on predatory. She had been born the same fall as had Mari, so they were of an age—but age is where their resemblance ended. Mari was tall, with a body more slender and graceful than was normal for an Earth Walker. Sora was shorter even than petite Leda, but her body was lush with a fullness to her breasts and hips that signaled to Mari that, unlike the rest of the woman of the Clan, the girl did little work.

Is Sora already accepting the tribute due only to a Moon Woman? Mari made an irritated mental note at the thought of a Clanswoman doing something so disrespectful. She'd bring up the subject with her mother. Perhaps a good part of Sora's apprenticeship should involve hard physical labor.

"Sora, I see you and acknowledge your willingness to serve your Clan. I hereby name you Moon Woman of the Weaver Clan, and my official heir. Do you accept my naming?"

"I do!" The excitement in Sora's voice shouted above Leda's.

Leda turned a complete circle as she asked, "Women of the Clan, do you accept my naming of Sora as Moon Woman?"

"We do," came the Clanswomen's joined cry. Mari thought it was interesting to note that the women seemed less exuberant in their response than the men, who stood and clapped and whistled.

"So I have proclaimed, and so the Clanswomen have agreed. Sora is my apprentice. Hereafter, the mystery of the moon's power will reveal itself to her so that the Clan may continue to be Washed of the madness and misery that comes with Night Fever." Leda, moving more stiffly than Mari liked to see, bowed to Sora as the girl seemed to glow with pleasure.

Mari was thinking about how much she would like to wipe the smug, victorious look from Sora's face when Rigel's body turned to stone.

"What is it?" she whispered.

Rigel's ears were pricked forward, as if he was still watching Leda, but as Mari studied him more closely she saw that his gaze was focused into the distance behind the gathered clan. Completely silent, Rigel moved out of Mari's lap. He stepped forward, pressing against the holly boundary. His tail lifted, and as it did, all of the fur along his neck and back raised. He turned his head and met her concerned gaze, and Mari was filled with an overwhelming desire to run away—back in the direction they had come—back to hide in the safety of their burrow.

Danger was coming to the Clan, Mari was absolutely certain of it.

She didn't hesitate. Within her mind she sketched a picture of their home with Rigel sitting before the entrance to the briar patch. "Go home, Rigel! Now!" she said.

Rigel trembled and whined softly, but he didn't leave her.

Mari held the image in her mind, adding herself and her mother to the sketch. "Go home! Now! Mama and I will be right behind you!"

With one last, miserable look at her, Rigel turned and crawled out of the concealing holly, sprinting back through the brush, retracing the way they had come. Mari made sure he was out of sight before she pushed through the prickly bush the opposite direction. Before she'd actually considered what she was going to say, Mari was already starting to pick her way down the treacherous bank. She squinted and stared into the grove of cherry trees behind the Gathering Site, trying to see through the fading light and catch sight of whatever danger Rigel had sensed.

A movement at the edge of her vision drew her attention. Mari paused, concentrating. Behind the Clan, just before the grove of cherry trees began, there was a thick patch of mature ferns that had begun to shake, as if a sudden gust of wind had blown through them.

But the wind had stilled until there was not even the slightest of breezes. As Mari watched in horror, the ferns burst apart so that men—tall and blond and carrying crossbows notched at the ready—sprinted forward, descending on the gathering.

Mari cupped her hands around her mouth and shouted, "Companions are coming! *Run!*"

Her mother's head whipped up, and her eyes instantly found her daughter. "Mari?"

"Behind you, Mama!" She pointed over her mother's head and repeated, "Run!"

Leda hesitated not a moment longer. "Earth Walkers, let night's madness fuel your flight. Flee to find safety!"

The Clan exploded into movement. There was no breath wasted on screams or cries of terror. Children ran silently to their mothers, and just as silently their mothers lifted them and raced off, fleet as clever deer, into the forest. Some men turned to face the intruders. Some men sprinted into the darkening forest.

Mari was sliding halfway down the bank when the first arrow struck through the neck of one of the Clansmen who had chosen to stay and face the Companions. His death cry gurgled through blood and he fell, twitching, not far from Leda.

"Mama! Hurry!" Mari cried, motioning for her mother to come to her. *We can hide in the holly. They won't expect any of us to stay that close. They'll pass by—they'll pass by!* Mari's mind worked frantically as her mother rushed into the creek, trudging laboriously through swift, thigh-deep water toward her.

A blond man jumped over a moss-covered log, saw Leda, and headed into the water. Close behind him another man paused long enough to yell, "Don't waste time with the old one. Get the girl on the other bank!" before he followed a mother and her infant daughter into the brush.

Girl on the other bank? He means me! Panic deadened Mari's reaction, and her body didn't seem to remember how to move.

The first man grunted in agreement with his friend, and plowed through the water past Leda. "No!" her mother cried. "Not my daughter!" With a thunderbolt of fear, Mari watched her mother grab at the man's clothing. She caught his shirt and pulled, causing him to pause in his headlong rush—but only long enough for him to backhand Leda so that she fell heavily, hitting her head against a rock. Leda crumpled and the swiftly flowing water lifted her, carrying her lifelessly downstream.

"Mama!" Mari cried. Her panicked freeze shattered. Shrieking rage and fear, she pulled the slingshot and a handful of rocks from her pouch. With a graceful, practiced motion, she sighted, whipped her arm back, and hurled the sling. The rock hit the man in his face, smashing his cheekbone and causing him to stumble so that he fell onto the steep bank only feet away from Mari.

Then Mari ran. Along the bank she rushed, keeping a loaded slingshot in her hand and dividing her focus between her mother's floating body, and the danger that searched the forest around her for captives.

Mari fought through the thickening underbrush, tripping over felled logs, her leaden feet finding leaf-filled holes in the forest floor that were camouflaged by dusk and her need to get to her mother before she drowned.

Mari was going to save her mother—she *had to* save her mother. Mari couldn't allow even the possibility of Leda's death to seep, poison-like, into her reality or her heart would crack and break and her legs would stop carrying her. Finally, the creek took a sharp right-handed turn, catching Leda's body in a jam of water-swollen logs and boulders. Mari half ran, half fell down the bank, leaping into the water and struggling against the current to her mother.

Leda lay, faceup, clothes and hair tangled in the water debris. Mari reached her and began wiping long hair and blood from her face, feeling frantically for a pulse in her neck. When she found the beat of her mother's heart, she sobbed in relief. "Mama! Mama! Wake up—talk to me!" Mari ran her hands over her mother's neck and arms, taking note of the hand-shaped bruise that was already darkening her cheek and the cut slowly weeping blood down her forehead. Mari forced herself to take deep, calming breaths as she began assessing her mother's injuries and pulling her free of the flotsam jam.

Leda moaned and began shivering, her eyelids fluttering. "Mari . . . Mari . . ." the Moon Woman murmured her daughter's name even before she was fully conscious.

"Shhh, I'm here, Mama, but we have to be quiet. I don't know where they are or how many of them there are," Mari whispered.

Leda's eyes opened. She tried to sit up and cried out, falling back into the water and clutching her side. "Ribs. Cracked or broken." Leda gasped and spoke quietly and quickly. "My head, too. Hit a rock in the water. My vision is blurred. Get me into the underbrush. I'll hide. You run for home."

"I will not leave you."

"Mari, do as I say."

"Leda, for once I don't care what you say. I will not leave you!" Mari enunciated each word carefully. "Now, stop talking and help me get you out of this water before you freeze." As gently as she could, she put Leda's arm around her shoulder and, grasping her mother's waist, began helping her wade through the water to the steep far bank.

"The other bank is closer and not as steep," Leda spoke between gasps of pain and chattering teeth.

"The other bank is also the direction they came from. The far bank is steeper, but it has more rocks and logs and places to hide. The underbrush is so thick I almost couldn't get through it to you. It held me up; it'll hold them up as well," Mari said grimly.

Leda didn't waste breath agreeing with her daughter—she just nodded and pressed her hand more firmly against her side, biting her lip to keep herself from crying out in pain. When they reached the rocky bank, Leda collapsed, trembling and trying to catch her breath in short, painful gasps.

"Just up there and a little way back I saw a dead cedar, choked by vines so that it still looks green—almost alive. I think it will hide us," Mari said.

Hand still pressed to her side, Leda lay against the damp, leaf-covered ground. "I can't. I'm too dizzy. I'll get sick if I move."

"Then we stay here and hope none of the Companions come this way."

"W-when did you become so stubborn?" Leda gasped, shaking her head at her daughter.

"I'm not sure, but I think I get it from my mother." Mari crouched beside Leda. "I can't lose you, Mama."

"Then it looks like I must make it up the bank to that dead tree."

Mari grasped her mother's hand and pulled her to her feet. Leda stood for a moment, only swaying slightly, and Mari thought it was going to be okay—and then the sickly white tinge of Leda's skin blanched almost colorless and a painful shiver skittered through her body, bringing with it a flush of silver gray.

"Oh, no," Mari murmured, looking frantically to the west, as if she could will the sun to stay in the sky.

"It's no use. Night comes, and with it more pain . . ." Leda shuddered again before her eyes rolled to show only whites and she crumpled slowly, almost gracefully, to the ground.

"I'm here, Mama. I'll help you. I'll always help you," Mari said. She gathered her mother into her arms and lifted her, so that as she began climbing up the bank she carried her mother close to her heart, thinking she was so light that it was as if her bones were hollow, and Mari was cradling a wounded bird.

Partway up a scream of pure terror had Mari freezing. Somewhere behind them in the distance, branches cracked and underbrush broke as careless feet trampled the delicate moss and ferns and the sacred idols of the Great Mother.

Gritting her teeth, Mari shifted Leda's weight so that she could climb faster, trying not to hear her mother's semiconscious moans of pain, and not dwell on the fact that her face had gone from the white of dead fish to the gray of moonlight and shadows.

Mari burst over the top of the bank. Clutching her mother in her arms, she sprinted to the ivy-choked cedar. It was an even better hiding place than she had imagined. The tree had half fallen, and the ivy had completely devoured it.

Another scream came from closer behind them. That and the pounding of feet coming toward them worked like a prod on Mari. She bent her head and, shielding Leda as best she could with her arms, pushed through the curtain of ivy and dead branches—and collided headlong into Xander and Jenna.

"Mari! Leda! You're—" Jenna's happy greeting was cut off when her father's big hand closed over her mouth.

Mari fell to her knees. She pressed a finger to her lips, miming for Jenna to be quiet. The girl and her father stared back and forth from Mari to her unconscious mother with eyes round with fear as heavy steps sounded from just outside their hiding space. Too afraid to move, Mari held her breath while she cradled her wounded mother in her arms.

"I saw a Scratcher run this way," said a male voice mere feet away from them. "She was the one that broke Miguel's cheekbone with a rock and knocked him unconscious."

"Nik, we already caught four Scratcher females. That's one more than the Farm needed replaced. And grabbing another Scratcher won't change the fact that Miguel's skin has been broken. All he can do now is to wait and see if he heals or if he—" The second man was farther away than the first, but his words carried to their hiding place.

"I want the one that hurt Miguel," insisted Nik, interrupting his friend.

"Look, Nik, that's not excuse enough to stay out here. The sun is setting. We've already gone way outside our usual hunting area because you want to search for the pup. Thaddeus has even less patience than usual, and he isn't going to allow the Hunt to continue, especially after one of us has been injured. We need to head back."

"O'Bryan, I want to look just a little more." Mari was surprised by the desperation in the man's voice.

"Cuz, have you seen any sign of the pup—a paw print, a tuft of fur, some scat? Anything at all?"

Mari felt the pressure of his words as if they were stones sliding into hidden pockets, weighting her, holding her down, drowning her in fear and worry.

"No, but that doesn't mean anything. We didn't see any sign of this being a Scratcher colony, but we just counted how many, close to one hundred of them? The pup might have been drawn here—might have thought the Scratchers were people."

"And if he was hanging around the Scratchers we'd have found some sign of him. But really, Nik, think about it logically. This will be the tenth night he's been gone. He has to be dead."

"He doesn't have to be!" Nik's voice exploded with frustration. "If I had more help—*canine* help—I could find him."

"Cuz, Sol had the Terriers, Laru, *and* Jasmine, the pup's own mother, search for him the entire day after he went missing, and they found nothing—no trace of him."

"Because those damn roaches swarmed and destroyed his trail so that there was nothing to find."

"Or because there was no trail to find because those damn roaches fed off him and left no trace of the pup at all." O'Bryan's voice was firm, but kind, and even through her fear and worry Mari noted that there was a very real friendship between the two men. "I'm sorry to say this to you, but the swarm eats everything in its path. You know that, Nik."

"The only thing I know for sure is that I can't stop looking for the pup. Not yet, O'Bryan. We had a connection. *He almost chose me.*"

O'Bryan sighed deeply. "If I ever go missing, I hope you search for me with half of the tenacity you're using to search for that pup."

"I will, but don't go missing," Nik said.

"All right then. Go ahead and keep looking through some of that deep underbrush along the bank. I'll make an excuse to Thaddeus, but we're already out later than we should be, and once he calls for the Hunt to be over, there's nothing I can—"

"Nik, there you are!" O'Bryan's words were cut off by an excited third man. "Come quickly! Thaddeus's Odysseus just alerted on a big holly bush. It looks like there's a paw print under the foliage—a Shepherd pup's paw print."

"Yes! I told you! I told you all!" Nik's shout was victorious. He and the other two men's voices faded as they raced back to Mari's first hiding place.

No one moved within the concealing vines for several long moments, then as all remained quiet in the forest surrounding them, Xander and Jenna crouched down, putting their heads near Mari, staring fearfully at Leda.

"Is she dead?" Jenna's voice trembled.

"No," Mari whispered reassurance. "She's going to be fine. She's just resting."

In the distance there were more shouts. Mari listened carefully, but none seemed to be coming closer to them.

"A missing canine has caused this misery?" Xander spoke so low that Mari had to strain to hear him. "It makes no sense."

"No, it doesn't, but the Companions make no sense," Mari spoke quickly, wishing that the man named Nik had never spoken. "Thankfully, the sun will set in moments and night will chase them back to their city in the trees." Mari spoke to Jenna, who was still staring with wide-eyed fear at Leda. "Then I will carry Mama home where I can take care of her properly. She'll be whole and well again soon. Don't worry, Jenna. We only need to hide here a little while more."

Mari heard Jenna's father grunt, as if in agreement, but there was something about the sound that had Mari's attention turning from Jenna to Xander. He was staring at Leda with a pained expression on his face, and as Mari watched, his skin began to flush with the sickly gray that signaled the setting of the sun and the coming of the Night Fever that cursed Earth Walkers.

I I

"N o! No! No! Not here, Daddy—not now!" Jenna crawled back, pressing against the rotting trunk of the dead tree and watching her father with eyes that were frantic with fear. She wrapped her arms around her knees and seemed to curl within herself, muttering over and over, "Not here, Daddy—not now!" Mari saw that the moonlight-colored tinge was creeping over Jenna's skin as well.

But the girl wasn't a threat—Mari understood that. If left alone for the night, Jenna would fall into despair, would cry inconsolably and lose part of herself to melancholy. That was sad and difficult, and left alone without the healing touch of a Moon Woman every Third Night, Jenna's spirit would begin to struggle to find happiness even during the daylight. It would only be a matter of time before the despair of the night smothered any respite the day might bring. Without the aid of a Moon Woman, Jenna's will to live would erode, leaving her to spend her short life in loneliness and depression. But Jenna wouldn't attack anyone, nor would she hurt anyone except, eventually, herself.

Mari couldn't say the same about Jenna's father.

"Jenna! When was the last time your father was Washed?"

"Tomorrow is Third Night!" Xander answered for his daughter, his voice rough and low.

"Usually we'd be in our burrow, resting, and the Night Fever wouldn't

131

be bad on a second night, but out here—under the open sky." Jenna shivered. "You have to help him, Mari! Please!"

Xander's breathing had increased. Tremors quaked through his body, and with each tremor his skin became more and more gray and his breathing more and more erratic.

"Wake Leda!" Xander hissed.

"I can't! She isn't asleep—she's unconscious." Moving slowly, she positioned herself between Xander and her mother. "You should leave, Xander. Get back to your burrow and rest. I'll watch over Jenna and Mama. You being here doesn't help them. Not now. Not after dark." She kept her voice low and soothing as she carefully reached into her pouch, feeling for a smooth stone. The slingshot was useless in such close confines, but she might be able to smash a rock in Xander's face, and hope she could knock him unconscious long enough for them to get away.

"No! Daddy can't go out there. They'll kill him."

"Wake her! Heal me!" Xander's voice had gone so guttural that his words were little more than a growl.

"Xander, listen to me! Mama's not asleep. She's hurt. She can't heal you." Mari tried to reason with Xander, knowing that every moment that passed brought night more fully to their world, and with the darkening night, so, too, darkened Xander's mind, causing his hold on sanity to slip further and further from him.

"Must. Heal. Me!" Xander's body seemed to grow until the barely contained violence he personified filled their hiding place.

"You can do it, Mari. I know you can." Jenna's tear-filled gaze held Mari's. "You have Leda's eyes. You are her daughter."

"Jenna, it's not that easy," Mari said. Then, with a snarl, Xander started to close the small space between them. Mari lifted the rock in her hand and drew herself up, glaring at him. She pitched her voice low, and tried to funnel her fear into ferocity. "Get out of here, Xander, before you make me hurt you."

With a snarl that was filled with a father's despair, Xander turned and began to push away from them through the concealing vines.

"No," Jenna sobbed. "He's all I have."

Mari made the decision that altered all of their futures quickly, with only a fleeting thought for possible regrets. With one hand she grabbed Xander's forearm, pulling him back within their hiding place. The other hand Mari raised. Xander whirled around, growling menacingly.

"On your knees!" Mari commanded, and was shocked when Xander obeyed and dropped roughly to his knees. She closed her eyes, letting the chaos and fear around her—Jenna's sobs, her father's terrible feral panting, and Leda's frightening stillness—be apart from her. Deep within herself, in the calmness where Mari held the beautiful images she translated into sketches, she imagined the moon as it would be this night, rising a half crescent, white and glowing above the sleeping pines.

When the picture of the moon, bright and newly risen, was set in her imagination, Mari began speaking while she continued to sketch with the power of her mind.

"Moon Woman blood is within me
Become that which I see
Mind and heart your image will be
Salvation for these beloved three"

The words flowed from Mari as the power of the moon swelled above her. They were not her mother's words, but Mari's alone—in a new cadence spoken with equal parts desperation and love.

In the sketch she created in her mind, Mari drew the crescent huge, so that it dominated the night's sky and the silver white light that cascaded down to the forest was like a dam had been opened—power, cool and calming—cascaded down.

Mari followed the power, making the cascade a waterfall that poured down, down, down finally finding the small figure that was not Earth Walker nor Companion, but was a matted-haired girl who was a mixture of them both. When she knew she was as ready as possible, Mari finished with her own version of the ancient language that called down the healing power of the moon.

*"By right of blood and birth channel through me
that which the Earth Mother proclaims my destiny!"*

Mari gasped as power poured into her. Keeping her eyes closed so that she didn't lose the picture in her mind, she stretched out her open hand. "Xander! Take it!"

The hand that grasped hers was hot with fever, and Mari sketched the moonbeam waterfall flowing through herself and into Xander, filling him—cooling him—calming him. She gritted her teeth against the residual pain she expected from the unbound energy that poured through her body, but no pain came. And as Xander's hand in hers cooled, he said, "Help Jenna now, please."

Mari could only nod. In her mind she busily replaced Xander's picture with his daughter's, just as her little hot hand replaced her father's.

Seconds or hours could have passed before Jenna squeezed her hand and released it and whispered, "You did it. You healed Daddy and me. Now I think you should heal Leda, too."

Mari nodded, but kept her eyes tightly shut. *Don't lose the picture! I can't lose the picture!* She bent and started to blindly reach for her mother when Xander's strong hands were there, guiding her to find Leda's crumpled body. "She's right here," Xander said in a perfectly normal, perfectly rational voice.

Her hand pressed against Leda's unresponsive body, Mari began to add to the picture in her mind, making the moon even bigger, more beautiful, more brilliant. She sketched shining ropes of silver power pouring down to Wash into and through her, and to pool within the sketch Mari created of her mother. First, her face, drawing it without the seeping cut on her forehead and the swollen, angry bruise on her cheek. Then her mind sketched the rest of her mother's small body, making her strong and whole again. Finally, Mari turned her mother's lips up into a welcoming smile, and sketched her eyes, open and clear.

"Oh, Leda, you did it!"

With a happy cry, Mari opened her eyes to see her mother smiling up at her.

"She did, Leda! Mari saved us!" Jenna cried.

"Shh, child," Xander said, giving a nervous glance over his shoulder at the forest beyond their concealing vines. "The Companions are still there—still searching for their lost canine."

"Lost canine?" Leda whispered, her sharp gaze meeting Mari's.

"We heard the men talking. One of them searches for a pup," Mari explained. "And it seems they found sign of him not far from here."

"Then it isn't safe to remain here, not even hidden," Leda said.

"And now the tree dwellers do not simply steal us away if we are forced to forage too close to their Tribe. They find reason to encroach on our lands and kill our people." Xander's voice was low but bitter. "May each of them and their canines be cursed."

Their canines, not mine. Mari kept her thoughts to herself, but now that her mother was better, Rigel's absence weighed on Mari. *Where was he? Waiting safely at home, or trapped somewhere between there and here by the seeking Companions?*

How could I bear losing my Rigel?

"Mama, I have to get back to our burrow. I—I don't feel well," Mari said.

"It can't be safe to leave yet," Xander said.

"Safe or not, Mari needs to return to our burrow and regain her strength. Drawing down the moon is exhausting, especially for one such as Mari," Leda said, watching her daughter closely.

"Thank you, Mother. I knew you'd understand." Mari met her mother's gaze, grateful that they were in agreement. At that moment finding Rigel was everything.

"Xander, you and Jenna wait here until the moon has risen above the eastern pines. Surely the Companions will have returned to their trees by then, but have a care with how you move through the forest. Do not pass through the Gathering Site," Leda said.

"Leda, perhaps it is time you shared with Jenna and me where your burrow is located. We could follow you and check to be certain you returned safely," Xander said. "And I give you my oath that I would never betray your trust."

"Xander, the location of a Moon Woman's burrow is forbidden for many reasons, none of which am I willing to break—especially as now it is home to *two* Moon Women," Leda said.

"Then you *will* name Mari your heir," Jenna said, grinning happily.

Mari found she was holding her breath as she waited for her mother's reply.

"Well, Jenna, it seems our Earth Mother has spoken for me, as after tonight there is no doubt that Mari carries my gift."

"Sora won't be happy to hear that," Xander said.

"Sora is young. She'll have many winters to discover that the path to one's destiny is rarely straight or clear of obstacles," Leda said.

Mari let out a long breath, not entirely sure of what to make of her mother's response, but her growing worry for Rigel was like an itch beneath her skin, and she found it more and more difficult to concentrate on anything else.

"Mama, are you ready?" Mari asked, offering a hand to help her mother stand.

Leda took it and stood. At first she moved slowly, carefully, as if expecting the dizziness and pain to return. Tentatively, she drew a deep breath, and let it out with a smile. "Thanks to you, my gifted daughter, yes I am ready. My bones are healed, as is the injury to my head."

Before Mari could respond, Jenna and Xander faced her.

"Thank you, Moon Woman," Jenna said formally, bowing to Mari.

"Thank you, Moon Woman," Xander mimicked his daughter's actions. "As is proper, Jenna and I will gather walnuts to bring as tribute to you next Third Night," Xander said. "I remember Jenna saying that you use their shells for your ink."

Leda lifted her brow and gave Mari a little nod of encouragement.

"Th-thank you, I do. And I will gratefully accept your tribute next Third Night," Mari spoke the words she'd heard her mother say countless times in the past, though it felt odd, almost as if she was trying to dress up in Leda's precious fur-lined cape and pretend to be someone she was not quite grown up enough yet to be.

"Fare thee well until we meet again," Leda said formally, hugging

Jenna and grasping Xander's hand. Then she turned to Mari. "I will follow your lead, daughter."

Mari nodded and paused at the ivy curtain, listening intently. All was silent beyond, so she parted the vines and crept from their hiding place. Mari stopped, waited, listening and looking—and when the forest remained silent and safe, she motioned for her mother to join her.

Leda slipped through the curtain and fell into step beside her daughter.

"Are you really well, Mama?" Mari tilted her head down to her mother and whispered the question.

"Yes," Leda whispered back. "I am so proud of you, Mari. What you did back there was extraordinary." Head still bowed to her daughter's, Leda asked, "Rigel?"

"I sent him home just before the attack. Rigel warned me they were coming."

"I thought as much," Leda said.

"Mama, one of the Companions talked about Rigel. I heard him. They came here because a man named Nik is searching for a Shepherd pup. It has to be Rigel. What are we going to do?"

Leda squeezed her daughter's hand. "We'll figure that out at home. Right now focus on reaching out with your mind and sending Rigel reassurance. Your canine must be frantic without you."

Mari did exactly that—she imagined Rigel sitting in front of their burrow and focused on her connection to the pup, and then she sent waves of reassurance and love to him through that connection, sketching a happy homecoming scene between the three of them in her mind's eye.

It was then that Mari made her biggest mistake. The first lesson of the forest was to never, ever take your concentration off of your surroundings. From the time she had been old enough to toddle about, Leda had been teaching her warnings with rhyme and repetition:

> *Be safe! Concentrate!*
> *Where old logs lie there are dangers to spy!*

Always prepare to beware!
Eyes on the trail—eyes ahead—
If you are to return safe and sound to your bed!

But that night was different. For the first time since Mari had been a small child, she was out in the forest, well after full dark, and her focus was not on the dangers that surrounded her. Leda, too, was unusually unfocused. Worry for Mari and Rigel, Jenna and Xander, as well as the Earth Walkers who had been taken and killed filled her thoughts, distracting her so much that her mind did not note the low, warning hum until she and Mari were already surrounded.

A skittering of leaves and forest debris had Mari pausing. Her instincts screamed danger at her and had adrenaline surging through her body, heightening her senses and shifting her focus, before her conscious mind fully processed what was happening.

And then the hum registered in both women's minds and the night changed irrevocably.

"Wolf spiders! Back-to-back, Mari! Wait for my signal!"

Leda was shouting and all thoughts of stealth flew from Mari's mind as surely as did the homey, perfect picture of reassurance she was transmitting to Rigel. Thankful for the years of drill and practice Leda had insisted on, Mari automatically pressed her back against her mother's as she and Leda moved in tandem, unstrapping the goatskin bags from over their shoulders, breaking the wax seals, and lifting them to their mouths.

"Hold, Mari. Hold. Ground yourself. Be apart from the danger and madness—just as you've practiced—just as you've done. And remember, I have your back. I'll always have your back."

Mari breathed deeply and slowly as the horrible humming vibrated through her body. Her mother's signal seemed as if it was never going to come, but Mari felt oddly calm, almost detached as she waited. Mari took a deep pull from the goatskin bag, holding the strong mixture of saltwater and lavender oil in her mouth. Using the preternaturally sharp night vision that she had inherited from her mother, Mari scanned the area around them, trying to see through cloaking night to the predators that were stalking them.

Then the humming stopped and the world around Mari exploded into chaos and danger.

Leda nodded, but Mari didn't need her signal. What had looked like a clump of fallen leaves only seconds before had shifted, turned, changed, and become a spider the size of a squirrel that gathered itself and then leaped at Mari's face.

With a cry that was equal parts rage and fear, Mari spat her mouthful of saltwater and oil at the creature, soaking its face and all eight bulbous eyes. The spider fell harmlessly past Mari as it writhed in agony and hissed like a hot coal being doused with water and she stomped on it, feeling the satisfaction of crushing its pulsating body.

"More coming!" Leda warned her.

Mari drew another mouthful of the concoction that blinded the hunting spiders and managed to fumble in her pouch to draw out her knife before the next creature hurled itself at her. Mari spat the spider poison, hitting two of them, and followed by quickly kneeling and stabbing the flint knife through each of their writhing bodies.

"Remember, no running. That's what they want us to do." Leda spoke quickly but calmly before drawing another mouthful of the liquid. "Keep walking. Slowly. Together. I've got your back. You've got my back. Do you have a full skin of repellent?"

"Yes," Mari assured her.

"Then we have enough to hold them off if we don't panic."

"I'll move with you, Mama. We'll make it home—I know we will."

"Get ready. More are coming," Leda said.

Mari readied herself as the sickening humming vibrated through the forest around them. She was lifting the goatskin to her mouth as the next wave of arachnids materialized from the darkness.

There was a ferocious snarling and snapping, and Rigel was suddenly there, fighting through the tightening noose of spiders to press against Mari's side.

Leda spit a spray of repellent at the attacking horde, soaking three of the creatures and knocking a fourth from her arm and stomping it into the ground. Mari did the same, stabbing two with one swipe of her blade.

"Stand over Rigel," Leda said, wiping her mouth with the back of her hand. "Don't let them lure him away from you. They get Rigel alone and they'll wrap him in their web so the nest can devour him."

Mari stole one moment to hug the pup to her before she positioned herself so that she was standing over Rigel, her back still pressed against her mother, telegraphing *don't leave me, don't leave me, don't leave me . . .* over and over to the pup. Rigel growled low in his throat. His attention was riveted on the skittering darkness around them, but he was pressed against Mari's legs reassuringly. "Don't you worry, Leda. He's not going anywhere."

A new wave of arachnids descended on them, and Rigel fought with Mari, snapping up any spider that got past the repellent and Mari's knife.

"As one, we move forward. Slowly, carefully, Mari. Between attacks on my word," Leda said, but before she could signal her daughter, light bloomed on the path ahead of them and first one man carrying a torch, then a line of them, rushed toward them, batting at the spiders with clubs.

"There are female Scratchers in the path! Grab them and let's get the hell outta here!" came a Companion's command.

For half a heartbeat Mari froze, then *they will not take Rigel away from me!* screamed through her mind and she bent to scoop the pup into her arms. She was already moving as she grabbed her mother's arm, pulling Leda with her off the path, when something big and powerful shoved her, so hard that Mari fell forward, taking Leda and Rigel with her. She curled into a ball around Rigel, so that as she hit the ground she was protecting the pup. Before she had even stopped rolling, Mari was reaching for her mother when the shout cut through the night to them.

"Run!"

Scrambling to her knees, Mari looked up to see the big man standing where she and her mother had been. Spiders swarmed over him as he used his fists to batter them away. And beyond him the torches drew ever closer.

With a sense of unreality, Mari watched Xander's gaze find her. Then his eyes grew huge with disbelief and disgust, and she remembered that she was clutching Rigel in her arms. Xander's head began to shake, back and forth, back and forth as he stared at her incredulously.

"It's a male! Kill it!" a Companion shouted at the same time a frightened scream split the night.

As one, Mari and Xander turned toward the scream in time to see a Companion holding a torch high, and dragging Jenna behind him.

With an inhuman cry of rage, Xander raced for his daughter. He ignored the spiders that sprang on him, covering his back, neck, and head. He ignored the Companions that sighted crossbows at him. And, even for a while, he ignored the barbs that struck him, over and over. Mari counted a dozen arrows buried to the feathers in his body, but he was still running toward the man holding his daughter.

"We can't help him. Run, Mari! Now!" Leda's frantic whisper brought Mari back to herself.

"But they have Jenna," Mari sobbed.

"And if we stay they will have us, too. *Run, Mari! Now!*" Leda repeated. She grabbed her daughter's hand and pulled, forcing Mari and Rigel to sprint into the darkness with her as Xander's cries of rage and pain faded with the glow of torchlight and the scent of blood.

12

N ik had never been to Farm Island after dusk, and he didn't relish the thought of a visit now, but at least he would be rid of the
crying female once they got there. For what seemed like the thousandth
time, Nik glanced over his shoulder at the captive Scratchers. The five
of them were tied together, wrists to waists, so that they could march,
one after another, in a line. The crying girl, the one that they'd captured
just as the Scratcher male attacked them, stumbled along last in line,
weeping inconsolably. The small group of Hunters, led by Thaddeus and
his Terrier, Odysseus, surrounded the females, keeping well-lit torches
held high so that they wouldn't be surprised by any more spiders, and
prodding the captives to keep up a fast jog. By now it was well past sunset, and the last thing the already battered group needed was for a roach
swarm to catch them before they reached safety.

"That last female is in bad shape." O'Bryan caught Nik's glance. "I
know she's just a Scratcher, but man, Nik, her crying is getting to me."

"Yeah, I know what you mean," Nik said as his cousin fell into a
steady jog beside him. "I'm used to them being depressed and pretty
much out of their minds, especially at night. Who isn't? That's why they
need us to take care of them like we do. But this female's crying is
weird."

"It's like she's mourning that big male we killed last," O'Bryan said.

"They do form attachments, a lot like children," Nik said, glancing behind them again at the sobbing female as she stumbled to keep up with the others, who jogged, blank-eyed and completely silent, with the Hunters. "Males try to steal the females from the island. And some of the females actually seem to go with them willingly. Two did just that a week or so ago. They were shot coming out of the Channel with the male who was leading them away."

"Well, this one must have been attached to the male who attacked us. Do you think he might have been trying to protect her?"

"Hell, O'Bryan, is that even possible? You know how the males are—they get so violent and out of their minds that they can't even be domesticated like the females. Would it know that it was protecting the girl?"

"You're right. It's probably not possible," O'Bryan said, wincing as the female drew a breath and then began sobbing even louder.

"She's younger than the others. She's just afraid. The forest terrifies *me* at night, and I'm not a childlike Scratcher. I imagine being out here is doubly frightening to a half-wit. She'll be fine when we get her to the island and the floating homes where it's safe," Nik said.

"Yeah, I'll be glad to get rid of her, too. Not far to the bridge now," said Miguel, breathing heavily. The man was obviously in pain—his left cheekbone was bloody and swollen, and he'd fallen back to the rear of the Hunters with Nik and O'Bryan.

"Miguel, that cheek looks bad. You sure you're okay?" Nik asked.

"Fine. I'm fine. Wish we'd got that bitch who hit me, though."

"Heal up and come back out with me. Maybe we'll get lucky and run into your Scratcher again," Nik said.

"You're going to keep searching?" Miguel said.

"Of course I'm going to keep searching. You saw the tracks as clearly as I did," Nik said with no hesitation, though a good measure of irritation. *Why the hell did the pup seem important only to him?*

"Yeah, and I also saw that the spider pack crossed over his tracks. A half-grown canine, even a Shepherd pup as big as that one was, can't survive an attack by an entire pack of those things," said Miguel.

"Oh, really? That's the same half-grown canine who can't have survived the fucking bloody beetles and damned swarming roaches—yet those were his tracks, I'm sure of it," said Nik.

"I'm with Nik—the pup should be found," O'Bryan said before Miguel could respond. "If he's still alive, he has to be a truly special canine."

Miguel shrugged and then winced painfully. "Hey, I hear you. I'm in, too. As soon as this is healed, I'll go out with you again."

"I'll hold you to it," Nik said, choking down the comment he wanted to make—the one where he told Miguel that he *really* needed Hunters who were also Companions. Using a Terrier's nose to track would help him far beyond what humans could discover. And, of course, there was also the fact that Miguel's skin had been broken—badly. It was doubtful he would heal enough to Hunt, or be chosen as a Companion, ever.

"Halt!" Thaddeus called back at the group, and the Hunters pulled the Scratchers to a ragged stop.

Nik looked around them and could see that they'd come to the edge of the pine forest. Before them the torches illuminated an ancient stretch of broken asphalt, and as they paused clouds scudded across the face of the moon, veiling the feeble, milky light. Then, with a sudden gust of wind, rain began to drizzle through the canopy, making a comforting pitter-patter on the fronds of the ferns and causing the broken road to glisten like a shattered mirror.

Nik gritted his teeth and muttered a curse. The rain would dilute the pup's trail. He had to get back to that big holly bush early tomorrow *with* hunting Terriers before the scent was completely untrackable.

"In the lookout! Hunters to enter the island!" The shout pulled Nik's attention up to the observation blind that had been built into the last of the massive pines that bordered the asphalt.

"Go ahead. I have you covered," came the answer from the tall Companion who moved out on the wooden deck, crossbow notched and ready, and his Shepherd by his side.

Thaddeus waved to the guard, and then motioned for the group to follow him. They jogged onto the broken road, following it up to the bridge. Thaddeus lit the torches that framed the entrance.

"First, Miguel, I don't like the way that wound looks. I give you leave to return to the Tribe and get it tended. Lawrence and Stephen—accompany him," Thaddeus said. "The rest of you watch the Scratchers as we cross the bridge. Don't let them misstep. They fall into the Channel at night and we've lost them and wasted a Hunt." Thaddeus caught Nik's gaze as his Hunters began cutting the thick ropes that bound the females together. "Nik, you're responsible for the last girl."

"Me? Why?"

"Because your puppy chase made us late."

"We found sign of him!" Nik tried to keep his tone reasonable, but he was just so damn sick of explaining the obvious.

"Sign, but no pup. What we did find was a hunting pack of wolf spiders, a grown male Scratcher who needed killing before he killed us, and a female who won't shut up." Thaddeus went to the crying female, cut the rope that connected her to the Scratcher in front of her, and with a rough jerk pulled her forward, handing the tether to Nik. "Like I said, you're responsible for her."

The female stumbled and Nik had to grab her arm to keep her from falling to the ground. She gave a little sobbing shriek and scrambled as far away from him as the rope would allow, then stood there, crying and looking at Nik through large, liquid eyes.

"I think you should try talking to her," O'Bryan said.

"Talk to her?"

"You know, like you would a scared pup."

Nik snorted sardonically. "A scared pup has more sense than a Scratcher."

"Oh, come on. You know that they can understand us just fine, even though they don't talk much—or at least during the day they can."

"All right! Let's move out!" Thaddeus called from the front of the group, and they began to shuffle forward.

The Scratcher girl's crying increased and she kept backing away, pulling Nik with her, as if she thought she could drag him into the forest.

Nik sighed and wrapped the rope around his fist, planting his feet.

"Come on now," Nik said, as gently as he could while he pulled on the rope, trying to coax the female forward. "You don't want to go back there. It's dangerous."

"Nik, you gotta get her moving. Thaddeus is already pissed. He's going to skin you if she holds us up anymore," O'Bryan said.

"Go on! We'll catch you." Nik shooed away his cousin and then faced the female. She was just so pitiful and ugly! Like all the Scratcher females, she was small. Actually, this one was even smaller than usual. Her dark hair was full of ivy and leaves, and her flat-featured face was smeared with dirt and snot, tears and blood.

"You don't have to be afraid. You'll be safe on the island." Nik gestured toward the bridge and the group that was moving away from them and onto it. "Everything will be okay once you get there."

The Scratcher met his gaze, and spoke. "Nothing will be okay again. You shot my daddy."

Her voice was small, and choked with emotion, but her words were completely clear—perfectly understandable. Nik had a sudden flashback to when she hurled herself at the dead Scratcher's body, clutching it and keening. Thaddeus had had to drag her away from the corpse. Her emotional response had been strange—there was no doubt about that. And now she was speaking to him? At night? *She really had been connected to that Scratcher male.*

"What is your name?" Nik surprised himself by asking.

"Jenna."

"I'm Nik. Jenna, would you let me help you across the bridge to your new home?"

Jenna hesitated, wiping her face with the back of her hand. She looked from the bridge to him, her face suddenly alight—bright and burning. "Would you let me go? Please?"

Nik felt as if she had just gut-punched him. "Jenna, I can't!" he blurted. "And even if I could, you can't go into that forest alone at night. You'd be killed."

"You don't know everything, Nik." Tears began to leak down her face again.

"Okay, sure, you're right. I don't know everything, but I do know that if you don't go over that bridge with me, Thaddeus will drag you over it."

"Is he dead?"

"Thaddeus? No, he's right up there and he's going to—" Nik began, purposely misunderstanding, but the innocence in the girl's big eyes stopped his words. He drew a deep breath, ran a hand through his hair, and began again. "Yes. Your father is dead. I—I'm sorry," he added, feeling as if he was trying to balance on shifting sand.

Jenna's slender shoulders drooped. "Why?"

"He attacked us. We had to kill him."

"Not that. Why are you sorry?"

Completely taken aback, Nik had no answer for her. He just stood and stared at the girl, until finally she wrapped her arms around herself as if trying to physically hold her small body together, and slowly started up the broken road to the bridge, leaving Nik to follow her.

They caught up to the group easily. Nik was shocked by how agile Jenna was, which was totally unlike the other Scratcher females who moved as if they were not really aware of the world around them. During the daylight hours they worked slowly, silently, but meticulously in the fields where something mysterious about their touch made each crop thrive and each harvest bountiful. At night they could only be led, prodded, goaded, or herded. Left on their own, it seemed to Nik as if the other captives would have behaved like normal Scratcher females, or any other burrowing animal, they would try to find a cave-like hole and crawl into it. If a hole wasn't readily available, they'd scratch one into the dirt and then hide in it.

They didn't take care of themselves.

They didn't converse.

They didn't weep for their fathers.

They didn't ask questions in small, knowing voices, or stare at him with big, tearful eyes.

Nik watched Jenna from the corner of his eye as they moved carefully down through the last of the rusted skeleton of the bridge and to the road that wound around the eastern edge of the island along the

Channel River. Jenna was still crying, though softly now. The rain mixed with her tears, washing the blood and dirt from her pale face, and leaving her looking very young and very sad.

"You caught up before Thaddeus noticed you were lagging. Good thing, too. He definitely got up on the wrong side of the nest today," O'Bryan said. He glanced at Jenna. "And she's not making so much noise now. Nice job, Cuz."

"I don't feel so nice." Nik hadn't realized he'd spoken aloud until O'Bryan gave him a stunned look, saying, "Did one of those spiders bite you? Damnit, Nik. You should have—"

"No, no I'm fine," Nik said hastily, not looking at Jenna. "Just real ready to be home."

"Cuz, I second that. But no worries, there's the dock. It'll be no time now." O'Bryan clapped him on the back. "And you did finally find sign of that pup of yours."

"Yeah, I did. It's been a great night." Nik's voice sounded flat to his own ears and when he glanced to the side he saw that Jenna was staring at him. "Come on." He gave her rope a little tug. "Let's get you to your new home." Looking away from her, Nik picked up his pace, leading the girl through the Hunters to the other Scratchers who were standing silent and empty-eyed on the wide wooden dock. She followed him with no further protestations until he reached the dock, then she stopped as if she'd run into an invisible wall. Nik glanced back at her to see her staring out at the Channel and the row of floating houses that bobbed lazily with the current.

Nik hesitated, and then instead of pulling her onto the dock, he went to her, speaking low in what he hoped was his best calming voice. "It's okay. The houses are where the Scratchers—" He paused and then corrected himself. "—I mean, they are where your people live. The water keeps them safe. No bugs can get to them, not even swarming roaches. Just, uh, pretend like they're floating caves."

"Nik, you know they're mindless! Stop wasting time trying to talk to it. You're holding us up. Again." Thaddeus glowered at Nik from the boat they would row out to the floating houses. The other four Scratchers had been lifted aboard, and they sat silently, staring down at their hands.

Nik took Jenna's elbow and gently, but firmly, guided her to the boat where Thaddeus promptly grabbed her by the waist and tossed her in with the others.

"Hey, watch it," Nik heard himself protesting. "She's littler than those others. I don't think she's very old."

"Damn, Nik, you're turning into a champion for lost causes!" Thaddeus's laughter was sarcastic and infectious, and the group, except for O'Bryan, joined him.

Nik would have turned away. He would have started immediately back for the bridge, but Jenna's face was tilted up toward him. It caught the light of the torches and it seemed to glow like a full Hunter's moon. Her eyes met his and he couldn't look away. Without saying anything, Nik stepped into the boat, taking the seat across from Jenna and lifting an oar.

"All righty then—let's deliver these Scratchers and go home. Row!" Thaddeus commanded.

The Channel was wide, and had dangerous hidden currents that swirled beneath its surface. Nik thought it would be tough to row the ferry, but it felt like it only took a few minutes and they'd docked alongside the closest of the twelve floating houses. Through the bars that covered the windows, dirty hands reached out and Nik could hear an unrelieved cacophony of madness and melancholy. It was difficult to make out individual words, as most of what they were saying was gibberish, but one word lifted over and over again from the chaos of voices: *"Help . . . help . . . help . . . help . . ."*

Nik shuddered. He knew she was looking at him, and for a moment Nik wished he was a coward, or as hard-hearted as Thaddeus. He wouldn't have made himself meet her eyes and smile encouragement. Not caring what the others would think, Nik told Jenna, "Don't worry. You'll be safe in there."

Jenna said nothing, but Nik blocked Thaddeus's way so that he could gently lift her to the deck of the house himself.

She stood there as if she'd been frozen. Then, slowly, she turned to stare at the closest house. Nik didn't think he'd ever seen anyone look so frightened. Her pale, terrified face made his stomach feel hollow. By now Thaddeus and the Hunters were lifting the other captives from the boat, and their appearance had the Scratchers inside the houses pressing their faces against the barred windows, their cries for help more easily understood from so close. Jenna began walking toward one of the windows, as if she really did want to help the females within.

Nik glanced quickly at Thaddeus, who was, thankfully, busy with lifting the largest of the captives onto the deck. Then Nik vaulted out of the boat and went to the girl, taking her arm again, and leading her away from the window.

It was while he was near the window that he heard it, as clearly as he'd heard Jenna speaking to him earlier.

"She has been Washed!" Then another voice added, "Moon Woman!" And yet another, "Where is our Moon Woman?"

Jenna reacted faster than Nik. Her head whipped around, so that she faced the window again. *"Forbidden!"* The girl practically spat the word at the females. The staring Scratchers went utterly still. Then Jenna turned and marched ahead of Nik back to dockside.

"Hey, Jenna, what's a Moon Woman?" Nik asked softly.

But Jenna didn't pause to answer him. Instead she took her place among the other four women. Nik watched and kept watching as Thaddeus led the five of them down to the wooden walkway that ran the length of the group of houses, unbarred the door of one of them, and shoved Jenna inside. The last glimpse Nik had of the girl was as she craned her head around so that she was staring at him when Thaddeus slammed and barred the door in her pale, stricken face.

Nik couldn't get the image of Jenna's face out of his mind. It stayed with him as he jogged with the Hunters back to the Tribe and the sanctuary of their homes in the sentinel pines.

It stayed with him after he had said a weary good-bye to O'Bryan and collapsed upon the sumptuous pallet in his cozy bachelor's nest. It haunted him as he closed his eyes, hoping that escaping sleep would claim him. But instead of sleeping, Nik sat abruptly upright; finally realizing what it was about Jenna's face that he couldn't forget.

The rain had washed away the dirt and blood from her cheeks to reveal the mystery beneath. Jenna's skin had been pale—almost as pale as moonlight. It hadn't been the gray color every Scratcher's skin turned from sunset to sunrise.

"What the hell is going on?" Nik spoke aloud to himself as he raked his fingers through his tousled hair. Had he been imagining things?

Nik's mind searched back through the events of the night, this time paying attention to *everything* and not just to the small, but real signs of his pup.

He hadn't put any real effort into chasing Scratchers. He truly had used the need for a few more captives as an excuse to join the Hunters out in the forest—and to encourage them to seek farther to the south than they usually hunted. He hadn't really cared whether they captured the female who had struck Miguel—he'd used that as an excuse as well. Not that Nik was ashamed of what he'd done. He'd do it all again and again. He'd do whatever it took to keep searching for the pup. Even if it meant killing more Scratcher males and capturing more females.

Nik stared down at his hands, suddenly not liking the feeling in his gut. "He was her parent—her father," he said softly. "Jenna's father." He cringed as his memory replayed the small girl throwing herself on the big man's bleeding body. She'd keened and cried as if her heart had broken. And her father had been protecting her. Nik realized that now. He remembered the Scratcher male standing in the middle of the path, covered by spiders, but not moving. Not attacking. Not until they'd grabbed Jenna. *Then* he'd charged them.

And as he sifted through his memory another vision had him sitting upright and shaking his head in disbelief—the big male had been bloody and pale, *but like his daughter his skin had not been Scratcher gray.*

13

Nik got almost no sleep that night, which was fine with him as it allowed him to be awake well before sunrise. He did spend a good amount of time on making himself presentable. Sol was his father, but he was also Sun Priest, Leader of the Tribe of the Trees, and to present himself disheveled and sleepy-eyed would not impress Sol or put him in the right mood to hear what Nik needed to say to him.

Freshly washed and groomed, Nik made his way along the suspended bridges and graceful wooden walkways to the heart of the Tribe and the large, beautiful nest that housed their Leader, the Sun Priest. Everything the Tribe created was made with an emphasis on form as well as function—artists were as revered by the people as were Hunters and Leaders, perhaps more, and that reverence had produced generation after generation of talented artisans—who had, in turn, created a city in the trees filled with beauty and grace.

In the dove-colored predawn Nik paused just outside the closed door of his father's nest, collecting himself and appreciating the glorious carvings of guardian Shepherds and beaming suns that decorated the arched entryway. Almost of its own accord, Nik's hand lifted so that he could stroke one of the carvings. His smile was poignant as he remembered his mother's golden head bowed over this very piece of wood that she had, two decades ago, so lovingly crafted for their home.

Though she had been gone for many years, Nik often missed her and wondered how his life might have been different had she not died that terrible day ten winters ago.

"Oh, Nik! You startled me. Good morning."

Hand still raised Nik stood there blinking in surprise, hardly knowing what to say or do, as Maeve and her pup, Fortina, filled the doorway in front of him. The older woman's hair was long and loose, spreading down her slim back, and she was wearing only a thin sleep shift. As he stared at her, Maeve's cheeks flushed a bright pink.

Fortina's young voice warbled, as if to ask Nik a question, and that had him unfreezing. "Oh, sorry, Fortina. You must need to go out." Nik stepped aside so that Maeve and Fortina could move past him.

"Thank you, Nik," Maeve said, then she hesitated and added, "Did you find sign of the pup during last night's hunt?"

"I did," Nik said.

"Oh, I am so pleased for you! I don't care what anyone says. I think he's still alive, too. Keep looking, Nik." Then Maeve patted his shoulder gently and followed her impatient canine.

Nik watched her go, his feelings warring between embarrassment at catching his father's lover leaving his nest, and pleasure that she actually agreed with him and believed the pup was still alive.

"Are you going to stand there forever, or are you going to come in?" Sol's voice boomed from inside the nest. Nik drew a deep breath, and stepped into his father's home, and the home of his childhood.

The Sun Priest's nest was larger than any other single-family home. Like the other nests, it had been beautifully woven, form following function, into a great, round structure. But unlike a normal family nest, Sol's had three levels to it. The entry room was outfitted with a gleaming pinewood table and benches that hugged the curve of the room and allowed an area for more intimate meetings with Tribal members than would take place in the public Forum. Curving stairs led up to the second-level landing, off of which had been Nik's sleeping room until he had passed sixteen winters and graduated to his bachelor pod. It was now his father's library, and held the largest private book collection in the Tribe. From the second-floor landing another stairway slanted up, wide and sturdy enough for a massive canine to traverse, and it was from the top of those stairs that Laru sounded three welcome barks and then hurried down, wriggling like a pup, to greet Nik.

"How are you doing, big guy? You're looking pretty spry for it being so early," Nik said, stroking the Shepherd lovingly and enjoying the feel of his thick, soft coat.

"Don't let him fool you. He's tired. Maeve's pup kept him up most of the night. If you come back by after midday you'll find him curled in a sunny spot sound asleep." Sol chuckled as he emerged from his third-floor bedchamber pulling on his shirt.

Nik slanted a knowing look at his father. "You're looking a little tired, too. Did *Maeve's pup* keep you up as well, and will you be napping with Laru later?"

"That is none of your business, Nikolas." His father's widening grin took the sting from his words and Nik returned the smile.

"Hey, you know I don't want you to be alone," Nik said, still petting Laru. "And Maeve is nice."

"She is, indeed. Tea?" Sol asked as he moved to the small brazier that had been carefully situated near the corner of the nest. Lined in shale the coals and tinder were in a miniature upraised brazier, over which hung one of the Tribe's most cherished artifacts, an iron pot.

Nik nodded. "Absolutely. I've missed your tea."

"You should visit my nest more often." Sol smiled over his shoulder at Nik before going to one of the small openings woven in the upper side of the nest. Though the sun had not yet risen, the sky was already blushing with dawn, and as Sol stared at the sky, his father's green eyes began to glow amber. He lifted his hands, and with a deft, practiced movement, flicked his fingers at the tinder, and small sparks, like tiny fireflies, leapt and crackled, lighting the coals and merrily burning the tinder pile.

Nik liked living on his own, but his bachelor's nest was definitely lacking the luxury that filled his father's home, especially as only a Sun Priest had the ability to harness the might of the sun as a fire starter. Lulled into relaxation by his father's familiar morning routine, Nik settled on a bench seat and Laru stretched out beside him, resting his head on Nik's lap.

His father poured two wooden mugsful of strong, steaming tea, handed one to Nik, and then sat across from his son. "It must be important. You even beat Thaddeus here."

"We found sign of the pup," Nik said without preamble.

Sol sat up straighter. "Truly? What sign did you find?"

"Paw prints under a holly hedge near a place where a bunch of Scratchers had gathered."

"Scat? Did you find scat as well?"

"No."

"So there is no way to judge how old the prints are."

"Father, if you give permission for me to return today *with Terriers* I will prove to you and everyone else that the tracks are fresh and my pup is alive."

"Nik, I want the pup to be alive as much as you do, but logic must dictate our actions, and it is not logical to believe that a half-grown canine has survived for nine nights unprotected in the forest."

"He's been in the forest ten nights now." Nik pointed at Laru. "This is his sire. Why is it so hard to believe that with such strong blood flowing in his veins the pup is still alive?"

Sol's expression saddened. "Not all sons are as strong as their fathers."

Nik gritted his teeth against the old pull of his father's disappointment. He was supposed to be Sun Priest after Sol, but that would never happen if he wasn't Companion to a Shepherd.

"Don't you see, Father? That's it exactly. I can't be what you want me to be unless I find this pup—*my* pup."

"Nikolas, I did not mean to disparage you. I was talking of pups and sires, not of you and me."

Nik met his father's moss-colored eyes and saw the lie there, but chose not to challenge him on it. Instead he deftly changed the subject and his tactics.

"We captured five Scratchers last night and killed several males."

Sol gave a resigned nod. "It is planting season and the Scratchers need to be replenished, especially in light of how rapidly the Tribe has been growing."

"Father, have you even known a Scratcher not to go gray at night?"

Sol shook his head, giving his son a confused look. "No, of course not. What are you talking about?"

Nik recounted the events that happened, beginning with the first sight of Jenna's father on the trail, and ending with his realization about the girl's pale skin and her father's.

Sol sipped his tea contemplatively before speaking. "I must admit that the Scratchers have long been on my mind. Their lives are so sad, so pitiable. I have often argued with myself about whether keeping them as we do is inhumane. Perhaps something you discovered last night could help them—could make their lives better."

"But everyone knows they're like big, walking babies. They can't take care of themselves. All they can do is make plants grow and live in mostly silent misery. We keep them safe, even from themselves, though their lives are so short. All we ask in return is that they tend our crops, which is already like second nature to them."

"We enslave them, Nik. And we do not ask that they tend our crops. They are our captives. They must do as we command," Sol said.

"But they don't seem to care," Nik said.

"True, but they don't seem to care about much of anything *after* we capture them." Sol shook his head slowly. "It's baffling. They must care for themselves in the wild, otherwise Scratchers would quickly become extinct, but on Farm Island they act like they're unable to protect themselves or do anything except eat, sleep, and tend crops."

"You really think they're that different in the wild?"

"I do, son. Actually, I believe they're drastically different."

"Why would you say that?"

"Because it is the truth. How many Hunts have you been on?"

Nik shrugged. "Counting last night, I think almost a dozen."

"I have been on fifty-seven Hunts. In that time I have seen many Scratchers, male and female, young and old. Very old. Women more often than men, but I have seen stooped, gray-haired grandmothers.

The Hunters do not capture them, as they are less likely to have the strength to tend our crops, but I have seen them," Sol repeated.

Nik thought about the faces he had seen last night pressing against the bars that covered the windows of their floating houses—their floating cages—and tried to remember if he had noticed any grandmother-aged women at all.

"They don't live long enough to grow old on Farm Island," Sol said. "They die of sadness instead."

"Father, we don't know exactly why they die. It's like they decide to quit living—and then that's it."

"Tell me, Nik, what did you feel last night while you were there, hearing the females call for help?"

Taken aback by the question, Nik hesitated, considering. "Well, I was tired and worried about the pup because—"

"I don't mean what did you feel about yourself," his father interrupted. "I mean what did you feel from the Scratchers, especially this young one you say spoke rationally to you."

"Well, I don't know if I felt Jenna's sadness, but I understood it." He met his father's gaze. "She'd just watched one of her parents die."

Sol closed his eyes and bowed his head. Nik could see his father's pain, and he shared it. Laru moved from Nik's side to his father, resting his head against his Companion's knee.

"I'm sorry. I didn't mean to remind you of Mother's death," Nik said softly.

Sol opened his eyes. "Son, your mother is never far from my thoughts, but it is not only in memory of her that I bow my head. I believe what happened last night was a sign."

"Really? A true sign?" Nik sat forward, waiting eagerly for his father to continue. Signs held great import for the Tribe. Where once their ancestors ignored omens and portents—so much so that they became completely detached from nature and the living earth—today's Tribe believed that the earth was ensouled, that animals, trees, and rocks and the earth herself were filled with unique energy and spirit, and that if the Tribe listened nature spoke to them of wonders and warnings.

"Really," Sol said. "The Scratchers have been often on my mind. I believe what you observed last night, whether an anomaly or not, is a sign that there is more to them than is convenient for the Tribe to admit. Thusly, I will make a deal with you, Nikolas. I will grant you permission to use one Hunter and his Terrier to keep searching for your pup for as long as you feel the need to search, but you must do two things for me in return."

"Anything, Father!"

"First, as you search for your pup, observe any Scratchers with which you cross paths. Take note of anything unusual about them, but do not capture them, and only report to me of what you observe."

"I will do that for you, Father. What else?"

"As you know, the Tribe's numbers have grown drastically over the past several winters."

Nik nodded. "The Tribe is strong. Almost all of the babies survive the winters."

"They do, and that pleases me, of course. But it also has made many of the family nests overly crowded," Sol said.

"The Gathering to celebrate Maeve's being chosen by Fortina was definitely overly crowded," Nik agreed.

"Exactly, which brings me to the second thing I would ask of you. Wilkes and his Odin are preparing to lead a foraging party into Port City. If we are to accommodate the fertility of the Tribe we must build new nests, as well as new pulley systems to lift and lower along the expanded city. We need the metal that can only be found in the ruins of the city. I want you to lead the party with Wilkes."

Nik blinked at his father, surprised by the request. "Father, you know that the Warriors will never follow someone who isn't Companion to a Shepherd."

"It is undisputed that you are the best bowman the Tribe has seen in many winters. The foraging party will need your talents."

"The Warriors appreciate my skill with a bow. I'll join the party to Port City. But they don't need to follow me for that."

"They do need to follow you—or at least listen to you—to benefit from your other skill."

Nik's brows furrowed. "My *other* skill? You want me to carve something during the foraging party? I'm sorry, Father, but that makes no sense."

Sol chuckled. "Outside your mother, you, my son, have the sharpest powers of observation I have ever known. The foraging party needs that particular skill very badly. You do remember what happened to the last group sent to Port City?"

Nik shuddered. "I do." Two of twelve Companions had returned alive. They had been carrying their mortally wounded Shepherds. Both had died within a double handspan of days, and their Companions had followed them to the grave not long after, but before they died they told a horrific story about how they had been lured into a trap and how Skin Stealers had flayed the captured Companions alive and begun wearing their skin while they were still conscious—

"I need your powers of observation to ensure this foraging party does not suffer the same fate as the one before it," Sol interrupted Nik's horrific remembrance.

"I get it, Father, and I'm willing to do as you ask, but that doesn't change the fact that I am not a Companion and the Warriors will not follow me," Nik said.

"But they will follow Wilkes, and Wilkes appreciates your skill. He will listen to you, thus the others will inadvertently be following you."

Nik's jaws clenched. *So, I'm to risk my ass without being granted the respect I deserve for it.*

"Is there a problem?"

Nik drew a deep breath. "No. There is no problem."

"Thank you, son," Sol said. "It is like an itching beneath my skin, this pity that I have for the Scratchers."

"Father, I'll do as you ask, but I have to know—you aren't actually considering setting the Scratchers loose, are you?" Nik asked.

"Would that I could, son. The Tribe would argue that the captive Scratchers need to be cared for—that what we do by keeping them on Farm Island is really a kindness. But you know as well as I what would happen if we were forced to tend our own crops. The harvests would decrease drastically without whatever earth magick the Scratchers use, but more importantly the accidents that would take place would be unavoidable." Sol shook his head sadly. "As would the deaths that would follow."

Nik shuddered. "Has there been no breakthroughs made by the Healers?"

"None whatsoever," Sol said somberly. "If our skin is broken we become vulnerable to the blight, and once it shows symptoms it cannot be cured—it can only be endured. And there is but one ending for the disease."

"Death." Nik shuddered. *And a horrible death at that.* Nik met his father's gaze, knowing they both were thinking of the beautiful woman who had been wife and mother to them, and who had slipped one day as she was carving a new lute to be played for the Mother Plants. She'd cut her wrist. Not a bad cut. It hadn't been deep or long. But the blight had infected her, using the vein at her wrist to spread quickly throughout her body. The disease had ravaged her in weeks. *Such a simple accident. Such a small cut.* Nik's thoughts turned to accidents and the tragedy that followed too often, turning small things into horrors. "A Scratcher hit Miguel last night with a rock."

Sol's sharp gaze pierced him. "His skin was broken?"

Nik nodded. "Yes."

Sol sighed. "I will go to him after sunrise. Nikolas, if Miguel is infected you should ready yourself. His family may blame you."

Nik bit back his angry excuses. His father was right. That he hadn't actually caused the Scratcher to strike Miguel wouldn't be important to a grieving family. The entire Tribe knew that Nik was still searching for the pup, and that because of that search the Hunters had roamed outside their normal territory. "I'll be ready. I'll keep a low profile."

Sol's brows lifted sardonically. "That might be a nice change."

Nik frowned at his father. "I don't usually cause trouble."

Sol's laughter was a little more sarcastic than Nik might have liked, but he joined him, glad that it broke up some of the sadness that had begun to settle between them.

"Come with me to welcome the sunrise?" Sol asked.

"I'd like to, but I need to get back to that holly bush as soon as possible, and I need to let a Hunter know he's going with me."

"Thaddeus and his Odysseus are one of the most talented tracking pairs that I've seen in many winters," Sol said.

"Actually, I'd rather not take Thaddeus," Nik said. "I prefer the company of Davis and his Cameron."

"They're young and a lot less experienced."

"Then searching for my pup will help them gain experience."

"Might I make a suggestion?"

Nik motioned for his father to continue.

"I'd like to suggest that if I was in a situation where an older, more experienced Tribe member like Thaddeus was, well, for lack of a better way to put it—rather condescending about something I believed strongly in . . ." Sol paused and Nik gave a weary nod of agreement. "Ah, I thought so. Let's say that I had a chance to prove directly to this condescending Tribe member that my belief was valid, and that his was rather shortsighted, I would take the opportunity to show him; thereby showing the entire Tribe."

"He's so arrogant! He completely dismisses the possibility that the pup still lives, even after we found sign of him."

"Thaddeus is definitely arrogant, and he can be rather caustic, but he takes immense pride in his tracking skills, which are indeed vast."

"I still don't like him."

Sol smiled. "What if I give permission for you to include Davis and Cameron with Thaddeus and Odysseus in your search? They could use the experience. It would help the Tribe, and make your searching more pleasant. Agreed?"

Nik let out a long, relieved breath. "Agreed." He paused and then, before Nik could talk himself out of speaking the words aloud, he said in a rush, "Father, have you ever thought that maybe the Tribe's Law about only allowing bonded Companions to serve in leadership positions is flawed?"

Sol's brows shot up to his hairline. "Whatever are you talking about, Nikolas?"

"It's acknowledged by the entire Tribe that Mother was the best carver to have lived in generations."

"Yes, that is truth," Sol said with a quizzical smile. "What are you getting at, son?"

"Yet she was not allowed the title of Master Carver because no canine chose her, even though she deserved the title and basically served as Master Carver for most of her adult life."

"Well, yes, but—"

"And you just said that I am the best bowman in the Tribe, and have excellent powers of observation, but I can't lead the Warriors because no canine has chosen me. It just doesn't make much sense to me."

His father studied him silently for several breaths before finally saying, "This is the hard truth, Nikolas—if you were chosen by a canine our laws would make sense to you. Son, you only question tradition because you are *not* bonded."

Nik didn't look away from his father's gaze. Instead, with a sad sense of resignation, he said, "You may be right, Father. We'll only know if I *am* chosen and I still feel the same then as I do about it now. So, if I may have your blessing on my venture I will go find Davis and Thaddeus and let them know we'll be heading back to Scratcher territory this morning."

"You will always have my blessing, Nikolas," Sol said. "And I do appreciate your keen, questioning mind—as would your mother."

"Thank you, Father."

Nik knelt before Sol. The Sun Priest put one hand on his son's bowed head and lifted the other to the window opening that was letting in more and more light. "I bless you with the Sun's touch, Nikolas, son of Sol. May you carry warmth and strength and light with you in your quest, and may you return home safely before darkness extinguishes day."

Nik closed his eyes as the warmth of the sun cascaded into his body, but instead of concentrating on the pup he so desperately wanted to find, all he could see against his closed eyelids was Jenna's pale, tear-streaked face.

14

Even after they were safely in their burrow with the bramble thicket protecting and camouflaging them, and the door barred firmly behind them, Mari and her mother at first spoke in hushed tones, their heads near one another. Though they knew little about canines and the specifics of their tracking abilities, both women understood that something had to be done to confuse Rigel's trail so that any returning Companions, especially the one named Nik, would have a difficult, if not impossible, time tracking the pup.

"I wish I knew more about what canines can and cannot track," Leda said.

"I wish we had time to test Rigel—to find out how to make him lose a trail," Mari said. "But we don't, Mama. I have to go back as soon as it's close enough to dawn to be sure that any swarming roaches will have finished." Mari paused, shuddering. The roaches would, for sure, have followed the wolf spider pack and the deadly raid of the Companions at the Gathering, looking for the leavings of death.

"Do you have a plan, Mari?"

"I have an idea. I know what makes it most difficult, impossible even, to track deer or wild boar. I'm going to try to duplicate as many of the circumstances that have messed up a day of hunting for me—and for you."

Leda nodded slowly. "Interesting, and it just may work."

"It will. It has to. So, let's finish eating, and then try to get a little sleep." Rigel stayed so close to Mari that she had to be careful not to trip over him as she got up to replenish the hearty rabbit stew that seemed to disappear from their bowls. While they ate, Mari studied Leda, not liking how pale she looked.

"Don't go with me in the morning. Stay here and rest, Mama. Rigel and I will be just fine, and back in no time."

"Absolutely not. *We* will make sure Rigel is safe. Together."

Mari nodded slowly as she ladled more stew into their bowls and fixed Rigel another bowl of the raw rabbit mixed with grasses and grains that he preferred over cooked food. Mari was worried about her mother, but she did need Leda's help if they were to be sure that nosy Nik wouldn't be able to track Rigel back to their burrow.

"He's not going to give up. No matter what we do in the morning, that Companion is going to keep searching for my Shepherd," Mari said.

Rigel whined and Mari opened her arms so that he could try to curl as much of his growing body as possible on her lap.

"From what you told me it seems this Nik Companion believes Rigel was going to choose him," Leda said.

"Well, he's dead wrong!" Mari snapped, and then gave her mother an apologetic smile, and petted Rigel soothingly. "Sorry. I didn't mean to take that out on you." She sighed as she took her seat beside Leda. "It was so bizarre to hear him talking about Rigel like he belongs to him. Bizarre and scary."

Leda patted her knee. "What you heard answers one of our questions about how the Companions could have lost a treasured Shepherd pup." Her mom smiled for the first time since Jenna had been taken. "Clever Rigel escaped so that he could find you!"

Mari grinned back at her. "Yes, he did!" She hugged Rigel around his neck and the pup licked her enthusiastically. Then Mari's expression sobered. "And that's why I know that man won't stop searching for him. They weren't being careless. They haven't stopped cherishing their canines. I'll bet Rigel is the first pup to have escaped them in a long time."

"I'd wager in forever," Leda said. "And I am in complete agreement with you. That Companion won't stop looking for your Rigel—not as long as he has not found evidence of his death."

"And that's something we can't fake. Isn't it?"

"I don't know how we could make it seem to a Companion that the pup has died. Your father told me that Shepherds are used to track people, and Terriers are used to track game. Either way, they are sure to have a canine involved in the search for Rigel, and a canine nose is not easily fooled, even if we could figure out a way to have his fur and some canine bones discoverable."

Mari's jaw tightened with anger. "Wait, you said they use Terriers to track game, but I heard that friend of Nik's say that a Terrier found Rigel's paw prints."

"That simply means the Hunters were searching for Rigel all along."

"No, Mother. That's not what it means. I also overheard that they were hunting for captives, and that Nik had talked them into searching outside their usual territory *because* he was looking for Rigel." In answer to her mother's confused look Mari continued bluntly. "Leda, they don't consider Scratchers people. That's why the Terriers were hunting us, and not the Shepherds."

"Oh. Oh dear." Leda looked faint.

"Well, let's look at the positive." With a Herculean effort, Mari brightened. "If they didn't think of us as animals they would have had Shepherds with them, and Shepherds would have been searching only for Rigel. They would have found him, Mama. I know it. So, *arooooow!*" Mari leaned back her head and, much to Rigel's amusement, howled happily. The pup joined her until Mari collapsed breathlessly beside him as he wagged his tail and smiled his tongue-lolling canine grin. "Tonight I don't mind being an animal with Rigel! Not one bit."

But Leda's mood would not lighten. "It worries me, Mari. Your father never told me that they thought of us as animals. He only said their Tribe thought of us as childlike, unable to care for ourselves. They enslave us under the pretense of protection, but they also need us to labor for them on their island. But if they see us as less than human, then what is to become of you after I'm gone?"

"Mama." Mari took Leda's hand. "We don't need to worry about that. You're strong and healthy and young still. We will have many, many more winters together. Let's just focus on how we're going to fix the problem of the Companions tracking Rigel. And—" Mari broke off, not wanting to add more worries for her mother.

"And what, Mari?" Leda prodded.

Mari sighed. "And Jenna. What do we do about Jenna?"

Leda met her daughter's gaze and spoke slowly and distinctly, as if she wanted her words to be imprinted on Mari's mind. "There is *nothing* we can do about Jenna. Not now. Not ever."

"But Mama, she's only known sixteen winters! Without a Moon Woman to Wash the sadness from her, she's going to die. She'll never fall in love. She'll never have her own daughter. She'll never know happiness ever again."

"Mari, you must listen to me." Leda gripped her daughter's hand tightly. "Unless they find a way to escape, all Earth Walkers captured by the Companions go mad with despair and die early. You already know this."

"I do," Mari said, choking back a sob. "And that's why we have to help Jenna escape."

"At what cost? I don't believe it possible that Rigel could get close to a Companion Tribe and *not* be discovered. After what happened tonight I have no doubt that the Companion named Nik would forcibly take your pup away from you. If they see us as no more than animals, then I am afraid they would consider you unworthy of a Leader canine . . ." Leda's words faded as her face paled. She shook her head as if trying to dislodge the disturbing thoughts forming there. "Are you willing to sacrifice Rigel and possibly yourself to save Jenna?"

A terrible chill shuddered through Mari's body and her free hand reached down to touch Rigel reassuringly. "No. I can't." Mari whispered her response. "I *won't* give up Rigel."

"And I do not fault you for that. Rigel is meant to be with you for life. Your bond with him is as deep as your soul, as strong as your heart. I would go. I would try to save our little Jenna, but if I was unsuccessful—if they captured me—"

"No! You can't! And not because you're a Moon Woman and the Clan needs you. Because you're my mama and my best friend. *I* need you."

"I know, Mari. I know." Leda pulled her daughter into her arms. "Remember, my sweet girl, these bodies of ours are but our shells. It is only Xander's body that has died. His true self—his spirit—has moved on, just as Jenna's body is all that has been captured. Her spirit will be free again."

"Mama, I don't think I'll ever quit seeing Xander's face just before Jenna screamed. He saw Rigel. He knew that we were together, that I was the cause of the Companions trespassing so far into our territory, and he looked at me like he hated me."

"Sssh, Mari. Nothing can be done to change what happened tonight, and Xander is now free of pain—free of the madness Night Fever brings—reunited with his beloved mate."

"But I was *glad* when they started shooting him," Mari sobbed into her mother's shoulder. "Because he'd seen Rigel, and I knew he was going to tell everyone. I hate myself for it. I hate myself for it. Poor Jenna! Xander was right to look at me with disgust. It's because of me that she's an orphan and a slave."

"It's not because of you. It's because of this world. And what this world has become is *not* your fault."

"I want to change things, Mama," Mari said between sobs. "Even if it means I have to leave this place and start over."

"I know, sweet girl. I know . . ."

Mari and Leda hugged each other tightly, while they cried for Xander and Jenna and the others of the Clan who were killed or captured, and wished that their world was different—was easier—or at least was just.

Mari didn't sleep at all that night. She lay snuggly between her mother and Rigel, and even though sleep eluded her, she drew comfort from the nearness of her family, glad Leda had fallen asleep on the pallet with her and not retreated to her own room. While Rigel snored softly Mari studied her mother's face. When had those lines overtaken the smoothness of her forehead? And how had she gotten so thin so suddenly? Her skin was still quite lovely, but it was also almost transparent. How many winters had her mother known? Almost forty? That wasn't old! She'd always seemed so young to Mari. Sometimes, especially when they were laughing together about something silly—like Mari's purposely silly illustrations—it seemed to Mari that she and Leda were closer than just mother and daughter. It seemed they were sisters and best friends, as well as each other's only family. Leda seemed many things to Mari, but until that night she had never seemed old.

Mari felt a sharp, cold stab of fear. Leda's mother had died just before she had seen forty winters. That had been two years before Leda met Galen and conceived her, but she often told Mari stories of her grandmother. *Why exactly had she died? Mama had only said that she had sickened, grown weaker and weaker, and died not long after Leda had finished her apprenticeship.* She tended to not ask her mother questions that brought Leda sad memories, but Mari vowed silently to find out what had happened to her grandmother. *Would it happen to her mother, too? Was it something all Moon Women had to suffer?*

No! That would not happen to Mama. Not now. Not ever. If that means Sora or I or both of us have to remain apprentice Moon Women for all the winters to come—then so be it. The thought echoed through Mari's mind so furiously that Rigel stirred restlessly in his sleep, turning to whine questioningly and lay his head across her, waking Leda. Her mother peered blearily at her through sleep-fogged eyes.

"Is it time?"

"I'll check." Mari untangled herself from Rigel, who grumbled, and then stretched and yawned. She hurried to the little hole that served as a window to the upper world. The black of night was lightening to gray and the palest of pinks. She turned back to her mother. "Yes, it's time."

Silently, Leda and Mari broke their fast, feeding Rigel as well. They dressed carefully, making sure Mari's arms and legs were fully covered, her hair was completely dyed, and reapplying the concealing clay and mud to her delicate features. Mari brought her slingshot and a pouch filled with smooth stones. Together they replenished the skins with the lavender oil and saltwater that blinded wolf spiders. When all was ready, they paused before the door.

"We need to move quickly and silently," Leda said. "The sun hasn't broken the horizon, but when it does—when it has vanquished the fog—you will be vulnerable. I do not doubt that other members of the Clan will be out today searching for loved ones gone missing."

"We'll stay off the trails, and we'll be quiet."

"And vigilant. Remember that you are not simply vulnerable because of your skin. If any Earth Walker saw you with Rigel, I do not know what they would do."

Mari knew what they would do. She'd seen it in Xander's eyes last night. "I won't let them see Rigel. He knows what hide means—we practice it whenever I take him out to relieve himself. I don't even have to give him the command anymore. I just point and think about him being so quiet and still that he becomes invisible, and Rigel understands." She stroked her pup affectionately, kissing him on his nose before nodding to her mother.

Leda opened the door. With her walking stick she held the razor-edged brambles aside as Mari and Rigel followed her around the winding, hidden pathway that led away from their burrow.

Mari hesitated just outside the bramble thicket, staring back at their camouflaged home and worrying her lip between her teeth.

"What is it?" her mother asked.

"I wish I knew how to cover Rigel's scent. If the Companions ever get near our burrow, whether they have Terriers or Shepherds, he is going to be scented."

"Then let us be quite certain they have no reason to come anywhere near our home," Leda said.

Mari nodded tightly. "Okay, I'm going to carry Rigel all the way back there. I don't want them to find one more pup-sized trail leading here."

"I think that's wise," Leda said.

Mari lifted Rigel in her arms, feeling his warmth and his solid weight, and thinking that it wouldn't be long before he'd be too big for her to carry very far. Keeping a tight hold on her pup, she moved with her mother through the ash and willow trees that dominated the damp, stream-filled forest that was Earth Walker territory. This close to their burrow, Mari and Leda kept the forest floor cleared of any edible plants that might draw others—be they Earth Walkers or Companions—and encouraged wild brambles, stinging nettles, poison oak, and devil's club to flourish, making their little section of the forest as unappealing as possible. There were no obvious pathways through the mixture of unpleasant and dangerous plants, but Mari and her mother made their way confidently and quickly through the area.

As agreed upon before they left their burrow, they did not go directly back to the Gathering Site and the holly bush under which Rigel's paw prints had been discovered. Instead they made their way to the site of Xander's murder, and the last place Rigel had been before the three of them had raced for home.

Leda was leading when they came to a spot where the ferns were trampled and broken. Rigel suddenly became restless in Mari's arms, whining and sniffing the air.

"Xander's there, isn't he?" Mari said.

Leda motioned for Mari to stay where she was, and she walked ahead, stopping abruptly and pressing her hand against her throat.

"Mama?" Mari whispered.

Leda bowed her head and mouthed a prayer before she returned to her daughter. "You were right. The roaches were here last night." Taking Mari's arm, she guided her in a wide circle around the horrific leavings. "This is it. I can smell the lavender. This is where we fought the spiders."

"And this is where we fell." Mari pointed at the dip in the forest floor where Xander had pushed them when he was trying to save them. "Okay, I'm going to put Rigel down now." She did so, wiping the sweat from her face and stretching to relieve the soreness in her back. "And now we circle all the way back to the cedar we hid under."

The women moved swiftly and silently. The ground was wet from the rain that had fallen late the night before, and Mari was glad to see that Rigel's oversized paws were leaving distinct prints. She and her mother were, of course, leaving prints as well, but Mari consistently threw twigs and pinecones for Rigel to chase, sending him out away from them while Leda used a mature deer fern as a broom to muddle and make much of their tracks indistinct.

When they arrived at the dead cedar, Leda went within and Mari kept Rigel outside the curtain of vines while her mother smoothed the tracks left by the four of them. She rejoined her daughter and Mari pulled the ivy aside, pointed, and told Rigel, "Hide!"

Wriggling happily, the young Shepherd ran within, spinning around and lying down to look up at Mari, his tail thumping against the floor of dead leaves and dirt, thoroughly enjoying the game. She let him stay where he was for a moment, hoping that his scent would be trapped within the hiding spot.

"That should be an easy find for anyone tracking Rigel. From here we walk straight back to the holly bush, and I'll tell him to hide in there, too."

The three of them closed the distance between the cedar and the holly bush. As they drew closer, Mari saw that the area was a disaster of trampled ferns, smashed logs, and destroyed undergrowth. There were a few places where Mari had spied the feathers of an arrow, and she had quickly averted her gaze.

"Another Earth Walker. Yet another male gone," Leda said softly. "I wonder how many they killed?"

"Xander, this one, and at the Gathering Site below I saw Warren shot and killed as they attacked," Mari said.

"Warren. I am sorry to hear it. Cyan will be grieving his loss."

Mari said nothing, though not because she was too callous to let death and the grief that followed it affect her. She simply didn't understand how a woman could grieve a man who spent so little of his life with her. Xander had been different. He had actually raised Jenna—had been more of a mother than a father to her. But Warren? Mari would have liked to have asked her mother how often he had come to her to be Washed of his madness. Had he bothered to retain his sanity for his mate, or had he, like many of the Earth Walker males, simply given in to Night Fever more often than not?

Mari shook herself mentally and pointed at the holly bush. "Rigel, hide!"

The pup dashed within, spun around, and mouth open in a grin, waited for whatever game would come next.

"We go from here to the creek?" Leda asked.

"Yes, but first I'm going to throw this for him and have him bring it back to me from a bunch of directions." Mari lifted the last stick she'd picked up. "Here you go, Rigel. Get it!" She tossed the stick and Rigel sprinted after it, happily carrying it back to her. A dozen times Mari threw the stick for Rigel—in a dozen different directions. Finally she nodded at her mother. "I think that's good. Now to the creek."

Mari called Rigel to her and the three of them made their way carefully down the steep bank.

"Watch your step, Mari," Leda said, taking her daughter's hand. "There are many holes and sharp, broken branches hidden beneath the leaves here. This bank is much more treacherous than it appears, which is why the crossing to the Gathering Site is quite a way downriver."

Mari squeezed her mother's hand and helped her pick her way down the steep bank while Rigel careened past them, all oversized legs and paws, making the two women smile.

"I think he's going to be even bigger than your father's Orion was," Leda said, breathing hard as they paused at the bottom of the bank to catch their breath.

"I think Rigel is going to be magnificent! I also think we're going to be successful today. After what we do, no Companion is going to be able to track Rigel back to our burrow," Mari said, hoping by saying the words she would make them real. "And I'll be more careful from today on. I'll never take a straight path back to our burrow, and I'll carry him whenever we get close to home."

Leda raised a brow. "Even when he's full grown?"

Mari nodded determinedly. "Even when he's full grown. I'm already strong, and my strength will grow with him."

Leda smiled at the gangly, frolicking pup and then at her daughter, her expression filled with love and pride. "Sweet girl, I believe you can accomplish anything if you work hard enough at it."

Holding hands, Mother and daughter slogged through the creek together. The late-night rains had continued to swell the creek and had the already treacherous current sucking at their legs. Mari kept a tight hold on her mother's slim hand while she glanced at Rigel, who had paused at the edge of the water and was whining piteously.

"Come on, Rigel. You can do it!"

The pup instantly stopped whining, pricked his ears at Mari, and then launched himself into the creek, sputtering and sneezing, but swimming strongly after them. The three of them reached the opposite, gentler bank together, and the women laughed softly as Rigel shook himself vigorously, and then began rolling in the moss in front of the nearest Earth Mother idol.

The women's laughter stopped abruptly as their gazes went from idol to idol. The Gathering Site was wrecked. The Hunters had taken no notice of the lovingly tended statues, and had trampled anything that had been in their path. Mari watched her mother wander from one desecrated statue to another. At first Leda tried to repair smashed ferns and torn moss, but finding one of the Goddess's carved sandstone faces that had been knocked from its rightful place and shattered, had her becoming still in her sadness. She sat with the broken rock in her lap, her fingers trailing over the cracked carving as if she could smooth away the damage.

Mari glanced at the sky. To the east of them it had lightened from gray and mauve to the colors of fire mixed with the cerulean of true morning.

"Mama." She went to Leda and touched her shoulder gently. "Rigel and I have to go upstream, toward the Companions' forest, and leave false trails. I can do it quickly and then return if you want to stay here and try to fix the Earth Mothers."

Leda looked up at her daughter, her eyes swimming with unshed tears. "Don't you need me to help you make the false trails?"

"No, Mama. Actually, I think it would be faster if just Rigel and I went." Mari paused and added. "There aren't any burrows upstream, are there?"

"No. There are no burrows in that direction. None would have been built heading toward the Companions' forest."

"Then I don't need to worry about Earth Walkers surprising me with Rigel, right?" Mari asked.

"Right again, sweet girl, which seems the norm these days." Leda smiled up at her daughter, though Mari thought her expression was shadowed with sadness. "You are growing into a fine woman, Mari. I am so proud of you."

Mari blinked in surprise. "Well, thank you, Leda," she said, trying to lighten her mother's mood.

"You are welcome. You deserve the compliment. And stop calling me Leda." She began shooing away Mari. "Go on. I'll stay here and ground myself—find my calm true self in the midst of this chaos. Then I will put to right this desecration." Leda paused and looked around her, sounding overwhelmed. "Or perhaps I should better use the time to go downstream to the burrows closest to here and warn the Clan that they must move."

Mari smoothed her mother's hair back from her face, noticing as she did so that there seemed to be an unusual amount of silver framing her temples. "Mama, weren't most of the Clanswomen present yesterday?"

"Yes. There had to be a majority present to witness and accept my choice as apprentice. The only people missing were out hunting or gathering," she said.

"Then the Clan has already been warned. I think you should wait here for me and care for the Earth Mothers."

"You're right, I'm sure. And you won't be gone long, will you, Mari?"

"No, of course not. The sun is rising in a clear sky. Rigel and I need to get back to our burrow, and you need to come with us. Be watchful, Mama. The Companions came through the cherry grove." Mari pointed behind them at the bud-filled trees. "Listen carefully. If you hear *anything* get across the creek and run home. If you're not here when I return I'll know you're waiting for us there."

"You be vigilant, too, Mari. You have to watch for Companions as you lay your false trail, and then when you return here you must watch for any of the Clan who—" Rigel, bumping her thigh with his wet nose, interrupted her and had Leda laughing softly. "Ah, I see clever pup. You will warn our Mari of danger."

"Yes, he sure will," Mari said, stroking the pup and kissing him on his damp head affectionately. "Don't you worry about us, Mama. I'll come back quietly and listen carefully. If I hear your voice I'll know you're talking to someone from the Clan and I'll be sure Rigel hides."

"If anyone from the Clan is here I'll be sure my voice is raised so you can hear me easily." Leda smiled at Rigel. "I mean so Rigel can hear me easily and warn you." Leda petted the damp canine, who wriggled happily.

"That sounds like the perfect plan, Mama." Mari bent and kissed her mother on her head, just like she'd so recently kissed her pup, making both women grin and the pup wag his tail in shared happiness. "We'll be back safely and soon. Then we can go home and rest for the entire day."

"I will be here waiting for the both of you," Leda said.

"I love you, Mama," Mari heard herself speaking aloud the words she was thinking.

Leda smiled as she looked at her daughter. "And I love you, too, my sweet girl." She turned her attention to the pup. "Rigel, I'm counting on you to take care of our Mari." The pup galloped to Leda, licking her face and wriggling happily as she petted him. "Good boy, good boy," she murmured. "And I love you, too." Then, smiling and humming softly, Leda turned to busy herself with the first of the Earth Mother idols.

Mari watched Leda begin to gently remold the moss that had been ripped from the idol's voluptuous, earthy body. Leda's expression had shifted from sad to serene. As always, tending the Goddess idols seemed to soothe her and help her find her center. Mari was glad of it, even if the idols had never had the same effect on her. *Maybe when I'm older. Maybe then the Earth Mother will speak to me like she does Mama.* Mari sighed. *Or maybe my father's blood has ensured the Great Earth Mother will never speak to me at all.*

Mari shook her head, scattering her gloomy thoughts, and waving a final time to her mother, motioned for Rigel to follow her into the creek so that they could begin trudging upstream.

15

Had the business of creating false trails not been so important to their existence, Mari would have been thoroughly enjoying herself. Rigel certainly was! While Mari threw stick after stick for Rigel to run after and then return to her, she walked through the creek, watching the pup sprint into the forest and return to her, plunging into the water and swimming to her as if he could never tire of their game. As the sun climbed the sky the spring morning grew warmer and warmer, and the cool creek water felt wonderful against Mari's legs. She daydreamed about how she would have loved to take off her clothes and submerge herself, washing the dirt and clay and dye from her arms and face and hair. Then she'd choose one of the wide, dark boulders positioned directly in the sunlight and she would lie there—naked—and soak in the heat of the sun. *If only,* Mari thought.

As the creek began to bend to the right, Mari waded to the nearest bank and sat on a sunny log, dabbing sweat and water carefully from her face. Rigel came to lie by her feet, and set about tearing up a pinecone he'd fished out of the creek.

Mari stretched mightily, and her palms, pointing skyward, tingled as unimpeded sunlight beamed down on her. Mari glanced around her. The creek had taken a sharp turn to the east, creating a covelike area where the water pooled in the shallows and glistened like a forgotten promise made new. She and Rigel were absolutely alone in a little bubble of sunlight and beauty. Hesitantly, Mari lifted her hands over her head again. Opening her palms, she held them up so that they could catch the morning sun.

Through her palms, warmth swept into her body. Mari welcomed it, noting the difference between the golden power of the sun, and the cool, silver strength of the moon. She couldn't say which she preferred—she hadn't had enough experience with sunlight, which sounded silly. The sun did rise every day, and it wasn't like she was a child anymore. It had been many, many winters since that first morning when she and Leda had been gathering berries in a clearing a little deer path had led them to. The sun had burned away the morning fog, leaving the clearing in brilliant, golden light. Mari remembered every moment of what had happened next. She had been so young that her features were as yet indistinct enough that she hadn't needed the camouflaging clay, though Leda had already been working dye into her fair hair. The sudden sunlight had filled Mari with an indescribably giddy feeling, and she had flung wide her arms and done a little impromptu dance around the berry grove, singing happily to herself until she'd heard her mother's horrified, *No, Great Mother! Not Mari!*

Mari had run to her mother, asking what was wrong—what had happened. Leda had been crying, Mari was sure of it even though her mother had carefully wiped her face and smiled before facing her inquisitive daughter and pointing to her bare arms. *Nothing is wrong, sweet girl. You are your father's daughter, and there is nothing wrong with that, nothing at all.*

But Mari had understood. Earth Walkers weren't fair-haired, nor did delicate, frondlike patterns of gold rise from beneath their skin when sunlight touched them. Mari had to pretend to be an Earth Walker, or according to Law she and her mother would be rejected by the Clan. That sunny day had been the official start of Mari's life of hiding.

"But I steal moments," Mari whispered. Purposefully, Mari spread the fingers on her raised hands wide, and let her head fall back so that her eyes could stare up at the clear morning sky. By her side, Rigel mimicked her actions, staring up at the sun. She knew without looking at him that his eyes, along with hers, had begun to glow, intensifying the warmth that filled and invigorated her. "Oh, Rigel! It feels so good, and the sun isn't even at mid-sky yet." And then Mari realized what she had just said, and she dropped her hands and shook her head, ordering her thoughts. This time when she looked around she saw more than the tranquil beauty of the cove. Mari saw the tall pines that the fat sun seemed to sit just above.

"Rigel, let's go!" Mari was up and moving into the creek before she'd taken two breaths. *Too far! I've gone too far and come too close to the Companions' forest!*

Wading into the creek with the pup swimming beside her, Mari turned downstream, glad that she could make up time going with the current. Then, as a floating log bumped against her, she had a wonderful idea. Snagging the log with one hand, she grabbed Rigel by his scruff and helped the soggy canine scramble up so that he was clinging to the piece of wood half in, half out of the water. Then, careful to stay low so that someone glancing at the creek would only notice floating flotsam with a log, but not so low in the water that she submerged her face and washed away the concealing clay and dirt and dye, Mari hugged the log to her, keeping one arm wrapped around Rigel. The current took them, and they began to float swiftly down the middle of the creek.

Mari kept her attention focused on the forest around them. She'd been gone too long—let too much time pass. Companions would certainly be on their way to continue their search, and maybe their hunt as well. Earth Walkers would definitely be stirring by now, and they couldn't know that the Companions would be returning so soon. They couldn't know that Nik and the other Hunters had only been there because of Rigel. Mari could imagine the Clan making their way back to the Gathering Site to look for evidence of lost loved ones and, like her mother, to care for the desecrated Earth Mother idols.

"Yeah, and they'll be there, like moles peeking their heads up after a hard winter. They won't be expecting enemies to come after them again," Mari muttered to Rigel. "Of course Mama will be right there in the middle of them, trying to save everyone, but only succeeding in putting herself in danger." As soon as she'd spoken the words, a terrible clenching fear fisted around her gut. "We need to get back and be sure Mama's safe. Hang on, Rigel, I'm going to start kicking."

Mari's kicks added to the current and propelled them swiftly downstream, and except for bumping her knees on submerged rocks, Mari was feeling pretty good about her plan to make up time when the sound of women's voices drifted across the water to her.

Instantly Mari released the log. Rigel close beside her, Mari swam to the shallows, and then, with a grunt and a huge effort, lifted the soaked Shepherd in her arms. She sent him soothing *all is well—stay still and quiet—all is well* thoughts as she picked her way slowly and silently through the forest underbrush.

"Xander dead and Jenna taken? It's so horrible!" Sora's distinctive voice lifted above the others, causing Mari to freeze in place. The pink, fragrant cherry blossoms were perfuming the air as she searched the area, trying to find somewhere she could hide Rigel. Remembering a huge willow positioned not too far upstream from the Gathering Site, Mari cut back toward the creek as her mother's answer was drowned by water and wind.

The willow was easy to find, and more perfect than Mari had expected. It sat by itself on a little bump of ground that lifted it and made the tree, with its graceful draping of thick boughs, look as if it was there to oversee the creek and the Gathering Site. Crouched low and still carrying Rigel, Mari approached the tree from the rear, slipping within the curtain-like branches.

She put Rigel down, whispering "Hide" before she crawled to the edge of the circle of gently swaying branches, parted them just enough to peek through, and went very silent as she studied the scene before her.

Leda had made her way into the creek with the stone face of another of the idols. She was still bent over it, her hands scooping water to wash away the muddy footprints left by uncaring Companions as they had trampled through the sacred site.

On the opposite bank, not far from the holly tree Mari and Rigel had hidden beneath the evening before, were several Clan members—all men except for Sora. She seemed to be doing all the talking while the men watched her silently as she and Leda carried on an animated discussion. Just as Mari was sighing in frustration at not being able to hear what was being said, the wind shifted, carrying the women's voices to her.

"Yes, Sora, I do insist that you abandon your burrow. First, because it is not far enough from here to be safe. As you know, my Mari was here last night. She overheard the Companions speaking to one another. They will return. One of their canine pups is missing and they think it became lost in our territory. They do not intend to stop looking for him. Quite simply, it is not safe for you to remain in this part of our territory, just as it is not safe for *any* of our Clan to remain nearby."

Mari's gaze went to Sora, who started to speak, but Leda's raised hand silenced her. "I have not finished, Sora. Second, you agreed to be apprenticed to me last night, which means you will someday—should our Great Earth Mother grant it—become a Moon Woman. You know it is forbidden for the location of a Moon Woman's burrow to be known to the Clan. You would eventually have to find a new spot for your home. Is now or later really that important?"

"Yes, it is important to me!" Sora said, sounding petulant.

"As it should be. A Moon Woman's choice of burrow is of extreme importance, as is the keeping of it secret." Mari smiled at her mother's response. *Sora is definitely out of her league.*

"I know that I have to find a new home, and keep it secret." Then, as if an afterthought, Sora added, "I just don't understand how I'm supposed to make my new burrow without the help of anyone. After all, *my* mother wasn't a Moon Woman. *I* don't have a burrow already hidden by silence and mystery."

Mari's eyes narrowed just as did Leda's. Sora's tone wasn't just whiny, it was disrespectful.

Leda had stopped washing the face of the idol, and had straightened. She faced Sora, and as she spoke her words were amplified by equal parts anger and love.

"Sora, I was going to wait until I could call another Gathering to tell you this, but now seems the perfect time. I have decided to break with tradition, which is always a Moon Woman's prerogative, and to announce that I claim two apprentices."

"Two? No, I—" Sora began, but Leda sliced her words off.

"Silence, apprentice! You may speak when I have finished. I proclaim that my daughter, Mari, will also apprentice as the Clan's Moon Woman." Leda paused and, smiling serenely, added, "Apprentice, now you may speak, but be wise with your words. I have the right to take away apprenticeship as easily as I give it."

Mari's heart was hammering so hard that she almost didn't hear Sora's next words.

"But the entire Clan knows Mari is too sickly to be a true Moon Woman!"

"Until the Companions attacked us last night, I thought Mari was too frail to be Moon Woman, too, but what she did proved me wrong. You see, the reason I know Xander was killed and Jenna taken, is because just before the Companions overran our hiding place, Mari called down the moon and Washed them both clean of Night Fever."

Sora's black brows shot up. "That is hard to believe."

"And yet I witnessed it," Leda said.

There was a long silence where Sora looked from Leda to each of the four men, her expression clearly saying what her words could not without invoking Leda's wrath. Finally, one of the men spoke up. It was, of course, Jaxom, the young Clansman Sora had been sharing looks with at the Full Moon Gathering. Slowly, with obvious reticence, he said, "Moon Woman, why would Mari have Washed Xander and Jenna, instead of you Washing them?"

"Jaxom, are you questioning my word?"

Mari shivered at the tone of her mother's voice. She had rarely heard it, but on those few occasions she knew what followed would not be pleasant.

Jaxom's eyes flicked to Sora, who quickly went to him, touching his arm intimately. "Of course Jaxom isn't questioning your word, Moon Woman. He is simply asking aloud the question we are all thinking."

"Then I will answer him just as simply. I was injured last night. Badly. Mari saved me from drowning, and got me to a hiding spot, where we met Xander and Jenna. I had a severe concussion. I had cracked ribs. I could not call down the moon, and the Companions were close by, so when Xander began to be consumed by Night Fever, Mari did what I could not. She Washed him. She Washed Jenna. Does that answer your question?"

"Almost," Sora said, making a big show of seeming to be embarrassed that there was more she needed to ask. "But if your injuries were so great that you couldn't call down the moon, couldn't even aid your daughter in calling down the moon, then why do you seem uninjured today?"

Leda lifted her chin, and in a voice so filled with love and pride it had Mari's eyes tearing, said, "I am uninjured today because after Mari Washed Xander and Jenna free of madness, she Washed me free of my wounds. And *that* Sora, is why I proclaim my daughter, Mari, my apprentice and heir in addition to you."

Mari didn't think she'd ever stop smiling. Sora's mouth was actually hanging open, and Jaxom was nodding—practically bowing—to Leda while he muttered something that sounded like an apology. The other three men looked equally chagrined. Mari was so filled with happiness that it took several breaths for her to realize that the sound she was hearing, a low rumble, was coming from Rigel. Reluctantly she turned her attention to the pup. He had been curled beside her on the mossy ground, semi-asleep after his exertions in the creek, but now he was standing. His body almost hummed with tension. The fur up and down his spine was lifted. His tail curled up over his back, scorpion-like, and his ears were pricked forward. He was growling softly, all of his attention focused on the cherry grove behind the creek. Suddenly Mari was filled with the desire to *run, escape, go go go*!

Mari moved fast, but not fast enough. As she parted the curtain of boughs and shouted, "Mama, run!" Companions and their canines burst from the cherry grove.

Sora didn't hesitate. Without so much as a glance at Leda, she grabbed Jaxom's hand and yelled, "Save me! Save me!" The young man half dragged her up the steep bank and then the two of them sprinted into the forest. The other three men followed closely behind.

Not one of them helped Leda.

Leda glanced over her shoulder, searching wildly for Mari. Stepping from the concealment of the willow, Mari gestured for her mother to go—run! She meant to go to her—to leave Rigel there, hidden and safe at least for the moment—and to rush to her mama. But her Shepherd had other ideas. With a strength that utterly surprised Mari, Rigel clamped his teeth into her tunic and pulled, jerking her off her feet and dragging her backward so that she fell to the ground within the safety of the willow.

"Rigel, no! I have to go to Mama!" Mari scrambled to be free of the pup, but it was too late. The voices of strangers filled the Gathering Site like the rumbling of thunder just before lightning strikes.

On her stomach, Mari crawled to the edge of the willow's sweeping boughs. With shaking hands she parted the long, green tendrils.

Her mother was almost across the creek. Mari's fingers dug into the moss. *Hurry, Mama! Hurry!*

Ferocious barking came from the center of the Gathering and a too familiar voice carried easily over it. "Thaddeus, Sol said there's no need to capture any Scratchers today. Calm Odysseus down before he breaks a blood vessel or something."

Mari tore her gaze from her fleeing mother to look at the group of men. It was with a sense of detached shock that she noted there were only three of them. Two were standing beside small, wiry-haired canines that must be Terriers. The third had no canine, but Mari recognized his voice and easily put a name to his tall, handsome form—Nik. The man who believed Rigel was his.

"Nik, the more time I spend with you, the more you remind me of a neurotic old woman. Odysseus is just having some fun. Actually, let's let Odysseus *and* Cameron have some fun. Davis, get ready. I'm going to send my boy after that Scratcher. You send Cameron, too."

"No, we're not supposed to catch any Scratchers," Nik said, obviously irritated. "Ignore the woman and let's get back to tracking my pup."

"We can do both, and Cameron needs the experience. Right, Davis? That's why he's here, isn't it? We'll release her after we catch her. No big deal." Before the younger man could respond, Thaddeus nodded, in a self-satisfied way, and commanded his canine, "Odysseus, capture!"

Mari watched helplessly as the first Terrier shot away from Thaddeus, arrow-like, and plunged into the creek after Leda. The second canine followed behind, barking enthusiastically.

"This is wasting time we don't have, Thaddeus!"

Nik was speaking, but his words weren't making any sense to Mari. The only thing that made sense to her was Leda. Her mother had reached the far bank and had begun climbing up it. Mari could see that she was trying to hurry, trying to climb quickly, but the ground rose too steeply and was too filled with rocks and broken branches and brambles. She was going to slip—going to fall, and just as Mari thought it, it happened.

Later, when Mari replayed the terrible scene over and over in her mind, she realized Leda's foot must have found one of the many holes that the dead leaves and forest debris so easily covered. But then, as Mari watched it happen, all she saw was her mother's body suddenly tilt alarmingly to one side so that, off-balance, arms flailing madly, Leda fell backward. The steep bank acted like a slide, and Leda's body careened down with a terrible momentum, head over feet, twisting and turning, until she landed in a broken heap half in, half out of the creek.

"Great. Now you've hurt one of them," Nik said. "Call off your canine, Thaddeus. Davis, grab Cammy. I promise you, this isn't the kind of experience my father meant for him to have."

Mari couldn't seem to make her body move. She couldn't breathe. She couldn't think. All she could do was to watch the three men wade through the creek. Thaddeus called his Terrier to him. The other man picked up his smaller, younger canine.

"Good thing we didn't need to capture this one. She's too damn old—too damn weak to be any good on the Farm," Thaddeus said, turning his back dismissively on Leda's still form. "Okay, so, the holly bush was just up this bank, correct?"

But Nik didn't answer Thaddeus. Instead he was looking at Leda.

"Hey, what are you doing? I thought you were in a big hurry to start tracking your phantom pup."

Nik rounded on Thaddeus. "Shut up! I think she's dead, and there was no reason for it."

"Dead?" Mari's lips mouthed the word and her body started to tremble. Rigel whined softly and pressed against her. "No no no no no."

"Who cares about another Scratcher? One less to infest this forest," Thaddeus said. "Come on, Davis. Bring Cameron up to the bush and we'll start doing Nik's job for him."

The two men and their Terriers started up the bank, but Nik didn't follow them. Instead he walked slowly to Leda.

"No no no no no," Mari whispered the only word she seemed able to form.

Nik crouched beside Leda. Hesitantly, he brushed her hair from her face. Mari could see Leda's face then, and she realized that she shouldn't have been able to. Her head was at a strange angle—it shouldn't have turned the way it did.

"No no no no no."

And then her mama moved! Mari let out her breath in a gasp, and began to scramble to her feet, to push through the curtain of green and run to Leda. But before she could move away from the tree, her mother's voice carried clearly, easily, over the water.

"Galen! My Galen. I knew we would be together again." She smiled serenely at Nik, and then a spasm of pain twisted her features. Leda coughed and blood spewed from her mouth, down her chin, across her twisted neck. She closed her eyes, and with a long, rattling exhale, Mari's mama died.

Mari felt her world dissolve. Her grief was so great that it was like a pounding fist within her, breaking her apart. She stumbled forward into a shaft of sunlight and the heat of it engulfed her.

"No. No! NO! *NO! NO!*" Mari screamed.

Still crouched beside her mother, Nik turned to look at her, and Mari saw his eyes widen in shock. It was as if she had stepped into the heart of the sun, and she knew it. Understood it. Wanted it and used it. She raised her arms and her despair exploded from her body in a stream of fire, so pure, so hot, that it was golden. With a ghastly *whoosh* the forest around Mari burst into flame.

16

The *whoosh* of the flames and the wall of heat that followed snapped Mari from the trancelike state that had gripped her since the moment her mother had landed, broken, on the rocky bank. Mari lifted her hands, trying to shield herself from the heat that threatened to engulf her.

Mama is dead.

The forest is on fire. I did it. Somehow I did it.

Smoke was roiling around her. She could hear the men shouting to one another, but the voice of the fire as it fed on the dry underbrush was deafening. Mari couldn't see them, nor could she make out what they were saying. She could not see Leda, either.

Mama is dead.

Mari simply stood there, rooted in place by despair and loss as the fire intensified around her. To her right a huge old log was fully engulfed in flame. The heat was causing her skin to redden and her hair to smolder. Mari stared at the log. A small pine next to the log caught fire like a candle's ripe wick. The long, tendril-like branches of the willow behind her began to curl inward and sway madly on the currents of expanding heat.

Very soon that will be me. I will burn high and hot. Maybe, maybe,

I will be with Mama again then. She believed that. She believed we all return to the earth, and to the Great Earth Mother.

It was easy, really. She could just stay where she was. It would be over quickly, almost as quickly as it had been over for her mama. Mari's shoulder's drooped. Her eyes closed. She wrapped her arms around herself, pretending for just a moment that she could feel her mother's comforting embrace.

She felt his presence then—against her left leg. Mari opened her eyes. Blinking through smoke and tears she looked down. Rigel was there, sitting quietly at her side, pressed against her leg. He did not whine. He did not grab her tunic and try to pull her away. He simply waited with her. Mari knew then beyond any doubt that if she chose to end her life, it meant the end of Rigel's life as well.

"No! Not you, too!" Mari cried and scooped the pup into her arms. She bolted through the willow tree and jumped over a smoldering log. And then Mari ran downstream. She didn't look back. She focused only on holding Rigel close to her, shielding him with her body from the heat of the fire as well as the prying eyes of the seeking Companions.

When they reached the creek Mari splashed into the water. Only then did she glance back, but the Gathering Site, and the bank where her mother lay, were completely obscured by smoke. She let Rigel swim beside her, keeping a hand on his wet fur, wanting to touch him—to be sure he was safe, alive, still with her. When they reached the far bank he scrambled up it, staying at her side—as if he, too, needed the comfort of her closeness. When they climbed to the summit of the bank, she ignored her weary muscles and lifted the Shepherd in her arms again and then, not knowing what else to do, Mari began to jog home.

She didn't slow until she reached the edge of the brambles. There she collapsed with Rigel on her lap. He stayed curled there, panting with stress, but otherwise not moving, only watching her with amber eyes that suddenly seemed bottomless and wise.

Mari could feel his love—feel their bond.

That was all Mari could feel.

A tremendous sense of numbness sank through her veins, pumping through her body in time with her heartbeat.

"Mama is dead," Mari told Rigel, speaking the words aloud. Tasting them. Trying to digest them.

Rigel didn't respond. He didn't even tilt his head with the playful listening pose he usually took when she talked to him. He just watched her with wise, old eyes.

She'd said the words. She'd seen Leda die. But it was just so fantastical—so very, very hard to comprehend—harder to comprehend even than one of her mama's stories. Mari squeezed her eyes closed. *I'll sketch her alive! I'll sketch her alive! I'll make it my reality.*

"Rigel!" Mari opened her eyes to peer intently at her canine. "What if I misunderstood? What if the reality is different from what I thought I saw? *What if Mama is just hurt and not dead?*" Rigel made no sound. "I have to go back. I have to see. If she's hurt I can heal her tonight when the moon is fully risen—I know I can! And even if she really is dead I can't leave her out there, by herself, to be eaten by the swarm." The more she spoke, the more Mari believed. She had no choice. Whether Leda was dead or alive, Mari had to go back for her mama.

Mari gently moved Rigel off of her lap, and then stood slowly on legs that felt liquid. Acting more on instinct than true understanding, Mari turned to the west and faced the sun.

"With me, Rigel. I need your help." Rigel turned with her and stared up at the midday sky. His eyes immediately began to glow. Mari stretched her hands over her head, reaching for the burning, yellow orb, and, for just a moment, felt its warmth and power sizzle through her body. It was over as quickly as it had begun. Feeling stronger, she dropped her arms and found Leda's staff. Leading Rigel, she parted the brambles so that they could follow the labyrinthine path to the burrow's entrance. Inside she set to work immediately. First, Mari gave Rigel water and drank long and deeply herself. She felt as if the fire that had somehow exploded from within her had left her utterly parched. Then she went to her mother's room. Mari didn't allow herself to think of anything except checking the Healer's pack that Leda took with her every night. Within the neat woven bag were bandages and ointments, herbs and liniments. Mari made sure there was plenty of numbing salve, as well as her mother's most powerful internal pain relievers. Then she drew a deep breath, and faced Rigel.

"You have to stay here. I don't know if the Companions will be gone. I—I can't let them see you. I can't lose you, too, Rigel." Mari began strong and sure, but as she spoke the pup began to whine and pant in distress, and her voice broke. She went to her knees, cupping his face in her hands and staring into his eyes, willing him to understand. "Please don't be sad. Please don't make any noise. Please just wait for me. I promise I'll come back to you. I promise. You're all I have left. I can't lose you, too, Rigel," she repeated. Still holding his gaze, Mari sketched within her mind a picture of Rigel curled on their pallet, watching the door, waiting for her.

She hugged him then and, before she began to shatter from the inside out, Mari kissed him, stood, and hurried to the door. She knew he followed her. She knew that she closed the door in his face, but she couldn't look back. She only hesitated long enough to mimic her mother's actions by touching the Earth Mother image carved into their arched doorway. Mari stared at the lovely Goddess and prayed silently and earnestly. *You don't have to speak to me, Earth Mother. I understand that I'm different from your people, but Mama isn't different. She belongs to you. So for her, not for me, I ask it of you. Please—please save Leda—your Moon Woman—my mama—my best friend.*

Mari didn't allow her thoughts to wander as jogged along the little deer path. She could not think of Rigel back in the burrow, filled with worry and sadness. She could not acknowledge that in leaving him behind she had also left behind a part of herself—perhaps the best part of herself. She would not think of might have beens or maybes. She would not feel. There would be time enough for thinking and feeling afterward—after she'd brought her mama home.

Mari smelled the smoke before she heard the voice of the creek. She slowed and left the path, creeping silently forward, pausing often to listen. She heard men's voices and slowed even more, concentrating on using the plentiful underbrush to conceal herself.

Finally she reached the edge of the steep bank. On her stomach, Mari crawled forward and slowly, slowly, looked down.

The forest wasn't ablaze as she thought it might be, though smoke still darkened the Gathering Site, obscuring much of her vision. As the wind shifted and the smoke eddied, Mari caught glimpses of the three men. They had taken off their shirts and were beating at the smoking foliage with their clothes. She could see that her willow was charred, and the brush and bushes closest to it were completely burned, but that was the worst of the fire. It seemed as if the men had contained it and were now working to defeat it. The two small Terriers were by their Companions' sides, busy digging fresh earth and letting it fly up behind them to cover what the men had already beaten out, as if they knew to be sure even any coals were smothered.

Of course the Terriers know. Rigel would know. Rigel would be working beside me to put out the fire, too.

As soon as the thought came to her mind, Mari's hand went to the space beside her, seeking the warmth and comfort of her Companion. His not being there was an open wound in her battered heart.

Mari dug her hands into the damp earth and steadied her thoughts. Then she looked down to her side of the creek's bank. She found Leda right away. She hadn't moved at all. Mari couldn't see her face. Leda's neck was twisted too far in a wrong-looking angle.

It doesn't matter. She might still be alive. And all I need is just the smallest spark of life and I might still be able to heal her.

Mari focused all of her attention on her mother, willing her to move—even a tiny bit.

Leda remained still.

"Nik! Thaddeus! I need your help over here. I'm losing this tree."

Mari's gaze was pulled from her mother as the youngest of the men motioned frantically to the other two as a broken cedar tree near the charred bones of the willow burst into flame. Nik and Thaddeus rushed to help him battle the fresh blaze.

Mari didn't hesitate. Staying as close to the ground as possible, she scrambled over the edge of the bank and half ran, half slid, down to Leda. She reached her mother and knelt beside her, touching her shoulder gently.

"Mama?"

Leda's shoulder was cold and already stiffening.

Her mother was dead.

"Come on, Mama. I'm going to take you home."

Mari emptied her mind, focusing only on lifting Leda—gently, carefully. She didn't try to carry her up the bank. Instead she moved quickly and silently with the current, following the creek downstream in the shallows, until she emerged ghostlike from the drifting smoke.

Mari paused then, breathing heavily. The day that had begun so bright and warm had turned overcast and cool. All around her mist began to lift from the warm, damp forest floor until, looking behind her, Mari couldn't tell what was smoke and what was fog. With a start of surprise Mari realized it was well into the evening, and not too many hours until sunset. She shifted her mother in her arms, collecting her limbs. Leda's head tilted close to Mari's to come to rest on her shoulder. For a moment Mari let her forehead tilt down and she breathed in the familiar scent of the rose water Leda always used to rinse her hair.

"It's okay, Mama. I have your back. I'll always have your back," Mari whispered. "It's getting late, but you don't have to do anything but sleep tonight. You finally don't have to do anything but sleep."

Resolutely, Mari stepped out of the creek, easily climbing the soft lip of the bank. She turned to the south, found the deer trail, and began the long, slow journey that would bring Leda home forever.

At first her mother's weight had seemed childlike and easy to manage, but it wasn't long before Mari's arms began to ache, her legs became heavy and awkward, and her breath came in gasps. The sun was veiled by clouds, and Mari didn't know how to reach its burning power. Leda's unrelenting stillness was a gnawing pain within her daughter's heart that soon grew to be an almost unbearable burden on the rest of her body. Mari stumbled on, forcing her legs to keep carrying her forward, afraid if she stopped, even just a moment to rest, she would never begin again. Night was coming, and though Mari didn't want to think about it, the truth was that after dusk her mother's body would become a beacon for the worst of the slithering, swarming forest scavengers.

There was a very real temptation that played with Mari's grief-numbed mind. As if observing herself from afar, Mari considered what would happen if she were caught out in the open forest after dark, carrying death in her arms. Mari wouldn't have to do much of anything. She could just sit down and hold her mother close. She could close her eyes and finally rest. Maybe even sleep. She was so, so tired. Darkness and the forest's insects would take care of everything else. If she didn't reach their burrow—didn't get within their shelter—Mari would never have to know what one dawn, then another and another without Leda, would bring, because her life would end with her mother's.

But if she didn't make it back to the burrow she knew what would happen to her pup. As surely as if Mari had sealed him within a tomb, Rigel would die—slowly, alone, frightened and in despair.

Mari couldn't do that to her Shepherd.

So Mari stumbled on, even after her aching arms became numb and her leaden feet were hardly able to move forward. The little path branched and Mari found herself standing still, breathing heavily and trying to rub the sweat out of her eyes. Which way? Which way? She blinked, orienting herself. Of course she knew where she was. She knew the forest as well as she knew her own home. To the right. She must keep moving always to the right.

Mari turned to the right, and as she did her foot was caught by an exposed root and, with a cry, she fell forward heavily, automatically twisting her body to try to shield Leda from the fall. A sharp pain splintered through her left wrist, and Mari cried out, collapsing in a crumpled pile—her mother's body twisted around her.

Mari tried to get up. She rearranged Leda's heavy, motionless limbs, collecting her in her arms like a beloved child—like Leda had so often held Mari and comforted her after she'd fallen and scraped her knees, or cried because she wasn't like any of the other Earth Walkers and needed her mother's reassurance and love.

But Mari couldn't stand, and Leda couldn't comfort her.

"I'm not ready, Mama." Mari smoothed Leda's hair back from her pale, cold face. "I'm not ready to lose you. What do I do now?"

Not far up the trail a branch snapped and Mari's heart fluttered with a primal rush of fear. Supporting her mother with one trembling arm, she felt frantically inside her pack with the other, trying to find her slingshot and to ready herself for whatever further horrors this terrible day would bring.

The young woman who emerged from the foggy path didn't see Mari at first. She was too busy glancing nervously behind her. When she did finally notice Mari, crumpled on the ground, holding her mother's body, she stumbled to a halt, eyes wide and startled.

"Oh, no! That can't be Leda. It simply can't be!"

Mari's anger felt pure and righteous, and so, so much more bearable than her grief.

"Sora, what are you doing here?"

The young woman ran forward, her gaze riveted on Leda's still, pale face.

"Oh, Goddess! She's dead? No, please no!" Sora's face twisted in a mixture of horror and disbelief and she leaned down, staring at Leda and ignoring Mari.

Something within Mari snapped. Of its own accord her hand snaked out, clamping around Sora's wrist. With a little shriek, the girl's gaze met Mari's, and what Sora saw there had her trying to pull away, face flushed with shock.

Mari held on to Sora's wrist, twisting it purposefully, painfully.

"Answer my question, Sora. What are you doing here?"

"I—I was looking for Leda, of course," Sora said, obviously trying to recover some measure of the arrogance that usually was so prevalent in her manner. "I *am* apprenticed to her, and dusk is nearing."

"No one is apprenticed to her anymore. Go away, Sora." Mari let loose her wrist, shoving her away.

Sora stumbled, but righted herself quickly. Gentling her voice until it was almost a whisper, she asked, "Mari, what happened?"

Mari met Sora's eyes. "You left her to die, *and she died.*"

Sora blinked. "What are you talking about? I didn't leave your mother to die."

"Do *not* lie to me!" Mari shrieked her rage at Sora. "I was there. I saw *everything.* When the Companions overran the Gathering Site you called the men to you, telling them to save you. *Then you ran, all of you, and left Mama to die!*" Spittle spewed from Mari's lips as her anger bubbled over.

"But I thought she'd run, too! I didn't mean for anything to happen to her. How could I?" Desperation crept into Sora's voice. "The Clan needs Leda. I *need* Leda."

"*You* need Leda?" Mari shook her head. "Sora, you're a selfish bitch. And guess what—you're not going to get everything you need, especially now that my mama is dead."

Sora drew herself up to her full height and thrust out her chin. "You're upset. I understand that. So I'm going to forget most of what you just said."

"Don't!" Mari hissed at her. "Don't ever forget what I just said. Remember it, and remember to stay away from me."

"But who's going to Wash the Night Fever from the Clan? Tonight is Third Night! Who's going to train me?"

"Figure it out yourself." Mari turned dismissively from Sora and began gathering Leda into her arms. She closed her eyes for a moment, concentrating and readying herself, and then she struggled to her feet.

She almost made it, but her weariness was too great. Mari would have dropped Leda had Sora not suddenly stepped forward, steadying Leda—lifting—resituating her still body over Mari's shoulder so that she could hold her more easily.

Mari's head lifted and she was looking into Sora's gray eyes.

"I'll help you carry your mama home. Then I'll help you bury her," Sora said softly.

"Where are all those men who like to follow you around?" Mari's voice was equally soft, but filled with venom.

Sora looked surprised at the question, but answered quickly, matter-of-factly, "Dusk is near. I don't allow men around me after dusk on a Third Night—not unless . . ." Her words trailed off as her gaze dropped to Leda.

"Not unless Mama's there to Wash the madness from them. That's what you were going to say, isn't it?"

Sora squared her shoulders. "Yes. That is what I was going to say. I'm not ashamed of it. I'd have to be more insane than them to want Clansmen filled with Night Fever near me."

"Then you better get used to being insane, or being alone at night because with Mama gone there's no one to save you or them." Mari started to stumble past Sora, but the girl moved to block her path.

"I said I'll help you bury Leda."

"You don't want to help me. You want to use me. I understand the difference. Get out of my way."

"Mari, you can call down the moon. Leda said so. You have to help me. And us—the Clan. You're all we have left of Leda."

Mari narrowed her eyes. "You need to listen carefully to what I'm going to tell you. I do *not* care what happens to you. I do *not* care what happens to the Clan. You used Mama until you used her up, and then you threw her away. You won't do the same to me. Don't try to find me. Don't try to follow me. Leave. Me. Alone." Mari stepped forward, bumping Sora hard with her shoulder and knocking her off the path.

"Mari! Wait! You can't just leave me out here like this. It's almost dusk!" Sora cried after her.

Without turning to look at her, Mari said, "Sora, if you follow me I will kill you."

———

Mari couldn't be sure that Sora wasn't following her, so instead of taking the most direct way back to the burrow she chose to circle around and around, following one of the mazelike routes that her mother, her mother's mother, and her mother's mother before her had spent their lifetimes creating, ensuring their home, and the Moon Women it protected, would remain hidden and safe. Mari worried about Rigel, and the extra time it was taking her to return to their burrow, but as she drew closer and closer to the burrow she held her mother more tightly, with more desperation.

This is the last time Mama and I will come home together. It's the last time we'll take this turn—walk this trail—circle around this path.

Finally, Mari stood before the entrance to the burrow. Still holding Leda, she stared at the carved Goddess that served as protector of the entrance to their home.

Why didn't you save her? Mari stared at the Goddess. *She loved you so much, probably as much as she loved me.*

As usual, the Goddess didn't answer her.

"You're nothing but a pretty piece of art. Nothing more than one of my sketches." Mari shook her head, dismissing the protective statue. She stumbled forward, opening the door with her shoulder.

Rigel was there, sitting just inside the doorway, exactly where Mari had left him hours ago. With maturity far beyond his short life, he came to Mari, went up on his haunches to sniff Leda's body, and then he dropped back down to all fours, his head low, waves of sadness rippling from him.

"I know, sweet boy. I know. But we have to put Mama to rest before we can grieve."

Afraid if she put Leda down she would not be able to lift her again, Mari carried her mother into the burrow and took the digging tool from the tidy pile of Leda's well-kept gardening implements. Then, with Rigel following silently, she slowly climbed the labyrinthine pathway through their bramble thicket up and around to their little clearing.

Mari sank to her knees and gently lay Leda in the soft grass, arranging her arms so that they were folded over her chest, and carefully straightening her neck so that it looked like she might be sleeping.

She approached the image of the Great Mother. This statue was probably the most beautiful, most carefully tended statue in the forest. Her face was lovely, carved from obsidian the color of a moonless, midnight sky. The ferns that made up her hair were lush and bright green. The moss that carpeted her body was soft and thick.

Mari spent no time looking at the statue. She took the tool and, choosing the spot directly in front of the Earth Mother image, she dug.

Soon Rigel was beside her. He dug with Mari, tearing the damp, fertile earth easily, but not with the puppyish enthusiasm he usually showed. Rigel was as silent and somber as was Mari. Both worked until their bodies trembled with exhaustion, and then worked more.

Finally the grave was deep enough and Mari went back to where her mother lay. She crouched next to her and Rigel stayed close, leaning into Mari's side. Mari touched her mama's face.

"She's cold, Rigel. That's why we have to cover her with the earth. Mama would want it that way. She'd especially want to rest beside her favorite Earth Mother statue."

Rigel whined softly and nuzzled Leda as if he could get her to move again.

"She's not going to wake up," Mari said to herself more than to the pup. "Mama's going to sleep now. Forever."

Mari bent and kissed Leda's forehead, and then one last time she lifted her mother into her arms. Staggering, she carried Leda to the grave and then, oh so carefully, placed her within. She went to the Goddess statue then and picked several of the delicate, lacelike ferns, arranging them gently over her mother's face before she began to fill in the grave.

When Mari was finished, she sat before the newly broken earth, resting her hands, palms down, on the damp ground. Rigel sat beside her, watching her carefully.

Mari cleared her throat, and her eyes lifted to the face of the Earth Mother's image.

"Earth Mother, this is Leda, Moon Woman to the Weaver Clan, my mama. My best friend. She loved you and believed in you, and I've brought her home so that she can rest with you. Mama said you spoke to her—that she often heard your voice in the wind and rain, trees and ferns, even in the music of the creek. I'm going to believe that you didn't save her because you love her so much that you wanted her with you. I can't blame you. I wanted her with me, too. I s-still want her with m-me. P-please take care of her."

Mari's voice broke completely then, and as dusk settled over the forest the gray sky opened and rained night's tears to mix with Mari's while she sat beside her mother's grave, and pressed her face into Rigel's warm, soft neck. Finally, Mari allowed the pain of her loss to engulf her as she sobbed, mourning the loss of her beloved mother while her Shepherd gave voice to his sadness as well and howled his grief into the night.

17

Nothing had gone the way Nik had intended. The day that had begun so bright and full of hope had turned cold and wet and confusing.

"Bloody beetle balls, I hope I never see this particular part of the Scratcher forest again." Thaddeus shook his head in disgust as he used his filthy shirt to wipe sweat from his face, leaving a streaky trail of soot and dirt smeared across his cheek.

"We caught a break with the rain, though. I don't think fire's a threat anymore. Should be safe to leave," Nik said, putting his own shirt back on and squinting up at the darkening sky. "Good timing, too. If we hurry we'll be back just before dusk."

"Good? I don't think there's been much good about today," Thaddeus grumbled. Without another word to Nik, he motioned for Odysseus to follow him and the two of them—sooty, sweaty, and disgruntled Terrier and Hunter—moved toward the trail that would lead them back to the Tribe.

Davis, Cameron, and Nik trailed after him more slowly.

"Too bad about not finding sign of the pup," Davis said not unkindly.

"Well, we didn't actually get to look for him," Nik said. "If we had and not found any sign—*that* would have been too bad."

"Keeping the forest from burning is a good thing." Davis grinned and cut his eyes to the trail before them at Thaddeus's back. He dropped his voice to a mock whisper and added, "And that's two goods today, but don't tell Thaddeus."

"I won't," Nik assured Davis, though he couldn't quite make himself joke and grin like the younger man. The whole damn fiasco was because Thaddeus had refused to listen and set the dogs on that old Scratcher. From that moment on the day had gone completely to shit.

There had been no reason for that Scratcher to die. Nik didn't think he was being sullen or brooding—he certainly wasn't as ill-tempered as Thaddeus—but he was having a tough time getting the image of the woman out of his mind. Her twisted neck had been horrible. She'd made him think of a battered and broken doll. But her injury wasn't what was so branded into Nik's mind. What he couldn't stop seeing was the joy that had transformed her thick-featured face from ugly to strangely sweet when he'd bent over her. What he couldn't stop hearing were her final words, spoken with such utter joy that the echo of it had reverberated through his mind as he fought beside Davis and Thaddeus to stop the fire from engulfing the forest. *Galen! My Galen. I knew we would be together again.*

What was she imagining as she lay there dying? What had her fading vision seen?

He hadn't had time then to give it much consideration because directly after the woman had died the girl had appeared—the girl on fire.

Who was she? *What* was she?

Nik had only seen two things before the fire had roared to life. One was the girl's dirty, grief-twisted face. The second was her eyes. They had glowed amber, blazing across the distance between them, oddly frightening in their familiarity.

She had been a Scratcher. He'd been sure of that when her cries had pulled his attention from the dead woman. Her hair had been dark and matted—her skin the dirty, earthy color of all Scratchers.

But those eyes. Those glowing amber eyes had definitely not been Scratcher.

Her eyes were Tribe of the Trees, as was her command of fire.

No! What the hell is wrong with me? That couldn't have been what I saw. Only the most powerful, carefully trained members of the Tribe ever attained the ability to channel sunlight into fire.

The girl was a Scratcher. The fire had to have been an accident. Hadn't it? How was anything else even possible?

But the events of the day kept replaying again and again in Nik's mind, each time ending with a blaze of amber and the roar of flame being birthed.

"Okay, now that we're out of that mess, what the hell happened back there?" Davis interrupted the cacophony of questions that filled Nik's mind.

Nik lifted his hands and dropped them with a shrug. He didn't hide his confusion or frustration, but he was very careful as he chose his words. He'd already decided the less he said about what he might have seen to anyone except his father—the better. "Davis, like I told you and Thaddeus before, the Scratcher died and then I heard someone yelling. I looked up in time to see a Scratcher girl standing by the willow where the fire started. Then everything around her burst into flame, and she disappeared."

Davis shook his head. "I know Scratchers aren't smart. I mean, they're great with crops and plants and such, but they need to be taken care of—protected really, especially from each other. Even so, I've never heard of them doing anything as stupid as setting fire to their own forest. Have you?"

"No. Never. That grove is obviously some kind of a gathering place for them. Seems likely that in the confusion an untended campfire must have—"

"They're fucking animals," Thaddeus interrupted, calling over his shoulder. "No, they're worse than animals. Animals don't destroy where they live. That's what those Scratchers tried to do today."

"What do you mean?" Nik asked.

"It's obvious! They set a trap for us. They musta heard you blabbing about that stupid pup and knew we'd be back. They rigged a fire to try to fry us, not giving a shit about what it would destroy if it had gotten out of control."

"I don't know, Thaddeus. They're really just big children. I don't think they're capable of that kind of planning, are they?" Davis said.

"Ask Nik. Last night he was chatting up a female Scratcher like she's a real person."

Nik scowled at Thaddeus, but in response to Davis's surprised look said, "She was young and scared. I talked to her to calm her down on the way to the Farm."

"You looked pretty chummy with her."

"Thaddeus, you're out of line. Last night I did what you told me to do—I took charge of the newest captive and stopped her crying. Nothing more. Nothing less."

"Well, I can tell you that after today I'm not going into Scratcher territory without Warriors and Shepherds backing me up. That is unless our Sun Priest, *your father*, commands it. Then I won't have any choice. Just like I didn't have any choice today." Thaddeus sent Nik a disgusted look.

"You smartass bastard, you had a choice today!" Nik's temper finally broke and the words he'd kept swallowed and silent exploded from him. "You could have *chosen* to stick to the plan. You were only supposed to track the pup. Instead that chip you carry around on your shoulder—the one that's bigger than your canine—got in the way and you *made the wrong choice*. Because of your choice there's a dead female Scratcher—at least one. Because of your choice we had to spend the rest of the daylight hours containing a fire instead of what we were really supposed to be doing. Because of your choice my pup's trail is one day colder and one day harder to track."

Thaddeus stopped and faced Nik. "That's roach shit and you know it."

It was Nik's turn to lace his words with disgust. "Why? Because of the big, bad Scratcher trap?" He laughed sarcastically. "That'll make perfect sense to my father and the Hunters who have been tracking and capturing Scratchers through more winters than we can count and who have *never been trapped by them before.*"

"Well we were trapped by them today!" Thaddeus shouted into Nik's face.

"No! What happened today was a Scratcher died. A girl screamed. A campfire burned out of control. None of those things would have happened if you had just done what you'd been told to do, which is exactly what I'm going to report to our Sun Priest, *my father.*"

"That's right, you spoiled fucking child, run to Sol and hide behind him. The whole Tribe knows you have no power of your own, just like you have no canine of your own."

Nik lunged for Thaddeus, but Davis was there between them, holding them apart, shouting, "No fighting among the Tribe!"

Thaddeus smiled and stepped back, holding his hands up in mock surrender. "Hey, I'm not breaking that rule. It's Nik who's having trouble controlling himself. Maybe someone should mention that to Sol when we give our report."

"No damage was done. No one struck any blows," Davis said, sounding nervous.

"Only because you were here." Thaddeus chuckled humorlessly and clapped Davis on the back. "You two ladies can stay back here and gossip. Odysseus and I are out of here." Then he turned and, whistling for his Terrier, took off down the path at a fast jog.

"I wouldn't have hit him," Nik said to Davis. "I would have liked to, but I wouldn't have."

Davis ran a hand through his hair and sighed. "Imagine him being your mentor for the Hunt. Believe me, from time to time *all* young Hunters have wanted to hit him."

"He shouldn't be mentor to anyone," Nik said.

"He's the best Hunter of the Tribe. That's undisputed."

"He's an arrogant ass."

"That's undisputed, too."

Nik exhaled a long, tense breath and then laughed softly. "We'd better catch up with the ass."

"Let's do one better. We're younger and faster. Let's beat him back."

Living high in the ancient Sugar Pines, far above the dangers of the forest floor, surrounded by people who were more than family—who were Tribe—made it easy to forget, or maybe take for granted, the serenity and beauty that infused almost every aspect of the Tribe of the Trees. Returning to the Tribe that evening, covered with soot and dirt and sweat, exhausted and frustrated by the unexpected events of the very long day, Nik felt a surge of gratitude as the three men and two Terriers jogged wearily up the well-worn trail that led to the uppermost ridge of the forest. The sun had just dropped below the gray western horizon and the light rain that had begun earlier at the Scratcher site had steadied itself into a comforting rhythm of pattering against the thick canopy of pine green.

Nik paused, breathing hard, taking in the loveliness of the torches being lit above them so that, within just a few moments, the pines stretched before them decorated with light and warmth and laughter.

"Hey, hear that?" Davis grinned as he turned to Nik.

Nik paused, listening. Then he blinked in surprise as he realized he was hearing celebratory music drifting from the Tribe, in perfect accompaniment to the spring rain. "It sounds like the whelping song."

"That it does, which means Fala has whelped. You ladies can stay here catching your breath and checking your hair. Odysseus and I are going to join the party." Thaddeus paused and, with a sarcastic smile to Nik, added, "You'll be glad to hear this means I won't be seeking out Sol tonight to give my report, so you'll have plenty of time to give your excuses to the Sun Priest." Laughing humorously, Thaddeus sprinted toward the lift, leaving Davis and Nik to frown after him.

"Fala?" Nik asked Davis.

"The little black Terrier who is Rose's Companion. No one's completely sure, well, no one except Thaddeus, but rumor has it that Odysseus could be the sire of the litter."

"Well, I'm glad to hear that a new litter has whelped, even if Odysseus could be the sire." Nik smiled at Davis, who returned the grin.

"You know it's true the canine is reflected in the Companion. I think Odysseus bit Cammy twice for every time Thaddeus yelled at you or me today." Davis knelt and scratched Cameron under the chin. The little blond Terrier wagged his tail.

Nik bent and patted the likable canine's head. "Sorry about that, Cammy."

Cammy jumped up, making the breathy *ah! ah! ah!* that was the Terrier version of laughter.

"Aw, we're used to it. Odysseus is as big a control freak as Thaddeus. Plus, Terriers may not have the pelt Shepherds do, but their skin is every bit as thick."

"Davis, how 'bout I give you my word that if I ask you to go on another tracking mission with me that it will *just* be you and Cammy— no others."

"Especially not Thaddeus?"

"Especially not Thaddeus," Nik agreed.

"Sounds like a better deal than we got today. But, hey, Cammy likes you. I like you. And I, for one, don't think you're wasting your time looking for that pup. If Cammy had disappeared, even before he'd chosen me, I would have never stopped looking for him," Davis said.

"Thanks. I appreciate you saying that." Nik offered Davis his hand, and the younger man grasped it warmly while Cameron danced around them huffing happily.

"Well, Thaddeus is going to tell everyone that you led us on another ghost hunt, but the truth is we didn't get to Hunt at all, and I plan to tell people the truth," Davis said stubbornly.

"Don't get yourself in trouble. Thaddeus doesn't like to be contradicted."

"Thaddeus doesn't like much of anything," Davis said with a wry smile. "And don't worry about me. He'll be too busy gloating over the pups he says are Odysseus's to bother with anything I might or might not say about what happened today."

"Just watch yourself. Don't cause problems with Thaddeus because of me." Nik gestured at the lift. Light from a torch was glinting off the metal links of the heavy chain as it lowered to the forest floor. "Lift's back." Cammy started nipping playfully at Davis's and Nik's ankles, herding them forward. Both men laughed good-naturedly at the canine's insistence.

"He wants to join the party," Davis said when he beat them to the waiting lift.

"Looks like out of the three of us Cameron's the smart one," Nik said, closing the lift door and signaling that it could begin the journey up.

"I've suspected as much since he chose me." He opened his arms and called, "Come on up here, Cammy!" The Terrier sprang up so that Davis caught him easily, and then he and Nik laughed while Cammy covered his Companion's dirty face in enthusiastic licks.

"Ugh, Davis, that is *not* how you're supposed to wash up."

Nik and Davis peered through the wooden slats of the cagelike lift as it came to rest in its roost above ground. She was standing on the landing, hand on her curvy hip, young Shepherd by her side. It seemed to Nik that both girl and canine were looking at the three of them as if they'd been rolling in scat.

"Cammy is just being friendly. That's all. This isn't how I wash up. I know better than that. Mostly." Davis put Cameron down and tried to sound nonchalant, but Nik could see that his freshly licked cheeks were now pink, where they weren't covered with Terrier spit and soot.

Nik stifled a sigh. Claudia was sexy and beautiful, and had been chosen two years before by Mariah—the largest, smartest canine in the only Shepherd litter to whelp that spring. She was also very aware of the effect she had on the men of the Tribe. Just then the effect she was having on Davis was to turn him mute.

"Hello, Claudia." Nik sent her his most charming smile. "Nice of you to welcome a Hunter home."

Claudia raised a golden brow sardonically. "It's my turn at the Lift Watch. I welcome *everyone* home. And, just so you know, there are no decent seats left at the celebration. The landing was overcrowded within a few minutes of the whelping announcement. Might as well take your time getting washed up—properly."

"Thanks for the info, and Davis and I appreciate seeing your pretty face, especially after how hard we worked putting out that fire. Don't we, Davis?"

Claudia's expression changed instantly, turning from smug to genuinely concerned. "Fire? In the forest? Thaddeus said nothing about that."

"Huh, that's strange. He must have been too distracted by the news of Fala whelping," Nik said, shrugging.

"That's no excuse to keep such important news to himself," said Claudia.

"We're definitely in agreement about that," Nik said, nodding at Davis until he nodded jerkily along with him. "Hey, Davis, you should make the report to the Elders about the fire. You know, since Thaddeus is busy."

"Someone certainly needs to, and soon. Where was the fire?" Claudia asked.

Nik sighed internally and sent the blushing Davis an *answer the woman* look, which worked on the young Companion like a prod.

"Oh, uh, over in Scratcher territory by that creek they were gathered at yesterday." Davis glanced at Nik, who nodded almost imperceptibly. "We, uh, think a Scratcher girl must have knocked over a campfire and started the fire accidentally."

"Scratchers really shouldn't be allowed to live on their own. They're sullen children. I'll bet the fire wasn't on their side of the creek, was it?"

Davis and Nik shook their heads in tandem.

"No, of course not. Was anyone hurt?" Claudia was studying Davis with new interest as she spoke.

"My hands are a little blistered, and Cammy's fur got singed," Davis said, holding out his dirty hands, palms up.

"A Scratcher woman fell and broke her neck. She died," Nik heard himself say.

"I meant people, not Scratchers," Claudia said, throwing a dismissive glance in Nik's general direction before she turned back to Davis.

"Then Davis and Cammy got the worst of the injuries." Nik quickly changed the subject, not liking the hollow feeling of *wrong* that had begun to settle in his gut when people talked about Scratchers.

"Are you sure Cameron is okay?" Claudia knelt and held her hand out to the Terrier, who eagerly trotted to her, licked her hand, and then almost licked the big, watching Shepherd, too, but at the last instant tucked his tail and raced back to Davis. Claudia's soft laughter was melodic and almost as lovely as her lush body and thick mane of golden hair. "Oh, little guy, don't worry. Mariah likes Terriers." Still smiling, she stood. "Your Cammy seems to be moving just fine, but you better keep an eye on him. I assume by all the dirt on his feet that he was helping smother the fire. Burned paws can be pretty sore, and take a long time to heal."

Looking worried, Davis knelt, picked up Cammy and held him so that he was on his back, dirty paws splayed. "Would you take a look at his paws?"

"Yes, of course," Claudia said.

"Davis, Claudia, I need to find Sol and let him know what happened today. I'll tell him that you're going to report to the Elders about the fire, right, Davis?" Nik said. Too busy with Cameron to pay much attention to him, Nik nodded absently. "Yeah, yeah, no problem. I'll do that as soon as Claudia's done checking Cammy."

"Okay, good. See you later, Davis." The two Companions, their heads bent together over Cammy's paws, waved absently.

Nik hurried away thinking that Claudia would do well to see the value in Davis. He wasn't Companion to a Shepherd, but he was kind and brave, and the kid had a sense of humor—unlike Claudia most of the time. The sound of Cammy's huffing and Claudia's soft laughter drifted after him with the rain and Nik's smile was self-satisfied.

Good luck, Davis. You're going to need it.

———

Thaddeus hated Nik. He'd only recently realized just how much. Nikolas, son of Sol, was soft and spoiled and useless.

"That's what happens when your daddy makes sure you have everything your little heart desires," he told Odysseus, who panted up at him in complete accord. "Oh, but that's right—even his Sun Priest daddy can't force a canine to bond with him. Poor, poor Nik." His voice was thick with sarcasm and hatred. "What I wouldn't give to put poor, poor Nik in his place!"

Odysseus whined and Thaddeus stopped his tirade to bend and ruffle the Terrier's ears. It was as he straightened that the dizziness hit him. Thaddeus staggered, clutching at his head. He fell to his knees, trembling.

"Hot," he murmured. "I'm so damn hot. Must be coming down with something."

Odysseus pressed himself against his Companion's body, shivering in fear.

"Hey, I'm fine. I just need to get rid of this damn headache. Had it on and off the past couple of days. Putting out that damn Scratcher fire didn't help it, that's for sure." Thaddeus scrubbed at his eyes with his palms. Damn eyes had been burning almost as long as he'd had the headache. "Yeah, the smoke was probably *real good* for whatever has been bothering my eyes," he continued to mutter. "Nik's fault. All Nik's fault!" Anger boiled within him, rising with his body temperature.

Odysseus whined again pitifully.

Thaddeus patted his head. "Hey, I said I'm fine. Relax boy. Actually, I'm better than fine. Forget the headache and the eyes—I'm thinking with real clarity for the first time in my life, and I'm telling you, O, it's time for a change in the Tribe of the Trees." His hand left the wiry fur of his Terrier and he began scratching his arms as he stared off into the distance. He blocked out the waves of worry Odysseus was blasting him with—he blocked out the strange headache and his burning eyes. He blocked out everything except the anger that seemed to pulse through his body along with his heartbeat. "No, it's not right. Not right at all that someone like Nik has it better than us just because his daddy bonded with a Shepherd. I've never known one Shepherd who had your nose, O. Not one. But do you get credit for that? Hell, no. If I don't do something to change it, you and I will never be anything but Hunters, taken for granted by the Tribe." Thaddeus scratched ferociously at his arms, not noticing that his skin had begun to slough off. "Well, I'm going to do something to change it. When I'm done you and I are going to finally get what we deserve, that I promise you."

As he spoke the promise, something within Thaddeus shifted. There was a great, blasting pain that radiated through his head that felt like his mind was splitting apart. Thaddeus vomited, suddenly and violently, spewing black-flecked blood and bile all around him.

On all fours now, Thaddeus gulped air, trying to steady himself. Odysseus was licking his face almost hysterically. With a shaking hand, Thaddeus pushed the Terrier aside, murmuring wordless reassurance to the little canine.

And then, as quickly as the nausea had hit him, it dissipated, taking with it all remnants of the headache and burning eyes.

Thaddeus sat back on his heals, drawing in a deep breath.

The pain didn't return.

He wiped his mouth on his sooty shirt.

The pain still didn't return.

He drew another deep breath. He felt better. A lot better. Good, actually, really good.

Thaddeus stood. He began to walk, then jog, then, with a feral grin, he kicked into a run and sprinted down the path, fleet and powerful as a stag.

He didn't notice that Odysseus was struggling to keep up with him. He didn't notice anything except the new power that coursed through his veins.

18

Nik knew his father would be easy to find, even during a crowded whelping party, so he took his time washing off the smoke and dirt and sweat and changing into clean clothes. Then Nik simply followed the sounds of celebration.

Claudia had been right. The Tribe didn't just fill up the huge landing area that surrounded the Mother Trees that served as hosts for the precious Mother Plants, they filled it up and spilled over, finding seats all along the walkway system that circled through and around family nests, artisan pods, lookout landings, and a plethora of bachelor pods. Nik paused, grabbing a thick bough and hefting himself up so that he could take in the happy chaos that was the thriving Tribe celebrating the birth of a litter of Terriers.

Music and scents of pots of simmering wild rice, mushrooms, and vegetables heavily seasoned with garlic and spring onions competed with laughter and cheers as the Sky Dancers performed from the aerial bars and ropes tethered to the uppermost branches of the trees surrounding the landing. The dancers were dressed in brightly decorated costumes. Their hair—both men and women—was dyed all sorts of colors, everything from beet red to camellia pink and dogwood blue. Nik watched them gracefully dive from perches to twirl and twist and grab a swinging bar, just long enough to lift and then dive again—always in time with the music. They looked like beautiful birds, and Nik cheered along with the rest of the Tribe as the music came to a crescendo and the dancers seemed to defy gravity with their grand finale. Then he made his way through the crowd, smiling and returning greetings as partiers who had obviously been partaking of the much beloved spring ale jostled him.

Sol was at his usual place on the landing. Seated beside him in the place of honor Nik recognized the very happy and very clearly drunk Rose, Companion to Fala. With a great sense of relief Nik did not see Thaddeus, though most of the Elders were present and seated just behind Sol.

Noticing his son approaching, Sol waved and smiled a welcome. Nik nodded respectfully to his father, and then greeted Rose. "Congratulations on Fala's whelping. How many pups did she have?"

"Five!" Rose slurred. "Sssshe had five! Big, black, and healthy. By all the gods, my girl did a good job." Rose raised her mug, which Nik noticed was almost as big as a pitcher.

"To Fala!" she yelled.

"To Fala!" Nik and those closest to them repeated the cheer. Then he stepped closer to his father. Sol scooted aside so that Nik could sit beside him.

"Bring my son a mug of ale!" Sol called.

Almost instantly a mug of foamy spring ale was shoved into his hand. "Nice celebration," Nik said after taking a deep drink.

"I think new pups are the best type of celebration," Sol said.

Nik raised a brow at his father. "How much *celebrating* have you been doing?"

Sol mirrored his son's look. "Not too much to interfere with hearing your report. That is, if you have anything to report to me."

Nik lowered his voice and leaned into his father. "I do, but not here."

Sol nodded once before turning to Rose. "Companion, duty calls me. But again I congratulate you on Fala and her pups. May the Sun bless you and them, and help you all to thrive."

"Thank you, Ssssol," she slurred.

Sol looked over his shoulder at the Lead Elder. "Cyril, would you take my place? I need to speak with Nik."

"Of course!" The white-haired man moved with a litheness that would put much younger men to shame as he and his gray-muzzled Shepherd moved forward. "Should I take your ale for you as well?"

Sol smiled. "That, my friend, I shall take with me. I have a feeling I'll need it after Nik and I talk."

Cyril's moss-colored gaze went to Nik. Nik nodded and smiled at the old man. "Greetings, Cyril."

"Greetings to you, Nikolas. Do you really need to speak with our Sol, or is he using you as an excuse to find his bed early?" Cyril dropped his voice in the pretense of a whisper. "You know, he is getting old."

Nik grinned. "That's what I keep telling him." Out of the twelve Elders who made up the ruling Council of the Tribe, he'd always liked Cyril best. He was the only Elder who seemed to care to stay in touch with the younger Tribe members—and he was the only Elder who had kept his sense of humor after he was appointed to the Council.

"If I'm finding my bed early, it's because of the lovely, shapely Companion who so often joins me there," Sol said. And while Cyril laughed, the Sun Priest cuffed Nik gently and said, "Come on, you."

"Yes, sir. I'm coming," Nik said. "Cyril, Thaddeus should be along shortly. He's going to report to you about a fire that we put out today in Scratcher territory."

"Fire?" Sol paused, moving back to stand close enough to Cyril that his voice wouldn't carry far. "Was anyone injured?" Sol asked.

"No Companion was hurt badly. Davis and his Cameron are a little singed. I don't think Thaddeus or Odysseus were hurt at all."

"That's right! Let's drink to Thaddeus and his Odysseus! The sire to my Fala!" Rose raised another sloppy mug and the crowd cheered.

Sol sighed. "I see now why Thaddeus didn't report."

"Being the Companion of a sire is no excuse," Cyril said.

Nik kept his face carefully neutral, but concerned, as he mentally put a check on the side of the good guys. Now Davis would be thanked for reporting while Thaddeus would be given a much deserved reprimand. *Mission accomplished,* Nik thought.

"Go on with Nikolas. I will be here waiting for Davis and his report. Shall we call a Council meeting after dawn?" Cyril said.

Sol glanced at Nik, who almost imperceptibly shook his head.

"I don't think it's necessary to call the Council to admonish Thaddeus," Sol said.

"You're right. I'll listen to Davis and then talk with Latrell. I'm sure he can come up with a proper reprimand for that mischief maker," Cyril said.

"But not tonight. Tonight send Davis to his cups and then you return to yours, old friend. Tomorrow is time enough for unpleasantness," Sol said.

"Agreed," Cyril said.

"Come, Nik."

Nik was surprised when his father didn't lead him back to his nest. Instead he spoke softly to Laru, who trotted ahead of them so that the revelers parted for the big Shepherd as they crossed the wide platform and headed up the winding stairs to Sol's landing.

For a moment neither man spoke. They stood side by side, with Laru sitting between them. Nik stroked the Shepherd's thick fur while his gaze took in the winking lights and flashing mirrors that glittered, firefly-like, across the city in the sky.

"I've moved up the foraging trip to Port City. You'll need to be ready to go by the next full moon."

Nik blinked in surprise. "So soon? That's in, what, two more weeks or so?"

"Yes, a little over. I wanted to wait until the days were longer, but—" Sol broke off, gesturing around them.

"Yeah, I get it. The Tribe's too crowded."

"From overcrowding comes dissension," Sol said.

"Speaking of dissension I need to tell you what happened today."

Sol turned and leaned against the carved balustrade facing Nik so that he could meet his son's gaze. "All right. Tell me."

Nik drew a deep breath and let it out in a rush saying, "It's going to sound unbelievable, and maybe I'm wrong. Maybe I misunderstood what I saw. But, Father, I give you my oath that I am telling you what I believe is the truth."

Sol studied his son carefully. "Nikolas, you have never given me reason to doubt your veracity, and I do not doubt it now. Tell me everything,"

And Nik did. He left out nothing. He described the site by the creek and how Thaddeus had insisted that he and Davis send the Terriers after the Scratcher woman.

"Sun's fire! I told Thaddeus clearly that he was *not* to hunt Scratchers," Sol said.

"I did, too. It didn't do any good. So, the woman panicked."

"Which is understandable. We'd just taken captives the night before," Sol said.

"And in her panic, she fell down a steep bank, breaking her neck," Nik said.

Sol shook his head, intoning softly, automatically, "May the Sun light her way to the World Beyond."

"Father, she spoke to me before she died."

"Truly? What did she say?"

"It was so strange. I went to her to see if there was anything I could do to help her. She looked at me like she was happy to see me. Incredibly happy. She said she knew I'd come back to her. Then she died."

"Why would a Scratcher be happy to see you?"

"I don't think she was seeing me. She called me Galen, like she was seeing him instead of me."

Sol's reaction shocked Nik. His father's face drained of color, and he closed his eyes as if he'd felt a sudden pain. The hand that he passed over his face trembled. Laru stirred, whining softly and pressing himself against his Companion's side.

"Father? What is it?"

"I—I know the name."

"Galen? You know a Scratcher named Galen?"

Sol met Nik's gaze. "No. I knew a Companion named Galen. So did you."

"Father, what are you talking about?"

"Tell the rest of it and I'll explain. How did the fire start?" Sol said.

Nik swallowed past the dryness in his throat, wishing he'd brought up his mug of ale. "This is the unbelievable part."

"Go on, son."

"The woman died and then from across the creek I saw a Scratcher girl. She'd just stepped out of the cover of a big willow. She was scream-ing no, and staring at me. Before I could say or do anything, her eyes changed, Father. They glowed *our* color—the color of sunlight. She lifted her arms, and then the brush on either side of her exploded into fire. *She* did it. I didn't imagine it—I swear to you I didn't. That Scratcher girl can call down sunlight and channel fire, like you can." Nik went very still, waiting for his father to scoff or laugh or patronize.

"Who else knows about this?"

"Thaddeus and Davis were there, but they didn't see the girl. As soon as the brush caught fire she disappeared."

"How do they think the fire started?"

"Thaddeus thinks the Scratchers set a trap for us. Davis doesn't think so, though. He agrees with what I told him."

"Which was what?"

"I said that there must have been other Scratchers around and that as they ran from us they scattered a campfire, catching the dry brush around the willow on fire."

"You said Davis agrees with you?"

Nik nodded. "That's what he's going to report to Cyril."

"Good. Good." Sol wiped a trembling hand across his brow.

"Father, you believe me?"

"Completely," Sol said.

"You even believe me about the girl on fire? The Scratcher girl?"

"I especially believe you about her, Nik. And I don't believe she is a Scratcher girl, or at least not a full-blooded Scratcher girl."

"I don't understand."

"I'm afraid I do," Sol said. "And it has to do with Galen."

"Who is Galen?"

"Not is, but was," Sol said. "He *was* my friend. Until I killed him. And I believe he was also that girl's father, which makes her part Scratcher and part Companion."

19

Utterly shocked, Nik stared at his father. *How could it be true? Father was a good man—a kind man—the spirit of the Tribe. How could he have killed his friend?*

"It was a long time ago." Sol spoke quietly, his voice weary with old regret. "Almost twenty years now. You were so young I'm not surprised you don't remember Galen, but I'll bet you do remember his Shepherd— Orion."

Nik blinked in surprise. "Orion! Of course I remember him. He was huge! Or at least my child's imagination remembers him as huge."

"Orion was the biggest Shepherd the Tribe had ever known. Even Laru isn't quite as massive as was that big male."

"Wait, I do remember his Companion. He left to join a more northern Tribe. I remember crying because I hadn't been able to say goodbye to Orion." Nik met his father's gaze. "You told me Orion and Galen had to go north because that Tribe needed a Shepherd to sire a new line."

"That was what we told everyone," Sol said. "That he never made it to the northern Tribe was a tragedy his family, and I, mourned."

"But you didn't kill him, right? He died making the trip north."

Sol drew in a deep breath and seemed to age before Nik's eyes. "I killed him. I killed Orion. And it has haunted me for almost twenty years."

Nik passed a hand over his face, eerily mimicking the gesture his father made when he was deeply disturbed. "I don't understand."

"Galen committed Sacrilege."

"Sun's fire! He destroyed a Mother Plant?"

Sol shook his head. "No, he stole swaddling fronds. Often and many of them."

"Father, this makes no sense. Why would a Companion steal swaddling fronds unless there was an infant that—" As realization came to Nik he felt as if he'd been punched in the gut. "The girl. He took the fronds for the Scratcher girl."

"They call themselves Earth Walkers, not Scratchers," Sol said slowly. "Nik, what I'm about to tell you I haven't spoken of to anyone in almost twenty years. Cyril knows. Your mother knew. Anyone else who knew is as dead as Galen and Orion."

"Okay, Father, go on. I'm listening, and I'll keep your secret."

"Thank you, son."

Sol stared out at the dark horizon and began to speak. At first his voice was rough, hesitant, as if he was having trouble finding the words to tell the story, but as he talked he fell into a rhythm as if he had traveled into the past with the retelling.

"Galen and I were of an age—we grew up together. We were made Companions within the same year. We even fell in love with the same woman." Sol smiled at his son's shocked expression. "Yes, Galen loved your mother, and she him. Luckily for me, her love for him was as a sister loves her brother—and her love for me was much more."

"Did Galen resent you because Mother chose you?"

"No, or at least not for long. It wasn't part of Galen's personality to hold resentment. He was the kindest person I have ever known. I only saw him angry once, and that wasn't over your mother."

"Was it when you caught him stealing from the Mother Plant?"

"No. He wasn't angry then. He was silent. And brave. He forgave me. He even forgave me for killing Orion." Sol wiped his face with his hand again, brushing away tears. When he continued speaking, his voice had found its rhythm and he did not falter. "Galen was the best forager I have ever known—possibly that the Tribe has ever known. He didn't lead Warriors into Port City and other ruins, though. He and Orion preferred to forage alone. The two of them had the ability to move in almost complete silence. It was remarkable, really, the way that big Shepherd could make himself a ghost. Baldrick, the Sun Priest before me, put restrictions on Galen, decreeing that he was too valuable to the Tribe to go off on his own, but when I was anointed in his place I removed the restrictions." Sol sighed and shook his head. "I was young and thought I knew better than the old man before me. I was wrong. Had I insisted Galen team with another Companion it couldn't have happened."

"Father, did Galen rape a Scratcher?"

"No, son. I believe Galen fell in love with an Earth Walker."

"The woman who died today?"

"Yes."

"How could it have happened?"

"I don't know the details. When he would be gone from the Tribe for days and days on end, no one questioned him about his absence because it was the norm for him. Galen and his Orion foraged alone. He always returned with treasures. And I was always glad to welcome him, and the gifts he brought." Sol stroked Laru, as if needing the comfort of his canine's touch. "But even then I knew something had changed with Galen. Once he and I were on lookout duty together and two Scratchers tried to escape the Farm. I shot and killed them quickly, as Law dictates. That was the one time I saw Galen angry. He ranted at me— saying how if we were in their place, if we were slaves held captive, we would be trying to escape, too. I'd reminded him that Scratchers aren't able to protect themselves, that they need to be cared for like children who don't grow up. I've never forgotten what he told me then. He'd said that they aren't Scratchers, they're Earth Walkers, and they are *different* from the Tribe, but no less than us. He said their lives have a connection to the earth, a simplicity and beauty we lack, and that they have true courage."

"Did he explain what he meant?"

Sol shook his head. "Once his anger was spent he apologized to me, and said that he just couldn't stand the killing. I didn't press him. I should have, but I didn't."

"He must have sounded crazy," Nik said.

"Then he did. Over the winters that have passed since, I have come to believe differently."

"But he didn't say anything to you about being with a Scra—I mean, Earth Walker female?"

"Not until just before I killed him." Sol's gaze moved from the horizon to his son. "Even after all these years it's difficult for me to think of that day, though it is never far from my mind. Galen forgave me. I hope you will forgive me. But I don't believe I'll ever truly forgive myself."

"How did it happen?" Nik prompted.

"Galen would have gotten away with it if Cyril hadn't seen him carrying the fronds into the forest. Galen was smart about it. He only took one frond from each plant. It wasn't enough to cause suspicion. The loss was barely noticed. One woman, the oldest of the group who tended the Mother Plants, mentioned to Cyril that she was concerned that the frond count was off. Cyril had just been named to the Elder Council then, and he was diligent in his duties. Though the old woman didn't believe someone was committing Sacrilege and stealing from the plants, Cyril was just pragmatic enough to wonder. Without sharing his suspicions with anyone, he began watching the Mother Trees. One night, during the quietest hour between midnight and dawn, he saw Galen sneak to the Mother Plants and, from each mature plant, take a single fat frond."

"It's almost unbelievable," Nik said. "Didn't Cyril stop him?"

"Cyril was an Elder, not a Warrior. It wasn't his place to carry out a death sentence. Also, he knew the jolt it would cause to the very heart of the Tribe if Galen was publicly accused and executed. And he found it as unbelievable as you."

"So Cyril told you," Nik said.

Sol nodded. "He did. We wanted to give Galen a chance to redeem himself—to explain why he was stealing from the Tribe. We followed Galen, Cyril with his Argos, and me with Sampson." Sol's gaze found the distant horizon again. "Galen's trail was ridiculously easy to track. I've often thought he must have wanted to be caught, though that may just be a reflection of my guilt. We caught him at a pool with a run-off-fed waterfall. He didn't have the fronds with him, but he admitted to taking them. He said he'd do it again. He said he wasn't sorry—would never be sorry.

"Cyril questioned him—tried to get him to lead us to the child he'd stolen the fronds for. Galen refused. He accepted his death sentence. Just before I carried out the sentence he whispered to me, *Sol, I love her. I love them both.*

"Then he looked me in the eye and told me he forgave me. He asked me to end Orion after him so that the canine wouldn't pine and die slowly. He told Orion to lie down—to be still—to be comforted—that all was well and they would be together again soon. I cut my friend's throat and then his canine's." Sol stopped speaking and bowed his head. Nik saw that his father was weeping.

"It must have been terrible," Nik said softly, wiping away his own tears.

"It's the worst thing I have ever done. Not one day has passed since that I haven't regretted it."

"But you felt as if you didn't have any choice," Nik said, trying to understand.

"That's no excuse for such a heinous act. I should have taken Galen back to the Tribe and made him stand trial before the Elders. Maybe the outcome would have been different," Sol said.

"Did the rest of the Elders know the truth?"

"Cyril told them Galen admitted stealing from the Tribe. That he'd shown no remorse and given no explanation as to why he had begun stealing Mother Plant fronds. Cyril reported passing sentence and then witnessing that sentence being carried out. The Elders were completely shocked. They debated about what could happen to the morale of the Tribe should they discover that a Companion as respected and loved as Galen had gone mad, and then been executed by their new Sun Priest. In Council they voted to cover up what happened. Cyril concocted the story about Galen and Orion going north. There was a semblance of truth to the lie. A northern Tribe had sent out a call for Shepherd sires to relocate with them."

"And the journey is dangerous, especially if a Companion and his Shepherd insist on traveling alone," Nik concluded for him.

Sol faced his son again. "That is the lie we told. I am sorry for it. I will eternally be sorry for it."

Nik studied his father, trying to imagine him killing a good man and his bonded canine, and it seemed the world had suddenly shifted and was tilted sideways. He felt nauseated and his head throbbed.

"Nikolas, can you forgive me?"

This time Nik hesitated before answering. "I forgive you," he said slowly. "Father, I have no right to judge you. You did what you believed you had to do, and the Elders did what they believed was best for the greater good of our Tribe. It's just so horrible. I can't imagine what it's been like for you carrying around this secret for all of these years."

"It has been a burden, one you now share with me, son. I am sorry for that."

Nik straightened his back, feeling the weight of the burden, wishing he could turn back time so that he didn't know now what he hadn't known moments before. But he couldn't tell his father that. The guilt and remorse in his father's gaze plainly said how close to unbearable keeping the secret had been for Sol.

Then he closed the few feet between them and took his father in his arms, hugging him tightly, surprised to realize he was several inches taller than Sol. When had that happened?

"Thank you, son. Thank you," Sol said, stepping out of Nik's embrace and wiping his eyes. "You do know why I had to tell you, don't you?"

Nik nodded slowly. "The girl on fire is Galen's daughter."

"She must be."

Then the thought hit Nik with such force he almost staggered.

"Father, the pup. My pup. Could he be trying to find this girl and bond with her?"

Sol's shocked expression told Nik far more than his words. "Sun's fire, Nik! If that is the truth there is a young canine out there looking for an orphan girl who has been raised as a Scratcher."

"Will she even accept him if he finds her? Will the other Scratchers kill him, or maybe even kill her?"

"I don't know the answers to those questions. I don't know the rules to their society—none of us do," Sol said. "You have to find her, Nik. You have to find her soon."

"And if I do, I'll find my pup," Nik said.

Sol rested his hand on Nik's shoulder. "Son, if you find him with her you need to understand that he'll be *her* pup, not yours."

"Well, at least he'll be found," Nik said, feeling hollow and sick. "It's ironic that I'm in much the same position as Galen." His father gave him a questioning look. Nik explained, "I have to search by myself, just as he did."

"Absolutely not, Nikolas. The tragedy with Galen happened because I bent the rules and allowed him to forage by himself. I won't let that happen again, especially not to my son."

"Father, be reasonable."

"I am being reasonable. I'm learning from my past mistakes. You will not be alone."

"Are you ready to share your secret with the rest of the Tribe?" Nik asked.

"No. But I'm also not ready to lose you. I don't want you out there alone. Who do you trust, Nik?"

"With a secret of this magnitude? No one!"

"Not the entire secret, Nikolas, only a portion of it. Just the fact that you saw a Scratcher girl who appeared to have the power to draw down sunfire, and that I have tasked you—confidentially, so as not to cause panic within the Tribe—with learning more about this girl on fire. At the same time you'll be looking for the pup."

"O'Bryan. I trust him," Nik said. "After him I'd say Davis."

"I'm more confident of O'Bryan's trustworthiness. You've been more big brother to him than cousin. But Davis is a good second choice, and I can imagine that you'll need the tracking skills of a Terrier. Start with O'Bryan, but I'll let Latrell know that I've given permission for Davis and Cameron to search with you as needed."

"I'll begin tomorrow morning."

"I'm afraid the best place for you to search is to go back to that Gathering Site," Sol said.

"I think so, too."

"Take O'Bryan tomorrow. See what the two of you can discover on your own."

"I will," Nik agreed. "I'll only call on Davis for help if O'Bryan and I can't find any trace of either the girl or the pup."

Sol took Nik's shoulders in his hands and gave his son a little shake. "Be smart, Nik. And be safe." Then Sol hugged him with a tightness that seemed almost desperate to Nik. Before he released him the Sun Priest whispered, "I'm sorry you have to carry this with you. I'm sorry you know."

Nik closed his eyes and returned his father's embrace. Aloud he said, "That's okay, Father. That's okay." But to himself Nik admitted silently, *I'm sorry I know, too. Very sorry . . .*

20

In the weeks following Leda's death Mari would have died had it not been for Rigel. It's not that she actively contemplated killing herself. She didn't think about jumping off a cliff, drowning in a river, or walking into Port City and letting the monsters who ruled the ruins flay the skin from her living body until it lived no more. No, Mari wouldn't have done any of those things.

She simply would have stopped living.

She wouldn't have struggled to get out of bed and feed herself so that she had the energy to feed Rigel. She would have just stopped everything—eating, drinking, and, eventually, living. Mari would have curled up on Leda's pallet and stayed there until she joined her mother in death.

But Mari couldn't sentence Rigel to the same death. She knew he would die with her. She'd known that since the fire at the Gathering Site. If she wished it, her Shepherd would lie on the pallet beside her and the two of them would sleep forever.

Mari couldn't ask that of Rigel. He'd escaped the Tribe of the Trees and fought his way through hell to find her—to choose Mari as his Companion for life, and he hadn't even really lived yet. He deserved better than being entombed with her.

So Mari lived for Rigel.

The morning of the first day was the worst. She woke up in Leda's bed with Rigel beside her. In that moment between awake and asleep, her mama was still alive, and for a few heartbeats Mari was just confused about why she'd slept in Leda's bed and why she was so sore and achy—and dirty.

"Mama?" she'd called, yawning and stretching stiffly. Rigel had whined and nuzzled her, waking her more fully, and cruel memory came alive.

Leda was dead.

She and Rigel were alone.

Mari curled into herself and began to sob. *Where do all the tears come from? Will they run out? They should. They really should.*

She wasn't hungry at all, just thirsty. Mari made her way slowly to the big stone water trough that she and Leda had just filled together yesterday—right before they'd left to hide Rigel's tracks. She stood staring at the water, her reflection indistinct in the otherworldly light cast by glowshrooms and glowmoss. Mari's fingers touched the surface of the water, cool and inviting. She used the small ladle to fill Rigel's wood water dish first, and the pup began lapping almost frantically. Then Mari drank, and drank deeply—once, twice, three ladles full.

Wiping her mouth she went to the viewing hole and peered up at darkness.

"We slept all day. Or maybe more than one full day." Mari talked to Rigel, as she normally did, though she tried not to think about the truth—that her pup was all she had to talk to, all she had to live for.

He'd gotten done with the water, and was circling around her, huffing and looking at the door expectantly.

"Okay, you have to go out. We have to do this differently now. We have to be even more careful than before—before when Leda was alive." Mari led Rigel slowly through the brambles, and then made him remain concealed within the thorny thicket while she went ahead and searched the night for dangers. The crescent moon was low in a clear sky. The forest was still. Mari hurried back to Rigel and held her arms open. "Up!" she called to him, and Rigel trotted quickly to her, springing up into her waiting arms. "We have to practice this a lot so that I can keep lifting you. I can't let you walk around outside our burrow. I can't take any chance of them finding you." She carried him far enough away from the burrow, putting him down so that he could relieve himself. Only then did she consider exactly from whom she must stay hidden. "Everyone," she told the young canine as he watched her with his intelligent amber gaze. "We have to hide from the Companions looking for you, and we have to hide from Sora and the rest of the Scratchers." Mari drew a long, sad breath and let it out slowly, feeling the weight of reality settling heavily on her shoulders. "We don't have any friends. Rigel, I don't think we can trust anyone."

The pup came to where she was sitting and put his head on her shoulder, sighing and leaning into her, flooding her with feelings of warmth and love and acceptance.

"You're right. We can trust each other, and that's enough." Mari put her arms around Rigel and buried her face in the thick, soft fur of his neck.

The pup held very still, sharing his warmth and his love with his Companion. It was only when his stomach growled ferociously that Mari stirred.

"Hungry. You have to be hungry. Mama smoked some rabbit for us. I can make stew and we'll—" Mari's words ran out. *We'll what? Mama's not here.* Mari shook her head. "No. I won't think about that. We'll eat. That's all I have to think about right now." A skittering sound in the brush behind them had Mari standing and calling, "Up, Rigel!" She held her pup close, drawing strength from him even though her body was exhausted and her mind mired in sadness.

It was while she was preparing their stew that Mari decided to change everything.

"We used to sleep most of the day and stay up, waiting for Mama, most of the night. We can't do that anymore, Rigel." Mari kept up a steady stream of her thoughts spoken aloud as she cut carrots and onions for the stew. "Only males mad with Night Fever go out alone at night. And—and we don't have Mama to wait up for anymore." Mari paused, blinking hard against the tears that threatened to drown her. "We'll set snares and check them during the day. We'll tend our gardens and harvest vegetables and fruits and herbs during the day. We'll do all the things we used to do with Mama at night during the day. And then, Rigel, at night we'll be here, in our burrow, asleep and safe."

Rigel sat close to her, watching her intently while she talked. Gone was the puppy-like mischievousness that used to have him poking his nose where it shouldn't be, and grabbing anything from a carrot to a slingshot rock to chew on. In the course of one day and night, Rigel had shed his puppyish playfulness; replacing it was the somber, listening demeanor of an adult Shepherd.

Mari told herself that the change in Rigel was a good thing, though the truth was that in the most secret part of her she mourned the loss of her puppy.

"Okay, your stew is ready. Here you go." Mari ladled out Rigel's portion, and then, noting his eagerness and the hollow look his belly suddenly had, she added more to the bowl, and kept filling the silence in the burrow with the sound of her voice as she continued to stir the stew, cooking it more thoroughly for her potion.

"So, where were we? That's right. We're going out during the day. Yes, I know that daylight has its own dangers. Someone from the Clan might see me, and if the sun is shining just right they might see my skin glow." She stopped mid-stir of the stew as a new and freeing thought came to her. "Rigel, I don't care if they see me!" The pup stopped eating and cocked his head at her. "Don't you understand? Mama always worried about the Clan finding out about me because she was afraid we'd be banished and she wanted me to be accepted by the other Earth Walkers. All of that has changed now. I'm not going to follow Mama as the next Moon Woman. I'm not part of the Weaver Clan. I've never really been part of Mama's Clan. So, I don't care if someone sees me and thinks my hair is too light or my skin glows in the sun because I've already banished myself!"

Mari stood there, holding the ladle and staring into the steaming stew while she tried to let her new life settle through her skin and into her soul. She wouldn't go out of her way to flaunt what she was to the Earth Walkers, but she also wouldn't avoid the daylight as she had been doing for most of her life. She'd be careful. She'd stay away from the Gathering Sites and the Clan's burrows, but she was finished with hiding from the sun.

A stray thought wound through her inner monologue. *I didn't hide from the sun at the creek, and fire came to me. I lit the forest on fire. How? How did I do that?* Mari shook herself. *Later. Think of it later. Not now.* She began dishing up stew for herself as she continued thinking aloud.

"I do have to be careful that no one finds us here, but this burrow is something that Mama and I have been hiding my entire life." There were all sorts of checks and balances for keeping their burrow's location secret, and Mari knew all of them as well as she knew how to make a two-dimensional sketch seem to live and breathe. "And I have to make sure that no one ever finds you—hurts you—takes you away from me." Mari drew several deep breaths to steady herself. "Hiding. You're going to practice hiding until you are so good at it that you can appear and disappear like smoke."

Rigel sneezed and went back to crunching rabbit bones. Mari would have smiled at him, but she wasn't able to make the corners of her mouth lift.

What's next? What happens after we hunt and gather and take care of the daily tasks of living? Then what do we do? How do we fill our lives?

Mari didn't realize she'd frozen again and had been staring motionless into the cauldron of stew until Rigel whined and pressed against her leg.

"Sorry," she said quickly, refilling his bowl. Then she sat beside him with her own dinner. "Here's what we'll do next. We'll move ahead one day, and then another, and then another. Together." Resolutely, Mari lifted her wooden spoon, forcing herself to take first one bite, then another, and then another. She ignored the tears that tracked down her cheeks and the terrible ache in her heart.

———

It was surprising how simple it was for Mari to change their sleeping pattern and the habits that went along with it. Perhaps part of the reason she slept so easily and soundly was because the only escape she had from the sadness that filled her days was in her dreams. Only when she dreamed was Leda still alive. Only when she dreamed was Mari happy and Rigel a playful pup again.

The screams began not long past dusk the seventh night after Leda's death. As had become her habit, Mari had closed and barred the door at sunset and was just completing the first of the new snares she had designed to catch live rabbits. Rigel was chewing contentedly on a venison bone Mari had scavenged from a fresh kill she'd made just that morning. The first scream was so feral that Mari almost discounted it as her brain automatically processed the sound as animal rather than human.

The second scream was closer. It was also more clearly human. Rigel dropped his bone, growling low in his throat.

"Stay close to me," Mari told him, though she needn't have said anything. Unless they were practicing his hiding skills, the Shepherd never strayed from her side, always keeping her in his sight. Mari unbarred the door and the two of them crept out, maneuvering through the winding, bramble-covered pathway that snaked around the burrow. Mari and Rigel didn't leave the protection of the thicket. Instead they paused just inside its boundary, listening.

The next screams were more distant, with each succeeding scream drifting farther and farther away. Mari kept listening until there was nothing left to hear, and then she and Rigel returned to the burrow, barring the door once more.

Mari took up her charcoal pencil and pulled out a fresh sheet of paper. The pencil felt almost foreign in her hand, and she realized with a start of surprise that she hadn't sketched anything since the day of Leda's death. Suddenly her vision was flooded with images of her mother—her smile, her gentle hands, the thickness of her hair, the tenderness in her gray eyes—and she shook with the effort not to put those images on paper.

"This first. Then Mama. Then I'll sketch Mama," Mari said. Clutching the charcoal she started making notes about the screams. She realized she should have counted them, and made a separate note to herself about that—COUNT THE SCREAMS NEXT TIME. Then she went on, writing about the direction the sounds seemed to come from, how long they lasted, and how it sounded like it was only one person screaming, and that it had definitely been a male voice.

"We'll stay away from the southeast tomorrow," she told Rigel. "We usually don't go far in that direction anyway because of the Gathering Site and burrows down there, but there are also wild berries that should be ripe about now. We'll find them in the north, or we'll do without them." Mari made an additional note about the berries, adding a reminder to search elsewhere for them.

And then she chose a new sheet of blank paper. She ran her hand over the smooth surface as she closed her eyes and let an image of her mother come to her. When she was ready, she opened her eyes and began to sketch.

Mari finished quickly. As if she'd just awakened from one of her dreams, she blinked, rubbed her eyes, and then looked down at her creation.

Leda smiled up at her. She was sitting near the hearth, at her favorite spot for basket weaving. Her expression was filled with the familiar warmth and joy with which Leda had looked at her daughter for as long as Mari had memory. Gently, Mari's finger traced the sketch, not realizing she was crying until her tears dropped with sad plopping sounds onto the paper. With fast, jerky movements, Mari wiped the dampness away and then, taking the sketch with her, she went to the pallet that used to be Leda's, and that she now shared nightly with Rigel. Hugging the paper to her, Mari curled up with Rigel pressed against her back.

Only this night she didn't fall so easily into an exhausted, dream-filled sleep. This night Mari remained awake for a long time, listening for screams and thinking . . . thinking . . .

21

Mari and Rigel woke at dawn. At first it had surprised her, how easy it was to align her waking and sleeping hours with the sun. If it was above the horizon—she was awake. If the sun had set—she and Rigel were heading to their bed. It actually made life easier, this ebb and flow of days that moved with the sun.

It was almost as if she'd forgotten the moon completely. Almost.

Mari fed Rigel and munched on dried apples while she worked on the live snares she'd been struggling with for the past several days. Weaving the last piece in place, she lifted a finished trap and smiled. "Rigel, I think I did it!"

The pup lifted his head from the bowl of rabbit stew and huffed happily at her, trotting to her as his whole body seemed to wag. Mari petted him and kissed the top of his head. "Go on—finish your breakfast. We're going to set this trap and then go mushroom hunting."

Rigel did as he was told, but his reaction to her smile and the excitement in her voice had Mari sighing and looking inward.

This is the first time I've smiled since Mama's death.

The thought shocked her, though Mari wasn't sure whether that was because she had actually smiled, or because Rigel's reaction made her realize just how sad she had been—how sad *they* had been.

"It's not fair for you," she told the pup, who stopped eating again to look at her, his tail wagging tentatively. "You deserve a happy family. You *had* a happy family." Rigel whined and, with an effort, Mari formed her lips into a smile again. *For Rigel I'll try. For Rigel I'll smile.*

As the Shepherd finished his breakfast he kept watching her while she applied the clay that thickened her features, focusing on her smile, his tail thumping against the floor of the burrow.

She almost didn't camouflage her features, but habit and fear had her sitting at her desk, meticulously changing her reflection. But she didn't reapply the hair dye.

"No more. I don't care that my hair is different. I just don't care," Mari told Rigel, who huffed and seemed to agree with her.

When she was ready, Mari took the satchel she'd begun packing every evening before they went to sleep. She had a cutting tool, her slingshot and smooth stones, the bladder newly filled with lavender oil and saltwater—just in case they got caught outside around dusk and wolf spiders tracked them. Mari also wrapped up some leftover rabbit for Rigel and for herself a collard leaf wrap filled with a mixture of sunflower seed paste, spring onions, sprouts, and the last of Leda's store of mushrooms.

"Okay," she told Rigel as they paused just outside the burrow door. "We're going to go away from the screams we heard last night. Good thing the early mushrooms are in the opposite direction, and not far from here. And I can set the live snare in the ash grove where we'll be mushroom hunting. When I was there with Mama, both of us said it was an excellent place to set the trap." Mari paused, letting the moment of pain pass that thinking of the everyday things she and Leda used to do always caused her. Then she brightened and tried, unsuccessfully, to smile at Rigel again. "But we're still going to be really careful. And we're going to practice a lot of this," Mari concentrated, imaging Rigel crouched quietly, hiding just inside the door to the burrow.

Before she could speak the command, Rigel padded swiftly and silently back inside the burrow and crouched just inside the door.

"Good job! I'm so proud of you!" Mari squatted beside him, petting and kissing him while his tail tapped a drumlike beat against the door and he licked her face.

Sweet girl, don't keep joy from him, Mari could almost hear her mother's voice as she took up the staff and began to lead Rigel through the bramble thicket. Mari shook herself. She needed to concentrate on reality. Daydreaming was dangerous. She needed to save the dreaming part of her life for when she and Rigel were safely tucked into bed with their door barred against the dangers of their world.

As always they paused just inside the edge of the brambles. Mari looked and listened carefully, but even more carefully she watched Rigel. The pup always knew before she did if there were dangers near. When he showed no sign of being concerned, Mari stepped out of the thicket, held her arms out, and called "Up!" Rigel jumped neatly into her arms and she shifted him around so that most of his weight rested over her left shoulder, leaving her right arm and hand free. "You're really getting heavy," she told him, and he licked her ear. "Don't! I'll drop you and you'll splat like a watermelon." The pup put his wet nose against her neck and Mari almost giggled, but squatting to get the snare, and struggling with it and her half-grown pup, had her groaning with effort instead.

"Seriously, Rigel. I'm going to start lifting you in the burrow. Lifting you and putting you down. Lifting you and putting you down. I have to keep building my muscles, or you have to stop eating and growing— and I don't think that's going to happen." Mari stepped out into the red cedar grove that edged their burrow, refusing to think about what she would do when Rigel was fully grown and weighed more than she did.

The morning was still foggy and cool, but by the time she was far enough away from the burrow that she could put Rigel down, Mari was sweating and breathing hard. "Uphill. The ash grove is downhill, but we have to climb up to get to the down part." She shook her head and wiped her face with the back of her sleeve. "Next time I'm going to be smarter about this. I'll carry you far enough away from the burrow *downhill,* then we'll circle around to start our climb. Okay, it's just around that far curve in the trail and over the top of the ridge." She wiped her face again and gestured for Rigel to follow her. "Let's go trap some fat, fertile rabbits and find a bunch of mushrooms for dinner."

As they made their way to the ash grove, Mari practiced sending Rigel images of tasks she wanted him to perform. First, and most important, was the hide command. Since Leda's death, Rigel seemed to truly understand the importance of hiding. He'd stopped his puppyish scampering about, and the chewing and digging he used to do when he was supposed to be silently blending into the forest. So Mari tried more commands with him. She imagined him lying down, sent him the image she sketched in her mind, and then was pleased when the Shepherd immediately dropped to his belly.

"Good boy, Rigel! Good boy!" Mari smiled, petting the pup, who wriggled and huffed joyously. From then on, whatever Mari sketched in her mind, Rigel did—*if* it made her smile.

"You're kind of like a little blackmailer," Mari told him, stroking his face. "And I know what you're doing. You're trying to make me be happy, and I love you for it." She kissed his nose then and hugged him close to her, hoping for his sake, if not for hers, that someday she would be happy again.

They came to the bend in the path, and Mari automatically sent Rigel the hide command. He ducked into the foliage inside the curve where he was hidden from anyone coming or going on the path, but he could still keep Mari in his eyesight.

She rounded the curve and was just about to release the pup when she heard the cry of relief above her.

"There you are!"

Mari froze and stared up into the branches of a mighty maple. There was a frantic rustling, muffled cursing, and Sora half dropped, half fell, from the tree.

"*Finally.* I've been trying to find you for days." Sora glared at her as she tried to smooth her dirty shift and pulled leaves out of her long, tangled hair.

"I told you if you followed me I would kill you."

"I know very well what you told me, and that's why I didn't follow you—though that was a very mean thing to say to me. But I forgive you because you were carrying your dead mother."

"I don't want your forgiveness. I don't want anything from you," Mari said.

"Well, I want something from you!" Sora paused, obviously trying to compose herself. When she began again the frantic edge in her voice had calmed, and she spoke slowly and rationally. "What I meant to say was *we* want something from you."

"No," Mari said. She pushed by Sora, glancing surreptitiously at the place in the underbrush where Rigel was hidden. Mari could just see the glint of his amber eyes.

Sora stepped in front of her, blocking her way and grabbing her wrist. Mari heard the warning growl that began deep in Rigel's throat. She shook off Sora's touch, speaking quickly and loudly, trying not to sound as frantic as she felt. "Good-bye, Sora. I'm not helping anyone. I'm mourning my mother."

"It's because of your mother that you have to help."

"No, I don't."

"The Clan needs you. They're going mad, Mari, especially the men. Without a Moon Woman to Wash them, the Night Fever stays with them, just like it stays with the women of the Clan, making them sadder and sadder every day."

"You don't seem too sad," Mari said. Studying Sora she added, "But I have seen you look much better."

"This," Sora pointed at herself, making a sweeping gesture that took in her dirty clothing and disheveled hair, "is how I look because I've been living in this Goddess be damned tree for the past five nights."

"Well, then, I suggest you go home."

"I can't! I don't have a home anymore!" The words exploded from Sora, followed by sobs that shook her shoulders. "The men know where I live. They destroyed my burrow during their madness. I—I have nowhere to go."

"Sora, I'm sorry about your burrow, but I can't—"

"Yes, you can! Only you can fix things—make them the way they used to be."

"I'm not a Moon Woman," Mari said.

"You're the closest thing we have to one."

"Then I'm sorry for you." Mari moved past Sora, sending Rigel a mental image of him following her off the trail, silently and hidden. But instead of staying by the maple tree, Sora fell into stride beside her. "Where are you going?"

"That's not your business. And you can't go with me. Stay here, Sora. Or don't. Go anywhere, just not with me." Mari stopped and looked back at the tree. "Why did you pick this place anyway?"

"I already told you. I was hiding and waiting for you."

"But why here?"

"This is the last place I saw you. You were carrying Leda's body. I assumed that this isn't far from your burrow, so when the men destroyed my home I made my way back here and I waited for you."

"Sora, make a new burrow like Leda told you to do. Someplace hidden. Keep it secret. And practice drawing down the moon. Mama believed in you. She saw your power, and since you don't seem mad—or at least not more so than usual—and you're obviously not depressed, Mama was right. Only Moon Women don't need to be washed of Night Fever. It's you the Clan needs, not me."

"I don't know how to do it! I've tried. I've tried every night. I can feel the energy of the moon. It's cold. It scares me. I can't make it do what I want it to do."

Mari sighed. "You have to focus, and that takes practice. Lots of practice."

"But how? I think I am focusing, and then that coldness fills me, and it's like I've broken through the ice in a frozen pond and there's no way out. I feel like I'm drowning. It's terrifying."

Mari nodded. "Yeah, I know. I've felt it, too. You just have to ignore the cold. Okay, you say it's like a frozen pond, then imagine the pond unfreezing and washing through you."

"All right, I'll try that. Then what?"

"Then you channel that energy into someone or something else," Mari said.

"Will you meet me tonight? Will you show me what you mean? Please, Mari."

"No, Sora. You'll have to figure this out yourself. I watched you at the last Full Moon Gathering. You should have been studying Mama, but you thought flirting with Jaxom was more important. You were wrong." Mari paused and then added, "Remember, *you* were Mama's first choice as her successor—not me."

"We all know Leda chose me over you only because there's always something wrong with you."

"There's nothing wrong with me! I'm different from the rest of you, that's all. Different doesn't mean wrong or sickly or less than. It just means different!" Mari realized she was shouting at about the same time she realized how good it felt to say what had been bothering her for years.

Then Sora spoke, and Mari wished she'd kept her mouth shut.

"Different? What do you mean? I thought you were sickly." Sora studied Mari. "What's wrong with your hair?"

Mari stifled the urge to lift the hood of her cloak and cover her hair.

"Nothing is wrong with my hair. What's wrong with yours? It looks terrible."

Sora put her hands on her curvy hips. "Mari, I have been hiding in a tree for days! What's your excuse?"

"My mother died," Mari said flatly as she walked away.

"Wait, Mari! I'm sorry. I didn't mean to offend you," Sora said.

"I'm done with this conversation. Do not follow me."

"Or what, you'll kill me? I don't believe you're a killer."

Mari turned to look at Sora. "There were only two people in this world I cared about—my mother and Jenna. Mama is dead. Jenna is worse than dead. I have nothing left to lose. Don't doubt that I will kill you." Then Mari kept walking, quickly, as she sent Rigel the release image.

As soon as Mari rounded the bend and was out of Sora's sight, she left the path, cutting down the ridge. Rigel burst through the under-brush beside her.

"Stay with me. Let's put some distance between us. Sora's never been much for physical exertion. No way will she catch us, even if she is stupid enough to try to follow me."

Mari clutched the rabbit snare and they ran, weaving a sinuous, con-voluted path. It was a simple thing for Mari to make her way through the forest she knew so well, eventually entering the low-lying ash grove from the southern, instead of the northernmost edge of it, where she finally collapsed on a bed of moss with Rigel panting beside her. She petted and made a fuss over the pup, telling him how clever he'd been, staying hidden so well. Rigel whined and sniffed her all over, es-pecially where Sora had touched her.

"Don't worry. We're not going to have anything to do with her—or with any of the Clan. We're our own Clan now. We're all each other needs."

After they'd rested for a little while, Mari went to the stream, which bubbled musically through the grove, and after she and Rigel drank deeply she began to seek the best place to set her live trap.

"Yes! I knew I remembered right. Look at this, Rigel—spring water-cress, lots and lots of it." Excited, Mari moved quickly along the edge of the stream. "And see these," she pointed, even though Rigel was busy tossing a stick in the air and catching it. "The two little tracks, one right after another, and the two bigger ones next to each other? Those are definitely rabbit tracks. And here are more, and more! This is the per-fect place to get our rabbits." Humming to herself, Mari set about pulling handfuls of wild grasses, which she rubbed all over the woven trap, hoping to dilute her scent. Then she placed it facing the water-cress, backed to a hedgerow-like line of young blackberry bushes.

Wiping her hands on her cloak, she called to Rigel, who galloped to her, stick in mouth. He skidded to a halt in front of her, sat, and, wag-ging his tail enthusiastically, offered her the stick, obviously hoping to lure her into a game of catch and toss.

"All right, but just for a little while. Mushrooms are waiting to be found, and you—my sharp-nosed boy—are going to help me find them." Mari took the stick from the pup and threw it across the stream so that Rigel had to leap over it. She watched him with pride as he easily found the stick, and then vaulted over the stream again, returning to sit in front of her.

Mari gazed down at him. He was getting so big! Sure, his paws still seemed awkwardly large for his growing body, and his face still had a puppyish look to it, but he must weigh fifty pounds—he sure felt like he weighed at least that much. Mari could see him changing, turning into a Shepherd who was majestic and handsome—smart and loving. She could see the adult canine he would become, and suddenly overwhelmed by the future vision of Rigel, she went to her knees, pulling him into her arms.

"I love you! I'm sorry it's just me, and that I'm not like I was when Mama was alive. But I'll try harder, Rigel. I'll try to make us happy." The young Shepherd dropped the stick and crawled onto her lap, though a good portion of him wouldn't fit. He lay his head against her shoulder, filling Mari with a flood of unconditional love.

"Get away from her you monster!" Sora's voice echoed through the grove. "Run, Mari! Run!"

Rigel reacted before Mari. He spun out of her lap to face the young woman, who was holding a stick over her head and brandishing it at him. He backed protectively against Mari, lifting his lips in a ferocious snarl, growling low and deep, and sounding nothing at all like a pup.

"Great Goddess! He's *your* monster!" Sora's voice was tinged with hysteria. Her gray eyes had gone huge. She dropped the stick and started to back away, but Rigel's growling increased, freezing her in place.

Mari felt numb. When she spoke her voice was utterly normal.

"He isn't a monster, but he is mine, and I am his."

Sora's wild-eyed gaze went back and forth between the canine and the girl. "Goddess be damned, that's what's wrong with you. You're a Companion!"

22

ctually, that's not accurate. I'm only half Companion. The other half is Earth Walker," Mari said.

"I—I have to sit down. Don't let him eat me," Sora said.

"He wouldn't *eat* you. He definitely would bite you, though, so sit slowly and don't try to run."

"I'd like to run, but my legs aren't working." Sora sat heavily where she was, unable to take her gaze from Rigel. "He's huge. Look at his teeth! Are his eyes always so buggy? Are you sure he won't eat me?"

Mari stroked Rigel affectionately. "I'm sure. Well, unless you try to run. Or try to hurt me. Then he'll bite you, and it'll be with my blessing. And he doesn't have buggy eyes."

"Are you always so unpleasant?"

Mari frowned. "I'm not unpleasant. You're the one who followed me. I told you not to."

"And now I know the truth about why. Did Leda know about this—this—" Sora broke off, gesturing at Rigel with a nervous shake of her hand.

"He's a canine. A Shepherd. His name is Rigel. And of course Mama knew about him. He lives with us." Mari paused, and then corrected herself sadly. "Well, now he lives with just me."

"Mari, how by all the levels of hell did this happen?"

"How did Rigel come to be with me, or how am I half Companion, half Earth Walker?"

"Why are you so calm?" Sora almost shrieked, and then when Rigel began to growl again she pressed her hand against her breast, as if to keep her heart from exploding, drew a deep breath, and said. "I cannot stand it when he shows his teeth at me and makes that terrible noise."

"Then don't yell at me."

"I'm trying not to!" Sora yelled, and then clamped her lips closed.

Mari sighed. "Okay, well, I don't know why I'm calm. I shouldn't be. You just discovered the secret Mama and I have been hiding for my entire life." She stopped, considering, and then continued as if she was reasoning aloud more than actually conversing with Sora. "It's a relief that you know—that someone finally knows. And since the day Mama died life hasn't been normal. You being here—seeing Rigel with me—that's just one more piece of kindling in the pile that is my life on fire."

"How did this thing find you?"

"Sora, don't call him a thing. Call him by his name."

"I'm sorry, but it's just so strange." She drew a deep breath and began again. "So, how did *Rigel* find you?" Sora was staring at the Shepherd again, and Rigel lifted his lips, showing her his teeth. "Can't you make him stop doing that?"

"Yeah, I can. But I'm not sure I want to."

"Well then I'll just sit here and be terrified," Sora said, trying to smooth her hair.

"That sounds like a good idea."

When Mari didn't say anything else Sora made a small, exasperated sound that had Rigel cocking his head and looking at her as if he wasn't quite sure what to make of her. "Mari, are you going to answer my question or not?"

"I suppose I might as well. The truth is I don't know how Rigel found me. He came to the burrow on the night of the last Full Moon Gathering. He was hurt pretty bad. I helped Mama draw down the moon, and healed him. That was the first time I was successful drawing down the moon."

"Just before Leda died she told me that she was going to announce that you would be apprenticing with her also, because you Washed Xander and Jenna."

"I know what she told you. I was there, hiding with Rigel under the willow tree at the Gathering Site."

"So you did Wash Xander and Jenna?"

"Yes. Mama wouldn't lie."

Sora scoffed. "Apparently Leda lied all the time about you! She said you were sickly and couldn't stand to be out in the sunlight."

"That's different. She was protecting me, not lying." Mari pulled up the sleeve of her cloak and scrubbed her dirty forearm against the damp, mossy ground. Then she took a few steps back where a wan ray of morning sunlight had found its way through the dissipating fog. Mari lifted her arm, as if reaching for the sun. She felt the warmth tingle through her body immediately. She met Sora's gaze at the same time she turned the bare spot on her arm toward her.

Sora gasped in shock. "Great Goddess! Your eyes! They're glowing. And—and your arm. That's so disgusting! Is your skin moving?"

Mari smoothed her sleeve down. "No, my skin's not moving. It's what happens when I draw in sunlight, and it's no more disgusting than drawing down the light of the moon."

Sora shook her head. "This is insane. Are you really Leda's daughter?"

"Of course I am!" Mari balled her hands into fists. "Don't ask that! Don't ever ask that again!"

Reacting to Mari's outburst, Rigel snarled and moved forward threateningly toward Sora. The young Clanswoman skittered backward, her heels digging furrows in the soft moss.

"Stop him! I didn't mean anything bad!"

Mari touched Rigel soothingly. "It's okay. Don't bite her. Yet."

"Yet?" Sora's voice squeaked.

"Yet," Mari said.

"Hey, I really am sorry. I didn't mean to upset you or him. I think we need to calm down and reason through this. And that's not me trying to tell you or your canine what to do. That's just me trying to make sense of a very strange situation," Sora said.

Mari drew a deep breath and then slowly she sat beside Rigel. She kept her arm around his neck, but that was more for comfort than control. Unless Sora actually attacked her, Rigel wouldn't do more than growl and snarl at the girl. Or at least Mari didn't think he would.

"Okay, let's make sense of it," Mari said. "Ask your questions. I'll answer them. Then we'll figure out what we're going to do."

"All right. Did a Companion rape Leda?"

"No! Mama and my father were in love," Mari said.

"That's impossible."

"And yet here I am, so it's obviously not impossible."

"Okay, if that's the truth then where is this Companion father of yours?" Sora asked.

"Dead."

"I don't want to offend you, but your Companion father being dead seems rather convenient."

"No, it's not. Had Galen lived he and Mama and me were going to leave here and find a place where we could be together as a family, but he was killed by his own people before we could get away," Mari said.

"How do you know that?"

"Mama told me all about it—how they fell in love—their plans to go away—and how Galen was followed by his people and killed when he wouldn't betray her or me to them. She watched it happen. I was just a baby, so I don't remember it. But Mama remembered. She remembered it every day of her life."

Sora studied Mari silently, and Mari saw something shift in the girl's eyes. "What?" Mari asked.

"The sadness of it surprises me, that's all," Sora said.

"Ask your other questions and let's get on with this."

"Right now I can think of only one more. So, the truth is you've trained your entire life as a Moon Woman, and the only reason Leda didn't name you as her apprentice and heir was because of that canine and your eyes and skin?"

"It's more than just my eyes and skin. My face is different, too, but I cover it." Mari's fingertips brushed her brow and her nose. "So is my hair. I dye my hair. Well, I used to dye my hair." She grimaced in disgust when she touched the matted mess. "I've stopped."

Sora squinted at her. "It's light colored, like a Companion's hair, isn't it?"

"Is that your last question?"

Sora frowned. "No, that's just an observation with a question attached to it."

"Yes, it's light. Or I think it is. I haven't seen it free of dye and clean for a long, long time."

"That's why you always look so dirty." Sora raised her hands, stopping Mari's words. "No, that's not a question. It's *just* an observation. And you haven't answered my original question—or at least not all of it."

"At first Mama didn't name me her heir because my powers were too unpredictable. That started to change when Rigel came to me, mortally wounded. And then I drew down the moon without Mama's help and Washed Xander and Jenna—and I healed Mama, too. Still, I was as surprised as you were when she told you she was naming me her apprentice in addition to you."

"You didn't know?"

Mari shook her head. "No. I had no idea she was going to do that. We'd talked about it, but she thought it would be too difficult for me to be parted from Rigel."

Sora's gaze flicked to the pup. "Why?"

"He and I are bonded. It's not good for either of us to be apart." Mari hugged Rigel, smiling at her pup as he thumped his tail and licked her. "When a canine chooses his Companion it's for life."

"Great Goddess! That monster is why the Hunters attacked the Gathering!"

"Don't call him a monster! And it's not Rigel's fault that some guy who doesn't have his own canine is obsessed with him," Mari said.

"But I'm right, aren't I? He's what the Hunters were tracking, and not us."

"That's another question, and you said you only had one more. I'm done answering. Now it's time to figure out what I'm going to do about you," Mari said.

Sora grinned. "That's easy! There's nothing to figure out because there's only one thing to do. I'm going to live in your burrow with you." She paused and her smile faded as she looked at Rigel. "Does he stay inside all the time?"

"Sora, you're *not* going to live with us. Yes, Rigel stays with me—all the time."

"Well, that's going to be inconvenient and more than a little frightening. I suppose it can't be helped, though. You're going to have to figure out a way to get him not to make those terrible sounds at me, or show his teeth, *or* bite me of course."

"Are you really a man? Do you have Night Fever?"

"Of course not and no."

"Then you're just crazy. There is absolutely no way you're going to live with Rigel and me," Mari said.

"Okay, I didn't want it to have to be this way, but you're not giving me any choice. Mari, If you don't let me live with you I'm going to tell the entire Clan who you really are—and about Rigel and how you and he are responsible for the latest attacks from the Companions. Your burrow is hidden, but how long do you think it, and you, will remain undiscovered if an entire Clan, mad with Night Fever, is searching for you?"

"I won't let you do that. I won't let you leave here," Mari said, getting to her feet. Rigel, always in tune with her emotions, stood beside her, growling menacingly at Sora.

"You'll have to kill me to keep me here," Sora said. "And, since the day you threatened me, I've been doing a lot of thinking. We've never been friends, and I don't know you very well, but I don't believe you're a killer."

"I may not be a killer, but I can't say the same about Rigel," Mari bluffed.

"You said he wouldn't eat me."

"I didn't say he wouldn't kill you," Mari said.

"I'm going to bet that he won't. Oh, I believe he can hurt me, maybe even kill me, but I don't think you'll let him," Sora said.

"And why wouldn't I?"

"Because you're Leda's daughter and you're better than that," Sora said. "Look, Mari, this can be a good thing for all of us. I'll only stay with you long enough for you to teach me what you know about drawing down the moon. Once I can be a proper Moon Woman for the Clan I'll leave."

"But you said your burrow was destroyed," Mari said.

"It was. Help me make my own hidden burrow. Please. I'll live there then, and go about the business of caring for the Clan. You can go about the business of whatever it is you want to do with the rest of your life."

"How do I know you won't betray me, won't tell the Clan about Rigel and me?"

"I won't betray you if you don't betray me. You'll be the only person in the Clan who knows the location of my new burrow. If you don't tell anyone my secret, I won't tell anyone yours."

Mari studied her. "Here's what I don't get—why are you so eager to be the Clan's Moon Woman? If you think it's an easy job, you're wrong. It's hard and exhausting and it never, ever ends."

"I'm aware of that. Or, at least I'm aware that working hard, being exhausted, and never, ever getting a break is the kind of Moon Woman Leda was." Sora raised her hands quickly, and continued before Mari could respond. "I respected your mother. She was a great Moon Woman. But here's the truth—I have no delusions about my greatness. Being a good Moon Woman is fine for me."

"Leda believed being Moon Woman was a calling—a responsibility."

Sora nodded. "Yes, I am well aware of that, too. I heard many lectures from Leda on that particular subject." She raised a dark, expressive brow at Mari. "Don't tell me she didn't lecture you about that, too."

"Mama was passionate about her Goddess-given gifts. You could have learned a lot from her." Mari realized she sounded defensive, but there was no way she was going to admit to Sora that she had shown disdain for her mother's dedication to being the Clan's Moon Woman.

"Well of course I could have learned a lot from her. Now I'm going to learn a lot from you. I'll try to be the best apprentice I can be, and you won't lecture me about my many, many responsibilities to the Clan. Will you?"

"No, I won't. I don't care about the Clan. I care about Rigel and me and keeping our secret."

"Then we should get along just fine," Sora said happily.

"You still haven't explained why you're so eager to be Moon Woman when you've made it clear you don't feel the way Mama did about it," Mari said.

Sora didn't say anything. She just chewed her lip and refused to meet Mari's gaze.

"Look, I'm not even going to consider this if you're not completely honest with me," Mari said.

Sora's gray eyes met hers, and within them Mari was surprised to see vulnerability. "Okay, that's fair." She drew a long breath, let it out, and then spoke in a rush. "I want to be Moon Woman because I want to be so important to the Clan that no one ever leaves me again."

Mari blinked, not sure she'd heard her correctly. She stared at Sora, who looked sad and shy. Where was the pretty, arrogant girl who hated to work and only had time for the young males of the Clan?

"Leave you? I guess I don't understand," Mari said.

"Of course you don't. You don't even know me." Sora sighed again. "My father was part of the Miller Clan. He met my mother at a Trade Gathering. After he and my mother mated, and she became pregnant with me, he left and went back to his old Clan. As soon as I was born my mother followed him. Without me."

"Your mama left you? Just like that?"

Sora looked away and nodded. "Just like that. And I don't ever want that to happen again. No one leaves a Moon Woman. No one. She's too important—too well loved."

"Oh," Mari said, shocked by this new version of Sora. "I'm sorry."

"You understand now, don't you? I won't be as good as Leda, but I will take care of the Clan."

"And in return they'll take care of you," Mari said.

Sora nodded. "I hope so. It's really all I've ever wanted."

"I do understand." Slowly, resolutely, Mari stood. "You can move in with us, but we're going to do things my way and not yours."

Sora's smile lit her face. "That's just fine with me. I'll be a good little apprentice. When do I start trying to draw down the moon?"

"Sadly, that'll be tonight when I would rather be sleeping. But first you are going to help me do some digging and hunting."

"Huh? Whatever for? Digging and hunting doesn't have anything to do with drawing down the moon!" Sora looked around the grove as if Mari had just asked her to begin building a burrow there, from nothing, with nothing.

"Well, first, you're going to find the biggest fern in the area and dig it up. We'll use it tonight while you're practicing drawing down the moon. No!" Mari stopped Sora's question before it left her mouth. "I'm not going to explain why right now. Second, you're going to help me gather mushrooms. For dinner. Until you're a true Moon Woman and you are paid tribute, you're going to have to hunt and dig and forage like any other Clanswoman." She patted Rigel on the head. "Come on, sweet boy, sniff out some of those mushrooms for Sora so that she can practice her gathering skills." Mari strode off, heading into the scrub pine where the mushrooms liked to hide with Sora trailing after her.

23

This bramble thicket is impressive," Sora said. They were standing just outside one of the hidden openings to the trail system that snaked around Mari's burrow. "How long did it take to get it this big?"

With a groan, Mari put Rigel down, and then picked up her walking stick so that she could move aside a thick, thorny bough. Rigel moved inside the cover of the thicket, and Mari used her foot to smudge away his paw prints. "It's been like this for as long as I can remember, but it doesn't stay this way without a lot of work, and the channeling of a lot of moon energy." Mari frowned, studying the brambles more closely. Leda hadn't even been gone for one full cycle of the moon, and already she could see that the new growth had slowed and some of the thorny branches were looking unusually sparse.

"Wait, you draw down the moon for these brambles?"

Mari looked at Sora. "You don't know much about being a Moon Woman, do you?"

"No. Leda died before she could begin training me."

"I thought you'd been working with Mama for a while now," Mari said.

Sora fidgeted restlessly, shifting the big fern Mari had made her dig up and carry with her from one arm to another, grimacing at the

streaks of dirt left on her skin and brightly colored tunic. "I was supposed to be observing her. You know, while she Washed the Clan. I'm
willing to admit that I could have been paying better attention, but I
don't remember seeing her do anything with any plants. Well," she
added quickly, "I know that Leda used plants to heal sickness and tend
wounds. But that's not the same thing as drawing down the moon *for*
a plant."

"Actually, it's exactly the same thing. I'll show you what I mean as
soon as the moon rises. The thicket is definitely in need of some care."

"Really? It looks good to me," Sora said. Tentatively, she touched one
of the unnumbered thorns that were on guard, pulling her finger back
with a little squeal and putting it in her mouth. "They're so sharp!"

Mari's gaze grew soft and far off. "Fireflies and moonlight. Mama
used to say the thorns are made of fireflies and moonlight."

"Well that's odd. Why would she say that?"

"I'll show you tonight." Mari motioned for Sora to move with Rigel
within the thicket. "Come on, you'll have to stay close to me, just like
Rigel does. We have another walking stick. Eventually you'll learn the
ways in and out of the thicket, but until then it's going to be pretty confusing, and even dangerous, for you."

"Ouch!" Sora squeezed a long, deep scratch on her arm.

"That's the point. And I told you to stay close to me. I have to hold
the branches aside for both of you."

"I don't want to get too close to him!" Sora said in a fierce whisper,
pointing at Rigel.

"You're going to have to get over that. Don't bother him—or me too
much—and he won't bother you," Mari said.

"He's just so big. And his teeth are ridiculous."

"Okay, stop whispering. Rigel can hear better than either of us. And
he understands way more than you'd believe. Plus, his teeth aren't
ridiculous. They're supposed to be big and bad. He's only going to get
bigger and badder, too. So get used to him and stop acting like a silly
Scratcher."

"Don't call me that!" Sora said, causing Rigel to give her a hard look as he bared his teeth at her. "See what I mean." Sora pointed at the pup. "We can't even have a conversation without him threatening me."

Mari lifted a shoulder. "Be nice and he'll stop doing that."

Sora blew out a long, frustrated breath. "I'm not being intentionally mean, but he is scary." Then she gave a little squeal of pain as a strand of her long, dark hair got caught on a bramble.

"You are giving me a headache," Mari said as she jerked Sora's hair free.

"That hurt!"

"Just keep up with me. And now you know why I keep my hair braided."

"Leda's hair wasn't braided," Sora said stubbornly, smoothing the strand back and rubbing her scalp.

"Leda was a lot more graceful than me—or you for that matter. Okay, watch out. We're taking a sharp turn to the right, and then an immediate turn to the left. Than we start climbing up in a zigzag pattern."

"Can I put this fern down?"

"No." Mari held another bramble branch aside. "It's not much farther."

"So, even if someone thinks they know where your burrow might be, they couldn't get inside this bramble thicket," Sora said, scooting past Mari carefully.

"That's the idea."

"Do you ever get used to coming and going through all of this?" Sora asked, looking up at the wall of thorns that, like the walls of an ancient labyrinth, almost blocked out the evening sky.

"All of this keeps us safe. Not only am I used to it—I appreciate it. You should, too."

"Oh, I do. I think it's magnificent! I just don't know how I'm going to re-create it," Sora said.

Neither do I, Mari thought, *but I'm going to figure it out. The sooner her burrow's ready—the sooner she's out of mine.*

"To the left here, and then we go down five paces, turn right, up five paces, and we're at the mouth of the burrow," Mari said.

"Finally! I'm exhausted and starving," Sora said. Then she almost bumped into Mari as she stared, openmouthed, at the entry of the burrow. Sora moved around Mari, careful not to let any of the thorns snag her, and approached the carving of the Goddess that seemed to hold up the thick wooden door. Reverently, she touched the image, reminding Mari for the space of a heartbeat, of Leda.

"She's so beautiful." Sora's voice was hushed. "Who created her?"

"The mother of my mother's mother. She was an artist," Mari said.

"It would make me very happy if the Earth Mother protected my burrow, too," Sora said. She looked over her shoulder at Mari. "Can you do this?"

Mari blinked in surprise at the question. "I don't know. I've never tried. I, um. I draw things."

Sora turned to face her. "Then you're an artist, too?"

"Yes. I suppose I am."

"Why didn't anyone in the Clan know that?" Sora asked.

"Jenna did."

"Jenna's a child. Why didn't anyone who was important know?"

"Mama knew. No one was more important than her," Mari said.

Sora looked at her for a long moment without speaking. Finally, she said, "The two of you kept many secrets."

"Because we had to," Mari said.

"I know the Law, but do you really believe two Moon Women would have been banished and shunned, especially for something that happened so long ago?"

"Leda didn't want to take the chance that I would be the one sent away from the Clan," Mari said.

"Leda was our only Moon Woman. She wouldn't have been shunned," Sora said matter-of-factly. "And had you shown that you were valuable to the Clan, you probably wouldn't have been shunned either." She paused and her gaze flicked to Rigel. "I can't say the same for him."

Mari lifted her chin. "The secrets Mama kept were to protect me. I'll protect Rigel the same way."

"How long are you going to carry him to and from your burrow?"

"As long as he breathes," Mari said without hesitation.

"And how much bigger is he going to get?"

"I don't know, but that doesn't matter. I'll still carry him."

Sora shook her head sadly. "You've chosen a hard life, Mari."

"I didn't choose it. I was born to it." Mari pushed past Sora. "Come in and I'll show you where you'll be sleeping for the short amount of time you'll be here. Oh, and you can leave that fern outside the door."

"I don't understand why you made me carry that thing all the way here."

"You will," Mari said tiredly. "Now, pretend to be a good apprentice and come in here so we can eat and get this evening over with."

"You're not a very nice mentor," Sora said with a whine that grated on Mari's nerves. Mari glanced down at Rigel, who looked up at her. They sighed in tandem, and she whispered to her pup, "Not surprising since I never planned on being a mentor at all . . ."

"Your burrow is lovely *and* clean. I can't believe you drew these. They are so good!"

Mari scowled at Sora. "The way you say it doesn't make it a compliment."

"You can't really blame me for being shocked." Sora kept leafing through Mari's pile of sketches as if they mesmerized her. "And I can't believe you have all this talent and you didn't share it with the Clan."

"What was I supposed to do? Draw pictures for them? I didn't know there was a big need for charcoal sketches amongst the Clan."

"Now you're being sarcastic," Sora said, not taking her eyes from the sketches.

"Actually, I'm not. I honestly didn't know anyone in the Clan would be interested in my drawings," Mari said as she stirred their stew and added another handful of mushrooms to the aromatic mixture.

"Have you never been in any other burrow than this one?"

"Yes. I've been in the burrow Jenna shared with her father," Mari said.

Sora scoffed. "That was little more than a male's hovel. You've *never* been in any of the females' burrows?"

Mari met Sora's gray-eyed gaze steadily. Even though the subject was not a pleasant one, she was finding that it was freeing to be able to tell the truth. "I was barely five winters old when the sun-colored pattern started appearing under my skin. Until then Mama had dyed my hair, but hadn't needed to do much else to cover what I am. I went everywhere with her then. Well, during the daylight I did. At night I would stay locked in here."

"All by yourself? Even when you were so little?"

Mari nodded. "Some of my earliest memories are of falling asleep by the door so that I'd be sure to hear Mama knocking when she came home at dawn."

"That must have been difficult for you, and for Leda," Sora said.

"It wasn't that bad. Mama and I had each other, and that was enough for us." Mari turned back to the stew. "So, I have been in the females' burrows, but I was too young to remember much. What sticks in my mind is that they seemed very big and full of lots of unusual things."

"Yes, like artistic decorations—carvings and tapestries and such. I'm really surprised that Leda didn't tell you about the beauty of the burrows. Your talent would be very much in demand if the Clan knew about it." Sora looked around the little cavelike dwelling. "I'm also surprised that your walls aren't decorated with murals you've painted. You can paint, can't you?"

"Of course I can. Mama and I talked about me painting scenes on our walls, but as you can see, we decided to fill them with extra glowmoss and glowshrooms instead so that the light is better for me at night while I waited up for her to come home." Mari pointed to the hearth. "I painted those."

"They're pretty." She studied the delicate blue flowers that seemed to be growing across the mantel.

"They're forget-me-nots. Mama's favorites."

"Like I said, they're pretty. You're an excellent artist. Your skills would be appreciated by the Clan—especially the teachers of the Clan. Those sketches of yours would really be helpful with teaching the children how to read and write."

Mari peeled and smashed another garlic clove with her fist, stirring it into the cauldron, and then began chopping spring onions. She thought about what Sora had said, turning the idea around in her mind and trying to see Leda's reasoning for keeping her talent a secret. Mari knew Leda had always thought first of her safety, and lived in terror that her secret would be discovered and Mari would be cast out of the Clan. She wondered, though, if maybe her mama had been *too* worried about her secret. For a moment Mari imagined being appreciated by the Clan for something that was unique to her, and not tied to her mother, and she was surprised at the rush of longing that washed through her.

Rigel whined and his warm, strong body pressed against her leg. She looked down at him, smiling.

"It's okay. I was just thinking about might-have-beens." She patted his head.

"You talk to him a lot," Sora said.

"Yep. He's a good listener," Mari said.

"You act like he can understand you."

"He can."

"Truthfully?"

"Truthfully." Mari glanced at Sora and saw only curiosity in her expression, so she added, "Rigel and I are bonded for life. He chose me as his Companion. That's more than just a title. It means that he and I are linked. I can feel his emotions and he can feel mine. And when I sketch a picture in my mind, and then imagine sending it to him, Rigel understands."

Sora arched her dark brows. "Are you making that up to tease me?"

"No! I'm telling you the truth."

"Can you show me?"

"How?" Mari asked.

"Well, sketch in your mind a picture of Rigel going over to the door and lying down," Sora said after thinking for a few moments.

"That's easy." Mari kept stirring the stew, and without looking at Rigel or saying a word, she imagined drawing a picture of Rigel lying in front of the door. Within a heartbeat or two, the Shepherd had left her side, padded to the door, and lay down.

"That's amazing. Do you think all of the Companions' canines can do that?"

"I don't know about *all*, but my father's Shepherd could. Mama told me about it."

"This is him, isn't it?" Sora held up the sketch of Galen, Orion, Leda, and Mari as an infant.

Mari glanced at it, and then quickly averted her gaze. It hurt to look at the sketches of her mama—hurt a lot. "Yes. That's Galen and his Shepherd, Orion, Mama, and me."

"The Shepherd is unfinished," Sora said.

"That's because until Rigel chose me, I hadn't seen a canine close up enough to draw one."

Sora sat heavily on the pallet that used to be Mari's, but was now—temporarily—hers. "It really is incredible."

"What is?"

"You—or rather your parentage. And him." She jerked her chin at Rigel, who was still lying by the door, watching Mari through sleepy eyes. "You know, his fur is very thick and surprisingly pretty colors. It would make a beautiful cloak."

Mari spun around, holding the ladle like a sword. "Don't you dare talk about skinning him!"

Sora laughed until Rigel's warning growl hushed her. She cleared her throat and then, eyes still sparkling but voice deceptively contrite, said, "I wasn't serious. It was a compliment."

Mari and Rigel snorted at the same time.

"It's very odd how in sync the two of you are," Sora said.

Mari ladled up a healthy portion of stew for Rigel, adding raw rabbit to his large wooden dish. She set it aside to let it cool while she dished up portions for Sora and herself. Then she gave the Shepherd his dinner and joined Sora, pulling up a chair to sit beside the pallet.

Sora tried the stew, nodded, and made a small, agreeable sound, and then through her second mouthful said, "No fresh bread?"

"If you want fresh bread feel free to bake some yourself," Mari said.

"I'll do that. My bread is light as clouds on the inside."

Mari snorted. "Like you can really bake."

"I can really bake. And well, too. Just because I don't like to root around in the dirt to gather things, and I loathe hunting, doesn't mean I don't understand how to turn what others hunt and gather for me into deliciousness." She took another spoonful of stew, tasting it thoughtfully. "This isn't bad, but you added too much garlic and too little salt."

"Are you complaining about my stew?"

"Absolutely not. I'm only making a truthful observation. Tomorrow I'll cook. You'll see. Do you have the makings for bread?"

"Yeah. It's all in the storage room in the rear of the burrow." Mari tried not to sound too interested, even though just thinking about bread as light as clouds was making her salivate. "Mama did the baking and I made the stews."

"I can do both and more. If you can hunt and gather it, I can cook it."

Mari bit back a quick retort. Why should she care if Sora knew how to find food or not? It *would* make her life easier if Sora did the cooking. "You have a deal," she said.

"Really?"

"Really."

"Thank you!" Sora said around another mouthful of stew. "You won't be sorry."

Mari laughed humorlessly. "I've been sorry since you found me under that tree."

"That was a mean thing to say." Sora stared into her stew, biting her lip.

Mari lifted a shoulder, surprised that Sora's comment made her feel uncomfortable. "I was being honest, not mean. I'm—I'm not used to spending this much time with anyone but Mama. Maybe you should stop being so sensitive."

"Do *you* want to change the way you are?" Sora asked.

"No. Why should I?"

"I won't go into that because it would be a really long conversation.

I'll just leave it at this—you don't want to change. I don't want to change. So instead of trying to change each other, why don't we just accept who we are and make the best out of our arrangement?"

"I guess that makes sense."

"So, is it a deal?" Sora said.

"It is," Mari agreed.

They finished the stew in silence and with at least the pretense of camaraderie together they cleaned the dishes. It was during the aftermath of dinner that Sora started rubbing her arms, reminding Mari poignantly of Leda.

Mari opened their window to the sky to see that dusk had, indeed, fallen. She drew a deep breath and turned to Sora. "All right, time for lesson number one. Do you know about earth writing?"

Sora was sitting on the pallet, working a wooden comb carefully through her long, thick hair. "No. I've never heard of it."

Mari sighed. "Did Mama teach you nothing?"

"Why don't you just assume that I know nothing about drawing down the moon, because like I told you earlier, *I know nothing about drawing down the moon.*" Sora paused and studied Mari before adding, "Why isn't your skin crawling? It's after dusk."

"I'm not like you. Sunset doesn't affect me," Mari said.

"Not at all? Your skin doesn't feel terrible?"

"No," Mari said.

"You have no pain whether or not you go out in the moonlight?" Sora was watching Mari with big, shocked eyes.

"The setting of the sun doesn't affect me. Neither does the rising of the moon," Mari said. "Now, about earth writing."

"Wait, are you sure you have the power to draw down the moon? I mean, how can you if you can't feel it in under your skin?"

"This is silly. Showing you is easier than telling you." Mari hesitated, and then she entered what had been her mother's room, but was now hers. She went to Leda's neat stack of cloths and took her cloak. She allowed herself a brief moment to hug the multicolored cloth close to her and breathed deeply of her mother's scent of rosemary and rose water. She put the cloak around her shoulders, tying it carefully into place before taking two thick clumps of dried sage, held together with brightly colored strips of cloth from Leda's basket of supplies, and then rejoined Sora in the main room of the burrow.

Mari paused to carefully brush a live coal from the hearth fire into a small tinderbox, and while she was bent to the hearth, Sora reached out and gently brushed her fingers down the sleeve of Leda's cloak.

"This is so beautiful."

Mari jerked in surprise, causing Rigel to lift his head and skewer Sora with his amber gaze.

"You don't need to be so shocked, especially when it makes *him* give me that look. I liked Leda. Plus, I've always envied her this cloak. The dyeing is lovely, as is the embroidery of flowers all around the edges of it."

"Thank you. I made this for Mama."

"If that's true you should try making some clothing for yourself. You really don't have to wear things that are so drab and dirty-looking. I can help you with your hair, too." Sora paused, studying Mari. "Well, I think I can help you."

"Sora, I'm tired. I'm sad. And I'm out of patience. Now follow me and try not to talk for a little while." Mari walked to the door, opened it, and handed Sora her old walking stick. "You're going to start by holding aside your own bramble branches. And remember—it's night. We're hidden here, but be mindful of what you say and how loud you say it. With Mama gone I have no idea where the Clan, or more specifically, the Clans*men* are at night."

"I know where they are. They're surrounding my lovely little burrow that is now all in ruins," Sora said in a broken voice. "I barely got out of there." She picked up her own cloak, grimacing at the dirt and stains that covered it. "Goddess, not having all of my tunics and cloaks and dresses is almost unbearable."

"Sora, focus. You're supposed to be my apprentice, and that means you should be thinking about attempting to draw down the moon—not your missing clothes."

"My clothes aren't missing. They're being held hostage," Sora muttered as she awkwardly brandished the walking stick. Just outside the door, she paused to gently touch the image of the Great Goddess.

"Hey," Mari said, glancing over her shoulder. "Don't forget to bring that fern."

With a groan, Sora slung the huge, wilted fern over her shoulder, causing dirt from its exposed roots to cascade down her back. Grimacing, she announced, "When I'm the Clan's Moon Woman I will never get dirty again. I mean it. Never! You might like dirt, but I absolutely, definitely do not."

Mari didn't bother to correct Sora. She simply strode forward, allowing a bramble branch to fall back over the path. Then she and Rigel shared an amused look at the muffled shriek that came from behind them.

24

This is lovely! And no one would ever guess that it's here," Sora said in a hushed, reverent voice. "May I approach the Earth Mother?" Mari made no response. She'd come to an abrupt halt half a step inside the clearing, and was just standing there, staring. "Mari? Are you okay?"

Rigel whined and licked her hand fretfully.

"What? Oh. Yeah. I'll be fine." Mari absently stroked Rigel, drawing comfort from his nearness.

"You don't look like you're going to be fine. You look like you're going to be sick."

Mari met Sora's gaze. "I buried Mama here—in the arms of the Earth Mother. I—I haven't been up here since."

"Oh. That explains your paleness. I'm sorry, Mari," Sora said quietly. "May I approach the Earth Mother?" she repeated, and then added, "I'd like to offer a prayer for Leda."

"Mama would like that."

Before Sora entered the clearing she squeezed Mari's hand briefly, saying, "I know we're not friends, but I am truly sorry about your mother."

Unable to speak, Mari nodded, blinking quickly. As Sora stepped into the clearing, she breathed deeply and called to Mari over her shoulder. "These flowers are incredible! They smell like honey. They look familiar, but I can't name them. What are they and how did you get them to grow here?"

"They're forget-me-nots, like what I painted on our hearth. I didn't get them to grow. They've never bloomed here before," Mari said. Sora had stopped and had turned to face her. Mari bent and brushed her fingers lightly through the delicate blue flowers that Rigel had buried his face in and was sniffing enthusiastically. "They don't usually bloom until midsummer, and never here."

"She sent them for you," Sora said.

"How do you know Mama did that?" Mari wiped at a tear that had escaped her eye.

"Not Leda." Sora nodded her head in the direction of the idol. "The Great Earth Mother sent them for you."

"Does she talk to you?" Mari asked as she studied the statue's serene face.

"Not with words, but I can feel the Goddess's presence. Can you hear her?"

Mari shook her head sadly. "No."

"But you feel her presence?" When Mari didn't respond Sora smiled at her and said, "Well, the Goddess obviously cares about you. Sending Leda's flower to comfort you is no small thing." Sora approached the Earth Mother idol. Mari watched as she knelt, raised her hands, and began murmuring something that she couldn't quite hear.

Feeling like she was eavesdropping on a private conversation, Mari shifted her attention to the ground, expecting to see the rawness of her mother's newly dug grave. But instead of broken earth the spot near the arms of the Goddess was exactly like the rest of the clearing— covered with grass and fragrant blue flowers.

Mari's gaze returned to the Earth Mother's face. She stared at the image of the Goddess, willing herself to be open to anything the Great Earth Mother might send her. Then she whispered, "If you did send these flowers, thank you. I'll never forget Mama. It would be like for-getting to breathe. But thank you."

"Oh, that is so much better!" Sora had risen from her knees and was standing in a white wash of moonlight, arms raised, head tilted back. The silver-gray color that had begun to taint her skin was gone, and when she turned to face Mari, she was smiling. "I'm ready for my first lesson in drawing down the moon."

"Do you know what direction is north?"

Sora cocked her head, thinking. Then she pointed at the idol. "That's north."

"Correct. We begin in the north. Do you know why?" Mari asked.

"It's the place of beginnings?"

"Well, yes. But the reason it's the place of beginnings is that we think of the earth as a living being, and her head rests in the north—thus we begin there."

Sora nodded. "That makes sense."

"What did you do with the fern?"

"It's right here." Sora picked it up from where she'd set it amongst the fragrant flowers.

"Put it in the center of the clearing." While Sora did as she was told, Mari positioned herself in front of the Goddess, opened the tinderbox, and lit both clumps of sage. "This one is for you." She held it out to Sora, who hurried to her and took it eagerly.

"Now what?"

"Back away from me several paces so that we both have room to move."

"How's this?"

"Good. Okay, this is how Mama described it to me when I was just a girl. Moon needs to know who her Women are, and like Earth, Moon appreciates beauty. So, we're going to introduce ourselves to Moon by dancing the pattern of our names over Earth in the moonlight."

Sora's look of nervousness changed to a pleased smile. "Really? I in-troduce myself as a Moon Woman by dancing?"

"Really," Mari said. "So, your feet are going to dance out the spelling of your name, and while you're dancing hold out the smoking sage stick. It should swirl around you, mimicking your pattern. Do you know why I brought sage instead of another dried herb?"

Sora swirled the lit stick around her and coughed softly. "Because it makes a lot of smoke?"

"No, I think that's just a nice coincidence. When you eat it, sage has vast healing properties, especially for women. Oils from its leaves can cure many ills. And when it is dried and burned, its smoke cleanses. It's good for new beginnings. Like tonight. Mama had me dance with a smoking bunch of it a lot like this the first time I introduced myself to Moon."

"I think I understand. Is there anything in particular I should do while I dance—I mean, besides following the pattern of my name?"

"Mama, what do I do while I dance my name?"

"Just be filled with joy, sweet girl. Show Moon how happy her future Woman is to be dancing an introduction. Dance all around the clearing—cover it with smoke and laughter and your unique beauty."

Leda's words drifted with the smoke around her. Mari smiled through the tears that trailed down her cheeks. "The only thing you need to do is to be happy. Show Moon how happy you are to be Her Woman. And use the entire clearing to dance. Fill it with smoke and dancing and happiness."

"I can do that. When do I start?"

"Start with me." Mari lifted her clump of sage, and then visualizing herself tracing the pattern of an M, she began to dance.

It was difficult for Mari to let go. More than ten winters had passed since she'd first introduced herself to Moon. Then she had been a giggling girl, her small bare feet twirling the pattern of her name in the lush earth, dancing with her mama to fill the clearing with happiness, fragrant smoke, and love. At first her movements were stiff, awkward even. But as the clearing filled with eddies of drifting sage smoke, and as Sora's breathless laughter accompanied her movements, Mari began to find comfort in the familiar path of her name. This she knew. She also knew the clearing. It was a safe place—a part of her home. It was her place with Mama, where she'd been born and grown up, and finally where she'd buried Leda. Her feet traced the pattern of her name through the fragrant blue flowers, and Mari felt the stirring of something that wasn't joy—not yet—but it was at least a letting loose of enough sadness, even if temporarily, that she spread wide both of her arms. Remembering the happiness she and Leda had filled the clearing with, Mari danced.

Suddenly a shriek was heard in the distance—feral and hate-filled—shattering the peacefulness of the grove.

"Oh, Goddess, no! Don't let them get me." Sora ran to Mari's side and clutched her hand.

Mari's gaze went to Rigel. The canine was still lying by the Earth Goddess idol. Except for his pricked ears and his sharp, distance-seeking eyes, he appeared to be relaxed and unaffected by the shrieks.

Mari felt the tension in her shoulders relax. "They're not threatening us. They don't know we're here, and even if they did it would be almost impossible for them to make it through the brambles," Mari said, adding, "Who are they?"

"Our Clansmen. They're why I've been hiding in that tree."

Another shriek echoed over the first one, coming from a different direction.

"Do you know where they are?" Mari asked.

"That first one, no. The second one, I have a good guess. Sounds to me as if he's coming from the direction of my burrow. Or, what used to be my burrow until a bunch of them destroyed it," Sora said grimly. "It's not just during the night that they're mad. They frighten me. I had to run from them *during the day*."

Yet another shriek sounded, closer than the other two.

"Is that coming from the direction of the tree I was hiding in?" Even in the moonlight Mari could see Sora's face had paled. She met Mari's gaze. "Do you understand how bad it is?"

"I have no doubt that it's bad. I heard the shrieks last night, too, but it sounded like only one man," Mari said.

"Well, it's not. It's all of them. All of them that are still alive anyway. Mari, I know you don't care about the Clan, and I'm not going to pretend to be as honorable and loving as your mother was, but if someone doesn't start Washing the Night Fever from them soon, there will be no Clan left."

Mari studied Sora. Her expression was frightened and earnest.

"All right. Then let's get on with your lesson while there's still a Clan left for you," Mari said.

"You could Wash them. I mean, just until I finish my lessons," Sora said.

"No. They're too unpredictable. Too uncontrollable. If something happens to me, Rigel would be inconsolable. I'm not sure exactly what he would do, but I don't think he'd live long if I didn't come back to him."

"And he means more to you than your Clan."

Sora's statement wasn't a question, but Mari answered it anyway. "Yes, he means more to me than *your* Clan. The Clan isn't mine, Sora. It's never been mine. Only Mama was mine." Mari turned away from Sora and began walking toward the fern, which waited, sad and wilted, in the middle of the clearing. "Come on," she said without glancing back at the girl. "Lesson number one is about healing."

"Healing? But shouldn't you just teach me about drawing down the moon to Wash the Clan? I can learn the rest later," Sora said, trailing along behind Mari.

"We do this my way, meaning Leda's way, or not at all," Mari said, putting her still smoking sage clump beside the fern and motioning for Sora to do the same as she joined her. "Sit by the fern." Mari pointed at the wilted green clump.

With a sigh, Sora sat. She lifted one of its limp fronds and let it drop. Glancing up at Mari she said, "It's in bad shape."

"Yeah, you're going to use the power of the moon to heal it."

"Why?" Sora said.

"Because a Moon Woman does much more than simply Wash her people of Night Fever. She is a midwife. She is a Healer. She is an herbalist—a counselor—a savior and sometimes even the one who hastens the comfort of death to the unsavable."

"Now *that* sounds like Leda," Sora said.

"It's going to sound like you, too. Or at least I'm going to teach you what Leda taught me. After that you can decide what kind of Moon Woman you want to be," Mari said. "Now, ground yourself and get ready to concentrate."

The night suddenly exploded with distant, hate-filled cries of men. Mari thought it sounded as if they were rabid wolves, howling their anger at the moon.

"I can't concentrate with *that* going on. It's horrible!" Sora said.

"You have to. How do you think they're going to be when they come to you? And I don't even mean just the first time. I mean *every time*. I Washed Xander on a second night—it hadn't even been the normal three days between Washings—and he was turning into a monster in front of me. Sora, you have to be able to ground yourself and concentrate in the midst of chaos and danger and fear or they will hurt you, maybe even kill you. That I promise."

"How did you do it? How did you get past your fear?" Sora asked, her eyes wide and liquid with unshed tears.

"In my mind I sketched the scene I wished was happening."

"But I'm not an artist! That makes no sense to me," Sora said.

"It makes sense to me, and maybe you can find some sense in it, too, if you just listen. When I draw I make real what's in my imagination. I didn't understand it until recently, but I think that's what every Moon Woman does. She imagines the power of moonlight channeling through her and into others, and her imagining is so great, so real to her, that the power follows her will. So, what you have to do is figure out how to make what you imagine seem real."

Sora chewed her bottom lip. "I have no idea how to do that."

"Well, let's try and see what happens. At least you'll have a starting point," Mari said.

Sora began to nod in agreement when another round of shrieks echoed through the night.

"They're getting worse," Sora said.

"They sound close together. That can't be good. I thought men were always solitary at night—at least unless they've been Washed," Mari said.

"It was a whole group of them that attacked my burrow. It was during the day. I think they may be traveling together." Sora's voice was ripe with fear.

"Hey, they won't find us here. We're safe. You're safe," Mari said.

Sora lifted her chin and nodded. "I'm ready now. I'm going to try to do this."

"Okay, first ground yourself. I think the easiest way to do that is to slow your breathing. Here, breathe with me on a count of six. Inhale first: one, two, three, four, five, six," she said breathily. "Hold it for one count, then exhale for six." Mari counted, watching Sora. The girl was following her instructions, but with a lackluster attitude—as if she was just going through the motions to appease her. *Mama, what do I do?* She searched her mind as she continued to count for Sora. *How do I get her to truly ground herself?*

Like a small, precious mourning dove, Leda's words lifted from Mari's memory. *Sweet girl, trust yourself and the Great Earth Mother. You are wiser than you know, and the Goddess is endlessly compassionate.* Mari's gaze wandered to the idol, wishing the Goddess would show some compassion and tell her what to do.

Then Mari's eyes widened in surprise. No, the Goddess didn't speak to *her*—didn't let Mari feel her presence. But Sora felt her presence—she'd already said so. And Mari had her answer.

"Sora, turn around so that you're facing the Earth Mother," Mari said.

Sora blinked up at her. "Are we done breathing?"

"No, not quite, but I have an idea. Sit facing the idol." Sora shifted around. "Okay, this time as you breathe with me, concentrate on the Earth Mother. Feel her presence filling this clearing. She's in the soft night wind. Her breath has the sweetness of the flowers around us. She's cloaked in Earth and veiled in night. She's everywhere."

Mari saw the difference in Sora instantly. Her shoulders relaxed. Her forehead lost the furrowed lines that were there only breaths before. She seemed to melt into the grass as she breathed deeply, easily, keeping her gaze on the Earth Mother.

"Now, let your breath return to normal, but keep your focus on the Goddess. Give me your hand."

Sora said nothing, but she lifted her hand. Mari took it in her own.

"Place your other hand on the fern."

Sora did as Mari instructed.

More shrieks rang through the night, and Sora's hand tightened on Mari's.

"Focus," Mari said quickly, finding her mother's words and sharing them with Sora. "Borrow serenity from the Earth Mother. You may be surrounded by chaos or sickness or injuries, but find the true you within. Release that which belongs to the world—fears, worry, sadness, so that the silver moonlight can wash through you. It is a waterfall at night. And this night the fern is the basin that must hold the waterfall. Think about the fern. Imagine it being filled with life, whole and thriving again."

Sora's grip on Mari's hand relaxed, and she said softly, "I'm ready."

"Good. You're doing well. When I start the invocation I want you to repeat after me and think about the moonlight washing through me—through you—and into the fern."

"Okay. I can do this," Sora said.

When Mari began the ritual invocation, it was as if Leda was there with her, smiling proudly and whispering lovingly in her ear.

"Moon Woman I proclaim myself to be
Greatly gifted I bare myself to thee."

Sora began repeating the lines in a small soft voice, but as Mari continued the invocation, and Sora continued the repetition, her voice grew in confidence until Mari could hear the beginnings of confidence within it.

"Earth Mother aid me with your magick sight
Lend me strength on this moon-touched night.
Come, silver light—fill me to overflow
So that those in my care, your healing will know.
By right of blood and birth channel through me
That which the Earth Mother proclaims my destiny!"

Mari raised her hand and closed her eyes, sketching in her mind a scene where the moonlight cascaded like water through her and into Sora. The cool, silver power rained down on her, swirling in her body—not with the cold, biting pain it used to bring, but with strength not yet familiar, yet sure enough that Mari could count on it, draw on it, channel it, and then release it into Sora.

"Oh! It's so cold!" Sora gasped and tried to pull her hand from Mari's.

"That's because it's not yours to keep. You don't need it. You're already Washed. Think of the fern. Focus, Sora!"

"I'm trying, but it hurts!"

"You can make the pain stop, but you have to release the power. Think of the fern. Imagine that the moonlight is water, and that you can channel it through your body and rain it over the plant," Mari said.

"It's—it's t-too hard!" Sora spoke around chattering teeth.

Mari gripped Sora's hand tighter and added a sharp edge to her words. "If I can do it—you can do it. Try harder!"

Mari saw Sora frown. Her shoulders hunched with the effort. Beads of sweat dotted her smooth forehead. The hand she'd placed on the fern was trembling, but just when Mari was considering stopping the exercise the limp fronds of the fern began to straighten and swell.

"Oh," Sora gasped. "It's happening! I'm drawing down the moon!"

And as quickly as that Sora's concentration broke. With a terrible convulsion she pulled her hand away from Mari's, fell to all fours, and vomited rabbit stew beside the half-healed fern.

"It's okay. This part will be over soon." Mari held Sora's thick hair back so she didn't soil it.

Sora was shaking. Between retches she said, "It felt awful. But then it was better. Then awful again."

"Yeah, I know. I've been there," Mari said.

Sora sat back, wiping her mouth on her sleeve and grimacing in disgust. "You got sick, too?"

"More times than I can count. I thought about making sure you didn't eat until we were done, but it's worse if there's nothing in your stomach to vomit. Dry heaves are horrible, and they last longer."

Sora shuddered. "Good to know. So, I didn't do too badly?"

"Actually, you did really, really well. Better than I did the first time I tried." Mari drew a deep breath and told Sora the truth. "You're gifted. Someday you're going to be a powerful Moon Woman. Mama was right to choose you as her apprentice."

Sora's gaze met Mari's. "Truly?"

Mari nodded. "Truly."

Sora's smile was bright and filled with happiness. "That almost sounded friendly."

"Hey, don't make me sorry for being honest with you," Mari said, getting up from where she was kneeling beside Sora, but the girl grabbed her hand.

"Wait. I didn't mean anything bad by that. What I should have said is thank you."

"Well, then, you are welcome," Mari said, seeing the sincerity in Sora's clear gaze. "Now plant your fern and then let's go to bed. I'm not used to being up all night anymore."

"Plant my fern? Where?"

"Wherever you want. You saved it. It's yours," Mari said.

Sora's smile widened to a grin. "Is that the rule? If you save someone or something it's yours?"

Mari opened her mouth to tell Sora not to get ahead of herself when a tidal wave of shrieks washed around them, filling the night with inhuman sounds of Night Fever–induced madness. Then, the terrifying howls and cries coalesced to form two words that the men began crying over and over, sending spider leg chills skittering across Mari's skin.

"MOON WOMAN! MOON WOMAN! MOON WOMAN!"

"Oh, Goddess! Where are they? They seem so close!" Sora curled in on herself, pressing her knees to her chest and rocking back and forth.

Mari looked to Rigel. He'd stood and was cocking his head, as if he, too, was trying to decide how close the men were. But his scruff didn't stand on end like it did when danger was near. He trotted to Mari and leaned against her side. Instantly she was filled with confidence—reassurance. She patted his head and bent to kiss him on his muzzle.

"What are we going to do?" Sora's voice was filled with fear and tears.

"They aren't a threat to us tonight. Or at least, not if we stay here, inside the bramble thicket. And I'm going to do what the Moon Women who have lived here for four generations have done. I'm going to channel power to the thicket to be sure we stay safe."

"Do you need my help?" Sora asked shakily.

Mari glanced at Sora. She was pale and sweaty and looked exhausted. "No. You're done for the night. I'll take care of the brambles. You take care of the fern."

Then, before Mari could think about the fact that she had never empowered the brambles by herself before, she walked quickly to the image of the Earth Mother. As she'd watched her mama do countless times, she stood before the idol and lifted her arms so that her palms were facing the sky, open to the silver light of the moon. She closed her eyes and checked her breathing—one, two, three, four, five, six, in. And then—one, two, three, four, five, six, out. She repeated the controlled breaths until her heart wasn't hammering against her chest and the cries of the Night Fever–mad Clansmen were as indistinct as the sloughing of the breeze through the thicket.

Then Mari began speaking. Her words echoed Leda's, but they were her own—unique and heartfelt. And as she spoke Mari sketched within her imagination a beautiful scene. In it the silver threads of power that cascaded from the moon and only answered a Moon Woman's call rained long, thick ropes down upon her beloved bramble thicket until the branches thickened and grew, and the sword-edged thorns multiplied and spread creating an impenetrable barrier from all who would harm Rigel and her.

"As my mother before me
It's your protection I seek.
Let the moon's powerful light
Swell thorns and branches this night.
By right of blood and birth channel through me
That which the Earth Mother proclaims my destiny!"

Cold power flowed into her palms with such ferocity that Mari had to grit her teeth to keep from crying out. She almost lost her concentration then, but she clung to the image in her mind, thinking over and over, *I am just a channel . . . I am just a channel.* With a sweeping gesture, Mari threw her arms wide, ridding herself of the cold power by sending it—like wildfire—into the bramble thicket.

The strange familiarity hit her with a force that almost dropped her to her knees.

The moon's power coursed through her and into the plants surrounding her like wildfire . . .

Like fire from the sun. The feeling was so similar! Except that moonlight was cold and it healed. Sunlight—the sunlight grief and despair had caused her to channel the day of Leda's death—was hot and it destroyed.

How could I have not thought about what I did? I set the forest on fire. Me!

It was then that Mari began to wonder about not *who* she was, but *what.*

She heard Sora's exclamation of surprise behind her, and Mari opened her eyes slowly, still managing to hold the image in her mind. All around her the brambles sparkled with glittering silver light. Each thorn glistened, firefly-like, as they swelled, lengthened, strengthened.

"Just like it used to do for Mama," Mari whispered. "Even though I am definitely not my mama."

Then, as quickly as it had begun it was over and the thicket settled back into the waiting darkness of a true protector.

Mari stared at the idol's face. It was as serene as ever. Mari listened as hard as she could, and opened herself completely.

Nothing. She felt nothing. Not even one small, precious hint of the Goddess's presence. With her mind in turmoil, Mari called Rigel to her, and while she waited for Sora to finish planting the fern, she took comfort in the unconditional love that came from her Companion.

25

Dead Eye was God. Of course the People called him Champion, or rather *some of* the people called him Champion. Some still respectfully acknowledged him as Harvester. Some avoided him completely, choosing to spread rumors and dissension. Dead Eye understood that the dissenters acted from confusion and anger. They were used to worshipping a dead god given false voice by selfish old women. Dead Eye knew what changes he must make so that he and those of the People worth saving could move into a new future.

His first step was to purge the Temple.

The Reaper's Temple was in the center of the ruined City. It was an unusual building, as was proper for housing a god. The buildings all around it had crumbled under the weight of time, but the Temple stood straight and tall. There was even some glass left in the dark windows. The skin of the building was also unique, and unlike anything else in the City. Slick green tile gave way to long, vertical stripes of red metal interspersed with broken glass and the cream-colored stone of the rest of the Temple.

The statue the People called the Reaper God perched above the covered entrance to the building, guarding it and the City in all of her fifty feet of magnificence. Dead Eye stared up at the statue, his fingertips stroking the trident scar on his arm contemplatively. As he met the cool, unwavering gaze of the Reaper, he was surprised to find that part of him still wished She would speak to him, even if it were to strike him down for trying to usurp Her.

But she did nothing. She wasn't a god. She was simply a magnificent, empty statue.

Yes, Dead Eye knew what he must do.

It was dirty, disgusting work. He'd killed several of the obsolete Watchers the night he'd announced to the People that he was the Reaper's chosen Champion, but within the Temple there was a nest of the vile old women that had been living there, sucking off the teats of the People for generation after generation.

Dead Eye entered the Temple, grimacing at the stale scent within. His eyes adjusted quickly to the murky daylight that filtered hesitantly in through the broken windows, and he headed to the stairway that led up to the God's balcony and the chamber beyond that housed the Watchers.

Dead Eye remembered what the Watchers' Chamber had look like when he'd been a boy and he'd been brought by the Caretakers to be presented to the God for the first time. It had been frightening and magnificent and mysterious.

Today the chamber he entered held almost no similarity to the one in his memory.

There were only two fires burning within the Watchers' Chamber. The other metal pots were cold and filled with moldy ashes. The curtaining vines had grown untrimmed and untended so that they seemed to pour from the ceiling and form waves of green that threatened to drown the filthy pallets that held the sleeping bodies of Watchers. Bones were scattered in messy mounds all around the chamber. They hadn't been cleaned. They hadn't been arranged in patterns pleasing to the eye. Flies buzzed fretfully around the room, moving lazily from rotting pile to pile.

Dead Eye stared around him in disgust. He felt his anger begin to burn and build and build and build . . .

"You may not enter!" croaked an old woman as she dragged herself up from a dirty pallet and limped toward him. "This chamber is sacred to our Reaper!"

Dead Eye glared down at the old woman in disgust. "It is sacred, and that is why I am going to set it to right." He lifted his triple-tipped dagger, and began the work he knew was best for the People. The Watchers tried to run from him, but they were weak and old and sick. Dead Eye took no pleasure in killing them. It was a simple culling. Best done quickly.

"Kill them all. Purge the Chamber of the God. It is the only way."

He was throwing their bodies from the Reaper's balcony when the voice came from behind him. It was so musical, so lovely, so strong, he thought it was the God, finally, *finally* speaking to him. Dead Eye spun around, dropping to his knees beside the mammoth statue and bowing his head in supplication.

"I will always do as you command, my Reaper," he said.

"Then we will always be in accord." Her voice did not come from the statue. It came from the Watchers' Chamber.

Dead Eye's head jerked up. A woman was standing in the middle of the bloody chamber. In an instant he was on his feet. His back to the metal statue, he faced the interloper, brandishing his trident. "Prepare to join the culling," he said.

"I already have. I choose to join it on the side of the Reaper's Champion." The woman took one step forward so that the light from the flames in one of the fire pits illuminated her face.

He stared at her. She wasn't actually a woman at all. She was a girl—a girl whose body was supple and pleasing—whose long, chestnut-colored hair fell loose and thick around the curve of her waist. She dressed like a Watcher, breasts and feet bared with a simple skirt decorated with a fringe made of the Others' hair, but when Dead Eye's gaze lifted from her body to her face, he felt a terrible shiver of shock.

Where her eyes should have been there were only dark, cavelike indention on her otherwise unlined, pleasing face. "Who are you?" he asked, though the question only bought him time to order his thoughts. He had never met her, but he knew her name. All of the People knew the sightless one's name. She had been taken to the God to be sacrificed when she was born, but the Watchers had said she belonged to the God, and spared her. That had been about sixteen winters ago, and this was the first time Dead Eye had glimpsed her.

"I am Dove," she said, cocking her head to the side. "But you already know that. Here is something you do not know, Champion. The God has called me to be your Oracle."

Dead Eye stared at her a moment longer, and then could contain himself no more. He threw back his head and laughed heartily.

"You laugh at your Oracle?"

"No. I laugh at an eyeless girl who has wit enough to survive."

"I am touched by our God, a divine Oracle."

Dead Eye gave sound to one more bark of laughter. "There is no need to pretend with me."

"I make no pretense."

"So, you have spoken for the God?"

"I have. I do."

"Tell me how that works," he said.

"I cannot see, but the God grants me visions," she said.

"Does everything the God show you come true?"

"Yes, but I do not always speak of everything I see. Sometimes the God wishes to teach a lesson, or to admonish or reward. Then I speak only of what the God allows."

"That is very convenient. If your visions don't come true, you can always say later that you saw something you left out—because the God asked you to, of course."

"You doubt me."

Though it wasn't a question, Dead Eye answered her. "I doubt you. Do you know why?"

"You wish to usurp my place," she said.

"No, not at all. I am already playing the part of Champion to a God I know is dead. Being Oracle to that same God does not interest me. Though you interest me. You interest me very much."

Dove went very still. Then slowly, knowingly, she began to smile. "You know."

"That the God is an empty statue and the Watchers have spent generations speaking for their own interests? Yes. I know."

"Then what are you playing at, calling yourself Her Champion and saying that you are following Her voice?" Dove asked.

"I *play* at nothing. I *am* going to lead those of the People who are worthy out of this City of disease and death, and into a new life. If I have to pretend at first that I am following a dead God, then so be it. The end will justify that one small deception."

"Because you deceive for the good of the People, and not simply the good of yourself."

"Ah, now I hear the Oracle. Did the God show you that?" he said sarcastically.

"No. My wits showed me that," she said. "There is no God. There are only petulant, self-absorbed old women and the People they have controlled for generations."

"Actually, Oracle, there are now only the People, you, and me. I have sent the petulant, self-absorbed old women to be with their dead God."

She smiled. "I hoped so. I smelled their blood and heard their cries. And now I would like to ask you a question."

"Ask," Dead Eye said, feeling uncommonly intrigued by this eyeless girl.

Dove walked toward him slowly. Instead of being hesitant or awkward, her steps were languid. Every motion she made was precise. Her body moved with a raw sensuality that had Dead Eye's stomach tightening with desire. She stopped within reaching distance of him.

"Is it true you absorbed the essence of a stag and that your skin sheds new, like a youngling?"

Dead Eye shrugged out of his blood-spattered shirt. "May I take your hand?" he asked her.

With no hesitation Dove offered him both of her hands, palms open. He took them, guiding her fingers over his thickly muscled arms and chest, allowing her to pause as she found the newly healed wounds where the stag's flesh and his had knitted to form one.

"Incredible," she whispered. "It is true."

"And it can be the truth for our People as well," Dead Eye said. "But not here. Not in this ruined City that is home to a dead God. We must leave this place and make a new City that isn't tainted by centuries of disease."

Her hands cupped his shoulders. Her eyeless face tilted up and he wondered at how he could find that face so expressive and so lovely.

"If you take me with you I will continue to speak for the God. I will reassure the People that it is Her will that we follow you, Her Champion. And I will begin by saying that the Reaper sent a vision to me showing Her dissatisfaction for what the Watchers had become, and calling for Her Champion to cull them from Her Temple."

"The old women were cruel to you, weren't they?" he asked softly.

Her head bowed and her long, dark hair swept forward, almost touching his naked chest.

"Until today, life has been cruel to me," she said.

"Then from this day on, your Champion will protect you from the cruelties of life."

It was as if his words had taken the breath from her. With a gasp, she went to her knees.

"Thank you, Champion," she said reverently. "I am yours to command."

"No," he said, gently taking her hands again and guiding her up. "Between us there should be no artifices, no unneeded ceremony, no false worship. You will not bow to me. Ever."

"But you are my Champion, and the Champion of the People. I wish only to show you the worship you deserve."

"It is not your worship that I desire, my Dove," he said.

Her sensual smile was back. "Tell me what it is you desire, Champion."

"I would rather show you."

Dead Eye took her into his arms and she did worship him, as fully and completely as his body worshipped hers.

Much, much later, after they had slaked the needs of their bodies, they worked together side by side, purging the Chamber. Dead Eye was amazed by Dove. Her skin was smooth and white—pure and rare as a snowfall. She had no eyes, but her steps never faltered. She moved around the Chamber, dragging the stinking pallets to the balcony so that he could throw them down into the courtyard below. She used a sacrificial trident to slice through the ropes of ivy that had not been tended in years, leaving mounds of green for him to scoop up and throw away.

Dead Eye found it difficult to keep his hands from touching Dove. She was so soft and warm and welcoming—more magnificent even than the ancient stories told of the God's Watchers before they deteriorated into diseased old women and were instead the pulse of the People.

As he paused in carrying armloads of reeking bones to throw from the balcony, Dove turned her eyeless face up to him, smiling and lovely. He stroked one finger down her smooth cheek. Wondering aloud at the flawless beauty of her skin, he asked, "Dove, has your skin never cracked? Never shed?"

"No, it hasn't," she said.

"Never?"

"Never," she assured him.

"Do you know why?" Dead Eye asked only out of vague curiosity. He didn't expect a true answer—though she shocked him by giving one.

"I believe I do know why. Since the day of my birth when the Caretakers brought me to the God to be sacrificed, I have never left this Temple—nor has my skin ever cracked. Nor has it shed."

"But surely you have never worn another's skin?"

Dove shook her head and her hair moved around her like a gossamer veil. "No. The Watchers would not waste the skin of the Others on me.

They said it was too precious—too rare, and that one such as me did not need it."

"Have you eaten the flesh of the Others? The last sacrifice was just a few winters ago when we captured several of the Others from that large foraging party. The Watchers did not share that sacrifice with you?"

"I remember well the last Others that were sacrificed. Their screams lingered in the air for many days. But, no. I was not allowed to eat of the flesh, either. The truth is, I was not allowed to eat meat of any kind." She paused and changed her voice to that of a waspish old woman. "Seeds, nuts, rice, and plants are good enough for the eyeless one!"

"Dove, listen! I, too, have never eaten of the Others' flesh! It has always disgusted me, so I only pretended to partake, though I have taken their flayed flesh and placed it over mine—but my body did not absorb it as it did the stag's." Dead Eye felt a great jolt of excitement. "And I choose to make my home in one of the buildings at the very edge of the City, and prefer to hunt from the forest for my table."

"The People say you spend an unusual time in the forest," Dove said.

"The People are right."

"The stag you absorbed. You didn't find it in the City, did you?"

"No. The beasts found within the confines of the City are never quite right. Away from here, in the forest, you understand that the animals are stronger. I rarely find the oddities seen here—the missing limbs—the great, bulbous masses growing just beneath their skins— the twisted bodies." Dead Eye took Dove by the shoulders and spoke fervently. "Dove, that is why I am so drawn to the forest! Because it is clean there—untainted by whatever killed the City, and still kills us."

"We must leave this place," she said.

"I knew it! I've known it since I was a youngling!"

"And now the People will know it. You truly are our Champion." She leaned forward and he bent to capture her soft, seeking lips with his own, loving how perfectly Dove fit against his body and thinking, *it is good to be a God.*

The firepots were lit, filling the newly cleansed Chamber and the God's balcony with the fragrant scent of cedar. While below in the courtyard Dead Eye gathered the bodies of the Watchers and the odoriferous rubble their lives had become into a great pile atop dead pine boughs, above Dove prepared a huge cauldronful of the vegetable stew she had perfected without the Watchers' sacrificial meat. When all was ready, Dead Eye lit the pyre and then returned to the balcony with Dove to wait for the People.

They did not have long to wait.

The burning pyre drew the People. They crept from the shadows, clutching the rodents and birds they brought as sacrifice to the God. As they reached the pyre, Dead Eye watched them peer into the flames and then recoil in horror when they realized what scented the pine with roasting meat.

"The People are below," Dead Eye spoke quietly to Dove. "It is time."

With no hesitation she held out her hand. He grasped it, guiding her up to the lip of the balcony. "Be brave," he whispered. "The ledge is wide, and I am here. I will not let you fall."

Her smile flashed in the firelight. "It is easy to be brave with you beside me, my Champion." Then Dove spread her arms wide. In a strong, pure voice, she called down to the People. "The God has sent me a vision and commanded that I share it with Her People!"

"Dove is speaking! It is the eyeless one, Dove! She speaks for the God!" The murmurings of the People lifted from below.

Dove waited for their restlessness to still before continuing. "The God has been displeased!"

Horrified gasps came from the People. Dove raised her hands and instantly they quieted.

"Do not fear. The Reaper has sent me a vision to show how the People may regain Her pleasure. Your Champion has already begun to obey Her commands. He has purged the Temple of the infestation known as the Watchers." Dove pointed below at the flaming pyre. "The old women and their filth are being purified by fire. The God is pleased by this, but the next steps must come from Her People."

"Tell us what we must do! Tell us how we regain the God's pleasure!" the People cried with one voice.

"Behold your Champion! He knows the God's will," Dove said, gesturing to him with a graceful flourish of her smooth, white arm.

Dead Eye leaped onto the lip of the balcony beside her.

"Hear the will of the God!" he shouted. "She commands Her People no longer eat of the beasts they find in the City. She commands Her People no longer eat of the flesh of the Others. She commands Her People live a purer life."

"How? Where do we find food? Where do we find sacrifice? How do we hope to renew our skins?"

The voices of the People verged on hysteria. Dead Eye waited patiently for them to still. When they were finally silent, all with up-turned, listening faces, he spoke.

"Know that the Reaper has spoken to me though Her Oracle, Dove. I asked the God how to lead Her People to find strength again, and She has answered! Our God tells us it is our right to have more because for so long we have had so little." He pointed toward the distant hills filled with the deep, verdant green of the thriving pine forest that protected the Others. "Why are they better than us?" Dead Eye paused to let the excited whisperings beneath him grow, and then his voice silenced their murmurings. "They are not better unless they can hold what they have! The Reaper reminds Her People through their Champion that might is right, and compassion is best found on the triple points of a three-edged sword." His wide gesture took in the distant city in the trees. "In the land of the Others the People will find new life!"

Into shocked silence the old man's voice was a rusty blade. "Leave our City? The City of the God? Perhaps that is your way, but it is not the way of the Reaper's People!"

Dead Eye found the speaker easily. It was, of course, Turtle Man. He had stepped forward from the clustering group of People and was glaring up. Dead Eye thought of rebutting his archaic statement with fact—the same facts he and Dove had discovered between them—but no. The People were used to the reality of death and sacrifice. With no further hesitation, Dead Eye grasped the trident spear used to burn the God's mark into the flesh of younglings, and flung it down, skewering Turtle Man in the middle of his chest.

The old man collapsed like his bones had gone to mush, stumbling and falling onto the pyre so that his body fed the flames into a roaring frenzy.

The People remained very quiet, their eyes all upturned toward Dead Eye and Dove.

"You killed him?" Dove whispered.

"I did."

Dove lifted her arms again. "Thus our Champion culls dissension from the People."

As if speaking on cue, Dead Eye added, "Who wishes to move into a new future? A future a strong, mighty People deserve?"

With no hesitation a young Harvester known as Iron Fist stepped forward. "I wish that!"

There was only a small pause, and then another and another of the People moved forward to join Iron Fist, each shouting their affirmations. Dead Eye saw that far from all of the People stepped forward—that many of them faded back into the shadows and rubble of the City. *So be it. They are dead to me. Soon I will send them to be with their dead God.* But for now it was enough to focus on the People who waited below.

"Come to me!" Dead Eye shouted joyfully. "All Harvesters and Hunters join me on the God's balcony."

As if finishing his thought, Dove added, "And women of the People, join me in the Chamber that is no longer the Watchers', but now belongs to the People!"

As the People entered the Temple, Dead Eye lifted Dove from the balcony ledge and kissed her fiercely.

"It is all coming to pass, my Champion," she murmured against his chest. "The women and I will feed you and your Hunters and Harvesters."

"And I will explain the new will of the God to them."

"Yes, my Champion. Yes!" She kissed him again, only moving re-luctantly from his arms when the footsteps of the People sounded outside the Chamber. "Welcome them," Dove said, smiling up at Dead Eye as if he truly was her God. "This night marks the beginning of your new life."

"*Our* new life." He corrected her, gently stroking her smooth cheek and kissing her soft lips once more before he strode to the entrance of the Chamber to greet his People.

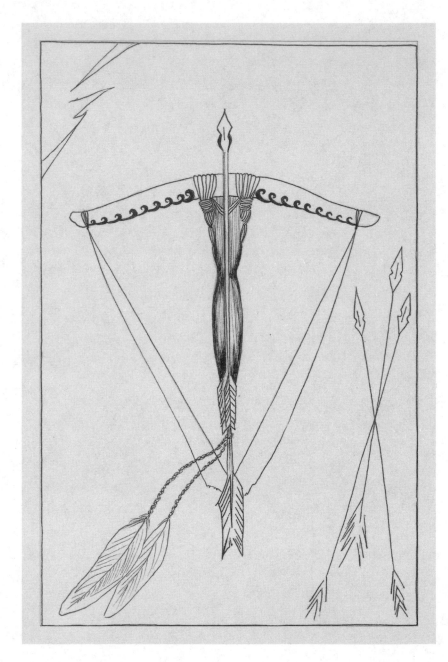

26

Nik, I'm telling you—there are no new tracks. No new signs. Nothing," Davis said. "I'm sorry, man. I know you have to leave with the foraging team tomorrow, and I wanted to send you off with some good news, but there's nothing here that even hints at your pup or a girl. We just keep finding sign of those big, crazy Scratcher males and the destruction they're leaving behind them. No women's tracks. No canine tracks."

"Cuz, I know you don't want to hear this. Hell, I don't want to say it. But I think we've run into a dead end," O'Bryan said. "And it's not that Davis and I don't believe you. We know you saw that mutated Scratcher girl somehow start a fire. We know that the pup is alive—or at least he was a couple of weeks ago. The three of us found his tracks. But they led to nothing. Went nowhere. I know it's still early today, but I think—well, I think it might be time to call it quits."

Nik thought he'd be ready to hear that Davis and O'Bryan wanted to quit searching for the pup and the girl, but the reality of it hit him hard—right in the gut. He swallowed past the knot of frustration that had threatened to choke him for the past two weeks, and with a supreme effort kept his voice calm. He pulled out the skin of fresh water he'd filled at the last stream they'd crossed and tossed it to O'Bryan, then nodded for him to share it with Davis. Taking collard rolls filled with nut paste, rice, and vegetables from his pack he passed them to the two men, giving Davis extra for the hardworking, always hungry Cameron, he motioned for them to join him on a fallen log.

"I hear you. I hear both of you. Do we all agree that something strange has happened with the Scratcher males?"

O'Bryan and Davis nodded as they chewed their makeshift meal.

"Yeah, something real weird is going on," Davis spoke around a mouthful of roll. "I know I'm new at this, but I've never seen or heard of signs like we've been finding."

"Hey, I'm not a Hunter, but, Nik, you know I've been tracking since I was barely old enough to leave the nests, and I'm telling you—whatever's going on with the Scratchers isn't good. It's changed things, and not for the better," O'Bryan said.

"I've been thinking about this. A lot, during the past week especially," Nik said, careful to begin by agreeing with his two friends. "I want to take a shot in the dark. Just one. Just today. If we still don't find anything I'll reevaluate while I'm with the team in Port City."

Nik watched O'Bryan and Davis share a glance. Davis shrugged and O'Bryan smiled, though Nik was pretty sure it was forced.

"What's your plan, Cuz?"

"Okay, we've searched patterns on the Tribe side of the Scratcher creek, expanding out from where we found the new tracks of the pup two weeks ago." The two men nodded in agreement. Nik continued, "And we searched the same pattern expanding out from the holly bush on the opposite side of the creek, as well as around the area where the wolf spiders attacked and we killed the male Scratcher that night." *Jenna's father,* Nik added, but only silently.

"Yeah, and the same thing happened over and over," Davis said. "The sign just stopped."

"Exactly!" Nik said. "It's strange, don't you think?"

"It's frustrating, that's for sure," O'Bryan said as Davis took another bite of roll and nodded. "Maybe what's going on with the Scratcher males has something to do with it."

"Well, I suppose that could be, but what if the signs stopped purposely?" Nik said.

The two men sent him questioning looks.

"Hear me out," Nik said quickly. "We're looking for a girl who is unusual—who, for whatever bizarre reason, has some vestige of Tribal power, correct?"

"Maybe. I mean, none of us know for sure. Not even you, Nik, and you're the only one who saw what she did," Davis said.

"You're right. This is just supposition, but *if* she's special, and *if* the pup is with her we've got to at least consider the possibility that she could be intelligent enough to hide the pup's tracks and be trying to throw us off their trail."

O'Bryan and Davis stared at him dumbfounded. Nik hastily added. "I know it seems crazy, but the whole thing is crazy."

"It is that," Davis said.

"So what do you propose?" O'Bryan asked.

"Let's change the way we're thinking about tracking them," Nik said.

"What do you mean?" Davis said.

"Up until now we've been assuming we're tracking a Scratcher and a pup. Maybe together. Maybe not. But certainly not anyone who could be covering their trail and making any concerted attempt to confuse us. What if we think of tracking her, and the pup, as if they're part of the Tribe?"

"How so?" Davis sat up straighter, intrigued.

Nik explained. "Let's pretend like the girl and the pup are Companions, and they've run away from the Tribe."

"Run away from the Tribe? That's crazy," O'Bryan said.

"Yep, it is. But we've already said this whole thing is crazy, right?" Davis said. "Go on, Nik. You may be on to something."

Feeling relieved that the Hunter was willing to listen to his odd idea, Nik spoke quickly. "Well, the question is what would you change about the way we've been searching if you knew that the person and canine you're tracking were actively trying to mislead you?"

Davis leaned back, chewing thoughtfully before answering. "Well, I'd stop chasing their tracks, because they were left only to throw Cammy and me off. Instead I'd try to think like whoever was misleading me, and then I'd head in the direction my mind told me to search instead of the direction the tracks were misleading me to go."

"That's what we have to do!" Nik said, clapping Davis on the back and causing Cammy to jump around them in excitement. "I think it's pretty easy to narrow down where we *shouldn't* look anymore." He opened his pack again and took out the map they'd been following. The two men huddled around him, pointing as they spoke.

"You mean no more looking on the Tribe side of the creek," O'Bryan said.

"Also no more looking south along the creek at all, even heading into Scratcher territory," Davis said. "We only found just a few tracks there, mostly in and out of the creek. If we're imagining that the girl's trying to mislead us, I'd say those tracks were made to try to draw us in the wrong direction."

"Now you're thinking!" Nik said.

"I'd say the same about the tracks going north," Davis said.

"How so?" Nik asked.

"We found a lot of very concentrated signs around the area of the attack, and then—zip—gone. Nothing at all. Following your supposition, I'd say from the signs that two women were attacked and a pup was with them. They returned and tried to confuse the trail, and us, but they didn't count on Cammy's nose." Davis patted the little blond Terrier fondly. "So when that nose tells us that the trail led north and west, and even south after it returned to the creek—I'd say that those are three directions we shouldn't be searching."

"Even though we have been searching those directions for the past two weeks," O'Bryan said.

Nik smiled. "I like the way you two are thinking. That leaves east. The one area we found no sign at all. And no need to run a circle pattern. We've already done that. Let's just go out past the eastern edge of our search area and then start zigzagging."

"We'll need to do this quickly, Nik. We can't get caught out here anywhere near dusk. Not with whatever's going on with the Scratchers," Davis said.

"Agreed," Nik said. "Then let's move and move fast."

They finished their rolls as they headed east, going through a section of the forest so filled with maidenhair ferns that Nik thought it looked like it had been covered with the delicate lace the artisans crocheted from sheep penned on Farm Island, but lovingly tended only by members of the Tribe.

"I never cared much for Scratcher territory," Davis said. "The pines aren't mighty enough, and there's too much mud and scrub and rot. But this section is pretty. We should pull up some of these ferns on the way back. If they're planted near one of our waterways they might take and spread like they do here."

"It's damn wet. That's why the maidenhairs grow so well here in this mess," O'Bryan said, grimacing as he knocked sticky black muck off his boot. "Scratchers love these lowlands, though I don't know why."

"I do," Nik said. "They love them because we hate them."

"Guess that does make sense," Davis said. "As far as I'm concerned they can have them. Do you smell that? Something really stinks."

"Probably the damned mud." O'Bryan sounded unusually grumbly. "Cuz, I love you and all, but you're going to owe me a new pair of boots after this."

"Done," Nik said. "But that doesn't smell like mud."

"Cammy's on it," Davis said, pointing at the Terrier's blond butt as it disappeared into the ferns.

The men jogged after the little canine. Coming over the crest of a ridge in the lowlands, they peered down at a stream, running through a cedar grove. The breeze shifted and increased, wafting up to them an odor so thick and fetid it almost made Nik gag. Excited barking also drifted up to them.

"Cammy, hold!" Davis shouted the Terrier's command, jogging down into the grove with Nik and O'Bryan close behind.

All three men piled to a halt as they reached the center of the grove and the Terrier, who was sitting under the desecrated carcass, barking an alert.

"Good job, Cammy. Well done," Davis praised his Companion as they stared up at the thing hanging from the boughs of the cedar.

"I don't understand this waste. Deer are rare, precious. It's been left to rot. All of that meat. All of that hide and gut. All ruined," Nik said. "Cut it down. Let the forest absorb it."

O'Bryan found the end of the rope that held the carcass in place. With a quick chop of his knife, the body was free, falling with a sickening thud to the forest floor.

"The heart and liver are gone, and all of the flesh from the deer's flank, chest, and neck. But that's it. That's all they've eaten," Davis said.

"And why the hell would they eat such thin strips of flesh and leave the rest," O'Bryan said.

"Look at the throat," Davis said.

Holding his sleeve to his nose, Nik crouched beside the deer. "I don't see any arrow or knife marks on it at all. Its head has been bashed in, and its throat and belly torn open by what look like bite wounds."

"Those aren't animal bites," Davis said.

"No. They're human," Nik said grimly. "I don't like this. I don't like it at all. I hate to say it, but this reminds me of Skin Stealers."

"Skin Stealers! Cuz, no! They never leave Port City," O'Bryan said.

"I know, but there's no denying that part of this deer has been flayed." Nik paused, looking more closely at the body before adding, "—possibly while it was still alive."

Davis was studying the tracks around the clearing. "Males. Several of them. Nik, I hear what you're saying about Skin Stealers, but these are definitely wide, flat tracks typical of Scratcher males. Though I don't get why they'd waste an entire carcass."

"They're mad," O'Bryan said. "How can anyone understand why Scratcher males do what they do?"

"But this hasn't happened before, right?" Nik said.

"No, never heard of anything like this," O'Bryan said. "You, Davis?"

"Nope. Never. Not even Scratchers waste a deer carcass. They're too precious—too hard to find."

"The forest is changing. The Scratchers are changing," Nik said, feeling a strange, crawling sensation under his skin. "This is just more proof of it. We need to get out of here. Now. My gut says we won't find sign of the girl or the pup near here. If they have enough sense to hide their tracks from us, they certainly have enough sense to stay away from anywhere rabid males hunt." Nik was giving one last sad look at the wasted deer when Cammy began to growl.

"Something's coming," Davis said. "Something bad."

The three men lifted their crossbows and began to retrace their path out of the grove when five Scratcher males seemed to materialize from the shadows.

They were moving with a feral grace, their bodies hunched, their hands clawed. One, larger than the others, bared his teeth at them as he spoke, his voice so guttural it was almost unrecognizable as human.

"Now you are the hunted!" His snarl worked like a goad on the other Scratchers. As one, the creatures attacked.

"Get to that ridge!" Nik yelled as he let fly an arrow, skewering the male that had targeted him. "We can pick them off from there."

"Cammy! Up!" Davis shouted, and the Terrier sprinted up the incline, well out of reach of grasping Scratcher claws.

Nik saw that Davis was halfway up the ridge with O'Bryan close behind him. He turned and took a stand. "Go on, O'Bryan! Get out of here!"

"Won't leave you!" O'Bryan cried.

Nik felt rather than saw his cousin hesitate. "You're not leaving me! Just get up there and start shooting them!"

"Got it! I'll—" O'Bryan's words were cut off with a shocked cry. "Ahhh!"

Nik pierced another Scratcher through the neck with an arrow. Gurgling and writhing, the big male went down, causing the other three behind him to hesitate, and giving Nik enough time to see that his cousin was wrestling with another Scratcher.

"O'Bryan! I'm coming!" With a motion as smooth as water over river rock, Nik lifted his crossbow, sighted, and took down two of the three Scratchers with one shot. The third male, one who looked younger and slightly less bestial, gave a shriek filled with anger before disappearing into the forest.

Nik turned and sighted his bow at the male who was in hand-to-hand combat with his cousin. But he couldn't get a shot. They were too close together. Instead of using his bow, Nik ran, pumping his arms and using all of his strength to reach O'Bryan. As easy as breathing, Nik took the dagger from its resting place threaded through his leather belt. The creature's back was to him, and he plunged his knife into it, all the way to the hilt. The male crumpled to his knees, screaming in agony, but before he could breathe his last breath, he sank his teeth into O'Bryan's leg.

"No!" Nik's cry echoed O'Bryan's scream of pain. He flung the twitching Scratcher aside, sending its body rolling down the ridge. Then Nik grabbed O'Bryan around the waist, supporting him, and yelled, "Go! Go! Go!"

Thunk! Thunk! Two arrows found their marks behind Nik. As he and O'Bryan reached the top of the ridge Davis was there with Cammy growling beside him, crossbow in hand.

"I got both of them," Davis said. "I don't see any more."

"Didn't see the one that attacked me until it was too late." O'Bryan spoke between gasps for breath as he leaned heavily on Nik. "He raised up from the forest floor. They were hidden, Nik. They ambushed us."

"We're out of here. Now!" Nik said. "Davis, send Cammy ahead. Tell him to warn us if he scents any more Scratchers." With his free hand Nik held his own crossbow at the ready. "You watch our back."

"Done!" Davis said grimly. "Cammy—home! Watch!"

Connected by blood and friendship, the three men fought their way forward. Two more males attacked them, and those two more males died—one from Davis's bow and one from Nik's. They didn't stop to rest or reevaluate until they reached the creek where it had all begun more than two weeks before.

Nik's dagger cut through O'Bryan's blood-soaked pant leg, exposing the nasty bite wound in his calf.

"Put your leg in the creek. Wash it out. Hurry, O'Bryan!" Nik said. "Davis, keep Cammy on guard. Tell him to warn us if any more of them are near."

Davis murmured to his smart little Terrier, and the canine jumped up on a boulder near the creek bank. From there he kept scenting the air in all directions as his sharp eyes searched the brush for danger. "He's got it! What can I do to help?"

"Gather moss from that statue-thing over there, and then rip a strip of fabric from your shirt. I'm gonna pack this, tie the moss on, and then we head for home," Nik said.

"Will do!" Davis ran to the Scratcher idol that looked oddly like a woman rising from the earth.

"Bloody beetle balls, Nik! My skin is broken!" O'Bryan began to claw at the wound, as if he could tear it and the death sentence it probably contained from his body.

"Stop it, Cuz! Stop!" Nik grabbed O'Bryan's hands, keeping them from causing further damage to his skin. "It's not that bad. Let me pack it, and then we'll get you to the Healers."

O'Bryan collapsed back, legs in the creek, and the rest of him trembling on the bank. "There's nothing they can do—you know that. I'm done."

Nik shook O'Bryan by his shoulders. "Don't you give up!"

"Here! Here!" Davis tossed a clump of thick green moss to Nik.

Nik packed the moss into the wound, trying to ignore the deep, bleeding pit of missing flesh. "It's going to be okay. No bleeders were cut."

Davis covered his eyes with his arm. "It's not okay. You know that. It'll never be okay again—not for me."

"I said don't give up!" Nik said, still packing the ugly wound. "Davis, I need that strip of cloth."

There was a ripping sound. "Got it." Davis handed him a long, thin strip of cloth.

Nik wrapped the cloth around the moss-packed wound, tying it securely. "Drink this," he said, handing his cousin the water skin.

With trembling hands, O'Bryan did as he was told.

"Cammy's alerting! There are more of them coming. We gotta get out of here," Davis said.

"Go without me. Just leave me a crossbow. I'll keep them busy," O'Bryan said.

"Absolutely no chance of that," Nik said grimly. "Now give me your hand and get your ass up out of that water. We're going home."

They did not see the big man and the two smaller, though no less dangerous, men, watching them from the deepest shadows of the forest. They did not see Dead Eye's look of satisfaction as he stroked the trident-shaped scar on his arm and imagined the new future that was beginning to unfold before him.

"You were right, Champion," said Iron Fist. "The Scratcher males have been infected."

"Which means the Others will be infected as well. All we need do is to keep flaying the forest creatures, but as you said, not so far as to take them to the Sacred Place of death," said the second man known as Stalker.

"No, we must do as you command, and stop while they still have strength to live—to travel—to be taken by the forest people," said Iron Fist.

"And they will destroy one another even more beautifully than they did today," said Stalker.

"Exactly. It pleases me that the both of you understand now," Dead Eye said. "And all is ready with the lure?"

Iron Fist nodded. "It is as you commanded."

"We made sure the Others' foraging team saw no sign of us, but has been lured to the ambush site," said Stalker

"You have done well. Very well," Dead Eye said. He lifted the snare that held several fat turkeys. "Now, let us take our untainted catch back to Dove and the God. The People feast tonight in celebration of what bounty the morrow will bring!"

27

It took until well after dusk—after Nik had seen O'Bryan to the Healers' Nest, and had Davis and Cammy checked over to be sure they hadn't sustained any skin-breaking wounds—for his hands to stop trembling.

"It's my fault. O'Bryan was only there because of me."

"Son, drink this." Sol placed the mug of warm, herb-infused ale in his son's hands.

Nik shook his head. "No, I can't sleep. I need to get back to the Healers' Nest and sit with O'Bryan."

"Nikolas, drink. Rest. Tomorrow you must go with the foraging party, and you can't go on no sleep—not if you expect to return, and *I* expect you to return," Sol said.

"Father, I can't leave O'Bryan here like this."

"There's nothing you can do for him. Only time will show whether he's blighted or not. I'll ask the Sun's blessing on him and tend to him while you're gone, but the foraging party cannot wait, and you must go with them."

"But O'Bryan—"

"One person is not as important as the Tribe!" Sol interrupted. "O'Bryan knew the risks of hunting with you. He agreed readily. You did your best to protect him. You managed to get a young Hunter, his

Terrier, and yourself back to the Tribe, even though you were ambushed and tracked by feral Scratchers. The foraging party needs you, and the Tribe needs the foraging party. You'll leave with them tomorrow."

Nik met his father's eyes. "Why are we doing this? Is it because of your guilt?"

"Answer that question yourself."

"I don't know the answer. I don't know anything anymore except that because I was chasing ghosts my cousin, my best friend, the man I consider a brother, will now probably die a terrible, blighted death after only knowing eighteen winters!"

"Nik, something has been set in motion here—something that reaches far beyond finding a young canine you wished would choose you, and finding the truth out about a hybrid girl. Whatever that *something* is—it's responsible for your cousin's wound. You saved him, son. You brought him home."

"For what? You know what awaits him. We watched Mother die of it. Maybe I should have let the Scratcher kill him—at least his pain would be over."

"What if the blight doesn't infect him? What then?"

"Father, the wound is deep. You know how slim his chances are," Nik said.

"But he does have a chance, and that is because you got him home. Drink," Sol repeated. "And stay here tonight. Together we'll visit the Healers' Nest in the morning before you leave."

Nik sighed and gave in to his father, tipping the mug against his lips and drinking deeply. The herbs flushed through his system quickly, causing his vision to blur and his speech to thicken.

"I wish it'd been me instead of him," he murmured as his father led him to the pallet he'd prepared by the hearth fire.

"And I will be eternally thankful that it wasn't," Sol said. "Laru, stay with Nik."

The big Shepherd curled up next to Nik, sending warmth through his body, and soothing him with his love and loyalty, making it impossible for Nik to fight against the blackness. Finally, nestled against his father's canine, he closed his eyes and gave himself over to dreamless sleep.

"He looks good," Sol said as he and Nik made their way from the Healers' Nest to the lift. "As the Healer said, no sign of infection or inflammation. That means O'Bryan has a chance. Plus, your cousin's positive attitude may very well pull him through this whole and well."

"I hope so, Father." Nik didn't want to talk about O'Bryan and the truth—that a good attitude or lack of inflammation or infection could not save him. The *truth* was that six out of every ten Tribe members who sustained an injury great enough to break their skin contracted the blight. The more serious the injury—the better the chances of being infected with blight. The Scratcher had bit a human-mouth-sized hunk of flesh from O'Bryan's calf. The odds were definitely against him, and Nik didn't want to discuss false hope with his father. He changed the subject. "How many pairs did you decide to send on the foraging trip?"

"Six pairs—Wilkes leading with his Odin, of course. I also okayed Monroe and Viper, Sheena and Captain, Crystal and Grace, Winston and Star, Thaddeus and Odysseus. And, of course, you."

Nik frowned at his father. "Wait, you approved Thaddeus joining the team, even though you knew I was going?"

"Nik, because he annoys you isn't a good enough reason to leave behind the best Hunter in the Tribe," Sol said.

"But because he's an arrogant ass who won't listen to me at all *is* a good enough reason."

Sol stopped and faced his son. "Thaddeus is arrogant, and the two of you don't like each other, but he won't do anything to jeopardize Odysseus's safety. Besides that, Wilkes is in charge of this trip. He will listen to you."

Nik sighed and ran his hand through his hair. "All right. I don't like it, though. And what about the two women? Should we be risking both of them?"

"Son, who do you think mapped out the preliminary route for this trip?"

Nik shrugged. "Figured it was Wilkes."

"No. Sheena and Crystal have been teaming up to map the ruins for the past several cycles of the moon. Don't underestimate them. They know that river better than the Fishers. Fishers avoid Port City. Sheena and Crystal know the waterway there and back as well as they know their own nest. Don't worry about them needing protection. They're petite, but that means they can get into places you and the rest of the men can't squeeze through. And their Shepherds are two of the toughest canines in the Tribe. They'll protect their Companions."

"Okay, you know best," Nik said, though he couldn't escape the gnawing sense of wrongness that already seemed to shadow this trip.

"Son, don't let what happened to O'Bryan slant your judgment. Use those powers of observation I know you have, as well as the crossbow skills the entire Tribe knows you have—and work with Wilkes to bring the team back safely."

Nik blew out a long breath. "You're right. This thing with O'Bryan is really messing with my head. Father, there are such strange things going on in the forest. Doesn't it concern you?"

"Of course it does. But the truth is there is always something strange going on in the forest. We live in an odd, dangerous world. Son, I think not finding the pup has you down."

"Yeah. I thought with Davis's and Cameron's help—and having O'Bryan along in the Hunt—they'd ensure that we'd find him. And the girl. Or at the very least we'd find substantial sign of them by now. But all we found was a Scratcher ambush and chaos."

"Will you keep looking when you return?" Sol asked.

"Honestly, Father, I haven't decided. And maybe that's what really has me down. I don't want to give up on him—on the pup. But I'm starting to believe my search may be as foolhardy as the rest of the Tribe believes it to be."

"Not all of the Tribe thinks you're foolhardy. Some of them think you're loyal and tenacious. Should you ever wonder, I'm part of that group, though I am increasingly concerned with the new behavior the Scratcher males are exhibiting."

"So no one else has ever known them to set up an ambush?" Nik said.

"No. Even Cyril has never heard of that happening. He went through the archived Hunter logs last night, and found no annotation there, either. It seems their strange behavior is unique to the present." Sol's eyes looked haunted. "I'm getting increasing pressure to order a clean-out of the Scratcher population. And in light of this new attack, I don't know how long I'm going to be able to logically tell the Elders no."

"A clean-out? They really mean to kill all the males they can find?"

"Yes. The idea sickens me," Sol said.

"What are you going to do?"

He sighed. "I'm going to pray that we are dealing with a handful of rogue males, and that you and your team killed most of them yesterday."

"And if the night screaming and the ambushes don't stop?"

"Then I'm very much afraid I'm going to be responsible for the annihilation of the Earth Walker males."

Nik put his hand on his father's shoulder. "You won't be responsible for it. It'll be the will of the Tribe."

"I'm Leader of this Tribe, Nik. That makes it my responsibility." They'd come to the lift. Waiting within were Wilkes and his Shepherd, Odin, who exchanged greetings with Laru.

"There you are, Nik. Good day, Sol," Wilkes said.

"Good day to you as well, Wilkes. Odin is looking in excellent flesh," Sol said, shaking the tall man's hand.

"Thank you, Sun Priest. He is indeed."

"Good to see you, Wilkes." Nik shook his hand and gave Odin a friendly pat.

"The rest of the team's already at the dock. Thought I'd wait for you," Wilkes said. "I assumed you were seeing to O'Bryan?"

"We were," Sol answered for Nik. "And he's doing well."

"Glad to hear it. Ready, Nik?"

"I am," Nik said.

"Son, I'll say my good-bye to you here," Sol said. "I must lead the Sunrise Celebration, and then Cyril needs me with the Council to discuss the Scratcher issue further." He pulled Nik into a tight hug. "Stay safe, son. Return home soon."

Nik returned his father's hug. "I love you, Father."

"And I you, Nikolas." With a nod to Wilkes, Sol and his Laru strode off in the direction of the Council nest.

"The Scratcher thing is weird, isn't it?" Wilkes said conversationally as the lift lowered.

"Yep. Weird," Nik said, hoping his shortness would stop Wilkes's questions.

"They really set up an ambush?"

Nik stifled a sigh. "Yes."

"I had no idea they were that smart," Wilkes said.

Nik shrugged dismissively. "Apparently they are."

"Smart and mean. That's a dangerous combination. A lot like my last mate." Wilkes chuckled and elbowed Nik.

Nik mentally leaped at the change of subject. "You and Ethan have called it quits?"

"No! I say my *last mate* because I think he'll be the death of me. If I called it quits with him, I *know* he'd kill me." Wilkes laughed good-naturedly, and Nik joined him—glad that the lift had made it to the forest floor and that they'd left the talk of Scratchers behind, even if just temporarily.

"So, what's the plan for the team?" Nik asked while they made their way through the forest, heading downhill toward Farm Island and the mighty river they would follow to the ruins of the great city they called Port.

"It's going to be a good trip. Sheena and Crystal discovered a building in the southwest, right on the waterfront, that we've never had access to before."

"Right on the waterfront?" Nik said. The Tribe had been foraging in the city for uncounted generations. They tried to stay as close as possible to the escape path provided by the wide waterway, known formally as the Willum River, and less formally but more morbidly as the Killum River. But as the winters passed and the decades rolled on, the Tribe had had to forage farther and farther inside the dead city, which meant fewer and fewer foraging parties had been allowed to go out, as Port City was Skin Stealer territory, and far too dangerous to justify risking the loss of life for pots or pans, mirrors or chains. "A find near the Killum is unusual. How'd it happen?"

"Apparently what we've long believed was just another mound of vines and rot was in truth a long metal building that had, until two days ago at the end of their reconnoitering, been so completely covered that no one bothered to look too closely at it."

"What changed?" Nik said.

"Looks like that big thunderstorm that passed through a few nights ago caused a section of the roof to cave in—almost like a lightning strike. The opening isn't large, but it's viewable from the river. The girls checked it out. They said inside is a wealth of steel cables, chains, and even some glass."

"Sounds too good to be true," Nik said, feeling a crawling under his skin.

"Well, it's happened before. Remember back about ten winters? That team, led—if memory serves me correctly—by Monroe's father, found a way inside the stone station by the train tracks. Damn place had been sealed up for as long as anyone could remember, and then one day—there it was—a fallen wall that opened to a king's hoard of mirrors and pots and pans."

"Yeah, I remember. My mother got one of the mirrors. Sol still treasures it," Nik said.

"And all that was just sitting there, practically in spitting distance of the river. Looks like this time the find will be even better—especially as it seems it's exactly what we need for building more nests," Wilkes said.

"Sounds promising." Nik shook off his sense of foreboding. The ruined city was a living being—one that changed, grew, died, and was reborn over and over. It was a good thing that the reconnaissance team had found what the Tribe needed so close to the river. It meant easy in—easy out—and less danger.

"Yes it does!" Wilkes smiled, obviously in high spirits. "We shouldn't even need the full moon light to paddle by tonight. I predict we'll be back in time for sundown and celebrations."

"I like your prediction," Nik said.

"Doesn't look like we'll need your observation skills, but don't worry. I'm still glad you're coming along. Hey, maybe we'll spot some game from the river and you can give us all a demonstration of your vast skill as a marksman. Tonight we bring home metal and glass *and* fresh meat," Wilkes said. "I'm telling you—this is a blessed mission."

"I'll do my best for you," Nik said, feeling foolish for the trepidation he'd been feeling. He knew his dark mood was more about O'Bryan, the lost pup, and the mysterious girl than Wilkes's foraging team. With an effort he mentally shook himself. He'd get his head on right and be a real part of this mission—and he'd decide what to do about everything else afterward.

The launching dock was near the base of the Farm Island Bridge. As Nik and Wilkes jogged down the final part of the sloping hill, the team was facing east and opening their arms to the newly risen sun.

"Ah, good. We're in time to soak in the dawn. That's always a good beginning to a foraging trip," Wilkes said.

He and Nik quickly joined them, raising their faces and arms to the clean, golden light of a new day. Nik breathed in deeply, allowing the power of the sun's rays to burn away the last of the sense of foreboding that had been haunting him since he'd entered the grove with the desecrated deer. Delicate frond patterns lifted just beneath the bare skin of his arms as warmth filled him, giving him a much needed jolt of energy.

"'Morning, Nik," Winston said. "Sorry to hear about your cousin."

"Thanks," Nik said, giving Winston's Shepherd, Star, a quick pat.

"How's he doing?" Winston asked.

"Holding his own," Nik said. "I appreciate you asking."

"Hey there, Nik! Glad you and your crossbow are joining us." Monroe clapped him on the back and his pure black Shepherd, Viper, greeted him with a friendly sniff.

"My crossbow and I are glad to be with you, too, Monroe," Nik said. "Though from what Wilkes has told me it looks like this is an easy in, easy out mission."

"That's what we're counting on," Sheena said. "Hi, Nik."

"Nice to see you, Sheena, and you, too, Crystal. Your Shepherds are looking good." Nik paused, really looking at Captain and Grace, who were sprawled together on the dock. "Grace looks particularly good."

Crystal's smile was joyous. "She should."

"That's right. She definitely should. She's carrying the future within her." Sheena gave Crystal a quick, intimate kiss, and then tossed a provisions pack into their kayak.

"Grace is pregnant?" Nik said.

"Don't fret, Nik," Crystal said, patting him on the cheek in a surprisingly motherly fashion. "It's still early enough that there's no harm in her coming with us."

"No harm at all," Wilkes agreed. "And fertility brings good luck."

"Does Sol know?" Nik asked. It was hard for him to believe that his father would give permission for a pregnant canine, even one in the early stages of pregnancy, to join a mission that had such potential for danger.

"Well, no. Not yet. Sheena and I thought we'd announce after—" Sheena began, but Thaddeus's sarcasm bit off her words.

"Nikolas, it's only you who feels like they have to tell your daddy everything."

The group fell silent, watching Nik and waiting for his response. It was no secret that Thaddeus had spent the past two weeks on latrine digging duty because of his behavior on Nik's tracking mission. Up until that moment, Nik hadn't been sure how many Tribe members had been aware that he had had rather more to do with Thaddeus's punishment than was supposed to be general knowledge.

Nik schooled his face into an expression of amusement. "I haven't seen much of you lately, Thaddeus. Oh, that's right. It's because you've been busy digging shit holes."

"Because of your mouth, you bast—"

"Enough!" Wilkes stepped between the two men. "I won't have dissension on this mission. You two bury what's bad between you until we're back, or I'll leave you both behind."

Nik make himself relax. He smiled at Wilkes. "I don't have any problem with that. I'm here to help. That's all."

"Thaddeus?" Wilkes asked pointedly.

"I've been on five other foraging missions. Odysseus and I will do our job, like we always do. You need something tracked—we'll do it. No need for Sol's boy to change that," Thaddeus said.

"Good. Then let's finish loading the kayaks and move out," Wilkes said.

Thaddeus walked past Nik, calling to his Terrier, Odysseus, and motioning for him to get into his kayak. As he brushed a little too closely by Nik, he spoke under his breath. "This isn't over between us."

Nik met his eyes and smiled humorlessly. "Good to know," he said in the same low voice.

"Nik, you'll be riding with Sheena and Crystal," Wilkes called from the dock. "They have the most room in their kayak."

"That's fine with us." Sheena grinned at Nik. "We'll make him do most the paddling."

"No problem. You two are so light, it'll be like floating on water," Nik said, grinning back at her.

Nik decided to ignore the still scowling Thaddeus, thinking, *let the team see what a pain in the ass he is. Maybe he'll manage to piss off Wilkes enough that he'll earn another two weeks on latrine digging duty.* The thought had Nik smiling and whistling as he helped the women finish loading their kayak. It might, after all, be a successful mission in more ways than one.

28

The six kayaks were loaded in short order and buoyant litters were secured to the aft of each small boat, all ready to be filled with the much anticipated spoils of their mission. Then Wilkes called them to huddle around the map he unrolled on a big, flat boulder dock side.

"One last time so that we're all clear—we follow the Willum all the way through Port City to the southwest waterfront. That means we have to pass all of the bridges, so stay alert and aware. Remember, what you don't see around those hulks is worse than what you do see. So, the find is just before these islands, here." Wilkes pointed at a spot on the map that showed a teardrop-shaped grouping of small islands centered in the river. "On the western bank." Wilkes's gaze flicked to Sheena. "You said there's a spot nearby to beach the kayaks?"

"Yeah, simple. It's right about there." Sheena pressed her finger to a place on the map.

"And it was a short climb to the opening of the building. You can see it from the river," Crystal added.

"Should be easy to hook towlines around the metal and pull it to the water, load 'em, and off we go," Sheena said as she and her mate smiled at each other.

"I like the way that sounds," Wilkes said. "Questions?"

Nik almost kept his mouth shut, but his father's words niggled at his conscience, goading him to speak up. "Sheena, you said you could see the opening from the river?"

"Yep. Even though it's still pretty choked by vines and such. We might not have noticed it at all if it hadn't been for the glass."

"Glass?" Nik asked.

"Yeah, it musta got caught in the vines when the roof collapsed and it just happened to catch the sunlight as we paddled past," Crystal said. "That's why we didn't see it the other days. How many times do you think we passed that spot before the thing winked at us?" she asked her mate.

Sheena lifted a slim shoulder. "Lots. It was a real blessing that the Sun led us to it."

Except for Nik, the team nodded and smiled.

"Did you have another question, Nik?" Wilkes said.

"No. No, that was my question. I just think it's odd. It's been ten winters or more since there has been a substantial find so close to the river, hasn't it?"

"Yes, well, looks like we're getting lucky," Wilkes said with an easy smile.

"Like the girls said, the Sun blessed them. Shouldn't be hard for the Sun Priest's boy to accept that," Thaddeus said with a caustic smile.

"Oh, I don't have any problem accepting blessings from the Sun," Nik said. "If they are blessings."

"What are you trying to do—chase ghosts again?" Thaddeus's eyes glinted with malice.

"Nope, Thaddeus. I'm just trying to do my job—same as you. I'm here to shoot things and observe. There's nothing I'm allowed to shoot right now, so I'm observing."

"Well, let's hope observing is all you have to do until we return to the Tribe, loaded with metal," Wilkes said.

"And glass," Crystal added. "I spotted an almost perfectly round piece—totally uncracked. I'm going to bring it back and use it as a window for our new nest."

Sheena slipped her hand in Crystal's. "Our new *spacious* nest. I cannot wait until we don't have to crowd into that tiny bachelor's nest anymore. After all, we'll have pups soon!"

"And on that blessed note, let's launch," Wilkes said.

The six gleaming wooden kayaks skimmed easily over the waters of the Willum, slicing through the current like a hot dagger through a bucket of lard. The canines settled comfortably on the ballast mats. Soon they were dozing in the warm morning sunlight.

Nik was glad he'd been teamed with Sheena and Crystal. He liked them. They'd been mates for several winters and, unlike Wilkes and Ethan, rarely argued. Plus, they were half the weight of the men, even taking into account towing their big Shepherds, both of whom were currently snoring loudly.

"Pups, huh?" Nik called from his position in the rear of the boat as the three of them paddled. "That is good news. Captain and Grace will make a fine-looking litter of pups."

"We're so excited!" Crystal said.

"You'd think she's giving birth," Sheena said, sending Crystal a warm smile over her shoulder.

"Oh, don't pretend like you're not as excited as I am. She *cried* when Captain and Grace mated," Crystal said.

"Happy tears," Sheena agreed. "I admit it. I might as well. I'll cry again when they're born."

"Congratulations. I'm truly happy for you," Nik said. "And it's a good thing that more pups are on their way with how fast we're growing."

"Don't you mean it's a good thing that more pups are on their way so that you have another chance at one choosing you?" Thaddeus called out.

"There's no reason for that kind of comment," Sheena said, skewering Thaddeus with a dark look.

"No worries," Nik said, laughing with forced humor. "Plus, the truth is that I'd be honored if a pup from your Captain and Grace chose me."

Thaddeus's snort carried across the water. "You'd be honored if *any* pup chose you—even a ghost."

Nik looked at Thaddeus. He was glaring at him maliciously as he scratched at his arms and, in general, looked grumpy and uncomfortable. *Well it's hot. The idiot shouldn't be wearing that long-sleeved tunic.* But before Nik could open his mouth to tell Thaddeus he needed to cool off—literally and figuratively—Crystal spoke.

"Nik, let's put some muscle in it and show the rest of the boys the way," she said, frowning at Thaddeus. "And the company will be more pleasant than it is right here."

"Wilkes, do you mind if we forge ahead?" Sheena called.

"No, but stay in sight, and let us catch you before we pass the Triangle Bridge. You two know the waters better than all of us combined, and that's a pretty dicey section of the river."

"Will do!"

The three of them set to paddling and their kayak shot forward, easily leaving the heavier boats behind.

"I can't stand that arrogant ass," Sheena said.

"Yeah, if it wasn't for his Terrier's excellent nose, he wouldn't have any status with the Tribe at all," Crystal agreed.

"It's maddening, isn't it?" Sheena said.

"That he's an ass? Yep," Nik said.

"Well, yes, but what I meant was that it's maddening that he was chosen by a canine—even if it is a Terrier and not a Shepherd—and you haven't been," Sheena said.

Unused to anyone besides O'Bryan speaking so frankly about such a touchy subject, Nik stayed silent, searching for words.

"Sheena, hon, Nik doesn't want to talk about that," Crystal told her mate gently.

"No, that's okay. I don't mind. I know people talk about me—talk about *it*. That I haven't been chosen and that I'm foolishly fixated on chasing the trail of a pup who's long gone."

"We don't think you're foolish. We agree with you," Crystal said. "I'd never stop looking for Grace, and Sheena would never stop looking for Captain."

"Thanks. That means a lot," Nik said, and then quickly changed the subject. "So, tell me about this new nest you'll be building."

Crystal latched on to the subject like a Shepherd with a hide ball, and soon she and Sheena were having an animated discussion about where their glass-enclosed window should be and whether they wanted a one- or two-story nest. Thankful that he didn't have to input anything to their conversation, Nik concentrated on paddling and studying the river.

His mother used to love watching the river. Nik remembered that she talked about it as if it were a living being who kept uncounted secrets, and though she'd respected its might, with the remnants of a dead world hidden beneath the innocent mask of its surface, it intrigued rather than frightened her.

Silently, Nik had disagreed with her when he was a child, and he still disagreed with her. It didn't intrigue him. It thoroughly frightened him, though that truth had died with the only person who had known about his fear—his mother. The tribe called the Killum a mystery, one that ended too often in death for those who spent too much time on it. Nik had watched that death be meted out. The first time had been when he'd been so young he shouldn't have any memory of it, but the image of a clear, summer day and the fishermen kayaking leisurely and casting wide, lazy nets was burned into his mind. Or rather, what was burned into his mind was the memory of the fisherman who had cast his net too close to a semi-submerged log they called a sweeper. The net had caught on the log, and before the fisherman could right it, he'd lost his balance and fallen into the river where the tangled web of currents that eddy around the sweeper pulled him under so that its roots, hidden beneath the murky, spring-swollen water, snagged him, and like a demon lover held him close until he drowned.

Nik suppressed a shudder at the still vivid memory of the Tribe dragging the sweeper to shore to free the pale, bloated corpse.

But the truth was it wasn't the sweepers or the unpredictable currents or the remnants of once mighty ships that had become rusted hulks, capsized and useless, clogging the waterway in the heart of the ruined city that haunted Nik. It was the death traps called bridges that terrified him the most.

From Tribal archives, and the puzzle-solving skills of the Builders of the Tribe, it was believed that Port City used to boast twelve massive bridges, spanning the wide expanse from one bank of the Willum to the other. Not one of the bridges had survived the death of the City intact, though to varying degrees all had left their footprints on—or beneath—the river.

"Heads up!" Crystal called from her position at the front of the kayak. "Arch Bridge ahead."

Nik set his teeth and wiped his sweating palms, one at a time, on his pants before he began stroking the water with renewed vigor. Since his was the position in the rear of the kayak—the main steering position—he was damned sure not going to let them drift anywhere near the enormous broken green arches that jutted out of the water like the rotting teeth of a drowned giant. He forced himself to breathe deeply, slowly, and repress the panic that was too close to his surface as he followed Sheena's shouted directions to go more to the left or to the right—faster or slower.

"Good job, Nik! Almost past it. Steer us closer to the middle. This bridge isn't bad, but the run-off will suck us in if we're not careful," Sheena said.

Nik bent into the paddling, propelling them to the center of the river and shooting past the deadly run-off. As they passed, well away from it, Nik glanced to his right in time to see a huge sweeper caught in the undertow, upended and tossed around the white-topped rapids like it weighed no more than a Shepherd's throwing stick, before it was sucked under and disappeared.

Nik shivered and kept paddling.

All that remained of the next bridge were oblong-shaped pillars of crumbling stone that tended to break off unexpectedly. Two winters past a Companion and his Shepherd had been killed when they'd paddled too close to one of the edifices, trying to stay away from the run-off current. The slide of stone had buried them so thoroughly that the Tribe was never able to recover their bodies.

"Let's hold here," Sheena said after they'd made it safely past the stone hulks. "We should pass the Triangle as a group."

"Some of the Triangle has shifted again," Crystal explained as they paused the boat. "Sheena will guide us through it. The others should follow pretty close."

"Okay. No problem." Nik hoped he sounded nonchalant, even though he couldn't stop wiping his sweating palms on his pants and rolling his shoulders, trying to work some of the tension out of them before they had to continue.

"The run-offs make my skin crawl, too," Crystal said.

"They're a pain in the ass, and the prime reason the damn river changes so much," Sheena said.

"I thought nothing about the Killum ever rattled you river types," Nik said.

"Are you kidding? They rattle me!" Crystal said. "They're unnatural."

Sheena laughed. "They're just water that's found a strange way to escape."

"You know what they remind me of?" Crystal asked Nik, though she didn't wait for his answer. "It's like the bridges pierced the skin of the earth, causing it to bleed from underneath the floor of the river. The run-offs are the earth's cut veins, shooting currents of water and dirt and sweepers and bodies," Crystal paused to shudder with disgust, "into the land."

"I can't say I disagree with you." Nik's gaze found the frothing water that marked the foundation of the next bridge. Even from this distance, he could see the whitecaps spouting off of the river and cutting a swatch of turbulent, flotsam-filled water shooting inland. "I've never seen anything like the run-offs in any other part of the river."

"They're just here, at what's left of Port City's bridges. I talked with one of the Elders a little over five winters ago when I really got interested in understanding the river. He said the theory is that the run-offs were created during the last of the major earthquakes. He didn't have a theory for why they're only here, and only near the bridges," Sheena said. Then she shrugged. "I see them as just one more problem that needs to be handled when we're scouting the river."

Crystal sent her mate a lingering smile. "It's Sheena who's brave about everything."

"Just because you're beside me," Sheena said.

Nik looked away while they kissed sweetly and intimately, giving them some small measure of privacy, and wondering what it would be like to be mated to someone who believed he was brave about everything.

"All caught up and ready to take on the Triangle!" Wilkes called as he led the rest of the group to join them.

"It's shifted some, probably during that last big storm," Sheena said.

"But Sheena knows how to get us through. Stay right behind us and you'll be fine," Crystal said. "Okay, Nik, give us some manpower!"

"Will do!" Nik bent to the task of paddling, keeping his focus on Sheena and the directions she called out to him. Nik respected and appreciated the confidence with which both women navigated the river, even if he did wish vehemently that he were elsewhere.

They approached the Triangle with practiced care. There was little left of the original bridge that was visible, but much that waited, just below the surface. It had been named Triangle for the shape of the huge steel fragments that littered the river. Deadly and sharp, they shifted and drifted, as if the shattered bridge was sentient, and it stalked those who dared to pass over its watery den.

"It's going to look like we're getting too close to the run-off," Sheena shouted over the sound of rushing water. "But we're just going to head toward it so we can get around a big piece of metal there, to the left of us. When I say *Now,* Nik will break and turn us—fast—toward the center of the river. But put your backs into your paddles. Don't want that run-off to snag any of you."

Nik swallowed hard, feeling sick to his stomach.

"Now, Nik!" Sheena yelled. Nik did exactly as she commanded, and they shot past the sharp edge of the rusted metal as well as the frothing run-off.

"Well done, Sheena!" Wilkes said after they were all free of the Triangle's territory. "Take us through the rest of them."

"Will do!" Sheena shouted back.

"That's my girl!" Crystal smiled and, half asleep still, Captain's tail thumped, brushing the surface of the water and waking him fully so that, with a start that almost sent him over the side, he tucked his tail up under him, causing the two women to laugh and tease the big Shepherd about being scared of a little water.

Nik didn't say anything. He only wiped his palms again and silently agreed with the canine. If he had a tail he'd be keeping it tucked up and away from the seething river, too.

The next bridge had broken apart in huge steel plates the color of old blood. The only ones that had not sunk to the bottom of the river were the two that had been caught on the hull of a ship, capsized against what was left of an enormous stone column. As they glided past, Nik thought he'd be eternally grateful that those who'd come before him had long since scavenged anything of use from the rusted corpses of all the ships in the Port City waterway.

They were entering what was considered the heart of the ruined city and as Sheena had him slow the pace so that the others could keep up with them more easily, Nik's gaze roamed over what was left of Port City.

A thick, living blanket of green covered everything. Storytellers still told tales about the ancients and their cities of glass and concrete and metal. It was known that Port City had been different—or at least different enough for the ancients to note. It was an accepted fact that those who built the city, and the people who had lived there, had at least some measure of appreciation for the forest, so that they included in their world of metal and glass and concrete trees and green space within the city itself. The Elders even agreed that the first Tribe members had, indeed, come from Port City, fleeing into the forests because they believed the trees could succor them.

Nik studied the city. Once in a while he caught a flash of sunlight on something that could be glass or metal, but mostly all that was left of Port City was great mounds of rubble that had been shrouded by plant life. Nik shivered again. The verdant vines and overgrown ferns, brambles, and trees were like sweepers in the river. Beneath them held countless ways to die, and not simply from the ruins under the plants and the mutated beings who chose to live there. In the city, the plants themselves were changed. Much like the treacherous run-offs, they were deadly and unnatural.

"All right, everyone ready to move on?" Sheena called.

"We'll be right behind you," Wilkes said.

Nik bent to his paddle and readied himself as the Steel Bridge loomed before them. It was the bridge that had survived the most fully intact. The only section that was entirely missing was from the center of the thing. Its two towers had fallen sideways, severing one side of it from the other so that dark water lapped around black metal trusses, looking like a diabolical mouth missing front teeth. It made Nik's skin shiver, but it was the safest bridge to pass, as all he had to do was to keep the kayak centered in the middle of those missing teeth, and they glided easily by the sucking run-offs.

Too soon afterward, they approached the next bridge. It had been near the ruins of the railroad and the building that ten winters before had provided such a wealth of loot that the Tribe still told stories about it. This bridge was completely gone, leaving only thick, square columns of stone above the water, though Nik knew that below were steel girders waiting to hook anything that dared to trespass too far beneath the lapping surface. As they passed between two of the enormous columns and entered the part of the river that was choked by the rusted bodies of ships, Nik felt a prickling of the flesh up and down his spine, as if behind him were the stone guardians of a watery graveyard, waiting only for one small misstep on his part to close and seal their escape route.

Only one remaining bridge still had life above the water—and Nik's gaze, as if on its own, turned upward to the towers that jutted more than one hundred feet above the river. Attached to the towers were thick steel cables—some had snapped, twisted, and half fallen with the center of the bridge, giving the thing the macabre but graceful look of the skeletal ribs of a dancer who had collapsed centuries before after one too many failed pirouettes.

"Strange that this one's still white, isn't it?" Crystal spoke in a hushed voice, as if she was afraid of waking the dead.

"It always looks like bones to me," Sheena said.

"Exactly what I was thinking," Nik agreed.

"The run-off for this one isn't too bad, but stay sharp. Just around this next bend is the last bridge and then we get to the site of the find," Sheena said. "And even though there's next to nothing much left of the bridge, the run-off is almost as bad as the Triangle. Don't let the curve of the river draw us too near the bank or we'll be sucked in."

"Did you hear that, Wilkes?" Crystal called.

"Got it!" Wilkes replied. "We're right behind you."

Nik ignored everything except Sheena's directions, so he was surprised when Crystal turned around and, with laughing eyes, said, "Okay, okay, we're past all of it now. You're going to paddle us all the way to the falls if you don't slow down."

"Oh, sorry," Nik said, trying to relax his white-knuckled grip.

"There! Can you see it?" Crystal called, pointing at a place just above the west bank.

Everyone's gaze followed Crystal's finger. Nik spotted the opening easily, but only because there was a flash of brightness that caught his eyes. Once he'd gotten a fix on the glinting light, he could see that it appeared that the vines had imploded, leaving a dark pit in the greenery.

Like a grave, Nik thought, and the crawling beneath his skin returned.

"Nik," Sheena said, gesturing to the western bank of the river. What wasn't covered with water-loving scrub and choking vines was rocky and littered with tree debris. "Do you see where those reeds and cattails start?"

"Yeah, I see them."

"Beach us close to them. The way up to the find is near there."

Nik propelled them there swiftly. Though he had no desire to crawl into the hole the others were so eager to explore, he did look forward to getting off the river, even if only for a short reprieve. The other five kayaks slid into place beside them, and the canines jumped eagerly off their mats, fully awake and obviously as happy as Nik to be on firm ground again.

"Sheena, good job getting us here safely," Wilkes said. "When we get back I'm going to propose to the Council that your and Crystal's nest be the first one built."

"And I think it should be a two-story nest," Monroe added. "Especially if your Captain and Grace are going to continue to gift the Tribe with litters."

Crystal gave a girlish squeal and hugged Sheena, who grinned happily. "We don't expect that—we're just doing our part for the Tribe, like the rest of you," Sheena said.

"But we'll take the two-story nest!" Crystal added quickly, causing the group to laugh.

"Well, then, let's get what we need and go home!" Wilkes said. "Weapons up. Especially you, Nik." He tossed Nik an additional quiver filled with crossbow arrows. "I want everyone else to carry towing ropes. Nik, you keep that bow aimed and those sharp eyes open. Remember, even though Skin Stealers live farther inside the ruins, they do come to the river to fish and forage. Stay alert unless you want one of them to be wearing your skin suit."

Crystal shuddered delicately. "Just thinking about them disgusts me."

"Did you see any of them while you and Sheena were on recon?" Nik asked her.

"No, thank the blessed Sun."

Nik narrowed his eyes and stared up at the hulking clumps of green that rose like gigantic burial mounds, covering the ruined remnants of what once had been tall buildings all along the waterfront.

"Wilkes, did any of you see sign of Skin Stealers when you were heading here?" Nik said, rubbing his forearm where his flesh was prickling like a frigid breeze had just blown across it.

"Nope, can't say that I did," Wilkes said. "Any of you see sign of those bastards?" The other men shook their heads. Wilkes smiled and clapped Nik on the shoulder. "See, it's like I told you—this is a blessed mission."

Nik said nothing. Instead he kept studying the area surrounding them.

"Winston, you and Star stay with the boats and watch our backs. We'll be in and out as fast as possible," Wilkes said.

Winston nodded, holding his crossbow in the crook of his arm. "If you find a pot, any kind of pot, I'd appreciate first dibs on it. My Allison's birthday is next week, and she would sure love to stop borrowing the boiling pot from her mother."

"The first pot found is yours," Wilkes said.

"All right, the way in is just over there." Sheena led the group, picking her way carefully through the rocks and rubble. Each Tribe member, except for Nik, kept his canine close, well aware that their senses would warn them far before human senses could begin to decipher danger. Nik kept his eyes and ears open and his crossbow at the ready as he tried to tell himself that the sick feeling that kept crawling over his skin was due to the close proximity of bridges and run-offs, and nothing else.

In just a few yards the bank cut sharply inland, with an unnatural slant that had Nik frowning in confusion. Shaped like a long rectangle, the river slashed into the bank. The water was quieter here and brackish, with water reeds choking the area. Coming out of the river were two long, thick strips of rusted metal. River water lapped beneath the rails, reminding Nik too much of another bridge. Though they jutted above the water, they were accessible from the bank by the half-broken remains of metal supports and concrete blocks.

"Are those rails?" Monroe asked.

Sheena nodded. "They are. See how they lead up to the find and then stretch all the way out there into the river proper?"

Nik did see—and he didn't like what he saw.

"Man, this is sweet!" Thaddeus said. "We can use the rails to climb up to the opening, and when we're done we can paddle the kayaks over here and slide the heaviest pieces of metal down these things and load them right up."

"That's what I thought, too," Sheena said.

"Yeah, Sheena and I used them to climb up and check out the find. It was a nice change from slogging through those terrible vines and undergrowth." Crystal shivered. "You never know what's hidden beneath that stuff."

"Why isn't it covered in vines?" Nik said, causing everyone to turn to look at him. "Did you and Sheena clear them off before you climbed up there?"

"Nope, they looked just like this when we found them," Crystal said.

"How about the area around them?" Nik gestured at the blocks and supports. Except for the choking river reeds that were in the water, the rails were eerily free of plants and debris.

"Nope again," Crystal said. "We didn't do much of anything except use the rails to get up there."

"What's the problem, Nik?" Wilkes asked.

"I don't know. It feels wrong to me."

Wilkes shrugged. "There are lots of rocks here, and lots of water. Maybe vines can't grow on the rails."

Nik pointed at the rest of the bank. "Same rocks and water there, and there, but lots of vines."

"I see that," Wilkes said, rubbing his chin. "Maybe the things are toxic. You never know what kind of crap is leeching out of them."

Nik carefully stepped up onto a wide cement block and followed it to a rail, then crouched beside it. It was big—really big—and now that he was closer he could see that the rails had been fashioned with a thick groove, as if to hook a giant something into them so that it could slide down and into the river. Easily three feet across they were rusted, but looked solid—as if they had been used yesterday. Nik thumped the top of the first rail with his knuckles. "It's just metal. No different from train tracks or bridge supports. They're big." He paused, looking up at the vine-choked building the rails led to. "Might have been a place where they built ships, what with this access to the water. Doesn't seem like it's toxic. Those other plants are flourishing."

"What are you getting at, except wasting our time?" Thaddeus said.

Nik ignored him and kept talking to Wilkes. "It's like the rails have been cleared so that we'd use them." He pointed up at the section of green from which a piece of glass winked enticingly. "Up there feels as wrong as this does down here."

"Wrong?" Wilkes asked.

"Like we're being led here by a strategically placed mirror and conveniently cleared vines," Nik said.

"Oh, come on! That's ridiculous. He's chasing ghosts again," Thaddeus said, throwing his arms up in disgust.

"Nik, Sheena and I climbed up there. We looked into the hole. It's just an eroded roof to some kind of huge warehouse—that's all. Like you said, it's probably where they built the ships and then used these rails to launch them into the river," Crystal said.

"I hear you, Nik, and I agree we should be cautious, but there's lots of metal rods and chains and glass inside," Sheena added. "And no sign of anything else. The inside's covered with dust and debris. Nothing's been in there except rodents and insects for centuries."

"I believe you," Nik told her. "I still don't like how this find is adding up. I think we should torch the place before anyone goes inside."

"Great bloody beetle balls! You've got to be fucking kidding," Thaddeus exploded. "That'll set us back days, maybe even weeks."

"Being dead will set us back even further," Nik said. He turned to Wilkes. "You know why you brought me along, and I'm telling you I'm seeing something here the others aren't. It won't hurt anything to torch it—let it burn—and then come back with more Warriors to stand guard while we scavenge the glass and metal."

"Except the glass will most likely be ruined from the fire." Thaddeus shook his head. "No. We do it Nik's way and days will be wasted. The Tribe needs new nests now, not whenever Nik decides it's safe enough to forage."

"Nik, what is it you fear?" Wilkes asked.

"Yesterday Davis, O'Bryan, and I were ambushed by Scratchers. This," Nik swept his arm out, taking in the big rusted rails, the strange rectangular pool, and the building that hulked above them, "feels like another ambush to me."

"Nik, you know Scratchers never go in the city," Crystal said gently.

"I don't mean Scratchers. I mean Skin Stealers."

"But we haven't seen any sign of them," Monroe said. "None at all."

"That's one of the things that has me worried," Nik said. "Usually we catch at least a glimpse of one of their fires—or some poor dead creature they trapped, flayed alive, and then nailed up the leftover corpse like a trophy. Did anyone see any of those signs on their way here?"

As a group they shook their heads.

"Which could mean those carrion eaters have moved on—or inward—or just haven't hunted near here lately," Wilkes said. "That's actually a good thing, Nik." The Leader went to Nik and put his hand on his shoulder. "I understand what you've just been through. This was probably bad timing—to go back out so soon. I think it's clouding your judgment, son."

"I hope you're right," Nik said.

"I am. But let's all stay aware. Listen to your canines. If they sense danger, alert everyone and get back to the kayaks," Wilkes said. "Okay, Sheena, Crystal, this is your find. You get to lead the way."

"Yippee!" Crystal cheered, causing Grace to jump around her joyfully. "Come on, my girl! Let's go get our new window."

29

Doing a little happy dance, Crystal stepped onto the first rail with Grace right behind her. The metal was so wide that the canine didn't bobble at all, but padded easily after her Companion.

"We climbed up using this one, and down using the other," Sheena explained. "So both are safe."

"Okay, Monroe, you and Viper follow them, then Thaddeus and Odysseus. Odin and I will bring up the rear." Wilkes glanced at Nik. "Are you coming or would you rather stay here?"

"I'll go where you want me," Nik said, scanning the area around them for any sign of what was making his skin crawl. *Maybe Wilkes is right—maybe I did come out too soon.*

"We have enough bows up there. Stay down here in case anything tries to sneak up on us," Wilkes said.

"Will do," Nik said.

"Hey, what's the holdup, Sheena?"

Nik and Wilkes turned at Monroe's question to see that Sheena's Captain was pacing nervously back and forth beside the wide rail. His Companion was already standing on the rail, but the big Shepherd kept sending nervous looks down at the murky, reed-clogged water that lapped thickly below them.

"Come on, Captain, let's go, big boy!"

Captain whined fretfully and didn't follow her.

Sheena frowned, obviously baffled by her canine's behavior. "What is it? You climbed up there like a champ just yesterday." Sheena sent Wilkes a confused look. "I have no idea what's going on with him. He's not a big fan of water, but he's never balked like this before."

"What's wrong?" Crystal called. She was midway up the rail, over what looked to be the deepest part of the pool.

"He feels worried—confused—even scared," Sheena said. "But I don't know why."

Nik moved closer to Wilkes and said low, for his ears only, "Get Crystal and Grace back here. Captain is feeling what I am. Something's wrong. We have to—"

Nik's words were cut off as the brackish pool below the rails erupted into a nightmare of chaos and death. Dropping the reeds through which they'd been breathing, Skin Stealers emerged from the water, their deadly triple-tipped spears weeping water as they shrieked their terrifying battle cry and attacked.

The first spear struck Grace, skewering the canine behind her shoulder. The force of the blow knocked her from the rail, and with an agonizing yelp the beautiful female Shepherd fell into the water.

"NO!" Crystal shouted, pulled a knife from the leather sheath around her waist, and with no hesitation jumped into the water after her Companion—landing in the middle of the Skin Stealers.

"Crystal!" Sheena was screaming and pulling her own knife free when Wilkes tackled her so that she fell to the bank instead of leaping to her death after her mate.

Nik went to his knees and began firing arrow after arrow down into the pit of water and death while spears whizzed past him. He tried to sight Crystal, but there were too many reeds and too much roiling water.

Another canine screamed in agony, but Nik didn't look around. He kept firing and firing. There were so many of them! And they'd all been hiding in wait, just below the surface of the water.

"They're targeting the canines!" Wilkes shouted. "We have to get back to the boat or they'll kill them and take us! Go now! Nik, cover us."

"Will do!" Nik shouted.

"Not without Crystal and Grace! I won't leave them!" Sheena was screaming and thrashing as Wilkes tried to drag her away.

"Then you and Captain will be as dead as they are!" Wilkes shouted back.

"Don't let them take me alive!" The horrible cry came from the pool. Nik saw Crystal then. She was in bloody, brackish water to her chest. One arm was wrapped around the body of Grace, and with the other hand she was brandishing her dagger, slashing and jabbed at the circle of Skin Stealers who were closing around her.

Nik shot once, twice, and two more Skin Stealers disappeared under the water. Two more immediately swam to take their place in the closing circle.

They wouldn't kill her, Nik knew. Not right away. Skin Stealers believed they could absorb the power of a Companion through the wearing of their skin, and that power was transferred to them only if the Companion was alive when the skin was stolen. They would take Crystal to their Temple in the heart of the ruined city, and there they would flay the skin from her body carefully, meticulously, keeping her alive as long as possible. Then they would feed on what was left of her body, eating the raw flesh from her in ravenous, bloody bites.

"More of 'em are coming from the find!" Monroe shouted.

Nik spared a glance up. Skin Stealers were pouring from the hole in the building.

"Crystal!" Sheena screamed.

"We can't save her!" Wilkes said. "Nik, end it for her and follow us."

Time seemed suspended. Nik stood, and as spears hurled past him, he sighted down into the pool. Crystal looked up and met his eyes. She threw her dagger, catching the closest Skin Stealer in his neck. Then she hugged Grace's body tightly to her, smiled, and nodded to Nik.

He didn't let himself think. He pulled the trigger of his crossbow and watched his arrow bury itself to the feathers in the middle of

Crystal's smooth white forehead. With a sigh that Nik would hear in his nightmares for the rest of his life, she collapsed over Grace's body and the two of them disappeared together under the water.

Then Nik was backing after Wilkes and Sheena, firing arrow after arrow into the horde that converged on them from above and below.

All of the boats except for the ones carrying Wilkes and Monroe, and him and Sheena had already launched when Nik got to the beached kayaks. From his peripheral vision he could see that Monroe's Viper had been struck, and he was half dragging, half carrying his Shepherd, who had a spear protruding from his haunch, into the ballasting mat.

Then, not twenty yards from him, Thaddeus cried, "Odysseus!" Nik watched as the biggest male he'd ever seen emerged from beneath Thaddeus's kayak. The little boat rolled dangerously, sending the Terrier sliding off the ballast and into the water, where a Skin Stealer instantly grabbed him. "No!" Thaddeus screamed again, and then his cry was cut off when the huge man backhanded him. Thaddeus fell backward, hitting his head against the wooden seat, knocked unconscious. The Skin Stealer grabbed the back of his tunic like it was a puppy's scruff, easily pulling him from the boat.

A spear sizzled past Nik's ear and he fired four more arrows, trying to aim for the big man swimming toward shore with Thaddeus under his massive arm, but Skin Stealers seemed to multiply from beneath the water, surfacing to form a living wall between his arrows and the retreating male.

"Go, Nik! Go!" Wilkes shouted as Odin leaped onto the other mat, balancing the kayak. He and Monroe pushed it into the river, jumping aboard as the current caught it and they shot into the river.

"Here, Nik! Help me!" Sheena called. He glanced behind him. Tears streaming down her face, Sheena was trying to wrench free the ballasts from the sides of their kayak. Captain was aboard already, crouched near what had been Crystal's seat. Instantly Nik knew what was happening. Without Grace as balance to Captain's weight, they'd capsize. They had to get rid of the ballasts if they were to escape.

Nik didn't waste time with words. He surged through the shallow water to the kayak. Using the heel of his boot, he kicked violently at the arm of the ballast, splintering it at the same time Sheena managed to wrench the other one free.

"Get in! I'll launch," Nik said.

Sheena scrambled into her place in the front of the kayak and Nik bent, using all of his strength to propel the little boat out into the river. As his feet lost contact with the riverbed and he hurled himself over the end of the kayak, a spear caught him, embedding itself in his upper back.

White-hot pain blasted through Nik's body. He struggled to sit— struggled to lift the paddle that was tied to the body of the boat. Moving on pure adrenaline, he sliced the water with the paddle, biting a bloody gouge in his lip to keep from crying out in pain. Around them it rained spears. One thunked into the wooden side of the kayak. Another buried itself just behind Nik.

Ignoring the pain—ignoring the fact that he could feel the strength leaving him with the blood that was washing hot and fast down his body, Nik paddled.

Dimly, Nik realized that the rain of spears was no longer all around them, but instead was falling short. They'd been caught in the current, and it was pulling them swiftly out of reach. But Nik kept paddling. Even as his vision began to tunnel, growing dim and gray around the edges, Nik paddled.

"Nik, help me turn us! We're too close to the run-off!"

He was vaguely aware that Sheena was shouting at him—vaguely aware that the small boat had begun heaving and spinning. Blinking his eyes and trying to clear his vision, he was briefly able to focus on Sheena. She was turning to look back at him and her eyes were huge in her pale, tear-streaked face.

"I'm sorry," Nik tried to tell her, but he'd lost command of his words.

"We're going to capsize!" Sheena shouted over the roar of the rapids. "Try to hold on to the boat. We might make it if we stay with the boat."

The current spun them around again, causing the bow to tilt

sickeningly to the side. Before he went into the water Nik looked up to see that they were being sucked down into a narrow passage between the barely submerged metal arch of what once was the underbelly of the ruined bridge.

He lost sight of Sheena and Captain and the kayak immediately. The current propelled him violently forward, so that his body smashed against the metal truss. He screamed in agony as the tail of the spear snapped off, leaving the head still embedded in his back. The whirlpool captured him then, sucking him down.

He tried to hold his breath. He tried to fight the current, but an almost sweet lethargy began filling his body with the cold, black water. As blessed darkness finally claimed him, Nik's last thought wasn't of his mother—or of his father—or of his too brief life. His last thought was of the pup—his pup. *I'm sorry I let you down. I'm sorry I didn't find you. But I'm glad, so glad, that you won't die with me today.*

30

"Light the firepots! Gather the People! Our Champion brings sacrifice!" Iron Fist bellowed as the surviving Harvesters and Hunters entered the Temple courtyard.

From the ledge of the Reaper's balcony, Dead Eye saw Dove. She was standing there, just as she had been when he and the People had left to ambush the Others. He could see her taut, listening expression and it gave him a rush of pleasure to realize that she had been waiting, was still waiting, to hear his voice and to know he was safe.

"Dove! I bring sacrifice!" he called.

Her face—her beautiful, smooth, eyeless face—lit up with a smile that blazed as hot and fierce as the firepots of the God. "Our Champion returns! Gather in the courtyard so that the God may witness the sacrifice!"

He saw the hands of the women—young girls, actually—Dove had recruited to be her Attendants reach for and guide her from the ledge of the balcony. Eager to be near her again, Dead Eye hefted the Other more securely across his back and hurried forward.

"Erect the sacrificial scaffold!" Dead Eye commanded.

The Hunters and Harvesters returning from the ambush with him instantly began to obey, dragging the stained wooden platform from just inside the Temple to the soot-marked place in the center of the courtyard where not long ago he had built the pyre that had purified the Temple. Dead Eye nodded in pleasure as he examined the scaffold. Dove and her Attendants had done just as she'd said they would do. While he and the men were setting the ambush and battling the Others, they had scrubbed the old platform with water and then beeswax so that its wood gleamed with a rich rusted color that spoke of generations of bloodletting, and the iron circles glistened silver as the light of the brightly burning firepots.

When all had been made ready Dead Eye waited patiently, only moving forward to place the still unconscious Other on the scaffold when Dove finally appeared. She stood beneath the Reaper's balcony, looking serene and godlike, surrounded by a perfect dozen young women. They were all bare breasted, dressed only in long skirts decorated with the human hair of Others who had been sacrificed to the People throughout the ages. Dead Eye appreciated the picture they made, especially as a girl with no eyes had created it.

"Shackle him and then lift the scaffold!" Dead Eye ordered. As the People scrambled to do his bidding, Dead Eye went to Dove. Unlike within the Chamber she had not left for the sixteen winters of her life, Dove did not move with the independent confidence here that she did above. But when he offered her his arm, saying, "Oracle, may I lead you to the sacrifice?" she did not hesitate. She placed her soft, white hand on his thickly muscled forearm, allowing him to guide her forward to the steps of the scaffold. Together they climbed the four steps, stopping before the man who now hung, spread-eagle, from the T-shaped structure.

"Who has his canine?" Dead Eye asked the People.

"Here! He is here!" The People parted, allowing Iron Fist to make his way to the platform. He was holding the little black Terrier, who was bound and muzzled.

Dead Eye noted the intelligence in the animal's eyes, and that he did not struggle or whine. He simply stared at the unconscious man bound to the platform.

"Wake him!" Dead Eye commanded.

Two of the Harvesters came forward carrying rusted buckets filled with water, which they dumped on the man. Instantly, he sputtered and began to struggle, trying to break free of the iron circles that held his wrists and ankles.

"You will only damage yourself if you continue to struggle," Dead Eye told him.

The man stopped moving. He blinked hard several times, obviously clearing his vision. He glanced at Dead Eye, but his gaze didn't remain on him. It rested on Iron Fist and the canine in his arms.

"Do anything you want with me, but let Odysseus go." He growled the words from between clenched teeth.

"You are in no position to bargain," Dead Eye said.

"Of course I am, you mutant bastard. I know that you think living flesh has some kind of magickal property that will save you from your disgusting life, so you want me to stay alive as long as possible. I give you my oath that I will fight death, even as you flay the flesh from my body, but only after you let my Terrier go."

"If not you will what?" Dead Eye asked, honestly curious about what the angry man would say.

"Simple. I give up. I focus on the pain and the blood, and I will myself to die so that I can join Odysseus in the next world. Sooner rather than later." He finished, then he spat a glob of phlegm at Dead Eye's feet.

"Is this canine so important to you?" Dead Eye said.

The man's eyes flashed with barely controlled rage. "You seem to be leader of these mutants, so I'm going to assume you have more brains than they do and you know the importance of a bonded canine-Companion pair. So, yes, Odysseus is so important to me that I would make many sacrifices to save him."

"Interesting . . ." Dead Eye mused. Then he lowered his voice and whispered to Dove. "You were right, my precious one. We needed to capture the canine with the man. This will be perfect."

She smiled serenely and stroked his arm. "Continue with our plan, Champion. I will make sure the God is with you. The People will follow your lead—now and always." She turned to face the crowd that waited with almost palpable excitement. "This will not be the type of sacrifice you are used to, but the God has shown me what must be done to please Her, and your Champion will make it so."

There was a stirring among the People, and then the Harvesters dropped to their knees, followed by the Hunters, and finally the older men and women who had begun to emerge from the shadows surrounding the Temple.

"They show reverence," Dead Eye whispered to her.

She nodded almost imperceptibly, and then she lifted the ritual trident from its sheath at her slender waist and shouted, "Let the sacrifice begin!"

"Let the sacrifice begin!" the People echoed.

Dead Eye took the trident from her, bowing reverently to Dove. Then he motioned for Iron Fist to join him on the platform. Flanked by the Harvester who held the canine on one side, and the eyeless Oracle on the other, Dead Eye approached the bound man.

"I would have your name before I begin," Dead Eye said.

"Will you free Odysseus?"

"I will. You have my word that your canine will be allowed to leave the City alive."

The man seemed to deflate with relief. "My name is Thaddeus."

"Thaddeus, I am the Champion, and I honor you for what you will bring to my People." Then Dead Eye reached out, grasped the front of Thaddeus's soaked tunic, and ripped it from his body.

Dead Eye stared at the man's naked torso, hardly believing what he was seeing, and then he threw back his head and began to laugh. Behind him the People stirred restlessly, questioning murmurs spreading throughout the crowd. Dead Eye stepped aside, so that the People could get a clear view of Thaddeus. There were gasps of shock and cries of amazement as the People saw the cracked, shedding skin that decorated his arms and torso.

"He is one of us!" Dead Eye shouted, then he turned back to Thaddeus, who was watching him with hard, cold eyes. "So, you ate the meat of the stag." He hadn't framed the sentence as a question, but the Other answered anyway.

"I didn't eat it. Its blood got in my eyes and my mouth."

"Then your skin began to crack and shed," Dead Eye said, unable to stop smiling.

"Yes. Look, enough of this useless chitchat. Let Odysseus go and get on with it. I'm actually looking forward to getting this fucking disgusting skin off my body and being rid of this pain-in-the-ass world."

Dead Eye laughed again. "Oh, no! No! You misunderstand. I'm not going to kill you. I'm going to save you." He gestured at Iron Fist. "Bring the canine to me."

Iron Fist came to him, holding out the little Terrier. Dead Eye took the canine, flipped him over, so that his side and belly were exposed. With a motion so smooth and practiced that Odysseus did not begin to scream or struggle until the first strip of bloody flesh had been sliced cleanly from his body, Dead Eye made the first cut.

"No! Fucking stop hurting him, you bastard! You swore to let him go!" Thaddeus shrieked and struggled against his shackles.

"And I will keep my oath, but only after I complete the sacrifice." With the same dexterity, Dead Eye cut two more slender, bloody strips from the struggling canine, handing each to Dove, who held them reverently in her soft, white hands. Finally, he told Iron Fist, "Bind the canine's wounds."

Then he turned to Thaddeus, who was sobbing and shrieking with the same hysteria the canine had been showing.

"Ssssh," Dead Eye soothed. "Your Odysseus will recover. He has served my purpose. And you will recover, too." Then he took the ribbons of scarlet flesh from Dove, one at a time, carefully shaping them into smaller pieces before he began packing them into the angry cracks in Thaddeus's skin.

"What are you doing?" Thaddeus said between teeth gritted against anger and pain.

"Saving you," Dead Eye said.

Meticulously, Dead Eye packed each of the cracks in Thaddeus's skin with the Terrier's still warm flesh. When he was finished, Dove called her Attendants to wrap strips of cloth over the wounds, and then, once more, Dead Eye turned to face the People.

"Now you see what the God has shown Dove. Bring Thaddeus water and his canine. They are free to return to their city in the trees!" Dead Eye unshackled Thaddeus, so that the man slumped to the floor of the bloody platform. Iron Fist returned then with the bandaged Odysseus, whom Dead Eye took from the Harvester and gave to Thaddeus. The man clutched the little canine to his bloody chest, rocking back and forth and staring through pain-slitted, wary eyes at him.

There was a restless silence, and then one of the senior Hunters, a man known as Serpent, spoke. "Champion, we hear and will obey the will of the God, but we do not understand."

Dead Eye smiled, pleased that the People did not falter in their support for him, even though they did not share his vision.

"Because you are faithful, I will explain," Dead Eye said. He turned to Thaddeus. "Tell me, Thaddeus, what would the Others do if they knew about your cracked, shedding skin?"

Thaddeus's neck moved convulsively as he gulped the last of the water Dove's Attendants had brought him. He wiped his mouth with the back of his shaking hand and met Dead Eye's gaze over his Terrier's head.

"I don't know what the Tribe would do."

"Oh, come now. You can do better than that," Dead Eye said.

Thaddeus stared down at his canine. He drew a deep breath and when he looked up, his expression had completely changed—hardened—turned flat and angry. "They would isolate me. If they couldn't cure me they would put me and Odysseus to death."

Dead Eye nodded, satisfied. "Yes, because killing you would be what is best for the Others."

"That's how they would see it," Thaddeus said.

"But that is not how I see it," Dead Eye continued. "I do not believe you are sick. I believe you are changed, made better, and that once you understand exactly what you are becoming, you will shun any so-called *cure.* But that will be your decision and yours alone. Now you are free to go—to keep your secret."

"Why?" Thaddeus asked.

"Because the Reaper God commands it, and we do not question Her." Dead Eye tossed his tunic to the bloody man, saying, "Return Thaddeus and his Odysseus to the river and their boat. Set them free."

The People responded, surging onto the platform and helping Thaddeus to stand, then supporting him as they led him from the courtyard to begin the trek through the ruined heart of the City. He looked back only once, and that was to stare at the huge statue of the God as She loomed above them.

Dead Eye stroked a finger down Dove's smooth cheek. "That was even simpler than I expected. What a fortuitous surprise to see that he was already infected. And now it has truly been set to motion."

"It will be just as you said." Dove took his hand, guiding it to her waist and stepping eagerly within his arms.

"Yes, he is already filled with anger just as surely as he has been filled with the infection of this tainted City. Thaddeus will sow dissension and destruction throughout the Others, and when his poisonous fruit finally ripens we will Harvest a new City, a new life, a new world!" Dead Eye bent and captured her lips with his, and then, in perfect accord, the two of them went into their Temple where, surrounded by Dove's Assistants, they feasted and made merry.

3 1

Mari made her decision just after she woke. She was yawning and stretching and enjoying the warmth Rigel generated as he lay beside her on what used to be Leda's pallet. She was thinking about the fact that she really, *really* needed to do laundry, which wasn't something she'd ever looked forward to, and thinking of washing her dirty clothes led to thinking about washing in general. As Mari stretched again and began to climb over Rigel her hair flopped into her face—her dirty, stinking, disgusting hair.

Mari lifted the matted hunk and tried to comb through it with her fingers. Then she noticed the dirt under her fingernails—and on her hands—and her arms. Of their own accord her grim-colored hands lifted to touch her face. It was dirty. She knew that. Much of the makeup had worn off, but out of habit Mari stood, ready to head to the pot of clay and reapply it to conceal her features. While she was at it she thought she'd better boil up some more dye for her hair. She didn't need to look in the mirror to know that its true color was bleeding through the dirt and dye. Just the thought of spreading the vile mixture on her already stinking hair had Mari's shoulders slumping. It made her want to crawl back into bed and sleep forever.

It would be so wonderful if I didn't have to cover myself in clay and filth and dye.

Then Mari froze.

Why not quit all of the camouflaging? Why not just be herself?

Feeling the change within her, Rigel woke fully. He jumped off the pallet, stretched, and then padded to her, looking up with a funny, quizzical expression.

She grinned down at her Companion. "I covered how I look before because it was best for Mama and me. But Mom is gone. Sora's going to be Moon Woman. That means I'll never have to be accepted by the Clan—ever!" Rigel wagged his tail and barked in agreement. Mari poked her head out of the little room that had been her mother's and peeked at Sora, who seemed to be sound asleep. She turned back to Rigel. "Okay, then that's it. I've decided. No more dirt. No more dye. No more clay. I'm done pretending to be someone I'm not."

Humming to herself Mari searched for clean clothes. Then she went to the pantry and pulled out an entire bulb of soaproot. While she was there she fingered the knives resting on their pantry shelf and chose the sharpest of them all. Then she set about feeding herself and Rigel while she daydreamed about what it would be like to have her own skin and her own hair showing, with nothing covered or hidden or dyed.

It would be glorious!

Her mind made up, Mari went into the main room of the burrow and bumped Sora's leg—once, twice. The girl muttered and curled up in a ball, pulling her legs close to her. Mari sighed, went to the door, and retrieved her walking stick. Then, smiling mischievously, she poked Sora right in the butt.

Sora flailed her hand about as if trying to knock aside an insect, muttering, "Stop it."

"I'm going out and you should probably come with me."

Sora rolled over, peering through narrowed, sleepy eyes at her. "No. I should probably sleep. Go away."

Mari almost grabbed the pelt Sora had cocooned herself in and pulled her off the pallet, but thought better of it. *Just like Mama used to say—I need to use my brains before engaging my brawn.*

"Okay. Stay here. But later when you're complaining about the smell you'll be talking about yourself and not me."

Sora's gray eyes opened wider. "*You're* going to wash?"

"Don't sound so surprised."

Sora sat up. "Of course I sound surprised. I've never seen you clean."

"You've seen me clean plenty of times. You've just never seen my skin or my face or my hair free of what I've had to cover it with for most of my life to keep me safe. I'm not dirty, Sora. I'm different," Mari said.

Sora sniffed in her direction and then wrinkled her nose. "You smell dirty."

"My mother died. I've been in mourning."

"People in mourning don't bathe?" Sora tried unsuccessfully to stifle a giggle.

"Sora, you are not funny. Get up and come with me. I'm going to wash all this stuff off me, and I'm sorry to say it, but I need your help."

"Really?" Sora brushed back her hair and began to plait it into a thick braid.

Mari watched her deft fingers. "Really, and I need your help with my hair."

"Finally! I'm glad for you, Mari."

"Well, there's no reason for me to try to fit in with the Clan anymore, so there's no reason for me not to be myself." Mari wondered why speaking the words to Sora made her feel so hollow when she'd been thinking them for weeks with no remorse at all.

"You know it doesn't have to be like this. You and I could help each other out. A lot."

"How so?"

"Why not have two Moon Women in the Clan?" Sora said. "That means half the effort for both of us."

"No. I just said I'm going to be myself, and who I really am and the Clan do not mix," Mari said.

"It was just a thought."

"Are you coming with me to the bathing pool or not?"

"I'm coming—I'm coming." Sora got up and as if she'd been living there forever, she went to the herb bin and began filling her mug to brew her morning tea.

Mari sighed and sat on her mother's chair. "If you're using chamomile, you might as well make me a mug, too."

"Is there stew left, or did your creature devour it all?"

"Rigel prefers his rabbit uncooked so, yes, there is stew left. It's in the cauldron."

"Want some of it, too?" Sora asked, heaping chamomile into a second mug.

"No, we already ate. You sleep a lot," Mari said, rubbing Rigel's ears.

"I have a feeling I'm going to go out there and see that the sun has barely risen. That's *not* sleeping a lot. You wake up at an unnaturally early hour."

"That's what the rest of the Clan thinks of dawn, too, which is why I get up and go out then. Unless someone is lurking about—like you—trying to find me, I'm pretty much guaranteed that I won't see anyone from the Clan," Mari said.

"If there's anyone left to see," Sora said. "The screams were terrible yesterday—like they were killing somebody. Lots of somebodies."

"Another good reason to get up early," Mari said.

"No, another good reason that our Clan needs two Moon Women," Sora said.

"Leave it alone," Mari said. "Please."

Something in her eyes had Sora turning away and closing her mouth in a sad, thin line.

Mari sipped her tea silently while Sora finished breaking her fast, then they divided up the dirty clothes between them, grabbed their packs and their walking sticks, and began picking their way through the bramble thicket.

"Are we going the right way?" Sora asked.

"We're going the right way to the stream. It's in the opposite direction from the front of the burrow." Mari used her stick to lift another thick branch of knife-tipped thorns so that Rigel and Sora could come up beside her. "We're going to leave the brambles after this next turn, but stay right behind me. Don't touch anything—not until I tell you it's okay."

"Why? What's going on?"

"It's easier to show you than tell you." Mari followed another bend in the bramble maze and lifted aside a branch that looked like a thorned wall. She stepped out of the thicket into a low, scrubby dip in the land.

Sora swatted at a huge mosquito, grimacing at the spot of blood it left on her arm. "I don't see any stream. Just mosquitoes and a lot of mud and weeds in a grove of weird maple trees."

"That's all you're supposed to see. And the weeds aren't just weeds—same as the weird maples aren't trees. Look closer."

Sora sighed, but did as Mari told her. "Ugh! Those low vines that are *everywhere* are poison oak. And those bushes are stinging nettles. I've never seen them so big!" She squinted, studying the closest of the odd-looking plants with disproportionately large maple-shaped leaves. Then she cringed back with a grimace. "Sweet Mother Goddess, those aren't trees! They're devil's club! Touch their stalks or step on their shoots and you'll be covered in spiny thorns. This place is awful. I don't see a stream and I don't want to walk through that. Can't we go another way?"

"Your reaction is perfect. It's exactly why Mama and I have nurtured this particular thicket for as long as I can remember. Transplanting the devil's club was the hardest of everything, but this grove of them stops anyone from exploring this area. The stream runs just a little west of here, and the poison oak and nettles flourish all along it. There's only one safe way through all of this, so stay close."

"We have to go through this every time we go to the stream?"

"It's easy once you know the path. When you see the stream and the bathing pool you'll understand that it's worth it."

Mari picked her way easily around the devil's club, nettle bushes, and past—without touching—the mounds of poison oak, heading down to a wide, shallow stream. Its waters were swollen with spring rains, but clear and sparkling in the early-morning sunlight. Mari stepped into the stream, wincing a little as the cold water lapped around her calves.

"How are we going to bathe in this? It's way too shallow," Sora said.

"This isn't where we bathe, or at least not when we want to take a proper bath. This is mainly where we fill our water buckets. The pool is up there." Mari pointed. "It's fastest and safest to walk in the stream to it. That way you avoid all of that." Mari gestured to the spread of poisonous ivy and nettles that crowded each bank of the stream. "When you find the site for your own burrow you'll have to transplant some of these there, as well as the bramble and the devil's club, of course."

"How am I supposed to do that without sticking or poisoning myself?"

"You use gloves, common sense, and the power of the moon," Mari said, sounding eerily like her mother. "Come on. It's not far."

They didn't see sign of any living being except for lots of squawking jays and several gray squirrels who barked at Rigel and then disappeared into the trees.

"We'll have to check the snares later today. We're running low on meat," Mari said.

"I'm just glad I don't have to wade through another nettle patch to get to them," Sora said, scratching her leg and wincing. "I got too close to one of those bushes."

Mari was about to tell her that she'd get used to picking her way successfully through them when the sound of a waterfall carried to them. She picked up the pace, and soon they were standing below a triple waterfall and the clear, round pool into which it fed. Rigel ran to the pool, lapped up some of the sparkling water, and then he stretched out on a sun-kissed rock, sighed contentedly, and closed his eyes.

"Isn't he supposed to be on guard?" Sora asked.

"He can guard with his eyes closed. Try grabbing me, and see what he does," Mari said.

"Never mind, I'll take your word for it." Sora studied the cascading water and the waiting pool. "This is incredible. I had no idea it was here," she said.

"That's because up there our nice little stream is a frothing mess that cuts between a rocky gorge. It's almost impossible to reach the water for quite a ways because the sides of the gorge are so slick. A dam was formed, probably from a rock slide ages ago, and that's what made the series of waterfalls tame enough to form the pool and the spill-off that's our little stream. It can get crazy if it rains too much, especially in the spring, but the dam has always held, and even if it didn't the water would just flood the nettles and ivy, and once it receded again everything would grow right back." Mari trudged through the stream, heading to the lowest part of the pool. On a wide, flat rock she laid out her clean clothes and the soaproot bulb. "Bring the dirty clothes up here. We can soak them while we wash. It'll make it easier to get them clean, and if the morning stays nice we can dry them in no time on these rocks."

Sora joined her, following her lead as she dunked the dirty clothes in the shallow part of the pool. Then Mari pulled the little paring knife from her pack and handed it to Sora.

"I want you to cut my hair," she said.

Sora gave her a quizzical look. "Are you sure?"

"Look at it. It's disgusting. I want it off."

"How short?"

Mari thought for a moment, then she lifted her hand, placing it against her neck just below her jawline. "Here. Cut it to here."

"That's pretty short," Sora said.

"It'll grow. And this time it won't be matted with dye and dirt. Just do it," Mari said.

Sora shrugged. "Okay, it's your hair. Your really, really dirty hair." She made a face as she lifted the mass of it, held it like a tail, and started sawing through it.

Mari closed her eyes and ignored the pulling pain. When Sora was done Mari's hands went automatically to her hair. Her head felt light and strange, like she wasn't quite herself.

"I got it pretty even. It was actually easy to cut once I got rid of that matted mess. Go wash it. I want to see what it really looks like," Sora said.

Mari stood, stripped, tossed her dirty clothes in the soaking pile with the rest of them. Then she cut the soaproot and, taking a generous piece with her, headed out into the deep part of the pool.

She felt Sora's eyes on her back, but she didn't turn to face her until she could sit on the bottom of the pool and submerge up to her shoulders. Sora was still standing beside the pool.

"You're staring at me. It makes me uncomfortable," Mari said.

Sora blinked and Mari saw her cheeks flush pink before she turned away. "Sorry. It's just that your skin under your clothes is a different color."

"I already told you that," Mari said.

"Well, telling and seeing are different things. Plus, the sunlight is hitting you and those weird glowy patterns are showing."

Mari looked down at herself, seeing the delicate filigree patterns of the frond of the Mother Plant lift from deep under her skin. She held out her arm, marveling at the miracle that lived within her.

"Does it hurt?" Sora asked in a hushed voice.

"No, not at all." She looked from her arm to Sora. "I've never talked about it before, not even to Mama."

"Why not?"

"It made Mama nervous. She was always afraid someone would see me. I—I think she wanted to forget this part of me," Mari said, blinking against tears that had begun to pool in her eyes.

"Hey, Leda wasn't denying who you are," Sora said. "She was just keeping you safe."

Mari smiled tentatively at her. "Yeah, that's right. Thanks for reminding me."

"Any time, teacher."

Mari dunked under the water and came up sputtering and scrubbing with the sticky, frothy root. She closed her eyes and rubbed a big hunk of it between her hands, and then she washed her face—over and over. She worked from her face to her arms and hands, scrubbing off the layers of clay and dirt that had been concealing the true color of her skin. Lastly, Mari attacked her hair. She didn't count how many times she soaped it up, rinsed it, and repeated, but she didn't stop until it squeaked between her fingers and there were no more snarls in it. Shivering, she waded from the pool, heading to Rigel's sunny rock to dry.

Sora hadn't taken so long to wash herself, and was already dried and dressed, sitting comfortably on another wide, warm rock.

Mari didn't look at her until she was seated beside Rigel. She wasn't modest—that was foolish. As Leda had taught her—a naked body was nothing to be ashamed of. It was a gift from the Great Goddess, and whether short or tall, fat or thin, all bodies had merit. Mari waited to look at Sora because she couldn't guess what her reaction would be. No one except Leda had seen Mari bare skinned and clean haired. Ever. So she sat in the sun, soaking up the warmth of the light, feeling equal parts of excitement and nervousness.

"You're glowing again," Sora said. "And I'm not staring, but it's hard not to notice it."

Mari studied herself. Her naked skin was still pink from the scrubbing she'd just given it, but the flush was overshadowed by the golden glow that spread in a frondlike pattern all across her body. She looked up and met Sora's gaze.

"Your eyes are different, too. They're shining really bright and are the color of the sun in summer. Your creature's eyes are doing the same thing. I don't mean to offend you, but it's strange," Sora said. She paused and then added. "But your hair is nice. The color of wheat and curly. And your face is different, definitely not like someone from the Clan, but I will say I think you look a lot better clean."

"Thanks," Mari said. She ran her fingers through her hair, loving the soft bounciness of it. "It feels good."

"What's it feel like when the sun shines on you like that?" Sora asked slowly.

"Warm," Mari said. "Nice. It makes me feel like I could run all the way to the ocean and back without even breathing hard." Mari started to think about the fire that had coursed through her and set the forest ablaze, but her mind skittered away from that image. She couldn't think about that now. She'd think about that later—after she was more used to her new self.

"Maybe you can do that. Who knows what Companions can do?"

"I'm not a Companion," Mari said.

"Well, you sure don't look like an Earth Walker anymore."

Mari bit her lip. She didn't know what to say—she didn't know who, or what, she was becoming. Mari dressed silently, wishing she had answers to the questions that flooded her mind.

As the sun climbed in the clear sky, she and Sora got to work washing the clothes and laying them out on the sun-drenched rocks that surrounded the pool. When they'd finally finished, Sora yawned hugely, and Mari was just going to suggest they nap while they waited for the clothes to dry when Rigel, who had been napping lazily all morning, suddenly bounded over to her. He was whining and yipping as he paced restlessly back and forth, back and forth. Mari didn't need their bond to know that something had the young canine seriously agitated.

"What is it? Are there males coming? Or Companions? What?" Sora was scanning the forest around them, looking as if she was ready to sprint back to the burrow.

"It's not danger. He's not warning me. He's anxious, like it's hard for him to sit still."

Sora snorted and relaxed a little. "Well, maybe that's because he slept the morning away. I think he's actually a little lazy."

"He's young. Young canines sleep a lot," Mari said, though she had no idea whether it was true or not. Mari crouched in front of her pup. "What's wrong? What's bothering you?"

Rigel barked twice and sprinted several feet away, as if he was heading up the rocky climb to the top of the waterfall. He stopped there, looked back at Mari, whining pitifully.

"Looks like he wants you to go with him. Does he do this a lot?"

"No. I usually understand exactly what he's trying to tell me." Mari walked to Rigel, but the pup sprinted off again, this time actually climbing partway up the steep bank. There he stopped again, and barked at her. "All right, I'll follow you." Mari turned to Sora. "You can stay here, but I'd better see what he's trying to show me."

"I'm not staying here by myself. If I lose you there's no way I'll find that path back through those poison, sticking things—not to mention back to the burrow. Nope, where you go—I go."

"All right, well, the clothes need to dry anyway." Mari made an encouraging motion to Rigel. "Go on! I'll follow you."

Rigel scampered up the rocks easily. When he reached the top he stood near the edge, looking down at Mari and barking encouragement.

"Sssh! Not so much noise!" Mari told him, and the pup instantly stopped barking, though he did keep up a steady, plaintive whine.

"This better be good. Climbing up here is no easy thing," Sora said, panting behind Mari.

"He's never done this before. I don't know what he could want to show me," Mari said. Then, with a groan, she hefted herself over the top edge of the ridge. Offering Sora a hand, she helped her up.

They'd only taken a few breaths when Rigel dashed off again, whining and looking back at them. The girls followed, which set up a tedious pattern. The pup would wait for them to catch up with him, and almost catch their breaths, then he'd rush off, leaving them to come after him.

"How far do you think he's going to go?" Sora wiped sweat from her face and lifted her thick hair to fan her neck.

"I can't tell," Mari said, picking her way around rocks, careful to stay clear of the edge of the gorge and its slick sides. "But I can feel that his anxiousness is getting worse. I hope that means we're almost to whatever it is he wanted me to see."

"I hope so, too," Sora said. "At least the bank isn't so terrifying here. It's more like Crawfish Creek, except the current is wilder."

"Yeah, it's not hard to get down to the water along here. This is where Mama and I come to see what's washed up from the city."

"The city? Is that where this stream comes from?" Sora said.

"Yeah, this is one of the rapids that broke from the river that flows through it."

"You and Leda followed this to the city?"

"No! Mama never let me anywhere near that awful place. We only know it comes from there because things have washed downriver to us that had to come from the city—things like the iron cauldron we make the stew in. Mama and I found that a few winters ago, not far from here. And one time we—"

A flurry of barking cut off Mari's words. Rigel was out of sight, and she sprinted to catch up with him. When she got to the young pup he'd made his way down to the water and was barking riotously at a clump of debris that had gotten snagged on the skeleton of a felled tree.

"Rigel, shush! You're making too much noise, and I'm right here. What did you want to show me?"

The young canine shifted his body, giving Mari a better view of the pile of debris, and her breath caught in her throat. Snagged with the logs and vines and the usual spring run-off river junk was the body of a man.

"Tits of the Mother! It's a Companion!" Sora gasped from behind Mari.

Mari stepped closer, staring at the man's face. With a sick start, she recognized him. It was Nik! The Companion who had been tracking Rigel.

"He's dead," Sora said. "We should get his knife. See, there? It's belted to his waist. And let's look around. Maybe we can find something else that floated here with him."

Mari nodded. "Okay, yeah. Let's do this." It seemed grisly, but she had to agree with Sora. Wasn't that why Rigel led them to this body? Knives were precious, especially as this one looked to be an actual metal knife. His leather belt was worth taking, too. She glanced at his feet. Mari wouldn't strip him—she couldn't make herself do that—but she could take his boots. Mari steeled herself, ignoring the queasy feeling in her stomach, and bent for the knife, which was when Nik coughed, and with a pain-filled groan puked water down his shirt.

"Great Mother Goddess, he's alive!" Sora said, and then she fainted.

32

When the Companion vomited river water all down his shirt, Mari scrambled back, slipping on rocks to get away from him. He didn't open his eyes, though. He just lay there in a broken heap, breathing in short, shallow pants and trembling.

From the corner of her eyes Mari saw Sora stir. "Are you okay?" she asked, not taking her focus off the man.

Sora sat, rubbing her elbow. "What happened?"

"You fainted."

"I fainted?" Then her eyes flicked to the flotsam pile and the man and they widened. "Oh, Goddess. I didn't dream it. It's real and it's alive."

Rigel padded up to the Companion, whining softly.

"Rigel! Stay back!" Mari said, moving forward to grab the pup and pull him back.

The Companion opened his eyes. Mari watched him blink several times, as if he was having trouble focusing his vision, then he saw Rigel and his lips tilted up. "I found you." His voice was weak and it sounded as if he was speaking through gravel. He lifted his hand, reaching for Rigel. Pain flashed across his face, which blanched so white that it made his lips look blue. He squeezed his eyes closed and breathed in short, panting gasps. Rigel sat, looking back and forth between the Companion and Mari with a plaintive expression in his intelligent eyes.

"Kill him." Sora was standing beside Mari, staring at the wounded man with ferocious disgust. "He's hurt. He can't stop you. Take his knife and slit his throat."

"I can't do that," Mari said.

"Then I'll kill him." Sora started forward, but Mari snagged her wrist. "No, wait."

Sora stopped and cocked her head, studying Mari. "It's crueler to leave him here to suffer. Come sunset the roaches will find him. They'll eat him alive. It's a mercy to end him before they get him."

Mari moved past Sora and approached the man. Rigel was sitting beside him. She patted his head and murmured softly to her pup, not liking the anxiety that radiated from him. She studied his face. Yes, she was sure it was the Companion named Nik—the one who had been searching for Rigel. While his eyes were closed she reached out and took his knife. Slipping in and out of consciousness, he made no response.

"Is it metal?"

Mari passed the knife to Sora. "I don't know. You check."

"It is! And it's amazingly sharp. This is a really lucky find." Sora inhaled deeply and then let the breath out in a rush with her words. "Okay, I'll do it. I'll kill him." She moved around Mari, striding to the fallen man with a no-nonsense attitude.

Mari was going to stop her, but Rigel was faster. He stood between the man and Sora, then he backed a few steps and lay across the man's legs, baring his teeth threateningly at the girl.

"Your creature has lost his mind," Sora said as she stepped back several paces.

Mari went to Rigel, who whined piteously and thumped his tail, but he didn't move from his protective position across the man's legs. Mari crouched in front of Rigel and looked into his eyes. The young canine flooded her with emotions—anxiety, excitement, and worry—lots and lots of worry.

Mari cupped Rigel's face between her hands. "We shouldn't. Plus, he's in bad shape. He may die anyway."

Rigel whined again and licked her face. He didn't have to use words to communicate clearly with Mari, and she was growing more and more certain about why he'd led her here, and what he wanted her to do.

"All right. For you I'll check him out."

"What? Why would you do that?" Sora asked.

"Sora, by now you should know that I'd do anything for Rigel. He led me here. He won't let you kill this man. I don't think he could make it much clearer that he wants me to help. So *that's* why I'm going to examine him—for Rigel."

Rigel moved then, but only enough so that Mari could examine Nik, and he remained between Sora and the man, shooting Sora menacing looks whenever she moved.

Mari didn't see the spearhead at first. She only saw that Nik had a wicked gash on his head, which was spreading scarlet-colored water down his face and body. She took a quick inventory of his legs and arms. His right thigh was cut. But the wound was a simple tear. It would need stitching, but it appeared to be a simple laceration. His left shoulder had been battered terribly, and it was already purpling. It was as she was trying to lift him that she saw the extent of the shoulder injury.

"Oh, this is bad," Mari told Rigel. "Most of it has broken off, but the head of the spear is buried in the back of his shoulder."

"Most merciful thing you can do is to take this really sharp knife and slit his throat," Sora said.

Rigel growled at her.

"Tell your creature that I'm just being logical," Sora said.

"Yes, I know how tempting it is to think about biting her," Mari told Rigel. "But I can't handle two wounded people right now."

"Two wounded *people*? Mari, he's not a person. He's a Companion—our enemy. Do you think he would give a second thought to helping either of us if we'd washed up wounded by his bathing pool? And I'll answer that for you—NO. No, he wouldn't."

Mari squatted back on her heels and looked up at Sora. "I've seen this Companion before. He's been looking for Rigel."

"Great Goddess! That's even more reason to kill him," Sora said.

"He was there when Mama died," Mari said softly. "He was kind to her."

"Him? Are you sure?"

"I'm sure." Mari wiped away a tear. Then, decision made, she stood and brushed her hands on her pants. "Sora, I'm not going to kill him. You're not going to kill him. And we're not going to leave him out here to be eaten by the swarm."

"You can't be serious! Think logically. Where are you going to nurse him?"

"In my home, of course," Mari said.

"That's ludicrous! You can't bring a dying Companion into our home!"

"Sora, it's not *our* home. It's *my* home. Mine and Rigel's, and that's exactly where I'm going to bring him."

"Because he seemed to show some compassion for your dying mother and your crazy canine is attached to him? Don't you hear how ridiculous that sounds? Companions have tracked us, enslaved us, and killed us generation after generation. Letting this one into your home and your life is a mistake that could cost you—and me—*our* lives! I told you the Clan would accept you because of your talent, and I still believe they would. But I *know* what they'd do if they found out you saved a Companion. You have to know the stories, too, about how our ancestors tried to help them. Earth Walkers did a kind thing, and Companions repaid us with death and slavery."

"Sora, I'm half Companion. I've had questions my whole life that my mother could only guess at the answers to. This man—this Nik—he can answer my questions. All of my questions. So he's coming to the burrow and I'm going to heal him. If you don't like it then you can live somewhere else," Mari said.

"I don't have anywhere else to live, and you know it," Sora said.

"Then help me. I'll find out what I need to know from him and then I'll send him on his way," Mari said. "Please, Sora."

"And you don't expect that he'll bring down the force of his Tribe on us after you send him on his way?"

"I won't give him the opportunity. I won't let him know where the burrow is," Mari said stubbornly.

"How are you going to do that?"

"The same way Mama did when one of the Clan was so severely injured that she had to stay at our burrow to be nursed. It didn't happen often, but when it did Mama covered the woman's face and walked her around until her sense of direction was completely confused."

Sora chewed her bottom lip, staring at the still form of the wounded man. "I don't have much choice, do I?"

Mari sighed. "Sora, I'm sorry about this. I do understand that it's dangerous, but what I need from him outweighs the danger. Rigel knew it—that's why he led me here. I have to try to save him. I have to try to find out about the other part of me." Mari raised her newly washed arm. The delicate fernlike patterning wasn't glowing, but her skin was a tanned, sun-kissed color. "I don't even know why my skin glows sometimes in the sunlight—and then, like now, doesn't. I don't know how big Rigel is going to get or even exactly how I'm supposed to take care of him. I don't know who part of me is at all."

Sora met her eyes. "Is it that hard—that not knowing?"

"It's terrible. It makes me feel like I'm a stranger to myself."

"A stranger to yourself—that would be a terrible feeling. All right. I'll help you."

Mari smiled at Sora. "Thank you."

"You are welcome, teacher. What do we do first?"

"We get him back to the burrow."

"Only that?" Sora said sarcastically.

"Well, not only that. We need to drag him out of that water, stop the worst of those wounds from bleeding out, and get him dry and warm so that he doesn't die of hypothermia or shock before we can get him home."

"Okay, but if he wakes up and tries to attack us I say we drop him and run."

"Rigel won't let him attack us," Mari said.

"You mean *you*—Rigel won't let him attack *you*."

Mari's lips tilted up. "Actually, I meant us. Rigel will protect the both of us. Right, sweet boy?"

Rigel's tail thumped.

Sora grinned. "Huh. That's, well, that's nice to hear."

"Let's get him out of the water first, then we can run back to the pool and get some clean things to wrap him in—the clothes should be dry by now."

"How are we going to carry him back to the burrow?"

"On Mama's litter."

"He looks heavy," Sora said.

"Good thing we're strong," Mari said.

Sora frowned and said nothing.

"Okay, I'll take the front of him and you take his legs. Let's get him out of the water and onto that mossy area just over there. Then I'll see what I can do to get him ready to be carried home," Mari said. "Rigel, you need to move." The Shepherd obediently made way for her, moving over to sit beside Sora.

Mari went to the man and crouched beside him. "Nik, can you hear me?"

The man didn't stir.

"Nik?"

The man's eyelids fluttered, then opened. He stared at Mari. "Who, *what* are you?" Then he tried to sit up, but collapsed back on the flotsam with a painful groan.

"Don't try to sit up again. You've been hurt badly," she told him. "You are Nik, though, aren't you?"

His eyes didn't open, but he nodded weakly.

"Okay, well, Nik, who I am is Mari." She decided to ignore the *what are you* part of the question for now, adding, "And that's Sora. We're going to move you out of the water. It's going to hurt. Probably a lot." She paused and added. "Just stay still. I'll try to do this fast, but if I leave you in this water you're going to die."

Nik's eyes slit open again and he nodded painfully, whispering, "Okay."

"He's ready. Take his legs." Mari climbed onto the pile of dirty leaves and roots, bent, and put her hands under his shoulders—trying to avoid the spearhead. "Okay, lift!"

Nik cried out, but only once. Then his face went the white of dead fish bellies, and Mari was pretty sure he lost consciousness.

"Hurry! He passed out. Get him to that moss," Mari said, struggling with his weight. He was a lot taller than an Earth Walker male, and his muscles were long and lean rather than thick and squat—but he was definitely as heavy as any Clansman.

Once he was out of the water and on the bed of moss Mari worked quickly. "Give me his knife." She began cutting his pants to expose the wound in his leg and then ripped his shirt open. "I need you to run back down the path. I'm almost positive I saw yarrow just around that last bend. Pull a bunch of it and bring it back here. I'll have the strips of moss ready and can bind these wounds so that he won't bleed out while we transport him."

"Yarrow about this tall, right?" Sora raised her hand three feet from the ground. "It has lots of small white flowers, smells funny, and its leaves look like a miniature version of a maidenhair fern?"

"Yes, good," Mari said as she continued to work on Nik. "I saw a big bunch of it spilling out onto the path. Go get it. Fast!"

"I'll be right back." Sora hurried toward the path.

"Am I dead?"

Mari startled at the sound of his voice and her gaze flew to his. "No. Not yet you're not. Don't talk. Save your strength. I'm going to have to move you again, but I want to pack your wounds first."

"The pup—safe?"

"Yes. Rigel's safe."

"Rigel?"

Mari nodded. "That's his name."

"You're his Companion."

He didn't phrase it as a question, but Mari was quick to answer, "I am his Companion."

And then Rigel was there, putting his head between them and sniffing Nik's face. The wounded man smiled weakly. "Glad he didn't die."

"Well, he's the reason you're not dead. You can thank him later—if you're still alive," Mari said.

She shooed Rigel out of the way, but the pup only moved a short distance, and lay down by Nik's feet, watching Mari intently. She wondered at Rigel's devotion to this man who obviously knew her pup—who had probably lived with him in their elaborate city in the trees—and she felt the sharp sting of jealousy. Was she going to lose Rigel to him? Would her Shepherd want to return to his Tribe and live the life they'd planned for him?

Mari stared down at the moss. Her hands stilled and she felt as if her heart was breaking.

Rigel moved then, coming quickly to her side. He leaned against her, looking up at Mari and nuzzling her with his muzzle as he filled her with love—unending, unconditional love. Mari threw her arms around his neck and buried her face in his warm, soft fur. "I'm sorry. I won't doubt you again. I'm sorry."

"Ugh, I'd forgotten how much yarrow stinks!" Sora said, then she frowned. "I thought we were in a hurry, so I *ran* back here, and I do not like running, to find you hugging the creature. Doesn't seem like you're doing much hurrying."

"Just give me the plants and keep gathering hunks of this moss. Oh, and he's awake. Sort of. Don't let that surprise you."

"After today I don't think there's anything left that could surprise me."

Mari smiled grimly at Sora and then began chewing a hunk of yarrow leaf. She spit the leaf mash into her hand and then pressed it to the weeping wounds, motioning for Sora to follow behind her and pack moss over the yarrow. Nik didn't open his eyes, nor did he make a sound until Mari lifted him to reach the spear wound, then he moaned and his eyes fluttered open.

Mari shook her head at the wound, and spoke more to herself than to him or Sora. "I can't care for this properly until we get him back to the burrow. I take this spearhead out now and he's going to bleed too much. It'll have to be cauterized."

"What are you going to do about it until then? It looks terrible, all bloody and swollen and disgusting. I'll bet that river water didn't help it at all," Sora said.

"No, it didn't. It's going to have to be cleaned and watched carefully, even after I cauterize it. But right now I'm just going to pack it with yarrow and moss. Gotta get him out of here. The more time that goes by since the spear struck him, the worse it's going to be getting it out and the worse the infection could be."

Mari chewed the last of the yarrow, spit it around the bloody spearhead, and packed moss over it, laying him back down on the bed of moss. She stood and went to the river to wash her hands.

"What now?" Sora asked.

"Now Rigel is going to stay with him while you bring back dry clothes. Make him as comfortable as you can," Mari said.

"And where are you going to be?"

"At the burrow getting Mama's litter. I'll be back as soon as I can." Mari squatted beside Rigel. "Stay here. Watch him and don't bite Sora." Mari glanced at the girl and added, "And if Nik wakes up and tries to hurt Sora, *bite him*."

"Really?" Sora grinned.

Mari smiled back at her. "Really. But don't get too excited. I'm pretty sure Nik can't even sit up, let alone attack you."

"Well, it's a nice sentiment anyway." Sora reached over and tentatively patted Rigel on the head. Once. The pup's tail thumped the ground. Once.

Mari crouched beside Rigel. "Watch Nik and Sora, but if anyone comes, you *hide*." She stared into Rigel's eyes, sketching pictures in her mind to illustrate what she needed him to do—and not to do. The young canine wagged his tail and made generally agreeable noises, sending soothing, warm feelings to her. "Okay, I believe you. I'll be back soon. Real soon. And I love you." Mari kissed him and then sprinted past Sora, calling, "Come on!"

She stayed ahead of Sora on the way back to the bathing pools, which wasn't difficult to do. The girl seemed to have no stamina at all.

"Don't you ever do anything physical?" Mari asked as Sora stumbled down the bank and bent over, gulping air.

"Not—if—I—can—help—it!" she gasped between breaths.

"Take these to him." Mari tossed one of her oldest tunics and a sleep dress to Sora. "Rub him dry with the tunic, but stay away from those wounds. Then cover him with the shift. I'll meet you back there with the litter and something to, hopefully, make him sleep until we get him to the burrow."

"Wait, we're carrying him on a litter all the way back?" Sora glanced pointedly behind them at the steep rocks that led up to the path. "Down that?"

Mari smiled. "Well, it's better than having to carry him *up* that." Without waiting for Sora's response, she finished gathering the clean clothes and then jogged for home.

33

All the way back to the burrow Mari sifted through her mind, trying to recall everything Leda had taught her about caring for someone as badly injured as Nik. The spearhead stuck in his back was going to be tricky. It made Mari feel queasy just thinking about what she was going to have to do—pull it out—wash it out—and then use one of Leda's cautery rods to burn the bleeding veins and kill whatever terrible infection might have already settled within the wound.

That was bad, but not as bad as an internal injury would be. Her mama had called internal injuries the silent death. Mari knew how to check for them—she'd given Nik a cursory once-over and hadn't seen any sign of internal bleeding. "But I'm not a real Healer. I could have missed something." Mari chastised herself as she came to the bramble thicket, grabbed her walking stick, and quickly traversed the maze that led to the burrow.

Mari tried to shake off her fear and her feelings of inadequacy. Moving with much more confidence than she felt, she went to her mother's medical pantry and began choosing carefully while she recounted aloud what she needed so that she wouldn't forget anything.

"Valerian root to, hopefully, help him pass out on the trip here." Mari began quickly brewing a thick, strong tea that she would pack in the medicinal skin and carry back to Nik. "A blanket and ropes—need to tie him to the litter so we can slide him down those rocks." Mari paused and shook her head, muttering to herself. "That's going to hurt." She went back to the medicinal pantry and stood there staring, feeling helpless, and missing Leda with such force that it almost knocked her to her knees. She wanted to give in to the despair. She wanted to curl up within herself and cry and cry and cry . . .

But she couldn't. No one would save her. No one would help her, or Rigel, or Sora, or even the Companion, Nik. *Think, Mari! Mama was a great teacher. She taught you everything you need to know—now you just have to remember.*

And then, feeling foolish and very young, Mari turned from the medical pantry and rushed to the lovingly carved wooden chest that sat at the end of her mother's sleeping pallet, and had been passed down from one Moon Woman to another for more generations than even Leda could remember. Mari paused. She hadn't opened the chest since Leda's death. Slowly, she lifted the lid and breathed deeply of the fine rosemary scent that would, for the rest of her life, remind Mari of her mother.

Sitting atop neatly folded blankets and winter clothes was her mother's Healer's journal. She touched it gently, feeling the texture of its aged cover with the tips of her fingers. All children of the Clan were taught to read and write and to discover their individual talents as they grew and matured. Clanswomen encouraged creativity and hard work, and whenever a child displayed a particular talent—like for poetry, carpentry, hunting, weaving, or dyeing—that child was given further instruction, even if it meant fostering them with a neighboring Clan. But from birth the daughters of Moon Women were trained differently. They were nurtured specially by their mothers because in their future they could hold the key to the Clan's health, sanity, and, ultimately, the Clan's history recorded in their Healer's journals.

"Mama's journal—Mama's magickal journal," Mari murmured. "No matter how many times you explained to me that your journal wasn't full of fantastical stories, but of nothing more, or less, than the truth of the Clan, I always thought of it as your special magick." She opened it, and it fell to a page that was marked by the brilliant blue feather of a jay. Mari's trembling fingers traced Leda's familiar handwriting.

"Mari, my sweet girl, do your best, but don't second-guess yourself. Indecision is as deadly as not doing anything. If you believe in yourself half as much as I believe in you, all will be well. I love you."

For just a moment it was as if Leda was there with her, standing beside her, lending Mari confidence through the strength of the belief she always had in her beloved daughter. Mari hugged the journal to her. Then she wiped her eyes, collected herself, reopened the book, and began to thumb through the pages.

The Skin Stealers led Thaddeus through their ruined City at a pace that had him struggling to carry Odysseus and keep up with them. Then a very strange thing began to happen. About the time the waterfront came into view, it seemed to Thaddeus that he found his second wind. Suddenly Odysseus didn't feel heavy. The pain and burning that had been his secret companion for the weeks since the stag's blood had soaked into his body from his eyes and mouth stopped.

Just like that. As it had begun—the pain ended.

Thaddeus drew a deep, pain-free breath and in that breath he smelled something. A lot of somethings. He could smell the water, though it was barely close enough to see. He smelled something sharp and dirty—and at the edge of his vision he saw a rodent the size of a rabbit dart from one of the ruined buildings to another.

I smelled the rodent! How the hell did I do that?

He caught the scent of something sweet and fragrant when the wind changed direction. It seemed like jasmine, but he saw none in the vines around him. Then they turned the corner, and another. He almost missed it because it was so damn small. Just two little vines being choked out by ivy, but the two vines together had four small white flowers.

I smelled jasmine well before I should have, even if it had been a huge, blooming bush and not four tiny, wilting flowers. What is happening to me?

"This way. We beached the little boat down there." The Skin Stealer called Iron Fist pointed at the river.

Thaddeus nodded and changed direction to where he was pointing. The Skin Stealers moved in almost complete silence. All of them wore only pants made of roughly tanned animal skins. Their heads were shaved and their bare torsos were painted with strange splashes of lines and symbols that decorated their arms, chest, and even necks and heads. As Thaddeus studied them he noticed that all of the designs were re-peated in threes—like the triple tip of the huge spear the statue of their God carried. There were only men in the party that surrounded him, but he would not soon forget the women that had stood watching him on the scaffold, silent and strangely alluring. The oddest of all of them had been the eyeless girl who was obviously mated to their Cham-pion. The caverns that should have been her eyes would haunt his future dreams as surely as would the memory of her nubile breasts, full lips, and the thick fall of glossy brown hair that brushed the slender curve of her waist.

"There. Your boat is there." Iron Fist had come to a halt at the top of the bank that led down to the river.

Thaddeus nodded and began to pick his way carefully down the bank, holding his wounded Terrier close. He reached the kayak easily, as he moved much more quickly than he'd realized. He looked back then, not sure what he was supposed to say to the Skin Stealers—almost expecting them to change their mind at the end and pull him back through their dead City to the bloody scaffold.

They were gone.

Thaddeus didn't pause to wonder. He hurried to the kayak, settling Odysseus as comfortably as possible in the belly of the boat, broke off the one ballast that had made it through the battle, took the paddle that was still tied to the rear seat, and with a mighty push launched it from the bank, jumping in with an athletic ease that seemed remarkably Terrier-like.

He bent to work, paddling against the current. At first he was wor-ried that he wouldn't be strong enough to guide the kayak past the bridge debris and run-offs, but Thaddeus soon realized that he was beyond strong enough. He paddled the kayak with ease. It shot down the river as if a team of Hunters propelled it forward.

Surely this is just adrenaline. Surely as soon as my body realizes we escaped it will wear off.

But it didn't. Thaddeus was filled with a tightly wound strength that mirrored the anger that seemed ever present within him. It didn't fade. It didn't wear off. It only increased.

Odysseus whined plaintively, and Thaddeus paused a moment to stroke the little Terrier, murmuring reassurances. As he did so, Thaddeus looked down at his arm. At his wrist and elbow creases the bandages had dried. Slowly, he unwrapped the cloth from around his wrist.

The wound had already begun to heal. It was closing around the strip of flesh the Champion had cut from Odysseus. Old, dead skin was sloughing from around it. Thaddeus brushed at it in disgust, and it shed from him, revealing healthy, pink skin beneath. Thaddeus stared, enthralled by what he was seeing. With hands that shook with haste, he unwrapped the next bandage around his elbow. It was the same there! His cracked skin was mending, absorbing Odysseus's flesh, and the infected skin was shedding from him.

Thaddeus lifted his arm, flexing it, feeling powerful and whole.

"Cure me? No. I don't need a damn cure. I don't need a damn cure at all." Thaddeus bent to pick up the paddle again, thinking, *The Champion was right. I'm not sick. I'm changed. And I like it. I like it a lot.*

When Mari finally made it back to Rigel and Sora and Nik she was sweating and thoroughly tired of trying to maneuver the light, but ungainly, litter. With a relieved sigh, she put the litter and Leda's well-worn medicine satchel down close to where Nik was lying, and then went over to Rigel, telling him how brave and good he was to have kept watch.

"You know, I was watching, too," Sora said.

"Thank you," Mari said. Then she grinned at Sora. "Do you want me to pet you?"

Sora giggled. "I think you should save your energy for him."

"Is he conscious?" Mari asked as she knelt beside Nik.

Sora shrugged. "I don't know. He was awake while I was drying him and covering him up with your shift—which is, by the way, entirely too small for him. But he didn't say anything except to groan a little. He opened his eyes a few times since, but all he did was stare at your creature."

Mari pressed her fingers to Nik's wrist, finding his pulse easily. It was strong, but faster than she'd like it to be, and his skin felt cold and clammy. She was about to call his name when he opened his eyes.

"Gray," he said softly, his voice sounding as if he wasn't quite awake. "Your eyes are gray."

"How are you doing, Nik?" She ignored his comment about her eyes.

"Been better," he said. "Back hurts. Skin Stealer's spear got me."

"I see that. I brought you something for the pain. Drink this and it'll help." Mari nodded at Sora. "Lift his shoulders a little so that he can drink, but be careful of that spear wound." While Sora held him Mari put the skin to his lips.

Nik looked at her, hesitating. Then his lips curved up slightly. "Easier ways to kill me than poison."

"I voted for slitting your throat with your very sharp knife, but Mari and her creature outvoted me," Sora said.

"Ignore her," Mari said. "I mostly do."

As Nik drank his eyes smiled up at Mari. When the skin was empty, she helped Sora lay him gently down.

"All right, I'm going to get you ready to be moved while that tea's working," Mari said.

"Moved?" Nik said.

"Can't stay here. The swarm will eat you," Sora said. "Not that I think that's a bad thing, but again, I've been outvoted."

"I'm taking you to my burrow—my home," Mari said. "It's not far from here, but that doesn't mean it's going to be an easy trip. We're up high, and to get you home we have to go down low."

"How?" Nik asked.

Mari cut her eyes at the litter she'd put beside him. "Well, I'm going to strap you to that, and then Sora and I are going to carry and, possibly, drag you down there."

"Sounds like it's going to hurt," Nik said.

"Oh, it's going to hurt for sure. A lot," Sora said gleefully.

"You'll be fine once the tea starts working. Let me know when you feel numb."

"Why?" Nik asked.

Mari frowned at him, wondering if she'd underestimated the severity of his head injury. "Because I don't want to jostle you around until the painkiller starts working."

"No, I mean why are you saving me instead of killing me?"

"That was my vote," Sora said.

Mari sent her a *shut up* look, and then faced Nik. "I'm not a killer."

"Don't have to be a killer. You could leave me here to die."

"Let's just say Rigel wouldn't like it if you died, and right now that's good enough reason to at least attempt to save you," Mari said. Then she motioned for Sora to follow her to the litter. She started to go through the hemp ropes, and rummaged through the satchel to find a biting stick. Sora followed her, peering over her shoulder. "First, we're going to slide him onto the litter." Mari spoke softly for Sora's ears alone. "Then we need to tie him to it—securely. He can't fall out when we lift him down the waterfall."

"Why don't we just put him in the litter and float him to the waterfall. Actually, we could float him *over* the waterfall. If he lives it'll be the Goddess's will. If he doesn't," she shrugged, "then it's not Her will that he lives and he dies."

"No to the floating, but only because I don't think he can tolerate the cold of the water again. And I'm not going to talk about sending him over the waterfall because it would definitely kill him, which I don't think is a sign from the Goddess. I think She's too busy to worry about one half-dead Companion and a couple almost Moon Women." Mari rolled her eyes and shook her head. "It would be more helpful if you actually *helped*."

"All right. I'm sorry. I was just teasing. Mostly. Tell me what to do."

Mari glanced back at Nik. "How are you feeling now?"

He looked at her, his moss green eyes looking unfocused and glassy. "Ssssleepy."

"Good. Sora and I are going to get you on this litter. We're going to tie you down so you don't fall off. We'll be as gentle and quick as possible, but, well . . ."

"Let'ssss hope I passss out?" Nik slurred.

"I'm counting on it," Mari muttered. She moved the litter so that it butted up to Nik's body, then she motioned for Sora to take his legs. "On three lift and slide him over. One, two, three!" Nik closed his eyes and moaned, but Mari was quick about it and set to using the woven ropes to tie him securely to the litter.

When he was tied as tightly as she and Sora could manage, Mari knelt beside him. "Nik?"

His eyes fluttered and then slitted open. "Are we there yet?" He spoke as if his tongue was too big for his mouth.

"No. Uh, not yet. But we will be pretty soon. I need you to bite down on this. It's willow bark, so besides not letting you bite through your tongue it'll help with the pain. I also need to wrap this around your eyes." Mari pulled a strip of bandaging from her pocket.

"Why cover my eyes?"

"Because I'll heal you, but I won't let you see where I live. Do you understand?"

Nik nodded weakly. "You're really sssssmart—not like an overgrown child at all."

Mari frowned at him.

"That's a weird thing to say," Sora said, peeking over her shoulder at Nik.

He started to answer, but Mari shut him up by putting the stick to his mouth. Obediently, he opened and then bit down on it. Then she quickly tied the cloth around his head and over his eyes.

"All set, Nik?"

He nodded again.

"Okay, good. Sora, I'll lead. Let me know when you need to rest, but don't make it too often," Mari told Sora.

"What if I get tired often?"

"Look at the sky," Mari said.

Questioningly, Sora glanced upward, then looked back at Mari.

"Where's the sun?" Mari prompted her.

"Oh, Great Goddess! It's moving down the sky. If we get caught outside at dusk with him, his blood will bring roaches, and beetles, wolf spiders, and—"

"And that's why you're not going to rest often," Mari said. She took hold of her end of the litter, telling Sora, "Remember to lift with your legs."

Mari would never forget that terrible journey back to the burrow, though out of it came two promises she made to herself. The first was that she was going to figure out how to get Sora into decent shape. The girl was all curves and softness with, Mari was sure, not one single muscle beneath her smooth facade.

The second promise she made to herself was to simplify her life—no Sora. No Nik the Companion. No nothing that would cause stress and confusion and angst. She was going to patch Nik up—get answers to her questions—send him on his way. Then she was going to be sure Sora could call down the moon—and send her on her way as well. *Then* she and Rigel were going to find some much deserved peace.

"I can't," Sora gasped, dropping the foot end of the litter and causing Nik to groan through the biting stick—again. "I'm sorry, but I can't carry him any farther."

Behind her, Rigel whined softly. More carefully than Sora, Mari put her end of the litter down and caressed the pup, reassuring him wordlessly that they were almost safe—almost home.

Mari looked at Sora, assessing the truthfulness of whether her energy was really spent or not. The girl was dripping sweat. Her thick, dark hair was plastered to her face and neck. Her arms were shaking and her breath was coming in gasps.

Thankfully, she'd dropped the litter just before the entrance to the bramble thicket. More carefully, Mari bent to speak to Nik. "Do you think you can walk? It's not far now."

He was so pale and still that with half of his face covered Mari wondered for a moment if he'd died during the last part of the trip. She was reaching to check his pulse when he mumbled, "Don't know."

"Well, you're going to have to try. Sora, get my stick. I'll help Nik walk. You'll have to listen to my directions, and we'll get through the brambles. I hope."

"Anything to be able to sit down and rest and have a nice cup of tea," Sora said.

Mari almost told her that resting wasn't going to be on the agenda for either of them that night, but when she met Sora's gray gaze and saw the honest exhaustion there, she thought better of it. Instead she smiled and said, "You've done a really good job helping me. We're almost there. Sit over there near the entrance and out of the poison oak. Rest while I untie him."

Sora nodded wearily and dropped to her butt. Mari worked the knots undone quickly. Then, murmuring encouragement to the semiconscious man, Mari draped his arm around her shoulders as she grasped him around the waist.

"Once you're inside turn immediately to your left. When you lift up the first branch you'll see the path. Follow it about ten paces, then it'll look like it turns to the left again, but it won't. It dead-ends into more brambles. Instead, go to the right."

"Okay," Sora said, reluctantly stepping into the brambles.

"Nik, lean on me. We're walking now."

It was harder than Mari had thought it would be. Nik kept stumbling and swaying. Mari was positive he almost passed out a couple of times, but she kept talking to him, and calling directions to Sora and, to her surprise, they actually made it to the door of the burrow with only a few scratches.

"Where are you putting him?" Sora asked as she collapsed in front of the hearth, poking the fire tiredly so that it flamed to life.

"On my bed. He needs to be close to the fire."

"I thought that was my bed now," Sora said.

"You sleep in Leda's bed. I'll make up a pallet for myself by the hearth. He's going to need tending all night." *And I need to be sure he doesn't wake and try to find his way out of here,* Mari added silently to herself. She guided Nik to the narrow pallet she'd slept on for most of her life. With a long sigh he lay back. "I'm going to take the blindfold off now," she told him. She unwrapped the cloth, and he blinked blearily up at her.

"Where am I?"

"Home. Well, my home. Rest while I get things ready to take care of that wound in your back." Mari went to Sora. "Start boiling water."

"Oh, Goddess, yes! Time for tea."

"Not really. It's time for tea for him. You and I are going to have to wait. I have to get that spear out of his back."

Sora frowned and her shoulders drooped in disappointment, but she filled the pot with fresh water and hung it over the hearth to boil. Mari hurried to her mother's pantry. She'd left the medical journal there, with the pages marked that held the instructions she needed to follow. Working quickly and with growing confidence Mari retrieved her mother's cautery rods from the chest, as well as several lengths of clean bandages and the little wooden box that held Leda's porcupine quill needles and rabbit gut thread she'd used to stitch wounds. Then she went to the basket filled with goldenseal root and carried the root, the cautery irons, and three large bowls to Sora.

"Cut three thumb-sized portions of this root and muddle them with some hot water, one piece for each bowl. Then fill the bowls with boiling water and submerge these irons in the biggest one of the three."

"Why?" Sora asked.

"The root is goldenseal. It gets rid of infection. The irons are for cauterizing his wound after I take the spear out, so they need to be as clean as possible. I'm going to wash my hands thoroughly in the mixture once it cools enough to touch and you're going to wash your hands in one of the other bowls. The third one is for rinsing his wound after the spear is out.

Be sure you refill the water in the pot and keep it boiling, though. I'm going to put together something for you to steep for him—something stronger than the valerian tea I gave him before." Mari lowered her voice. "It should knock him out, but I don't know how long he'll stay out, so we're going to have to work fast."

"We?" Sora whispered.

"Do you still want to be a Moon Woman?"

"Of course," Sora said.

"Then it's *we*," Mari said.

"Okay, that's logical, but I'm going to heat up some stew. We need to eat so that we're as alert as possible." Sora glanced questioningly at Nik, who was unconscious again.

"No, he doesn't need to eat now. He'll more than likely puke it up. He will need a broth, though, for later, which you can also make for him. Pick the meat off the last of the rabbit bones and—"

"Stop. Cooking I understand. You worry about him. I'll worry about feeding all of us."

"Thank you, that's a help." Mari sent Sora a grateful smile. Then she stood, brushed her hands on her tunic, and hurried back to the medical pantry to gather the precious glass bottle filled with the liquid Leda kept on supply for emergencies. Made from the juice of a poppy, it was a powerful potion. Mari reread Leda's instructions about dosage, and then decided how much to add to the cannabis tea that her mother's journal said should be brewed for antinausea, antianxiety, and pain relief.

"That should knock him out," she said to herself. "If it doesn't kill him." Then she gathered more bandages, and flipped to the entry in her mother's journal about a particularly deep puncture wound she'd cared for several winters before. Leda had taken meticulous notes about the cautery, what she did directly afterward, and how she packed the wound with a poultice made of honey, witch hazel, sage, and calendula flowers. Mari smiled at her mama's final note: *Wound healed nicely—no infection—thank the Great Earth Mother and the power of positive thinking!*

Trying to only think positively, Mari gathered honey, witch hazel, sage, and calendula flowers. Putting generous portions of each in the bottom of her mother's largest stone muddling bowl, she returned to the main room of the burrow while she mixed all of the ingredients together.

"His tea's ready, and I added the boiling water to the three bowls with the goldenroot stuff," Sora said.

"Golden*seal* stuff," Mari corrected, sounding exactly like her mother. "I'll take the tea. Keep muddling this mixture for me." She paused and then added, "Please."

"I'd be happy to." Sora gave her a tired smile. "Here's his tea. Give it to him then come back here and sit down for a moment and eat your bowl of stew."

Mari nodded her thanks and then went to Nik. His eyes opened as she called his name and sat beside him on the pallet. "Drink this. It tastes terrible, but it's going to make you sleep. While you're asleep I'm going to get that spear out of your back and sew you up."

"Good thing I'll be asleep." His eyes were clearer than they'd been since they'd left the river, and he was able to lift himself up enough to gulp the bitter mixture. He lay heavily back on the pallet, but when Mari stood he reached out with surprising strength and grabbed her hand. "Could the pup come over here to me? Just until I sleep?"

Mari didn't answer him. Instead she stared down at her hand trapped within his. After a breath, he let go of her.

"Rigel can sit with you," she said. Mari glanced at her pup. He was lying in his usual place in front of the door. She noticed that his big wooden food bowl was near him, looking recently licked clean. Mari looked questioningly at Sora.

"Yes. I fed your creature while you were taking care of the other male creature in our burrow," Sora said. "I knew you wouldn't let us eat until he'd eaten. I mean the canine, not the man."

"Huh," Mari said, too surprised to formulate a real response. Then she turned back to Rigel and made a slight nod of her head. Instantly he padded to her. Mari hugged him and buried her face in the thick, soft scruff around his neck, borrowing strength and security from him. She kissed his nose. He wagged his tail and licked her before going to the pallet and curling up beside it. Mari watched Nik's hand drop until it touched Rigel. Eyes closed, he slowly stroked the young canine.

Mari joined Sora at the hearth. The girl handed her a bowl. "Thank you," she said. They ate silently and ravenously. Halfway through the bowl of stew Mari glanced at Sora. "And thank you for feeding Rigel."

"You are welcome. I'm just glad he didn't take a bite out of me instead of the rabbit."

"I'm glad, too," Mari said, and with a jolt of surprise she realized she really was glad Rigel hadn't taken a bite out of Sora. "I'm going to need your help with what comes next, and it's going to be a lot harder than carrying him here was."

Sora held Mari's gaze. "Well, then, I guess it's a good thing that I'm here to help."

"Yeah," Mari heard herself admitting the surprising truth. "I guess it is a good thing you're here after all."

34

Sora poked Nik's shoulder hard with the tip of her finger—once, twice, three times. The man didn't stir. She looked up to meet Mari's gaze. "He's gone. Completely."

Mari nodded grimly. "Okay, then we need to work fast. Help me turn him on his side so that we can slide the mat under him." Together Sora and Mari took one of Leda's woven mats that she'd used for everything from something to sit on when they picnicked to protection from the rain and wind when they had to hunt and gather during bad weather. "Let's roll him onto his belly, and I think it would be a good idea to tie his arms and legs down. If he wakes up while I'm cauterizing the wound he could cause a lot of damage to himself if he doesn't hold still."

"Tying him up sounds good to me," Sora said.

"You do that and I'll start washing my hands. You need to join me as soon as he's secured." Mari went to the bowl filled with the hot goldenseal water, took the irons out and put then carefully in the fire, and then she began to wash her hands, remembering what her mother had told her over and over—*Sweet girl, wash your hands until you think they're clean, and then double it and wash them again. Don't forget under your fingernails.*

Sora joined her, and Mari poured some of the hot water into another bowl, telling her, "Wash them a lot longer than you imagine you'd need to, and don't forget under your fingernails." Mari smiled secretly to herself. Hearing the echo of Leda in her words had begun to reassure her more than make her sad. It was as if her mama was still there, in the burrow, watching and loving her.

"All washed. Now what?" Sora said, hands on hips looking at Nik.

Mari had already laid out the needles, gut thread, her mother's smallest, sharpest knife, and bandages. While she'd placed them near the pallet, Mari had named them for Sora and explained what they were used for. The girl had listened to her attentively, which had helped calm Mari's nerves, though she felt as if she should have waited on eating the stew as her stomach was rumbling dangerously already.

"Now you're going to sit at his head and hold his shoulders. When I ask for something give it to me as quickly as you can."

"What if he starts moving? Do I let him go to get something for you, or keep ahold of him?"

"That depends on what I'm doing. If I have a knife, hot rod, or a needle in his flesh—hold him. Anything else you can let him go."

"Got it."

"Are you ready?" Mari asked.

"Are you?"

"Absolutely. Couldn't be more ready. I'm going to start now," Mari said, standing by Nik and staring down at him.

"You can do this."

Mari blinked in surprise, and met Sora's gaze. "Are you sure?"

"Yes. I'm sure," Sora said with no hesitation. "You're a Moon Woman, daughter of generations of Moon Women. I don't think there is anything you can't do."

"Thank you, Sora." Mari blinked away unexpected tears, and then, buoyed by Sora's belief in her, she sat beside Nik on the pallet and began unpacking his wound.

"That looks bad," Sora said when the moss and yarrow were cleaned from the area.

"That's why we needed to hurry. It's already so swollen that I may have to cut him to get the spearhead out of there." Mari drew a deep breath, reminding herself that he wasn't going to feel a thing—until afterward—if she hurried. So Mari hurried.

At first she was tentative, but the spearhead was lodged in there around a lot of swollen, bloody flesh, and being gentle was getting her nowhere except in a mess of more swollen, bloody flesh.

"Give me the knife!"

Sora handed it to her. Mari cut around one side of the piece of iron, slid her fingers down the bleeding skin, and managed to hook them around the spearhead. With a grunt she pulled, and the nasty, triple-pointed thing came free with a sickeningly wet sound.

"Goldenseal water and bandages, quick!"

Sora handed her one, and then the other. Mari rinsed and rinsed and rinsed the wound, being careful to watch from where the worst of the bleeding was seeping. Her mother's notes had been clear on that. She had to know where the bleeders were to burn them closed.

"Okay, now I need the medium-sized rod. Be sure you wrap the end in cloth before you grab it. Those things get really hot."

Sora nodded, and rushed to the hearth, coming back holding the glowing rod gingerly through a swatch of what Mari thought might be one of her clean shirts.

"Now I need you to wash the wound out one more time, press a bandage to it, hard, and when I tell you take it off and grab his shoulders. If he's going to wake up, it'll probably be now."

Sora poured the yellow disinfecting water on the wound, and then just as Mari had instructed, held pressure on it, watching Mari closely.

Mari didn't hesitate. She was afraid to—afraid if she hesitated at all she would give up.

"Now!"

Sora lifted the bandage and, before the wound could fill with blood again, Mari pressed the glowing cautery rod against the area of the worst bleeding.

A guttural scream was torn from Nik, and Sora held him firmly down. Within moments his body sagged into unconsciousness again.

"Get me the other one. The smaller one," Mari said, breathing a sigh of relief and brushing her sweat-dampened hair out of her face with the back of her forearm. Sora quickly offered the other rod to her, and Mari exchanged it for the cooling one, pressing the newly glowing head against the other bleeders.

Nik's body jerked then, but spasmodically, an automatic response to the cauterizing. He made no sound and as soon as Mari took the iron from the wound his body stilled again.

"Bring me the poultice," Mari said.

Sora gave her the wooden bowl in which they had muddled her mother's concoction of honey, witch hazel, sage, and calendula flowers. Mari had added some of the goldenseal root to it because she was so worried about infection. Working quickly, she packed the cauterized wound with the sticky, fragrant mixture.

"Okay, now I just have to sew it up."

Sora handed her a threaded needle, and Mari set to work stitching up the wound. She was surprised how little it bothered her to sew flesh. She had, of course, watched Leda do it countless times, but she had only practiced on dead rabbits and pelts. *I'm good at this,* Mari realized with a happy little jolt of surprise. *I'm really good at this.*

Together Mari and Sora wrapped the sutured wound carefully with clean bandages before laying him on his back and moving to his leg wound. Mari had already decided against stitching up the head wound. Once it had quit bleeding she'd realized that it hadn't been as bad as all the blood had made it appear. But the leg wound was something else.

"That's really deep," Sora said, moving to hold Nik's ankles, though he remained unconscious and still.

"Yeah, I'm going to clean it out and pack some of the leftover poultice I used in his back in it before I sew it up. But it worries me almost as much as his back."

Mari set to work, and time seemed to pause. She was so focused, so in a little bubble of concentration, that she didn't notice Sora's growing agitation until her hands were trembling so hard that she made Nik's legs shake.

"Sora, you have to hold still. I can't—" Mari glanced up. Sora's face was pale with pain, which contrasted eerily with the silver flush that was spreading across her skin.

"I'm sorry. I've been trying to fight it, but—"

"It's not your fault. Go. You need the moonlight. Go now."

"But you need my help," Sora spoke through teeth she'd gritted together against pain.

"I need you to be whole and not filled with pain and depressed."

"I think I'm going to be sick." Sora pressed a silver-tinged hand over her mouth.

"Go on. You need to get outside in the moonlight." Mari glanced at the pup, who had taken his spot in front of the door. Hands pressed against Nik's leg wound, she shifted her concentration, imagining her young canine finding his way through the maze of brambles with Sora following him. "Rigel, lead Sora above."

"But he won't!" Sora said.

"Of course he will." Mari turned back to sewing the nasty leg wound, sparing only one small glance at her pup as Sora opened the door for him and he went out, then turned and waited for the girl to follow. *Thank you—you're so smart and handsome and brave and kind. Thank you, Rigel!* Mari sent the thought, along with a wave of love, to her Shepherd. Then, knowing Rigel wouldn't let her down, she bent over Nik's leg and resumed her work.

"That went better than I expected," Mari said. Sora and Rigel had returned in time to help Mari bandage the newly sewn leg wound. They'd arranged Nik as comfortably as possible, half on his side, half on his back. And after putting the instruments in a goldenseal bath and gathering the bloody bandages, the two women were finally taking a moment to relax by the hearth, sipping tea and staring at the still body of their patient.

"Me, too. I thought for sure he'd wake up and thrash around," Sora said. "What was in that tea you gave him?"

"Poppy juice and cannabis." She glanced at Sora and felt herself smiling. "I wish I could take some myself right about now."

"Ha! Usually I would encourage you to make yourself a lovely sleeping potion, and then drag him out of here while you're unconscious, but I'm so proud of all of that work we just did that I don't think I could make myself do anything to mess it up."

"Well, that's encouraging," Mari said, and she meant it. Then she drew a long breath and turned to face Sora. "You did a good job tonight. I appreciate your help."

"Thank you!" Sora said, obviously surprised by Mari's compliment.

But Mari wasn't through. "You're going to make an excellent Moon Woman."

Sora's face flushed pink. "That—that means a lot to me—you saying that." Then, almost shyly, she added, "You reminded me of Leda tonight. She would have been proud of you."

Mari smiled. "She wouldn't have let you kill Nik either."

"I realize that. Still, I would have recommended that she slit his throat."

"I'm sure you would have, and Mama would have given you a lecture on kindness and humanity that would have blistered your ears."

Sora's gaze drifted back to Nik. "I don't doubt that at all." She turned back to Mari. "It'll never work."

"It might work. If I can stay ahead of the infection I'm pretty sure he'll heal. Well, that and if he doesn't have a deadly internal injury that I've missed."

"No, I don't mean that. I mean Earth Walkers and Companions will never coexist in peace. *That* will never work. There's too much pain, too much violence between us. How could you ever trust them?"

"Mama and a Companion fell in love. They made me. They wanted to coexist in peace," Mari said.

"And your father was killed for it. Mari, you can't have both. You can't be an Earth Walker and a Companion."

Mari's gaze went to Rigel, who was lying beside Nik's pallet sleeping soundly.

"But that's what I am—half one and half the other," Mari said.

"You're going to have to choose which world is yours," Sora said.

Still looking at Rigel, Mari said, "I made my choice when Rigel found me."

"No, just because you have a canine doesn't mean you have to live like a Companion. You can be part of the Clan. Mari, I believe they'll accept you—as you are—because of your talents."

Mari snorted. "You're going to be their Moon Woman, not me."

"But you could be, too! I'm not just talking about your Moon Woman talents. If you don't want to draw down the moon, then fine—don't draw down the moon. There's a lot more to you than that. Your sketches are beautiful. You're a gifted Healer, really you are. And even though you can be grumpy, you're an excellent teacher. The Clan values all of those talents. I think they'll overlook the fact that you're part Companion and you have that creature if you share your talents with them. It's not like it's your fault, and with both of your parents gone there really isn't anyone left to banish."

Mari sipped her tea, considering.

Nik moaned, and Mari was on her feet instantly. "Sora, strain that mixture I've been brewing and bring it to me as soon as it's cooled down enough to drink." She went to Nik's bedside and put a gentle hand on his shoulder. "Nik, you have to try to be as still as possible. The spearhead is out, and I've sewed up your wounds, but you could break them open and restart the bleeding if you move too much."

He turned his head and his bleary eyes met hers. "Hurts like a fire in my back."

"I know. I'm sorry." Sora hurried to her, handing her the wooden mug of pungent-smelling tea. "Drink this. It'll help."

Sora had to help Mari lift Nik, and he choked, coughing and sputtering, but he drank the entire mug. Then he collapsed back, moaning with pain.

"Thirsty," Nik said weakly.

"I'll refill this with water." Sora took the mug and went to the drinking bucket, returning in a moment and handing it to Mari. Again, they held Nik so that he could drink. Afterward, they settled him as comfortably as possible.

Mari watched the herbs begin to take affect as the tension in his body relaxed. Just before his breathing deepened into sleep, Nik's hand reached down to find Rigel. With a sigh of contentment, he fell asleep touching the pup.

"Does that bother you?" Sora spoke softly as she poured the fragrant chamomile and lavender tea she'd been brewing for them, and sat with her feet curled comfortably beneath her in what was becoming her usual place beside the hearth.

"Does what bother me?"

"That he's obviously obsessed with your creature."

"You know, you could call him Rigel. It is his name," Mari said.

"I could, but Creature is growing on me." Rigel pricked his ears at Sora, and the girl grinned. "I think it's growing on him, too."

"How do you know that's not his *I want to eat her* look?" Mari teased.

"Because he didn't show me those horrible teeth of his. And you didn't answer my question."

"Rigel and I are bonded for life. Nothing and no one can change that. I know that much from what my father told Mama, and Mama told me. The rest I know from here." Mari touched her chest, just over her heart. "And here." She moved her hand from her heart to her head. "So, I'm not bothered as in jealous. I'm bothered because of the obsession itself."

"I knew we should have killed him."

"You may be right," Mari said.

"What? Did you actually admit I'm right?"

"Don't get all excited. It's just this once that you *might* be right," Mari teased, smiling so that her words held no sting before she continued. "The truth is we won't know if we made a colossal mistake in saving him until after he's healed and gone."

"Are you sorry we didn't kill him?"

Mari considered before she answered. Finally deciding, "No. I'm not sorry about that. Sora, I've watched Companions kill our people with less thought than I give to gutting a rabbit. Even if my choice to save Nik was wrong, what wasn't wrong was to value life more than they do."

"If we act like them, we're no better than them," Sora said slowly. "I agree with you in theory, I just hope you're right in practice. Our Clan can't take much more."

Mari sighed. "I miss Jenna."

"I know you two were close."

Mari nodded. "I saw them take her. Sora, Nik was part of that hunting group, which has me thinking . . ."

Sora's brows shot up, and when Mari didn't continue, she prodded, "What are you thinking?"

"I'm thinking one favor should lead to another."

35

Had it not been for the fire in his back, Nik would have been sure he was dead and had been sentenced to a particularly bizarre level of hell. From the moment he'd regained consciousness after the river vomited him from the rapids onto the pile of flotsam, his world had become a decidedly strange place.

At first it seemed too dreamlike to be true. The pup found him! Along with a Scratcher female who wanted to kill him, and the pup—his name was Rigel—Rigel's Companion, a girl named Mari.

Mari was also too dreamlike to be true. At first glance she looked like she could belong to the Tribe. She was tall and slender. Her sun-colored hair was cut short so that it curled, childlike, around her face. But it was her face that gave her away. Her features weren't all Tribe-like. She did have the fine, high cheekbones and full, bow-shaped lips of the Tribe, but her eyes were wrong. They were bigger and almost almond-shaped. And the color was all wrong. Instead of any of the varying shades of green that marked a member of the Tribe, they were a gray so bright and clear that they were almost silver.

Her eyes reminded him of something, but that something kept skittering away from Nik's pain-fogged mind.

Though Nik drifted in and out of consciousness while the two women transported him from the river to their home, he was aware of the tension between them—and of the fact that Mari was definitely in charge.

After they reached their home, which they called a burrow, Nik's memory faltered like a half-remembered childhood incident where you're not really sure if you actually experienced the incident, or if you just "remembered" it because of being told the story over and over again.

It couldn't be possible that Scratchers had saved him.

It couldn't be possible that they had carried him on a litter to the neat, attractive little burrow they called home, removed the spearhead from his back, and tended to all of his wounds.

It couldn't be possible, and yet there he was, finally fully awake on a comfortable pallet in an underground burrow with the half-grown Shepherd pup he'd spent weeks searching for lying within his reach, and that pup's Companion, who was also a Scratcher, dozing by the homey warmth of a hearth fire.

"And yet here I am," Nik whispered to himself.

The pup lifted his head to look at him. Nik smiled and stroked his soft fur, not caring that the movement sent shards of pain through his back.

"Are you really awake?"

Nik looked from the pup to the girl. She rubbed her eyes sleepily and stretched before she poked the fire into life and ladled more water into a pot to boil.

"Yes, I think I am. Unless you tell me I'm dreaming," Nik said.

"You're not dreaming. How are you feeling?"

"I'm feeling confused," Nik said honestly.

She cocked her head as she studied at him. Her eyes seemed to smile, but her expression remained serious. "Confused isn't bad. I'd expected you to say something more like 'I'm in agony,' or ask me if you're dead for about the hundredth time."

"Well, my back hurts. So do my leg and my head. But my confusion is bigger than my hurts. Um, I have you to thank for that."

"For being confused?"

"Yes and no. You are the reason I'm confused, but I have to thank you for helping me," Nik said.

"You're welcome," she said.

"Is your name really Mari?"

"Yes."

"I thought so. But remembering yesterday is a little like trying to recall a dream. Well, a nightmare if I'm going to be completely honest," Nik said.

"Yesterday?"

"Yeah, when you pulled me out of the run-off and brought me here."

She poured the steaming water into a stone bowl and swirled it around before saying, "The yesterday you're remembering happened five yesterdays ago."

Nik felt a sizzle of shock. "I've been here five days?"

"Actually, you're heading into day seven. Dawn isn't too far away," she said.

"I don't feel like I've been unconscious for almost seven days," he said.

"You haven't been—not completely. You've been in and out of consciousness, mostly because you had a fever. But that's broken now. You did a lot of talking about someone named O'Bryan."

"He's my cousin and my best friend," Nik said.

"Your fever self was worried about him."

"My awake self is worried about him, too. He was wounded not long ago."

"You were talking to your father, too."

"What did I say?" Nik asked, feeling strangely violated and curious at the same time.

She shrugged. "It was pretty difficult to understand you, but I could make out the words father and O'Bryan."

"Father probably thinks I'm dead." Nik spoke more to himself than to her.

"You're healing well. I'm especially pleased that you're fully conscious. Finally. You'll be back with your father soon." She lifted the stone bowl and poured the steaming mixture within through a delicate cloth and into a large wooden mug. Then she brought the mug to him. "Drink this. It'll take the edge off your pain."

"Can you help me sit up first?"

She nodded and he leaned on her while she arranged pillows behind him to prop him up. When he lay back again, Nik was shocked to realize that just that small exertion left him panting and weak with pain radiating from the wound in his back.

"Drink the tea," she repeated, handing it to him.

Still Nik hesitated. "It'll make me sleep again, won't it?"

"You should hope so," she said.

He put it on the ledge beside him. "Can we talk a little first?"

She lifted her shoulders. "It's your pain—so it's your decision."

"Mari, where am I?"

"You're in my burrow—my home."

"Where's the other girl who was here before? There was a girl with you, wasn't there?"

"You mean Sora. Yes, she was here. She's outside right now, but she'll be back soon."

"She wanted to kill me?" Nik said.

The smile in Mari's gray eyes briefly reached her lips. "Yes, she did. Well, she probably still does, but she won't."

"Why not?"

"She'd say because I won't let her, but the truth is because it would be inhumane to kill you, and we aren't inhumane," she said, meeting his gaze steadily, almost as if her words were meant to challenge him.

"But she's a Scratcher!"

"Don't call her that. Don't ever use that word around me," Mari snapped at him, her gray eyes flashing with anger. "We're Earth Walkers. If you're going to call us something, even after you get back to your people, call us that."

"But the pup chose you, which means you are definitely not a—"

"I am!" Mari interrupted. "I'm an Earth Walker, just like my mother before me was an Earth Walker, and her mother before her."

Reacting to her agitation, Rigel padded over to the girl. She had returned to her place by the hearth, and the young Shepherd leaned against her, gazing up at her with adoration. And all the puzzle pieces fell into place.

It was her! She's the girl on fire. And she has bonded with the pup, just as Father and I guessed. Nik studied Mari while she murmured softly to the canine and began brewing tea for herself.

Was he remembering wrong what she'd looked like that day she'd set the fire, or had she changed drastically? No, he hadn't been wrong. He hadn't needed to see her up close to know that she'd looked like any other Scratcher female. Her hair had been long and dark, and her features had been unrefined.

What had happened to change that, or was he truly stuck in a nightmare and going mad because of it? Nik decided there was only one way to know for sure. He blurted, "Did you set that fire in the forest the day that old woman fell and broke her neck?"

"She wasn't old." Mari's voice had lost all emotion.

"I'm sorry. I didn't mean to be insulting," Nik said, choosing his words carefully. "That was you, though, wasn't it?"

"It was me," she said. "The woman's name was Leda. She was my mother."

The truth of it settled through Nik's blood. That was what had been familiar to Nik—the girl's eyes! They were the same color as the woman's who had died. Mari was truly a half-breed—the child of a Companion and a Scratcher—or rather an Earth Walker, Nik corrected himself silently. He met her gaze. "I'm sorry about your mother."

"So am I," she said.

"I didn't mean for it to happen. It was an accident."

"I know. I was there." She paused and then added, "I saw you go to her. Did she say anything to you before she died?"

"She called me Galen. She—she thought he'd come back for her," Nik said.

Mari looked away, blinking rapidly. Before she spoke she cleared her throat, though her voice was still rough with emotion. "Galen was my father's name."

"He was one of the Tribe—a Companion," Nik said.

Mari met his eyes again. "Yes, he was. And you killed him for loving my mother."

"Mari, I didn't kill him," Nik said.

"What are you doing out here in our territory, Nik?"

Nik hesitated, but the decision wasn't difficult to make. He didn't want to lie, and this girl—this part Companion, part Earth Walker girl who had saved his life—deserved better than a web of lies and half-truths. His father would agree with him, even if no one else in the Tribe would. So he'd tell her the truth—or as much of it as he could—but he needed information in return.

"I'll answer any questions you have for me, but I need something from you in return," Nik said.

Her brows went up. "That's a pretty arrogant thing to say to the girl who just saved your life."

Nik sighed and then grimaced at the pain the movement caused and shifted restlessly trying to find a more comfortable position. Finally, he said, "I didn't mean it to sound arrogant. I know I'm in your debt. But I think you can imagine that I have questions for you, too."

Mari nodded her head slightly. "Yeah, I can imagine that. Fine. I'll trade you question for question. What do you want to know?"

"Why aren't you childlike or filled with melancholy? Why are you and Sora normal?"

Mari blinked in surprise, and then laughed—heartily and loudly—causing Rigel to jump and bark with joy around her. She had to settle the pup and wipe her eyes before she answered him, and when she finally did her gray eyes still sparkled with suppressed amusement.

"Sorry about that. It's just that thinking of Sora and me as *normal* is actually pretty funny."

"So the rest of the Scra—um—I mean Earth Walker females are depressed and listless, even catatonic?"

"No, of course not. But Sora and I are, well," she hesitated, obviously choosing her words carefully. "I suppose the best way to describe what we are is to call us Healers. And there is usually only one Healer per Earth Walker Clan."

"That's why you're unusual? Because there are two of you for your Clan?" he asked.

"Kind of. There was only one Healer for our Clan, and she was my mother. She died without having fully trained an apprentice. You could say that Sora and I are working together to try to take Mama's place—and neither of us knows as much as we should. That's unusual because Healers usually only have one apprentice."

"I'm still alive, so it seems to me that you're doing well," Nik said.

"I'm doing my best, and that isn't as good as Mama, but it's all I can do," she said.

"I'm sorry, I'm still confused. You're talking with me normally, as if you're just another member of the Tribe. And I don't remember all that happened during the past several days, but I think I would have remembered if Sora was mortally depressed. All I remember is her being angry and wanting to kill me."

"That sums up how Sora feels about you. And, nope, she's not depressed."

"But why not?" Nik flung out his hands and then had to freeze, squeeze his eyes shut, and breathe through a wave of pain and nausea. When he opened his eyes, Mari was beside his pallet, peering down at him with concern.

"I think you should drink the tea and quit moving around. Seven days ago you came very close to dying," she said.

"I will, but this is important." He hated how weak his voice sounded. "Could I have a drink of water?"

Mari went to the drinking bucket, filled a wooden mug, and brought it back to him.

"Thank you." He drank deeply before he continued. "Here's why I'm so confused. The only, ur, Earth Walkers I've known couldn't carry on an intelligent conversation because of their depression. They're also childlike in their inability to care for themselves. Or, if they were men, they actively tried to kill me, and I don't mean like Sora who said she wanted to kill me, but didn't actually attack. So, why? Why are you two different? And look at this burrow! It's lovely. The art is incredible. Who did it? Are all your homes like this?"

She met his eyes and shook her head, sending him an incredulous look. "First, that's way more than one question. Second, let me guess— the only Earth Walkers you've known, except for Sora and me, were your prisoners."

"Well, yes. I mean, they were all on Farm Island," Nik said, feeling very uncomfortable, and this time not from his wounds.

"Farm Island? That's what you call the place where you hold our people in slavery?"

"They—um—work for us there. Yes."

"No, Nik. If they *worked* for you they could leave at any time. But if they try to leave, *your people kill them*. Holding people against their will and forcing them to work for you is slavery."

Nik didn't look away from her angry gray gaze. "You're right. Yes. Farm Island is where we keep the women who tend our fields. They're all depressed. So depressed that they eventually just lie down and die. But they're not like you. They don't—"

"They would be like me if they were free again!" The words seemed to explode from Mari's mouth. "We can't be caged. It kills us. Your people kill us. Why would our men not attack you on sight? They're protecting us, just like Xander did Jenna when your group captured her. You killed him for it, and he was her father."

"I—I know." Nik couldn't continue to meet Mari's eyes. "I was with her that night. She's like you. She actually talked with me."

Mari rounded on him. "Have you seen Jenna since you captured her?"

"No. My job isn't to tend the Farm or the Scratchers, ur, I mean Earth Walkers. I'm really a Carver. I—"

"Go see Jenna after I get done saving your life and return you to your Tribe. I promise you she'll be depressed and seem vacant in her mind. She's a slave, and it will end up killing her just as surely as you killed her father. Do you know how old she is?"

"No, I don't."

"She's only known sixteen winters. Sixteen," Mari said.

"I'm—I'm sorry," Nik said.

"Being sorry won't save Jenna from dying from despair. Being sorry won't bring Jenna's father back. It's my turn to ask the questions now. What were you doing in our territory?"

"I wasn't wounded in your territory. I was part of a foraging team to Port City. We were ambushed by Skin Stealers. I don't know if any of the others made it back to the Tribe. I was caught in a run-off after taking a spear." Nik paused as images of Crystal and Grace flashed through his memory.

"Not then. Before, when you were with the Hunters. The night you captured Jenna and the next day when Mama died. Why were you in our territory then?"

"I was tracking Rigel." At the sound of his name, the young canine's ears pricked up and he cocked his head, listening to Nik. Nik mentally shook himself, pushing aside thoughts of those who had been lost during the ambush. Later—he'd deal with all of that later—if this girl actually let him return to the Tribe. If he actually lived.

"That's what I thought," Mari said.

"You covered your tracks—his and yours—trying to throw us off your trail. Didn't you?" Nik asked.

"Yes, Mama and I covered Rigel's tracks and ours. That's why we went back to the creek that day."

There was an awkward silence as the realization hovered between them that because he had been tracking the pup, Mari had lost her mother. Feeling miserably guilty, Nik tried to change the subject. "Rigel looks good—really good."

That had Mari's expression changing, almost warming. "Do you really think so? I never know for sure how much or what to feed him. And his fur—it's so thick and it gets everywhere. I worry that I'm doing something wrong because it's started to shed off him in hunks."

Nik chuckled, and then had to grit his teeth against a stabbing pain in his back. Sweat broke out over his body, and he thought he might be sick. Mari was beside him in a moment, lifting the mug of drugged tea to his lips. He shook his head.

"Not yet. There—there are more questions. I'm okay. It hurts, but it's nice to actually be able to think." He hesitated, and then added. "Could I maybe have something to eat?"

"I'll heat up some broth for you, but you need to drink the tea soon. If you don't stay ahead of the pain you're going to regret it," Mari said.

Nik nodded. "Just a little while more."

She went back to the hearth, and changed out the boiling pot for a small skillet that was black with age. As she stirred it, the mouthwatering scents of meat and garlic and onions drifted to him, making Nik swallow thickly and try to sit up a little straighter.

"The shedding is normal, especially around the change in seasons. You're not doing anything wrong. We use small fishbone combs to groom the Shepherds, and they need to be groomed daily. What are you feeding him?"

"Rabbit mostly."

"Feed it to him raw, that's what's best for a canine. Add any raw eggs you can find, shell and all, as well as leafy greens. Add apples, carrots, and celery when you can. And don't feed him as much as he'll eat. Some of the big Shepherds will eat themselves to death if you let them, and he's from a long line of very big Shepherds who are very big eaters." Nik grinned at the pup, who was splitting his attention between Mari and him. "The general rule of canine health is that you should see the indentation of his ribs, but not each rib individually. Rigel's looking in good flesh—not over or under fed."

"You know his mother and father?"

"Of course! His mother is Jasmine. She's almost completely black and is as big as many male Shepherds. His father is Laru. I know Laru very well."

"Is Laru big, too?"

Nik's grin grew. "He's the biggest Shepherd in the Tribe. His Companion is my father."

"Your father! So that's why you kept tracking Rigel."

Nik opened his mouth and then closed it, not sure what, or how much he should say to this strange girl. When he looked at her again, Nik saw that Mari had quit stirring the broth and was watching him carefully.

"That's not why I kept tracking Rigel," Nik heard himself admitting. "I wouldn't stop tracking him because . . ." He trailed off, unable to admit the embarrassing truth.

"You don't have a canine, do you?"

"No. I don't," Nik said.

Mari's brows shot up. "Oh! You wanted Rigel to choose you."

Nik hesitated, and then blurted, "Yes, I did. It was my fault he got away that night. Almost everyone in the Tribe thought I was crazy for believing he could live through the bloody beetles and the roach swarm, but I never gave up on him."

"He was hurt badly when he showed up here," Mari said.

Nik blinked in surprise. "So, he did track you all the way to your home?"

"He did." She caressed the young canine as his tail thumped against the floor of the burrow. "And then Mama and I healed him."

"Has your family always been Healers?" Nik was asking as the door to the burrow opened and the other young woman rushed inside.

"Don't tell him anything about us," she snapped, sending him a glare. "Mari, I did it! The fern is alive!"

Mari's face split into a wide grin that made her gray eyes sparkle and two little dimples appear in her cheeks. "That's awesome! And now you're ready for the next step."

"People?"

Mari nodded. "People."

"Sora, I'd like to thank you, too." Nik said. "For saving me."

The Scratcher sent him a dark look. "I didn't save you. Mari saved you. I was just helping her." She turned to Mari. "Let me know when he passes out again and I'll come out and have dinner with you." Then she disappeared into the back of the burrow.

Into another awkward silence Nik said, "Yes, I remembered correctly. That one wanted to kill me. Are you sisters?"

"Like I told you before, that one's name is Sora. No, we're not sisters." After a pause Mari added. "We're friends."

"She doesn't seem very friendly."

"Actually, she's a lot friendlier than me. She just doesn't trust you." Mari poured the broth from the skillet into a small wooden bowl and brought it to him.

"Thank you," he said, then all of his attention went to sipping the delicious liquid and the warmth it spread throughout his battered body. It seemed as if the broth was gone in no time, and Nik leaned back carefully, feeling full and exhausted.

"Now this." Mari handed him the cooled tea, which he finally took, gulping the bitter mixture quickly. "Okay, before you fall asleep again I need to change your bandages."

Grunting, Nik rolled a little on his side, giving Mari access to his back. He gritted his teeth, steeling himself for more pain, but her touch was amazingly gentle and he felt little except a tug on the skin around the bandage.

"No, no, no. That's not supposed to be happening."

"What?" Nik tried to twist his head around, but a sharp look from Mari had him holding still and asking into the pillow. "What's not supposed to be happening?"

"It was healing well—really well. No sign of infection except for your fever, which broke earlier today. But now the flesh around the wound is discolored, dusky even, like it's dirty. But it couldn't be. And there are small, raised black spots that look like scabs attached to the wound."

"Does it have a scent?" Nik's stomach felt hollow. Sweat had begun to bead his face.

He felt Mari lean down. She sniffed at the wound, and then he heard her gag. She turned away from him, but he craned his head around and saw her wiping her mouth and shaking her head. More to herself than to him she was muttering, "The flesh appears to be rotting. It has a rancid scent." She placed the bandage back on the wound and said, "Let me see your leg."

Without saying anything, Nik rolled carefully over, giving her access to the wound on his leg.

When she lifted the bandage he smelled it—the sickening familiar scent of blight and death. He lay back and closed his eyes, trying to calm the panic and fear that threatened to choke him.

"I just don't understand." Mari bent over the wound. "I see ulcerations appearing on this one, as well as the discoloration of the flesh and the foul scent. It makes no sense. I changed the bandages yesterday and there was absolutely no sign of this."

"It's not your fault." Nik felt as dead as his voice sounded. "And there's nothing you can do about it."

"What do you mean?"

"I mean this will kill me, and there's nothing you can do to stop it. It's called the blight, and it has been cursing the Tribe for many winters now, and taking more and more lives with each passing season." Nik met Mari's gaze. "Would you help me get home? I want to see my father before I die."

Mari put both hands on her hips and her eyes narrowed stubbornly. "I'm not taking you anywhere until you tell me exactly what the blight is and how you caught it."

"The only thing we know for sure about the blight is that it's a type of fungus. It can infect us when our skin has been broken."

Mari's eyes widened. "Anytime you get a scratch you can catch it?"

Nik nodded wearily. "Yes, there's a possibility of catching it whenever our skin is broken, but the truth is the deeper the wound, the better chance of catching the blight." Now that the first shock had passed he felt tired and sad and sick, and he just wanted to crawl inside another mug of Mari's sleeping potion and sleep forever.

"Your Tribe is dying?"

Nik looked at Mari. She didn't seem to be gloating. She also didn't seem to be upset. She only seemed curious.

"Actually, the Tribe is growing, but the blight is getting worse. It used to infect only the very young or very old. And it used to infect only about a third of everyone who was injured. That's been changing, though. More people get the blight. My mother died of it just after my tenth winter."

"I'm sorry. I know what it's like to lose your mother," Mari said.

"Thank you. Will you help me get back to the Tribe before this kills me? I don't have long. Once it starts to stink and ulcerate it's in the blood. It'll take over my body soon. If I'm lucky the spear wound is close enough to my heart that it'll kill me fast."

"Nik, I haven't given up on healing you," Mari said.

"I appreciate that, Mari. Truly I do. But you don't understand. Our Healers have been trying to cure the blight for generations. They can't even slow it down. It's why we started capturing your people and making them tend our crops. Too many of the Tribe were dying of blight after small injuries in the fields."

Mari stared at him as if he had just sprouted a tail and begun to bark at her.

"You enslave us because your Healers can't figure out how to cure a disease?"

"Well, yes. Or mostly yes. That's why we started taking, ur, Earth Walkers captive. And then once they became our captives it was obvious that they were unable to care for themselves."

"Only because we die if we're enslaved!"

"We—we didn't know that. None of us knew that." Nik didn't add that today he wasn't so sure that was the only reason for keeping them slaves. He thought about Thaddeus and Claudia and even Wilkes, and couldn't imagine them plowing and planting, weeding and harvesting.

"That's just ridiculous, and it's going to end now. No wonder Rigel led me to you. Nik, I'm going to change your world," Mari said. Then she strode to the closed curtain that sectioned off the back rooms of the burrow, pulled it aside, and called, "Sora! Don't get comfortable in there. We have work to do."

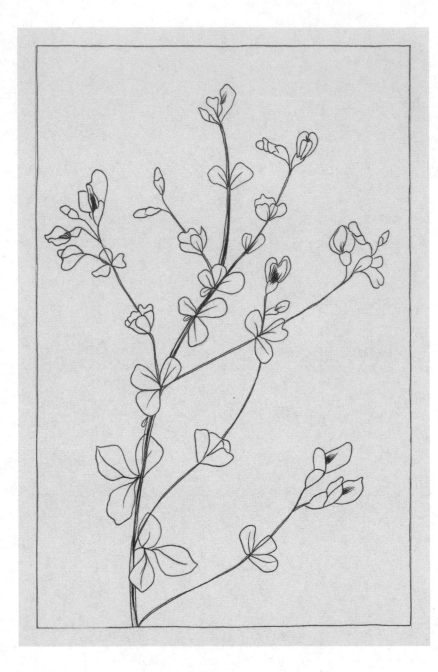

36

I'm really sssssleepy!" Nik's shout was slurred.

Mari and Sora exchanged a look. From the medical pantry, Mari called, "Good. Being sleepy is good. Just don't fall asleep. Yet."

"Not ssssure I'm in control of that," he shouted again.

Mari went to the doorway to the front room of the burrow and stuck her head through the curtain. "Nik, I'm right here. You don't have to yell. I told you that I'm going through Mama's journal to find a way to cure you. And you need to stay awake."

"But I want to sssssleep."

Mari rolled her eyes. "You can sleep afterward." She glanced behind her where the young canine was sitting, as usual staying close to her side. "Rigel, go to Nik." As the pup padded to his pallet, Mari said, "Pet Rigel. Or talk to him. Or whatever. Just stay awake."

"Okay!" he said, and then he saluted her.

Mari rolled her eyes again and disappeared behind the curtain. She hurried back to her mama's chest where she and Sora had been sitting as she searched through Leda's medical journal hunting for cures for anything that sounded remotely like Nik's blight.

"Why don't you let him sleep? He makes too much noise when he's awake," Sora said.

Mari looked up from the page she was reading. "Can you carry him?"

Sora snorted. "Of course not. We already tried that and I failed miserably. Plus, my arms and legs are just now starting to feel normal again instead of screaming with soreness."

"Your pain tolerance is low," Mari said.

"I know that, but I don't see it as a bad thing. Really, Mari, who *wants* to be in pain?"

"Sora, sometimes you do make a good point or two."

"Thank you!" she grinned.

"Can we get back to healing Nik now, please?" Mari said.

"Okay, but I still don't understand why you're so adamant about it. I don't mean to sound inhumane, but even he says he's dying. Why not ask him all of your questions, and then give him something to stop his pain long enough for him to return to die with his Tribe?"

"The excuse his Tribe uses for capturing Clanswomen is because they have the blight and can't tend their own crops. I'm going to cure the blight, so they have no excuse to enslave us."

"I guess I'm not as optimistic as you about the Tribe suddenly setting our people free."

"I think this might be it!" Mari jumped up and sprinted into the other room. "Nik! Open your eyes."

He blinked blearily at her. "Are they open?"

"Yes, now they are. Okay, listen to this." She read from the journal entry, "*Callie had a terrible fungal infection. It reminded me of tree blight, which is why I'm making a special note of it here. Small black spores were attached to what was a cleanly healing wound. Then the flesh began to turn a dusky color, ulcerations appeared, along with a rancid scent.*" Mari looked up from the journal. "Does this describe what happens with the blight?"

Nik grinned at her and nodded. "Yes indeedy it does. So, Scratchers—oops, I mean Earth Walkers—they get it, too?"

"Got it. Past tense," Mari said smugly. "My mother cured it, just like I'm going to cure it. I'll be back."

Mari hurried back to Sora. "This is it!"

"I heard. What else does it say?"

"Mama writes:

"*I tried several poultices, to no avail. Finally, I remembered a strong remedy my mother had used on a dire fungal infection. I tried it, and the infection was cured, though not without the power of the moon, and the grace of our benevolent Earth Mother. Poultice is as follows: Muddle a fresh indigo root with boiling water. Mix with warmed honey and apply sparingly to the wound. Healing is quick, but NOTE—take care! Large doses are toxic, inducing nausea, diarrhea, heart palpitations, paralysis of breathing, and death. One poultice was enough to cure the disease. I'm very much afraid more than one application would be toxic.*"

"Sounds simple. Do you know what an indigo root is?" Sora asked.

"Of course. I use it for dye. It's the plant with the beautiful blue flower that grows by streams. After it's done flowering it makes blue pods that rattle in the wind."

"Oh, I know what flower you're talking about!"

"Good. Go pull some up and bring me the roots."

Sora frowned. "You didn't answer my question about why he can't be asleep for this. What does carrying him have to do with making that poultice?"

"Mama wrote that her patient was cured with *the power of the moon*."

Sora's mouth fell open. "No. You cannot mean to draw down the moon for him."

"I absolutely do, and you're going to help me. It's your next step, remember? You healed the fern," Mari said.

"But he can't know that we're Moon Women!" Sora's whisper was more of a hiss.

"And that's why I'm going to brew another potion just like the one I gave him before we pulled out that spear, only I don't want him to pass out until he's walked himself outside and up to the clearing."

Sora's forehead wrinkled in confusion. "So, you're going to have him walk outside—give him the potion—he'll pass out—and then we'll draw down the moon and heal him. Then what?"

Mari grinned at Sora. "Then we'll drag him back in here."

"Well, there's a bright spot in the evening. I'll go get you that indigo root." Sora paused at the door. Quietly, she said, "After this—after you heal the blight—can he leave then?"

"Yes. He can leave then."

"Finally. I'll be quick."

"'Splain this to me again," Nik slurred.

Mari took firm hold of her patience and answered him. Again. "I've repacked your wounds with the poultice my mother said cures the blight. But she also notes that the patient needs to spend time in the moonlight. So Sora and I are going to blindfold you again, and guide you to a place outside where you'll be safe. I'll give you a potion out there, and you can sit in the moonlight and cure the blight. Understand?"

"Nope," he said sleepily. "Don't. Understand."

"How about this—you do what Mari says and you live. You don't and you die. It's really that simple," Sora said. "Understand?"

Nik squinted at Sora, blinked several times, and then said. "You don't like me."

"Like has nothing to do with it. Trust does," Sora said.

"I like Mari more than you." Nik spoke slowly and carefully.

Mari covered her laugh with a cough. "What we're asking you to do might seem strange to you, but my mother was a great Healer. Trust me, Nik. I know I can heal you."

Nik's mossy gaze met hers, and for a moment his eyes were completely lucid. "I trust you, Mari."

Mari swallowed through the sudden dryness that filled her mouth. He was telling her the truth. Nik did trust her.

"I'm not going to let you down," Mari said. "I am sorry that you're going to have to walk. I know you're in pain."

"Hhhhhardly at all!" Nik slurred happily.

"Well, that's good," Mari said. "Okay, let's get you to the door." Nik leaned on her and they made their way slowly to the door. Before Sora opened it, Mari propped Nik against the wall of the burrow while she lifted the strip of cloth that she would tie around his head, covering his eyes.

"Don't really need to do that," Nik said, grinning at her. "Won't tell anyone where you live."

"No one can know where Healers live," Mari told him. "Not even the Clan."

"Sssseems fair I can't either then. Okay! Blind me."

He swayed forward so that Sora and Mari had to right him before he toppled over. Then, quickly, Mari tied the cloth around his face.

"Can Rigel come?" Nik asked, moving his head blindly around.

"Yes, of course. He'll be right there with you while you soak up the moonlight," Mari assured him.

"And soak up the potion," Sora said in an exaggerated whisper.

"Sssssora, I do not trust," Nik said.

"Sssh," Mari told him. "Concentrate on staying upright and walking. Keep your arms close to me or to your side. We're going to be walking through a lot of brambles. Got it?"

Nik nodded, which made him stagger—which also made him groan with pain as he stepped down too hard with his wounded leg.

"Hold tight to me." Mari put his arm around her shoulder and slid her arm around his waist, taking weight off his leg.

"That'ssss better," Nik said. "I like holding tight to you."

Sora shook her head and looked like she was close to taking her walking stick and hitting Nik with it. Mari quickly said, "I'm ready, Sora."

Sora led the way through the brambles. She only hesitated twice, and both times chose the correct path before Mari had to remind her. Mari was surprised at how good the girl had gotten at finding her way through the mazelike thicket, and made a mental note to tell her so—later.

It was slow going and they had to rest often, but they made it up to the clearing where Mari led Nik to the Goddess statue and helped him take a seat on the thick grass carpeting the ground in front of it. She untied his blindfold and while he was blinking and rubbing his eyes, she took the mug of tea laced with cannabis and juice of the poppy from Sora.

"Okay, Nik. Drink this and then make yourself comfortable."

Nik reached for the mug, but stopped as his vision cleared. He stared around them, wide, blurry eyes taking in the neat little clearing, the bramble walls, and the Goddess image that seemed to be emerging gracefully from the ground.

"Am I dreaming?"

"Yes, you are," Sora said.

"Can Rigel be part of my dream?"

Mari frowned at Sora, but answered Nik. "Yes, he can." Without her having to say anything to him, the young canine padded to Nik and lay down beside him. The man smiled and rested a hand on the pup's soft coat. Mari felt a little unexpected jolt at the picture they made together. In the moonlight Nik didn't look so pale and sick. His blond hair was mussed and fell over one of his eyes. He tried to brush it away—unsuccessfully—and then he sighed heavily, reminding Mari of a young boy—a very handsome young boy. She mentally shook herself. "Drink the tea, please, Nik," she said.

Blinking hard, Nik looked from Rigel to Mari. "Rigel trusts you. I trust you," he finally said. "I'll drink anything you give me." Then he took the mug from her and gulped the bitter potion. He lay back, looking up at the Goddess and petting Rigel slowly. "Beautiful," he said in a dreamy voice that was oddly free of slurring. "She's so beautiful. Reminds me of you, Mari. Solid. Trustworthy. But strange. Very strange . . ." His voice trailed off as his hand stilled, his eyes closed, and his breathing deepened to soft snores.

Sora walked up to him and poked his foot with her walking stick. When he didn't react, she smiled at Mari. "That was really fast. How much of that stuff did you give him?"

"Enough to make sure he won't wake up in the middle of us drawing down the moon." Mari wiped the sweat from her forehead with the back of her sleeve. "He's a lot heavier than he looks."

"Yes, he is. Also, he's got a thing for you," Sora said.

"He does not! He's sick, in massive pain, and I've filled him full of drugs. Nothing he said means anything."

Sora snorted.

"Are you ready to do this?" Mari asked.

"If it gets him out of our burrow—yes. I'm more than ready."

"All right." Mari went to Nik and sat beside him, close to Rigel's warmth. Gently, she turned Nik so that she could press her hand against the poulticed and bandaged spear wound. The other hand she held up for Sora to take. "Let's start."

"But you should be here and I should be where you are," Sora said.

Mari smiled at her. "You can do this. Just like with the fern, only imagine that I'm the fern and you're drawing down the moon to flow through you and pool into me. I'll take it from there and send it into Nik."

"Are you sure you shouldn't—"

"I'm sure you can do it. Just like you can pick your way through a forest of brambles and lead us up here. I believe in you, Sora."

Sora blinked quickly and looked away from Mari. Mari thought she saw the sheen of tears in the girl's gray eyes, but when she looked back at her Sora was smiling. "I'm ready. And I can do this."

Sora clasped Mari's hand and began the incantation. Mari closed her eyes, listening with pleasure to Sora's steady voice. She didn't falter one time. She'd memorized the entire drawing-down spell. As Sora repeated the familiar words, Mari deepened her breathing. Easily slipping into her imagination, she drew within her mind a scene that showed silver moonlight cascading like a magnificent waterfall into Sora's raised palm. She sketched Sora glowing with light and then made that light pour into herself, Washing through her body as well, to pool within Nik so that he was illuminated with the moon's majesty. She kept her eyes squeezed shut, seeing in her mind the wound on Nik's back turning from putrid and rotting to healing pink flesh. Then, keeping her eyes closed and maintaining the drawing in her mind, she walked her hand down Nik's body, from the wound on his back to the wound on his leg. She pressed her palm to it, imagining it, too, healing.

Mari had no idea how long the three of them stayed like that, connected through touch and power and imagination. She only knew when Sora sank to her knees beside her and pried their hands apart.

"It's done. I can't hold it anymore," Sora said quietly, sounding utterly exhausted.

Mari opened her eyes, coming back to herself. She was ravenous and thirsty. Her gaze went to Nik. He was sound asleep.

"Do you think it worked?" Sora asked.

"Let's drag him back to the burrow and see."

"I'm so glad you said drag," Sora said. "I'm not taking his head, though. I don't like being close to his face."

"What's wrong with his face? I don't think he's ugly," Mari said, struggling to her feet. *Actually, I think he's handsome,* she thought, but refused to say aloud.

"He's a Companion. They're all ugly. Except you, of course. You have some Earth Walker in you, which saves you from looking completely like one of them."

"Thank you. I think."

Mari bent and took hold of Nik's limp body under his arms while Sora hefted his legs.

"You know what we need to figure out?" Sora said as she panted and pulled with one hand, and with the other she used the thick walking stick to hold aside the thick bramble boughs.

"What?" Mari asked.

"We need to figure out how to wrap a rope around your creature's chest so that he can help us drag bodies and whatnot."

"Actually, that's not a bad idea," Mari said and then laughed at the expression on her young Shepherd's furry face.

"It worked!" Sora exclaimed. Nik stirred and murmured something unintelligible. She frowned at him and dropped her voice to a whisper. "The black things are gone, and so are those pus things."

"They're called ulcerations. And the black things were spores." Mari closed the bandage over the poultice on Nik's leg, and then straightened, stretching her back.

"Ulcerations and spores. Got it. Can we eat now?"

"I hope so. Is the stew ready?"

"Yes it is, and I added more spice to it this time." Sora hurried to the hearth and began ladling fragrant stew into their bowls. Mari's mouth was watering in expectation of Sora's increasingly delicious cooking when she sat next to the girl and began eating enthusiastically.

"This is good. Really good," Mari said between bites.

"Thank you," Sora said. Then she threw Nik a sideways glance. "How long is he going to stay asleep?"

Mari shrugged. "Last time he was out for an entire day. Hard to tell this time, but his body is healing quickly. Sleep will only help, but awake means he'll be leaving soon. Sora, he knows Jenna," Mari said.

Sora's eyes widened. "What? How?"

"He told me that he was with the group of Hunters that captured her." Mari glanced at Nik. He looked like he was soundly asleep. Still, she scooted closer to Sora and kept her voice low. "He wanted to know why we're not helpless and dying of sadness like the others they capture, and why Jenna talked to him."

"Talked to him? Huh?"

"That night—that awful night Xander was killed and Jenna captured—it was just after I'd Washed both of them. So Jenna was totally herself when they took her."

"Just like Xander knew exactly what he was doing when he attacked them and tried to save Jenna."

Mari took a big bite of stew and nodded, not wanting to remember that Xander had tried to save her, too. Not wanting to remember Xander's look of disbelief and hate when he'd realized Rigel was with her.

"What did you say?"

"Say?" Mari shook herself mentally.

"When he asked you why we're normal?" Sora said.

"I told him slavery kills us."

"Well, that's a version of the truth. Do you think there's any way you can talk him into setting Jenna free?" Sora asked.

"I don't know, but I'll try."

"You can't let him know we're Moon Women," Sora whispered.

"I won't," Mari said.

"It's forbidden. You know it's forbidden for a Companion to know anything about Moon Women," Sora insisted.

"I know that. Sora, don't be crazy. I'm going to find out everything I can about Rigel and Jenna, and then, once his wounds have healed enough, I'm going to blindfold him and lead him out of here." They ate in silence until Mari added, "You really did good tonight. I'm proud of you."

"Thank you!" Sora covered her mouth when her exclamation had Nik stirring restlessly. Then, whispering again, she told Mari, "It was so much easier tonight. I did what you said—I pictured the moonlight traveling through me and filling you up, just like the fern, and it actually happened."

"You're doing it," Mari said. "You're becoming a Moon Woman."

Sora's smile was brilliant. "Because of you. All because of you."

"Not really. I'm just following Mama's teachings. She'd have been better at this than me."

"I'm not sure you're right about that, but I don't want to argue with my teacher," Sora said.

"Since when?" Mari teased.

"Since now. Don't worry, though, I'm sure that'll change."

The girls grinned at one another. With a jolt of surprise, Mari realized that she was actually smiling. A lot. And enjoying Sora's company. *I'm not so alone anymore,* she thought, and then, not sure she wanted to be attached to anyone except Rigel, Mari pushed the thought aside, saying, "I didn't hear any shrieks from roaming males tonight, did you?"

"Early, when I was healing the fern I heard some, but only faintly. They came from the southwest and it sounded like there were maybe two or three different voices, and not the half dozen or so we've been hearing until now."

Mari wiped her hands and retrieved the journal she'd begun what seemed like so, so many nights ago when she'd first heard the cries. "Three different voices, distant, coming from the southwest. That's it?" She glanced up from the page at Sora.

"Yes, that's it. Except for . . ."

Mari put the quill down and returned to sit next to Sora. "Except for what?"

"Mari, I think it's time we try to find some of the Clanswomen." When Mari opened her mouth to speak, Sora cut her off. "Wait, hear me out." Mari sat back, crossing her arms over her chest, and Sora continued, "You said my next step is people. So, I need people to heal."

"Which you helped me do tonight."

"I said hear me out."

Mari nodded and motioned for Sora to continue.

"I've been thinking about this a lot lately. It's been long enough since Leda's been gone that the Clanswomen will be overwhelmed with sadness. I could try to wash the sadness from them. That's all—nothing fancy. It wouldn't be much different from what we did tonight, right?"

"Well, it's a little more complicated than that, especially if there's a whole horde of melancholy Clanswomen swarming you and begging to be Washed."

"Then I'll make sure I'm not swarmed. Here's my plan—I'll go to the birthing burrow today, *before* sunset. There are what, four women in the Clan who are near their time?"

Mari moved her shoulders. "I'm not positive, but that sounds about right."

"I'll talk with them and see what kind of shape they're in. Then I'll come back here and explain to you what I found, and you can tell me what I need to do."

"They're all going to need to be Washed," Mari said. "And they might need other healing. I just don't know what happens to one of the women if she has had no Moon Woman, and she goes into labor. Sora, I'm not sure if a woman would have the will to give birth if she hasn't been Washed regularly of the Night Fever."

"Then come with me. Bring Leda's medicine bag. Between the two of us we can handle whatever might happen in the birthing burrow," Sora said.

"I need to stay here."

"You said you were done hiding."

"I'm not staying here because I'm hiding. I'm staying here because of him." Mari jerked her chin in Nik's direction.

"Make Rigel watch him and come with me. The Clanswomen are more important than him," Sora said.

"Why don't we get some sleep and then I'll see how he's doing?" Mari said.

"Okay, yes, we need to get some sleep. If he's awake when we're ready to leave, drug him again. Then you can come with me without worrying about him getting past your creature." Sora glanced at Rigel, who was lying beside Nik's pallet. "I can see why you're worried, though. Your creature really seems to like him."

Rigel lifted his head, looking from Mari to Sora, obviously understanding that they were talking about him. Mari smiled at the young canine. "I told you before, Rigel would never leave me, if that's what you mean about me being worried. I just don't want Rigel to have to try to stop Nik from leaving. I mean, what would Rigel do to him?"

"The creature could bite him. I'd give a lot to see that," Sora said.

"I don't want Rigel to bite him. I just want Nik to get well enough to walk out of here—after he's answered all my questions."

Rigel stood, stretched, and then padded over to squeeze between Mari and Sora, who were still sitting close enough that they could whisper to one another.

Sora grimaced and tried to scoot away. "Every time I get near him your creature gets his fur all over me."

"Nik says it's because of the change of seasons, and after questioning him today I know how to comb out his coat."

"Well, that's a relief."

Rigel looked up at Sora and then sneezed all over her mostly empty bowl of stew.

"Oh, yuck. The creature is disgusting." She plopped the bowl in front of the pup. Wagging, his tail, he gulped the rest of her sneeze-covered stew.

"He's smart about getting more food, that's for sure. And that's something else Nik told me about today. Gotta watch how much he eats," Mari said, patting Rigel affectionately. She stood then, putting her empty bowl by the hearth. "Okay, let's get a little sleep, then I'll see what kind of shape Nik is in."

"I hope he's drugable," Sora said, waggling her fingers at Mari and Rigel. "Sweet dreams."

"Sweet dreams," Mari whispered as she curled up with Rigel before the hearth on their makeshift pallet. As the firelight faded to a red glow, Mari watched Nik and began cataloguing questions for him in her mind, but the questions kept slipping away as she studied him, distracted by the way his blond hair gleamed in the dim firelight. She looked from his hair to his face, and was even more intrigued. His features were so different from those of the Clansmen. Nik was more refined, with strong cheekbones and full lips. Had his jaw not been so square and his neck and shoulders not so powerfully built, Mari would have been tempted to call him pretty.

He moved fitfully, brushing one of the coverings from him so that his arm, golden tan with long, lean muscles, lay naked against the pelt. Mari felt a fluttering low in her stomach as a warm rush of desire flowed through her body.

Almost without thought, Mari went to Nik. She rearranged the pelt so that it covered him again. Then she glanced surreptitiously at the empty doorway to the back room. Sora was definitely in bed. Slowly, Mari reached out until just the tips of her fingers caressed his hair.

Soft—it's so soft!

A muffled snore from the back room had Mari retreating to the fireside where Rigel joined her, resting his head on her knee while they both continued to watch Nik.

"Want to know a secret?" she whispered to the pup. "I think he's beautiful. But do *not* tell Sora."

Rigel huffed several doggie laughs before stretching out beside her and falling asleep. Mari found sleep more slowly, and when she did she dreamed of gleaming blond hair, long, tan muscles, and softly waving pine trees . . .

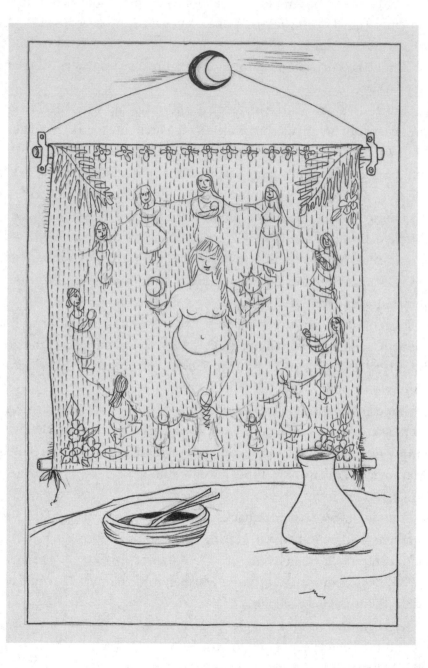

37

"I can't believe this. It's gone! It's really gone!" Nik was staring at the wound in his leg. Just the night before it had been putrid and black with deadly blight, and now it was pink with health and obviously healing. "And the one in my back? That one, too?"

"I already told you it's free of the blight." Mari smiled at him as she finished packing his wound with more of the indigo poultice and closed the bandage.

"But will it come back?"

Mari met his gaze. "Trust me, Nik. It's gone for good."

"I do trust you. I promise I do."

Nik's bright gaze went from Mari to Sora, who was watching Mari with a strange, knowing expression in her gray eyes. He ignored the Scratcher and focused on Mari.

"You won't be gone too long, will you?" Nik asked.

A loud snort came from Sora. "Oh, don't pretend like you wouldn't relish the opportunity to grab Mari's creature and run back to the Tribe." The young Clanswoman frowned severely at him and Nik frowned back at her.

"I can't *run* anywhere. I can barely walk. And I wouldn't do that. I would never steal someone else's canine!" he said.

"Right, just like you wouldn't kill someone's mother? Or father?

Wait, you don't think *Scratchers* are someone. You think they're some*thing*, so killing them is fine," Sora said.

"I don't think you're a thing, and I—" Nik began, but Mari cut him off.

"Nik, I'll be back soon. We'll both be back. But you're going to need to drink this so that I don't have to worry about whether you'll be here when we do return." As usual, Mari sounded rational and reasonable, unlike Sora, who he had silently dubbed her crazy Scratcher friend. So when she handed him a mug full of a noxious-smelling potion, he drank it in several long gulps.

"Whoops, I might have put some nightshade in that tea. Was that the wrong herb, Mari?" Sora said with mock innocence.

Nik's stomach clenched. Nightshade wouldn't kill him, but it would definitely make him vomit, and the wound in his back would hurt bad enough that he might wish he were dead. He stared into the mug, wondering and worrying.

"Stop it," Mari told her crazy friend, then she turned to him. "She wouldn't really do that, but I made the tea. There's nothing in it that will hurt you, though you are going to sleep. You know we're Healers. We have to check on our other patients. We won't be gone long." She bent and hugged Rigel. "Stay here with Nik. Don't let him leave."

The young Shepherd licked her face and thumped his tail. She kissed his muzzle and then she and Sora, carrying packs filled with herbs and poultices, left the burrow.

Rigel went to the closed door and sat, whining fretfully.

"Yeah, I know how you feel, boy. But at least you know where we are." Rigel looked over his shoulder at Nik, and then turned back to the door, whining again. The tea was going to kick his ass soon, but at that moment he felt completely invigorated. *Mari had healed the blight! He wasn't going to die! No one in the Tribe would ever have to die again— all he had to do was to talk Mari into sharing her poultice secret with him.*

"And that's something I'll talk to Mari about when her crazy friend is out of hearing range. That woman is a thorn in my side," Nik grumbled. But not even the Scratcher could dampen his mood today. *He wasn't going to die of the blight!* "Hey, Rigel, how about we explore a little. And I do mean a little. I definitely have enough energy to hobble to that desk. Sitting at a chair, even for a few minutes before Mari's awful tea knocks me out, will seem like a great adventure."

He could feel Rigel's eyes on him as he used the edge of the sleeping pallet to steady himself. Nik managed to shuffle the few feet to the desk, and then sat heavily with a groan. His wounds felt better, but the movement had caused stabbing pain to return to his back and a dull throbbing in his leg that pulsed in time with his heartbeat. He sat very still, trying to slow his breathing and fight the dizziness that was already tugging at him.

The pup's muzzle was wet and cool, and wonderfully familiar when it poked him. Nik smiled and opened his eyes.

Rigel was, indeed, a handsome boy. Nik caressed his sable-colored head and smiled into his intelligent eyes.

"I haven't had the opportunity to thank you for saving my life. I don't know how you got your Mari to come to me, let alone to bring me to her home and heal me, but I thank you. My father, Sol, would thank you, too. You remember Sol? The Sun Priest?" Rigel wagged his tail and smiled the panting, tongue-lolling version of a Shepherd smile, which had Nik grinning in response. "I'll bet you do remember. I'll bet you remember everything, and still you choose to be here—to stay with her." Nik's grin turned bittersweet. "I wouldn't expect anything less of you. Your Companion is a lucky woman." Rigel licked Nik's hand before padding back to the door, yawning, and lying down in front of it at his normal, watching position.

"Well, I guess I've had enough adventure. Time to make my way back to my pallet." Nik put a hand on the desk to help himself up, accidentally scattering the papers on which he'd seen Mari writing notations. Nik sat back down, meaning to straighten the pile and leave it as it was. He glanced at the neat writing. It was a journal entry about his wounds and what Mari had packed them with, how often she'd changed his dressings, as well as comments about the extraction of the spearhead and the potions she had been brewing to help him sleep and, he noted with surprise, help him heal.

Feeling a prickle of excitement, he quickly read through the annotations, looking for any mention of the ingredients to the poultice she'd used to cure the blight. Nik sighed in frustration. "She hasn't written that part yet," he mumbled to himself. "But she will, and all I need to do is to read and remember what she writes."

Steal it—all I need to do is to steal it and get back to the Tribe with the recipe.

Nik felt a hot flush of guilt. No, he wouldn't do something so dishonorable. He would *ask* Mari to share the poultice with him and his people. It was only if she said no that he would consider a less trustworthy alternative.

He had to have that poultice recipe. For the Tribe. He had to have it.

Nik's attention went back to the stack of notes. He read through them again, making sure he hadn't missed anything, and from beneath the blank pages waiting to be filled with Mari's neat handwriting, he saw the corner of something that didn't look the same as the others. He pulled the thick sheet of paper free and sucked in a quick breath of surprise.

It was a sketch of Rigel, and it was exquisitely drawn with such talent that it could have been created by one of the Tribe's Master Artists. Trying to fight off the dizziness that Mari's tea was causing, Nik quickly paged through the rest of the papers, hardly believing the beauty they held. He looked up at the paintings that decorated the hearth's mantel, and the few others that were scattered between sections of glowmoss and glowshrooms.

"Those are good, but not as good as these." His gaze went back to the sketches. There was a small, almost unnoticeable signature at the bottom of each sketch. Nik squinted and made out the name, *Mari*. He kept looking through the pile, eventually coming to the last sketch— the one that had him holding his breath. It was of a Scratcher woman clutching an infant swaddled in the fronds of a Mother Plant. She was smiling up at a tall, handsome Companion and his Shepherd, who gazed at her with an expression that was filled with love.

"That's Galen. It has to be. And that's Mari's mother, with Mari as an infant." Nik shook his head. "I see this—and I see the grown-up Mari—and I know the truth, but it is hard to believe. All of this is just so hard to believe." Slowly, Nik reorganized the papers, stacking them as neatly as they had been. Then he hobbled carefully to the pallet and collapsed there, breathing heavily and feeling ridiculously weak.

As his eyes closed he was thinking of Mari and wondering what his father would say when he told him all that he'd learned about her, and about the Earth Walkers.

Nik knew what his father would say. He could almost hear his voice there in the burrow as he fell into a drugged, painless sleep. *Bring her home to the Tribe, son. Bring her home to the Tribe.*

"It's really hot today." Mari paused, wiping the sweat from her face and taking a drink of water from the skin they'd brought with them. "And summer isn't even here."

"It hasn't rained for days. It's nice not to have to trudge through mud, but this heat is terrible," Sora said.

"Well, the birthing burrow is always comfortable and cool, and there's that nice little stream that runs down beside it. I can't wait to dangle my hot feet in it."

"Sounds wonderful. The women in the burrow always have the best food, too. Have you noticed that?" Sora said.

"I guess I haven't thought about it, but you're probably right. Pregnant women eat a lot, so it figures their food would be extra good," Mari said. She smiled at Sora. "And that just made me want to hurry."

"Well, we're almost there. Hey, I have a thought. I'm going to see if I can get shoots from their herb garden. Yours is sadly lacking for edible herbs, which means what I've been cooking for us is sadly lacking in seasoning," Sora said.

"I'm fine with whatever you want to cook and however you want to cook it. You're a good cook," Mari said.

"Thank you. I like to cook, probably because I'm a big fan of eating."

"Whatever the reason—I'm glad. Mama was better at it than I am, but you're *really* good."

"Yes, I am!" Sora grinned, then her expression sobered. "Hey, what are you going to tell the Clanswomen about all of that?" She made a finger-fluttering gesture that took in Mari's short blond hair, her delicate features, and her clean, uncamouflaged skin.

"I'm going to tell the truth," Mari said resolutely.

"The whole truth? As in telling them about your creature, and by creature I mean Rigel and not Nik."

"Nik isn't mine, but no. I'm not going to tell them about Rigel or Nik. At least not right now. I think finding out about me will be enough for them to take in without adding a canine and a wounded Companion," Mari said.

"You might never want to tell them about Nik," Sora said.

"What I'm hoping is that one day very soon I'll have to tell them about Nik because they'll need to know the reason why the Companions aren't enslaving the Clan anymore."

"You know, I thought you were a complete pessimist at first, and you can be. But you're also oddly idealistic. I think you must get that from your father," Sora said.

"I don't know, Leda always looked at the positive in every situation," Mari said.

"So, you're actually an idealist. Well, I try to be a realist, so do you mind if I'm the teacher for once and give you a little advice?"

"I don't mind," Mari said.

"Don't tell Nik how to cure the blight. Ever. Don't ever tell him or anyone from their Tribe," Sora said.

"But they can't cure it anyway, even if they know how to make the poultice. They can't draw down the moon," Mari said.

"What if they can draw down the sun, though? I watch you do something like that when your skin glows. Aren't you just drawing down the sun then?"

"Maybe, but I haven't asked Nik about that yet." Mari thought about the jolt of heat and energy that had sizzled through her the day her mother had died and she'd accidentally set the forest on fire. "I think you're right, though. The glowing is a reaction to the power of the sun. I just don't know anything about controlling it."

"I'll bet the Tribe does," Sora said.

"You're right. I'll take your advice. I won't tell Nik what I used to make his poultice. At least not yet I won't," Mari said.

"If it was up to me, you'd never tell him or any of them. Knowledge is power, Mari. Keep your power."

Mari nodded in somber agreement.

They walked on in silence, both lost in their own thoughts, until Mari heard the happy sound of water bubbling over smooth stones. "Oh, look—there's the stream. The burrow is just around the bend. Do you smell food? I don't smell food yet." Mari sniffed the air.

"I don't. I've never been here when there hasn't been something delicious all ready to eat." Sora sniffed the air, too.

The two women rounded the bend and then began climbing up the boulders that had been arranged as wide steps, making the door to the burrow easily accessed. Mari looked up, smiling in anticipation, and the smile slid off her face.

The door to the burrow was broken. It hung drunkenly, as if a giant had flung it open. The fecund Goddess that was carved into the door-frame had been cracked as the door had shattered so that it looked disturbingly as if she had been cut in two.

Sora hurried up the last of the stairs, stopping at the doorframe. Her fingers traced the ruined image gently, as if she could smooth away the destruction with a touch.

"Wait, Sora." Mari spoke softly, taking out her slingshot and several smooth stones. "Let me go in first."

"Oh, Goddess!" Sora whispered, sending frightened, furtive looks inside the darkened burrow. "You don't think there are Clansmen in there, do you?"

"Don't know," Mari whispered back. "Wish Rigel was here, though."

"I never thought I'd say it, but I wish he was here, too." Sora stepped aside and let Mari go before her.

Mari had been to the birthing burrow many times with Leda. It was basically one huge, cavernous room with a large hearth and many comfortable pallets. The burrow was usually filled with the sounds of women and infants, but all was silent and still within. Like all Earth Walkers, Mari's eyes quickly adapted to the dim light inside. She saw that the hearth fire was unlit, then she cast her eyes around the room. The entire place was a disaster. Beds had been thrown against the curved walls of the burrow so that their splintered wooden frames littered the floor along with the thick pelts and blankets that should be cradling birthing women.

"I don't see anyone. Do you?" Sora whispered from several feet behind her.

"No, but there's a large pantry back there. I need to check it."

"Not alone you're not." Sora strode forward, pausing only to pick up the broken leg of a bedframe, which she brandished like a club.

Together the two women walked through the devastation of the burrow until they came to the rear of the room. The best artisans of the Clan had woven the tapestry that was used as a curtain to divide the main room from the pantry. It had depicted a scene that showed a group of Clanswomen circled around an exquisite, fertile Earth Mother idol that was rising from the mossy ground, bedecked in flowers and ferns. All of the women were smiling and holding healthy, happy infants. Now the tapestry clung to the wooden rod by a few strands of cloth—its lovely woven scene had been ripped and shredded. Mari brushed aside the ruined cloth.

"No, please, don't hurt me. I'll do anything you want, just don't hurt me!"

"Oh, Goddess," Sora said in a hushed voice. "It's Danita."

Mari stared at the girl, hardly recognizing her as the young woman her mama had so recently called before the Clan as a candidate for Moon Woman apprentice. But she looked up at them with gray eyes, glassy with shock, proving she was, indeed, that same young woman.

Sora pushed past Mari to go to the girl, who was cowering in the far corner of the pantry, wedged between broken, empty shelves and the rubble that violence and theft leaves in its wake.

"No! No!" The girl screamed, covering her face with her arms and curling into a tight little ball.

"Sssh, Danita, it's me, Sora. And Mari's with me. You're safe. Everything is going to be okay now." Sora knelt by her. The girl peeked up through her arms at Sora. She started to drop her arms from her face, but her frantic gaze found Mari and she began to cry in little panting sobs, scrambling back, attempting to wedge herself farther into the corner.

"Hey, it's just Mari!" Sora said, touching the girl's trembling shoulder gently. "I cut her hair for her—that's why it's short. And she washed it and herself. Finally. Remember how dirty she used to be?"

Mari frowned down at Sora, but didn't say anything because Danita had stopped sobbing and was gazing up at her with big, frightened eyes.

"I—I remember," Danita said, her voice trembling.

"Well, when her hair's clean, it's a strange color." Sora caught Mari's frown and hastily added, "Not strange. I didn't mean strange. I meant different—and different isn't anything for you to be afraid of, right?"

"Right," Danita said tentatively, studying Mari.

"Hi, Danita. See, it's just me. How about you come out of the pantry and tell us what happened?" Mari said gently.

Danita met Mari's gaze. "I don't think I can." Her gray eyes were awash with tears that were leaking down her cheeks. It was then that Mari noticed the blood that spotted her tunic along with the tracks of her tears.

"Danita, honey, are you hurt?" Mari asked.

The girl's face crumbled and she nodded. "They hurt me."

"They?" Sora said.

"Clansmen," Danita whispered the word, and then she hugged her legs to her chest and began to rock back and forth. As she rocked Mari got a glimpse of the girl's naked thighs. They were purpled with bruises and smeared with dried blood.

"Danita, are the Clansmen still here?" Mari asked quickly.

"No. I haven't seen them for days. No one is here."

"We're here now," Sora said, stroking her shoulder. "We'll take care of you."

"Sora and I are going to fix a pallet for you and get a fire burning in the hearth." Mari uncorked her water skin and held it out to Danita. "Why don't you drink some water and wait here while we do that."

Danita's hand was dirty and it shook badly, but she took the water and began to gulp it. Mari motioned for Sora to follow her back to the main room.

"I think she's been raped," Mari whispered as soon as they were out of Danita's range of hearing.

"What!"

"There are blood and bruises all over her thighs." Mari started going through the medicine pack she'd brought. "Can you get that fire going? I need boiling water."

"Yes, of course." Sora rushed to the hearth.

"I'm not going to try to put a bedframe together. I'll just pile up these pelts and blankets, and make a quick pallet. Sora, I couldn't tell if she's still bleeding."

Sora looked over her shoulder at Mari. "You can do this. You can help her."

Mari nodded and finished making the pallet. Then she gave Sora a small bundle of herbs. "Brew this for her. Damnit! I didn't bring hardly any medicines with us. That pantry is usually filled with them. All I brought are things for nerves and melancholy."

"What is this?" Sora sniffed the herb pack Mari had given her. "Smells like something you'd give Nik."

"It has valerian in it. It should calm her." Mari pawed through her satchel, scowling in frustration at her lack of choices. "Well, maybe there's something useful left in that mess of a pantry."

"What do you need? The herb garden is near the stream."

Mari thought for a moment, and said, "Sage would be great if you can find it. The bigger the leaves, the better. It stops bleeding."

"I hope I can find it. I hope even more that you don't need it," Sora said.

"I'll coax Danita out here."

"And I'll get water and sage," Sora said.

"Keep that club with you, and I'll keep my slingshot close. If you even think you hear or see a Clansman, scream. Loudly."

"Oh, don't worry. Rigel will probably be able to hear me all the way back at the burrow."

As Sora hurried outside, Mari drew a deep, calming breath, and then headed back to the pantry.

Danita's body jerked in terror and she tried to scramble backward again, as if she could make herself disappear into the burrow's wall while she made small, panicked sounds.

"Danita, it's just me again, Mari." She squatted in front of the girl, careful not to get too close too fast. "Sora is going to brew some tea for you and I have a pallet all made up so that you can be more comfortable. Would you come out into the other room with me?"

"What if they come back?"

Mari pulled the slingshot from the front pocket of her tunic. "I will shoot them with this. I'm an excellent shot."

"Shoot to kill," Danita said.

Mari swallowed hard. "I will. Sora and I won't let anything bad happen to you."

"It already has."

"Will you let me examine you? I can help."

"Where's Leda?"

"Mama is dead," Mari said.

"That's what they said, but I didn't want to believe it—I didn't want to!" Danita shook her head back and forth, back and forth, and covered her face with her hands, sobbing brokenly. "Then this won't end."

Mari moved closer to Danita and gently pried her hands from her face, holding them securely in her own. "Mama trained me. I can help you. I'm training Sora. She can help you, too. It's going to be all right—I promise. Will you please come into the other room with me?"

"I don't think I can stand up," Danita said.

"Then we'll stand up together." Mari stood, pulling Danita up by her hands. Then she put her arm tightly around the girl, noting how thin she felt and how cold and clammy her skin was, and helped her walk slowly to the pallet.

Danita cried out in pain as she sat back on the mound of blankets and pelts. Carefully, Mari lifted her legs, arranging pillows under her knees.

Sora walked briskly past them, handing Mari a fistful of fragrant sage plants. She was carrying a dilapidated bucket that sloshed water on the floor from several of the holes in its battered metal. "This is the only thing I could find to boil water in. There's not one kettle or skillet anywhere. Oh, and I didn't see sign of anyone out there—man or woman."

"They're gone. They're all gone," Danita said.

"The Clansmen?" Mari asked.

"I—I hope so." Danita pulled the blanket up to her chin, trembling again. "But I don't know about them. It's the women who are gone. All of them."

"Wait, what?" Sora turned from hanging the bucket over the hearth fire.

"The Clanswomen left. They said Leda was dead. They said you're dead, too, Sora."

"Me? I'm definitely not dead."

"Some of the women went to your burrow, hoping that maybe you could draw down the moon for them. They said your burrow was destroyed."

"They were right. The men did it, but I wasn't in it when they did it. I've been with Mari."

"They think Mari's dead, too. And Jenna."

"Jenna's captured, not dead," Mari said. "Danita, are you sure all of the women left?"

"Positive. There was nothing to stay for except sadness and Night Fever. Some of the women went south to the Miller Clan. Some went to the coast to the Fisher Clan. And the men—the men are all completely mad. We had to get away from the men." Tears started leaking down Danita's face again, and Mari sat on the pallet beside her, smoothing back her hair.

"Why didn't you go with them?" Mari asked gently.

"I did!" Danita hiccupped a little sob. "I was going with the group who chose the coast, but then I remembered the beautiful tapestry, there." Her trembling hand pointed at the shredded curtain. "My grandmother wove it specially for the birthing burrow. I miss her—my grandmother."

"Of course you do," Sora said as she steeped Danita's tea. "She was a wonderful weaver and a good Clanswoman."

"See, you understand. When I realized the women had forgotten to bring it with them, I volunteered to go back for it." She curled her trembling hand over her heart, pressing her other hand over it as if she was trying to calm the frantic beating inside her chest. "They came in while I was taking it down. They—they screamed at me to draw down the moon—to Wash them. It wasn't even night!" Danita's wide, liquid gaze flicked from Mari to Sora. "I told them I couldn't. Not even if it had been night. And—and they—they attacked me." Her shoulders shook with the force of her wrenching sobs. "They hurt me."

Without speaking, Mari pulled the girl into her arms and, just as Leda had done so many times for her when she was hurt or sad or scared, Mari rubbed Danita's back and held her close, letting her know she understood, she was safe, she wasn't alone.

"The tea's ready," Sora said softly.

"Danita, Sora has a nice tea for you. It'll help you feel better. Will you drink it?"

The girl hiccupped and nodded. Her hands were trembling badly, so Mari held the cup to her lips, then she helped her lie back.

"Do you mind if I wash you a little? Sora has warmed water over there."

"I hurt," Danita said. "Especially there." She pointed between her legs.

"I know, honey," Mari said. "I'll be careful."

At Mari's nod, Sora dunked strips of bandages into the hot water and gave them to Mari before she went to Danita's head and took her hand. While Mari washed and examined the girl, Sora kept up a steady stream of chatter, talking about everything from recipes for flatbread to the lack of rain until the girl's eyelids fluttered and finally closed.

Mari motioned for Sora to follow her to the hearth, and they tiptoed to the other side of the room and tilted their heads together.

"How bad is she?" Sora asked quietly.

"Bad. She's torn, but the wound's several days old—too old to stitch. I washed and bandaged her with the sage leaves, but they abused her horribly. Sora, I don't know if she'll be able to have children."

"What else can we do for her?"

"She needs rest and poultices to fight infection."

Sora shook her head. "I can only imagine what kind of pain she's been in. Mari, she can't stay here. She has to come back to the burrow with us."

"I know," Mari said.

"She can't know about Nik. If the Clan found out you'd saved a Companion, I don't know what they'd do—to either of us."

"I know," Mari repeated.

"So, what are you going to do about him?"

Mari let out a long breath and made her decision. "I'm going to send him back to his Tribe. Now."

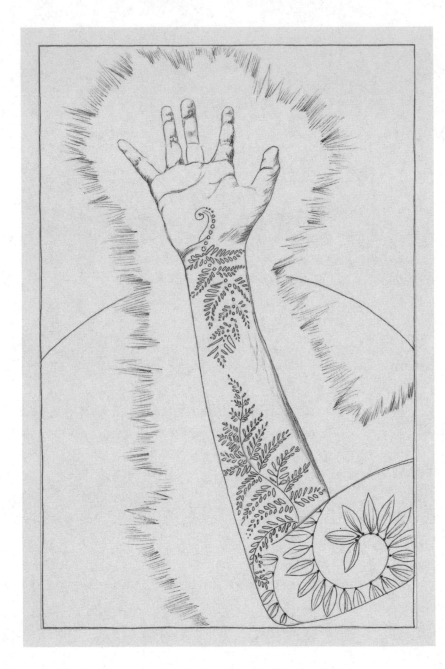

38

"Nik, wake up. You have to wake up!" Mari shook his shoulder hard enough to jostle his wound.

Nik frowned and pushed her hand away. "I don't need any more tea. I'm already sleepy."

"You can't be sleepy. Nik, you have to wake up. You have to go back to the Tribe. Now."

His eyes opened. "Back? Now?"

She nodded, handing him the biggest clothes she could find. "Yes. Now. Get dressed or you won't make it back before dark, and that's not going to be good for you."

Stiffly, slowly, Nik sat. "Then why can't I wait until morning? Then I'll be sure to make it back."

"Because you have to go. Sora's bringing a girl here. She's been hurt pretty badly and there's no where else for her to go."

"And she's an Earth Walker?"

"Of course she's an Earth Walker, and her seeing Rigel is going to be hard enough to explain. I'm not going to let her see you, too."

"Why not? You're a Healer. She'll understand that you've been healing me, just like you're going to heal her."

"Nik, there's a chance that the Clan would kill me if they found out I saved you—me *and* Sora."

"Oh. I didn't think of that."

"I know you're still weak, and you really shouldn't be making this trip for several more days, but there's nothing I can do about it." Mari talked as she helped him put on the tunic. "I'll go with you until we reach Crawfish Creek, then you'll have to go the rest of the way by yourself."

"Is it cloudy or sunny today?" he asked.

"Sunny and hot," Mari said.

"Good. That'll help."

"How?"

Nik's smile curved up on one side more than the other. "Take me outside and I'll show you."

Mari made Nik say his good-byes to Rigel at the burrow.

"I know it's a lot easier for you to track Rigel than it is to track me. So, will you give me your word that you won't come back and try to track him?" Mari asked when Nik complained about leaving Rigel behind at the burrow.

Nik blew out a long breath. "I might not tell you *everything*, but what I do tell you is the truth, so I can't make that promise to you without lying."

Mari shook her head, giving him a dark look. "I saved your life and you're still after my Rigel?"

"No! A canine and his Companion should never be parted. Mari, did it not occur to you that I know if I find Rigel I'll find you again, too, and I might want to find you again?"

Mari's forehead scrunched. "No, that didn't occur to me."

"I thought we were becoming friends. I don't put my friends in danger, or at least I try not to. I'd never lead the Tribe into your territory to try to find you."

Mari fidgeted. "I believe you, Nik. Or I guess what I really believe is that you're telling me the truth right now, but after you're back with your own people, the truth could easily change."

"I promise I will never do anything that would cause you and Rigel to be separated. No matter where I am or who I'm with I will keep that promise."

"Even after you return and show everyone that your blight has been healed by a Scratcher woman?" Mari said.

"They're called Earth Walkers, not Scratchers," Nik said and grinned cheekily at her, then he sobered and added, "Mari, please share with me the recipe for the poultice and the tea you used to cure me. It would saves lives and drastically change my entire Tribe."

"Absolutely, but only after all of the Earth Walkers you keep as slaves are released and your Tribe agrees never to hunt us again."

"I can't promise that I can make that happen. That's something the Elders and the Sun Priest must decide."

"Then I will keep the cure for the blight to myself. When you can make that promise to me or, better yet, when I see the captive Clanswomen returning to their burrows, then I'll reconsider sharing with you and your Tribe," Mari said. "So, say bye to Rigel inside because I'm not going to let him follow us."

Nik was sitting in the chair by the desk. "Rigel, come here, little man." Rigel looked at Mari, who nodded, and then he trotted to Nik. He bent, petting him and staring into the young canine's eyes. "I'm so glad I found you alive and well. I never forgot you—I never will forget you. Take care of your girl. She seems to need a lot of care. And it would be nice if you bit Sora, just a little, for me."

Nik hugged Rigel and ruffled his thick scruff. She could see that tears were tracking down Nik's cheeks and she looked away while he wiped his eyes and collected himself.

"Okay, I'm ready."

She went to him and wrapped the blindfold around his head, completely covering his eyes before she led him out of the burrow. She was pleased to see that he was able to walk by himself, though he leaned heavily on one of the walking sticks. Mari had told him to follow close behind her, reminding him about the brambles. With a hand resting on her shoulder, Nik limped slowly after her.

Once they were free of the bramble thicket, Mari put his arm around her shoulder, helping to take some of the weight from his injured leg. It was slow going, and they were both sweating and breathing heavily by the time they were far enough away from the burrow for Mari to turn Nik around and around, completely disorienting him, before taking off his blindfold.

He wiped the sweat from his face and blinked against the light. "Good, we're not under the canopy yet. This will be easier out here." Nik glanced up at the sky, and then turned so that he was facing the sun. "You should do this with me. You'll probably need the energy to doctor the wounded girl. I can't imagine you've been getting much sleep."

"What am I doing with you?"

"Soaking up the power of the sun, of course," Nik said. "Have you never done that?"

Mari moved her shoulders. "I'm not sure."

"But you set the forest on fire with the power of the sun," he said.

"I didn't mean to," Mari said. "Can you set the forest on fire?" she asked tentatively.

He laughed, and then grimaced at the pain in his back. "No. I can't. Not many of the Tribe can actually call down sunfire. My father can. A few of the Elders can. But that's it. If we had more time I could help you—show you how Father does it."

"I wish we did, but we don't have more time. Actually, we don't have *any* time," Mari said. "So, do what you need to do quickly. Your wounds are still too fresh for you to be safe, and if you get caught out in the forest after dark the swarm will find you quickly, and all of my healing will have been for nothing."

"Okay, I hear you. This is all I need to do." Nik tilted back his head and spread wide his arms. "Fill me, blessed Sun. Lend me your strength so that I can return safely to the Tribe."

Entranced, Mari watched Nik's eyes begin to change color, shifting from a deep, moss green to a shining amber that reminded her of Rigel. Then, starting on his palms, which were lifted and opened to the sunlight, a delicate and familiar pattern began to rise to the surface, glowing golden.

And suddenly Nik didn't look like a wan, wounded stranger. He looked strong and tall, and surprisingly handsome. Disconcerted by the sudden change in her perception of him, Mari forced her gaze from Nik, glancing down at her bare arms where the same filigree pattern was beginning to glow.

"You do it, too, Mari! You, too!"

Feeling strangely shy, Mari couldn't meet Nik's eyes. "I don't know how."

"It's the easiest thing ever. Just open your arms and accept the gift that is your right to claim through your blood."

Tentatively, Mari opened her arms. They were glowing faintly, but nothing else happened, and she didn't feel anything except the warmth of the sun.

"Your eyes aren't changing. Turn your face to the sun and raise your arms. Hold your palms out and open, like this." Nik did an exaggerated demonstration.

Mari mimicked him. "Okay, I'm doing what you're doing, but it's not working the same with me as it does with you. Maybe I can't do it."

"Of course you can! Absorbing the sun is simple compared to calling down sunfire, but you have to accept it, Mari. And that means you have to accept the part of yourself that belongs to the Tribe of the Trees."

Mari dropped her arms then. "That might take some doing."

"Not if you think about it like this—if you weren't part Companion, Rigel wouldn't have sought you out and chosen you to bond with. That's not hard for you to accept, right?"

"Right." Mari drew a deep breath, spread and lifted her arms again, opening her hands and turning her palms up. Then she stared up at the glowing ball of fire in the sky and thought, *I accept the part of me that gave me Rigel. By right of my blood, fill me.*

Heat and power sizzled into her body through her palms, causing her to gasp.

"That's it exactly! Well done, Mari!"

Mari looked at her bare arms, fascinated by the detail of the swirls and patterns that glowed up through her body as it absorbed the rays of the sun and began changing heat into energy.

"It feels incredible!" she said.

"Your eyes are glowing like you've harnessed pieces of the sun in them. You have a gift. I've only seen a few people be able to absorb sunlight as fully as you do. Mari, there is so much the Tribe could teach you about yourself!"

Reluctantly, Mari dropped her arms and turned her face from the alluring sun.

"I'm not going with you," she told him.

"Okay, I understand. But don't close yourself off from an entire world that you could be a part of."

"You said you'd only tell me the truth. So, tell me truly, Nik, would the Tribe completely accept me?"

Nik stared at her, and Mari could see warring emotions in his eyes. Finally, he answered, speaking with reluctant honesty. "I don't know. The Tribe has never had to accept anyone like you. I don't know what they would do."

"Thank you for telling me the truth."

"I'll never lie to you, Mari."

Their gazes met and held until Mari felt a nervous fluttering in her stomach. She was the first to look away.

"Come on. Let's get you to the creek. I need to go back to the burrow. Sora will have the girl there by now, and she needs my attention."

Nik slid his arm around her shoulder, which felt oddly intimate to Mari, though she told herself sternly that that was silly. She'd been this man's Healer. She'd seen *all* of him, for days and days. It hadn't been awkward then. Why should it be awkward now?

Mari wrapped her arm around his waist and they kept walking.

They made better time than Mari had anticipated. Nik was visibly invigorated after he absorbed the sunlight and even though walking was difficult and slow, it was possible. Mari led him to the southern part of Crawfish Creek, where the eastern bank wasn't treacherously steep. They crossed very carefully, and Mari breathed a huge sigh of relief when Nik stepped firmly on dry land.

"You can find your way back to the Tribe from here, right?"

Nik nodded. "Right."

"Okay. Well. Good-bye, Nik." She started to turn away from him, but he touched her hand, stopping her.

"Mari, may I see you again?"

"Nik, let's not make any plans or promises. You're a Companion. I'm an Earth Walker. Being friends is not natural for us."

"It was for your mother and father."

"That's different. Galen loved Mama." The words came out of Mari's mouth before she could stop them. She felt her cheeks flush with heat. "I didn't mean anything crazy like you're supposed to love me. I'm just saying that Galen and Mama were different than us, and that's a good thing because their relationship cost that Companion and his Shepherd their lives."

"But you're not just an Earth Walker," Nik said.

"*Just* an Earth Walker? See, that's the problem. You might have stopped calling us Scratchers, but you don't think we're equal. How am I supposed to be friends with someone who thinks half of me is less than human?"

"I don't think Earth Walkers are less than human. Not anymore—not after meeting you and Sora."

"Oh, so now you like Sora?" Mari unsuccessfully tried to keep a smile from tilting her lips up.

"Bloody beetle balls no! I don't like Sora. But I also don't think she's less than human. I think she could take on many Warriors of the Tribe and probably defeat them."

"She's actually not a very good fighter. She doesn't believe in physical exertion."

"She could definitely nag them to death," Nik said.

"That I'd agree with." They smiled at each other, and Mari couldn't stop herself from adding, "Nik, if you ever really need me Rigel will bring me to you."

"Just like he did before," Nik said.

"Yes, just like that." Mari found herself not wanting to turn away from Nik. Unsettled by the strangeness of her emotions, she blurted a question that had been circling through her mind for several days. "Nik, now that you know Rigel has chosen his Companion, won't you bond with another Shepherd?"

"I wish it was that easy. The truth is Rigel didn't stop me from bonding with another Shepherd, or a Terrier, either. No one knows why a canine chooses his or her Companion, only that the choice cannot be changed or undone. I've been waiting to be made a Companion for as long as I can remember, but it seems that's not what fate has planned for me."

"What do you mean? Is there a shortage of puppies?"

"No, nothing like that, but canines choose their Companions from Tribe members who have seen between sixteen and twenty-one winters. There are some exceptions to this, but mostly that's because some Companions are chosen again after their canine died."

"Dies?" Mari went pale.

Nik touched her shoulder in gentle understanding. "Be sure you and Rigel soak up a lot of sunlight. It doesn't just give our canines and us energy—it lengthens our lives. Your Rigel can live thirty or more winters."

Mari felt herself relax a little. Thirty winters! That was a long time. She met Nik's gaze. "So, are you saying the only exception to the rule of a canine choosing a Companion after he's older than twenty-one winters is if he's already been made a Companion?"

Nik nodded and looked away from her.

"How old are you?"

"Last winter was my twenty-third. You see, it doesn't appear that a canine is going to choose me."

"I didn't know. I'm—I'm sorry, Nik. Really sorry. Does that make things hard with your Tribe?"

"Yes, not being bonded to a canine keeps me in a strange, limbo state."

"What do you mean?"

"Well, one example is that I'm the best archer in the Tribe, but because no Shepherd has chosen me I'll never be allowed to be a Leader, so I'll never be acknowledged as Head Archer. Mari, I haven't told anyone this, but sometimes it feels like I'm not sure who I am."

"Can't you just be yourself?" Mari said, acknowledging to herself the irony of giving this particular advice to Nik when she was not completely sure who the new Mari was, either.

"That's what I've been trying to do, but who I really am doesn't fit into what's normal for the Tribe."

"Well, I can't help you with that one because I've never felt normal."

Nik grinned. "That's probably why we make such a good team."

Mari grinned back at him. They stood there like that, smiling at each other, until it became awkward. Then Mari stuck out her hand and, in her best copy of Leda's brisk, no nonsense voice, said, "I wish you health and happiness, Nik. Good-bye."

Nik grasped the hand she offered, but instead of shaking it he turned it gently, holding it in both of his, and then he bent and kissed the pulse point at her wrist.

When he looked up their eyes met and held.

"Why did you do that?" Mari asked, feeling breathless.

"I'm not sure," Nik said.

She pulled her hand from his. "Well, good-bye." This time when she turned away, he didn't try to stop her.

Mari made it quickly to the other side of the creek. Pausing for just a moment, she turned, expecting to see Nik's back as he hobbled away. He was standing exactly where she'd left him, and he was watching her. Self-consciously, she lifted her hand, waving at him.

Instead of waving back, he cupped his hands around his mouth and shouted across the water. "I said I'd tell you the truth, and here are two truths! One—I would give my world to have a Shepherd like Rigel choose me. And two—I *will* see you again. That I promise!" Then he turned and limped into the waiting forest.

Mari didn't allow herself to watch him, or at least not for very long.

39

The rest of Nik's journey home was exhausting, painful, and entirely too silent. He should have been excited to get back to the Tribe, but the truth was the closer he got, the more his mind was at war.

He'd found the pup, but he didn't have the pup.

He'd found the cure for the blight, but he didn't have the cure.

And he'd found the girl on fire, but he didn't have her, either.

"Sure, yeah, I could announce the truth to everyone. Then what happens?" Nik reasoned aloud. "The entire Tribe demands I find Mari and bring her, the pup, and the cure to them." He shook his head. "*If* I found her again, and that's a big if unless Mari wants to be found, she wouldn't agree to come to the Tribe." Nik scowled to himself, imagining what men like Thaddeus would do. "They'd bring her to the Tribe, willing or not. Rigel would protect her. Who knows where that would lead?" He shuddered, remembering too well the terrible story his father had told him about Galen and his Orion. They'd both been killed—both. And they had been full members of the Tribe, Companions, respected by all. "What would they do to Mari?"

No. There had to be another way. Mari was smart and compassionate. Once he earned her trust, made her understand that he and his father would fight to change things for the captive Earth Walkers, then he believed she would share the cure for the blight with him.

"I need time. Father will help me. He and I will figure this out." And that meant he couldn't tell anyone except Sol about Mari's ability to heal the blight. "So, where have I been? How do I explain not being dead?" Nik limped forward, thinking . . . thinking . . .

He found the answer as he topped the ridge on which spread the Tribe of the Trees. Standing there, catching his breath and admiring the majesty of the Tribe, Nik understood what he had to do.

Nik had to tell the truth. Or at least as much of it as he could without putting Mari's whole world in danger.

He limped to the lift and tugged on the chain. From far above a voice called, "Who goes there?"

"Davis?"

There was a long pause. "Nik?"

"Yes! It's me!"

The lift immediately began to lower, and as Nik climbed in it and ascended he could hear Cammy's excited barking. As soon as the door to the cagelike lift opened, a blond blur ran to him, leaping around and huffing as the little Terrier greeted him.

"Cammy, it's good to see you!" Nik bent stiffly, petting the canine.

Then Davis grabbed him in a bearlike hug, making Nik laugh while he grimaced in pain.

"Sorry! Sorry. Are you hurt? They said you'd been killed, so you have to be hurt. Sorry, didn't mean to grab you like that!" Davis babbled and he pumped Nik's hand in a less painful greeting.

"I'm okay, or at least I am now. It's really good to see you, Davis."

"Sol's going to be beside himself when he sees you. Come on! Let's get you to your father."

"Wait, Davis. Where is Father?"

"Oh, bloody beetle balls, what's wrong with me? You need to see the Healers first. You're standing, but you look like you could fall over any second. And what are you wearing? Can you walk? How badly hurt are you?"

"Okay, one thing at a time. I can walk, but not very much farther.

I can make it to Father's nest, though. Do you know where Father is?" Nik repeated.

"I think he's on his platform, taking in the last rays of the setting sun."

"Could you get him for me?"

"Of course, Nik!"

"And can I borrow your cloak?"

"Sure. Are you cold? In shock? You look bad," Davis said, pulling off his cloak and handing it to Nik.

"No, I just don't want anyone else to see me before Father does." Nik pulled the hood of Davis's cloak over his head. If he kept his face down, no one should recognize him—especially since they thought he was dead.

"That makes sense. It's been bad, Nik. Really bad since the survivors got back from the foraging trip."

"Who did we lose besides Crystal and her Grace?"

"Monroe's Viper died two days ago. Yesterday Monroe followed him."

"Suicide?" Nik felt sick.

"No. He caught a spear in his side. It killed him. It just took several days," Davis said.

"What about Sheena and Captain?"

Davis shook his head sadly. "They're barely hanging on."

"They made it back!"

"Yeah, Captain's front leg is broken. It's too early to tell if he's going to heal. If he dies, Sheena will follow him."

"Was she hurt?"

"She almost drowned, but wasn't wounded. She managed to avoid being sucked into the run-off. She and Captain clung to the bridge ruins long enough for Wilkes to paddle back for them. Captain's leg got caught in the truss, and it snapped. I don't know how Sheena kept ahold of him and the bridge, but she did." He paused and then put his hand on Nik's shoulder. "That thing with Crystal. It was pretty terrible, huh?"

Nik nodded, not trusting his voice enough to speak.

"You did the right thing, though, ending her before those bastards took her away."

Nik nodded again, blinking hard and looking away. He cleared his throat. "Did the rest of the team make it home? What about Thaddeus? I saw a Skin Stealer grab him from his kayak, and tried to stop him, but I couldn't get a good shot."

"Yeah, it was really bad. Skin Stealers captured him and Odysseus and started flaying the flesh from the little Terrier's body."

"Bloody beetle balls, that's awful! I don't like Thaddeus, but I wouldn't wish that horror on him or his Odysseus."

"Hey, don't get too sad. Thaddeus managed to escape with Odysseus, and he's back to being even more arrogant and asinine than he was before."

"Odysseus is alive?"

"He is! And healing remarkably well. Seems that the Skin Stealers started on him, and were so distracted by how hard the little guy fought them that Thaddeus somehow managed to get free, kill a bunch of them, grab Odysseus, and escape on the river."

"I'm glad to hear it. It was awful—truly awful. I'm glad any of us made it out of there, though we were all in the same amount of danger."

"How Wilkes tells it the team wouldn't have been in danger had they listened to you."

"It's too late for second-guessing. And Wilkes had good reason to make the decisions he did." Nik passed a shaking hand through his hair.

"Well, shit! Here I am blabbing on and on, and you're about to fall down. Go to your father's nest. I'll get him for you."

"Thank you, Davis."

"Welcome home, Nik. It's really, really good to see you alive."

Laru burst into the nest, tackling Nik just seconds before Sol. Nik was laughing and groaning in pain and telling Laru to get off him when he was lifted from the chair he'd gingerly sat himself in and engulfed in his father's arms.

"Father, careful! My back's hurt."

Sol loosened his grip, but didn't release his son. Nik felt his father trembling, and realized the big man was sobbing. Feeling unexpectedly childlike, Nik rested his head on his father's shoulder, returning his embrace with as much strength as he could muster.

Eventually, Sol leaned back, holding Nik by his shoulders. His face was wet with tears, but his smile blazed with joy.

"You scared me, son. You scared me."

"Didn't mean to. And I scared myself, too," Nik said.

"I love you, boy. Too much for you to do that again," Sol said.

"I'll try not to almost die again anytime soon," Nik said. "Father, I have to sit down before I fall down."

"Of course! Of course! Laru, move, so that Nik can get comfortable."

Gratefully, Nik sank back on the chair. Laru sat beside him, leaning against him and whining softly.

"He's fine, Laru. He's fine," Sol gently scolded the big Shepherd, but then he squatted in front of his son, studying him carefully. "You are fine. Aren't you?"

"Yes, but the truth of it is a long, crazy story."

"I'll brew you a big mug of tea while you tell it to me," Sol said.

"That's a deal, but do you have anything stronger than tea?"

"Thankfully, yes. " Sol collected two wooden cups and a big pitcher, filling the cups and handing one to Nik before he pulled a chair from the other side of the table to sit beside his son. "All right. Tell me."

Nik felt his father's fingers gently probed the skin around the wound in his back.

"You're right. There's no sign of blight at all. It's obviously a serious wound, but it's hard to believe it happened only a week ago. The healing that's taking place is incredible. Just like the cut on your leg." Sol stepped back and Nik pulled down the tunic top. "It's unbelievable."

"But it's the truth. The blight had taken hold enough that the wound on my leg had started to fester and stink."

"That's a death sentence, and a quick one," Sol said.

"Not anymore it isn't."

"This girl, Mari, she didn't give you the remedy, though."

"She will, Father. I know she will. I just need time to get her to trust me."

"I hear you, son, and I'm even in agreement with you, or as much in agreement as I can be without having met this girl. What you described to me is someone the Tribe could possibly accept, especially if she brings with her Laru's son and the cure for the blight. The problem is time. You don't have much of it," Sol said.

"I'll have all the time I need if we don't tell anyone that Mari can cure the blight. We just tell part of the truth for now—that some Earth Walker women found me and saved my life, and that they did it to show their humanity. We'll tell the rest of it after I've earned her trust and brought her and Rigel here. I don't understand the problem with that."

"There isn't any problem with your plan. There's only a problem with time. Nikolas, I'm sorry I have to tell you this, but O'Bryan is dying."

"What! The wound wasn't that bad. It was only—" Nik stopped himself as realization caught up with his racing mind. "O'Bryan has the blight."

"He does. And it's advancing rapidly."

"How long does he have?"

"Days. He wants to end it, Nik. He's been begging the Healers to give him the dram of monkshood."

"No! That's not going to happen. I won't let it happen."

"What are you going to do?"

Nik rubbed his shoulder, wishing he had a mug of Mari's noxious tea to ease his aches and pains. "I'm going to find Mari and convince her to cure O'Bryan. Now."

"We could go to the Elders and petition them to allow a group of

Scratchers to go free. We'd have to tell them about Mari's ability to cure blight, but that would be enough to get them to agree, though I can't promise that they'll continue to free the Scratchers after we do have the cure."

"Father, you have to stop calling them Scratchers. They're Earth Walkers." Then Nik sat up straighter. "And we don't need to go to the Elders because I don't need a group of Earth Walkers freed. I only need one." He met his father's questioning look with a relieved grin. "Jenna is Mari's friend! I'll offer Jenna's freedom in exchange for O'Bryan's life. Mari doesn't have to give me the recipe for her poultice right now, so long as she cures O'Bryan."

"I don't think the boy can travel, Nik. He's pretty bad off," Sol said.

"Then I'll need your help twice—once sneaking Jenna off Farm Island, and again sneaking Mari here to cure my cousin."

"Son, I'll help you once, twice, a thousand times. Just don't almost get yourself killed again."

"Father, that's a deal."

"What's this daughter of Galen like really?" Sol said.

"She's smart and strong. She's also kind, but I don't think she'd describe herself that way. As tough as she is, calling her kind might actually be an insult to her." Nik found himself smiling as he thought about Mari. "She's an incredible artist. She even sketched a picture of Galen, Orion, and her mother."

"I'd like to see that someday," Sol said.

"I hope you will, Father." Nik sipped his ale, thinking about Mari. "There's a sadness about her. Every time she smiled it was like she'd forgotten how, and wasn't sure if she even wanted to remember."

"Well, she's lost both of her parents. Her mother recently. You know how that feels, son."

"I do, but I think it's more than that. I recognize the sadness that comes with being an outsider in your own skin," Nik said.

"You've never told me you feel like an outsider," Sol said.

"It's not an easy thing to tell, and I don't want to disappoint you any more than I already have."

Sol leaned forward, taking his son's shoulders in both of his hands. "Nikolas, you don't disappoint me. That's something you've created in your mind. I don't care if you are chosen by a dozen magnificent Shepherds at the same time, or no canine at all—I wouldn't love you any more, and I'll certainly never love you less."

Nik blinked through tears, trying for a smile. "Father, are you just saying this because you thought I was dead?"

Sol's expression didn't lighten. He held his son's gaze. "I'm saying it because it is the truth. Son, I want you to make your own choices, and if that takes you down a path I could never have expected for you, then follow it and know that you will always have my love as well as my respect."

"Thank you, Father." Sol hugged him, and for a moment Nik rested there, safe in his father's embrace.

They parted, each wiping at their eyes. When their gazes met again the two men laughed.

"It is so good to have you back," Sol said. "Wilkes gave a full report about what happened out there. He made it clear that your instincts were absolutely correct, and had they listened to you the outcome would have been much different."

"I had to kill her. I couldn't let them take her, but Father, it was the hardest thing I've ever had to do."

"You did Crystal a great kindness."

"I wish that task had fallen to someone else."

"I know, son. Sometimes it is our greatest kindnesses that are the most difficult to bear."

"I want to see O'Bryan."

"Son, wait. Stay here tonight. You've been through so much. You need to sleep and to continue to heal. At dawn I'll go with you to the infirmary."

"I can't wait. If it was me in that deathbed, O'Bryan wouldn't wait either," Nik said.

"Your loyalty is impressive, son. It's one of your best qualities. Would you like me to come with you?"

"That's not necessary. Relax, finish the ale. I will take you up on your offer for me to stay here tonight, though. I don't feel like being alone."

"Actually, you being alive has breathed life back into me, and I have something to do, too." Sol stood, wiping his hands on his pants. Nik saw shadows under his father's eyes, and the lines on his face looked deeper than they had before he'd left, but Sol was smiling at him and it seemed he was newly energized. "I could walk partway to the infirmary with you."

"Can I borrow some of your clothes? I'm going to cause enough lifted brows and ten thousand questions without appearing in the castoffs of a Scratcher," Nik said.

"Absolutely!" Sol took the stairs to his bedroom two at a time, and was back in moments with pants and a woven tunic, thick enough to keep out the nighttime chill.

"Where are you off to, Father? Going to see Maeve?" Nik asked as he changed his clothes.

"No, yes, well—I imagine she'll be there already."

"There?"

"We have a member of the Mercenaries visiting us," Sol said.

Nik's brows shot up. "A cat man is here? Really?"

"Really. It has been interesting, though I admit I have not been a proper host. I was mourning the loss of my son."

"Not anymore!" Nik grinned at Sol.

"Which is why I am going to join the gathering for him when earlier I excused myself," Sol said.

"Well, tell him not to allow his Lynx to mark the visitors' nest. Remember the last time one of the Mercenaries came through here and his cat marked the nest?"

Sol shuddered. "The stench was unbelievable, especially after our canines felt they needed to add their markings to try to cover what the cats did. Dreadful, just dreadful. But we don't have to worry about that with Antreas's Lynx—females don't mark like males."

"What? Are you saying a male Mercenary bonded with a female Lynx?"

"That's what I'm saying," Sol said.

"I didn't think that could happen," Nik said. "Male Lynxes choose a male human to bond with, and females choose a female. Or have the childhood stories of the cat people completely misled me?"

"You haven't been misled. This bonding is unusual—the first I've known. I don't believe it's a particularly polite subject to question a Mercenary about, though."

"No doubt," Nik smiled. "What's the cat man doing here?"

"Looking for a mate."

Nik laughed. "From among the Tribe? I can't see many of our young women wanting to go from living in the sky surrounded by beauty and canines, to living in a den surrounded by cats."

"You know *surrounded* by cats is an exaggeration. With how solitary they are, it can pretty much be guaranteed that the only cats that would surround them are kittens the female births, and then only until they bond with their humans."

Nik shook his head. "They're an odd people, aren't they?"

"They reflect their Companion animal, as do we. Lynxes are different from canines, and so are their people. No matter how strange they seem to us, they are excellent guides and fighters."

"You mean excellent guides and *assassins*," Nik said.

"I think calling them assassins is as impolite as questioning them about the sex of their cats," Sol said, smiling at his son. "But there is no doubt about their skill with blades."

"And that those skills are for hire. That's never sat well with me, Father. Where's their loyalty?"

"To their Lynxes and themselves, I believe," Sol said. "They do know the only paths through the mountain passes, which makes me glad their skills are for hire."

Nik laughed. "Father, I can't imagine you wanting to trek through the mountains."

"Well, not me. The time for roving has passed for me, but there is a whole other world beyond the mountains. I hear that the grasslands stretch on forever, and are a thing of great beauty," Sol said.

"And don't forget the Wind Riders!"

Sol laughed heartily. "How could I forget them? When you were a boy you could never get enough of the stories of the magickal horsewomen of the prairie. Do you know I saw you riding a stick and pretending it was a horse when you were about six winters old?"

Nik felt his face flush with heat. "Can we change the subject now?"

His father grinned at him. "I think you named that stick Lightning, if I remember correctly."

"Old man, your memory is totally fading," Nik teased. "Let's go before you're completely senile."

Sol laughed again and clapped his son on the back. "All right, all right, are you ready?"

"As I'll ever be," Nik said.

Just before they left the privacy of the nest, Sol turned to Nik. "Son, I applaud your decision to tell as much of the truth as you can about what has happened to you. I want you to be prepared, though. If all goes as we hope the Tribe will, eventually, know the full truth about Mari. I cannot predict how our people are going to react. They believe Scratchers are little more than underdeveloped children with a strange, magickal ability to grow things. They need to be cared for, as we do our sheep. Losing that belief will change our world, and I just don't know how the Tribe is going to accept that change." Sol paused and then added, "Though if they want to stop dying of the blight, they have little choice."

"Father, that is exactly what I'm counting on."

40

Nik was relieved to see that the gathering for the Mercenary was small, and mostly made up of the Elder Council and a group of single women who were young enough still to consider mating, but old enough that the chance of a canine choosing any of them was pretty slim. *Which means,* Nik thought, scowling to himself as he and his father approached the group, *that most of the women are my age.*

"Nik! Oh, Nik! You're back! You're alive!" Maeve jumped up from her place beside Cyril and hurled herself into Nik's arms as she laughed through happy tears.

"Hello, Maeve. And Fortina. It's good to see you, too." Nik disentangled himself from Maeve and bent to rub the growing canine behind her ears, thinking how very much she looked like Rigel—and then feeling a pang. Not of envy, as he would have felt before he found Rigel, but a pang of yearning. He missed Rigel. He also missed Mari. The realization of that missing left him crouched beside Fortina, staring at the pup with his mind in tumult.

"Nik, are you well? Are you whole? Sol, is he really okay?" Maeve was asking.

Nik shook himself mentally, patted Fortina once more, then he stood, smiling at his father's lover. "Sorry, Maeve. Yes, I'm fine. Completely fine."

"Nikolas! I cannot express how good it is to see you returned to us." Cyril grasped Nik's hand, shaking it warmly.

"Thank you, Cyril. It was a close thing."

"How did you get back? Sheena said you were mortally wounded when the run-off took you under," Cyril said.

"That's a complicated story, my friend," Sol began. "Nik can tell it after—"

"Father, I don't mind telling Cyril." Nik made himself smile, as if he had absolutely nothing to hide. "The sooner the Tribe hears what happened to me, the less complicated the telling will be."

"Go ahead then, son," Sol said.

Nik drew a long breath and then dove directly into the deep end. "Sheena was right. I was mortally wounded." Nik moved so that his back was to Cyril and Maeve. Then Sol helped to lift his sweater so the neatly bandaged wound was visible to all.

"You've already been to the infirmary?" Cyril and the rest of the group that had left the Mercenary to join Nik shared confused glances, which Nik understood. Gossip traveled like summer forest fire in the Tribe. If he'd been to the infirmary, the Tribe would have already known he'd returned.

"I'm on my way to the infirmary right now," Nik explained, pulling his sweater down. "My wound was bandaged by Earth Walker Healers."

"Earth Walker Healers?" Maeve's tone was incredulous as she looked from Nik to Sol for an explanation.

"He means Scratchers." Thaddeus's voice, laced with sarcasm, came from the rear of the group that had joined them.

There was a sudden, complete silence, and then Nik nodded and smiled at Thaddeus as if the man had just helped him. "Good to see you alive and well, Thaddeus. And what you said is correct. Earth Walker is what they call themselves. The name Scratcher is an insult."

Thaddeus barked laughter. "Leave it to Nik to worry about insulting a Scratcher."

Nik's smile was gone. He skewered Thaddeus with a sharp, honest gaze. "The Earth Walkers saved my life. I think to repay that with insult is wrong."

"But why would they save you?" Cyril spoke quickly before Thaddeus could monopolize the conversation.

"That was one of the first questions I asked the two women," Nik said. "And the truth is one of them wanted to slit my throat and leave me floating with the river trash where they'd found me."

"If that is the truth, why didn't they?" said Rebecca, another of the Elders, who was studying Nik carefully.

"The other Healer, Mari is her name, wouldn't allow it. Luckily for me, Mari was in charge. She said to kill me would make them as inhumane as the people who make up the Tribe of the Trees."

The outcry that followed Nik's words was so great that other members of the Tribe started poking their heads out of nearby nests.

Sol lifted his hands, motioning for silence. "Nikolas simply repeats the words he was told. Shouting will not change the experience. I say we listen to Nik and learn from what has happened to him."

"You were actually in a Scratcher burrow this past week?" Rebecca asked.

"Earth Walker burrow, and yes, that is where I have been."

"What was it like?" called one of the young women from the back of the group.

"Are you saying they were actually taking care of themselves?" said someone else from the gatherers.

Nik looked through the growing crowd until he saw who had asked the first question, and addressed her directly when he answered. "Evelyn, the burrow was comfortable and clean, as well as beautiful in a unique way. As to the second question—yes, they were most definitely taking care of themselves, and me as well."

"Yeah, and your answers prove how delirious you had to have been," Thaddeus quipped. "Well, at least Nik knows where the burrow is. A Healer or two will be a nice addition to the Farm. Maybe they can keep the other Scratchers from dropping dead so often."

"I don't know where the burrow is. The women blindfolded me, but even if I did know, I wouldn't lead you to them," Nik said.

"Are you no longer part of the Tribe of the Trees? Are you now an *Earth Walker*?" Thaddeus asked the question as if he was concerned for Nik's answer, but his eyes were shining with a shallow, mean victory light and his words were laced with anger.

Nik ignored Thaddeus, turning to Cyril instead. "Those two women saved my life, and all the Earth Walkers asked in return was for me to share my story with the Tribe. So, this is what you should know—the Earth Walkers we keep captive here seem unable to care for themselves, are filled with melancholy, and die early because being caged is deadly to them. Out there, in the wild, they are very different. They are not morbidly depressed. They have families they love. They value loyalty and their Healers. They have an amazing understanding of herbs and how to use them to heal. They appreciate art. They're smart and inter- esting. They are as human as are we.

"And that's the story they wanted me to bring to the Tribe. Now, you'll have to excuse me. I need to visit my cousin in the infirmary." Nik hugged his father and then pushed his way through the swiftly form- ing crowd, bumping Thaddeus with his shoulder. He had to suck in a painful breath as it felt as if he'd run into a stone wall.

"Watch yourself." Thaddeus's voice was low and mean. "There's more to some of us than what can be seen."

"Obviously, as you somehow managed to escape from a gang of Skin Stealers with the only wounds being sustained by your canine," Nik said in an equally low voice. Then he turned his back to Thaddeus and walked away.

As he passed the Mercenary where he sat on a carved wooden bench, Nik nodded a greeting to the man. The Mercenary nodded slightly in return, his face as inscrutable as the still, yellow-eyed Lynx at his side.

Behind him the voices of the Tribe, raised in passionate discussion with his father, began to fade, eventually mixing indistinguishably with the susurrus of the night wind through the mighty pines.

"Well," Nik said to himself. "There's no going back from that." And even though he was on his way to see his best friend who was dying, Nik felt as if a great burden had been lifted from his life.

The infirmary was a series of simple nests built in a circular fashion and connected by a bridge system that was wide and sturdy enough that the ill and infirm could be easily transported to and from them, even if it meant being carried on a litter. The infirmary was used for humans and canines, with no differentiation between the two, as both were of equal importance, which is why Nik saw Sheena before he found O'Bryan. He'd entered the first nest, meaning to ask the Healer on duty where he could find his cousin, to find the nest empty except for Sheena and Captain.

She'd been humming what Nik recognized as an old lullaby as she gently groomed her big Shepherd, who was lying on his side, front right leg swathed in a massive splint and bandage. Sheena looked up when he entered the nest, and her body went completely still. All color drained from her face.

Nik tried to smile, but was overwhelmed by memories of Crystal—her exuberance on the foraging trip—her kindness and humor—her love for Sheena—and, lastly, the ghastly way she had clutched Grace's dead body as she had begged him to end her life.

"Nik? Is it really you, or did Captain and I finally die, too?"

"It's me. And no one else is going to die." Nik went to her and knelt next to her, locking his gaze with hers. "Can you forgive me?"

Tears filled Sheena's eyes, but she didn't look away from him. "Forgiveness is not needed. You did the right thing. Had we listened to you, my Crystal would be here and we would be getting ready for a new litter of puppies." The tears overflowed, tracking down Sheena's wan cheeks. Captain stirred restlessly then, and his Companion automatically stroked him, murmuring soothingly. When he'd quieted, Sheena motioned for Nik to follow her to the other side of the nest. "Captain hasn't been able to sleep, so they drugged him." Sheena kept her voice low, trying not to wake her canine. "They drugged me, too, but that's not working so well. Every time I close my eyes I see her pull her knife from her belt and jump into that cesspool after Grace." A tremor went through her body. "I can't stop seeing it, and I can't sleep."

"She smiled at me right before I shot her." Nik's voice shook and he had to force himself to keep meeting Sheena's tortured gaze. "She was holding Grace. She looked up at me—smiled, nodded, and then when it was done, she and Grace disappeared under the water together."

Sheena reached out and grasped Nik's hand. "Thank you for telling me. It makes it a little easier that she and Grace were together."

"Neither of them suffered. I promise you that," Nik said.

"Then don't you suffer either, Nik. Crystal wouldn't want you to, and she would have suffered, suffered greatly had you not ended it before those monsters could take her away with them."

Nik nodded, squeezing her hand before releasing it. "How is Captain? I hear the break is pretty bad."

"I don't know yet. It isn't infected, but they're still not sure if he'll keep the leg." Sheena shook her head, staring at her sleeping canine. "He's not doing well without Crystal and Grace—neither am I."

Nik swallowed down the platitudes he'd heard so many times after his mother's death: *it'll get easier with time, she'd want you to go on and be happy, she's in a better place.* None of those words had helped, and worse—they'd seemed to take away from the depth of his loss. So Nik said to Sheena what he'd wished someone had told him.

"You and Captain had Sheena and her Grace for a lot of years. Your love was true and strong. It's going to be hard to live without them, and when it gets really bad, try remembering that you shared something that some people live a lifetime without experiencing. I don't know if that'll make it better, but it might make it bearable."

Sheena wiped her face. "I'll remember. I'm just not sure what to do without her."

"You have to keep moving forward. Life will take care of the rest." Nik glanced at the sleeping Shepherd. "So will Captain. You have each other, and that's something worth living for."

Sheena sobbed a little more and then Nik watched her straighten her shoulders and wipe her face again. Suddenly she seemed to really see him.

"Hey, why are you alive?"

Nik smiled. "I might be too stubborn to die."

"No, really. What happened?"

"Healers from the Earth Walkers found me and took me in. I would be dead if it hadn't been for them." He paused and then added. "Earth Walkers are Scratchers."

"I know. I'm good with growing things. Before Crystal and I started going on foraging runs I spent quite a bit of time on Farm Island. The women call themselves Earth Walkers." Sheena leaned against the wall of the nest and crossed her arms, hugging herself as she watched her Shepherd sleep. "Did you actually stay with an Earth Walker?"

"Yep, with two. They're Healers. That's why I'm alive. They pulled out the spearhead and stitched me up."

"No sign of the blight?"

"None," Nik said.

"What did you think of the Earth Walkers?"

"They surprised me. One of them I liked. One wanted to kill me, so it was harder to like her."

"I've always wondered what they're like in the wild. They're so sad on the island, but sometimes—not often, but sometimes—I caught a glimpse of something different in them. When they're first captured they weave mats and baskets and such—you know, things that would make those floating cages they're housed in at night more homelike than jail-like. It doesn't last, though. They fall into the melancholy fast and stop doing anything except tending the crops during the day and weeping inconsolably at night."

Nik studied her, and then took a chance. "What if I told you they're completely different in the wild? That it's the captivity that makes them melancholy and kills them."

Sheena glanced at him, and for a moment Nik saw a spark of interest in her despair-filled eyes. "I'd say that doesn't surprise me. Not everyone in the Tribe believes they're helpless idiots, especially those of us who have spent time on Farm Island." She shrugged, and the spark died. "But what can we do? The blight makes working in the fields a death sentence."

"Change isn't easy," Nik said as his mind whirred with possibilities.

Sheena looked at him. "You're different than you used to be."

He nodded.

"Is that going to be a good or bad thing?" She sounded like she was musing aloud, rather than asking him a question, but Nik answered.

"I can't tell yet. I'll let you know when I figure it out."

"That's a deal. Hey, you should know that Thaddeus came back changed, too, though I'm pretty sure his change is more bad than good."

"What do you mean?"

"Well, he's never been very likable, but since he and Odysseus made it back from the ambush, his attitude has been even worse than what was normal for him. Whatever he saw, whatever happened, it took away any kindness he might have had before. He's mean, and angry. All the time. And he hates you, Nik. Watch out for him."

"I will. Thanks for the warning."

"If you ever need anything, come to me, Nik. I owe you."

"No you don't!"

She rested her hand on his arm. "Yes, Crystal and I do. Your cousin is in Nest Three. You know he's bad off, don't you?"

"I do."

"I'm sorry," Sheena said. Then her lips tilted up ever so slightly. "Change is hard."

"It is." He smiled sadly at her. "Sheena, try to let go of that picture of Crystal, and get some sleep. Captain needs your strength."

Sheena nodded. "I'll try." Then she walked wearily back to Captain's bedside. Just before Nik left the nest she called, "I'm glad you came back."

"I'm glad you did, too."

Nest Three was across the platform, and Nik was there in seconds. He stood outside the opening, breathing deeply of the night air and reminding himself that whatever he saw inside—however bad it was with O'Bryan—Mari could heal him. Mari *would* heal him.

He stepped in the nest. The fetid stench of advanced blight was so thick that he could taste it. The smell brought back memories of his mother's painful last days and he had to steady himself to keep from either running from the nest or gagging. It seemed like a very long time, but it could have only been seconds when a Healer approached him.

"How may I help—" Her eyes widened in surprise as she recognized Nik. "Nikolas! You've returned. Are you injured? Do you need care?"

Nik took her offered hand, smiling with sincere warmth. Kathleen was the oldest of the Healers, and Nik thought she was also the kindest. She'd been at his mother's side when she died, and he would forever be grateful for the gentle care she'd given her.

"Kathleen, I'm fine. I'm here to see O'Bryan."

The old Healer frowned up at him, and the grizzled Terrier that was never far from her mimicked her expression so completely that Nik almost laughed.

"Fine? How could that be? Sheena said you were speared and sucked into the run-off."

"That's true, but I was also tended by a great Healer, so I'm fine."

"Healer? From what Tribe? How?"

"Not Tribe, Clan. Earth Walkers tended me," Nik said, and then waited for the old woman's reaction.

"Scratchers?" She looked completely mystified.

"Earth Walkers," Nik corrected.

"Nik?"

He looked around Kathleen at the sound of his name to see O'Bryan trying to struggle to a sitting position. Nik hurried to him.

"Cuz, how are you feeling?"

"Nik! It is you. Thought you were part of my dream."

Kathleen pulled a chair next to O'Bryan's pallet and motioned for

Nik to sit before whispering, "Don't stay long. He hasn't much strength." Nik nodded absently and took the seat, leaning in so that he could catch his cousin in a hug.

Nik was shocked to feel O'Bryan's bones through his tunic, and when he lay back on the pallet, he saw that his face had taken on the bloodless blue tinge that signaled his death was frighteningly close.

"I hope it was a good dream."

O'Bryan smiled up at him. "It is now." He clutched his cousin's hand. "I can't believe you're here. They said you were dead."

"I almost was." He leaned forward and dropped his voice, even though Kathleen had moved to the other side of the large nest to tend the patients there. "Listen to me. I have to say this fast. She found me—the girl on fire."

"What!"

"Sssh!" Nik hissed. "Her name is Mari. The pup was with her, just as we suspected. He's chosen her."

"Like she's a Companion?" O'Bryan's eyes were fever bright, but his mind was still sharp.

"She's part Companion. Her father was one of us." Nik made a sharp gesture to cut off O'Bryan's instant questions. "I'll explain everything later. All that's important now is getting you well."

"Cuz, I'm dying. Everyone knows it. There's nothing that can be done. I'm so glad you're here, though. Will you stay with me when I drink the monkshood?"

"You won't be drinking that damned monkshood. And you will be healed and whole again." Nik leaned closer so that O'Bryan wouldn't miss anything he said. "There was a spearhead buried in my back and my leg was slashed open. Blight set in yesterday." Moving carefully, Nik lifted his pant leg and pulled the bandage aside so that O'Bryan could see the pink, healing flesh.

His cousin's brow furrowed. "But there's no sign of blight."

"Exactly. And yesterday putrid ulcers covered the wound."

"Then it couldn't have been the blight," O'Bryan said.

"Oh, it was the blight. I'm positive about it. O'Bryan, Mari healed it. And she's going to do the same for you."

O'Bryan stared up at him disbelievingly. "Now I know I'm dreaming."

Nik grinned. "Leave everything to me. All you need to do is not tell anyone, and I mean *anyone*. And be ready to get out of here."

"Nik, I can't do much walking." O'Bryan moved the blanket that covered the bottom half of his body. His right leg was elevated and swathed in bandages from his knee down. His naked thigh was dusky and swollen to twice it size.

Gently, Nik pulled the blanket back over his cousin's ruined leg.

"It was a good idea, though," O'Bryan said. "It just didn't come in time."

"You're not giving up because I'm not giving up. If you can't go to her, Mari's going to have to come to you," Nik said.

"I know my thinking isn't too clear anymore, but how is that ever going to happen?"

"I'm going to trade a life for a life—that's how."

41

Isn't it strange that something as important as sleep is taken for granted so easily—until you don't have enough of it?" Mari rested her head against the side of the burrow and closed her eyes in exhaustion.

"Sorry, did you say something? I was asleep."

Mari opened her eyelids a crack and shared a tired smile with Sora. "You did it all by yourself tonight."

Sora's smile brightened, making her weariness fade and her beauty blaze. "I was spectacular."

"If you do say so yourself?"

"Well, if you're not going to say it, I certainly will."

"You were good tonight—really good. Spectacular even," Mari said. Her gaze went to the pallet that used to hold Nik, but now was a temporary home to the small, sleeping form of Danita. "Her body will heal. It's her mind I'm worried about."

"Did Leda write anything in her journals about helping with something like what's happened to Danita?"

"Rape. Let's call it what it is. Danita was raped."

"It's an ugly word," Sora said.

"Then it fits the deed."

Sora shook her head. "Things can't stay like this. We have to do something."

"We are. Danita's body is healing. You've Washed her with the moon tonight. I'll look through Mama's journals. I'm sure there is something I can brew that'll help her mind recover, too."

"I don't mean something has to be done with Danita. I'm talking about the males. You heard them tonight. They're close again. Too close."

Mari sat up a little straighter and put another log on the hearth fire. "I heard them."

"They need to be Washed. There's no reasoning with them until they're free of the Night Fever."

Mari stared at Sora. "No."

"No? What are you talking about? Of course they need to be Washed."

"I'm not doing it."

"But Mari—"

"You saw what they did to Danita! They brutalized her. She's torn, bloody, and bruised. Sora, *she has bite marks on her breasts and thighs.* They're animals, and they need to be put down."

"They're only like that because their Moon Woman died! If we Washed them they would go back to being normal."

"And then what? Once they're normal again are they going to just live with what they've done?" Mari said.

"Maybe it's a burden they should bear forever, but they shouldn't be left to grow madder and madder—and not only because it has to be terrible for them." She shook her head. "I don't understand how you can show so much compassion for someone like Nik, whose people have killed and enslaved us for generations, but you aren't willing to help the men of our Clan."

"I'm from both, Companions and Earth Walkers. Sora, I'm doing my best to figure out where I fit in. Maybe I'm wrong, but what they did to Danita is so terrible, I just don't have any desire to help them," Mari said.

"I hear you, and the men *are* dangerous, but they don't seem to be moving on from here like the rest of the Clan. Something has to be done about them. Are you willing to track them and kill them?"

Mari grimaced. "I don't think so."

"Well, good. So, we have the ability to help them. Let's help them," Sora said.

"You're ready, you know. You're strong enough now to Wash them by yourself."

Sora caught Mari's gaze and held it. "I'm afraid of them."

"That's smart."

"Will you please come with me? Help me to help them?"

"Sora, I don't want to be Moon Woman," Mari said.

"But you are!"

"No, I'm not!"

Sora and Mari glanced at the pallet, but Danita had fallen into a deep, exhausted sleep and she didn't so much as twitch.

"I'm not," Mari insisted, lowering her voice.

"Why do you hate the Clan so much?" Sora asked bluntly.

Mari opened her mouth to deny it, but stopped herself. Slowly, thinking aloud, she tried to answer Sora honestly. "Because I've never been a part of the Clan—never been accepted by them. Mama had to keep me at a distance. Sora, for as long as I can remember, I've hidden who I really am and known that if I don't hide and disguise myself and lie, Mama and I could pay for it with our lives."

Sora turned to face her. "Danita accepted you today without any problem. She even petted your creature and said the fur around his neck was as soft as a rabbit—which I find hard to believe, but it was nice of her to say. Did you ever think that maybe you and Leda made too much of your differences, and not enough of your similarities with the Clan?"

"Please don't say anything against Mama."

Sora touched Mari's arm gently. "I'm not. I wouldn't. Leda did what she thought was best. She protected you. All I'm saying is that she might have *overprotected* you. I accepted you. Danita accepted you. I think the rest of the Clan would, too, especially if they knew that you are even more gifted than your mother."

"I'm definitely not more gifted than Leda."

Sora raised a dark brow sardonically. "I know about the fire."

"Huh?"

"You caused it. That day Leda died. You did it by using your sun power," Sora said. When Mari didn't respond, she prodded. "Hey, you know you can tell me the truth. I'm right about the fire, aren't I?"

"Yeah," Mari admitted softly.

"How did you do it?"

"I have no idea. Nik said he could help me with it, but he left too soon."

"Well, then you have nothing to worry about. That particular male will definitely be back," Sora said.

Mari said nothing.

"And when he comes back he can tell you how to use your sun power. Then if the males try anything—or, actually, if anyone from the Clan tries anything—just zap them with a little fire. I think that would settle the question of you being accepted by the Clan," Sora finished with a self-satisfied smile.

"I think there's a difference between acceptance and intimidation," Mari said.

"Small difference, and what do you care if you get what you want?"

"What is it you think I want?" Mari asked.

"To be part of the Clan without being isolated and judged," Sora said.

Mari was mortified to feel her eyes filling with tears. She blinked rapidly and turned toward the hearth. "I'm going to make some chamomile tea. Want some?"

"Not if you make it." Sora took the herbs from Mari and forced her to meet her eyes. "You're an excellent Moon Woman, but a really abysmal cook. And you don't need to be ashamed that you want to be accepted. We all do."

"Really?"

"Really. Wipe your face. I'll make the tea. There's also some bread left." Rigel lifted his head and padded over to Sora, sitting in front of her and whining softly. "I shouldn't have fed you. Now you'll never leave me alone."

"It's a compliment to your cooking that he already understands the word *bread*," Mari said.

"I suppose you're right." Sora broke off an end of the long, slim loaf and tossed it to Rigel, who caught it neatly. She split the rest of the loaf in half and handed one hunk to Mari. "So will you help me?"

"Are we back on the males again?"

"Yes, we are," Sora said.

"Let me think about it," Mari said.

"While you're thinking, consider this—you are part of both worlds—the Tribe and the Clan. I think you should use your powers for good, for both of them."

Mari's eyes widened in surprise. "You realize that means you're okay with me helping the Tribe?"

"If you'll also help the Clan then I think it's an even trade," Sora said. "*If* your precious Tribe doesn't take you captive or kill you because you're part Scratcher."

"There is that," Mari said.

"I guess that's something you can discuss with your Companion when he comes back around here looking for you."

"You're pretty sure about that," Mari said.

"You can cure the blight that has been killing his people for years. He'll be back," Sora said.

Mari stared into the fire. "I suppose you're right."

"Hey." Sora bumped her shoulder. "There's also the way he looks at you. That'll bring him back."

"He likes Rigel, too," Mari said.

"That he does. But he doesn't look at Rigel like he looks at you."

"Now *that* would be creepy," Mari said.

"Drink your tea and think positive thoughts about your Clan. You hear me, Mari? *Your* Clan," Sora said.

"Oh, I hear you perfectly. *My* Clan has either fled or is completely, brutally, mad."

"Well," Sora said, smiling at Mari. "It is *your* Clan, Moon Woman."

"Father, wake up!" Nik shook Sol's shoulder. Laru was sleeping beside his Companion. He raised his graying head, giving Nik a few sleepy thumps of this tail. "Father, it's important. You have to wake up."

Sol blinked several times, recognized his son, and came instantly awake. "What is it? What's happened?"

"I have to find Mari. Now. O'Bryan doesn't have any time left. I might already be too late," Nik said.

"How much of the night is gone?"

"They just rang the midnight bell," Nik said.

Sol sat up and began pulling on his clothes. "Here's what we're going to do—you're going to sleep for a few hours, and then—"

"Sleep? Bloody beetle balls, Father! Didn't you hear me? I don't have time to sleep."

"You don't have time *not* to sleep. How far do you think you'd get alone in the forest at night with your injuries and your state of exhaustion?" Sol said.

"I can't sleep while my cousin is dying," Nik said.

"Nik, you can't drag that girl through the forest at night, even if you were rested and unhurt. You still need daylight to find your way to Mari. Here's what I propose—you sleep for a few hours. Just before dawn go to the Channel side of the island, close to the bridge. I'll have a kayak waiting there for you. Take it to the floating houses. Find the girl and get her in the kayak, then I want you to beach as close to the blind as you can."

"But, Father, the lookout in the blind will see me for sure."

"He would see you for sure on any other dawn. On this morning, though, he will be praying with his Sun Priest and accepting the rays of the rising sun," Sol said. "I'll be sure the lookout will be able to completely focus on his prayers and accepting the sun because I'll watch the island for him."

"If the Tribe finds out you helped me steal a woman from Farm Island, you could lose your position as Sun Priest," Nik said.

"The Tribe can replace me as Leader. They can never take my calling from me," Sol said. "So, you're going to beach the kayak by the lookout blind, and then take the most direct route into the forest."

"I'll circumvent the Tribe and head straight for Earth Walker territory."

"Do you know how you're going to find Mari?"

Nik ran a hand through his hair. "I'm going to hope Jenna can help me with that, but if she can't I think I know the general area of where her burrow is located. The truth is I'm counting on Rigel's help."

"The pup? You think he'll lead Mari to you like he did before?" Sol asked.

Nik nodded. "I hope so."

"Okay, so, let's say you do find Mari and manage to talk her into trading Jenna's life for your cousin's. Then what?" Sol said.

"Then I'll bring her here to heal O'Bryan, *if* I can assure her safe passage. Can you help me with that?"

"Well, she's bonded with a Shepherd. Her father was one of our Tribe. Violence against a member of the Tribe is taboo. Our own laws should protect her, but if they don't I'm willing to take her under my personal protection. That's the least I can do for her father."

"What are you going to do when the Tribe finds out her father was Galen? She knows how he died. She doesn't know it was you who killed him, but she knows he was killed by the Tribe," Nik said.

"Cyril will probably disagree with me, which is why I'm not going to ask his advice, or permission, on this. I believe it is time for the truth to be told."

"That could go badly for you, Father," Nik said.

"It will be no worse than keeping that terrible secret for all these years."

"You're a great man, Father. I love you," Nik said.

"What's the old saying? The cone doesn't fall far from the pine?" Sol smiled at his son. "Sleep for a few hours. I'm going to put a kayak in position for you, and provision it. I'll send Laru to wake you before dawn. Do you have a plan to get the girl and, I assume, her Rigel, to the infirmary?"

"I hadn't thought that far yet. I expected to have more time to figure this all out."

Sol stroked his chin, thinking. "I think I can help you with that as well. Time your return for dusk or right afterward. Go to that old meditation platform to the east. You know the one I'm talking about?"

"The one Mother spent so much time carving?"

"That's it. It's rarely used after mid-evening because of its distance from the Tribe. I'll be sure there's a candle and tinderbox there. Light the candle and put it on the railing. When I see it I'll know you've returned with Mari. Wait there until after the dinner lights are extinguished. Then bring Mari to the base of the infirmary trees where the emergency block and tackle lift is situated. I'll be above, ready to hoist the three of you up."

"That's a great plan, though I have a feeling we're going to get into a lot of trouble over this," Nik said, looking at his father with newfound respect.

"I haven't been in any real trouble for decades, and I'm finding the possibility of it makes me feel young again."

Nik smiled at Sol and shook his head. "And they call *me* a troublemaker."

"They call you more than that!" Nik and Sol chuckled. Then Sol clapped his hands together, causing Laru to wag his tail and trot around his Companion in expectation. "Ha! It's keeping Laru young, too," Sol said. Then he sobered and pulled his son into his arms for a fast hug. "Nikolas, try not to almost die again. It's hard on my heart."

"I'll do my best, Father." Nik crawled into the pallet warmed by his father and his Companion Shepherd, and was asleep before Sol left the nest.

It seemed only minutes had passed when Laru's cold muzzle poked his neck and Nik's face was covered with licks.

"Laru, okay, okay! I'm awake—I'm awake!"

The big Shepherd gave Nik one more lick, and then sprinted from the room and out of the nest. Nik wished he could follow his example, but his body ached. For a moment he felt a terrible sinking in his gut and he hastily unwound the bandage on his leg, sure he was going to see the pus and ulcers had returned along with the deadly blight. He had to sit heavily on the pallet as relief made him weak.

There was no blight, only a tender wound that needed rest. He went to his father's water bucket and splashed his face and chest with the cool, clean water. Fully awake, he hurried from the bedroom to find that Sol had left a new crossbow and a full quiver of arrows for him, as well as two words, written in his fierce cursive: *Return Safely.*

Nik smiled, grabbed a pair of his father's thick leather gloves, the cloak Davis had let him borrow, pulled up the hood, and hurried from the nest.

Nik didn't go to the lift. It would be too easy for another Tribe member to see him, and to ask questions about where he was off to so early, especially as everyone by now must know he was newly returned from the dead.

But the city in the trees had been designed with a myriad of ways for the Tribe to get safely and quickly to the forest floor, and Nik took advantage of the easiest of those. Not far from his father's nest was one of the many static rappelling stations the Tribe could use in case of emergency. Every member of the Tribe, from the time they were small children, trained until they were proficient in rappelling. It was second nature for Nik to pull back the cape, put on the gloves, and step into the leather harness, lowering himself swiftly and silently to the dark forest floor far below.

Nik tried to jog down the ridge to the Channel, but his battered body could only be coaxed into a limping walk. He gritted his teeth against the pain and the frustration—O'Bryan didn't have time for this!

By the time he made it to the broken asphalt that used to be a road, the sky was beginning to lighten with the gray that was the harbinger of dawn and he was sweating with pain and effort.

He found the kayak easily. His father had left it right where he'd promised—beached near the bridge to Farm Island. Nik didn't allow his eyes or his attention to shift to the bridge. He didn't think about the terror the water held for him. He focused on the task at hand, which was far more difficult than it would have been had Nik's body been well. First, he checked the kayak. The paddle was tied inside the little boat, along with a basket filled with food and water. There was also a still warm mug of tea nestled in the middle of the basket. Nik smiled and mentally sent a *thank you* to his father, and then gulped down the tea. It was sweet and strong, and it sizzled energy through his body, which he definitely needed as dragging the kayak into the water had his wounds screaming in protest. When he finally was able to jump into the boat and begin paddling for the floating houses, he could feel a warm line of blood tracking down his back.

More work for Mari, Nik told himself, refusing to let his wounds cost him any more precious time than was absolutely necessary. *They're nothing compared to what my cousin is going through—nothing.*

The current in the Channel was unpredictable and could be difficult to traverse, but it hadn't rained for almost a week and the river was down and sluggish. Nik made good time to the dock, where he quickly tied the kayak, and then hurried to the first of the floating houses.

All was dark and quiet within. He glanced at the door and the thick metal rod that barred it shut from the outside. No, he wouldn't open it unless he knew Jenna was inside. Nik went to the window and peered inside between the wooden bars.

He'd been wrong. All was dark, but *not* quiet within. This close, he could hear soft sobs, muffled moans, and low keening that sounded as unending as the wind.

"Jenna? Jenna, are you in there?" Nik called.

There was a scrambling sound from within as the mounds on the floor shifted and formed into individuals. Pale, silver-tinged faces turned in his direction.

"Jenna! Is there a Jenna inside?"

"Not our male!" Came an angry voice. "Go away!"

"I'm looking for an Earth Walker named Jenna. I have to find her," Nik said. "Please, it's an emergency."

The women turned their backs to him and the muffled sounds of despair began anew. Nik was moving away from the window when a whispered voice stopped him.

"Are you going to hurt her?"

Nik grasped the wooden bars in his hands and squinted through the darkness to see the small, round face of a girl looking at him through gray eyes.

"No." He spoke softly so as not to rouse the other women. "I wouldn't hurt Jenna. I need her help."

"Do you keep your word?"

"I try to. What is your name?"

"Isabel. What is your name?"

"Nik." He smiled at her. "Isabel, I give you my word that I won't hurt Jenna, and I won't let anyone else hurt her either."

"I'll remember you, Nik. If you break your word the Earth Mother will know."

"I wouldn't have it any other way," Nik said.

"She's in the last house."

"Thank you!" Before he turned away he reached through the bars and offered his hand to her, which she took in her small, thin one. "Things are going to change for you. That I promise, too."

Isabel's smile was sad and disbelieving. Silently, she lay down and curled into herself.

Nik limped down the dock to the last house. He unbarred the door and stepped inside. Faces turned in his direction and he spoke quickly, with authority.

"Jenna! It's Nik. Where are you?"

There was a rustling sound as a mound of blankets moved, and then Jenna was blinking up at him.

"Nik?"

He hurried to her, stepping carefully over or around the scattered bodies of weeping women. Nik held out his hand. "Come with me."

She only hesitated for an instant, then she held up her hand. Nik grasped it, pulled her to her feet, and taking her elbow he began guiding her through the room.

They'd almost made it to the door when hands scrabbled for him, pulling at his pants, trying to stop him. Cries lifted from all around him.

"No!"

"Don't take her!"

"Stop!"

Nik pushed Jenna out the door and faced the room. "I won't hurt her. I give you my word."

The women began to keen and turned away from him. Feeling sick, Nik left the house, barring the door behind him. He guided the silent Jenna to the kayak. She didn't resist as he helped her sit in it. As he paddled away from the dock and made for the far shore, heading for the solitary lookout blind, the sky began to change from gray to the pale yellows and blushing peaches of sunrise. Nik ignored the burning pain in his back and paddled with all of his strength.

"Jenna, we'll be out of this kayak in a few minutes, then we're going to have to move fast. We need to get ashore before anyone sees us. Do you understand?"

When she didn't respond he glanced at her. Her arms were wrapped around herself and she was rocking slowly back and forth. As the sun climbed above the horizon, the silver-gray tinge was fading from her skin, but her eyes were wide and except for a pervasive sense of sadness, empty of reason or emotion.

Grimly, Nik paddled.

When he reached the bank just below the blind, Nik didn't hesitate. He rammed the kayak into the sandy ground, tossed the basket onto the bank, and then lifted Jenna by her waist and managed to half drag, half carry her to shore. There he picked up the basket and took Jenna's little hand in his, looking into her dark eyes and speaking quickly and earnestly.

"We have to hurry and be very quiet until we're out of Tribe territory. Just keep ahold of my hand, and I'll guide you. Once we're safe, I'll explain what's going on. For now, can you just trust me?"

Jenna blinked like she was breaking the surface after a long dive. "No one killed us."

"No one is going to kill us," Nik said. "Not today."

"Nik? It is you." The ghost of a smile lifted the corners of her lips, but only for a moment.

"Yep, it's me. Okay, stay close." He started forward, but Jenna pulled on his hand, holding him back.

"Where are you taking me?"

He smiled at her. "Home. Jenna, I'm taking you home."

42

The sun was partially up in the morning sky and it was already unusually warm when Nik finally decided they were far enough from Tribe territory to take a break. He sat on a moss-covered log, wiped the sweat from his face with the back of his sleeve, and handed Jenna the drinking skin before digging into the basket for the hard flatbread sandwiches his father had packed.

"Thank you, Father," Nik said gratefully, taking a huge bite of the first sandwich. "Here, there's plenty," he said around a full mouth, offering Jenna the basket.

Delicately, she took a sandwich and began to nibble on it. Nik watched her, trying to decide what to say. Their trip had been one of silence, relieved only when Nik said something. If it was a question, Jenna answered it monosyllabically. On her part, she'd not initiated conversation or asked questions.

Nik swallowed and cleared his throat.

"How have you been, Jenna?"

Her eyes met his. "How do you think?"

He looked at her—really looked at her. Jenna's dark hair was a matted mess. She was so thin she looked years older than when he'd seen her last. How long ago had that been? One month? Two? She was so pale that the dark circles under her eyes looked like dirty smudges.

"I think it's been hard for you," Nik said.

"Yes." She went back to nibbling on the biscuit. As if speaking to the sandwich and not to him, she continued. "Thank you for setting me free. Is this where you're leaving me?"

"No," Nik assured her hastily. "No, I want to leave you with Mari."

Like a trapped bird, her gaze darted to his and then flitted away, only to return again. "I—I don't know a Mari."

"Yes, you do. Mari told me you're friends."

She stared at him speechlessly.

Nik kept talking. "Mari saved my life. I was hurt and almost died. She found me and healed me, and now I need to find her again because I need her help to heal my cousin, O'Bryan. You remember O'Bryan? He was there the night you were taken."

Jenna shook her head, but Nik couldn't tell if it was from disbelief, or if she just didn't remember O'Bryan. He hurried on. "I was at Mari's burrow with Sora for almost a week. Of course they blindfolded me and didn't let me see where they lived. I was hoping that you could get me near enough to the burrow for one of them to find me again." Nik carefully didn't mention Rigel. It had been obvious that Mari led an unusual, hidden life, and he knew, of course, that Rigel was a recent addition to that life, and he wasn't sure how many Earth Walkers were aware that the pup even existed. "Then I'm going to ask Mari to trade your life for my cousin's."

Jenna shook her head again. "Did you say Mari and *Sora*?"

"Yeah, I don't like Sora much, though," Nik said.

"This—this doesn't make sense," Jenna said. "What about—" Then the girl pressed her lips into a white line and stopped speaking.

"Were you going to say what about Mari's mother, Leda?"

Jenna's pale face flushed pink with shock. "H-how do you know her name?"

"I told you—Mari healed me and I was at her burrow." He paused, and then in the kindest voice he could manage, added, "Leda is dead."

Tears filled the young girl's eyes and made slashes of a white trail down her dirty face. "No," she whispered brokenly. "Leda can't be dead."

"I'm sorry. I'm so sorry."

Jenna bowed her head and sobbed. Helplessly, Nik watched until, tentatively, he reached out and patted her back gently. When her sobs faded to small hiccups and she wiped her face on the edge of her shirt, Nik offered her the water skin again. She took it, and even though her hands trembled, drank deeply.

"Jenna, will you help me?" he asked.

She looked at him through puffy, red eyes. "No one can know where Mari lives."

"I won't tell anyone. I give you my word."

Jenna shook her head. "No. You don't understand. I don't even know exactly where she lives."

Nik ran his hand through his hair. "Can you get me close to her burrow?"

Jenna moved her shoulders restlessly. "Maybe."

"I promise you that I'm not trying to trick you or Mari. How about this—you get me as close to her burrow as you feel comfortable. Then we'll wait and see if she finds me. If she does, she can choose."

"Choose?"

"Yes. She can choose whether or not to help me," Nik said.

"But you said you would trade my life for your cousin's. If Mari says no—"

"If Mari says no you stay free," Nik interrupted. "You're not going back to Farm Island no matter what."

"Why? Why would you do this? You wouldn't free me that night. Why do you free me now?"

"Everything is different now." Then, with a small smile, he added, "Plus, I know Mari, and I believe she'll do the right thing."

Jenna stared at him for a long time, until Nik didn't think she'd answer him. But just as he was trying to figure out what else he might say to convince this girl to help him, she actually smiled and said, "You do know Mari! I'll help you."

———

"Hey, I can go get the snares. I know how much you hate doing that. And, plus, I've had a nap and—" Mari's words were smothered by a huge yawn.

Sora snorted. Mari's eyes were bruised with exhaustion. She was pretty sure the girl hadn't slept a full night for a week. "I see how rested you are. Do I hate checking the snares for rabbits? Yes. But you were up most of the night with Danita." Sora glanced at the pallet. "She's finally sleeping, and it's time for you to sleep, too. I'll get the snares today. It'll be your turn tomorrow."

"Really? You don't mind?"

"Well, I mind, but I'll do it anyway. Plus, you'll be fresh and rested so you can get up with her again tonight if she has more of those dreams." Sora shuddered and lowered her voice. "I thought she was going to cry herself sick."

"Yeah, it was bad, but I did find Mama's recipe for peaceful sleep. While you're out could you gather some more lavender? Mama's journal said to pack it around someone who is having troubled sleep. It soothes night terrors."

"She's definitely having night terrors," Sora said. "I'll get plenty. Anything else?"

"Yes, I need some fresh aloe for her wounds. If you cross the stream by where we set the snares and climb over the bank to that rocky area, you'll find a bunch of it there."

"Okay, no problem. Go back to sleep. I might be a little while. I want to harvest some wapato root for dinner, and I'm sure I saw some growing by the watercress."

Mari yawned again and said, "Whenever you talk about what you're going to cook for dinner you make me hungry."

"Good." Sora smiled, enjoying the feeling of being appreciated by Mari. Her smile widened as she teased. "And if you're going to be hungry, you might as well have something specific to think about. Tonight I'm going to mash the wapato root with garlic and mushrooms and

some of that precious salt that you like to hoard. That and strips of rabbit rolled in ground flax and fried, and I'll take care of that hunger."

"You know, sometimes I don't mind having you live here." Mari
smiled at her, and Sora thought that she had begun to look genuinely
happy sometimes. Mari was still smiling when she lay back down
beside Rigel—the lazy creature had hardly moved during their
conversation—and closed her eyes.

"Yep, I know! I totally know," Sora said, taking her walking stick
from beside the door. She kissed the tips of her fingers and touched
them to the Earth Mother carved into the arched doorframe.

Her mood light, even though she dreaded the thought of checking
the snares, Sora made her way with increasing confidence through the
bramble maze. Then she turned to the north and headed for the little
stream that was a breeding ground for rabbits.

It was early, but the day was already hot, and Sora found herself
wishing for rain. It was nice, really, in the spring when the rain made
everything seem washed clean and vibrantly green. Mari was easier
and easier to be around—she certainly appreciated good cooking. Soon
the big peppers should be ripening. Sora mentally crossed her fingers
that the crazy males were too crazy to think of destroying the Clan
gardens. They hadn't bothered the herb garden at the birthing burrow, so maybe that wouldn't be a worry.

Almost skipping, she scampered up the little ridge beyond which
was the clearing beside the rabbit stream. With happy thoughts of planning dinners for Mari and now Danita, too, Sora picked up her pace
and in what seemed like no time she was slipping and sliding downhill,
and looking forward to taking off her shoes and wading into the stream.

"Check the snares first. Get it over with," Sora told herself. She went
to the live snares, exclaiming in delight when both traps held bright-
eyed rabbits. "I'll have to crowd you both into one cage to carry you
home, but Mari is going to be so pleased!" Then she approached what
she thought of as the killer snares. Since she was alone, Sora held her
hands up in front of her eyes and peeked through her fingers. Two were

empty, but the third had trapped a fat turkey, which had Sora grinning, kicking off her shoes, and doing a little happy dance as she waded into the lazy stream. She bent and splashed water on her sweaty face, considering stripping down and taking a proper bath in the cool water before she started searching the marshy bank for the tasty wapato roots.

Sora was so preoccupied with thinking about how she was going to prepare the lovely turkey that she didn't know the males were there until they were almost upon her.

"Pretty Sora. Pretty, pretty Sora."

She spun around to see Jaxom standing just a few feet from her, staring at her with such intensity his gaze almost burned. Emerging from the tree line behind him were two more males. She recognized them as Bradon and Joshua—two men who were older than Jaxom by several winters—though *recognizing* them was sad. The men had changed drastically over the weeks since Leda's death. They walked with bestial, hunched movements that reminded Sora of the stories the Clan told of Skin Stealers who would come for bad children, particularly those who wouldn't sleep when they were told to go to bed. What was left of their clothes was little more than tattered rags, through which Sora could see strange, broken wounds and missing skin that left raw, oozing flesh.

Sora wanted to run—she might have even been able to outrun them, but her body wouldn't obey her mind. It was as if the males had forged iron nails from the ruined city and driven them into her feet, rooting her in place.

"What do you want?" She tried to sound confident and just the right amount of annoyed, but her hands were trembling so badly that she had to ball them into fists to keep them steady.

"Wash us!" Bradon demanded, his voice rough and scratchy, as if he'd become unused to speaking.

"I'm not a Moon Woman. You know that. I didn't even have time to apprentice before Leda died."

"Wash us!" Joshua shouted as he and Bradon entered the clearing.

"I told you, I can't!" Sora said. "And it's the middle of the day. There is no moon in the sky. Even Leda couldn't Wash you right now. Go away. I can't help you."

"Pretty Sora must Wash us!" Jaxom said, taking another step toward her. Sora could see that he was less hunched and feral than the other two males, but his gaze kept lingering on her tunic and her breasts that were too visible beneath the damp material.

"No! Stay back!" Sora bent and grabbed a fist-sized rock from the stream bed and held it up threatening. "Jaxom, I wish I could, but I can't help you. If you go away now I'll promise to practice drawing down the moon, and meet you back here, in this clearing, on the night of the next full moon. By then I should be able to Wash you."

"You will Wash us!" Bradon said.

"Wash us!" Joshua repeated as they began to close the distance between them and her.

Sora looked frantically around, trying to find anything else she could use as a weapon. Why hadn't she asked Mari to teach her how to use that slingshot? Mind whirring, she remembered the digging knife she'd put in her satchel—the satchel that was lying on the bank by Jaxom's feet.

Bradon and Joshua reached Jaxom, and then everything happened very fast.

"If you can't Wash us, then you will do other things for us!" Joshua said, and with a predatory snarl he lunged for Sora, grabbing her wrist and wrenching it so that she cried out and dropped the stone.

He began to pull her from the stream. Sora fought him, kicking, hitting and punching—though it felt as if she was struggling against a tree for all the effect she had on him. She fell, and Bradon took her other wrist, pinning her to the ground.

"Jaxom! Help me! Remember that we used to be friends? You used to like me!"

"Pretty Sora should stay with us. Pretty Sora can make us feel good." Jaxom's eyes were bright with lust as he captured her kicking feet by both ankles, and spread her legs.

It was then that Sora began to scream.

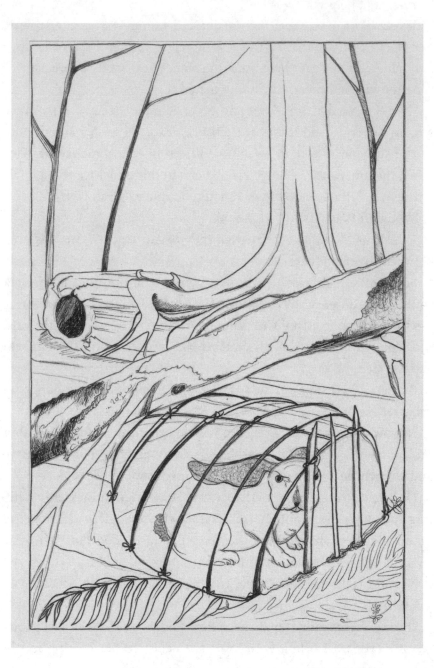

43

Nik suspected the girl was leading him around in circles. He understood why—she was showing her loyalty to Mari and whatever rules of secrecy her Clan followed, but he was out of time, patience, and energy.

"Jenna, how close do you think we are?"

"Not far now, and a little way from here there's a pretty stream and a clearing. I thought we could wait there. It might be cooler by the water," Jenna said, sending him a shy, sideways smile.

"Thank you, Jenna. That does sound nice. This part of the forest is pretty, even though there aren't any of our pines." Nik smiled at Jenna. "I suppose that's the point—that Earth Walkers don't build their burrows near Tribal groves." Jenna was opening her mouth to respond, when Nik hesitated, coming to a halt. He held up his hand, stilling Jenna. "Did you hear that? Someone's voice?"

Jenna cocked her head, listening along with Nik.

The scream, filled with terror and pain, pierced the serenity of the forest.

"Stay behind me. If I say run—then you run and try to find Mari. Tell her I need her. Tell her she knows who can find me."

Jenna's dark eyes were huge with fear, but she nodded. Nik notched his crossbow and held three more arrows to ready between his fingers.

Gritting his teeth against the pain in his leg, he began to run, following the sounds of fear.

He topped the rise with Jenna close behind him, and looked down at a clearing with a little stream bubbling through the middle of it. Sora lay beside the stream, arms and legs spread by three Scratcher males. The one between her legs was ripping her clothes from her as the two holding her arms bared their teeth and leaned down, licking and biting her arms and breasts. Sora was shrieking and struggling.

Horrified, Nik sighted and shouted. "Leave her alone you fucking animals!"

The males reacted exactly as Nik had hoped they would. They lifted their heads, searching for him.

Thawk! Thawk!

The two males that had been holding Sora's arms were easy targets and arrows buried to the feathers in each of their foreheads.

The one between Sora's legs began sprinting across the clearing, staying low, but running with superhuman speed. Nik sighted and shot, and then cursed loudly as the arrow went through the back of the creature's shoulder. It knocked the Scratcher to his knees, but he recovered with amazing quickness, and before Nik could sight again, he'd crawled on all fours and disappeared into the forest.

"Stay close to me!" Nik told Jenna, and then he surged over the ridge, slipping and sliding down to the clearing. He ran through the stream to Sora.

"No! No! No!" she shrieked when he reached her, scrambling back, over the body of one of the men. Her eyes were wide and unseeing with panic.

Jenna moved quickly around Nik. "Sora! Sora! It's Jenna. It's me."

"Oh, Goddess! Oh, Goddess! Jenna? Run! They'll hurt you! Run!"

"I'll check the forest for more of them," Nik told Jenna. "Talk to her. Try to calm her."

Nik hurried to the tree line. He found the bloody trail left by the wounded Scratcher, but saw no sign of more of them. He sniffed then, wondering what the hell that rancid smell was, and his eyes returned to the blood path. He bent, touched a scarlet drop to his finger and lifted it to his nose. He grimaced in disgust at the smell—it was the blood! Its scent reminded him of a long-dead carcass. He wiped his hand clean on a thick pad of moss, then, keeping a wary eye on the seemingly empty forest, he backed to Sora and Jenna.

Jenna was smoothing Sora's torn clothing and trying to get it to cover her body. Sora looked up as he got close, eyes filled with fear.

"It's just me—Nik," he said. "You know I won't hurt you."

"Nik, you saved me!" Sora said, and then her face crumpled and she began to cry—great wracking sobs that shook her entire body.

Jenna pulled her into her arms. "You're safe now. You're safe now," she murmured.

Nik crouched beside the two girls, eyes still scanning the forest around them. "Were there more than three of them?"

"I—I don't think so," Sora said through sobs.

"Okay, then let's get you out of here—now." Nik started to help Sora stand, but the girl cringed away from him. He met Jenna's gaze, and the girl nodded her head, understanding.

"Come on, Sora. I'll help you stand up," said the girl.

Nik retrieved the satchel that wasn't far from them. "Which way?" he asked Sora.

"I can't tell you," Sora said.

Her sobs had quieted, but tears still tracked down her cheeks, mixing with blood from a split in her bottom lip.

"You have to tell me," Nik said. "There could be more of them."

Sora's shoulders began to shake. "I can't, Nik!"

"Sora, I give you my word, sworn on Rigel's life, that I will never tell anyone from the Tribe where Mari's burrow is. You can trust me. You have to."

"He rescued me from the island." Jenna's voice was soft and sweet. "I think he's a good man, even though he is a Companion."

Finally, Sora nodded. "Go southeast."

Nik started to lead them from the clearing, but Sora stopped him.

"We have to bring the rabbits. And the turkey. I—I have to get wapato and lavender, too. For Mari. Mari needs them."

"Sora, there's not time for any of that. I didn't kill the third male, and if he brings more back in force, I won't be able to hold them off," Nik said.

"I'll get the turkey," Jenna spoke with a matter-of-fact attitude that seemed to belong to a woman much older than the pale, little girl he'd rescued from the island. "I'll wring the rabbits' necks and carry them, too."

"No! We need the rabbits alive." Sora met Nik's gaze. "Mari is breeding them."

Nik almost told Sora that Mari would have to come back and get them herself, but then he realized what Mari must be doing. She was raising rabbits because Rigel's rapidly growing body required constant fresh meat.

He sighed. "Jenna, get the turkey from the snare. I'll take care of the rabbits." He hurried to the traps, quickly grabbing one of the animals by its ears and shoving it into the cage with the other. Hefting it under his arm, he turned to Sora. "We're not digging for roots or gathering lavender. We're getting you safely home. Now. The two of you stay behind me, and stay close and quiet."

Thankfully, Sora didn't argue. Clutching Jenna's free hand, she followed Nik from the clearing and into the forest.

Mari was having a lovely dream about mounds and mounds of steaming roasted wapato mixed with all sorts of herbs and salt—lots and lots of precious salt—when Rigel jolted her awake. She sat up, rubbing her eyes and feeling anxious and confused. The young canine was at the door, barking frantically.

"What's happening? Help me, Mari!" Danita was sitting on her pallet, clutching a blanket to her chin and staring at the door with wide, panicked eyes.

"Everything is fine. No one can get to us here, Danita."

Mari hurried to Rigel. The young canine had stopped barking, but he was whining and scratching at the door. "Okay, I'm coming. Just a second." Mari rushed to throw across her shoulder the pack that held her slingshot. She grabbed several handfuls of the carefully chosen stones she kept in good supply near the hearth, tossing them into the pack. "Stay here. Bar the door behind me and don't open it unless Sora or I tell you to."

"No, Mari! Don't leave me here by myself!" the girl cried.

"You're safer here than anywhere in the forest."

"What if you and Sora don't come back?"

Mari almost assured her that they would, and then she thought of Leda, who she lost long before she should have. "If we don't come back you stay here until you're stronger. There are foodstuffs and supplies in the pantry—enough to last several days if you're careful. Then you have to follow the rest of the Clanswomen to the coast or south to Clan Miller. Only travel during the day. Find a big tree to hide in at night. Do you understand?"

Danita nodded.

"Bar the door behind me," Mari repeated.

She opened the door, and Sora fell into her arms, sobbing and speaking hysterically. "I'm sorry! I'm so sorry! I had to bring him here. Males are in the forest. They attacked me. I'm so sorry, Mari!"

Utterly confused, Mari looked behind Sora to see Nik standing in the doorway. He was holding a crossbow in one hand and a full rabbit trap in the other. He looked dirty and pale and soaked with sweat—and Mari's heart did a strange little stutter step of happiness as he smiled at her. Then he moved a little to the side, revealing Jenna.

"Surprise!" Nik said.

Unable to speak through her tears, Mari opened her arm to allow Jenna to come into her embrace. She stood like that, enfolding the two young women in her arms as Nik smiled into her eyes, for what seemed like a very long time.

She wasn't able to look away from him or find her voice until he crouched to greet Rigel.

"Hey there, good to see you again, big man. Good to see you." He scratched the wriggling canine behind his ears.

Mari glanced at Sora and really saw her—the tear-streaked face, the bloody lip—the torn clothing. "You're hurt!" She disentangled from the two girls and began quickly assessing Sora's injuries, adding bloody, bruising bites on the soft part of her upper arms to the list. "What happened? Tell me what happened!"

Nik came all the way inside the burrow, closing the door behind them, which is when Danita started screaming.

"Go to her. I'm fine," Sora said.

Mari rushed to Danita and took her face between her hands. "Danita, you are completely safe. That is our friend, Nik. He isn't an Earth Walker, so he has no Night Fever."

"He's a Companion! He'll take us away or kill us!"

"No, he won't. He's different," Jenna said, joining Mari. "Nik just helped me escape from the Companions."

"Jenna, take Danita into our back room and tuck her into bed." But before Jenna could do as she asked, Mari pulled her into a tight hug. "I'm so glad you're back!"

"Me, too, Mari." Jenna pulled back and looked into Mari's eyes. "What happened to your hair?"

"Sora."

Jenna giggled, then her expression sobered. "Nik told me about Leda. I'm so sad about it."

Mari hugged her again. "I know, honey. I know." When she finally let her loose, Jenna kissed her cheek before taking Danita's hand and leading her into the other room.

Mari went to Sora, who was trying to pour water into the pot for tea, but her hands were shaking so badly that she was spilling more than she was saving.

"I'll do that. Sit down." Sora sank down in her usual spot by the hearth and stared into the fire. Mari glanced at Nik, who was sitting on the chair by the little desk, petting Rigel, whose tail hadn't stopped thumping. "Are you hurt?" she asked him.

"Nothing new. I think I broke open the back wound, though."

"Is it bad?"

He shook his head. "Tend Sora first. She needs you."

Mari sat beside Sora. "What happened, and where are you hurt?"

"My—my arms hurt, and my breasts," she whispered. Then her voice began to rise. "My face. What happened to my face?" Sora looked frantically at Mari, her hand lifting to her bloody lip.

Mari caught her hand, gently holding it out of the way. "Your lip is cut, but not badly. Your cheek is swelling and already bruised." She hesitated before pulling off the remnants of Sora's clothing. Over her shoulder she said, "Nik, could you leave the burrow? Just wait right outside. I need to examine Sora."

Nik was getting stiffly to his feet when Sora spoke. "He doesn't have to leave. He saved me. But c-could he turn around?"

"Of course, Sora," Nik said, turning the chair so that his back was facing the women.

"All right, talk to me," Mari said as she began untangling the torn clothing from Sora's bruised body.

"I was in the clearing. I was so happy I was wading in the stream and thinking about what wonderful thing I was going to do with the turkey we'd snared." Sora smiled through new tears. "It felt good to be so happy."

Mari nodded and made an understanding sound, though she didn't take her focus from the nasty bite wounds on Sora's arms.

"Jaxom, Bradon, and Joshua came out of the forest. I didn't even know they were there until it was too late," Sora continued. "I tried to reason with them, but they're completely mad, and in terrible shape, worse than Night Fever, worse than anything I've ever seen. They wanted me to Wash them during the day . . . and when I couldn't they dragged me from the water and, and they attacked me." Tears slid down her face. "They held me down. Even Jaxom. Jaxom was going to rape me— they were all going to rape me." Sora's shoulders began to shake. "Then Nik was there. He-he killed Bradon and Joshua, and he shot Jaxom, but he got away."

Mari glanced at Nik's broad back. "Did you kill the third one, Nik?"

"Not sure," he said. "Not outright, but the arrow went through his shoulder. If I hit the right place he'll bleed out. If not, my guess is he'll die slowly of infection. Sora's right. There's something seriously wrong with those males."

"Jaxom and I used to be friends," Sora sobbed. "We even talked about being mates."

"Did he rape you?" Mari asked softly.

Sora shook her head. "No. Nik stopped him."

Mari breathed a long sigh of relief. "Good. That's really good. Okay, I'm going to get a wash ready to clean those bite wounds. Your skin is only broken in a few places, but you're going to bruise badly, and you'll be sore. I'll brew a tea for you that'll help with the pain and make you sleep."

"I don't want to sleep. Wash the wounds, but sleep won't make me better. And I have a turkey to roast. I'm sorry about the wapato and lavender. I should have gathered it before I played in the stream. I should have—" Sora broke off, putting her face in her hands while she sobbed.

Mari wrapped her arms around her friend and held on tight. "None of this was your fault. None of it."

"I—I led Nik here. I'm sorry, Mari," she said brokenly.

"She had to, Mari," Nik spoke up. "We didn't know how many more of them might be lurking in the forest. And the wounded one could have returned. I did swear that I would never betray your home to anyone in the Tribe. I meant it, Mari. You can trust me to keep your secret."

"It's okay—it's okay," Mari said to them both. "I believe you, Nik. What's most important is that we are all here and safe. We'll figure everything else out in time."

"He brought Jenna home," Sora said, raising her tear-streaked face and looking at Nik.

Mari had to blink hard to keep from crying. "Which means you need to consider two more mouths to feed for dinner," she said instead of dissolving into half-hysterical, half-happy tears.

Sora smiled tentatively. "It's good that the turkey is big and fat."

"It's good that we're all together." Mari hugged her. "Do you think you can brew us some tea while I check Nik's back and grind some goldenseal?"

Sora nodded. "You'll need more boiling water for the wash, won't you?"

"I will." Mari went to the empty pallet and got a blanket, giving it to Sora so she could wrap herself in it. Then, as Sora chose herbs for the tea and filled the pot, Mari went to Nik.

She stood in front of him and held out her hand. "Hello, Nik. Nice to see you again."

He grinned up at her, took her hand, turned it, and, as if he did it every day, kissed the pulse point on her wrist. "Hello, Mari. Nice to see you again, too."

Though her cheeks were flushing so much that they felt on fire, Mari somehow managed to speak calmly—as if she was used to Nik kissing her. "You need to take off that shirt so I can see how badly you've messed up my work."

"Sorry about that, but it was a little tougher getting Jenna free and getting here than I thought it was going to be," Nik said, as he pulled off his shirt.

Mari stepped behind him, frowning at the bleeding wound. "Well, there's no sign of infection, and you didn't completely rip out the stitches. It's going to be sore, but I'll clean it and bandage it tightly enough that it should continue to heal—though it is going to leave a pretty nasty scar."

"Scars add character," Nik said.

From the hearth Mari heard Sora snort, which made her smile. Sora was going to be just fine.

"Okay, just relax while I get what I need for the both of you together." Mari paused and then added, "Is Jenna hurt, too?"

"No. She was pretty bad last night when I took her from the island, but the closer we got to here, the better she's been," Nik said.

Mari smiled with relief. "That's good to hear." She made a mental note to be sure to Wash Jenna as soon after moonrise as possible. Then she put her hand on Nik's shoulder and looked into his green eyes. "Thank you for saving Sora."

"I couldn't have done anything else," Nik said.

"Yes, you could have," Sora said.

Mari and Nik turned to face her. Sora was standing by the hearth with a blanket wrapped around her, bruised and bloodied, but whole.

"If it had been up to me, that day we found you I would have killed you and left you for the roaches. You knew that, but you saved me anyway. I was wrong about you. I ask you to forgive me for that, Nik," Sora said.

"I willingly forgive you, Sora."

Sora blinked, wiping new tears from her cheeks, and turned back to the hearth fire.

"And thank you for freeing Jenna," Mari said. "It seems we have a lot to thank you for today."

Nik took her hand from his shoulder and held it gently. "Before you make me out to be too much of a hero, I have to tell you exactly why I freed Jenna."

"Okay, tell me," Mari said.

"I have a cousin who is like a brother to me. His name is O'Bryan. He was wounded by a pack of those males. While I've been gone his wound has blighted. He's dying, Mari. Soon. I freed Jenna to trade a life for a life—hers for my cousin's. Please return to the Tribe with me and heal my friend."

44

Mari felt as if Nik had punched her in the stomach. She pulled her hand from his. "You were right. We shouldn't make you out to be too much of a hero," she said.

"Don't do that, Mari." Mari looked up to see Jenna standing in the doorway. "He could have tied me up and dragged me to our territory, and then held me as a hostage until you agreed to help him, but he didn't. He was nice to me—really nice. He even tried to help me the night Father was killed. He might not be *as much* of a hero as you thought, but he's definitely not a villain." Then her gaze went to Rigel. "Mari, why is there a big Shepherd in your burrow? Is he Nik's?"

"No!" Mari and Nik said together.

"He's mine," Mari continued. "His name is Rigel, and he found me." Then she blurted, "Jenna, my father was a Companion from Nik's Tribe. That's why I look like this, and why Rigel bonded with me."

"Did your father rape Leda like the males were trying to do to Sora?"

"No. He loved Mama very much," Mari said.

"Well, then, where is he?" Jenna asked.

"He died when I was a baby."

"Oh. That's too bad. And that explains why you've always been so different," she said. "Danita says she could eat something, and so could I. I thought I'd start plucking that turkey for Sora."

"That would be nice. Thanks, Jenna," Sora said. "I'll boil more water for that."

"Okay, call me when it's ready. I'll sit with Danita until then."

When she was gone, Mari shook her head. "I thought it'd be a lot harder than that."

"What would be harder?" Nik asked.

"Telling people who she really is," Sora spoke with her back to them as she began their dinner preparations. "You see, Nik, our Mari thinks the Clan will hate her and banish her because she's part Companion."

"Maybe they will," Mari said. "Maybe it's just my friends who are willing to accept me."

"I say if someone's not your friend then don't waste your time on them," Sora said as she rattled pots and pans and began filling mugs with steaming tea.

"I'm your friend," Nik said. "I accept you for exactly who and what you are."

Mari looked at Nik. "Okay, okay! Get your cousin. I'll heal him."

"That was my first choice, too, but when I saw him last night I realized he's too far gone to walk. Mari, you have to come to the Tribe with me."

"No! I'm all for her helping you, especially after what you just did for me, but Mari can't go there," Sora said.

"You have to," Nik spoke directly to Mari. "Please. He'll die if you don't."

"And what if she saves him—cures him of this awful blight? Do you expect us to believe the rest of your Tribe is just going to let Mari leave?"

"No, I don't expect you to believe they'll let her leave. I do expect you to believe that my father and I will make sure she has safe passage—to the Tribe, and back."

"What does your father have to do with this?" Mari asked.

"He's our Sun Priest—the Leader of our Tribe," Nik said.

Into the shocked silence Sora spoke first. "I'll do it. I'll go with you and heal your cousin. You said a life for a life. You just saved mine. I'll save your cousin's in return."

"Can she do that?" Nik asked Mari.

"Probably, but she's not going to have to. I'll go."

"Mari, no! You're the closest thing to a true Moon Woman we have. You can't go," Sora said.

Mari went to Sora. "You are a true Moon Woman, too. If something happens to me, you have Mama's journals. This burrow would be yours. Take care of Jenna. Train Danita. Go to the Millers and the Fishers and bring our women back to their homes. Be who Leda believed you could be."

Sora brushed away tears. "I'll be who *you* believe I can be."

"I'll bring her back to you safely. That I promise you," Nik said.

Sora pulled Mari into her arms, hugging her tightly. Over Mari's shoulder she told Nik, "You'd better, because if you don't we'll come get her."

Mari and Nik left after Sora put together a hasty meal of leftover stew and bread for them. She complained all the while about how they were going to be missing the turkey feast she was in the middle of preparing, but Mari had agreed with Nik. With the symptoms he described even Leda's journals warned that the disease was advanced and without drastic measures would be fatal.

As they left the burrow and began the long, hot journey to the Tribe, Mari thought about the "drastic measures" she would have to perform, and then, according to her mother's notes, there was still no guarantee a case this far along could be cured.

"You look worried," Nik said.

"I'm thinking about your cousin," Mari admitted. "Nik, you do understand that he might be too sick for me to heal, don't you?"

"That was one of the first things I thought about when I saw him last night. It's why I left right away, even though I knew it could be bad for my own wounds," Nik said. "Mari, could the blight come back?"

"I didn't see anything in Mama's journals that said the blight reoccurred. She wasn't taking notes on Companions, of course, but you did respond to the treatment immediately. I think you're okay, Nik."

"That's good to hear," Nik said.

"And you know where I live. If your wounds start bothering you, come by the burrow and I'll take a look at them."

"That's better to hear." Nik grinned at her. "But do I have to be in pain to see you?"

"Why else would you want to see me?"

"Because I like you! And I like Rigel. And now that Sora doesn't want to kill me I like her okay, too."

"I don't know if we can be friends," Mari said slowly, surprised at how difficult it was to reject him.

"I thought we were already friends."

"Well, we are. But that doesn't mean we can keep seeing each other. Nik, my father was killed because of his relationship with an Earth Walker. I don't want that to happen to you," Mari said.

"It's a different world now than it was all those years ago," Nik said.

Mari met his eyes. "You're going to have to prove that to me when we get to your Tribe."

A squirrel bolted from the path in front of them and Rigel, barking with happy excitement, took off after it.

"Are you sure I shouldn't send him back to the burrow? Sora calls him a creature, but I can tell she secretly likes him. At least he'd be safe there," Mari said, watching the treed squirrel scold her pup.

"The Tribe would never separate a Companion from her canine. I told you that."

"I'm only half Companion," Mari reminded him.

"No, you're Rigel's Companion—his choice for life—and that's stronger than anything in your blood. Trust me, Mari. I won't let anything bad happen to either of you."

They walked on in silence for a little while until Mari's curiosity couldn't be still. "So, your father is Leader of your Tribe *and* a priest?"

"A priest, or priestess, is always Leader. There's also a Council of Elders that rules on Tribal business and upholds laws and such." Nik paused and then added. "So a Moon Woman is what you call your Clan's Healer?"

Mari had told herself she was ready for Nik's questions. He'd over-heard enough to make his curiosity dangerous, and before they'd left Sora had pulled her aside and vehemently reminded her that *no one* from the Tribe could know the extent of a Moon Woman's abilities. Mari agreed, but she wasn't looking forward to lying to Nik. She'd promised herself to tell him the truth—just not all of it.

"Mari?"

"Oh, I'm sorry. Yes, a Moon Woman is a Healer, but it's more com-plicated than that. Like I explained before there is usually only one Healer per Clan, and we always live apart from our people," she said.

"Why?"

"Safety." She sent Nik a pointed look implying what the Moon Women had to stay safe from was his Tribe and their Hunters.

"Oh, I see." He looked away from her and Mari breathed a mental sigh of relief. "I'm sorry."

"Don't be. It's not your fault." Guilt made Mari's response sound more abrupt than she'd meant it to, so she added, "It's the way our world is."

"Sometimes I think our world needs to change."

Mari mimicked Sora's sarcastic snort. "Just sometimes?"

"Yep, sometimes. When I was in your burrow watching Sora grum-ble about us not staying for her feast, and Jenna playing that strange card game with little Danita, and you buzzing from the front room to the pantry and back again and again while you loaded up your medi-cal pack—well, that's some of the times that I don't think the world needs to change," Nik said.

Mari stared at him, not knowing what to say.

"Do all of your Healers have gray eyes?"

His question surprised her and she scrambled for an answer that wasn't a direct lie.

"Why do you ask?"

"Your eyes are gray, and so are Sora's. You're Moon Women. That new girl, Danita?"

"Yes, that's her name."

"Her eyes were gray, too. I heard you tell Sora to train her. And the Earth Walker who told me where Jenna was being held last night was the only female who would talk to me—her eyes were gray, too."

"Did she tell you her name?"

"Yes—Isabel."

The knowledge that one of the girls Leda almost chose to apprentice was imprisoned settled within Mari like a sick secret.

What would Mama do? What would Mama do?

"Mari, is something wrong?"

"I know her. Isabel was a—a friend of Mama's."

"I suspect you know many of the Earth Walkers on Farm Island," Nik said.

Mari nodded.

"I don't know what to say about that."

Mari looked at him, meeting his gaze with a frank fierceness that caught her off guard. "You could say that you'll help me figure out a way to free them."

"Your friends?"

"Yes. No. All of them, Nik. All of the Earth Walkers. My friends— the women I don't know. *All of them.*"

"I think you're the key to that," he said.

His response utterly shocked Mari. "Me?"

"Absolutely. Hear me out. You don't know my Tribe, my people, but they aren't monsters. They aren't killers and slavers. They're just people—like Sora and Jenna and you. They justify enslaving the Earth Walkers because of the damned blight. Working the fields—planting, weeding, irrigating, and picking—that's a death sentence to people who can't survive a simple cut in their skin. But you can cure the blight! If you share that cure with my Tribe, they'll have no reason to enslave your people."

Mari stared at him. Was he really that naive, or was he trying to trick her into giving him the cure? Of course the irony was the added an- notation in Leda's medical journal: *the infection was cured, though not without the power of the moon.* Mari could give him the recipe for the

indigo poultice—that was simple. But without a Moon Woman drawing down the power of the moon, it would be as ineffective as whatever
the Tribe's Healers had been using.

And she couldn't tell him the full truth. Could she?

"Nik, healing the blight isn't as simple as you think it is. There are
things about Moon Women, and my people, that you don't know. It's—
it's complicated," she prevaricated.

"Oh, I know! I remember. You need moonlight to cure blight, too.
Lucky for us there's plenty of moonlight up in the trees."

"Well, that's good!" Mari said brightly. "But Nik, that's not all there
is to it."

"I understand. You don't want to give the cure to the Tribe. And
why should you?"

She hated the sadness in his eyes. "Nik, can we agree to talk about
it later?"

"Sure. Right now let's just get O'Bryan well. Everything else can
come later," Nik said.

"That sounds good to me," Mari said. Rigel ripped past them, barking wildly at another squirrel. Mari and Nik laughed. "So your father's
canine is Rigel's father?"

"Laru—his name is Laru. They look a lot alike." Nik smiled as Rigel
tried to climb a tree after the squirrel. "They act a lot alike, too. Or at
least Rigel acts like Laru used to when he was young. He's more mature
now, or at least he pretends to be, but you'll definitely see the similarities."

"I'll get to see Laru?"

"Of course! He's always with my father," Nik said.

"I'm meeting your father?" Mari felt a little dizzy.

"He wouldn't have it any other way. Plus, you'll be safe with him. I
can say I won't let anything happen to you, but Father has the power to
grant you safe passage."

"Does he know about me? Who I really am?"

"Yes."

"And he accepts me?"

"Completely," Nik said. "He helped me get Jenna from the island. He knows everything, Mari. You can trust my father as surely as you can trust me."

Mari gave Nik a nervous smile, and said nothing. Then she had a thought and asked, "Does the entire Tribe know I'm coming?"

"No! Just Father and me—and O'Bryan, of course."

Through measured, sideways glances, Mari studied him. "You're going to get in trouble for letting Jenna go free, aren't you?"

"I don't know," Nik said. "I don't think anyone has ever freed a Scr— ur, I mean Earth Walker before."

"You're going to get in trouble," Mari said.

"Most likely."

He didn't appear to be upset by the likelihood, so Mari teased, "Well, you can always hide in my burrow!"

He stopped and met her gaze, smiling. "That is an offer I may take you up on."

With her stomach feeling as dizzy as her head, Mari said, "Um, how much farther is it?"

"Not far now. We'll get there not long after sunset."

Mari glanced at the darkening sky and wiped her sweaty palms on her tunic.

"You don't need to be nervous. You're only going to meet Father and O'Bryan. Oh, and Laru, of course."

"Nik, did it feel like you were *only* meeting Sora and Rigel and me?"

He laughed. "No! It felt like I had been tossed upside down into a while new world."

"Okay, then. I'm going to be nervous."

His grin widened. "You are going to be fabulous."

45

Against the canvas of the setting sun, the Tribe of the Trees looked to Mari like a magickal painting created by sky gods. Having climbed the well-traveled ridge more quickly than they'd expected, Nik led her to a pine situated several hundred yards away from where the city began. There were wide, sturdy steps built into the tree so that it was easy for Rigel to follow Mari and Nik up onto a beautiful wooden platform, sanded smooth, with a railing decorated with carvings of flowers and songbirds.

"What is this place?" she asked him, running her hand over the intricate decorations as she stared to the west at the city in the trees.

"It was built a long time ago as a private meditation space. That's why it's not connected to the rest of the Tribe. It's also why my father knew no one would be here this close to dusk. It's too far away from the city to be used after sunset."

"Wait, did you say your father?"

Nik smiled. "It was his idea to bring you here." He searched the platform, looking under the wooden benches built around the circumference of the tree until he spotted a box. "This was his idea, too." Nik opened the tinderbox and set about lighting the thick beeswax pillar candle. "Father will be looking for this. We'll stay here until it's fully dark, and then—with his help—we'll get you to O'Bryan." Nik lit the candle and positioned it on the wide railing, facing westward. "That's it. Now we wait." Nik made a gesture that took in the massive pines and the city within them. "My part of the idea is that I thought you'd like to get a real view of the Tribe before sneaking into it."

Mari stared to the west. "It's incredible. I had no idea it was so big." Her hand was resting on the railing and her fingers traced its intricate decorations. "Everything is so beautiful. This carving—the birds and flowers look so real it's like I'm waiting to smell the jasmine while I watch the birds fly away."

"My mother carved it," Nik said.

"Really? She was very talented," Mari said. "How old did you say you were when she died?"

"It was just after my tenth winter."

There was a long pause, and then Mari asked, "Does it get easier to be without her?"

"Yes and no. The pain gets easier. It fades. Missing her doesn't fade, though. Sometimes it'll hit me when I don't expect it at all—like when I'm doing something as simple as choosing a new blanket for my nest. Her voice will suddenly be there, in my mind, telling me that that particular color of blue reminds her of the summer sky." He paused and cleared his throat before he continued. "When that happens I miss her so much it's hard to breathe for a while."

Understanding, Mari nodded. "I'll reach for something and all of a sudden my hand will look exactly like Mama's. It's so strange how that's a comfort and a sadness."

"At least you've drawn her. You won't forget her face," Nik said.

"You don't have any drawings of your mother?"

"I do, but they're not as good as yours. Your talent is impressive."

"I could draw her for you sometime, if you'd let me try," Mari said.

"How?"

"Well, show me a drawing you do have of her, and then tell me more—describe more about her to me, and not just how she looked. Tell me about the things she loved and the things she disliked. What was a normal day for her like? What were some of your favorite things to do together? Expression is important in getting a portrait right, and expression is ruled by a person's likes and dislikes."

"That would mean a lot to me, and to my father."

"I'd be happy to do it. When I sketch it's like I go to a different world," Mari said.

"Do you hate this world so much?"

Mari met his gaze. "I used to."

"And now?"

"Now I'm not sure. I'm not sure about a lot of things I used to think I knew," Mari said.

"Me either." Rigel padded to them and sat between them, lying half on, half off both of their feet. Nik grinned. "We make a strange team."

Mari laughed with him. "We can definitely agree on that."

"I wish you had met my mother. She would have liked you," Nik said.

Mari felt herself flush hot with unexpected pleasure. "That was a nice thing to say. Thank you."

"It was just the truth, but you are welcome. Thank you for coming with me."

They sat on the graceful platform for a long time, side by side, waiting for the world to catch up with them. They watched the sky go black, and then become dotted with the crystal dust of stars. The moon appeared, a fat crescent, glowing with a brilliance that caused Mari to squint against its brightness. Finally, the flickering lights from braziers and torches began to blink out and the Tribe became sleepy and still.

"Are you ready?" Nik asked her.

"Yes," she said firmly, hoping the word would become a self-fulfilling prophecy. "But how are you going to sneak me all the way up there?"

"Well, Mari, *that* is going to be a grand adventure for you. Um, you didn't mention it before, but are you afraid of heights?"

"Does it matter if I am?"

"Only if you scream or faint when you're afraid," he said.

"I know we're not up as high as the rest of the Tribe is, but I didn't mind climbing up the stairs to get to this platform at all. I don't think climbing farther up is going to be any problem for me at all," Mari said.

"Oh, you're not going to climb—you're going to fly." Chuckling to himself, Nik motioned for her to follow him down the stairs. Baffled, but intrigued, Mari followed.

"It's like a litter that's been turned into a strange cage that lifts." Mari crouched beside the contraption Nik had guided them to.

"All you and Rigel need to do is to climb in."

Mari looked up. And up. And up, up, up. Her stomach gave a sick flutter.

"Everything all right?" Nik asked.

"Yes. Just thinking. Nik, it's really far up there. Are you sure this is safe?"

"Safer than hanging out here on the forest floor at night with a guy who has unhealed wounds," Nik said.

"You're right about that." She looked at Rigel. "Is he going to be okay, or do we need to tie him in somehow?"

Nik grinned. "Rigel, let's go up!" He pointed to the litter. With zero hesitation, the young canine bounded into the litter and lay down, mouth open in a canine grin, tail wagging. "He's used to heights, remember?"

Mari sighed. She climbed in behind Rigel, clutching her medical satchel to her lap and trying to pretend that she was somewhere—anywhere—else.

Nik got in behind her. "Ready?"

"Absolutely not, but let's go up anyway," she said.

Nik chuckled and pulled on a thick hemp rope. There was a pause, and then the lift jerked up, causing Mari to gasp and flail for the sides of the litter and something to hold on to.

Nik's strong hands were on her shoulders in an instant. "Relax," he said into her ear. "We use this for people who have been so badly injured that they can't make it to the infirmary nests from any of the large lift cages scattered around the city."

"Does that mean I should be badly injured?"

"That means you should be confident that this little lift is absolutely safe," Nik said. "And open your eyes."

"How did you know they were closed?"

"Easy guess. Open them."

Mari did so, and then found herself looking around as they rose into the sky. The trees were massive. They were also beautiful with their drapings of moss and ferns. As they went higher, all around them things began to glitter, and Mari realized that the entire city was decorated with crystals and mirrors and beads and ribbons. Then, carried on the rising wind, came a musical tinkling and chiming in time with the night breeze.

"What kind of music is that? It sounds like the wind is playing glass and bells—but how is that possible?" Mari asked Nik.

"The wind is playing glass and bells—and beads and shells and hollowed reeds and all sorts of precious things hung in the branches of our pines."

"Wow. Mama would have loved this."

Moments later the litter was being pulled onto a wide platform by a man who looked like an older version of Nik. Beside him was a huge Shepherd whose face was eerily familiar. Rigel leaped out of the litter to greet the Shepherd. Nik took Mari's hand, helping her onto the platform. Then, with a sense of joy that had her spirit lifting, he presented her to his father.

"Father, this is my friend, Mari. You already know her Shepherd, Rigel. Mari, I'd like to introduce you to my father, Sol, Leader and Sun Priest of the Tribe of the Trees."

Mari wished she'd thought about what she was going to do when she met Nik's father—or at least wished she'd asked Nik what she was supposed to do. Then she didn't have any more time to be nervous because she was enveloped in the warmth of Sol's hug.

"Welcome, Mari! You are so very, very welcome," he said. Then he held her at arm's length, looking into her eyes. "Thank you for my son's life. That is a gift for which I will never be able to fully repay you, though I will try, Mari. I promise you I will try."

Mari smiled up at him shyly. He was so tall! Though when she glanced at Nik she realized that he was actually taller than his father.

"You are welcome, Sun Priest," she said awkwardly. "I'm glad Rigel led me to Nik, and I'll be glad to help with his cousin, too."

"Please call me Sol," he said. Then his Shepherd approached her. "And this is Rigel's sire, my Laru."

Mari reached her hand out to the huge Shepherd, who sniffed it, and then licked her, wagging his tail happily. "You're so handsome! And Rigel looks so much like you!" she said, then turned to Nik. "Is Rigel going to get this big?"

"Bigger, maybe. Don't you think, Father?"

Sol smiled. "Your Rigel is bigger than Laru was at his age. He looks good, Mari. You've done well for him."

"Thank you," Mari said, and added, "I hope I can help Nik's cousin."

Sol's smile slid from his face. "I hope you can help O'Bryan, too, but I'm afraid it may be too late. He fell asleep about midday and will not awaken."

"Then we need to go to him—now." Nik began to hurry toward one of the nearby nests, but Sol caught his arm.

"He's not there, son. He's been moved to the Transition nest."

"He drank the monkshood?"

"Nikolas, lower your voice before we're found out and any chance O'Bryan has is gone," Sol said.

"Sol, Nik, I can't heal someone who's taken the monkshood root. The poison cannot be stopped," Mari said.

"O'Bryan didn't drink of the root," Sol said quickly. "He simply went to sleep and didn't wake."

"Take me to him," Mari said.

"Put this on first." Sol handed her a long, hooded cloak. "It's late, so there is only one Healer on duty, but we can't be too careful. Nikolas, I had to enlist Maeve's help."

"Maeve?" Mari asked.

"She's a special friend of mine," Sol said.

"She's his lover," Nik explained.

"Well, I did say she's special," Sol said. "Maeve and I managed to convince my brother and his wife to leave O'Bryan's bedside, where they've been since he began to deteriorate earlier today. We sent them to their nest to eat and try to get some sleep. I promised to send for them if his condition changed. I'm hoping that when I do it's with good news instead of bad. Maeve's with O'Bryan now." He turned to Mari. "Are you ready, child?"

"I am."

"Then follow me."

Mari followed Sol and Nik across a wide wooden platform that enfolded four huge pines. Built into the trees were houses that looked like they could be nests for a species of beautiful, enormous birds. The nest they stopped at was the most exquisite of the group. It was swathed in diaphanous material that fluttered gracefully in the wind. Glittering lengths of sparkling objects—Mari recognized shells and crystals, as well as bits of mirrors—dangled from the branches from which the nest suspended.

The entrance of it was an easy step up from the platform. Once Mari was within, she was enfolded in soft, flickering lights thrown from candles that danced within glass cages hanging from the ceiling. The scent was thick with beeswax and putrefying flesh, and Mari immediately recognized the smell of blight.

A woman who appeared to be about Sol's age got up from the bedside of the single patient in the nest and hurried to them, but Mari's attention was captured by the Shepherd who bolted from her side to greet Rigel with such enthusiasm that she knocked the pup off his feet.

"Fortina, easy. Not here—not now!" The young canine immediately disentangled herself from Rigel and, looking chagrined, loped to her Companion.

Rigel padded back to Mari and sat by her feet. Mari could feel his happiness and excitement bubbling over from him into her.

"Mari, this is Maeve. Maeve, this is Mari and her Rigel—who you already know as Fortina's brother," Sol said.

"Hello, Mari. I've been very curious to meet you." Maeve took Mari's hand briefly in greeting, though with less warmth than Sol had shown. "Rigel is looking very well."

Utterly overwhelmed, Mari refocused on the only thing she could control—healing a new patient. "Hello, Maeve—thank you. That must be O'Bryan," she said, looking over the woman's shoulder at the still body of a young man on a narrow bed.

"Yes, this is my cousin." Nik took her arm and led her to the bed. "Tell me what you need to help him and we'll get it for you."

Mari opened her satchel and took out a woven pouch filled with herbs. "This needs to be steeped into a very strong tea."

"But Mari, he's not awake," Nik said.

Mari glanced up at Nik. "He will be, and he'll need that tea then."

"I'll brew it," Maeve said, taking the packet from Nik and hurrying from the nest.

Then Mari turned all of her attention to her patient. He was covered with a light blanket, and when she pulled it off him she had to hold her breath as she accustomed herself to the noxious stench. The wound was simple to locate. His entire right leg was black and swollen. Gently, Mari unwrapped the bandage from around his calf. She heard Sol retching somewhere behind her, but it meant nothing to her; Mari's entire world had narrowed to the man on the bed.

The wound was like nothing Mari had seen before. It was ulcerated and weeping pus and discolored blood. Striations of dusky, purpled disease spread from the site of the wound, and completely covered his leg. Mari lifted his tunic to see that they continued all the way past his waist, with fingers of darkness beginning to reach his chest. Where the disease didn't mar his skin, it was hot and damp to the touch.

He's dying—fast. He could stop breathing at any moment.

Mari squared her shoulders and pulled the basket filled with indigo poultice from her satchel. "I need some water to rinse this wound."

In moments Nik was handing her a bucket with a ladle and a towel. Quickly and efficiently she rinsed the horribly infected wound, and then packed it with the indigo poultice.

"I need fresh bandages," she said. Someone placed them in her hands and she wrapped them around the wound. She stood and faced Nik and Sol.

"Can you save him?" Sol asked.

"I'm going to try." She turned to Nik. "You said that there is plenty of moonlight up here in your trees."

He nodded.

"I need you to take your cousin and me to it, now."

"Take you to it? Do you mean you need us to carry O'Bryan outside the nest to the platform?" Sol asked.

"No. The trees are blocking too much of the moonlight there. I need a place where there is nothing between the moon and us except the sky."

"Is this completely necessary? Shouldn't we wait until your poultice has begun to work? Moving him now could kill him," Sol said.

"If he stays here the blight will kill him," Mari said.

"But your poultice?"

"My poultice is only one part of the cure for this disease. I need access to moonlight, and not the weak light that might filter in from those windows." Mari jerked her chin in the direction of the high, circular-shaped windows of the nest. "Without the full power of unhindered moonlight, he has no chance," Mari said.

"Your prayer platform. It's the highest place in the Tribe. There is nothing above it but sun and moon and sky," Nik said.

"Is it the only way?" Sol asked her.

"Yes."

The Sun Priest nodded solemnly. "Then, son, let's get your cousin up there."

Working quickly, Sol and Nik wrapped O'Bryan up, cocoon-like, in a light blanket.

"Maeve, you stay here. If the Healer or anyone else asks after O'Bryan tell them . . ." Sol trailed off as if searching in vain for words he couldn't quite capture.

"Tell them your Sun Priest has taken O'Bryan above to pray for healing," Mari said. When the three of them stared at her, she had to force herself not to fidget nervously. "Is that wrong? The Clan goes outside to pray to our Earth Mother. Wouldn't you pray to your Sun under the open sky, too?"

"We would—we do," Sol said.

"What you said wasn't wrong. It was perfect," Nik assured her.

"I'll go first. Keep to the shadows behind me and only move when I motion the way is clear," Sol said. "Laru—keep Fortina and Rigel here with you."

"No." The word broke from Mari at a visceral level before she willed it. "I won't be separated from Rigel. Not even for a moment. Not even for this. Nik told me I wouldn't have to be."

"Where Mari goes, Rigel goes," Nik said.

"Very well. Keep the pup quiet and close to you. The entire Tribe would recognize him, and that attention is something none of us needs right now."

Mari nodded, and then crouched beside her young Shepherd. "Stay with me and don't make any noise, Rigel. Like we're hiding—like we're back around the Clan." Within her mind Mari sketched a picture of the two of them, silent as shadows, creeping from the nest. Rigel licked her and thumped his tail briefly, then he stilled even that small, happy sound.

Mari kissed his nose, and then stood. "He understands. We're ready."

Nik lifted O'Bryan, holding him in his arms as if he was a small child who had fallen asleep and needed to be carried to his bed.

"He's so light. It's like there's nothing left of his body," Nik said.

Sol closed his eyes and bowed his head, and Mari saw his mouth moving as he offered a silent prayer.

"Follow me."

The journey to the Sun Priest's platform wasn't long, but later Mari would remember it with a kind of distracted wonder. She crossed bridges that swayed gently in the breeze and connected clusters of homes that were exotic and incredibly lovely—each similar in form, but completely unique.

Just before they got to the stairs and began ascending to the platform, they crossed over a huge deck area, bigger than Mari could ever have imagined. In the center of the deck there were six massive pines, grown so close together for so long that they had joined to form a heart. And from the very middle of the heart, growing directly on the stately trees, was an enormous cluster of ferns, so big that a single frond could cover Nik from head to toe.

She and Nik were huddled in the shadows, waiting for Sol's go-ahead signal. Mari whispered to Nik, "What are they?"

"Those are the Mother Trees," he whispered back. "Growing on them are the Mother Plants. I'll tell you all about them later."

"I know about them," she said softly. "They cost my father his life."

Before Nik could say anything more, Sol motioned and they hurried across the wide deck.

The artist within Mari wanted to stop and stare at everything—to take in the myriad of nest and pods and mazelike bridges and platforms that held it all together so that she could reproduce it on paper later.

The Clanswoman within her wanted to find the quickest escape route and flee.

And what did the Tribeswoman want? Mari glanced at Rigel. She didn't need to be connected to the pup on a Companion level to see how relaxed and at home he was. Her gaze slid to Nik's strong, broad back as he cradled his cousin in his arms and carried him so gently that it seemed Nik's own life depended upon it.

The Tribeswoman wants to belong, Mari thought. *And that, for a change, is exactly what the Clanswoman wants, too.*

They reached Sol's platform without crossing anyone's path. The circular stairs were narrow and steep, but Nik's steps were steady and his arms sure. Once on the upper deck, Mari moved to the railing, quickly orienting herself.

"Put him here, facing north," she said.

Sol helped Nik lay O'Bryan carefully on the platform. The young man didn't waken. Nor did he make any sound.

"You have to leave me alone now," Mari told Nik and Sol. "What happens next is for the Clan's eyes alone."

"But we would not—" Sol began, but a touch from Nik stopped his words.

"We'll be below. Send Rigel when you're ready for us to come back," Nik said.

Mari nodded. She caught Nik's gaze and held it, hoping that he could see how much his trust meant to her, though she couldn't seem to find the words then to tell him.

The two men were turning away when O'Bryan's body began to writhe in a violent seizure. Mari ran to him, turning him on his side so that he wouldn't choke if he vomited.

"I need a piece of wood for his teeth, so that he doesn't bite off his tongue." She shot out the command, her voice echoing through the night sky sounded eerily like Leda. Footsteps faded and then returned, and a stick was handed to her. She pried O'Bryan's mouth open and placed it, just as she had watched Leda do, holding it in there while she supported his head and murmured soothingly to the unconscious, dying man. *Mama, what would you do now? I need you! I need help!*

"Whatever you need, I'll do." Nik was on his knees beside her.

She looked at him. "I need you to hold him like I am so he won't injure himself, but you can't be here, Nik. You can't see what I'm going to do."

Nik locked his gaze with hers. "Then I will stay here and hold him just like you are, and I won't see anything you do. Mari, I swear on my love for my mother that I will not betray your secrets. Trust me. Please trust me."

I know what Mama would do. Mama would save O'Bryan and trust this man.

"Sol has to go below," she said.

"I'm going," Sol said, his footsteps fading as he descended the staircase.

"You must never speak of this," Mari told him. "The life of my Clan depends upon your silence."

"You have my vow and you will always have my silence."

"Hold O'Bryan, just like this. Be sure you keep him on his side. Talk softly to him. Soothe his fears. But don't let him go. Tell him it isn't time for him to transition yet."

Nik nodded, and took her place.

Mari turned so that the silver light of the glowing crescent flushed her face. She tried to concentrate. Tried to sketch within her mind a scene that would draw down the life-giving power of the moon and channel it through her and into O'Bryan, but she felt utterly disconnected.

Mari closed her eyes, focusing, slowing and deepening her breathing in and out, in and out, and trying to reach for the earth to find her center—her grounding.

But the earth was too far below. It couldn't find her, and Mari didn't know how to reach it.

"What is it? What's wrong?" Nik asked.

"This place is so strange to me, Nik. I can't—I can't find myself here! And if I can't find myself, how will the moonlight know me?"

Nik put his hand over hers. "It's the same you, Mari. Where you are doesn't matter, and what you're doing doesn't matter—it's who you are that matters. Know yourself, and I believe the Moon will know you, too."

"Oh, Nik! That's it! It is still me—all I have to do is reintroduce myself." Moving with increasing confidence, Mari stood and spread wide her arms. She found her mama's voice in the music that joined the wind blowing through the trees. *Joy, sweet girl! Remember to be filled with joy! And tonight, Mari, you must save some of the Moon's power for yourself.*

Mari's smile seemed to lift from her spirit to fill her body and spill over her face. *I hear you, Mama. For once, I'll do exactly as you say.*

Filled with joy and starting with M, so that the Earth and the Moon would recognize her, Mari began to dance her name among the Tribe of the Trees.

46

Holding his dying cousin as he writhed and fought to breathe, Nik waited anxiously for Mari to do something—anything—and save O'Bryan. What he didn't expect her to do was dance. But there she was, arms held wide, hands turning and fingers fluttering as if in accompaniment to the tinkling of the countless strands of crystals and glass and beads and shells that decorated the trees, Mari began to dance. She moved around him, tracing a pattern with her steps. Her face, that face that was such a unique mixture of Tribe and Clan, was alight with joy and moonlight, and her blond hair curled around it caressingly.

Nik thought she was the most exquisite woman he had ever seen.

When she started to speak it was in a hesitant, singsong voice that reminded him of a storyteller.

"Moon Woman I proclaim myself to be
Greatly gifted I bare myself to thee.
Earth Mother aid me with your magick sight
Lend me strength on this moon-touched night."

Still dancing around him, her voice became stronger and more confident.

"Come, silver light—fill me to overflow
So that those in my care, your healing will know."

She paused her dance before O'Bryan's ruined right leg and sank gracefully to her knees beside him. Gently, she rested one hand on his calf, directly over the wound. The other she lifted above her, holding it with her fingers spread wide, palm open to the moonlight. In a voice filled with power she spoke the end of her invocation.

"By right of blood and birth channel through me
That which the Earth Mother proclaims my destiny!"

For the rest of his life, Nik would be able to conjure the image of Mari, hand and face lifted to the moon, eyes blazing silver. She seemed to become a beacon for the moonlight as it poured down on her, suddenly illuminating Mari and, through their nearness, O'Bryan and even Nik. He felt his cousin's body jerk, as if she'd shot something into him. It touched Nik, too. He felt the cool power of it, as if he'd paddled too close to a waterfall. The wound in his back that had been throbbing with an ache in time with his heartbeat, especially after he'd carried O'Bryan, was suddenly gone. The pain in his thigh—the constant heat and pulling—released.

And suddenly Nik realized O'Bryan was no longer writhing with seizures. His body had gone completely limp. Instead of struggling for breath, he was breathing deeply and evenly. Actually, he seemed to be asleep.

Nik couldn't stop looking at Mari. Spotlighted by moonlight she was a goddess come to earth—powerful, alluring, and mysterious.

She moved then, turning her face from the sky to look at him. As he watched, the silver fire in her eyes faded until they returned to her normal gray again, but the joy didn't leave her face.

"I did it!" she said. "I drew down the moon!" She shook her head, and a little laugh bubbled from her. "I wasn't sure I could do it, but I did. He's healed, Nik. O'Bryan is going to be just fine now."

"What are you?" Nik asked in a hushed, reverent voice.

Mari smiled. "Like you said, it's just me."

"No, you're so much more than *just* anything. You're—"

O'Bryan coughed, spitting out the stick and wiping his mouth. He blinked several times, and then focused on Nik. "Cuz? Where am I?"

Joy blossomed inside Nik and he grinned at his cousin through happy tears. "You're with Mari and me. You're going to be okay now, O'Bryan. You're going to live!"

O'Bryan's forehead furrowed as he glanced around them, finding Mari kneeling next to his leg, her hand still resting on his calf.

He smiled tentatively at her. "Hi. I've heard a lot about you. It's good to meet you, girl on fire."

Mari dimpled. "Nice to meet you, too, O'Bryan. Let's take a quick look at this." With dexterity, she unwound the bandage and Nik stared in wonder at O'Bryan's leg. It was still swollen, but the striations were already fading. Mari removed the hemp wrap holding the poultice securely on the wound, and Nik gasped.

"The ulcers are completely gone!" he said.

"So is that terrible smell," Mari said. "I'm really glad that goes away fast."

O'Bryan used Nik to help brace himself, then he sat up, peering at his leg. When he looked at Mari, tears were streaming down his cheeks.

"How is this possible?"

"Moon magick and Nik refusing to take no for an answer," Mari said simply as she rebandaged the injury.

O'Bryan reached out and took her hand. "I owe you my life."

"Then make it count. Be kind. Be truthful. And most of all, don't ever harm an Earth Walker."

"You have my word on that," O'Bryan said. Then he grinned, looking like his old self. "Nik didn't tell me you were so pretty."

Nik watched Mari's cheeks flush pink. Then Rigel padded up to them, sticking his nose in O'Bryan's face and making them laugh.

"It's the pup! It's so good to see him."

"His name is Rigel," Mari said, shooing him away gently. She met

Nik's eyes. "You should carry him back now. He's going to need a lot of rest."

"Carry me? In front of a girl as pretty as you? I'm not dead enough to be okay with that—or at least now I'm not. Help me up, Nik."

"Cuz, I don't think—"

"Well, I know you don't always think, but maybe you should keep Mari from knowing that for at least a little while longer," O'Bryan teased, which made Mari laugh softly.

Nik sent his cousin an exaggerated scowl, but his heart was filled with happiness. "Fine. It's your leg and your pain. You know if you fall down those stairs and break it I'll just have to carry you back up here—in front of Mari—so she can fix you up again."

"Stop being such a worrier!" O'Bryan said.

He and Mari together helped O'Bryan stand, and then, leaning heavily on Nik and moving slowly and carefully, they descended the stairs with Mari and Rigel following them.

"O'Bryan! By the Sun's glory, you're alive!" Sol rushed to them, enfolding O'Bryan in a hug.

They stood there like that, Nik, his father, and his beloved cousin, linked through touch and love and gratitude, because of a girl who shouldn't have been born. As he gazed at Mari, Nik felt his world shift, expand, and change irrevocably.

"He needs to lie down," Mari said quietly, breaking the spell that surrounded the four of them.

"Of course—of course," Sol said. "I'll lead, just like on the way here."

Nik nodded and told O'Bryan quickly, "We snuck Mari in. We didn't have time to answer Tribe questions. It was too close with you."

"Bloody beetle balls, I almost died, didn't I!"

Nik shook his head at O'Bryan's excited tone. He and Mari exchanged a look, and she rolled her eyes.

"Yes, you almost died. Nik really should carry you back," Mari said.

"As usual, Mari's right," Nik said.

O'Bryan snorted. "No chance of that, Cuz."

"The three of you stop chattering and follow me," Sol said.

Barely suppressing relieved laughter, the three of them did as Sol commanded.

None of them noticed the figure in the shadows who slowly, stealthily, followed, too.

Mari made sure the hood of her cloak was pulled securely around her face and Rigel stayed close to her and quiet, but she couldn't help feeling light and almost giddy with happiness as she waited in a shadowy alcove outside the Transition nest for Nik, Sol, and Maeve to resituate O'Bryan within. The Tribe's Healer hadn't returned, but the consensus was that she would be making rounds soon, so Mari waited outside. And she did so happily. The city in the trees fascinated her. She wished it was day, and she could see everything—explore everything. For just that moment Mari allowed herself to imagine what it would be like to live in the sky among such beauty—to be accepted as Leader and to have a life that wasn't filled with struggle and Night Fever. She thought about Nik's eyes on her as she'd danced her name and drawn down the moon. It had seemed as if he'd looked within her and glimpsed her spirit.

The wind, which had picked up noticeably, whipped around Mari, making her shiver even as she enjoyed the sounds of the Tribe's chimes and bells tinkling in time with the elements.

Then, along with the delicate, windblown music, Mari heard another sound. She felt Rigel stir where he sat beside her, cocking his head as he, too, listened.

It was a woman crying. Mari was sure of it.

Rigel stood, took a few hesitant steps, and then looked back at Mari expectantly.

"Rigel, do *not* go anywhere!" she whispered sternly.

He whined plaintively, then jogged around the Transition nest.

"Rigel!" Mari's whisper sounded more like a hiss as she hurried after him.

Rounding the side of the Transition nest, Mari saw another, smaller, nest situated close by. Sitting just outside the entrance was a woman. Her face was in her hands and she was sobbing brokenly.

Rigel went to her and touched her with his muzzle. The woman jerked in surprise and then lifted her grief-ravaged face.

"Who are you?" she said, her voice thick with tears. "Wait, I know who you are . . ."

Mari hesitated, not sure whether she should step forward, or run back to the Transition nest for Nik. Thankfully, a strong hand touched her shoulder and Nik said, "I'll get him. Don't worry. Stay here."

Nik strode toward the woman and Rigel. Mari moved as close as the shadow would let her, listening intently.

The woman looked up at him, wiping at her eyes. "Nik! Isn't this Laru's pup? The one you've been looking for all this time?"

"Hi, Sheena. Yes, it is the pup," he said. Mari watched him hesitate, obviously searching for an explanation he could tell her, but Nik didn't need one. Instead of questioning him further, the woman began crying again with shoulder-shaking, body-wracking sobs. Nik sat beside her and put his arm comfortingly around her.

"I'm sorry, Nik. I'm sorry. It's Captain—he's failing. He won't fight. It's like his heart was broken along with his leg. He wants to follow Crystal and Grace. I can feel it. I can't blame him for that. I want to follow them, too."

"No, don't say that, Sheena. Shepherds are resilient, but you have to be strong for him."

The woman shook her head. "I've tried, but he's in so much pain. His leg—it's infected. He's dying, Nik."

Rigel slipped out from underneath Nik's hand and galloped to Mari. Sitting in front of her, he whined and gave a little encouraging bark. Mari looked into his amber eyes and felt his urgency and his confidence in her.

"Okay," she told him. "But I hope you know what you're doing."

Mari left the concealing shadows and went to Nik and the sobbing, broken Sheena.

"I can help," Mari said.

"Who are you?" Sheena asked.

"My friend," Nik said. "And the pup's Companion. She's also a Healer."

Sheena shook her head. "The Healers have given up. They say there's nothing they can do."

"Can you help him?" Nik said.

"Rigel seems to think I can," Mari said. "May I try?" she asked Sheena.

"Yes. Just don't do anything that will cause him more pain."

"I won't. I promise," Mari said.

Sheena went inside the little nest. Mari, Nik, and Rigel followed. Near the hearth on a thick pallet was a big male Shepherd. His front right leg was splinted and swathed in bandages. Sheena knelt beside his head, stroking him and murmuring his name. The Shepherd opened his eyes, moved his muzzle so that it rested against his Companion, and then he closed them again.

"May I touch him?" Mari asked.

Sheena nodded, wiping at the tears that continued to flow down her cheeks.

Mari crouched beside the big canine. She ran her hands over him lightly, feeling the unnatural heat that radiated from his infection-ravaged body. Even through the splint and bandages, she could see how much his leg was swollen, though he didn't seem to be injured anywhere else.

"Is it just his leg?" she asked Sheena.

"That and his heart," Sheena said softly, still stroking him.

"Sheena's mate, Crystal, and her Shepherd, Grace, were killed the day the Skin Stealers ambushed us," Nik explained.

"I'm so sorry," Mari said.

Sheena just nodded, never taking her gaze from Captain's face.

"Can you help him?" Nik asked.

"Yes," Mari said.

"Do you need me to carry him outside?" Nik asked.

Sheena began to protest, but Mari smiled and touched her arm gently. "It's okay. Nik doesn't need to take him anywhere, but I do need a moment alone with your Captain. I give you my word I will only help. I will not cause him any pain."

Sheena looked from Mari to Nik to Rigel, and then back to Nik.

"You can trust her," Nik said.

Sheena blew out a long breath, her shoulders slumping miserably. "I could use a mug of ale. I'll go get one." She bent and kissed Captain's muzzle, whispering, "I'll be right back. I love you." Moving slowly and stiffly, like a woman thrice her age, Sheena stood and shuffled from the nest.

"You really don't need me to carry him up to Father's platform for you? I will, you know, even though it'll be hard on him."

Mari smiled at Nik. "Usually, when I draw down the moon I am only a conduit for its power. It goes through me, but doesn't stay with me. Tonight I had, well, I'm going to call it a premonition, and I saved some of the moonlight for myself, but now I know it wasn't meant for me. It was meant for Captain." She closed her eyes and rested both hands on the canine's splinted leg. This time finding her center was easy, and once she was there she sketched a picture in her mind of her hands glowing and that glow spreading over Captain. Not just his leg, but all of him— his head, his body, and his heart—mostly his heart.

When she felt him stir beneath her hands, Mari quickly added a smiling image of Sheena to her picture. Then she opened her eyes to see that the Shepherd had raised his head and was staring at her. Mari smiled. "Hello, Captain."

The big canine's tail thumped—hesitantly at first, and then with more enthusiasm as Sheena entered the nest and rushed to his side. He greeted her, licking her face and trying to crawl onto her lap. Laughing and crying at the same time, Sheena hugged him, telling him how much she loved him and how strong and brave and wonderful he was.

Quietly, Mari stood. Nik took her hand and they left the nest together. They paused outside. Filled with gratitude, Mari turned her face to where the moon peeked through the thick boughs of the tall, watchful trees. Nik stood beside her silently, still holding her hand.

"Nik, Mari! There you are." Sol rushed up to them. "What are you doing over here? You were supposed to stay—"

"Wait, don't go yet!"

The three of them turned as Sheena rushed to Mari. She took her hands and held them tightly in hers. "Thank you isn't enough. I can't ever repay what you've done for me."

"What has happened?" Sol asked.

Sheena turned her tear-stained face to Sol. "You know Captain was dying?"

"Yes," he said solemnly, pain shadowing his kind eyes. "I am so sorry, Sheena." There was a rustling in the entryway to the nest behind them, drawing Sol's gaze. Mari watched his eyes widen and she knew what she'd see before she turned her head to look.

Captain was standing in the doorway. He swayed a little, but his eyes were bright and his mouth was open, tongue lolling, in a canine grin. Slowly, he limped to Sheena, leaning against her as she dropped Mari's hands to crouch beside him and put her arms around him.

"He's walking!" Sol blurted. His gaze shot to Mari. "You did this?"

"She did," Sheena said. "Somehow she brought my Captain back, but she didn't just heal his leg—she healed his heart, and by doing that healed mine as well." Her gaze went back to Mari. "Who are you?"

"She's a miracle," Sol said.

"She's a goddess," Nik said.

A tide of emotions washed through Mari, filling her to overflowing. When she spoke she heard her mother's voice mixed with her own. "I'm not a miracle or a goddess. I'm a Moon Woman."

"What Tribe is that?" Sheena asked.

"It's complicated," Nik and Sol said together.

Then Sol turned to Mari, taking her hands much like Sheena had so recently done. "Thank you is not enough, though I heartily thank you—for my son's life—for my nephew's life—and now for the lives of two more precious members of our Tribe. If there is anything you need—anything you want—ask it of me, my dear. If it is within my power, I will give it to you."

Everything around Mari got very still, and within that stillness she knew what she must ask for. In a voice that echoed with the authority of generations of Moon Women, Mari said, "What I want is for you to take me to Farm Island."

47

N o, Mari!" Nik grabbed her by the shoulders, forcing Mari to look into his eyes. "I don't care what you say, I won't let you go there. I won't let you turn into a sad ghost of yourself."

Mari put her hands over his. "That won't happen to me. It can't. I'm a Moon Woman, Nik. It's different for me."

"Why do you want to go there?" Sol asked.

Mari turned to him. "I can help my people."

"I won't let you stay there," Nik insisted.

Mari held Sol's gaze as she answered Nik. "That's not your decision to make. It's mine."

"Actually, it's mine," Sol said.

"Not if your word is good," Mari said. "You just offered to give me anything I wanted that's in your power to give."

"It is in my power to take you to Farm Island. It is even in my power to allow you to stay there, should that be your desire. It is not in my power to speak for the Tribe and release the Earth Walkers. That I cannot do."

"I'm not asking you to release my people. I'm also not asking you to lock me up with them."

"Then what are you going to do?" Nik asked.

"The right thing. I'm going to heal my people, just as I healed you,

Nik, and O'Bryan, and Sheena and her Captain. Sol, will you take me to Farm Island or not?"

There was a long pause as Sol studied his son. Then, with a deep sigh, he said to Mari, "I will take you there."

"Not without me you won't," Nik said.

Mari glanced up at the sky. "We need to hurry. The moon is waning."

"It's late enough that few of the Tribe will be stirring. Pull up your hood and stay close. We'll use the lift closest to the edge of the ridge," Sol said.

Mari nodded, pulled up her hood, and hurried after Sol with Nik close beside her.

Thaddeus waited until Sheena and Captain had gone back inside the nest before, quick as a Terrier, he sprinted away. His mind was reeling with what he'd just witnessed. He'd always known there was something about Nik that he hated, something besides the fact that everything came too easily for him. *Well,* he corrected himself smugly as he sent a self-satisfied look to the canine by his side, *everything except the ability to get a canine to choose him. Though it seems he might have done that— in a twisted, perverse version of how a true Companion was chosen.*

The girl was a mutant though he didn't understand how the mutation had happened. Her face was a bizarrely compelling mixture of Companion and Scratcher. It was obvious to him that she had been sent to the Tribe as a temptation. That much was abundantly clear. Thaddeus knew about temptation. Since he'd returned from the ambush, his body had continued to change and strengthen. His mind had begun changing, too. Everything seemed sharper, clearer to Thaddeus. He could see so many problems with the Tribe's archaic Law system. Why were Terriers less than Shepherds? It made no sense, and that was only one of the Laws Thaddeus saw as senseless or obsolete.

Odysseus had healed completely, seeming even stronger than he'd been before the Skin Stealers had wounded him—shared his flesh with Thaddeus—and drastically changed their lives. Their bond was more intimate, too. The Terrier had become more serious and more easily angered. At first Thaddeus had been concerned about the change in Odysseus, but after further reflection, he'd decided the canine wasn't actually that changed. He'd always been quick to temper, his sharp teeth keeping other Terriers focused during Hunts. Plus, he liked and appreciated Odysseus's edge. There was no reason a Terrier couldn't be as fierce as a Shepherd, just as there was no reason a Terrier's Companion couldn't lead like a Shepherd's Companion.

Thaddeus felt his anger building, his body heating, his blood pounding through his veins. He balled his fists, fighting the urge to hit something—anything. Odysseus, who had been trotting determinedly before him, turned and yipped impatiently.

"You're right. One thing at a time. Get rid of Nik and the Sun Priest. That's the beginning of the end of the old ways." Satisfied, Odysseus sprinted on with Thaddeus following. All that really mattered was that the two of them were tight, and strong, and in agreement that what had happened to them was a good thing—a very good thing. The rest would come. He would be sure the rest would come.

Thaddeus did wonder about the change in his dreams. Every night, every single time he fell asleep, his dreams were filled with strange visions, as disturbing as they were alluring. In each of them the predominant image was of an eyeless girl who beckoned to him with a smooth, soft, outstretched hand.

Thus far, Thaddeus had resisted the lure of that beguiling hand, though he fantasized endlessly during the day about sneaking back to Port City and the Temple of the Reaper God. With the amazing increase in his strength and sight and sense of smell, Thaddeus was sure he could manage to steal the sightless girl from them.

Just thinking about seeing her again—touching her, possessing her, had Thaddeus's hands trembling and his stomach tightening with excitement.

No! he told himself firmly. *I will not succumb to that temptation. Not now. Not until I know more about what is happening to me.*

Nik had, of course, succumbed easily to the lure of his mutant girl. That was no surprise to Thaddeus. Nik had always been desperate to fit in. What truly shocked him was how easily their Sun Priest had succumbed, though in retrospect he should have expected it. Sol had always been too liberal—too accepting of oddities. That dead wife of his was the perfect example. She had been an oddity. She'd had beauty and talent aplenty, but there had been something off about her—some kind of internal strangeness that kept any canine from choosing her.

Well, if his luck held, after tonight tiptoeing around Sol and his needy son would no longer be an issue. There were still Companions who would listen to reason—still Companions who believed in breeding strength and stability within the Tribe.

He reached the correct nest, and knocked on the doorframe. Nothing happened. He waited, and then knocked more insistently—again and again.

There was a shuffling from inside and the grizzled muzzle of an ancient Shepherd poked through the doorway curtain. The canine looked up at him and growled softly.

"Argos, who is it?" called an equally grizzled voice from within.

"I'm sorry to disturb your sleep, sir. But there is something you must know about," he said.

The curtain was pushed to the side, and Cyril, looking disheveled but typically bright-eyed, peered out at him, frowning. "Thaddeus, what is it you think is so important that it can't wait until after sunrise?"

"Well, sir, let me tell you what I've witnessed tonight."

With increasing concern Cyril listened to Thaddeus describe the mutant woman, the returned pup, and the role the Sun Priest and Nik were playing in her infiltration of the Tribe. Finally, the old man parted the curtain and motioned for him to come in.

"You were right to wake me. This must be stopped."

Smiling victoriously, Thaddeus entered the Lead Elder's nest and waited patiently while the old man dressed.

The short trip to Farm Island was a blur for Mari. Her mind was awhirl with conflicting thoughts about what was to come. She had to Wash the women. Her conscience wouldn't allow her to leave—to retreat back to her comfortable burrow and the friends waiting for her there—while knowing Earth Walker women were suffering and she had had the opportunity to relieve them of that suffering, even if it was only for a little while.

As they hurried down the ridge, heading for the channel and the island that lay like a green jewel between it and the mighty river, Mari studied Sol, considering . . .

That Nik was a good man was beyond any doubt. He'd proven himself to her over and over, even in the short time she'd known him. But was his father the same caliber of man? Or had power and leadership and popularity eroded him?

Mari decided tonight she was going to find out.

"Stay still. I'll do the talking. When I walk away, follow me quickly," Sol said as they approached the last huge pine before the ruins of an old road and the bank that framed the west side of the Channel broke the land. He walked to the base of the pine, cupped his hands, and shouted up, "Attention in the lookout! It's Sol. My group and I are entering the island."

Mari looked up to see the shape of a man, with a Terrier beside him, step out to the edge of the small deck and look down. Sol waved his hand. The man waved back and shouted down, "Go ahead, Sol!"

"That's Davis, and that's a really good thing," Nik spoke under his breath to his father.

Sol nodded. "Thank you, Davis!"

"Looks like you're pulling a lot of duty lately," Nik called up.

"Nik! Good to see you out and about! Let's get a drink later and catch up." Mari could hear the smile in the young man's voice, and she felt the tight knot of tension within her begin to loosen.

"Will do, Davis!"

Sol waved again, and then strode out onto the broken road. Mari and Rigel followed, picking their way carefully over the buckled, cracked surface. Mari glanced up and down the ancient road. It looked like a massive water serpent had slithered from the water onto the land, its spine breaking apart the earth as it departed.

Nik took her elbow, helping her over the last of the road. "Are you okay?"

Mari nodded. She met his gaze. He was worried about it, that was obvious, but he also looked angry. "I have to do this, Nik, even if it makes you angry."

"I'm not angry. I'm scared for you. I'm scared for me, too. I don't want to lose you, Mari. I just found you."

Mari smiled softly. "I'm scared, too. And if I have anything to say about it, you won't lose me. But things have to change for the Earth Walkers; you know that, Nik."

Nik kept her arm, linking it with his own so that they walked side by side, their heads tilted toward one another, to the rusted hulk of the only bridge on and off Farm Island.

"Then promise me you won't put yourself in danger if you can help it," he said.

"Nik, I'm all for not being in danger. I don't want to be hurt. I'm not crazy! I just have to do the right thing, and recently I've realized that sometimes the right thing seems crazy to those who don't want change."

"Okay, stay close," Sol said as they caught up with him just before the bridge. He took a torch from its holder at the entrance to the bridge and held it high. "This thing is rusted through in more spots than it's not. Keep ahold of Mari, Nik."

"That's my pleasure." Nik took Mari's hand, steadying her as they picked their way over the crumbling byway.

In the center of the bridge Mari paused, looking to her left. The night had started as still, clear, and warm, but as dawn grew progressively near, the wind had increased drastically, sending mounds of clouds scudding across the moon. The fat, glowing crescent broke through the billowy veil, turning the mud-colored Channel to liquid silver and illuminating a line of houses, connected by a long dock that appeared to be floating in the middle of it.

"That's where the women are kept, isn't it?" Mari said.

Nik stopped beside her. "It is."

Mari studied the area, and then nodded with satisfaction. "The moon will definitely have no problem finding me there."

"You'll be careful?"

Mari studied Nik. She felt something break loose and turn over within her. This man who had once seemed so strange, even danger-ous, now felt right by her side. He felt safe. He felt like family. She drew a deep breath, and spoke the words that would change her life forever. "You don't need to worry. Earth Walker women aren't violent. They're just sad. It's only our males who are violent if they don't have a Moon Woman to Wash the Night Fever from them."

Nik stared at her. "You mean their sadness isn't because they're cap-tives?"

"In a roundabout way it is. Because they're captives they don't have access to a Moon Woman. Without a Moon Woman to wash Night Fever from them, Earth Walker women fall into a terrible depression and, eventually, will themselves to die. With men it's not depression. It's violence."

"But the men who attacked Sora weren't captives. They had access to you, and yet they were violent."

"That's because I haven't been Washing the Clan. Nik, I wasn't the Moon Woman. Mama was. Sora was her apprentice. I was just her daughter."

Nik touched her face. "*Just* her daughter? It seems to me that you were her everything."

"And she was mine. Until Rigel. And Sora. And you." Mari stared out at the floating prisons.

"And now you have Jenna, Donita, Father, O'Bryan, and Sheena and her Captain, too."

"Nik, having them—having all of you in my life—it's taught me to be the Moon Woman Mama hoped I could be." She stared at him, wanting him to understand, but not sure how to reach him.

"That's why you have to go to them, isn't it? It's what your mother would want you to do."

"Yesterday I would have said yes, I'm doing this for Mama. I changed today. Your people changed me. Today I'm doing this for my Clan. We are every bit as human as your Tribe, and I believe if Sol sees that—if your people just see that—it will be the beginning of changing our world."

"And our world does need to change," Nik said.

"So you agree with me?"

"I do, Mari. You can count on me. I have your back. I'll always have your back," Nik said.

Mari stared at him, hearing the words she and Leda had shared echoed in his. With tears brimming her eyes, she stepped into his arms. Nik bent and pressed his lips to hers. Mari returned the kiss—tentatively at first—and then her hands slid around his strong shoulders and she clung to him, opening herself to the thrilling sensations that were coursing through her body.

"Nik, Mari, come on! There's time for that later! Sunrise is near!" Sol called from the island side of the bridge.

Mari's face felt hot as she and Nik disentangled. Embarrassed by the new feelings that were awakening within her, she tried to pull completely away from him, but he snagged her hand, coaxing her back to his side.

"Hey, I'm sorry if I moved too fast," Nik said, touching her face gently and brushing a blond curl from her cheek.

"You didn't move too fast. I—I just never kissed anyone before," Mari blurted.

"So you're not sorry?" Nik asked.

Mari met his amber eyes. "No. Never. I like it. I liked it a lot. I—I'd like to kiss you again, but I agree with your father. There will be time for that later. I hope." She sent him a nervous smile.

"That, my beautiful Moon Woman, is exactly what I hope, too. But first let's start changing our world." He grinned and then pointed to the closest of the floating houses. "You'll find Isabel in that house—the one nearest to where we'll dock the boat."

"Okay, I'm ready," Mari said.

Hand in hand, Mari and Nik crossed over to Farm Island.

As they walked along the Channel, Mari readied herself. She breathed deeply of the fecund fields, in awe of the acre after acre of growing things that stretched from the island side of the Channel over the width of the emerald isle. She grounded herself with the earth, holding in her mind the simple fact that though her people had been forced to till and plant and harvest for the Tribe, this land had been imprinted with the labor of Earth Walkers. The Earth would know. The Moon would remember.

Stairs built into the high bank of the channel led them down to water level and the small rowboat that waited there. Nik helped Mari aboard, and the two men rowed quickly to the floating houses.

All was still as they climbed onto the dock. Mari stood, gazing at the first of the dozen or so houses, wondering what should happen next.

Then she saw the thick wooden beam that barred the door, and the strong wooden poles that filled the windows—all ensuring that once closed within, the women could not get out. And Mari knew what to do.

She went to the first house, unbolted the door and began to open it.

Sol's hand reached from behind her, pressing against the wood, holding it closed.

Mari faced him. "Will you not hold to your word?"

"I will. I have. I brought you here, but I already told you that I do not have the authority to release your people."

Nik stepped up beside his father, gently taking his hand from the door. "My father taught me that I shouldn't let others control my actions, especially if I know I'm doing the right thing. Instead of waiting for the Tribe to act, to decide to do the right thing, I'm going to do it. It's what my father would expect me to do."

Sol stared at his son. Then, slowly, he placed the torch he had been carrying in the holder beside the house, and stepped purposefully away from the door. "When did you get so wise?"

Nik clasped his father's shoulder, but he looked past him to meet Mari's gaze. "When I stopped waiting for the world to change, and decided to create the change myself." Nik swung the door open wide, and then he retreated several paces back with his father, so that Mari was alone, silhouetted in the doorway.

Mari didn't allow herself time to hesitate. "Isabel!" she called within. "Isabel, are you there?"

There was the sound of movement inside, accompanied by a low moan, and a few broken sobs. And then a pale face lifted from the mounds that were women. Mari saw her blink, and then her eyes widened in shock.

"Mari?"

Mari held her hand out to the girl, who rushed forward, clasping it. "Oh, Mari! It is you! Where is Leda? What are you doing here?" Her wide, startled gray gaze focused over Mari's shoulder on Sol and Nik, and she started to cringe back inside. Mari tightened her grip on the girl's hand.

"Leda is dead." Gasps of shock and cries of despair came from within, and Mari had to raise her voice to be heard. "I am the Clan's Moon Woman, and I have come to Wash you."

As if a candle had been snuffed, all sound ceased from inside the house. Then, one by one, the women within began to stand.

"Moon Woman—our Moon Woman is here." The voices began softly and then the idea caught, and the women's cries blazed. "Moon Woman! Wash us, Moon Woman! Save us!"

Mari pulled Isabel from the house. "Stay close. I'm going to need your help." She turned her attention to the mass of women pressing around the doorway. They didn't leave the house. It was as if an invisible barricade held them. "Step out into the moonlight, and step out into a new world!" she shouted. Then Mari turned to Nik. "Help me open all the doors!"

Together they ran the length of the dock, unbarring and flinging wide the doors, and as they did so women began to spill out of the houses, crying, "Moon Woman! Our Moon Woman!"

And then they were surrounding her, and it seemed a million hands reached for her as voices cried, over and over, for her to Wash them—

save them. It was as if they each wanted a piece of her and she suddenly felt as if they would, truly, pull her apart.

Mari tried to back away. Tried to reason with them. "Wait, no. I'll help. I just have to—" But her words were carried away by the tidal wave of their need.

Then Nik was there, and his strong arms were pulling her as his body shielded her from their grasping hands.

"Nik! Mari! This will help!" Sol called. Mari glanced up to see that he had a big wooden water trough he'd retrieved from one of the houses. Dragging it with him, he strode to the middle of the widest part of the dock, and turned it over. Then he held his hand out to Mari.

Nik pulled her from the crowd and they ran to Sol, who helped her climb on top of the trough. She turned to the crowd of confused, excited women who clambered after her.

"Form a circle around me! Link hands! Everyone, link hands!" She found Isabel, who was still standing beside the door to the first of the houses. "Isabel, take my hand!" The girl didn't hesitate. She rushed to Mari, grasping her hand. "Like Isabel! Link hands like Isabel!"

Thrumming with barely contained hysteria, the women surged forward, spreading around Mari and down and across the dock. The first woman took Isabel's hand. Another stepped forward taking Mari's other hand, and then, like a ripple over water, all of the women joined hands.

Mari tilted her face to catch what was left of the moonlight. She closed her eyes and began to sketch within her imagination the most intricate, most beautiful drawing she had ever created. In her drawing she imagined the power of the moonlight to be like rain. She drew it falling from the sky in a beautiful, shining downpour, filling every woman below and Washing all sadness from them in a torrent of benevolent power.

Mari felt the wind whipping around her, lifting her hair and caressing her body as if to encourage her. Holding the image firmly in her mind, Mari spoke the invocation to the moon.

"By right of blood and birth channel through me
That which the Earth Mother proclaims my destiny!"

Power such as she had never before known flooded Mari, filling her . . . filling her . . . filling her until she overflowed—and that overflow spilled into the waiting women, Washing through them, and carrying away the despair that had clung to them like a rancid smell.

When the power was drained completely from her, Mari opened her eyes. Everyone was staring at her. The silence was so profound that it seemed to be deafening.

And then a woman whose face Mari recognized as one of the Clan, but who had gone missing so many winters before that Mari couldn't recall her name, let loose her neighbor's hands and stepped forward.

She spoke simply, though her face was alight with joy. "Thank you, Moon Woman." She bowed deeply, reverently, to Mari.

All around her the women mimicked her actions. Each spoke their gratitude, and then showed homage by bowing deeply to Mari.

Mari stood on the impromptu podium, tears of happiness overflowing her eyes, as she accepted their thanks as simply and honestly as her mother would have accepted them.

Then one woman spread wide her arms as more wind whipped around them. Laughing, she began to dance, her feet tapping a fast, joyous pattern on the dock. Other women joined in the dance, until the music of their feet vibrated across the dock, lifting into the wind with their laughter.

Mari searched over the sea of dancing women until she found Nik. Their eyes met and she felt the touch of his gaze like a caress. He smiled and nodded his head, mouthing the words *well done Moon Woman* to her.

"Get back in your houses immediately and no one will be hurt!"

At the sound of the shout, Mari whirled around. Kayaks filled with Companions and their canines surrounded the floating houses. Each had a crossbow lifted, aimed at the crowd of dancing women.

Sol began pushing his way through the crowd, heading for the far side of the dock facing the throng of boats. Nik hurried to Mari. He reached her as the women's dance faltered and they began to mill around in small clusters.

"Wilkes, I am in charge here!" Sol's deep voice echoed across the water, stilling the frightened voices of the women behind him. "These women, these captive women we call Scratchers, but who are really Earth Walkers, have been mistreated by the Tribe for generations. Their melancholy, which grows so great they will their lives to end, is un-natural, and only occurs because they are prisoners. It is unjust and inhumane. As your chosen Leader and Sun Priest, I cannot, in good conscience, allow their abuse to continue."

"So instead you would consign your own people to death?"

Sol searched the faces before him until he found Cyril. "No, my old friend, instead of allowing their abuse I would ask my people to do the right thing."

"Take me to your father," Mari told Nik. Without questioning her, he quickly guided her through the clustering women. They stepped beside Sol, Rigel and Laru flanking them. She faced the old man who had been speaking, and raised her voice so that it would carry over the wind and water to all of the watching Companions. "I can cure your blight."

One voice, fueled by hatred, could be heard over the disbelieving outcry. "That's her! The mutant who is not of the Tribe, but who has lured a canine to her!"

"Ah, so this group is here because of your poison, Thaddeus," Nik said. "I should have known."

"This group is here because Thaddeus had the presence of mind to come to me when he discovered you and your father had allowed an intruder among the Tribe—one who is here expressly to rob us of our Scratchers!" Cyril shouted.

"They're Earth Walkers! And they're people, not property. They can-not belong to you," Mari told the old man.

"Young woman, you should learn your place and not speak back to your elders," the old man said.

"Is that how you rule in the Tribe? Through intimidation and ignorance?" Mari's questions shot out.

"That's enough! Silence that creature and get the Scratchers back in their houses," Cyril commanded.

"Cyril, Mari is here by my invitation and under my protection," Sol said.

"Then you choose her over your own people!" Thaddeus sneered. "I see where your son gets his twisted propensities."

"By choosing to protect Mari I *am* choosing my own people," Sol said. "She is Earth Walker *and* Companion. She is both in one. You know my words are true, Cyril, and you know why they are true—even if you will not admit it. Mari can also heal the blight. I have witnessed it."

"If all that is true, why are you and Nik hiding her from us?"

Nik searched the faces until he found Wilkes, but before he could respond to the Leader of the Warriors, Mari spoke.

"They were hiding me because I told them if they didn't I wouldn't come—I wouldn't heal O'Bryan of the blight. There is such a history of violence and mistrust between our peoples that I was unwilling to share the cure with you."

"That's cruel!" shouted another Companion.

"More cruel than enslaving the women of my Clan and slaughtering our men?" Mari countered with.

"What does she propose?" Cyril asked Sol.

"She can answer for herself," Sol said.

Mari lifted her chin and faced the old man. "I don't *propose* anything. There is only one truth here, and it's a simple one. If you want the blight that infects your Tribe to be cured you will let the Earth Walkers go free, and swear never to enslave them again. If you don't, the blight can continue to kill you and I'll say good riddance to a people so driven by their own selfishness that they deserve to be culled from the earth!" Mari shouted at him.

"There's one other truth," Cyril's voice was granite. "You will not be allowed to destroy our world. Kill her and get those Scratchers back in their cages!"

"Cyril, you must do the right thing! We are not monsters! We cannot continue to—" Sol began, but in a motion blurred with inhuman speed, Thaddeus lifted his crossbow and fired. Sol surged forward, knocking Mari to the ground, and the arrow meant for her pierced him through the chest.

"No!" Nik cried and fell to his knees beside his father. "No! Father! Father!"

From the kayaks, men and canines began to leap to the dock, closing on the women, and on Mari, Nik, and Sol.

Suddenly Laru and Rigel were before them. Hackles raised, teeth bared, they formed a wall between them and the encroaching Companions, who hesitated, as even the angriest of Warriors could not abide harming a canine.

From her hands and knees, Mari watched in horror as panic rippled through her people. Screaming, they tried to flee the Companions, and in the midst of their hysteria the torch was knocked to the ground. Mari saw it roll into the straw-floored house and with a *whoosh* it caught flame.

Heart hammering, Mari turned her attention to Nik, who was sobbing over his father.

She crawled to Sol, feeling for his pulse, though when she saw that the arrow had gone through his body, skewering his heart, she knew she would not find one.

Nik was shaking his father's body. "Wake up! You have to wake up, Father!"

"Nik!" She took his face in her hands and forced him to meet her eyes. "He's gone."

He stared at her, at first unseeing, and then his vision focused. "Save him, Mari! Please, save him," he wept brokenly.

"I can't, Nik. Your father is dead. I can't save him any more than I could save Mama."

There was an explosion behind them that rocked the dock as the first house was engulfed in flames. The roof collapsed inward, and the walls began to blaze, setting the house beside it aflame as well. With an incredible rush of heat, the next house and the next caught as the fire roared.

The heat was terrible. It drove the Companions back to the Channel, and had the women milling around the edges of the dock in panicked groups.

Mari stood, and in a voice amplified by the horror of what was happening around her, she shouted above the blaze, "Earth Walkers, flee! Go to ground! Go to the burrows!" Her words were all they needed. The women leaped into the channel and began to swim for the far shore.

"You bitch! You caused this!"

Mari looked up to see the Companion called Thaddeus standing in his kayak, another arrow notched and aimed at her.

Growling fiercely, Laru and Rigel backed against her, shielding her with their bodies.

He fired his crossbow, but the young Companion who was paddling the kayak, and whose blond Terrier was barking fiercely at Thaddeus, had swerved the boat in time, and the deadly arrow flew harmlessly over the canines' heads.

"Thaddeus! What are you thinking? You can't kill the Shepherds!" the young man shouted at him.

Thaddeus ignored him. His sole focus was on Mari. "You have to stand up some time, and when you do, I'm going to kill you!"

There was another explosion, as more of the houses imploded, and the blast of heat forced Thaddeus and the other Companions to cringe away from the flaming dock.

"We have to get out of here, Nik," Mari said, pulling on his arm. "Come on! Get to the boat with me!"

Nik looked unseeing at her.

Behind him the wind suddenly whirled with a violence that was almost sentient, pulling at the ravenous flames, feeding them, encouraging them, and finally carrying their sparks up and up, until they paused there, hovering to form the voluptuous shape of a beautiful, earthy woman. The watching people, Companions and Earth Walkers alike, gasped in amazement. Then, with the sound of a sigh, the figure moved over the channel, re-forming into fire. All eyes followed the progress of the column of flame as it found the bank. There was a portentous pause, and then the bank erupted into a blaze that lifted, lifted, enveloping the first of the massive pines—then another—then another. As they watched, like a living being, the fire converged on the city in the trees.

"Go! Go! Go!" Cyril shouted. "Get us back there! We have to stop that fire!"

"Nik, listen to me! We will burn if we stay on this dock. Laru and Rigel will die with us."

His eyes met hers then. She understood the depth of despair she saw within them and her heart broke for him, and she said the only thing she thought might reach him.

"Your father would want you to live."

He nodded woodenly. "Go. I'll be behind you."

"Rigel, with me!" Mari called as she sprinted across the dock. She unwound the rope that tied the little rowboat to it. Rigel jumped into it, and then Mari followed him.

Nik was still crouched beside his father's body with Laru nearby. There was another terrible explosion, and the dock trembled. Then it, too, erupted into flame.

"Nik! Run for it!"

With flames licking at his feet, Nik ran, skidding into the boat beside her. Bending over the oars, Mari pulled with all her strength, trying to gain some space between them and the inferno that was the dock.

"Laru! Come to me!" Nik called.

The big Shepherd was standing over Sol's body, completely surrounded by flame. The Shepherd's head bent. He touched his muzzle to Sol's cheek and closed his eyes. Mari watched as the tips of his sable fur began to curl and singe and then she looked away, unable to bear to see the loyal canine's end.

"Laru, I can't lose you and Father! Please choose to live! Please come to me!" Nik roared in a voice that sounded so like Sol's that it sent chills skittering up and down Mari's arms.

Laru's eyes opened. And then, as if shot from a bow, the Shepherd gathered himself and leaped through the flames, ran across the deck, and dove into the water. Surfacing in moments, he swam for the boat.

An arrow plunked harmlessly into the water several feet in front of them, and as Nik wrapped his arms around Laru and hauled him into the boat, Mari saw Thaddeus.

All of the other Companions were paddling wildly for shore, determined to beat the fire to the Tribe—determined to save their families. Thaddeus was standing in his kayak, facing the opposite direction. Though his young partner in the little boat was paddling them toward the shore, Thaddeus continued sighting his crossbow at Mari and letting arrows fly, one after another, even though they were clearly out of range. She could see that his face was red with rage—his expression so twisted by hatred that he looked less human than monster.

"I'll get us out of here." Nik took her place and began rowing them farther into the Channel, farther away from the Companions and the burning forest.

"This isn't over!" Thaddeus shrieked his rage at them. "I will hunt you down and kill you! That I swear on my own canine's life!" Then smoke, black and thick, spread across the Channel, shielding them from more of his venom.

Nik continued to row, bending his back to the task as if he was attacking the water with the oars. Mari went to Laru, feeling all over the Shepherd for injuries. Finding nothing except singed fur, she sank to the bottom of the boat, trembling with relief and holding tightly to Rigel.

Minutes or hours could have passed as Nik continued to row. They were alone on the water. Mari looked to the east. Where the sun should have been rising there was a wall of flame.

Laru stood, and on legs that shook, he staggered to Nik. Nik dropped the oars and pulled the Shepherd into his arms, saying, "I know this choosing wasn't the same as when you bonded with Father, but thank you for answering my call and coming to me. Laru, I *accept you and I vow to love and care for you until fate parts us by death.*" The Shepherd rested his head across Nik's chest, sighed, and closed his eyes, nuzzling as close as possible to his new Companion.

Mari watch Nik look from Laru to the dock, which was completely ablaze, to the fiery ridge. As if he felt her gaze on him, his eyes found hers.

"My world is burning," he said.

She leaned to him, grasping his hand in both of hers. "Then let's build a new world. Together. Where everyone is accepted—where everyone can belong."

"I don't know if I believe that is possible," Nik said.

She moved forward and took him and the big Shepherd into her arms, holding them, comforting them. Rigel joined them then, completing their circle of love and loyalty.

"Then I'll believe it enough for both of us until you can, too. Trust me, Nik. I have your back. I'll always have your back."

Dove woke him with three words that changed everything. "Something is happening."

Dead Eye was instantly alert. "What is it?"

"I'm not sure. I sense a change. Can you smell that? The air has an odd quality to it. My Champion, we must go to the balcony. You must be my eyes."

"That I will always be," he said. Taking her hand they left their sleeping pallet and walked quickly through the chamber to the God's balcony. He helped her step up on the ledge with him as he gazed out at the morning, instinctively turning to the northwest.

At first it seemed something was wrong with the clouds—that they were being formed in the distant forest ridge instead of the sky and rising from it. Dead Eye stared, baffled. The wind shifted, allowing him to see a black column of smoke with an orange glow in the center of the billowing white. Thick and ominous, it spread, staining the perfect cerulean sky with darkness. Dead Eye was filled with excitement.

"What is it, my Champion? What do you see?"

"Our future. I see our future!"

With the grace and strength of a stag, he lifted Dove off her feet, pressing her naked body against his, twirling her round and round as the two of them laughed with delight while the Reaper God loomed silently behind them. Her copper eyes stared out at the distant forest as if she, too, was gazing at their future. In her frozen expression there was no delight, no anger, there was only a waiting, watching stillness frightening to behold.

The End. For Now.

EPILOGUE

B ast was the only reason Antreas didn't get trapped in the inferno. His Lynx saved him. Again. The big feline had pawed and pawed at him with her huge pads so insistently that she'd frightened the curvy Tribeswoman he had finally managed to convince to join him in the visitors' nest for a private drink. Antreas had been so irritated by Bast that he'd slipped into normal, denlike behavior and had hissed at the Lynx, which was when the girl had fled the visitors' nest, sending him and his feline horrified looks over her shoulder as she disappeared into the night.

"I suppose you're going to be smug about that," he'd muttered at Bast. "Because if she's scared away by a little pawing and hissing she's definitely not mate material."

Bast had rubbed against him then, twining around and through his legs, and purring mightily before padding to the door and looking back at her Companion expectantly.

Antreas sighed. "All right. Might as well hunt with you since my chances of any other kind of sport are over for the night. Truthfully, Bast, after that one spreads the word, we'll be lucky if any of the Tribes-women agree to be alone with me."

Bast had simply pawed at the doorway and made the unique, almost owl-like cough that signaled her impatience.

Sighing heavily, Antreas followed his feline.

It had been late, and the two of them, Lynx and Companion, hadn't seen anyone until they'd come to the main lift.

Antreas hadn't had to knock on the nest's doorway to get the lift sentry's attention. The low, warning growl that came from the Shepherd within had already alerted him.

"Oh. It's you," the man stepped from the doorway of the nest to frown with disdain at Antreas and Bast.

The Mercenary kept his expression placid, though the arrogance of the dog men was beginning to grate on his nerves. "Bast needs to hunt. I'd appreciate it if you lowered us to the forest floor."

"It may be different in the mountains, and by different I mean easier, but here it's not a good idea to spend time on the forest floor after dark."

"I'm aware of that. Bast and I can take care of ourselves," Antreas said.

Instead of moving to the lift controls, the man tilted his head, studying Antreas. "Is it true you can scale trees?"

"It is," Antreas said.

The man's smile was mocking. "Then why do you need the lift to get down? Or can you just scale up?"

At his side, Bast hissed. Antreas watched the dog man's eyes widen as his gaze went from him to the big feline and then back to him again. Antreas knew what he was seeing, and that knowledge had a slow, satisfied smile lifting the corner of his lips.

In the old language, Lynx meant light. The big cats had thus been named for the reflective power of their preternaturally sharp eyes—a power that passed to the human chosen by a Lynx—a power that outsiders said made the bonded Lynx and human look equally otherworldly, equally demonic.

"We can scale up *and* down trees. We can do many things your Tribe speaks of—and does not speak of—but in my home, my den, such questions posed to a guest are considered rude. Is that not so among the dog people of the Tribe of the Trees?"

The sentry blinked. His shocked expressed shifted back to one of forced disinterest. "Get in the lift. Wave the torch when you want to return."

Antreas and Bast entered the lift and closed the door. His smile was mocking, though his tone remained carefully neutral. "Thank you for your hospitality."

When they were still many feet from the forest floor, Bast clawed open the cage door and leaped from the lift, landing delicately on her wide paws. Grinning fiercely, Antreas followed her, so catlike in his movements that he, too, seemed to defy gravity.

And then Antreas was sprinting through the forest, following the silver streak that was Bast. With a teasing look over her shoulder at him, the big Lynx leaped up into the low arms of a young pine and crouched there, calling to her Companion with a rolling yowl. Nimbly, Antreas jumped from a nearby log, up and up, hurling himself at the tree Bast was perched in, catching himself easily by jabbing the spikes that protruded from the toes of his boots into the thick bark. With a practiced flick of his wrists, ten claws elongated from his otherwise normal-looking fingers, and with a satisfied grunt Antreas buried them into the skin of the tree so that he clung there with Bast, looking more feline than human.

"Not something dog men can do!" Antreas shouted at Bast, who bared her teeth in a fierce feline grin, and yowled in complete accord with her Companion. Then she gathered herself and leaped to another tree, not needing to so much as glance back at Antreas. Bast knew he'd follow her—Antreas would always follow her.

"You want a run and not a hunt! Okay, then, let's go!"

The human and feline appeared to fly through the forest, moving from tree to tree with a grace and speed that was as incredible as it was rare for outsiders to witness.

By the time they reached the bottom of the ridge, Antreas was sweaty and laughing, his good humor restored by the chase. Breathing heavily, he dropped from the last of the trees to the mossy ground beside Bast and neatly retracted his claws, wiping his damp face with the back of his arm.

It was close to dawn and the wind had picked up, swirling clouds across the angry-looking sky.

"Looks like a storm may be coming," he told Bast as he sat beside her, rubbing the downy silver fur at the base of the feline's tufted ears.

Instead of relaxing and purring, Bast's body suddenly became tense. All of the fur along her back lifted and she stared up into the lightening sky, growling low and deep in her throat.

"Hey, don't worry, Bast. I won't let a storm keep us here any longer than—" Antreas's words broke off as he followed his feline's gaze. High in the sky a wall of flame was taking form, roiling, boiling, and shifting to form the body of a woman. Then the wind whipped violently around them, and the body returned to flame. That flame descended on the ridge behind them.

The first pine was engulfed in seconds.

There was an ominous, almost sentient sound, and the flames began to feed on the next tree.

"By all the Realms of the Gods, it's going to destroy the Tribe of the Trees!" Antreas said. He stood then, feeling the urge to run for the river—to get as far away from the fire as possible.

He started to move—to back away from the distant inferno, even though it was obviously devouring the forest before him and not heading in his direction.

Bast's absence from his side had him halting.

The big feline hadn't moved—hadn't followed him. Instead she was staring at the burning city in the trees.

"Bast, we should go. We can't do anything to stop that fire. No one can. We can only die with those poor dog people."

Bast slowly turned her head so that she could meet his gaze. He felt her sorrow, and he loved her all the more for it.

"I know, my girl. I'm sorry for them, too." Antreas gestured for her to come to him, and she did. Side by side, human and feline walked slowly, sadly, until they were well out of the forest and had come to the bank of the Channel that ran beside the Tribe's island. The Lynx stopped there, turning to look back at the burning hillside.

"Bast, I don't think it's a good idea to stay here. If the wind changes we could be where the Tribe is—trapped in the middle of a wall of flame."

But Bast refused to go any farther. Still facing the direction of the burning Tribe, she curled onto a wide, flat rock.

Antreas recognized the stubborn set of his feline's ears. He knew her so well that he didn't need the psychic bond that existed between them to understand her choice.

"But if we didn't find my mate before that," he gestured at the flaming forest, "we definitely won't find her now—not here anyway."

Bast's ears flicked back once and Antreas was filled with a rolling tide of surety wrapped in his feline's stubbornness.

Antreas knew he was defeated. Bast had decided, and unless he was willing to bind her and drag her with him, the Lynx would be immovable.

With a sigh that was lost in the deafening roar of wind and distant flame, Antreas went to his Lynx and sat beside her.

As always, he would follow her lead and wait until her preternatural understanding of the ebb and flow of time and events converged, and it became clear to Antreas what his Lynx needed . . . wanted . . . waited for.

"Okay, we stay here and see what we can do to help them rebuild," Antreas said.

And as always, as Antreas sat and waited with Bast, he wondered what life-altering adventure following his Lynx would take him on this time.